D1111554

Patricia Cornwell is one of the world's major international best-selling authors, translated into thirty-six languages across more than fifty countries. She is a founder of the Virginia Institute of Forensic Science and Medicine, a founding member of the National Forensic Academy, a member of the New York OCME Forensic Sciences Training Program's Advisory Board, and a member of the Harvard-affiliated McLean Hospital's National Council, where she is an advocate for psychiatric research.

In 2008 Cornwell won the Galaxy British Book Awards' Books Direct Crime Thriller of the Year – the first American ever to win this prestigious award. Her most recent bestsellers include *Scarpetta*, *Book of the Dead* and *The Front*. Her earlier works include *Postmortem* – the only novel to win five major crime awards in a single year – and *Cruel and Unusual*, which won the coveted Gold Dagger award in 1993. Dr. Kay Scarpetta herself won the 1999 Sherlock Award for the best detective created by an American writer.

ALSO BY PATRICIA CORNWELL

SCARPETTA SERIES
Postmortem
Body of Evidence
All That Remains
Cruel and Unusual
The Body Farm
From Potter's Field
Cause of Death
Unnatural Exposure
Point of Origin
Black Notice
The Last Precinct
Blow Fly
Trace
Predator
Book of the Dead
Scarpetta
Port Mortuary

ANDY BRAZIL SERIES
Hornet's Nest
Southern Cross
Isle of Dogs

WIN GARANO SERIES
At Risk
The Front

NON-FICTION
Portrait of a Killer: Jack the Ripper - Case Closed

BIOGRAPHY
Ruth, a Portrait: The Story of Ruth Bell Graham

OTHER WORKS
Food to Die For: Secrets from Kay Scarpetta's Kitchen
Life's Little Fable
Scarpetta's Winter Table

Patricia
Cornwell

The
Scarpetta
Factor

sphere

SPHERE

First published in the United States in 2009 by G.P. Putnam's Sons,
a division of Penguin Group (USA) Inc.
First published in Great Britain in 2009 by Little, Brown
This paperback edition published by Sphere in 2010
Reprinted 2010

A CIP catalogue record for this book
is available from the British Library.

ISBN 978-0-7515-3876-2

Typeset in Garamond by M Rules
Printed and bound in Great Britain by
Clays Ltd, St Ives plc

Papers used by Sphere are natural, renewable and
recyclable products sourced from well-managed forests and certified
in accordance with the rules of the Forest Stewardship Council.

Mixed Sources
Product group from well-managed
forests and other controlled sources
www.fsc.org Cert no. SGS-COC-004081
© 1996 Forest Stewardship Council

FSC

Sphere
An imprint of
Little, Brown Book Group
100 Victoria Embankment
London EC4Y 0DY

An Hachette UK Company
www.hachette.co.uk

www.littlebrown.co.uk

We owe respect to the living.
To the dead we owe only truth.

VOLTAIRE, *Oeuvres Completes*, 1785

1

A frigid wind gusted in from the East River, snatching at Dr. Kay Scarpetta's coat as she walked quickly along 30th Street.

It was one week before Christmas without a hint of the holidays in what she thought of as Manhattan's Tragic Triangle, three vertices connected by wretchedness and death. Behind her was Memorial Park, a voluminous white tent housing the vacuum-packed human remains still unidentified or unclaimed from Ground Zero. Ahead on the left was the Gothic redbrick former Bellevue Psychiatric Hospital, now a shelter for the homeless. Across from that was the loading dock and bay for the Office of the Chief Medical Examiner, where a gray steel garage door was open. A truck was backing up, more pallets of plywood being unloaded. It had been a noisy day at the morgue, a constant hammering in corridors that carried sound like an amphitheater. The mortuary techs were busy assembling plain pine coffins, adult-size, infant-size, hardly able to keep up with the growing demand for city burials at Potter's Field. Economy-related. Everything was.

Scarpetta already regretted the cheeseburger and fries in the cardboard box she carried. How long had they been in the warming cabinet on the serving line of the NYU Medical School cafeteria? It was late for lunch, almost three p.m., and she was pretty sure she knew the answer about the palatability of the food, but there was no time to place an order or bother with the salad bar, to eat healthy or even eat something she might actually enjoy. So far there had been fifteen cases today, suicides, accidents, homicides, and indigents who died unattended by a physician or, even sadder, alone.

She had been at work by six a.m. to get an early start, completing her first two autopsies by nine, saving the worst for last—a young woman with injuries and artifacts that were time-consuming and confounding. Scarpetta had spent more than five hours on Toni Darien, making meticulously detailed diagrams and notes, taking dozens of photographs, fixing the whole brain in a bucket of formalin for further studies, collecting and preserving more than the usual tubes of fluids and sections of organs and tissue, holding on to and documenting everything she possibly could in a case that was odd not because it was unusual but because it was a contradiction.

The twenty-six-year-old woman's manner and cause of death were depressingly mundane and hadn't required a lengthy postmortem examination to answer the most rudimentary questions. She was a homicide from blunt-force trauma, a single blow to the back of her head by an object that possibly had a multicolored painted surface. What didn't make sense was everything else. When her body was discovered at the edge of Central Park, some thirty feet off East 110th Street shortly before dawn, it was assumed she had been jogging last night in the rain when she was sexually assaulted and murdered. Her running pants and panties were around her ankles, her fleece and sports bra pushed above her breasts. A Polartec scarf was tied in a double knot tightly around her neck, and at first glance it was assumed by the police and the OCME's medicolegal investigators who responded to the scene that she was strangled with an article of her own clothing.

She wasn't. When Scarpetta examined the body in the morgue, she found nothing to indicate the scarf had caused the death or even contributed to it, no sign of asphyxia, no vital reaction such as redness or bruising, only a dry abrasion on the neck, as if the scarf had been tied around it postmortem. Certainly it was possible the killer struck her in the head and at some point later strangled her, perhaps not realizing she was already dead. But if so, how much time did he spend with her? Based on the contusion, swelling, and hemorrhage to the cerebral cortex of her brain, she had survived for a while, possibly hours. Yet there was very little blood at the scene. It wasn't until the body was turned over that the injury to the back of her head was even noticed, a one-and-a-half-inch laceration with significant swelling but only a slight weeping of fluid from the wound, the lack of blood blamed on the rain.

Scarpetta seriously doubted it. The scalp laceration would have bled heavily, and it was unlikely a rainstorm that was intermittent and at best moderate would have washed most of the blood out of Toni's long, thick hair. Did her assailant fracture her skull, then spend a long interval with her outside on a rainy winter's night before tying a scarf tightly around her neck to make sure she didn't live to tell the tale? Or was the ligature part of a sexually violent ritual? Why were livor and rigor mortis arguing loudly with what the crime scene seemed to say? It appeared she had died in the park late last night, and it appeared she had been dead for as long as thirty-six hours. Scarpetta was baffled by the case. Maybe she was overthinking it. Maybe she wasn't thinking clearly, for that matter, because she was harried and her blood sugar was low, having eaten nothing all day, only coffee, lots of it.

She was about to be late for the three p.m. staff meeting and needed to be home by six to go to the gym and have dinner with her husband, Benton Wesley, before rushing over to CNN, the last thing she felt like doing. She should never have agreed to appear on *The Crispin Report*. Why for God's sake had she agreed to go on the air with Carley Crispin and talk about postmortem changes in head hair and the importance of microscopy and other disciplines of forensic science, which were misunderstood because of the very thing Scarpetta had gotten herself involved in—the entertainment industry? She carried her boxed lunch through the loading dock, piled with cartons and crates of office and morgue supplies, and metal carts and trollies and plywood. The security guard was busy on the phone behind Plexiglas and barely gave her a glance as she went past.

At the top of a ramp she used the swipe card she wore on a lanyard to open a heavy metal door and entered a catacomb of white subway tile with teal-green accents and rails that seemed to lead everywhere and nowhere. When she first began working here as a part-time ME, she got lost quite a lot, ending up at the anthropology lab instead of the neuropath lab or the cardiopath lab or the men's locker room instead of the women's, or the decomp room instead

of the main autopsy room, or the wrong walk-in refrigerator or stairwell or even on the wrong floor when she
boarded the old steel freight elevator.

Soon enough she caught on to the logic of the layout,
to its sensible circular flow, beginning with the bay. Like
the loading dock, it was behind a massive garage door.
When a body was delivered by the medical examiner
transport team, the stretcher was unloaded in the bay and
passed beneath a radiation detector over the door. If no
alarm was triggered indicating the presence of a radioac-
tive material, such as radiopharmaceuticals used in the
treatment of some cancers, the next stop was the floor
scale, where the body was weighed and measured. Where
it went after that depended on its condition. If it was in
bad shape or considered potentially hazardous to the living,
it went inside the walk-in decomp refrigerator next to the
decomp room, where the autopsy would be performed in
isolation with special ventilation and other protections.

If the body was in good shape it was wheeled along a corridor to the right of the bay, a journey that could at some
point include the possibility of various stops relative to the
body's stage of deconstruction: the x-ray suite, the histology
specimen storage room, the forensic anthropology lab, two
more walk-in refrigerators for fresh bodies that hadn't been
examined yet, the lift for those that were to be viewed and
identified upstairs, evidence lockers, the neuropath room,
the cardiac path room, the main autopsy room. After a case
was completed and the body was ready for release, it ended
up full circle back at the bay inside yet another walk-in
refrigerator, which was where Toni Darien should be right
now, zipped up in a pouch on a storage rack.

But she wasn't. She was on a gurney parked in front of

the stainless-steel refrigerator door, an ID tech arranging a blue sheet around the neck, up to the chin.

"What are we doing?" Scarpetta said.

"We've had a little excitement upstairs. She's going to be viewed."

"By whom and why?"

"Mother's in the lobby and won't leave until she sees her. Don't worry. I'll take care of it." The tech's name was Rene, mid-thirties with curly black hair and ebony eyes, and unusually gifted at handling families. If she was having a problem with one, it wasn't trivial. Rene could defuse just about anything.

"I thought the father had made the ID," Scarpetta said.

"He filled out the paperwork, and then I showed him the picture you uploaded to me—this was right before you left for the cafeteria. A few minutes later, the mother walks in and the two of them start arguing in the lobby, and I mean going at it, and finally he storms out."

"They're divorced?"

"And obviously hate each other. She's insisting on seeing the body, won't take no for an answer." Rene's purple nitrile-gloved hands moved a strand of damp hair off the dead woman's brow, rearranging several more strands behind the ears, making sure no sutures from the autopsy showed. "I know you've got a staff meeting in a few minutes. I'll take care of this." She looked at the cardboard box Scarpetta was holding. "You didn't even eat yet. What have you had today? Probably nothing, as usual. How much weight have you lost? You're going to end up in the anthro lab, mistaken for a skeleton."

"What were they arguing about in the lobby?" Scarpetta asked.

"Funeral homes. Mother wants one on Long Island. Father wants one in New Jersey. Mother wants a burial, but the father wants cremation. Both of them fighting over her." Touching the dead body again, as if it were part of the conversation. "Then they started blaming each other for everything you can think of. At one point Dr. Edison came out, they were causing such a ruckus."

He was the chief medical examiner and Scarpetta's boss when she worked in the city. It was still a little hard getting used to being supervised, having been either a chief herself or the owner of a private practice for most of her career. But she wouldn't want to be in charge of the New York OCME, not that she'd been asked or likely ever would be. Running an office of this magnitude was like being the mayor of a major metropolis.

"Well, you know how it works," Scarpetta said. "A dispute, and the body doesn't go anywhere. We'll put a hold on her release until Legal instructs us otherwise. You showed the mother the picture, and then what?"

"I tried, but she wouldn't look at it. She says she wants to see her daughter and isn't leaving until she does."

"She's in the family room?"

"That's where I left her. I put the folder on your desk, copies of the paperwork."

"Thanks. I'll look at it when I go upstairs. You get her on the lift, and I'll take care of things on the other end," Scarpetta said. "Maybe you can let Dr. Edison know I'm going to miss the three-o'clock. In fact, it's already started. Hopefully I'll catch up with him before he heads home. He and I need to talk about this case."

"I'll tell him." Rene placed her hands on the steel gurney's push handle. "Good luck on TV tonight."

"Tell him the scene photos have been uploaded to him, but I won't be able to dictate the autopsy protocol or get those photos to him until tomorrow."

"I saw the commercials for the show. They're cool." Rene was still talking about TV. "Except I can't stand Carley Crispin and what's the name of that profiler who's on there all the time? Dr. Agee. I'm sick and tired of them talking about Hannah Starr. I'm betting Carley's going to ask you about it."

"CNN knows I won't discuss active cases."

"You think she's dead? Because I sure do." Rene's voice followed Scarpetta into the elevator. "Like what's-her-name in Aruba? Natalee? People vanish for a reason—because somebody wanted them to."

Scarpetta had been promised. Carley Crispin wouldn't do that to her, wouldn't dare. It wasn't as if Scarpetta was simply another expert, an outsider, an infrequent guest, a talking head, she reasoned, as the elevator made its ascent. She was CNN's senior forensic analyst and had been adamant with executive producer Alex Bachta that she could not discuss or even allude to Hannah Starr, the beautiful financial titan who seemingly had vanished in thin air the day before Thanksgiving, reportedly last seen leaving a restaurant in Greenwich Village and getting into a yellow cab. If the worst had happened, if she was dead and her body turned up in New York City, it would be this office's jurisdiction, and Scarpetta could end up with the case.

She got off on the first floor and followed a long hallway past the Division of Special Operations, and through another locked door was the lobby, arranged with burgundy and blue upholstered couches and chairs, coffee tables and racks of magazines, and a Christmas tree and menorah in a window overlooking First Avenue. Carved in marble above the reception desk was *Taceant colloquia. Effugiat risus. Hic locus est ubi mors gaudet succurrere vitae.* Let conversations cease. Let laughter depart. This is the place where death delights to help the living. Music sounded from a radio on the floor behind the desk, the Eagles playing "Hotel California." Filene, one of the security guards, had decided that an empty lobby was hers to fill with what she called her tunes.

". . . You can check out anytime you like, but you can never leave," Filene softly sang along, oblivious to the irony.

"There should be someone in the family room?" Scarpetta stopped at the desk.

"Oh, I'm sorry." Filene reached down, turning off the radio. "I didn't think she could hear from in there. But that's all right. I can go without my tunes. It's just I get so bored, you know? Sitting and sitting when nothing's going on."

What Filene routinely witnessed in this place was never happy, and that rather than boredom was likely the reason she listened to her upbeat soft rock whenever she could, whether she was working the reception desk or downstairs in the mortuary office. Scarpetta didn't care, as long as there were no grieving families to overhear music or lyrics that might be provocative or construed as disrespectful.

"Tell Mrs. Darien I'm on my way," Scarpetta said. "I need about fifteen minutes to check a few things and look at the paperwork. Let's hold the tunes until she's gone, okay?"

Off the lobby to the left was the administrative wing she shared with Dr. Edison, two executive assistants, and the chief of staff, who was on her honeymoon until after the New

Year. In a building half a century old with no space to spare, there was no place to put Scarpetta on the third floor, where the full-time forensic pathologists had their offices. When she was in the city, she parked herself in what was formerly the chief's conference room on the ground level, with a view of the OCME's turquoise-blue brick entrance on First Avenue. She unlocked her door and stepped inside. She hung her coat, set her boxed lunch on her desk, and sat in front of her computer.

Opening a Web browser, she typed *BioGraph* into a search field. At the top of the screen was the query *Did you mean: BioGraphy*. No, she didn't. *Biograph Records*. Not what she was looking for. *American Mutoscope and Biograph Company,* the oldest movie company in America, founded in 1895 by an inventor who worked for Thomas Edison, a distant ancestor of the chief medical examiner, not sure how many times removed. An interesting coincidence. Nothing for BioGraph with a capital *B* and a capital *G*, the way it was stamped on the back of the unusual watch Toni Darien was wearing on her left wrist when her body arrived at the morgue this morning.

It was snowing hard in Stowe, Vermont, big flakes falling heavy and wet, piled in the branches of balsam firs and Scotch pines. The ski lifts traversing the Green Mountains were faint spidery lines, almost invisible in the storm and at a standstill. Nobody skiing in this stuff, nobody doing anything except staying inside.

Lucy Farinelli's helicopter was stuck in nearby Burlington. At least it was safely in a hangar, but she and New York County Assistant District Attorney Jaime Berger weren't going anywhere for five hours, maybe longer, not before nine p.m., when the storm was supposed to have cleared to the south. At that point, conditions should be VFR again, a ceiling greater than three thousand feet, visibility five miles or more, winds gusting up to thirty knots out of the northeast. They'd have a hell of a tailwind heading home to New York, should get there in time for what they needed to do, but Berger was in a mood, had been in the other room on the phone all day, not even trying to be nice. The way she looked at it, the weather had trapped them here longer than planned, and since Lucy was a pilot, it was her fault. Didn't matter the forecasters had been wrong, that what began as two distinct small storms combined into one over Saskatchewan, Canada, and merged with an arctic air mass to create a bit of a monster.

Lucy turned down the volume of the YouTube video, Mick Fleetwood's drum solo for "World Turning," live in concert in 1987.

"Can you hear me now?" she said over the phone to her Aunt Kay. "The signal's pretty bad here, and the weather isn't helping."

"Much better. How are we doing?" Scarpetta's voice in Lucy's jawbone.

"I've found nothing so far. Which is weird."

Lucy had three MacBooks going, each screen split into quadrants, displaying Aviation Weather Center updates, data streams from neural network searches, links prompting her that they might lead to websites of interest, Hannah Starr's e-mail, Lucy's e-mail, and security camera footage of the actor Hap Judd wearing scrubs in the Park General Hospital morgue before he was famous.

"You sure of the name?" she asked as she scanned the

screens, her mind jumping from one preoccupation to the next.

"All I know is what's stamped on the steel back of it." Scarpetta's voice, serious and in a hurry. "BioGraph." She spelled it again. "And a serial number. Maybe it's not going to be picked up by the usual software that searches the Internet. Like viruses. If you don't already know what you're looking for, you won't find it."

"It's not like antivirus software. The search engines I use aren't software-driven. I do open-source searches. I'm not finding BioGraph because it's not on the Net. Nothing published about it. Not on message boards or in blogs or in databases, not in anything."

"Please don't hack," Scarpetta said.

"I simply exploit weaknesses in operating systems."

"Yes, and if a back door is unlocked and you walk into somebody's house, it's not trespassing."

"No mention of BioGraph or I'd find it." Lucy wasn't going to get into their usual debate about the end justifying the means.

"I don't see how that's possible. This is a very sophisticated-looking watch with a USB port. You have to charge it, likely on a docking station. I suspect it was rather expensive."

"Not finding it if I search it as a watch or a device or anything." Lucy watched results rolling by, her neural net search engines sorting through an infinity of keywords, anchor text, file types, URLs, title tags, e-mail and IP addresses. "I'm looking and not seeing anything even close to what you've described."

"Got to be some way to know what it is."

"It isn't. That's my point," Lucy said. "There's no such thing as a BioGraph watch or device, or anything that might remotely fit what Toni Darien was wearing. Her BioGraph watch doesn't exist."

"What do you mean it doesn't?"

"I mean it doesn't exist on the Internet, within the communication network, or metaphorically in cyberspace. In other words, a BioGraph watch doesn't exist virtually," Lucy said. "If I physically look at whatever this thing is, I'll probably figure it out. Especially if you're right and it's some sort of data-collecting device."

"Can't do that until the labs are done with it."

"Shit, don't let them get out their screwdrivers and hammers," Lucy said.

"Being swabbed for DNA, that's all. The police already checked for prints. Nothing. Please tell Jaime she can call me when it's convenient. I hope you're having some fun. Sorry I don't have time to chat right now."

"If I see her, I'll tell her."

"She's not with you?" Scarpetta probed.

"The Hannah Starr case and now this. Jaime's a little tied up, has a lot on her mind. You of all people know how it is." Lucy wasn't interested in discussing her personal life.

"I hope she's had a happy birthday."

Lucy didn't want to talk about it. "What's the weather like there?"

"Windy and cold. Overcast."

"You're going to get more rain, possibly snow north of the city," Lucy said. "It will be cleared out by midnight, because the system is weakening as it heads your way."

"The two of you are staying put, I hope."

"If I don't get the chopper out, she'll be looking for a dogsled."

"Call me before you leave, and please be careful,"

Scarpetta said. "I've got to go, got to talk to Toni Darien's mother. I miss you. We'll have dinner, do something soon?"

"Sure," Lucy said.

She got off the phone and turned the sound up again on YouTube, Mick Fleetwood still going at it on the drums. Both hands on MacBooks as if she was in her own rock concert playing a solo on keyboards, she clicked on another weather update, clicked on an e-mail that had just landed in Hannah Starr's inbox. People were bizarre. If you know someone has disappeared and might even be dead, why do you continue to send e-mail? Lucy wondered if Hannah Starr's husband, Bobby Fuller, was so stupid it didn't occur to him that the NYPD and the district attorney's office might be monitoring Hannah's e-mail or getting a forensic computer expert like Lucy to do it. For the past three weeks Bobby had been sending daily messages to his missing wife. Maybe he knew exactly what he was doing, wanted law enforcement to see what he was writing to his *bien-aimée,* his *chouchou,* his *amore mio,* the love of his life. If he'd murdered her, he wouldn't be writing her love notes, right?

```
From: Bobby Fuller
Sent: Thursday, December 18, 3:24 P.M.
To: Hannah
Subject: Non posso vivere senza di te

My Little One,
I hope you are someplace safe and read-
ing this. My heart is carried by the
wings of my soul and finds you wherever
you are. Don't forget. I can't eat or
sleep. B.
```

Lucy checked his IP address, recognized it at a glance by now. Bobby and Hannah's apartment in North Miami Beach, where he was pining away while hiding from the media in palatial surroundings that Lucy knew all too well—had been in that same apartment with his lovely thief of a wife not that long ago, as a matter of fact. Every time Lucy saw an e-mail from Bobby and tried to get into his head, she wondered how he would really feel if he believed Hannah was dead.

Or maybe he knew she was dead or knew she wasn't. Maybe he knew exactly what had happened to her because he really did have something to do with it. Lucy had no idea, but when she tried to put herself in Bobby's place and care, she couldn't. All that mattered to her was that Hannah reaped what she sowed or eventually did, sooner rather than later. She deserved any bad fate she might get, had wasted Lucy's time and money and now was stealing something far more precious. Three weeks of Hannah. Nothing with Berger. Even when she and Lucy were together, they were apart. Lucy was scared. She was seething. At times she felt she could do something terrible.

She forwarded Bobby's latest e-mail to Berger, who was in the other room, walking around. The sound of her feet on hardwood. Lucy got interested in a website address that had begun to flash in a quadrant of one of the MacBooks.

"Now what are we up to?" she said to the empty living room of the town house she'd rented for Berger's surprise birthday getaway, a five-star resort with high-speed wireless, fireplaces, feather beds, and linens with an eight-hundred thread count. The retreat had everything except what it was intended for—intimacy, romance, fun—and Lucy blamed Hannah, she blamed Hap Judd, she blamed Bobby, blamed everyone. Lucy felt haunted by them and unwanted by Berger.

"This is ridiculous," Berger said as she walked in, referring to the world beyond their windows, everything white, just the shapes of trees and rooflines through snow coming down in veils. "Are we ever going to get out of here?"

"Now, what is this?" Lucy muttered, clicking on a link.

A search by IP address had gotten a hit on a website hosted by the University of Tennessee's Forensic Anthropology Center.

"Who were you just talking to?" Berger asked.

"My aunt. Now I'm talking to myself. Got to talk to somebody."

Berger ignored the dig, wasn't about to apologize for what she'd say she couldn't help. It wasn't her fault Hannah Starr had disappeared and Hap Judd was a pervert who might have information, and if that hadn't been enough of a distraction, now a jogger had been raped and murdered in Central Park last night. Berger would tell Lucy she needed to be more understanding. She shouldn't be so self-ish. She needed to grow up and stop being insecure and demanding.

"Can we do without the drums?" Berger's migraines were back. She was getting them often.

Lucy exited YouTube and the living room was silent, no sound but the gas fire on the hearth, and she said, "More of the same sicko stuff."

Berger put her glasses on and leaned close to look, and she smelled like Amorvero bath oil, and had no makeup on and she didn't need it. Her short, dark hair was messy and she was sexy as hell in a black warm-up suit, nothing under it, the jacket unzipped, exposing plenty of cleavage, not that she meant anything by it. Lucy wasn't sure what Berger meant or where she was much of the time these days, but she wasn't present—not emotionally. Lucy wanted to put her arms around her, to show her what they used to have, what it used to be like.

"He's looking at the Body Farm's website, and I doubt it's because he's thinking of killing himself and donating his body to science," Lucy said.

"Who are you talking about?" Berger was reading what was on a MacBook screen, a form with the heading:

Forensic Anthropology Center
University of Tennessee, Knoxville
Body Donation Questionnaire

"Hap Judd," Lucy said. "He's gotten linked by his IP address to this website because he just used a fake name to order . . . Hold on, let's see what the sleaze is up to. Let's follow the trail." Opening Web pages. "To this screen here. FORDISC Software Sales. An interactive computer program that runs under Windows. Classifying and identifying skeletal remains. The guy's really morbid. It's not normal. I'm telling you, we're onto something with him."

"Let's be honest. You're onto something because you're looking for something," Berger said, as if to imply that Lucy wasn't honest. "You're trying to find evidence of what you perceive is the crime."

"I'm finding evidence because he's leaving it," Lucy said.

They had been arguing about Hap Judd for weeks. "I don't know why you're so reticent. Do you think I'm making this stuff up?"

"I want to talk to him about Hannah Starr, and you want to crucify him."

"You need to scare the hell out of him if you want him to talk. Especially without a damn lawyer present. And I've managed to make that happen, to get you what you want."

"If we ever get out of here and he shows up." Berger moved away from the computer screen and decided, "Maybe he's playing an anthropologist, an archaeologist, an explorer in his next film. Some *Raiders of the Lost Ark* or another one of those mummy movies with tombs and ancient curses."

"Right," Lucy said. "Method acting, total immersion in his next twisted character, writing another one of his piss-poor screenplays. That will be his alibi when we go after him about Park General and his unusual interests."

"*We* won't be going after him. I will. You're not going to do anything but show him what you've found in your computer searches. Marino and I will do the talking."

Lucy would check with Pete Marino later, when there was no threat that Berger could overhear their conversation. He didn't have any respect for Hap Judd and sure as hell wasn't afraid of him. Marino had no qualms about investigating someone famous or locking him up. Berger seemed intimidated by Judd, and Lucy didn't understand it. She had never known Berger to be intimidated by anyone.

"Come here." Lucy pulled her close, sat her on her lap. "What's going on with you?" Nuzzling her back, sliding her hands inside the jacket of the warm-up suit. "What's got you so spooked? It's going to be a late night. We should take a nap."

Grace Darien had long, dark hair and the same turned-up nose and full lips as her murdered daughter. Wearing a red wool coat buttoned up to her chin, she looked small and pitiful as she stood before a window overlooking the black iron fence and dead vine-covered brick of Bellevue. The sky was the color of lead.

"Mrs. Darien? I'm Dr. Scarpetta." She walked into the family room and closed the door.

"It's possible this is a mistake." Mrs. Darien moved away from the window, her hands shaking badly. "I keep thinking this can't be right. It can't be. It's somebody else. How do you know for sure?" She sat down at the small wooden table near the watercooler, her face stunned and expressionless, a gleam of terror in her eyes.

"We've made a preliminary identification of your daughter based on personal effects recovered by the police." Scarpetta pulled out a chair and sat across from her. "Your former husband also looked at a photograph."

"The one taken here."

"Yes. Please let me tell you how sorry I am."

"Did he get around to mentioning he only sees her once or twice a year?"

"We will compare dental records and will do DNA if need be," Scarpetta said.

"I can write down her dentist's information. She still uses my dentist." Grace Darien dug into her handbag, and a lipstick and a compact clattered to the table. "The detective

I talked to finally when I got home and got the message. I can't remember the name, a woman. Then another detective called. A man. Mario, Marinaro." Her voice trembled and she blinked back tears, pulling out a small notepad, a pen.

"Pete Marino?"

She scribbled something and tore out the page, her hands fumbling, almost palsied. "I don't know our dentist's number off the top of my head. Here's his name and address." Sliding the piece of paper to Scarpetta. "Marino. I believe so."

"He's a detective with NYPD and assigned to Assistant District Attorney Jaime Berger's office. Her office will be in charge of the criminal investigation." Scarpetta tucked the note into the file folder Rene had left for her.

"He said they were going into Toni's apartment to get her hairbrush, her toothbrush. They probably already have, I don't know, I haven't heard anything else," Mrs. Darien continued, her voice quavering and catching. "The police talked to Larry first because I wasn't home. I was taking the cat to the vet. I had to put my cat to sleep, can you imagine the timing. That's what I was doing when they were trying to find me. The detective from the DA's office said you could get her DNA from things in her apartment. I don't understand how you can be sure it's her when you haven't done those tests yet."

Scarpetta had no doubt about Toni Darien's identity. Her driver's license and apartment keys were in a pocket of the fleece that came in with the body. Postmortem x-rays showed healed fractures of the collarbone and right arm, and the old injuries were consistent with ones sustained five years ago when Toni was riding her bicycle and was struck by a car, according to information from NYPD.

"I told her about jogging in the city," Mrs. Darien was saying. "I can't tell you how many times, but she never did it after dark. I don't know why she would in the rain. She hates running in the rain, especially when it's cold. I think there's been a mistake."

Scarpetta moved a box of tissues closer to her and said, "I'd like to ask you a few questions, to go over a few things before we see her. Would that be all right?" After the viewing, Grace Darien would be in no condition to talk. "When's the last time you had contact with your daughter?"

"Tuesday morning. I can't tell you the exact time but probably around ten. I called her and we chatted."

"Two mornings ago, December sixteenth."

"Yes." She wiped her eyes.

"Nothing since then? No other phone calls, voicemails, e-mails?"

"We didn't talk or e-mail every day, but she sent a text message. I can show it to you." She reached for her pocketbook. "I should have told the detective that, I guess. What did you say his name is?"

"Marino."

"He wanted to know about her e-mail, because he said they're going to need to look at it. I told him the address, but of course I don't know her password." She rummaged for her phone, her glasses. "I called Toni Tuesday morning, asking if she wanted turkey or ham. For Christmas. She didn't want either. She said she might bring fish, and I said I'd get whatever she wanted. It was just a normal conversation, mostly about things like that, since her two brothers are coming home. All of us together on Long Island." She had her phone out and her glasses on, was scrolling through something with shaky hands. "That's where I live. In Islip. I'm a nurse at Mercy Hospital." She gave Scarpetta the phone. "That's what she sent last night." She pulled more tissues from the box.

Scarpetta read the text message:

From: Toni
Still trying to get days off but Xmas so crazy. I have to get coverage and no one wants to especially because of the hours. XXOO
CB# 917-555-1487
Received: Wed Dec. 17. 8:07 p.m.

Scarpetta said, "And this nine-one-seven number is your daughter's?"

"Her cell."

"Can you tell me what she's referring to in this message?" She would make sure Marino knew about it.

"She works nights and weekends and has been trying to get someone to cover for her so she can take some time off during the holiday," Mrs. Darien said. "Her brothers are coming."

"Your former husband said she worked as a waitress in Hell's Kitchen."

"He would say that, as if she slings hash or flips burgers. She works in the lounge at High Roller Lanes, a very nice place, very high-class, not your typical bowling alley. She wants to have her own restaurant in some big hotel some-day in Las Vegas or Paris or Monte Carlo."

"Was she working last night?"

"Not usually on Wednesdays. Mondays through Wednesdays she's usually off, and then she works very long
hours Thursdays through Sundays."

"Do her brothers know what's happened?" Scarpetta
asked. "I wouldn't want them hearing about it on the
news."

"Larry's probably told them. I would have waited. It
might not be true."

"We'll want to be mindful of anybody who perhaps
shouldn't find out from the news." Scarpetta was as gentle
as she could be. "What about a boyfriend? A significant
other?"

"Well, I've wondered. I visited Toni at her apartment in
September and there were all these stuffed animals on her
bed, and a lot of perfumes and such, and she was evasive
about where they'd come from. And at Thanksgiving she
was text-messaging all the time, happy one minute, in a
bad mood the next. You know how people act when they're
infatuated. I do know she meets a lot of people at work, a
lot of very attractive and exciting men."

"Possible she might have confided in your former husband? Told him about a boyfriend, for example?"

"They weren't close. What you don't understand is why
he's doing this, what Larry is really up to. It's all to get
back at me and make everybody think he's the dutiful
father instead of a drunk, a compulsive gambler who abandoned his family. Toni would never want to be cremated,
and if the worst has happened, I'll use the funeral home
that took care of my mother, Levine and Sons."

"I'm afraid until you and Mr. Darien settle your dispute
about the disposition of Toni's remains, the OCME can't
release her," Scarpetta said.

"You can't listen to him. He left Toni when she was a baby. Why should anybody listen to him?"

"The law requires that disputes such as yours must be resolved, if need be by the courts, before we can release the body," Scarpetta said. "I'm sorry. I know the last thing you need right now is frustration and more upset."

"What right does he have suddenly showing up after twenty- something years, making demands, wanting her personal things. Fighting with me about that in the lobby and telling that girl he wanted Toni's belongings, whatever she had on when she came in, and it might not even be her. Saying such horrid, heartless things! He was drunk and looked at a picture. And you trust that? Oh, God. What am I going to see? Just tell me so I know what to expect."

"Your daughter's cause of death is blunt-force trauma that fractured her skull and injured her brain," Scarpetta said.

"Someone hit her on the head." Her voice shook and she broke down and cried.

"She suffered a severe blow to the head. Yes."

"How many? Just one?"

"Mrs. Darien, I need to caution you from the start that anything I tell you is in confidence and it's my duty to exercise caution and good judgment in what you and I discuss right now," Scarpetta said. "It's critical nothing is released that might actually aid your daughter's assailant in getting away with this very terrible crime. I hope you understand. Once the police investigation is complete, you can make an appointment with me and we'll have as detailed a discussion as you'd like."

"Toni was out jogging last night in the rain on the

north side of Central Park? In the first place, what was she doing over there? Has anybody bothered asking that question?"

"All of us are asking a lot of questions, and unfortunately have very few answers so far," Scarpetta replied. "But as I understand it, your daughter has an apartment on the Upper East Side, on Second Avenue. That's about twenty blocks from where she was found, which isn't very far for an avid runner."

"But it was in Central Park after dark. It was near Harlem after dark. She would never go running in an area like that after dark. And she hated the rain. She hated being cold. Did someone come up behind her? Did she struggle with him? Oh, dear God."

"I'll remind you what I said about details, about the caution we need to exercise right now," Scarpetta replied. "I can tell you that I found no obvious signs of a struggle. It appears Toni was struck on the head, causing a large contusion, a lot of hemorrhage into her brain, which indicates a survival time that was long enough for significant tissue response."

"But she wouldn't have been conscious."

"Her findings indicate some survival time, but no, she wouldn't have been conscious. She may have had no awareness at all of what happened, of the attack. We won't know until certain test results come back." Scarpetta opened the file and removed the health history form, placing it in front of Mrs. Darien. "Your former husband filled this out. I'd appreciate it if you'd look."

The paperwork shook in Mrs. Darien's hands as she scanned it.

"Name, address, place of birth, parents' names. Please

let me know if we need to correct anything," Scarpetta said. "Did she have high blood pressure, diabetes, hypoglycemia, mental health issues—was she pregnant, for example."

"He checked *no* to everything. What the hell does he know?"

"No depression, moodiness, a change of behavior that might have struck you as unusual." Scarpetta was thinking about the BioGraph watch. "Did she have problems sleeping? Anything at all going on with her that was different from the past? You said she might have been out of sorts of late."

"Maybe a boyfriend problem or something at work, the economy being what it is. Some of the girls she works with have been laid off," Mrs. Darien said. "She gets in moods like everybody else. Especially this time of year. She doesn't like winter weather."

"Any medications you might be aware of?"

"Just over-the-counter, as far as I know. Vitamins. She takes very good care of herself."

"I'm interested in who her internist might be, her doctor or doctors. Mr. Darien didn't fill in that part."

"He wouldn't know. He's never gotten the bills. Toni's been living on her own since college, and I can't be sure who her doctor is. She never gets sick, has more energy than anyone I know. Always on the go."

"Are you aware of any jewelry she might have routinely worn? Perhaps rings, a bracelet, a necklace she rarely took off?" Scarpetta said.

"I don't know."

"What about a watch?"

"I don't think so."

"What looks like a black plastic sports watch, digital? A large black watch? Does that sound familiar?"

Mrs. Darien shook her head.

"I've seen similar watches when people are involved in studies. In your profession, I'm sure you have, too. Watches that are cardiac monitors or worn by people who have sleep disorders, for example," Scarpetta said.

A look of hope in Mrs. Darien's eyes.

"What about when you saw Toni at Thanksgiving," Scarpetta said. "Might she have been wearing a watch like the one I just described?"

"No." Mrs. Darien shook her head. "That's what I mean. It might not be her. I've never seen her wearing anything like that."

Scarpetta asked her if she would like to see the body now, and they got up from the table and walked into an adjoining room, small and bare, just a few photographs of New York City skylines on pale-green walls. The viewing window was approximately waist-high, about the height of a casket on a bier, and on the other side was a steel screen—actually, the doors of the lift that had carried Toni's body up from the morgue.

"Before I open the screen, I want to explain what you're going to see," Scarpetta said. "Would you like to sit on the sofa?"

"No. No, thank you. I'll stand. I'm ready." Her eyes were wide and panicked, and she was breathing fast.

"I'm going to push a button." Scarpetta indicated a panel of three buttons on the wall, two black, one red, old elevator buttons. "And when the screen opens, the body will be right here."

"Yes. I understand. I'm ready." She could barely talk, she

was so frightened, shaking as if freezing cold, breathing hard as if she'd just exerted herself.

"The body is on a gurney inside the elevator, on the other side of the window. Her head will be here, to the left. The rest of her is covered."

Scarpetta pushed the top black button, and the steel doors parted with a loud clank. Through scratched Plexiglas Toni Darien was shrouded in blue, her face wan, her eyes shut, her lips colorless and dry, her long, dark hair still damp from rinsing. Her mother pressed her hands against the window. Bracing herself, she began to scream.

2

Pete Marino was unsettled as he looked around the studio apartment, trying to read its personality and mood, trying to intuit what it had to tell him.

Scenes were like dead people. They had a lot to say if you understood their silent language, and what bothered him right away was that Toni Darien's laptop and cell phone were gone, their chargers still plugged into the wall. What continued to nag at him was that there was nothing else that seemed to be missing or disturbed, the police by now of the opinion that her apartment had nothing to do with her murder. Yet he sensed someone had been in here. He didn't know why he sensed it, one of those feelings he got at the back of his neck, as if something was watching him or trying to get his attention and he couldn't see what it was.

Marino stepped back out into the hallway, where a uniformed NYPD cop was babysitting the apartment, no one allowed to go in unless Jaime Berger said so. She wanted the apartment sealed until she was satisfied she needed nothing more from it, had been adamant on the phone with Marino but also talking out of both sides of her mouth. Don't get too hung up on her apartment, and treat it like the crime scene. Well, which was it? Marino had been around the block too many times to pay much attention to anyone, including his boss. He did his own thing. As far as he was concerned, Toni Darien's apartment was a scene, and he was going to turn it inside out.

"Tell you what," Marino said to the cop outside the door, his last name Mellnik. "Maybe give Bonnell a call. I need to talk to her about the missing laptop, the cell phone, make sure she didn't take them."

Bonnell was the NYPD case investigator who'd already been through the apartment earlier today with the Crime Scene Unit.

"What, you don't got a phone?" Mellnik was leaning against the wall in the dimly lit hallway, a folding chair nearby at the top of the stairs.

When Marino left, Mellnik would move the chair back inside the apartment and sit until he needed a bathroom break or his replacement showed up for midnight shift. A fucking lousy job. Somebody had to do it.

"You're so busy?" Marino said to him.

"Just because I'm hanging around with my thumb up my ass doesn't mean I'm not busy. I'm busy thinking." Tapping his gelled black hair, a short guy built like a bullet. "I'll track her down, but like I was telling you? When I got here, the guy I relieved talked my ear off about it, about what the crime scene guys were saying. Like where's her phone? Where's her laptop? But they don't think someone came in here and took them. No evidence of that. I think it's pretty fucking obvious what happened to her. Why do people still jog in the park at night, especially females? Go figure."

"And the door was locked when Bonnell and the crime scene guys got here?"

"I told you, the super unlocked it, a guy named Joe, lives on the first floor, other end." Pointing. "You can see for yourself. There's no sign somebody jimmied the lock, broke in. The door was locked, the shades down in the windows, everything undisturbed, normal. That's what I was told by the guy here before me, and he witnessed what Crime Scene did, the whole thing."

Marino was studying the doorknob, the deadbolt, touching them with his gloved hands. He got a flashlight out of his pocket, looking carefully, not seeing any obvious signs of forced entry. Mellnik was right. Nothing appeared damaged or recently scratched.

Marino said, "Find Bonnell for me, get the dispatcher too so I can get it from her direct. Because I'm going to be asked about it fifty times when the boss is back in town, if not sooner. Most people who take their laptops off-site also take the charger. That's bothering me."

"Crime Scene would have taken the charger if they took the computer. They didn't take nothing," Mellnik said. "Maybe the victim had an extra charger, that occur to you? If she took her laptop somewhere and had a charger at that location or, you know, just an extra one. That's what I think happened."

"I'm sure Berger will send you a handwritten thank-you for your hearsay opinion."

"What's it like working for her?"

"The sex is pretty good," said Marino. "If she'd just give me a little more time to recover. Five, ten times a day, and even I get tuckered out."

"Yeah, and I'm Spider-Man. From what I hear, men aren't what wind her clock. I look at her and go, no way. Must be a vicious rumor because she's powerful, right? Any woman who's got her kind of power and prominence? You know what they say, doesn't mean it's true. Don't get my girlfriend on the subject. She's a firefighter. So right off, she's either a lesbo or wearing a swimsuit in a calendar, that's the assumption."

"No shit. She in the Female Firefighters calendar? This year's? I'll order me a copy."

"I said it was an assumption. So, my question. Is it an assumption about Jaime Berger? I got to admit, I'd love to know. It's all over the Internet about her and Dr. Scarpetta's—what is it, her daughter, her niece? The girl who used to be FBI and now does all Berger's computer investigative stuff. I mean, does Jaime Berger hate men and that's what motivates her to lock them up? Almost always it's men she locks up, that is true. Not that females commit most sex crimes, but still. If anybody would know the real story, I guess it would be you."

"Don't wait for the movie. Read the book."

"What book?" Mellnik sat down in his folding chair, slipped his phone out of the holder on his duty belt. "What book you talking about?"

"Maybe you should write it, you're so curious." Marino looked down the length of the hallway, brown carpet, dingy tan-painted walls, a total of eight units up here on the second floor.

"Like I was saying, I've been thinking I don't want to do shit work like this all my life, maybe I should go into investigations, you know." Mellnik kept on talking as if Marino was interested and they'd been friends for years.

"Get assigned to Jaime Berger's office like you, as long as she's not a man-hater, that goes without saying. Or maybe to the FBI's Joint Bank Robbery Task Force or Terrorism or something, where you go to a real office every day, get a take-home car, get treated with respect."

"There's no doorman," Marino said. "The way you get into this building is a key, or you have to buzz somebody to let you in, like you did for me when I showed up. Once in the common area where the mailboxes are, you got a choice. You turn left, walk past four apartments, including the super's, and take the stairs. Or you turn right and walk past the laundry room, the maintenance and the mechanical-systems closets, and a storage area, and take those stairs. Up two flights and conveniently here you are, not even six feet from Toni's door. If someone got in her apartment, maybe had keys for some reason, he could have come in and left and not necessarily been seen by the neighbors. You been sitting here how long?"

"Just got here at two. Like I said, there was another officer here before that. I think once the body was found, they dispatched someone right away."

"Yeah, I know. Berger had a little something to do with that. How many people you seen, you know, residents?"

"Since I got here? Nobody."

"You heard running water, people walking around, noise coming from any of the other units?" Marino asked.

"From where I've been, either right here at the top of the stairs or just inside the door? It's been real quiet. But I only been here, what?" Looking at his watch. "About two hours."

Marino tucked the flashlight back into his coat pocket. "Everybody's out this time of day. Not the building for you if you're retired or a shut-in. One thing, there's no elevator, so if you're old or crippled or sick, this is a bad choice. There's no rent control and it's not a co-op, not a close-knit community, no residents who have been here for a long time, the average stay a couple of years. A lot of singles and couples with no kids. Average age, twenties and thirties. There are forty units, eight of them empty at the moment, and my guess is there aren't a lot of Realtors showing up and buzzing the super. Because the economy sucks, which is one reason there are so many empty apartments to begin with, all vacated within the last six months."

"How the hell do you know? You got psychic abilities like the Medium?"

Marino pulled a wad of folded paper from a pocket. "RTCC. Got a list of every resident in this building, who they are, what they do, if they ever been arrested, where they work, where they shop, what kind of car if they own one, who they fuck."

"I never been over there." He meant the Real Time Crime Center, or what Marino thought of as the command bridge of the U.S.S. *Enterprise,* the information-technology center at One Police Plaza that basically ran NYPD's starship operations.

"No pets," Marino added.

"What do pets have to do with it?" Mellnik yawned. "Since they switched me to evenings, I'm so whacked. Can't sleep worth shit. My girlfriend and me are like ships in the night."

"In buildings where people aren't home during the day, who's going to take out the dog?" Marino continued. "Rents here start around twelve hundred. These aren't the type of tenants who can afford dog walkers or want to be bothered. Other thing about that? Brings me back to my point. Not much going on, no eyes or ears. Not during the day, like I'm saying. If it was me, that would be when I'd show up to get inside her apartment if I was up to no good. Do it in plain view, when the street, the sidewalk are busy but the inside of the building isn't."

"I remind you she wasn't attacked up here," Mellnik said. "She was murdered while she was jogging in the park."

"Find Bonnell. Get started on your investigative training early. Maybe you'll grow up to be Dick Tracy."

Marino walked back inside the apartment, leaving the door open. Toni Darien had lived like a lot of people just getting started, in a tiny space that Marino seemed to completely fill, as if the world suddenly had shrunk all around him. About four hundred square feet, he guessed, not that his apartment in Harlem was a hell of a lot bigger, but at least he had a one-bedroom, didn't sleep in the friggin' living room, and he had a backyard, a patch of artificial grass and a picnic table he shared with his neighbors, not much to brag about but more civilized than this. When he'd first showed up about half an hour ago, he'd done what he always did at a crime scene—gotten an overview without looking at anything in detail.

Now he'd pay closer attention, starting with the entranceway, enough space to turn around in and that was about it, with a tiny rattan table. On it was a Caesars Palace souvenir ashtray, maybe for Toni's keys, which had been on a silver dice keychain found in a pocket of the fleece she was wearing when she was killed. Maybe she was like her old man, liked to gamble. Marino had checked him out, Lawrence Darien, a couple DUIs, had declared bankruptcy, and a few years ago was implicated in an offshore gambling ring in Bergen County, New Jersey. There were hints of ties to organized crime, possibly the Genovese crime family, the charges dropped, the guy a scumbag, a loser, a former bio-electrical engineer from MIT who had walked out on his family, was a deadbeat dad. Just the sort to set up his daughter for getting involved with the wrong kind of guys.

Toni didn't look like a drinker. So far, she didn't strike Marino as the partying type or someone given to compulsions, in fact the opposite, controlled, ambitious, and hard-driven, a fitness freak, a health nut. On the rattan table just inside the door was a framed photograph of her running in a race, maybe a marathon. She was nice-looking, like a model, with long, dark hair, tall and on the thin side, a typical runner's body, no hips, no tits, a look of fierce determination on her face, pumping hard on a road packed with other runners, people off to the side cheering. Marino wondered who had taken the picture and when.

A few steps beyond the entranceway was the kitchen. A two-burner stove, a refrigerator, a single sink, three cabinets, two drawers, everything white. On the counter was a stack of mail, none of it opened, as if she'd walked in with it and set it down and got busy with other things or just wasn't interested. Marino looked through several catalogs and circulars with coupons, what he called junk mail, and a flyer on bright pink paper alerting residents in the building that the water would be shut off tomorrow, December 19, from eight a.m. until noon.

Nearby was a stainless-steel drain rack, and in it a butter knife, a fork, a spoon, a plate, a bowl, a coffee mug with a *Far Side* cartoon on it, the kid at "Midvale School for the Gifted" pushing on a door that reads "PULL." The sink was empty and clean, a sponge and bottle of Dawn liquid detergent, no crumbs on the counter, no food stains, the hardwood floor spotless. Marino opened the cabinet under the sink, finding a small garbage can lined with a white plastic bag. Inside were a banana peel that was brown and smelled pungent, a few withered blueberries, a soy milk carton, coffee grounds, a lot of paper towels.

He shook open a few of them, detecting what smelled like honey and citrus, like lemon-scented ammonia, maybe furniture and glass cleaners. He noticed a spray bottle of lemon-scented Windex, a bottle of a wood preserver containing beeswax and orange oil. It seemed Toni was very industrious, maybe obsessive, and had been cleaning and straightening up when she was home last. What did she use the Windex on? Marino didn't see anything glass. He walked to the far wall, peeked behind the shades, wiped his gloved finger over a pane of glass. The windows weren't filthy, but they also didn't appear to have been recently cleaned. Maybe she'd used the Windex to clean a mirror or something, or maybe somebody else had been cleaning in here, getting rid of fingerprints and DNA or thinking he was. Marino returned to the kitchen, which took him fewer than ten steps. The paper towels from the trash went into an evidence bag. Check them for DNA.

Toni had kept her cereal in the refrigerator, several boxes of whole-grain Kashi, more soy milk, blueberries, cheeses, yogurt, romaine lettuce, cherry tomatoes, a plastic container of pasta with what looked like a Parmesan sauce, maybe takeout, or maybe she'd eaten dinner somewhere and had carried the leftovers home. When? Last night? Or was the last meal she'd eaten inside her apartment a bowl of cereal with a banana and blueberries, and a pot of coffee—breakfast? She didn't eat breakfast this morning, that was for damn sure. Did she eat breakfast here yesterday morning, then was gone all day and maybe ate dinner out, some Italian place? Then what? Came home, put her leftover pasta in the refrigerator, and at some point during the rainy night went jogging? He thought about her stomach contents, was curious what Scarpetta had found during the autopsy. He'd tried to reach her a couple of times this afternoon, had left her several messages.

The hardwood floor creaked under Marino's big booted feet as he moved around, stepping back into the living area. Traffic on Second Avenue was loud, car engines and honking and people on the sidewalk. The constant noise and activity could have given Toni a false sense of security. It was unlikely she would have felt isolated here, one level above the street, but she probably kept her shades down after dark so no one could see in. Mellnik claimed the shades were down when Bonnell and the crime scene guys got here, suggesting the shades had been closed by Toni. When? If her last meal here had been yesterday morning, she didn't bother opening her shades when she got up? She obviously liked to look out the windows, because she'd set a small table and two chairs between them. The table was clean, a single straw place mat on it, and Marino imagined her sitting there yesterday morning, eating her cereal. But with the shades down?

Between the windows was a flat-screen TV on a single-arm wall mount, a thirty-two-inch Samsung, the remote control on the coffee table near a love seat. Marino picked up the remote, pushed the power button to see what she'd been watching last. The TV blinked on to *Headline News,* one of the anchors talking about the murder of "a Central

Park jogger whose name has not yet been released by the authorities," cutting over to Mayor Bloomberg making a statement about it, then Police Commissioner Kelly, the usual things the politicians and people in charge said to reassure the public. Marino listened until the subject turned to the latest outrage over the bailout of AIG.

He set the remote back on the coffee table, exactly where he'd found it, pulled his notepad out of a pocket, wrote down the channel the TV had been on, wondering if the crime scene guys or Bonnell had noticed. Probably not. He wondered when Toni had been watching the news. Was that the first thing she did when she got up in the morning? Did she turn on the news during the day or watch it before she went to sleep? When she'd been watching the news last, where had she been sitting? The way the wall-mounted arm was tilted, the TV was facing the double bed. It was covered with a light-blue satin spread, three stuffed animals on the pillows: a raccoon, a penguin, and an ostrich. Marino wondered if someone had given them to her, maybe her mother, not likely from a boyfriend. They didn't look like something a guy would give as a gift, unless maybe he was gay. Marino nudged the penguin with a glove-sheathed finger, looking at the tag, then checked the other two. *Gund.* He wrote it down.

Next to the bed was a table with a drawer. Inside were a nail file, a few double-A batteries, a small bottle of Motrin, a couple of old paperbacks, true crime: *The Jeffrey Dahmer Story: An American Nightmare* and *Ed Gein—Psycho.* Marino wrote down the titles, flipped through each paperback, looking to see if Toni might have made notes, not finding any. Tucked between the pages of *The Jeffrey Dahmer Story* was a receipt dated November 18, 2006,

when the paperback apparently had been purchased sec-
ondhand from Moe's Books in Berkeley, California. A
woman living alone reading scary shit like this? Maybe
someone had given them to her. He put them in an evidence bag. They'd go to the labs, check them for prints, for
DNA. Just a feeling he had.

To the left of the bed was the closet, the clothing inside
it hip, sexy: leggings, tunic sweaters with bright designs, low-
cut screen-print tops, spandex, a couple of sleek dresses. Marino
didn't recognize the labels, not that he was an expert in fash-
ion design. Baby Phat, Coogi, Kensie Girl. On the floor were
ten pairs of shoes, including Asics running shoes like she'd
been wearing when she was murdered, and a pair of sheepskin
Uggs for winter weather.

Linens were folded and stacked on an overhead shelf,
next to a cardboard box, which he pulled down, looked
inside it. DVDs, movies, mostly comedies and action, the
Ocean's Eleven series, another gambling theme. She liked
George Clooney, Brad Pitt, Ben Stiller. Nothing very violent, nothing scary like the paperbacks by her bed. Maybe
she didn't buy DVDs anymore, watched movies, including
horror if that was what she was into, on cable, had Pay-Per-
View. Maybe she watched movies on her laptop. Where the
hell was her laptop? Marino took photographs and more
notes.

It had entered his mind that so far he hadn't seen a
winter coat. A few Windbreakers and a long red wool coat
that looked out of style, maybe from high school, maybe a
hand-me-down from her mother or someone, but what
about a serious winter coat for when she walked around the
city on a day like today? A parka, a ski jacket, something
down-filled. There was plenty of casual wear, plenty of

running clothes, including fleeces and shells, but what about when she went to work? What about when she went out on errands or to dinner or ran in really cold weather? No heavy winter coat had been found on or near her body, just a fleece, which struck Marino as incongruous with the miserable weather last night.

He stepped inside the only bathroom, turning on the light. A white sink, a white tub and shower combined, a blue shower curtain with fish on it and a white liner. Several framed photographs on the white tile walls, more pictures of her running, not the same race as in the other photograph he'd looked at in the entranceway. She had on different bib numbers, must run a lot of races, must really be into it, and also into perfume, had six bottles of different fragrances on the counter, designer brands. Fendi, Giorgio Armani, Escada, and he wondered if she had gotten them in a discount store, or maybe ordered them online for seventy percent off like he had done about a month ago, shopping early for Christmas.

Only now he was thinking it was a bad idea to give Georgia Bacardi a perfume called Trouble that he'd gotten for $21.10, a huge discount because it didn't have a box. When he'd found it on eBay, it had seemed funny and flirty. Not so funny now, the two of them were having trouble, all right. So much trouble all they did was fight, their visits and phone calls less frequent, all the same warnings. History repeating itself. He'd never been in a relationship that lasted or he wouldn't be seeing Bacardi to begin with, would be happily married, maybe still be with Doris.

He opened the medicine cabinet above the sink, knowing one of the first things Scarpetta would ask was what he'd found inside it. Motrin, Midol, athletic tape, Band-Aids, sterile cushions, a friction block stick for blisters, and a lot of vitamins. There were three prescriptions, all for the same thing but filled at different times, most recently right before Thanksgiving. Diflucan. Marino was no pharmacist, but he knew about Diflucan, knew what the hell it meant if the woman he liked was on it.

Maybe Toni had a chronic problem with yeast infections, maybe she was having sex a lot, or maybe it had to do with all the jogging she did. Wearing tights or fabrics that didn't breathe, like patent leather or vinyl. Trapping moisture is the number-one enemy was what Marino had always been told, that and not washing laundry in hot enough water. He'd heard of women putting their panties in the microwave, and somebody he used to date back in his Richmond PD days had quit wearing them altogether, claiming that circulating air was the best prevention, which was fine by him. Marino took an inventory of everything in the medicine cabinet and under the sink, mostly cosmetics.

He was still in the bathroom, taking photographs, when Mellnik appeared, talking on his phone, indicating with a thumbs-up that he'd tracked down Detective Bonnell.

Marino took the phone from him and answered, "Yeah."

"What can I help you with?" A woman's voice, pleasant-sounding, low-pitched, the way Marino liked.

He didn't know Bonnell, had never heard of her before today. That wasn't necessarily surprising in a police department the size of the NYPD, some forty thousand cops, about six thousand of them detectives. Marino jerked his head at Mellnik, indicating for him to wait in the hall.

"I need some information," Marino said over the phone.

"I work with Berger and don't think you and me have met."

"I deal with ADAs directly," she said. "Which is probably why you and I have never met."

"Never heard of you. How long you been in Homicide?"

"Long enough to know better than to triangulate."

"You a mathematician?"

"If Berger wants information, she can call me."

Marino was used to people trying to bypass him to get to Berger. He was used to hearing all types of bullshit about why someone had to talk to her and couldn't possibly talk to him. Bonnell hadn't been in Homicide very long, or she wouldn't be so pushy and defensive, or maybe she'd heard rumors, had decided without benefit of directly dealing with Marino that she didn't like him.

"You know, she's a little busy right now," he said. "That's why she's got me answering questions for her, doesn't want to start her day tomorrow with a phone call from the mayor wondering what the hell she's doing to prevent further damage to the tourist industry, what's left of it. A week before Christmas a jogger in Central Park gets raped and murdered, and maybe you change your mind about bringing the wife and kids here to see the Rockettes."

"I guess she hasn't talked to you."

"Yeah, she's talked to me. Why do you think I'm in Toni Darien's apartment?"

"If Berger wants information from me, she's got my number," Bonnell said. "I'm happy to take care of whatever she needs."

"Why are you giving me the runaround?" Marino was already pissed and he hadn't been on the phone a minute yet.

"When did you talk to her last?"

"Why are you asking?" Something was going on. Something Marino didn't know about.

"Maybe it would be helpful if you'd answer my question," Bonnell said. "It works both ways. You ask me. I ask you."

"You guys hadn't even cleared the scene at the park this morning when I was talking to her. The second she was notified, she got on the phone with me, since she's in charge of this friggin' investigation." Now Marino was the one sounding defensive. "I've been on the fucking phone with her on and off all day."

Not exactly true. He'd talked to Berger three times, most recently about three hours ago.

"What I'm trying to say," Bonnell continued, "is maybe you should be talking to her again instead of talking to me."

"If I wanted to talk to her, I'd call her. I'm calling you because I've got questions. You got a problem with that?" Marino said, walking around the apartment, agitated.

"I might."

"What'd you say your first name is? And don't give me your initials."

"L.A. Bonnell."

Marino wondered what she looked like and how old she was. "Nice to meet you. I'm P.R. Marino. As in Public Relations, a special talent of mine. I'm just confirming you guys didn't take in Toni Darien's laptop and cell phone. That they weren't here when you showed up."

"They weren't. Just the chargers."

"Toni had a pocketbook or billfold? Other than a couple empty purses in her closet, I'm not seeing anything that she might have routinely carried. And I doubt she would have taken a purse or billfold with her when she was out jogging."

A pause, then, "No. Didn't see anything like that."

"Well, that's important. It would seem if she had a pocketbook, a billfold, they're missing. You collect anything in here for the labs?"

"At present we're not considering the apartment a crime scene."

"Curious why you would absolutely rule it out, categorically decide it's not connected in any shape or form. How do you know the person who killed her isn't someone she knew? Someone who's been inside her place?"

"She wasn't killed inside it, and there's no evidence it was broken into or anything's been stolen or tampered with." Bonnell said it like a press release.

"Hey. You're talking to another cop, not the fucking media," Marino said.

"The only thing unusual is her missing laptop and cell phone. And maybe her pocketbook and billfold. Okay, I agree we need to figure that out," Bonnell said in a less wooden tone. "We should get into details later, when Jaime Berger's back and we can sit down."

"Seems to me like maybe you should be more worried about Toni's apartment, maybe worried someone might have gone into it and taken these things that are missing." Marino wasn't going to let it go.

"There's nothing to say she didn't take these items somewhere herself." Bonnell definitely knew something she wasn't going to tell him over the phone. "For example, she could have had her cell phone with her when she was running in the park last night and the perpetrator took it.

Maybe when she went out running, she left from some other location, a friend's house, a boyfriend's house. Hard to know when she was home last. Hard to know a lot of things."

"You've talked to witnesses?"

"What do you think I've been doing? Hanging out at the mall?" She was getting pissed off, too.

"Like here in the building," Marino said, and after a pause that he interpreted as her unwillingness to answer, he added, "I'm going to be passing all this to Berger the minute I get off the phone from talking to you. I suggest you give me the details so I don't have to tell her I had a problem with cooperation."

"She and I don't have a problem with cooperation."

"Good. Let's keep it that way. I asked you a question. Who have you talked to?"

"A couple of witnesses," Bonnell said. "A man who lives on her floor says he saw her come in late yesterday afternoon. Said he'd just gotten home from work and was on his way out to the gym and saw Toni come up the stairs. She unlocked her apartment door while he was walking in the hallway."

"Walking in her direction?"

"There are stairs at either end of her hallway. He was taking the stairs near his apartment, not the stairs near hers."

"So he didn't get close, didn't get a good look, is what you're saying."

"We should get into the details later. Maybe when you talk to Jaime again you can tell her all of us should sit down," Bonnell answered.

"You need to be telling me the details now, and that's indirectly a directive from her," Marino said. "I'm trying to

picture what you just described. The guy saw Toni from his
end of the hallway, from about a hundred feet away. You
talked to this witness yourself?"

"An indirect directive. That's a new one. Yes, I talked to
him myself."

"His apartment number?"

"Two ten, three doors down from the victim's, on the
left. The other end of the hall."

"So I'll stop by on my way out," Marino said,
pulling out his folded report from RTCC, looking to
see who lived in apartment 210.

"Don't think he's going to be there. Told me he was on
his way out of town for a long weekend. He had a couple
of overnight bags and a plane ticket. I'm a little concerned
you're off track."

"What do you mean 'off track'?" *Goddamn it*. What
hadn't he been told?

"I mean your info and mine might be different," Bonnell
replied. "I'm trying to tell you something, one of your indirect directives, and you're not paying attention."

"Let me share. I'll tell you my info and maybe you'll tell
me yours. Graham Tourette," Marino read from the RTCC
data report. "Forty-one years old, an architect. My info is
what I find out by taking the time to look. I got no idea
where you're getting your info, but it doesn't appear to me
you're bothering to look."

"Graham Tourette is who I talked to." Bonnell wasn't as
prickly now. What she sounded was cautious.

"This Graham Tourette guy friendly with Toni?" Marino
asked.

"Said he wasn't. Said he didn't even know her name, but
he's sure he saw her go into her apartment yesterday around

six o'clock. He said she was carrying her mail. What looked like letters, magazines, and a flyer. I don't like getting into all this over the phone, and my call waiting's going crazy. I should go. When Jaime gets back, we'll sit down."

Marino hadn't said anything about Berger being out of town. It was occurring to him that Bonnell had talked to her and wasn't going to tell him what had been said. Berger and Bonnell knew something that Marino didn't.

"What flyer?" he then asked.

"A flyer on bright pink paper. He said he recognized it from a distance because everyone got one that day—yesterday."

"You check Toni's mailbox when you were here?" Marino asked.

"The super opened it for me," Bonnell said. "You've got to have a key. Her keys were in her pocket when she was found in the park. I'll put it to you this way. We've got a sensitive situation on our hands."

"Yeah, I know. Sexual homicides in Central Park tend to be sensitive situations. I saw the scene photographs, no thanks to you. Had to get them from the OCME, their death investigators. Three keys on a lucky-dice keychain that turned out not to be so lucky."

"The mailbox was empty when I checked it this morning, when I was there with CSU," Bonnell said.

"I got a home phone for this Tourette guy but no cell. Maybe e-mail me what you got on him in case I want to talk to him." Marino gave her his e-mail address. "We need to take a look at what the security camera recorded. I'm assuming the building's got one in front, or maybe there's one nearby and we can take a look at who was coming and going. I think it would be a good idea for me to talk to some of my contacts at RTCC, ask them to link to that camera live."

"What for?" Bonnell was sounding frustrated now. "We got a cop sitting in there twenty-four-seven. You think someone's going to come back for more, saying where she lived is somehow connected to her murder?"

"Never know who decides to walk past," Marino said. "Killers are curious, paranoid people. Sometimes they live across the friggin' street or are the boy next door. Who the hell knows? Point being, if RTCC can link up live with whatever security camera network is involved, we can make sure we capture the video ourselves, make sure it doesn't get accidentally recorded over. Berger will want the video, which is the bigger point. She'll want the WAV file of the nine-one-one call made by whoever discovered the body this morning."

"It wasn't just one," Bonnell replied. "Several people called as they drove past, thought they saw something. Since this has hit the news, the phones are ringing off the hook. We should talk. Let's you and me talk. You're not going to shut up, so we may as well have a face-to-face."

"We'll also be getting Toni's phone records, getting into her e-mail," Marino went on. "Hopefully there'll be some logical explanation about the cell phone, the laptop, like maybe she left them at a friend's house. Same thing with her pocketbook and billfold."

"Like I said, let's talk."

"I thought that's what we were doing." Marino wasn't going to let Bonnell call the shots. "Maybe someone will come forward, say Toni was visiting and went out for a run and never came back. We find her laptop and phone, we find her pocketbook and billfold, maybe I'll feel a little better. Because I'm not feeling so good right this minute. You happen to notice the framed picture of her on the little table when you first come through her door?" Marino stepped into the entranceway, picked up the photograph again. "She's running in a race, wearing bib number three forty-three. There are a couple others in the bathroom."

"What about them?" Bonnell said.

"She's not wearing headphones or an iPod in any of the pictures. And I'm not seeing anything like an iPod or Walkman in her apartment, either."

"And?"

"And this is what I'm talking about. The danger of having your friggin' mind made up," Marino said. "Marathon runners, people into running races, aren't allowed to listen to music. It's prohibited. When I was living in Charleston, it was front-page news when they had the Marine Corps Marathon. They threatened to disqualify the runners if they showed up with headphones."

"And this is leading to what point you're trying to make?"

"If someone came up behind you and hit you in the back of the head, maybe you'd have a better chance of hearing it coming if you weren't listening to music full blast. And it would appear that Toni Darien didn't listen to music when she ran. Yet someone managed to come up behind her and whack her in the back of the head without her even turning around. That bother you at all?"

"You don't know that the killer didn't confront her and she turned away, ducked, or whatever to protect her face," Bonnell said. "And she wasn't hit exactly in the back of the head, sort of on the left side, behind her left ear. So maybe she'd started turning around, was reacting, but it was too late. Maybe you're making some assumptions because you're missing information."

"Usually when people react and try to protect themselves, their reflex is to raise their arms, their hands, and then they get defense injuries," Marino said. "She doesn't have any in the scene photos I've looked at, but I've not talked to Scarpetta yet, and when I do I'll confirm. It's like Toni Darien had no idea and suddenly was on the ground. That seems a little unusual for someone running after dark, someone who maybe is used to being aware of her surroundings because she runs a lot and doesn't wear headphones."

"She was running in a race last night? What makes you think she never wore headphones? Maybe she had them on last night and the killer took her iPod, her Walkman."

"Everything I know about serious runners is they don't wear headphones whether they're in a race or not, especially in the city. Just look around. Tell me any serious runners you see in New York who are wearing headphones so they can drift in the bike lane or get run over by drivers not paying attention or get mugged from behind."

"You a runner?"

"Look. I don't know what information you have that you're obviously not sharing, but my information from eyeballing what's under my nose is we should be careful about jumping to conclusions when we don't know jack shit," Marino said.

"I agree. The same thing I'm trying to convey to you, P.R. Marino."

"What's L.A. stand for?"

"Other than a city in California, nothing. You want to call me by something other than Bonnell or asshole, you can call me L.A."

Marino smiled. Maybe she wasn't hopeless. "Tell you what, L.A.," he said. "I was going to head to High Roller Lanes in a few minutes. Why don't you meet me there. You bowl?"

"I think you have to have an IQ less than sixty or they won't rent you shoes."

"More like seventy. I'm pretty good," Marino said. "And I got my own shoes."

3

Scarpetta wasn't surprised that Marino had been trying to get hold of her today. She had two voicemails from him, and a few minutes ago he'd sent an instant message riddled with its typical typos and almost indecipherable abbreviations and complete lack of punctuation or capitalization unless it was done automatically by his BlackBerry. He'd yet to figure out how to insert symbols or spaces or more likely couldn't be bothered:

```
Berger OOT as you no but bak this pm
will want dets re Darien and I have some
to ad and a lot of quests so dall
```

Marino was reminding Scarpetta that Jaime Berger was out of town. Yes, Scarpetta was well aware. When Berger was back in New York tonight, Marino's hieroglyphics went on, she would expect to know autopsy results and any details about evidence Scarpetta might be aware of, since it would be Berger's Sex Crimes Unit that was in charge of the case. Fine. Scarpetta certainly didn't need to be told that, either. Marino was also indicating he had information and questions, and when she got a chance to call him. Also fine, because she had a lot to tell him, too.

She attempted to message him back as she walked into her office, annoyed all over again with the BlackBerry Lucy had bought for her two weeks ago. It was a thoughtful and generous surprise that Scarpetta considered a Trojan horse, something wheeled into the backyard that held nothing but trouble. Her niece had decided that Berger, Marino, Benton, and Scarpetta should have the same latest, greatest personal digital assistant that Lucy did and had taken it upon herself to set up an enterprise server, or what she described as a two-way authenticated environment with triple data encryption and firewall protection.

The new handheld device had a touch screen, a camera, a video recorder, a GPS, a media player, wireless e-mail, instant messaging—in other words, more multimedia capabilities than Scarpetta had time or interest to figure out. She wasn't on good diplomatic relations with her smartphone so far and was quite certain it was smarter than she was. She paused to type on the LCD display with her thumbs, every other keystroke needing to be deleted and retyped because, unlike Marino, she didn't send messages replete with errors:

```
Will call later. Have to meet with the
chief. We have problems—have things on
hold.
```

That was as specific as she intended to get, having a huge distrust of instant messaging but increasingly unable to avoid doing it because everybody else did these days.

Inside her office, the stale aroma of her cheeseburger and fries was revolting, her lunch well on its way to being of archaeological interest. Tossing the box, she set the trash can outside the door and began to close the blinds in the windows overlooking the OCME's granite front steps, where family and friends of the patients who ended up here often sat when they couldn't bear to wait in the lobby. She paused, watching Grace Darien get into the back of a dirty white Dodge Charger, a little less shaky but still disoriented and shocked.

At the viewing, she had almost passed out, and Scarpetta had returned her to the family room, where she'd sat with her for quite a while, making her a cup of hot tea, taking care of her as best she could until she felt it was safe for the distraught woman to leave. Scarpetta wondered what Mrs. Darien would do. She hoped the friend who had driven her would stay close, that Mrs. Darien wouldn't be left alone. Perhaps colleagues at her hospital would take care of her and her sons would get to Islip quickly. Maybe she and her ex-husband would put an end to their battle over the disposition of their murdered daughter's remains and belongings, decide life was too short for bitterness and strife.

Scarpetta sat at her desk, really an improvised work station surrounding her on three sides, and nearby were two metal file cabinets that served as a stand for her printer and a fax machine. Behind her was a table for her Olympus BX41 microscope, attached to a fiber-optic illuminator and a video camera so she could view slides and evidence on a monitor while capturing the images electronically or printing them on photographic paper. Within easy reach was an assortment of old friends: *Cecil*

Textbook of Medicine, Robbins Pathology, The Merck Manual, Saferstein, Schlesinger, Petraco, and a few other things she'd carried in from home to keep her company. A dissecting kit from her medical-school days at Johns Hopkins and other collectibles reminded her of the long tradition in forensic medicine that preceded her. Brass scales and a mortar and pestle. Apothecary bottles and jars. A Civil War field surgical kit. A compound microscope from the late eighteen-hundreds. An assortment of police caps and pins.

She tried Benton's cell phone. It went straight to voicemail, which usually meant he had it turned off, was someplace he couldn't use it, in this instance, the men's prison ward at Bellevue, where he was a consulting forensic psychologist. She tried his office, and her heart felt lighter when he answered.

"You're still there," she said. "Want to share a cab?"

"You trying to pick me up?"

"Rumor has it you're pretty easy. I need about an hour, need to talk to Dr. Edison first. What's it look like for you?"

"An hour should work." He sounded subdued. "I need to have a conference with my chief, too."

"You okay?" She wedged the phone between her shoulder and chin, and logged in to her e-mail.

"There may be a dragon I need to slay." His familiar voice, baritone and soothing, but she detected the flinty edge of anxiety and anger. She'd detected it a lot of late.

"I thought you were supposed to be helping dragons, not slaying them," she said. "You probably won't tell me about it."

"You're right. I won't," he replied.

He was saying he couldn't. Benton must be having problems with a patient, and it seemed to be a trend. For the past month, Scarpetta had gotten the impression he was avoiding McLean, the Harvard-affiliated psychiatric hospital in Belmont, Massachusetts, where he was on staff and where they had their home. He'd been acting more stressed and distracted than usual, as if something was really eating at him, something he didn't want to say, suggesting that legally he couldn't. Scarpetta knew when to inquire and when to leave it alone, having grown accustomed long ago to how little Benton could share.

The lives they led, filled with secrets like rooms that held as much shadow as light. Their long pilgrimage together was mapped by independent detours and destinations not always known to each other, but as difficult as it was for her, in many ways it was worse for him. There were few occasions when it was unethical for her to have case discussions with her forensic psychologist husband and seek his opinion and advice, but rarely could she return the favor. Benton's patients were alive and enjoyed certain rights and privileges that Scarpetta's dead patients didn't. Unless someone was a danger to himself or others or convicted of a crime, Benton couldn't discuss the person with Scarpetta without violating patient confidentiality.

"At some point we need to talk about when we're going home." Benton had turned to the topic of the holidays and a life in Massachusetts that was becoming increasingly distant. "Justine's wondering if she should decorate the house. Maybe string a few white lights in the trees."

"Good idea if it looks like someone's there, I suppose," Scarpetta said, skimming through e-mail. "Keeps the burglars away, and based on everything I hear, burglaries and robberies are going through the roof. Let's do some lights. In the boxwoods, maybe just on either side of the front door and in the garden."

"I take that as a no to doing anything else."

"With what's going on here," she said, "I have no idea where we'll be in a week. I've got a really bad case, and people are fighting."

"I'm making a note of it. Lights to scare away the burglars. The rest, why bother."

"I'll pick up a few amaryllises for the apartment, maybe a tiny fir tree we can replant," she said. "And hopefully we can get home for a few days if that's what you want."

"I don't know what I want. Maybe we should just plan on staying here. Then it's not a question anymore. How about that? Deal? Have we decided? Put together a dinner or something? Jaime and Lucy. And Marino, I guess."

"You guess."

"Sure. If you want him."

Benton wasn't going to say he wanted Marino. He didn't. No point in pretending.

"Deal," she said, but she didn't feel good about it. "We'll stay in New York." She started feeling really bad about it, now that it was decided.

She thought of their two-story bungalow-style house, built in 1910, a simple harmony of timber, plaster, and stone that reminded her daily of how much she adored Frank Lloyd Wright. For an instant she missed her big kitchen with its commercial-grade stainless-steel appliances. She missed the master bedroom with its deep-set skylights and exposed-brick flue.

"Either way. Here or home," she added. "As long as we're together."

"Let me ask you something," Benton said. "You haven't gotten any unusual communications, like maybe a greeting card, maybe something sent to your office in Massachusetts or the OCME here in New York or maybe to CNN?"

"A greeting card? From anybody in particular?"

"Just wondering if you've gotten anything unusual."

"E-mails, e-cards, mostly what I get from strangers is sent to CNN, and fortunately, other people go through it."

"I don't mean fan mail, exactly. I mean like a talking or singing card. Not an e-card. A real one," he said.

"Sounds like you have someone in mind."

"It's just a question." He had someone in mind. A patient. Maybe the dragon he had to slay.

"No," she said, opening an e-mail from the chief. *Good.* He was in his office, would be until five.

"We don't need to discuss it." Meaning Benton wasn't going to discuss it. "Call me when you're ready to leave and I'll meet you out front," he said. "I've missed you today."

Benton pulled on a pair of cotton examination gloves and removed a FedEx pouch and a Christmas card from the plastic evidence bag he had tucked them in earlier today.

It disturbed him that the unseemly holiday greeting had been sent to him here at Bellevue. How could Dodie Hodge, who had been discharged from McLean five days ago, know Benton was at Bellevue right now? How did she have any idea where he was, for that matter? Benton had considered a number of possibilities, had been obsessing about them all day, the specter of Dodie bringing out the cop in him, not the mental health practitioner.

He supposed it was possible she had seen the commercials on TV about Scarpetta's live appearance on *The Crispin Report* tonight and had assumed Benton would accompany his wife, especially this close to the holidays. Dodie might then deduce that if he was going to be in the city, he'd drop by Bellevue, at least check his mail. It was also possible that her psychiatric condition was deteriorating now that she was home, that her insomnia had worsened, or that she simply wasn't getting the fix of excitement she craved. But no explanation Benton had come up with satisfied him, and as hours had passed, he'd become more unsettled and vigilant, not less. He worried that Dodie's disturbing gesture was out of character, not what he would have predicted, and that she might not have acted alone. And he worried about himself. It seemed she had awakened certain inclinations and behaviors in him that were unacceptable to his profession. Not that he'd been himself of late. Because he hadn't been.

The card's red envelope was blank, nothing on it, not Benton's name or Scarpetta's or Dodie Hodge's. That much was consistent with what he knew about her, at least. While she was at McLean she'd refused to write. She'd refused to draw. At first she'd claimed she was shy. Then she decided the medication she was taking during her hospitalization had caused tremors and impaired her coordination, making it impossible for her to copy the simplest sequence of geometric designs or connect numbers in a certain order or sort cards or manipulate blocks.

For almost a month, all she had done was act out, stir up trouble, complain, lecture, advise, pry, lie, and talk to anyone who would listen, sometimes at the top of her lungs. She couldn't get enough of her self-aggrandizing dramas and magical thinking, was the star in her own movie and her own biggest fan.

There was no personality disorder Benton dreaded more than the histrionic, and from the moment of Dodie's arrest in Detroit, Michigan, for misdemeanor petty theft and disorderly conduct, it had been the goal of all involved to get her psychiatric care and as far away from them as possible. No one wanted anything to do with this bombastic woman who was shrieking and wailing in Betty's Bookstore Café that she was the aunt of movie star Hap Judd, that she was on his "free list" and therefore it wasn't stealing to stuff four of his action movie DVDs into the front of her pants. Even Betty herself was happy to drop the charges as long as Dodie never stepped foot in her store again or in Detroit or the state of Michigan. The deal was that Dodie had to be hospitalized for a minimum of three weeks, and if she complied, the case would go away.

She had cooperated with the stipulation that she was to be admitted to McLean because it was where VIPs, the rich and famous, go and was convenient to her estate in Greenwich, Connecticut, and also to Salem, where she liked to shop in various witcheries and do readings and rituals for hire and offer for a price the gifts of The Craft. She insisted that for the amount of money her private hospitalization would cost her, she was to be paired with the most established and prominent forensic expert available, a male with at minimum a Ph.D. and a background with the FBI, in addition to an open mind about the supernatural and a tolerance of other faiths, including the Old Religion.

Dodie's first choice was the forensic psychiatrist Dr. Warner Agee because he was a former FBI profiler, according to her, and on TV. The request was denied. For one thing, Agee had no affiliation with McLean, and for another, the Detroit DA's office wanted no association with the Dr. Phil of forensics, as they referred to him. Agee's name being introduced into the mix was enough to send Benton the other way, no matter who the patient was—he despised the man that much. But Benton had a professional obligation to McLean, and it was his bad luck to be the obvious candidate for the onerous assignment of evaluating this woman who claimed to be a witch with ties to celebrity. The goal was to keep her out of court and out of jail—not that any jail on the planet would want her.

During the four weeks she had been a patient, Benton had spent as much time as possible in New York, not only to be with Scarpetta but to be away from Dodie. He'd been so relieved when she was discharged this past Sunday afternoon, he'd checked several times to make sure she'd actually been picked up and driven home, not to an estate in Greenwich, because that was another lie. She'd been deposited at a small house in Edgewater, New Jersey, where she apparently lived alone, having gone through four husbands, all dead or having fled years ago. Poor bastards.

Benton picked up the phone and dialed the extension of Bellevue's chief of forensic psychiatry, Dr. Nathan Clark, and asked if he had a minute. While Benton waited, he looked at the FedEx envelope again, certain details continuing to perplex and concern him and prompt him to act in ways he knew he shouldn't. There was no return address on the airbill, and his address here at Bellevue was handwritten in a functional calligraphy that was so precise it looked like a printed typeface. Not at all what he would have expected from someone like Dodie, whose only writing while she'd been at McLean was a large, looping scrawl when she'd had to sign her name on various forms. He slid the thick glossy card out of its envelope, a big fat Santa on the front of it being chased by a furious rolling pin-wielding Mrs. Claus, and the caption "Who Are You Calling a Ho!" He opened the card and Dodie Hodge's recorded off-key voice began to sing, to the tune of "A Holly, Jolly Christmas":

Have a Ho-Dee, Do-Dee Christmas
And When You Think of Me
Stick Some Mistletoe Where It Ought to Go
And Hang an Angel from Your Tree
Merry, Merry Christmas, Benton and Kay!

Over and over, the same maddening lyrics and greeting in her childish, breathy voice.

"Not exactly Burl Ives," Dr. Clark said as he walked in with his coat, his hat, his beat-up leather satchel with its long strap that reminded Benton of a mailbag from the days of the pony express and covered wagons.

"If you can stand it, it will keep going until the recording time runs out," Benton said. "Exactly four minutes."

Dr. Clark placed his belongings in a chair and came over to where Benton sat, leaning close to get a look at the card, steadying himself by placing both hands on the edge of the desk. In his early seventies, he'd recently been diagnosed with Parkinson's disease, a cruel punishment for a gifted man whose body had always been as agile as his mind. Tennis, skiing, mountain climbing, piloting his own plane—there wasn't much he hadn't tried and succeeded at, his love of life boundless. He'd been cheated by biology, by genetics, by the environment, maybe something as mundane as exposure to lead paint or old plumbing that had caused free-radical damage to the basal ganglia of his remarkable brain. Who the hell knew how he'd ended up with such a scourge. But it was advancing rapidly. Already he was stooped, his movements retarded and clumsy.

Benton closed the card, and Dodie's voice abruptly stopped mid-lyric. "Homemade, obviously," he said. "The typical talking card has a recording time of as little as ten seconds, maybe as long as forty-five, but not four minutes. From what I understand, the way you create a longer recording is to buy a bare voice module that has more memory. You can order them on the Internet, then basically build your own greeting card. Which is what this particular former patient of mine did. Or someone did it for her."

He picked up the card in his white cotton-gloved hands and turned it at different angles so Dr. Clark could see the edges, see how it had been pieced together with exactness and care.

"She found this greeting card, or someone did," Benton continued to explain, "and made her recording on a module, which was glued to the inside, then a square of paper was glued over it, possibly the blank side of another greeting card that was cut out. Which is why the inside of her card is completely blank. She didn't write anything on it. She didn't write anything the entire time she was at McLean. She says she doesn't write."

"Graphophobic?"

"That and medication, so she says."

"A perfectionist who can't cope with criticism." Dr. Clark went around to the other side of the desk.

"A malingerer."

"Ah. A factitious disorder. For what motive?" Already Dr. Clark wasn't trusting what Benton was saying.

"Money and attention are her two strongest motivating forces. But maybe there's something else," Benton said. "I'm beginning to wonder who and what we had at McLean for a month. And why."

Dr. Clark sat slowly, carefully, the smallest physical act no longer taken for granted by him. Benton noticed how much his colleague had aged just since the summer.

"I'm sorry to bother you about this," Benton added. "I know you're busy."

"Never a bother, Benton. I've missed talking to you and have been thinking I should call. I've been wondering how you are." Dr. Clark said it as if they had things to talk about and Benton had been elusive. "So she refused pencil-and-paper tests."

"Wouldn't do the Bender-Gestalt, Rey-Osterrieth Complex Figure drawing, digit symbol substitution, letter cancellation, not even trail making," Benton said. "Nothing that required her to write or draw."

"What about psychomotor function tests?"

"No block designs or grooved pegboard, no finger tapping."

"Interesting. Nothing that measures reaction time."

"Her latest excuse was the medication she was taking,

said it gave her tremors, caused her hands to shake so badly she couldn't hold a pen and she didn't want to humiliate herself by trying to write or draw or manipulate objects." Benton couldn't help but think of Dr. Clark's own condition as he explained Dodie Hodge's alleged complaints.

"Nothing that requires her to physically perform on demand, nothing that might, in her mind, invite criticism, judgment. She doesn't want to be scored." Dr. Clark stared out the window behind Benton's head, as if there was something to look at besides beige hospital brick and the encroaching night. "What medication?"

"My guess, nothing now. She's not exactly compliant and has no interest in substances unless they make her feel good. Alcohol, for example. While she was hospitalized, she was taking Risperdal."

"Which can cause tardive dyskinesia. But atypically," Dr. Clark considered.

"She wasn't having muscle spasms or twitches except ones she faked," Benton said. "Of course, she claims her condition is permanent."

"Theoretically a possible permanent side effect from Risperdal, especially in older women."

"In her case, it's malingering, it's bullshit. She has some agenda," Benton repeated. "Thank God I followed my instincts, mandated that all of my sessions with her be recorded on video."

"And how did she feel about that?"

"She dressed the part. Whatever character came to mind, whatever her mood. Seductress or Salvation Army or Strega."

"Do you fear she could be violent?" Dr. Clark asked.

"She has violent preoccupations, claims to have recovered

memories of satanic cult abuse, her father killing children on stone altars and having sexual intercourse with her. No evidence that any such thing ever occurred."

"And what evidence might there be?"

Benton didn't answer. He wasn't allowed to check on a patient's veracity. He wasn't supposed to investigate. It was so counterintuitive for him to operate this way, it was almost intolerable, and the boundaries were blurring.

"Doesn't like to write but likes drama," Dr. Clark said, watching him closely.

"Drama is the common denominator," Benton said, and he knew Dr. Clark was already on the road to truth.

He sensed what Benton had done—or that he had done something. It occurred to Benton that subconsciously he'd orchestrated the conversation about Dodie because he really needed to talk about himself.

"Her insatiable need for drama and a sleep disturbance she's suffered from most of her life," Benton went on. "She was tested in the sleep lab at McLean and apparently has participated in a number of actigraphy studies over the years, clearly has a circadian rhythm disorder, suffers from chronic insomnia. The worse it gets, the poorer her judgment and insight, the more chaotic her lifestyle. Her fund of knowledge is extraordinarily good. She's within the bright-superior range of intelligence."

"Any improvement on the Risperdal?"

"Her mood was somewhat stabilized, not as hypomanic, reported that she was sleeping better."

"If she's stopped her medication, she's likely getting worse. How old?" Dr. Clark asked.

"Fifty-six."

"Bipolar? Schizophrenic?"

"Would be more treatable if she was. Axis-two personality disorder, histrionic with borderline and antisocial traits."

"Lovely. And why was she prescribed Risperdal?"

"On admission last month, she seemed to be suffering from delusions and false beliefs, but in fact, she's a pathological liar." Benton went on to give a brief history of Dodie's arrest in Detroit.

"Any chance she'll accuse you of violating her civil rights, claim the hospitalization was against her will, that she was coerced and forced to take a medication that permanently impaired her?" Dr. Clark asked.

"She signed a conditional voluntary, was given a civil rights packet and notice of her rights to legal consultation and all the rest. At the moment, it's not litigation I'm concerned about, Nathan."

"I didn't suppose you're wearing examination gloves because you're afraid of being sued."

Benton returned the card and its FedEx pouch back inside the evidence bag and resealed it. He pulled off his gloves and dropped them in the trash.

"When was she discharged from McLean?" Dr. Clark asked.

"This past Sunday afternoon."

"Did you interview her, talk to her before she left?"

"Two days earlier on that Friday I did," Benton said.

"And she gave you no token of affection, no holiday greeting at that time, when she could actually have done so in person and experienced the gratification of watching your reaction?"

"She didn't. She talked about Kay."

"I see."

Of course he did. He knew damn well the sorts of things Benton had to worry about.

Dr. Clark said, "Possible Dodie selected McLean because she knew a priori that you, the prominent husband of the prominent Kay Scarpetta, are on staff there? Possible Dodie chose McLean so she could spend some quality time with you?"

"I wasn't her first choice."

"Who was?"

"Someone else."

"Anyone I might know?" Dr. Clark asked, as if he had a suspicion.

"You'd know the name."

"Possible you have doubts that her first choice was really her first choice, since Dodie's motives and truthfulness seem to be a question? Was McLean her first choice?"

"McLean was."

"That's significant, since some other *first choices* might not have privileges there, not unless they're on staff."

"Which is what happened," Benton said.

"She have money?"

"Allegedly from all the husbands she's been through. She stayed in the Pavilion, which is self-pay, as you know. She paid in cash. Well, her lawyer did."

"What is that now? Three thousand a day?"

"Something like that."

"She paid more than ninety thousand dollars in cash."

"A deposit upon admission, then the balance in full when she was discharged. A bank wire transfer. Done through her Detroit lawyer," Benton said.

"She live in Detroit?"

"No."

"But she has a lawyer there."

"So it appears," Benton said.

"What was she doing in Detroit? Besides getting arrested."

"Says she was visiting. On vacation. Staying at the Grand Palais," Benton said. "Working her magic on the slot machines and roulette table."

"She's a big gambler?"

"She'll sell you a few lucky amulets, if you'd like."

"You seem to dislike her rather intensely," Dr. Clark observed with the same keen look in his eyes.

"I'm not stating as a fact that I didn't factor into her choice of hospitals. Or that Kay didn't," Benton replied.

"What I'm hearing is you've begun to fear it," Dr. Clark said, taking off his glasses, cleaning them with his gray silk tie. "Any chance that events of late are making you anxious and disproportionately suspicious of those around you?"

"Any particular events you're thinking of?"

"Why don't you tell me," Dr. Clark said.

"I'm not paranoid."

"Which is what all paranoid people say."

"I'll interpret that as your special vintage of dry humor," Benton said.

"How are you doing? Besides this? Been a lot going on, hasn't there," Dr. Clark said. "A lot happening all at once this past month."

"There's always a lot going on."

"Kay's been on TV and in the public eye." Dr. Clark put his glasses back on. "So has Warner Agee."

Benton had been anticipating for a while that Dr. Clark was going to say something about Agee. Benton probably had been avoiding Dr. Clark. Not probably. He had been. Until today.

"It's occurred to me that you must have a reaction to seeing Warner in the news, this man who sabotaged your career with the FBI, sabotaged your entire life because he wanted to be you," Dr. Clark said. "Now he's publicly playing the role of you—metaphorically speaking—taking on the persona of the forensic expert, the FBI profiler, at last his chance for stardom."

"There are a lot of people who make claims that are exaggerated or untrue."

"Have you read his bio on Wikipedia?" Dr. Clark asked. "He's cited as one of the founding fathers of profiling and your mentor. It says during the period you were at the FBI Academy, the unit chief of Behavioral Science, and just beginning your adulterous affair, and I quote, with Kay Scarpetta, he worked a number of notorious cases with her. Is it true he worked with Kay? It's my understanding Warner was never a profiler for the FBI or anyone else."

"I didn't realize you considered Wikipedia a reliable source," Benton said, as if Dr. Clark was the one spreading these lies.

"I took a look because often the anonymous individuals who contribute alleged factual information to online encyclopedias and other Internet sites also happen to have a vested and not so unbiased interest in the subject they're stealthily writing about," Dr. Clark said. "Curiously, it appears that in the past few weeks, his bio has been heavily edited and expanded. I wonder by whom?"

"Perhaps by the person it's about." Benton's stomach was tight with resentment and rage.

"I imagine Lucy could find that out or already knows and could have this misinformation removed," Dr. Clark said. "But maybe she hasn't thought to check on certain details the way I have because you haven't shared with her what you've shared with me about your past."

"There are better things to spend our time on than limited individuals desperately seeking attention. Lucy doesn't need to waste her forensic computer investigative resources on Internet gossip. You're right. I haven't told her everything I've told you." Benton couldn't remember the last time he'd felt this threatened.

"If you hadn't called me this afternoon, it wouldn't have been long before I would have trumped up some reason to talk to you so we could get it out on the table," Dr. Clark said. "You have every reason to want to destroy Warner Agee. I have every reason to hope you'll get over wanting that."

"I don't see what this has to do with what we were talking about, Nathan."

"Everything has to do with everything, Benton." Watching him, reading him. "But let's return to the subject of your former patient Dodie Hodge, because I have a feeling she's connected anyway. I'm struck by a number of things. The first being the card itself, the obvious suggestion of domestic violence, of a man degrading a woman by calling her a whore, the wife chasing the husband with the intent of beating him with a rolling pin, the sexual overtones. In other words, one of those jokes that isn't funny. What is she saying to you?"

"Projection." Benton had to will his fury toward Warner Agee to leave the room. "It's what she's projecting," he heard himself say in a reasonable tone.

"All right. What is she projecting, in your view? Who is Santa? Who is Mrs. Claus?"

"I'm Santa," Benton said, and the wave was passing. It had seemed as big as a tsunami and then receded and was almost gone. He relaxed a little. "Mrs. Claus is hostile toward me for something she perceives I did that was unkind and degrading. I, Santa, said, 'ho, ho, ho,' and Mrs. Claus interpreted it as my calling her a whore."

"Dodie Hodge perceives that she is falsely accused, degraded, unappreciated, trivialized. Yet she knows her perception is false," Dr. Clark said. "That's the histrionic personality disorder kicking in. The obvious message of the card is poor Santa is about to take a drubbing because Mrs. Claus grossly misunderstood what he said, and obviously Dodie gets the joke or she wouldn't have picked the card."

"Assuming she picked it."

"You keep alluding to that. To the possibility she might have had some help. Possibly an accomplice."

"The technical part of it," Benton said. "Knowing about the recorders, ordering them, assembling the damn thing. Dodie's impulsive and seeks instant gratification. There's a degree of deliberation that is inconsistent with what I saw when she was at the hospital. And when did she have time? As I said, she was discharged just this past Sunday. The FedEx was sent yesterday, Wednesday. How did she know to send it here? The handwritten address on the FedEx label is odd. The whole thing is odd."

"She craves drama, and the singing card is dramatic. You don't think that's consistent with her histrionic proclivities?"

"You yourself pointed out she didn't witness the drama," Benton said. "Drama's no fun if there's no audience. She didn't see me open the card, doesn't know for a fact I did. Why not give it to me before she was discharged, do it in person?"

"So someone else put her up to it. Her accomplice."

"The lyrics bother me," Benton said.

"Which part?"

"Stick mistletoe where it ought to go and hang an angel from your tree," Benton said.

"Who's the angel?"

"You tell me."

"It could be Kay." Dr. Clark held his gaze. " 'Your tree' could be a reference to your penis, to your sexual relationship with your wife."

"And an allusion to a lynching," Benton said.

4

The chief medical examiner of New York City was bent over his microscope when Scarpetta lightly knocked on his open door.

"You know what happens when you absent yourself from a staff meeting, don't you?" Dr. Brian Edison said without looking up as he moved a slide on the stage. "You get talked about."

"I don't want to know." Scarpetta walked into his office and sat in an elbow chair on the other side of his partner's desk.

"Well, I should qualify. The topic of discussion wasn't about you, per se." He swiveled around so he faced her, his white hair unruly, his eyes intense, hawklike. "But tangentially. CNN, TLC, Discovery, every cable network under the sun. You know how many calls we get each day?"

"I'm sure you could hire an extra secretary for that alone."

"When in fact we're having to let people go. Support staff, technicians. We've cut back on janitorial services and security," he said. "Lord knows where it will end if the state does what it threatens and slashes our budget by another thirty percent. We're not in the entertainment business. Don't want to be, can't afford to be."

"I'm sorry if I'm causing problems, Brian."

He was probably the finest forensic pathologist Scarpetta personally knew and was perfectly clear about his mission, which was somewhat different from hers, and there was no way around it. He viewed forensic medicine as a public health service and had no use for the media in any manifestation beyond its role of informing the public about matters of life and death, such as hazards and communicable diseases, whether it was a potentially deadly crib design or an outbreak of the hantavirus. It wasn't that his perception was wrong. It was simply that everything else was. The world had changed, and not necessarily for the better.

"I'm trying to navigate my way along a road I didn't choose," Scarpetta said. "You walk the highest of roads in a world of low roads. So, what do we do?"

"Stoop to their level?"

"I hope you don't think that's what I'm doing."

"How do you feel about your career with CNN?" He picked up a briarwood pipe that he was no longer allowed to puff inside the building.

"I certainly don't think of it as a career," she said. "It's something I do to disseminate information in a way that I deem is necessary in this day and age."

"If you can't beat 'em, join 'em."

"I'll stop if you want, Brian. I've told you that from the start. I would never do anything, at least not intentionally, to embarrass this office or compromise it in the slightest."

"Well, we don't need to go round and around this topic again," he said. "In theory, I don't disagree with you, Kay. The public is as badly misinformed about criminal justice and all things forensic as it has ever been. And yes, it's fouling up crime scenes and court cases and legislation and where tax dollars are allocated. But in my heart I don't believe that appearing on any of these shows is going to solve the problem. Of course, that's me, and I'm rather set in my ways and from time to time feel compelled to remind you of the Indian burial grounds you must step around. Hannah Starr being one of them."

"I assume that was the point of the discussion at the staff meeting. The discussion that wasn't about me, per se," Scarpetta replied.

"I don't watch these shows." He idly toyed with the pipe. "But the Carley Crispins, the Warner Agees of the world, seem to have made Hannah Starr their hobbyhorse, the next Caylee Anthony or Anna Nicole Smith. Or God forbid you're asked about our murdered jogger when you're on TV tonight."

"The agreement with CNN is I don't talk about active cases."

"What about your agreement with this Crispin woman? She doesn't seem to be known for playing by the rules, and it will be her shooting off her mouth live on the air tonight."

"I've been asked to discuss microscopy, specifically the analysis of hair," Scarpetta said.

"That's good, probably helpful. I do know a number of our colleagues in the labs are worried their scientific disciplines are fast being viewed as nonessential because the public, the politicians, think DNA is the magic lamp. If we rub it enough, all problems are solved and the hell with fibers, hair, toxicology, questioned documents, even fingerprints." Dr. Edison placed his pipe back in an ashtray that hadn't been dirty in years. "We're comfortable with Toni Darien's identification, I presume. I know the police want to release that information to the public."

"I have no problem with releasing her name, but I certainly don't intend to release any details about my findings. I'm worried her crime scene was staged, that she wasn't murdered where she was found and may not have been jogging when she was assaulted."

"Based on?"

"A number of things. She was struck on the back of the head, one blow to the posterior aspect of the left temporal bone." Scarpetta touched her head to show him. "A survival time possibly of hours, as evidenced by the large fluctuant and boggy mass, and the hemorrhagic edematous tissues underneath the scalp. Then at some point after she died, a scarf was tied around her neck."

"Ideas about the weapon?"

"A circular comminuted fracture that pushed multiple bone fragments into the brain. Whatever she was hit with has at least one round surface that is fifty millimeters in diameter."

"Not punched out but fragmented," he considered. "So, we're not talking about something like a hammer, not something round with a flat surface. And not something like a baseball bat if the surface is fifty millimeters and round. About the size of a billiard ball. Curious as to what that might have been."

"I think she's been dead since Tuesday," Scarpetta said.

"She was beginning to decompose?"

"Not at all. But her livor was set, the pattern consistent with her being on her back for quite some time after death, at least twelve hours, unclothed, with her arms by her sides, palms down. That's not the way she was found, not the way her body was positioned in the park. She was on her back, but her arms were up above her head, slightly bent at the elbows, as if she might have been dragged or pulled by her wrists."

"Rigor?" he asked.

"Easily broken when I tried to move her limbs. In other words, rigor had been full and was beginning to pass. Again, that takes time."

"She wouldn't have been difficult to manipulate, to move, and I assume that's what you're implying. That her body was dumped in the park, which would be rather difficult to do if she was stiff," he said. "Any drying? What you might expect if she'd been somewhere cool that had kept her well preserved for a day or two?"

"Some drying of her fingers, her lips, and tache noir—her eyes were slightly open, and the conjunctiva was brown due to drying. Her axillary temp was fifty degrees," Scarpetta continued. "The low last night was thirty-four; the high during the day was forty-seven. The mark left by the scarf is a superficial circumferential dry brown abrasion. There's no suffusion, no petechia of the face or conjunctiva. The tongue wasn't protruding."

"Postmortem, then," Dr. Edison concluded. "Was the scarf tied at an angle?"

"No. Mid-throat." She showed him on her own neck. "Tied in a double knot in front, which I didn't cut through, of course. I removed it by cutting through it from the back. There was no vital response whatsoever, and that was true internally, as well. The hyoid, thyroid, and strap muscles were intact and free of injury."

"Underscoring your speculation that she might have been murdered in one location and dumped where she was found, at the edge of the park, in plain view during daylight, perhaps so she would be found quickly this morning when people were up and out," he said. "Evidence she might have been bound at some point? What about sexual assault?"

"No contusions or impressions from bindings that I could see. No defense injuries," Scarpetta said. "I found two contusions on the inner aspect of each upper thigh. The posterior fourchette shows superficial abrasion with very slight bleeding and adjacent contusion. The labia are reddened. No secretions visible at the introitus or in the vaginal vault, but she has an irregular abrasion of the posterior wall. I collected a PERK."

She referred to a Physical Evidence Recovery Kit, which included swabs for DNA.

"I also examined her with a forensic light and collected whatever was there, including fibers, mostly from her hair," she went on. "A lot of dust and debris in her head hair, which I shaved at the edges of the laceration. Under a hand lens I could see several flecks of paint, some embedded in the depths of the wound. Bright red, bright yellow, black. We'll see what trace says. I'm encouraging everyone in the labs to expedite things as much as possible."

"I believe you always tell them that."

"Another detail of interest. Her socks were on the wrong feet," Scarpetta said.

"How can socks be on the wrong feet? Do you mean inside out?"

"Running socks are designed anatomically correctly for the right and left feet, and actually designated as such. An *L* on the left sock, an *R* on the right. Hers were on backwards, right sock on the left foot and left sock on the right."

"Possible she did that herself, didn't notice when she was getting dressed?" Dr. Edison was putting on his suit jacket.

"Possible, of course. But if she was that particular about her running attire, would she put her socks on the wrong feet? And would she be out running in the rain and cold and not wearing gloves, not wearing anything to keep her ears warm, and no coat, just a fleece? Mrs. Darien says Toni hated running in bad weather. She also can't account for the unusual watch Toni had on. An oversized black plastic digital watch with the name BioGraph stamped on it, possibly collects some type of data."

"You Google it?" Dr. Edison got up from his desk.

"And had Lucy do a search. She'll look into it further after DNA's done with it. So far no such watch or device called a BioGraph, it appears. I'm hoping one of Toni's doctors or someone else she knew might have an idea why she was wearing it and what it is."

"You do realize your part-time is turning into full-time." He picked up his briefcase and retrieved his coat from the back of the door. "I don't think you've been back to Massachusetts once this entire month."

"It's been a little busy here." She got up and started collecting her belongings.

"Who's running your railroad there?"

"The train tracks are fast leading back to Boston," she said as she put on her coat and they walked out together. "A repeat of the old days, which is a shame. My northeastern district office in Watertown will be shut down, probably by summer. As if the Boston office isn't over-whelmed enough."

"And Benton's going back and forth."

"The shuttle," Scarpetta said. "Sometimes Lucy gives him a lift on her helicopter. He's been here a lot."

"Nice of her to help out with the watch, the BioGraph. We can't afford her computer skills. But when DNA's done with it and if Jaime Berger agrees, if there's some sort of data in whatever the device is, I'd like to know what. I have a meeting at City Hall in the morning, in the bull pen with the mayor, et al. Our business is bad for tourism. Hannah Starr. Now Toni Darien. You know what I'm going to hear."

"Maybe you should remind them that if they continue to cut our budget, our business is going to be worse for tourism because we're not going to be able to do our job."

"When I first started here in the early nineties, ten per-cent of all homicides in the country were committed right here in New York," he said as they walked through the lobby, Elton John playing on the radio. "Twenty-three hun-dred homicides my first year. Last year, we had fewer than five hundred, a seventy-eight percent decrease. Everybody seems to forget that. All they remember is the latest sen-sational slaying. Filene and her music. Should I take away her radio?"

"You wouldn't," Scarpetta said.

"You're right. People work hard here, and there's not much to smile about."

They emerged into a cold wind on the sidewalk, First Avenue loud with traffic. Rush hour was at its peak, taxis careening and honking, and the wailing of sirens, ambu-lances racing to the modern Bellevue hospital complex several blocks away and to NYU's Langone Medical Center next door. It was after five and completely dark out. Scarpetta dug in her shoulder bag for her BlackBerry, remembering she needed to call Benton.

"Good luck tonight," Dr. Edison said, patting her arm. "I won't be watching."

Dodie Hodge and her Book of Magick in its black cover with yellow stars. She carried it with her everywhere.

"Spells, rituals, charms, selling things like bits of coral, iron nails, small silk bags of tonka beans," Benton was telling Dr. Clark. "We had some real issues with her at McLean. Other patients and even a few hospital employees buying into her self-professed spiritual gifts and seeking her counsel and talismans for a price. She claims to have psychic abilities and other supernatural powers, and as you might expect, people, particularly those who are troubled, are extremely vulnerable to someone like that."

"Seems she didn't have psychic abilities when she stole those DVDs from the bookstore in Detroit. Or she might have predicted she'd get caught," Dr. Clark said, moving along the road to truth, the destination just ahead.

"If you ask her, she didn't steal them. They were rightfully hers because Hap Judd is her nephew," Benton said.

"And this relationship is real, or another falsehood? Or, in your opinion, a delusion?"

"We don't know if she's related to him," Benton answered.

"Seems like that would be easy enough to find out," Dr. Clark said.

"I placed a call to his agent's office in L.A. earlier today."

Benton's statement was a confession. He wasn't sure why he'd just offered it, but he'd known he would.

Dr. Clark waited, didn't fill the silence, his eyes on Benton.

"The agent didn't confirm or deny, said she wasn't in a position to discuss Hap Judd's personal life," Benton continued as the wave of anger came back, only bigger this time. "Then she wanted to know why I was asking about someone named Dodie Hodge, and the way she said it made me think she knew exactly who I was talking about, even though she was pretending otherwise. Of course, I was extremely limited in what I could divulge, simply said that I'd been given information and was trying to corroborate it."

"You didn't say who you were or why you were interested."

Benton's silence was his answer. Nathan Clark knew him very well, because Benton had allowed it. They were friends. He might be Benton's only friend, the only one Benton permitted to enter his restricted areas, the only one other than Scarpetta, and even she had her limits, avoided areas she was afraid of, and this was all about the area she feared most. Dr. Clark was drawing the truth out of Benton, and Benton wasn't going to stop it. It needed to be done.

"That's the problem with being former FBI, isn't it?" Dr. Clark said. "Hard to resist going undercover, getting information any way you can. Even after how many years in the private sector?"

"She probably thought I was a journalist."

"That's how you identified yourself?"

No answer.

"As opposed to stating who you are and where you were calling from and why. But that would have been a HIPAA violation," Dr. Clark went on.

"Yes, it would have."

"What you did wasn't."

Benton was silent, allowing Dr. Clark to go as far as he wanted.

"We probably need to have a meaningful discussion about you and the FBI," Dr. Clark said. "It's been a while since we talked about those years when you were a protected witness and Kay thought you'd been murdered by the Chandonne family crime cartel, the darkest of times, when you were in hiding, living a horror beyond what most people can fathom. Perhaps you and I should explore how you're feeling these days about your past with the FBI. Maybe it isn't past."

"That was a long time ago. Another life ago. Another Bureau ago." Benton didn't want to talk about it and he did. He allowed Dr. Clark to keep going. "But it's probably true. Once a cop."

"Always a cop. Yes, I know the cliché. I venture to say this is about more than clichés. You're admitting to me that you acted like a law enforcement agent today, a cop, instead of a mental health practitioner whose priority is the welfare of his patient. Dodie Hodge has roused something in you."

Benton didn't answer.

"Something that's never really been asleep. You just thought it had," Dr. Clark continued.

Benton remained silent.

"So, I'm asking myself, what might have been the trigger? Because Dodie's not really the trigger. She's not important enough. More likely she's a catalyst," Dr. Clark said. "Do you agree with me?"

"I don't know what she is. But you're right. She's not the trigger."

"I'm inclined to think Warner Agee's the trigger," Dr. Clark said. "In the past three weeks or so he's been a frequent guest on the same show Kay's on tonight, touted as the forensic psychiatrist to the FBI, the original profiler, the supreme expert on all things serial and psychopathic. You have strong feelings about him, understandably. In fact, you once told me you had homicidal feelings toward him. Does Kay know Warner?"

"Not personally."

"Does she know what he did to you?"

"We don't talk about that time," Benton replied. "We've tried to move on, to start over. There's a lot I can't talk about, but even if I could, she doesn't want to, wouldn't want to. Truthfully, the more I analyze it, I'm not sure what she remembers, and I've been careful not to push her."

"Maybe you're afraid of what might happen if she remembers. Maybe you're afraid of her anger."

"She has every right to feel it. But she doesn't talk about it. I believe she's the one who's afraid of her anger," Benton said.

"What about your anger?"

"Anger and hate are destructive. I don't want to be angry or hateful." Anger and hate were eating a hole in his stomach, as if he'd just swallowed acid.

"I'm going to assume you've never told her the details about what Warner did to you. I'm going to assume that seeing him on TV and in the news has been extremely upsetting, has opened the door to a room you've done your best not to enter," Dr. Clark said.

Benton didn't comment.

"Possible you might be considering that Warner deliberately targeted the same show Kay is on because he relishes being in direct competition with you? I believe you've mentioned to me that Carley Crispin has been pushing to get both you and Kay on at the same time. In fact, I think she's gone so far as to say that on the air. Believe I saw or heard that somewhere. You refuse to go on that show, and rightly so. And then what happens? Warner is on instead. A conspiracy? A plot against you on Warner's part? Is this all about his competition with you?"

"Kay is never on any show when other people are, doesn't participate in panels, refuses to be part of what she calls *The Hollywood Squares* of alleged experts yelling at each other and arguing. And she's almost never on that show, on *The Crispin Report.*"

"The man who tried to steal your life from you after you returned from the dead is becoming a celebrity expert, is becoming you, the man he has most envied. And now he's appearing on the same show, the same network, your wife is on." Dr. Clark made his point again.

"Kay's not on that show regularly and is never on when other people are," Benton repeated. "Only a guest now and then on Carley's show—against my advice, I might add. Twice she's been on as a favor to the producer. Carley needs all the help she can get. Her ratings are slipping. Actually, this fall, more like an avalanche."

"I'm relieved you're not defensive or evasive about this."

"I just wish she'd stay away from it, that's all. Away from Carley. Kay's too fucking nice, too fucking helpful, feels she has to be the world's teacher. You know how she is."

"Easily recognized these days, I imagine. Somewhat difficult for you? Perhaps threatening?"

"I wish she'd stay off TV, but she has to live her life."

"As I understand it, Warner stepped into the limelight about three weeks ago, about the time Hannah Starr disappeared," Dr. Clark then said. "Prior to that he was behind the scenes over there. Very rarely a face on *The Crispin Report*."

"The only way someone uninteresting and uncharismatic, a nobody, can get on prime-time TV is to talk to Carley with gross inappropriateness about a sensational case. To be a fucking whore, in other words."

"I'm relieved you don't have an opinion about Warner Agee's character."

"It's wrong, completely wrong. Even someone as fucked up as that knows it's wrong," Benton said.

"So far you've been unwilling to say his name or reference him directly. But maybe we're getting warmer."

"Kay doesn't know the details of what happened in that motel room in Waltham, Massachusetts, in 2003." Benton met Dr. Clark's eyes. "She doesn't know the details of anything, not really, doesn't know the intricacies of the machine, the design of the machine that drove the operation. She thinks I masterminded the whole thing, chose to go into a protected witness program, that it was completely my idea, that I'm the one who profiled the Chandonne cartel and predicted I would be dead, that everyone around me would be dead, if the enemy wasn't led to believe I was already dead. If I were alive, they would have come after me, come after Kay, come after everyone. Sure. Well, get in line, and they came after Kay anyway, Jean-Baptiste Chandonne did, and it's a miracle she's alive. It wasn't how I would have handled it. I would have handled it the way I eventually did, take out the people trying to take me out, trying to take Kay and others out. I would have done what I needed to do without the machine."

"What is the machine?"

"The Bureau, the Department of Justice, Homeland Security, the government, a certain individual who gave tainted advice. That was the machine set into motion because of this tainted advice, because of self-serving advice."

"Warner's advice. His influence."

"There were certain people behind the scenes influencing the suits. One person in particular who wanted me out of the way, wanted me punished," Benton said.

"Punished for what?"

"For having a life that this individual wanted. I was guilty of that, it would seem, although anyone who knows my life might wonder why anyone would want it."

"If they know your interior life, perhaps," Dr. Clark said. "Your torments, your demons, perhaps. But on the surface, you're pretty enviable, would appear to have everything. Looks, a pedigree that includes money, you were FBI, their star profiler, and now you're a prominent forensic psychologist affiliated with Harvard. And you have Kay. I can see why someone might covet your life."

"Kay thinks I was a protected witness, went under deep cover for six years and, after I came out, resigned from the Bureau," Benton said.

"Because you turned on the Bureau and lost all respect for it."

"Some people believe that's the reason."

"Does she?"

"Probably."

"When the truth is you've felt the Bureau turned on you and lost all respect for you. That it betrayed you because Warner did," Dr. Clark said.

"The Bureau invited opinions from its expert and got information and advice. I can see why there would have been concern about my safety. Regardless of any biased influence, those in decision-making positions had very good reason to be concerned. I can see why they'd be concerned about my stability after the fact, after what I'd been through."

"Then you think Warner Agee was right about the Chandonnes and the necessity of faking your death? Then you think he was right about your stability and deciding that you were no longer fit for duty?"

"You know the answer. I was fucked," Benton said. "But I don't think television appearances are about a rivalry with me. I suspect it's about something else that has nothing to do with me, at least not directly. I could have done without the reminder, that's all. I could have done without it."

"It is interesting. Warner's been quiet, if not invisible, for the entirety of his rather lengthy and not particularly noteworthy career," Dr. Clark said. "Now, suddenly, he's all over the national news. Admittedly, I'm perplexed and possibly off base about what the real motive might be. Not sure it's about you, or at least not entirely about you and his envy or lust for fame. I agree with you. It's probably about something else. So, what might it be? Why now? Perhaps he's simply in it for the money. Maybe like a lot of people, he's in financial trouble, and at his age, that's damn scary."

"News shows don't pay for guest appearances," Benton answered.

"But guest appearances, if titillating and provocative enough, if they improve a show's ratings, can lead to other ways of getting paid. Book deals, consulting."

"It's very true that a lot of people have lost their retirement and are looking for ways to survive. Personal gain. Ego gratification. No way for me to know the motivation," Benton replied. "Except it's obvious that Hannah Starr has presented an opportunity for him. Had she not disappeared, he wouldn't be on TV, he wouldn't be getting all this attention. Like you said, before that, he was behind the scenes."

"*Him* and *he.* Pronouns. We're talking about the same person after all. This is progress."

"Yes. Him. Warner. He's unwell." Benton felt defeat and relief at the same time. He felt grief, and he felt drained. "Not that he was ever well. He's not a well person, never was, never will be. Destructive and dangerous and remorseless, yes. A narcissist, a sociopath, a megalomaniac. But he's not well, and at this stage of his miserable life, likely is decompensating further. I venture to say he's motivated by his insatiable need for validation, by whatever he perceives is his reward if he goes public with his obsolete and unfounded theories. And maybe he needs money."

"I agree he's unwell. I just don't want you to be unwell," Dr. Clark said.

"I'm not unwell. I admit I haven't enjoyed seeing his fucking face all over the fucking news and having him take fucking credit for my career or even mentioning my name, the fucking bastard."

"Would it make you feel any better to know my senti-
ments about Warner Agee, who I've met more times than
I'd like to remember over the years?"

"Knock yourself out."

"Always at professional meetings, when he'd try to
ingratiate himself somehow or, better yet, belittle me."

"What a shock."

"Let's just forget what he did to you," Dr. Clark continued.

"Will never happen. He should go to fucking jail for it."

"He probably should go to hell for it. He's a horror of a
human being. How's that for candor?" Dr. Clark replied.
"At least there's something to be said for being old and
falling apart, every day wondering if this day will be worse
or maybe a little better. Maybe I won't topple over or spill
coffee down the front of my shirt. The other night I was
flipping through channels and there he was. I couldn't help
myself. I had to watch. He was going on and on, spewing
all this nonsense about Hannah Starr. Not only are we talking about a case that isn't adjudicated, but the woman
hasn't even been found dead or alive, and he's speculating
about all the gruesome things that some serial killer may
have done to her. The pompous old fool. I'm surprised the
FBI doesn't find a discreet way to silence that lamb. He's
a terrible embarrassment, gives the Behavioral Analysis
Unit one hell of a black eye."

"He's never been involved in the BAU and wasn't
involved with the Behavioral Science Unit when I headed
it," Benton said. "That's part of the myth he perpetuates.
He was never FBI."

"But you were. And now you're not."

"You're right. I'm not."

"So I'll recap and summarize, and then I really do have to go or I'll miss a very important appointment," Dr. Clark said. "You were asked by the Detroit district attorney's office to conduct a psychological evaluation of this defendant, Dodie Hodge, which didn't give you the right to begin investigating her for other perceived crimes."

"No, I didn't have that right."

"Receiving a singing Christmas card didn't give you that right."

"It didn't. But it's not just a singing card. It's a veiled threat." Benton wasn't going to give in on that point.

"Depends on whose perspective. Like proving a Rorschach image is a squashed bug or a butterfly. Which is it? Some might say your perception of the card as a veiled threat is regressive on your part, clear evidence that your long years of law enforcement, of exposure to violence and trauma, have resulted in an overprotectiveness of people you love and an underlying and pervasive fear that the bastards are out to get you. You push too hard on this and you run the risk of coming across as the one with a thought disorder."

"I'll keep my disordered thoughts to myself," Benton said. "I won't make comments about people who are beyond repair and a plague."

"Good idea. It's not up to us to decide who's beyond repair and a plague."

"Even if we know it to be true."

"We know a lot of things," Dr. Clark said. "A lot of it I wish I didn't know. I've been doing this since long before the word *profiler* existed, when the FBI was still using tommy guns and was more hell-bent on finding Communists than so-called serial killers. Do you think I'm in love with all of my patients?" He got out of his chair, holding on to the armrests. "Do you think I love the one I spent several hours with today? Dear Teddy, who deemed it reasonable and helpful to pour gasoline into a nine-year-old girl's vagina. As he thoughtfully explained it to me, so she wouldn't get pregnant after he raped her. Is he responsible? Is an unmanaged schizophrenic, himself a victim of repeated sexual abuse and torture as a child, to blame? Should he get lethal injection, a firing squad, the chair?"

"Being blamed and being held responsible are two different things," Benton said as his phone rang.

He answered, hoping it was Scarpetta.

"I'm out front." Her voice in his ear.

"Out front?" He was alarmed. "Of Bellevue?"

"I walked."

"Christ. Okay. Wait in the lobby. Don't wait outside. Come inside the lobby and I'll be right down."

"Is something wrong?"

"It's cold out, nasty out. I'll be right down," he said, getting up from his desk.

"Wish me luck. I'm off to the Tennisport." Dr. Clark paused in the doorway, coat and hat on, bag slung over a shoulder, like a Norman Rockwell painting of a frail old shrink.

"Go easy on McEnroe." Benton started packing his briefcase.

"The ball machine is on very slow speed. And it always wins. Afraid I'm reaching the end of my tennis career. I was on the court next to Billie Jean King the other week. Took a spill, was covered with red clay from head to toe."

"What you get for showing off."

"I was picking up balls with a hopper and tripped on the

goddamn tape and there she was, hovering over me to see if I was all right. What a way to meet a hero. Take care of yourself, Benton. Give my best to Kay."

Benton deliberated about the singing card from Dodie, decided to tuck it in his briefcase, he wasn't sure why. He couldn't show it to Scarpetta, but he didn't want to leave it here. What if something else happened? Nothing else was going to happen. He was just anxious, overwrought, haunted by ghosts from the past. Everything was going to be fine. He locked his office door, walking fast, in a hurry, nothing to be anxious about, but he was. He was as anxious as he'd been in a very long time. A feeling of foreboding, his psyche bruised, and he imagined it as purplish and injured. *It's remembered emotions, not real anymore,* he said, hearing his own voice in his head. It was a long time ago. That was then, and nothing is wrong right now. The doors of his colleagues were shut, everyone gone, some on vacation. Christmas was in exactly one week.

He headed to the elevator, the entrance of the prison ward across from it, the usual noise coming from that direction. Loud voices, someone yelling, "Coming through," because the guard in the control room never opened the barrier doors fast enough. Benton caught a glimpse of an inmate in the blaze orange jumpsuit of Rikers Island, shackled and escorted, a cop on either side of him, probably a malingerer faking some malady, maybe something self-inflicted, so he could spend the holidays here. Benton was reminded of Dodie Hodge as steel doors slammed shut and he got on the elevator. He was reminded of his six years of nonexistence, isolated and trapped in the persona of a man who wasn't real, Tom Haviland. Six years of being dead because of Warner Agee. Benton couldn't stand the way he felt. It was hideous to want to hurt some-one, and he knew what it felt like, had done it more than once in the line of duty but never because it was what he fantasized about, a desire like lust.

He wished Scarpetta had called sooner, hadn't set out alone in the dark in this part of the city, which had more than its demographic share of the homeless, of indigents and drug addicts and psychiatric alumni, the same patients in and out until the overstrained system couldn't fit them anywhere anymore. Then maybe they pushed a commuter off a subway platform in front of a train or attacked a crowd of strangers with a knife, caused death and destruction because they heard voices and nobody listened.

Benton walked swiftly through what seemed to be end-less corridors, past the cafeteria and gift shop, weaving through a steady traffic of patients and visitors, and hos-pital personnel in lab coats and scrubs. The halls of Bellevue Hospital Center were decked out for the holidays, with cheerful music piped in and bright decorations, as if that somehow made it all right to be sick or injured or criminally insane.

Scarpetta was waiting for him near the glass front doors, in her long, dark coat and black leather gloves, and she didn't notice him yet in the crowd as he walked toward her, mindful of people around her, of the way some of them looked at her as if she was familiar. His reaction to her was always the same, a poignant mixture of excitement and sad-ness, the thrill of being with her tainted by the remembered pain of believing he never would again. Whenever he watched her from a distance and she was unaware, he relived the times he'd done it in the past, secretly and deliberately, spying on her, yearning for her. At times he wondered how life would have turned out for her if what she'd believed had been true, if he really was dead. He wondered if she would be better off. Maybe she would. He had caused her suffering and harm, brought danger to her, damaged her, and he couldn't forgive himself.

"Maybe you should cancel tonight," he said when he got to her.

She turned to him, surprised, happy, her deep blue eyes like the sky, her thoughts and feelings like the weather, light and shadow, bright sun and clouds and haze.

"We should go have a nice, quiet dinner," he added, taking her arm, keeping her close, as if they needed each other to stay warm. "Il Cantinori. I'll call Frank, see if he can fit us in."

"Don't torment me," she said, her arm tight around his waist. "Melanzane alla parmigiana. A Brunello di Montalcino. I might eat your share and drink the whole bottle."

"That would be incredibly greedy." He kept her protectively close as they walked toward First Avenue. The wind blasted, and it was beginning to rain. "You really could cancel, you know. Tell Alex you've got the flu." He signaled for a taxi and one darted toward them.

"I can't, and we have to get home," she said. "We have a conference call."

Benton opened the cab's back door. "What conference call?"

"Jaime." Scarpetta slid across to the other side of the backseat and he climbed in after her. She gave the driver their address and said to Benton, "Fasten your seat belt." Her quirky habit to remind people, even if they didn't need to be told. "Lucy thinks they can get out of Vermont in a couple of hours, that the front should have cleared south of us by then. In the meantime, Jaime wants you, me, Marino, all of us, on the phone. She called me about ten minutes ago when I was on the sidewalk, on my way here. It wasn't a good time to talk, so I don't know details."

"Not even a clue what she wants?" Benton asked as the taxi cut over to Third Avenue, headed north, the windshield wipers dragging loudly in a misty rain, the tops of lighted buildings shrouded.

"This morning's situation." She wasn't going to be specific in front of their driver, didn't matter if he understood English or could hear them.

"The situation you've been involved in all day." Benton meant the Toni Darien case.

"A tip called in this afternoon," Scarpetta said. "Apparently, somebody saw something."

5

Marino's was an unfortunate address: room number 666 at One Hogan Place. It bothered him more than usual as he and L.A. Bonnell paused in the gray-tile hallway stacked to the ceiling with banker's boxes, the three sixes over his door seeming like an indictment of his character, a warning to whom it may concern to beware.

"Uh, okay," Bonnell said, looking up. "I couldn't work here. If nothing else, it causes negative thinking. If people believe something's bad luck, it will be. Me, I'd definitely move."

He unlocked his beige door, dingy around the knob, the paint chipped at the edges, the aroma of Chinese food overwhelming. He was starved, couldn't wait to dig into his crispy duck spring rolls and BBQ baby ribs, and pleased that Bonnell had ordered similarly, beef teriyaki, noodles, and nothing raw, none of that sushi shit that reminded him of fish bait. She wasn't anything like he'd imagined, having envisioned someone tiny and perky, a spitfire who could have you on the floor, hands cuffed behind your back, before you knew what was happening. With Bonnell, you'd know what was happening.

She was close to six feet tall, big-boned, big hands, big feet, big-breasted, the kind of woman who could keep a man fully occupied in bed or kick his ass, like Xena the Warrior Princess in a business suit, only Bonnell had ice-blue eyes and her hair was short and pale blond, and Marino was pretty sure it was natural. He'd felt cocky when he was with her at High Roller Lanes, saw some of the guys staring, nudging each other. Marino wished he could have bowled a few and strutted his stuff.

Bonnell carried the bags of takeout into Marino's office and commented, "Maybe we should go into the conference room."

He wasn't sure if this was about the 666 over the door or the fact that his work space was a landfill, and said, "Berger will be calling on the line in here. It's better we stay put. Plus, I need my computer and don't want anyone over-hearing the conversation." He set down his crime scene case, a slate-gray four-drawer tackle box perfect for his needs, and shut the door. "I figured you'd notice." He meant his room number. "Don't go thinking it means something personal about me."

"Why would I think it's about you personally? Did you decide what number this office is?" She moved paperwork, a flak jacket, and the tackle box off a chair and sat.

"Imagine my reaction when I was showed this office the first time." Marino settled behind mountain ranges of clutter on his metal desk. "You want to wait and eat until after the call?"

"A good idea." She looked around as if there was no place to eat, which wasn't true. Marino could always find a spot to set a burger or a bowl or a foam box.

"We'll do the call in here and eat in the conference room," he said.

"Even better."

"I got to admit I almost quit. I really thought about it." He picked up where he'd left off in his story. "The first time I was showed this office, I was like, you got to be shitting me."

He'd honestly thought Jaime Berger was joking, that the number over the door was the usual sick humor of people in criminal justice. It had even occurred to him that maybe she was rubbing his nose in the truth about why he'd ended up with her to begin with—that she'd hired him as a favor, was giving him a second chance after the bad thing he'd done. What a reminder every time he walked into his office. All those years he and Scarpetta had been together and then he hurt her like that. He was glad he didn't remember much, had been fucked up, shitface drunk, had never meant to put his hands on her, to do what he did.

"I don't consider myself superstitious," he was telling Bonnell, "but I grew up in Bayonne, New Jersey. Went to Catholic school, was confirmed, was even an altar boy, which didn't last long because I was always getting into fights, started boxing. Not the Bayonne Bleeder, probably wouldn't have made it fifteen rounds with Muhammad Ali, but I was a semifinalist in the National Golden Gloves one year, thought of turning pro, became a cop instead." Making sure she knew a few things about him. "It's never been contested by anyone that six-six-six is the symbol of the Beast, a number to be avoided at all costs. And I always have, whether it's an address, a post office box, a license plate, the time of day."

"The time of day?" Bonnell questioned, and Marino couldn't tell if she was amused, her demeanor difficult to anticipate or decipher. "There's no such time as sixty-six minutes past six," she said.

"Six minutes past six on the sixth day of the month, for example."

"Why won't she move you? Isn't there some other place you can work?" Bonnell dug into her pocketbook and pulled out a thumb drive, tossing it to him.

"This everything?" Marino plugged it into his computer. "Apartment, crime scene, and WAV files?"

"Except the pictures you took when you were there today."

"I got to download them from my camera. Nothing all that important. Probably nothing you didn't get when you were there with the CSU guys. Berger says I'm on the sixth floor and my office is the sixty-sixth one in sequence. I told her yeah, well, it's also in the book of Revelation."

"Berger's Jewish," Bonnell said. "She doesn't read the book of Revelation."

"That's like saying if she doesn't read the paper nothing happened yesterday."

"It's not like that. Revelation isn't about something that happened."

"It's about something that's going to happen."

"Something that's going to happen is a prediction or wishful thinking or a phobia," Bonnell said. "It's not factual."

His desk phone rang.

He snapped it up and said, "Marino."

"It's Jaime. I think we have everybody." Jaime Berger's voice.

Marino said, "We were just talking about you." He was watching Bonnell, found it hard not to look at her.

Maybe because she was unusually big for a woman, super deluxe in every department.

"Kay? Benton? Everybody still on?" Berger said.

"We're here." Benton sounded far away.

"I'm putting you on speakerphone," Marino said. "I've got Detective Bonnell from Homicide with me." He pushed a button on his phone and hung up. "Where's Lucy?"

"At the hangar, getting the helicopter prepped. Hopefully we'll be flying out in a few hours," Berger said. "The snow's finally stopped. If all of you go into your e-mail, you should find two files she sent before she headed out to the airport. Following Marino's advice, we've gotten analysts at the Real Time Crime Center to log in to the server that operates the surveillance camera outside Toni Darien's apartment building. I'm sure all of you know that NYPD has an agreement with several of the major CCTV security camera providers so it can access surveillance recordings without tracking down system administrators for passwords. Toni's building happens to be covered by one of these providers, so RTCC was able to access the network video server and has gone through some of the recordings in question, focusing as a matter of priority on this past week and comparing images with recent photos of Toni, including her driver's license photo, and photos of her on Facebook, MySpace. Amazing what's out there. The file called *Recording One,* we'll start with that. I've already looked at it, and also the second file, and what I've seen corroborates information received several hours ago that we'll discuss in more detail in a few minutes. You should be able to download the video and open it. So let's do that now."

"We've got it." Benton's voice, and he didn't sound friendly. Never did these days.

Marino found the e-mail Berger was talking about and opened the video clip as Bonnell got up from her chair and came around to watch it, squatting next to him. There was no audio, just images of traffic in front of Toni Darien's brick building on Second Avenue, cars, taxis, and buses in the background, people walking past, dressed for the rainy winter weather, some of them holding umbrellas, oblivious to the camera that was recording them.

"Right about now she's coming into view." Berger always sounded like she was in charge, even if she was just talking normally, didn't matter about what. "In a dark-green parka with fur trim around the hood. She's wearing the hood up and has black gloves on and a red scarf. A black shoulder bag, black pants, and running shoes."

"Be good to get a close-up of the running shoes." Scarpetta's voice. "To see if they're the same ones she had on when she was found this morning. Asics Gel-Kayano, white with a red lightning flash and red accents on the heel collar. Size nine and a half."

"The shoes in this, whitish with some red," Marino said, aware of how close Bonnell was to him. He could feel her warmth next to his leg, next to his elbow.

The figure in the green parka was captured from the back, her face not visible because of where she was in relation to the camera and because of the fur-trimmed hood. She turned right and skipped up the wet front steps of the apartment building and already had her keys out, suggesting to Marino that she was organized and gave thought to what she was doing, was aware of her surroundings and security-conscious. She unlocked the door and disappeared

inside. The time stamp on the video was five-forty seven
p.m., December 17, yesterday. Then a pause, and another
recording of the same figure in the green parka with the
hood up, the same large black bag over her shoulder,
coming out of the building and going down the steps, turning right and walking off in the rainy night. The time stamp
was seven-oh-one p.m., December 17.

"I'm curious." It was Benton talking. "Since we can't see
her face, how do the analysts at RTCC know who it is?"

"I wondered the same thing," Berger said. "But I
believe it's because of earlier images that obviously are
her—ones you'll see shortly. According to RTCC, what
we're looking at now is the last image of her, the last time
she's recorded entering or leaving her building. It appears
she returned to her apartment and was there for a little
more than an hour, then left. The question is, where was
she after that?"

"I should add," and it was Scarpetta talking, "that the
time on the text message Grace Darien received from
Toni's cell phone was approximately an hour after this
second video clip. At around eight p.m."

"I left Mrs. Darien a voicemail," Marino said. "We'll get
the phone from her so we can see what else is on it."

"I don't know if you want to get into this now. But the
time on the text message and these video clips are in conflict with what I noted when I examined the body,"
Scarpetta said.

"Let's focus on what RTCC found first," Berger replied.
"Then we'll get to the autopsy results."

Berger had just said she considered what RTCC had
found more important to the case than what Scarpetta had
to report. One statement by one witness, and Berger had it

all figured out? But then, Marino didn't know the details, only what Bonnell had told him, and she'd been vague, finally admitting she and Berger had talked on the phone, and that Berger had instructed her to say nothing to anyone about what they'd discussed. All Marino had managed to coax out of Bonnell was that a witness had come forward with information that would make it "crystal clear" why Toni's apartment wasn't relevant to her murder.

"As I'm looking at the clips here," Marino said, "I'm wondering once again what happened to her coat. The green parka isn't in her apartment and hasn't showed up."

"If someone had her cell phone"—Scarpetta was still on that subject—"he or she could send a text message to anyone in Toni's contacts directory, including her mother. You don't need a password to send a text message. All you need is the cell phone of the person you want the text message to appear to be from—in this case, Toni Darien. If someone had her phone and reviewed messages sent and received, that person could get an idea of what to write and how to word it if the goal was to fool someone into thinking the message was from Toni, if the goal was to make people think she was still alive last night when she wasn't."

"It's been my experience that typically, homicides aren't as elaborately planned or as clever as what you're suggesting," Berger said.

Marino couldn't believe it. She was basically telling Scarpetta this wasn't Agatha Christie, wasn't a friggin' murder mystery.

"Ordinarily, it would be me making that point," Scarpetta answered, without registering the slightest insult or irritation. "But Toni Darien's homicide is anything but ordinary."

"We'll try to trace where the text message was sent from, the physical location," Marino said. "That's all we can do. It's a legitimate thing to raise, since her cell phone's missing. I agree. What if someone else has it and that person sent the message to Toni's mother? May sound far-fetched, but how do we know?" He wished he hadn't said "far-fetched." It sounded like he was criticizing Scarpetta or doubting her.

"As I'm looking at this video clip, I'm also asking, How do we know the person in the green coat is Toni Darien?" It was Benton who spoke. "I can't see her face. Not in either clip."

"Just that she looks white." Marino backed up the video to check again. "I'm seeing her jaw, a glimpse of her chin, because her hood's up and it's dark out and she's not facing the camera. It's catching her from behind, and she's looking down as she walks. Both when she's entering the building and leaving."

"If you'll open the second file Lucy sent with the name *Recording Two*," Berger said, "you're going to see a number of stills from earlier recordings, ones made days earlier, same coat, same figure, only we get a clear visual of Toni's face."

Marino closed the first file and opened the second one. He clicked on the slide show and began looking at video stills of Toni in front of her building, going in and coming out. In all of them she had on a bright red scarf and the same green parka with a fur-trimmed hood, only in these images it wasn't raining and the hood was down, her dark-brown hair long and loose around her shoulders. In several of the video stills she had on running pants and in others she had on slacks or jeans, and in one she was wearing olive-green and tan mittens, and in none was she wearing black gloves or carrying a big black shoulder bag. Each time she was on foot, except once when it was raining and the camera recorded her getting into a cab.

"It corroborates the statement her neighbor gave me," Bonnell said, brushing against Marino's arm, the third time she had done it, barely making contact but noticeable as hell. "That's the coat he described," she went on. "He told me she had on a green coat with a hood and was carrying her mail, which she must have gotten right after she entered her building at five-forty-seven p.m. I assume she unlocked her mailbox, got whatever was in it, then went up the stairs, which was when her neighbor saw her. She entered her apartment and placed the mail on the kitchen counter, where I found it this morning when I was there with CSU. The mail was unopened."

"She had her hood up when she was inside the building?" Scarpetta asked.

"The neighbor wasn't specific. Just said she had on a green coat with a hood."

"Graham Tourette," Marino said. "We need to check him out, check out the super, too, Joe Barstow. Neither of them have a record except traffic violations, failure to yield, invalid registration, a broken taillight, going way back, none resulting in an arrest. I had RTCC pull up everything on everyone in the building."

"Graham Tourette made a point of telling me he and his male partner were at the theater last night, someone had given them tickets to *Wicked*," Bonnell said. "So I'll just go ahead and ask Dr. Wesley . . ."

"Improbable," Benton said. "Highly improbable that a gay man committed this crime."

"I didn't see any mittens inside her apartment," Marino said. "And they weren't at the scene. She's not wearing black gloves or carrying a black bag in the earlier stills, either."

"It's my opinion this is a sexually motivated homicide," Benton added, as if Marino wasn't on the phone.

"Signs of sexual assault on autopsy?" Berger asked.

"She has injuries to her genitalia," Scarpetta answered. "Bruising, reddening, evidence of some type of penetration, of trauma."

"Seminal fluid?"

"Not that I saw. We'll see what the labs find."

"I believe the possibility the Doc's raising is maybe the crime scene and maybe the crime itself was in fact staged," Marino said, still feeling bad about saying "far-fetched" a little while ago, hoping Scarpetta didn't think he'd meant anything by it. "If so, it could be a gay guy, right, Benton?"

"Based on what I know, Jaime," Benton answered Berger instead of Marino, "I suspect staging is for the purpose of disguising the true nature and motive of crime and when it was committed and what the connection might be between the victim and the assailant. Staging in this case is for the purpose of evasion. Whoever did it fears being caught. And I reiterate, the murder is sexually motivated."

"Doesn't sound like you think it was a stranger who did it," Marino said, and Benton didn't answer.

"If what the witness says is true, sounds to me like that's exactly what we're dealing with," Bonnell said to Marino, touching him again. "I don't think we're talking about a boyfriend, maybe not even anybody she'd ever met before last night."

"We'll need to bring in Tourette for an interview. And

the super," Berger said. "I want to talk to both of them, especially the super, Joe Barstow."

"Why especially Joe Barstow?" Benton wanted to know, and he sounded a little pissed.

Maybe Benton and the Doc weren't getting along. Marino had no idea what was going on with either of them, hadn't seen them in weeks, but he was tired of going out of his way to be nice to Benton. It was getting old being dissed all the time.

"I have the same information from RTCC that Marino does. You happen to notice Barstow's employment history?" Berger was asking Marino. "A couple of livery companies, a taxi driver, in addition to a lot of other jobs. Bartender, waiter. He worked for a taxi company as recently as 2007. Looks like he's been doing a lot of things while going to school part-time, to Manhattan Community College, on and off for the past three years, based on what I'm seeing."

Bonnell had gotten up and flipped open a notepad, was standing next to Marino.

She said, "Trying to get his associate's degree in video arts and technology. Plays bass guitar, used to play in a band, would like to get involved in producing rock concerts, and still hoping for his big break in the music business."

Reading her notes, her thigh touching Marino.

"Of late, he's been working part-time at a digital production company," she went on, "doing odd jobs, mostly working the desk, being a runner, what he called a production assistant and I'd call a gopher. He's twenty-eight. I talked to him about fifteen minutes. He said he only knew Toni because of any contact he might have with her in the building, that he—and I quote—had never dated her but had thought about asking her out."

"Did you ask him directly if he'd ever dated her or thought about it?" Berger said. "Or did he volunteer it?"

"Volunteered it. Also volunteered that he hadn't seen her for several days. He says he was in his apartment all last night, had a pizza sent in and watched TV because the weather was so bad and he was tired."

"Offering a lot of alibis," Berger said.

"It would be fair to conclude that, but also not unusual in cases like this. Everybody figures they're a suspect. Or they have something going on in their lives they don't want us to know about, if nothing else," Bonnell replied, flipping pages. "Described her as friendly, someone who didn't complain a lot, and he wasn't aware of her being the party type or bringing people into the building, such as— and again I quote—a lot of guys. I noted he was extremely upset and scared. It doesn't appear he's a taxi driver now," she added, as if the detail was important.

"We don't know that as fact," Berger said. "We don't know that he doesn't have access to taxicabs, what he might do off the books so he doesn't pay taxes, for example, like a lot of the freelance drivers in the city, especially these days."

"The red scarf looks similar to the one I removed from Toni's neck," Scarpetta said, and Marino imagined her sitting somewhere with Benton, looking at a computer screen, probably their apartment on Central Park West, not far from CNN. "Solid red, a bright red made of a high-tech fabric that's thin but very warm."

"That's what it looks like she has on," Berger said. "What these video clips and the text message on her mother's phone seem to establish is she was alive yesterday when she left her building at one minute past seven and was still alive an hour later at around eight. Kay, you started to tell us you might have a different opinion about her time of death, different from what's implied by these video clips, for example."

"My opinion is that she wasn't alive last night." Scarpetta's voice, even keel, as if what she'd just said shouldn't surprise anyone.

"Then what did we just look at?" Bonnell asked, frowning. "An imposter? Someone else wearing her coat and entering her building? Someone who had keys?"

"Kay? Just so we're clear? Now that you've seen the video clips? You still of the same opinion?" Berger asked.

"My opinion is based on my examination of her body, not video clips," Scarpetta answered. "And her postmortem artifacts, specifically her livor and rigor mortis, place her time of death at much earlier than last night. As early as Tuesday."

"Tuesday?" Marino was amazed. "As in day before yesterday?"

"It's my opinion she received her head injury at some point on Tuesday, possibly in the afternoon, several hours after she ate a chicken salad," Scarpetta said. "Her gastric contents were partially digested romaine lettuce, tomatoes, and chicken meat. After she was struck in the head, her digestion would have quit, so the food remained undigested as she died, which I think took a little time, possibly hours, based on the vital response to her injury."

"She had lettuce and tomatoes in her refrigerator," Marino remembered. "So maybe she ate her last meal in her apartment. You sure that couldn't have happened when she was in there last night, when it appears she was there for an hour? During that interval we just watched on the video clip?"

"Would make sense," Bonnell said. "She ate, and several hours later, at nine or ten o'clock, let's say, she was out and was assaulted."

"It wouldn't make sense. What I saw when I examined her indicates that she wasn't alive last night, and it's very unlikely she was alive yesterday." Scarpetta's calm voice.

She almost never sounded flustered or sharp and never was a smart ass, and she sure as hell had a right to sound any way she wanted. After all the years Marino had worked with her, most of his career in one city or another, it was his experience that if a dead body told her something, it was true. But he was having a hard time with what she was saying. It didn't seem to make any sense.

"Okay. We've got a lot to discuss," Berger spoke up. "One thing at a time. Let's focus on what we've just seen on these video clips. Let's just assume the figure in the green coat isn't an imposter, is in fact Toni Darien, and that she also text-messaged her mother last night."

Berger didn't buy what Scarpetta was saying. Berger thought Scarpetta was mistaken, and incredibly, Marino wondered it, too. It entered his mind that maybe Scarpetta had started believing her own legend, really thought she could figure out the answer to anything and was never wrong. What was that phrase CNN used all the time? The exaggerated way her crime-busting abilities were described? *The Scarpetta Factor. Shit,* Marino thought. He'd seen it happen time and again, people believe their own press and quit doing the real work, and then they fuck up and make fools of themselves.

"The question is," Berger continued, "where was Toni after she left her apartment building?"

"Not at work," Marino said, trying to remember if Scarpetta ever made the kind of error that impeaches an expert, gets a case ruined in court.

He couldn't think of a single example. But she didn't used to be famous and on TV all the time.

"Let's start with work, with High Roller Lanes." Berger's voice was strong and loud over speakerphone. "Marino, let's start with you and Detective Bonnell."

Marino was disappointed when Bonnell got up and moved to the other side of the desk. He made a drinking motion, maybe she could bring out the Diet Cokes. He had a different feeling as he looked at her, noting the color in her cheeks, the brightness of her eyes, how energized she seemed. He could feel her against his arm even though she was nowhere near him, could feel the firm roundness, the weight of her against him, and he imagined what she looked like, what she would feel like, and he was attentive and awake in a way he hadn't been in a while. She had to know what she was doing when she was brushing against him.

"First off, let me describe the place because it's not your typical bowling alley," he said.

"More like something out of Vegas," Bonnell said, opening a paper bag, getting out two Diet Cokes, handing one to him, her eyes touching his briefly, like sparks.

"Right," Marino said as he opened the can, Diet Coke spurting up and running over, dripping on his desk. He mopped up the mess with several sheets of paper, wiped his hands on his pants. "Definitely a place for high-roller bowlers. Neon lights, movie screens, leather couches, and a glitzy lounge with a huge mirrored bar. Twenty-something

lanes, pool tables, a damn dress code. You can't go in there
looking like a bum."

He'd taken Georgia Bacardi to High Roller Lanes last
June for their six-month anniversary. It was highly unlikely
they'd be celebrating their twelfth. Last time they saw each
other, first weekend of this month, she hadn't wanted sex,
had about ten different ways to tell him the same thing,
which was forget about it. Didn't feel good, too tired, her
job at Baltimore PD was just as important as his, she was
having hot flashes, he had other women in his life and she
was sick and tired of it. Berger, Scarpetta, even Lucy.
Including Barcardi, that was four women Marino had in his
life, and the last time he'd had sex was November 7, almost
six damn weeks ago.

"The place is beautiful, and so are the women who wait
on you while you're bowling," he continued. "A lot of them
trying to get into show business, modeling, a real upscale
clientele, photos of famous people, even in the bathrooms,
at least in the men's room. Did you see any in the ladies'
room?" To Bonnell.

She shrugged, taking off her suit jacket, in case he had
any doubt what was under it. He looked. He openly stared.

"In the men's room there's one of Hap Judd," Marino
added, because Berger would be interested. "Obviously not
the highest place of honor, being on the wall above a
urinal."

"You know when it was taken and if he goes in there a
lot?" Berger's voice.

"Him and a lot of other celebrities who live in the city,
or maybe when they're filming here or whatever," Marino
said. "The inside of High Roller is like a steak house.
Photos of famous people everywhere. Hap Judd's photo

might have been taken last summer. No one I talked to could remember exactly. He's been in there, but he's not a regular."

"What's the attraction?" Berger asked. "I didn't realize bowling was that big with celebrities."

"You never heard of Bowling with the Stars?" Marino said.

"No."

"A lot of famous people bowl, but High Roller Lanes is also a hip hangout," Marino said, and his thoughts were sluggish, as if the blood had drained out of his head, was flowing due south. "The owner's some guy who has restaurants, arcades, entertainment centers in Atlantic City, Indiana, South Florida, Detroit, Louisiana. A guy named Freddie Maestro, old as Methuselah. All the celeb photos are with him, so he must spend a lot of time here in the city."

He pried his eyes away from Bonnell so he could concentrate.

"Point being, you never know who you're going to meet, is what I'm getting at," Marino went on. "So, for someone like Toni Darien, maybe that was part of the appeal. She was looking to make money, and tipping is good in there, and she was out to make connections, to hook up. Her shift was what I call prime time. Nights, usually starting around six until closing at two in the morning, Thursday through Sunday. She'd walk to work or take a cab, didn't own a car."

He took a sip of Diet Coke, fixing his gaze on the whiteboard on the wall near the door. Berger and her whiteboards, everything color-coded, cases ready for trial in green, those that weren't in blue, court dates in red, who's on call for sex crimes intake in black. It was safe staring at the whiteboard. He could think better.

"What type of hooking up are we talking about?" Berger's voice.

"My guess, in a high-rent place like that you can probably get whatever the hell you want," Marino said. "So maybe she ran into the wrong person in there."

"Or High Roller Lanes might have nothing to do with anything. Could be completely unrelated to what happened to her." Bonnell said what she believed, which was probably why she hadn't been particularly interested in the photographs or what was playing on the huge video screens over the lanes, or the sightings of the rich and famous.

Bonnell was convinced that Toni Darien's murder was random, that she was targeted by a predator, a serial killer on the prowl. She might have been dressed for jogging, but that wasn't what she'd been doing when she'd ended up in the wrong place at the wrong time. Bonnell said Marino would understand better when he heard the 911 call made by the witness.

"I'm assuming we still have no clue about what's happened to her cell phone and laptop." Scarpetta's voice.

"And her billfold and maybe her purse," Marino reminded them. "Appears they're missing, too. Not in her apartment. Not at the crime scene. And now I'm wondering about her coat and mittens."

"The missing items might make sense in light of the nine-one-one call, the information Detective Bonnell received," Berger said. "What a witness said. Possibly Toni got into a taxi, had those things with her for some reason because she wasn't out jogging. She was out doing something else, possibly going to make a stop and then jog later."

"What about any other types of chargers besides ones for the laptop and cell phone?" Scarpetta said. "Anything else in her apartment?"

"That was all I saw," Marino said.

"What about a USB dock, for example? Anything that might indicate she had some other sort of device that needed charging, such as the watch she had on?" Scarpetta asked. "It appears to be some type of data-collection device called a BioGraph. Neither Lucy nor I can find it on the Internet."

"How can there be a watch called that and it's not on the Internet? Someone has to sell it, right?" Marino said.

"Not necessarily." When Benton answered him, it was always to disagree or put him down. "Not if it's in research and development or part of a classified project."

"So maybe she worked for the fucking CIA," Marino shot back.

6

If Toni's murder was a hit by an intelligence-gathering agency, then whoever was responsible wasn't going to leave a data device on her wrist.

Benton made the point in the flat tone he used when talking to people he really didn't like. An arid tone, a bland tone, that reminded Scarpetta of parched earth, of stone, as she sat on the sofa inside a guest room he'd converted into his office at the rear of the apartment, a handsome space with a city view.

"Propaganda. To make us think something. In other words, planted," Marino sounded from the VoiceStation next to Benton's computer. "I'm just responding to your suggestion that it might be part of some classified project."

Benton listened impassively from his leather chair, a wall of books behind him, organized by topic, hardbound, a number of them first editions, some very old. Marino had gotten annoyed and finally had flared up because Benton had made him feel foolish, and the more Marino talked, the more foolish he sounded. Scarpetta wished the two of them would stop acting like adolescent boys.

"So, if you're going down that road? Then maybe they wanted us to find the watch because whatever's on it is disinformation," Marino said.

"Who's 'they'?" Benton said in a decidedly unpleasant voice.

Marino no longer felt he had a right to defend himself, and Benton no longer pretended he'd forgiven him. It was as if what had happened in Charleston a year and a half ago was between the two of them and had nothing to do with Scarpetta anymore. Typical of assaults, she no longer was the victim. Everyone else was.

"I don't know, but truth be told, we shouldn't discount anything." Marino's big invasive voice filling Benton's small private space. "The longer you do this, the more you learn to keep an open mind. And we got a lot of shit going on in this country with terrorism, counterterrorism, spying, counterspying, the Russians, the North Koreans, you name it."

"I'd like to move away from the CIA suggestion." Berger was no-nonsense, and the turn the conversation had taken was trying her patience. "There's no evidence we're dealing with some organized hit that's politically motivated or related to terrorism or spying. In fact, plenty of evidence to the contrary."

"I want to ask about the position of the body at the scene," said Detective Bonnell, soft-spoken but confident and at times wry and hard to read. "Dr. Scarpetta, did you find any indication that she might have been pulled by her arms or dragged? Because I found the positioning strange. Almost a little ridiculous, like she was dancing 'Hava

Nagila,' the way her legs were bent froglike and her arms straight up. I know that probably sounds strange to say, but it did cross my mind when I first saw her."

Benton was looking at the scene photographs on his computer, and he answered before Scarpetta could. "The position of the body is degrading and mocking." Clicking on more photographs. "She's exposed in a sexually graphic manner that's intended to show contempt and to shock. No effort was made to conceal the body but exactly the opposite. The position she's in was staged."

"Other than the position you've described, there was no evidence she'd been dragged." Scarpetta answered Bonnell's question. "No abrasions posteriorially, no bruises around her wrists, but you need to bear in mind that she wasn't going to have a vital response to injuries. She wasn't going to have bruising if she was grabbed by the wrists after death. In the main, the body was relatively injury-free, except for her head wound."

"Let's assume you're right about her having been dead for a while." It was Berger talking, broadcasting forcefully from the sleek black speaker Benton used for conference calling. "I'm thinking there might be some explanation for this."

"The explanation is what we know happens to the body after death," Scarpetta said. "How rapidly it cools, the way uncirculating blood settles to the dependent regions due to gravity and what that looks like, and the characteristic stiffening of the muscles due to the decline of adenosine triphosphate."

"There can be exceptions, though," Berger said. "It's well established that these types of artifacts associated with time of death can greatly vary depending on what the person was doing right before he or she died, the weather conditions, body size, and how the person was dressed, and even what sort of drugs someone might have been on. Am I correct?"

"Time of death isn't an exact science." Scarpetta wasn't at all surprised that Berger was debating her.

It was one of those situations when truth made everything immeasurably harder.

"Then it's within the realm of possibility there were circumstances that could explain why Toni's rigor and livor seemed so well advanced," Berger said. "For example, if she was exerting a lot of energy, was running, perhaps running away from her assailant, when he hit her on the back of the head. Couldn't that account for an unusually rapid onset of rigor mortis? Or even instantaneous rigor, what's known as a cadaveric spasm?"

"No," Scarpetta answered. "Because she didn't die immediately after she was struck in the head. She survived for a while, and in fact would have been anything but physically active. She would have been incapacitated, basically in a coma and dying."

"But if we're objective about it," as if hinting Scarpetta might not be, "her livor, for example, can't tell you exactly when she died. There are many variables that can affect lividity."

"Her livor's not telling me exactly when she died, but an estimation. It does, however, tell me unequivocally that she was moved." Scarpetta was beginning to feel as if she was on the witness stand. "Possibly this was when she was transported to the park, and likely whoever is responsible didn't realize that by positioning her arms the way he did, he offered an obvious inconsistency. Her arms were not above her head while her livor was forming, but closer to her sides, palms down. Also, there are no indentations or marks from clothing, yet there is blanching under the band of her watch, indicating it was on her wrist after livor was intensifying and becoming fixed. I'm suspicious that for at least twelve hours after death she was completely nude, except for her watch. She wasn't even wearing her socks, which were an elastic material that would have left marks. When she was dressed before her body was transported to the park, her socks were put on the wrong feet."

She told them about Toni's anatomically correct running socks, adding that typically when assailants dress their victims after the fact, there are telltale signs of it. Often mistakes are made. For example, clothing is twisted or inside out. Or in this case, an inadvertent reversal of left and right.

"Why leave the watch on?" Bonnell asked.

"Unimportant to whoever undressed her." Benton was looking at scene photos on his screen, zooming in on the BioGraph watch on Toni's left wrist. "Removing jewelry, except for purposes of taking souvenirs, isn't as sexually charged as removing clothing, exposing bare flesh. But it's all a matter of what's symbolic and erotic to the offender. And whoever was with her body wasn't in a hurry. Not if he had her for a day and a half."

"Kay, I'm wondering if you've ever had a case when someone has been dead only eight hours but it looks like he or she's been dead almost five times that long?" Berger had her mind made up and was doing her damnedest to lead the witness.

"Only in cases where the onset of decomposition is

dramatically escalated, such as in a very hot tropical or subtropical environment," Scarpetta said. "When I was a medical examiner in South Florida, escalated decomposition wasn't uncommon. I saw it often."

"In your opinion, was she sexually assaulted in the park, or perhaps in a vehicle and then moved and displayed as Benton has described?" Berger asked.

"I'm curious. Why a vehicle?" Benton said, leaning back in his chair.

"I'm posing the possible scenario that she was sexually assaulted and murdered in a vehicle, then dumped and displayed where she was found," Berger said.

"There's nothing I observed during the external examination or during the autopsy that would tell me she was assaulted inside a vehicle," Scarpetta answered.

"I'm thinking about the injuries she might have if she'd been sexually assaulted in the park, on the ground," Berger said. "I'm asking if it's been your experience when someone is sexually assaulted on a hard surface, such as the ground, that there would be bruises, abrasions."

"Often I will find that."

"As opposed to being raped, for example, in the backseat of a car, where the surface under the victim is more forgiving than frozen earth that's covered with stones and sticks and other debris," Berger continued.

"I can't tell from the body whether she was assaulted in a vehicle," Scarpetta repeated.

"Possible she got into a vehicle, was hit in the head, and then the person sexually assaulted her, was with her for a period of time before dumping her body where she was found." Berger wasn't asking. She was telling. "And her livor, her rigor, her temperature are, in fact, confusing and misleading because her body was barely clothed and exposed to near-freezing conditions. And if it's true she died a lingering death, perhaps lingered for hours because of her head injury—that maybe livor was advanced because of that."

"There are exceptions to the rules," Scarpetta said. "But I don't think I can offer the exceptions you seem to be looking for, Jaime."

"I've done a lot of literature searches over the years, Kay. Time of death is something I deal with and argue in court fairly frequently. I've found a couple of interesting things. Cases of people who die lingering deaths, let's say from cardiac failure or cancer, and livor mortis begins before they're even dead. And again, there are cases on record of people going into instantaneous rigor. So, hypothetically, if for some reason Toni's livor was already developing right before she died and she went into instantaneous rigor for some very unusual reason? And I believe that can happen in asphyxial deaths, and she did have a scarf tied around her neck, appears to have been strangled in addition to being hit with a blunt object. Wouldn't it be possible that she'd really been dead a much shorter period than you're assuming? Maybe dead for just a few hours? Fewer than eight hours?"

"In my opinion, that's not possible," Scarpetta said.

"Detective Bonnell," Berger said. "Do you have that WAV file? Perhaps you can play it on Marino's computer. Hopefully we'll be able to hear it over speakerphone. A recording of a nine-one-one call that came in at around two p.m. today."

"Doing it now," Bonnell said. "Let me know if you can't hear it."

Benton turned up the volume on the VoiceStation as the recording began:

"Police operator five-one-nine, what is the emergency?"

"Um, my emergency is about the lady they found in the park this morning, the north side of the park off One hundred and tenth Street?" The voice was nervous, scared. A man who sounded young.

"What lady are you referring to?"

"The lady, um, the jogger who was murdered. I heard about it on the news. . . ."

"Sir, is this an emergency?"

"I think so because I saw, I think I saw, who did it. I was driving by that area around five this morning and saw a yellow cab pulled over and a guy was helping what looked like a drunk woman out of the back. The first thing I thought was it was her boyfriend, like they'd been out all night. I didn't get a good look. It was pretty dark and foggy."

"It was a yellow cab?"

"And she was, like, drunk or passed out. It was real quick and, like I said, dark and a lot of mist and fog, really hard to see. I was driving toward Fifth Avenue and caught a glimpse. I had no reason to slow down, but I know what I saw, and it was definitely a yellow cab. The light on the roof was turned off, like when cabs are in use."

"Do you have a tag number or the identification number painted on the door?"

"No, no. I didn't see a reason, um, but I saw on the news, they said it's a jogger and I do remember this lady looked like she had on some type of running clothes. A red bandana or something? I thought I saw something red around her neck, and she had on a light-colored sweatshirt or something like that instead of a coat, because I noticed right away she didn't look all that warmly dressed. According to the time they said she was found, well, it wasn't long at all after I drove past that spot. . . ."

The WAV file stopped.

"I was contacted by dispatch, and I did speak to this gentleman over the phone and will follow up in person, and we've run a background on him," Bonnell said.

Scarpetta envisioned the yellow paint chip she had recovered from Toni Darien's hair, in the area of her head wound. She remembered thinking in the morgue when she was looking at the paint under a lens that the color reminded her of French's mustard and yellow cabs.

"Harvey Fahley, a twenty-nine-year-old project manager at Kline Pharmaceuticals in Brooklyn, has an apartment in Brooklyn," Bonnell continued. "And his girlfriend does have an apartment in Manhattan, in Morningside Heights."

Scarpetta certainly didn't know if the paint was automotive. It could be architectural, aerosol, from a tool, a bicycle, a street sign, from almost anything.

"What he told me is consistent with what he said on the nine-one-one recording," Bonnell said. "He'd spent the night with his girlfriend and was driving home, was headed to Fifth Avenue, planning to cut over on Fifty-ninth to the Queensboro Bridge so he could get ready for work."

It made sense why Berger was resistant to what Scarpetta believed was Toni's time of death. If a cabdriver was the killer, it seemed more plausible that he was cruising and spotted Toni while she was out, possibly walking or jogging late last night. It seemed implausible that a cabdriver would have picked her up at some point on Tuesday, perhaps in the afternoon, and then kept her body until almost five o'clock this morning.

As Bonnell continued to explain, "There was nothing suspicious about anything he said to me, nothing about his background. Most important, the description about the way the woman was dressed, his description of her as she was being helped out of the taxi? How could he possibly know those details? They haven't been made public."

The body doesn't lie. Scarpetta reminded herself of what she'd learned during her earliest days of training: *Don't try to force the evidence to fit the crime.* Toni Darien wasn't murdered last night. She wasn't murdered yesterday. No matter what Berger wanted to believe or any witness said.

"Did Harvey Fahley offer a more detailed description of the man who was allegedly helping the drunk-looking woman out of the taxi?" Benton asked, looking up at the ceiling, hands together, impatiently tapping his fingertips together.

"A man in dark clothing, a baseball cap, maybe glasses. He got the impression the man was slender, maybe an average-size person," Bonnell said. "But he didn't get a good look, because he didn't slow down and also because of the weather conditions. He said the taxi itself was blocking his view because the man and the woman were between it and the sidewalk, which would be true if you were driving east on One hundred and tenth, heading to Fifth Avenue."

"What about the taxi driver?" Benton asked.

"He didn't get a look but assumed there was one," Bonnell answered.

"Why would he assume that?" Benton asked.

"The only door open was the back door on the right side, as if the driver was still up front and the man and woman had been in the back. Harvey said if it had been the driver helping her out at a location like that, he probably would have stopped. He would have assumed the lady was in trouble. You don't just leave a drunk passed-out person on the roadside."

"Sounds like he's making excuses about why he didn't stop," Marino said. "He wouldn't want to think what he actually saw was a taxi driver dumping an injured or dead woman on the roadside. Easier to think it was a couple out drinking all night."

"The area he described in the nine-one-one recording," Scarpetta said. "How far would that be from where the body was found?"

"About thirty feet," Bonnell said.

Scarpetta told them about the bright-yellow paint chip she'd recovered from Toni's hair. She encouraged them not to place too much stock in the detail, because none of the trace evidence had been examined yet and she'd also found red and black microscopic chips on Toni's body. The paint could have been transferred from the weapon that fractured Toni's skull. The paint could be from something else.

"So if she was in a yellow cab, how could she have been dead thirty-six hours?" Marino voiced the obvious question.

"It would have to be a cabdriver who killed her," Bonnell replied with more confidence than any of them had a right to feel at the moment. "Either way you look at it, if what Harvey said is true, it had to be a cabdriver who picked her up last night, killed her, and dumped her body in the park early this morning. Or he had her for a while and then dumped her, if Dr. Scarpetta's right about time of death. And the yellow cab could connect Toni Darien to Hannah Starr."

Scarpetta had been waiting for that assumption next.

"Hannah Starr was last seen getting into a yellow cab," Bonnell added.

"I'm not at all prepared to connect Toni's case to Hannah Starr," Berger said.

"Thing is, if we don't say something and it happens again," Bonnell said, "then we're talking three."

"I have no intention of making any such connection at this time." Berger said it as a warning: Nobody else had better think of making that connection publicly, either.

"It's not necessarily what I think, not about Hannah Starr," Berger continued. "There are other factors about her disappearance. A lot of things I've been looking into point at her possibly being a very different type of case. And we don't know that she's dead."

"We also don't know that somebody else didn't see the same thing Harvey Fahley did," Benton said, looking at Scarpetta, saying it for her benefit. "Wouldn't be good if some other witness did the typical thing these days and instead of going to the police went to a news network. I wouldn't want to be within five miles of CNN or any other media outlet if this detail about the yellow cab has been leaked."

"I understand," Scarpetta said. "But whether it has or hasn't, I'd be concerned that my being a no-show tonight would make matters only worse. Would only escalate the sensational value. CNN knows I'm not going to discuss Toni Darien or Hannah Starr. I don't discuss active cases."

"I'd stay clear." Benton looked intensely at her.

"It's in my contract. I've never had a problem," she said to him.

"I agree with Kay. I'd conduct business as usual," said Berger. "If you cancel at the final hour, all it will do is give Carley Crispin something to talk about."

Dr. Warner Agee sat on the unmade bed inside his small suite of English antiques, the curtains closed to afford him privacy.

His hotel room was surrounded by buildings, eye-to-eye with other windows, and he couldn't help but think about his former wife and what it was like when he was forced to find his own place to live. He'd been appalled when he noticed how many downtown Washington apartments had telescopes, some decorative but functional, others for serious viewing. For example, an Orion binocular mount and tripod set in front of a reclining chair that didn't face a river or a park but another high-rise. The Realtor was crowing about the view as Agee peered directly into the condo across the way at someone buck naked, walking around, the drapes not drawn.

What purpose was there for telescopes and binoculars in congested areas of major cities like Washington, D.C., or here in New York unless it was spying, unless it was voyeurism? Obtuse neighbors undressing, having sex, arguing and fighting, bathing, sitting on the toilet. If people thought they had privacy in their own homes or hotel rooms, think again. Sexual predators, robbers, terrorists, the government—don't let them see you. Don't let them hear you. Make sure they aren't watching. Make sure they aren't listening. If they don't see or hear you, they can't get you. Security cameras on every corner, vehicle tracking, spy cams, sound amplifiers, eavesdropping, observing strangers in their most vulnerable and humiliating moments. All it takes is one piece of information in the wrong hands and your entire life can change. If you're going to play that game, do it to others before they can do it to you. Agee didn't leave blinds or curtains open, not even during the day.

"You know what the best security system is? Window shades." Advice he'd been giving his entire career.

Truer words never spoken, exactly what he'd said to Carley Crispin the first time they met at one of Rupe Starr's dinner parties when she was a White House press secretary and Agee was a consultant who traveled in many orbits, not just the FBI's. The year was 2000, and what a bombshell she'd been, outrageously attractive, with flaming red hair, edgy, smart, and a catbird when she wasn't talking to reporters and could say what she really thought. Somehow the two of them ended up in Rupe Starr's rare-book library, perusing old tomes on a few favorite subjects of Agee's, the flying heretic Simon Magus and the flying saint Joseph of Cupertino, who indisputably had the ability to levitate. Agee had introduced her to Franz Anton Mesmer and explained the healing powers of animal magnetism, and then Braid and Bernheim and their theories on hypnosis and nervous sleep.

It was natural that Carley with her journalistic passions

would be less interested in the paranormal and more drawn to the bookcase of photo albums, all bound in Florentine leather, the rogues gallery of Rupe's so-called friends, as Agee referred to the most popular section in the rare-book room. For a long stretch of solitary hours on the third floor of that massive house, Agee and Carley cynically perused decades of pictures, the two of them sitting side by side, pointing out the people they recognized.

"Amazing the friends money will buy, and he thinks they mean it. That's what I'd find sad if I could bring myself to feel sorry for a multi-fucking-billionaire," Agee said to someone who trusted no one because she was as amoral and just as much a user as anyone Rupe Starr might ever meet.

Only Rupe never made Carley any money. She was simply an attraction for the other guests, the same thing Agee was. You couldn't even get an interview at Rupe's special club without a minimum of a million dollars, but you could be a guest if he liked you and thought you were an amusement of one sort or another. He'd invite you to dinners, to parties, as entertainment for his real guests. The ones with money to invest. Actors, professional athletes, the newest wizards on Wall Street would descend upon the Park Avenue mansion, and for the privilege of making Rupe richer would get to mingle with other luminaries whose commodity wasn't cash. Politicians, television anchors, newspaper columnists, forensic experts, trial lawyers—it could be anyone in the news or with a good story or two who fit the profile of whomever Rupe was trying to impress. He researched his potential clients to find out what moved them, and then he would recruit. He didn't have to know you to put you on his B list. You'd get a letter or a phone call. Rupert Starr requests the pleasure of your company.

"Like throwing peanuts to the elephants," Agee had told Carley on an evening he'd never forget. "We're the peanuts, they're the elephants. Heavyweights we'll never be, even if we live to be as old as elephants, and the unfair irony is some of these elephants aren't old enough to join the circus. Look at this one." Tapping his finger on the picture of a ferociously pretty girl staring boldly into the camera, her arm around Rupe. The year written on the page was 1996.

"Must be some young actress." Carley was trying to figure out which one.

"Guess again."

"Well, who?" Carley asked. "She's pretty in a different way. Like a very pretty boy. Maybe it is a boy. No, I think I see breasts. Yup." Moving Agee's hand as she turned the page, and her touch startled him a little. "Here's another one. Definitely not a boy. Wow. Rather gorgeous if you get past her Rambo clothing and no makeup; she's got a very nice body, very athletic. I'm trying to remember what I've seen her in."

"You haven't and you'll never guess." Leaving his hand where it was, hoping she might move it again. "Here's a hint. FBI."

"Must be organized crime if she can afford to be in this Starr-studded collection." As if human beings were no different than Rupe's precious antique cars. "On the wrong side of the law, that's the only FBI connection she could have if she's filthy rich. Unless she's like us." Meaning the B list.

"She's not like us. She could buy this mansion and still have plenty left."

"Who the hell is she?"

"Lucy Farinelli." Agee found another photograph, this one of Lucy in the Starr basement garage, sitting behind the wheel of a Duesenberg, seeming intent on figuring out a priceless antique speedster she wouldn't hesitate to drive and maybe did on that particular day or some other day when she was in Starr Counting House, counting out her money.

Agee didn't know. He hadn't been to the mansion at the same time Lucy had, for the simple reason that Agee would be the last person invited for her entertainment or pleasure. At the very least she would remember him from Quantico, where as a high-school wunderkind she'd helped design and program the Criminal Artificial Intelligence Network, what the Bureau simply referred to as CAIN.

"Okay, I do know who that is." Carley was intrigued once she realized Lucy's connections to Scarpetta, and especially to Benton Wesley, who was tall with chiseled granite good looks, "the model for that actor in *The Silence of the Lambs*," in her words. "What's his name, who played Crawford?"

"Pure horseshit. Benton wasn't even at Quantico when it was filmed. Was off in the field somewhere working a case, and even he will tell you as much, arrogant prick that he is," Agee said, more than just ire aroused. He was feeling other stirrings.

"Then you know them." She was impressed.

"The whole gaggle. I know them, and at best they might know *about* me, might know *of* me. I'm not friends with them. Well, excluding Benton. He knows me rather intimately. Life and its dysfunctional interconnections. Benton fucks Kay. Kay loves Lucy. Benton gets Lucy an internship with the FBI. Warner gets fucked."

"Why do you get fucked?"

"What is artificial intelligence?"

"A substitute for the real thing," she'd said.

"You see, it can be difficult if you have these." Touching his hearing aids.

"You seem to hear me well enough, so I have no idea what you mean."

"Suffice it to say I might have been given some tasks, some opportunities, if a computer system hadn't come along that could do them instead," he'd said.

Perhaps it was the wine, a very fine Bordeaux, but he began to tell Carley about his ungratifying and unfair career and the toll it had taken, people and their problems, cops and their stresses and traumas, and the worst were the agents who weren't allowed to have problems, weren't allowed to be human, were FBI first and foremost and forced to unload on a Bureau-ordained psychologist or shrink. Babysitting, hand-holding, rarely being asked about criminal cases, never if they were sensational. He illustrated what he meant with a story set at the FBI Academy, Quantico, Virginia, in 1985, when an assistant director named Pruitt had told Agee that someone who was deaf couldn't possibly go into a maximum-security prison and conduct interviews.

There were inherent risks in using a forensic psychiatrist who wore hearing aids and read lips, and to be blunt, the Bureau wasn't going to use someone who might misinterpret what violent offenders were saying or had to continuously ask them to repeat themselves. Or what if they misinterpreted what Agee said to them?

What if they misinterpreted what he was doing, a gesture, the way he crossed his legs or tilted his head? What if some paranoid schizophrenic who had just dismembered a woman and stabbed out her eyes didn't like Agee staring at his lips?

That was when Agee had known who he was to the FBI, who he would always be to the FBI. Someone impaired. Someone imperfect. Someone who wasn't commanding enough. It wasn't about his ability to evaluate serial killers and assassins. It was about appearances, about the way he might represent the Almighty Bureau. It was about being an embarrassment. Agee had said he understood Pruitt's position and would do anything the FBI needed, of course. It was either do it their way or no way, and Agee had always wanted to get close to the fire of the FBI ever since he'd been a frail little boy playing cops and robbers, playing army and Al Capone, shooting cap guns he could barely hear.

The Bureau could use him internally, he was told. Critical incidents, stress management, the Undercover Safeguard Unit, basically psychological services for law enforcement with an emphasis on agents coming up from deep cover. Included in the mix were the supervisory special agents, the profilers. Since the Behavioral Science Unit was still relatively new to training and development, the Bureau should be more than a little concerned about what the profilers were exposed to on a regular basis and whether it interfered with intelligence gathering and operational effectiveness. At this point in the somewhat one-sided dialogue, Agee asked Pruitt if the FBI had given much thought to paper assessments of the offenders themselves, because Agee could help with that. If he could have access to raw data such as interview transcripts, evaluations, scene and autopsy photographs, the entirety of case files, which he could assimilate and analyze, he could create a meaningful database and establish himself as the resource he ought to be.

It wasn't the same thing as sitting down with a murderer, but it was better than being Florence Nightingale with a bedside manner, a support system while the real work, the satisfying work that was recognized and rewarded, went to inferiors who didn't have nearly the training or intelligence or insight he did. Inferiors like Benton Wesley.

"Of course, you don't need manual data analysis if you have artificial intelligence, if you have CAIN," Agee told Carley as they'd looked at photographs in Rupe Starr's library. "By the early nineties, statistical computations and different types of sorting and analysis were being done automatically, all of my efforts imported into Lucy's nifty artificial-intelligence environment. For me to continue what I was doing would have been akin to cleaning cotton by hand after Eli Whitney invented the cotton gin. I was back to evaluating agents—that's all I was good for in the eyes of the F-ing-BI."

"Imagine how I feel knowing the president of the United States is getting credit for my ideas." Carley, as usual, had made it about her.

Then he'd given her a tour of the mansion while the other guests partied several floors away, and in a guest room, he took her to bed, knowing full well that what had excited her wasn't him. It was sex and violence, power and money, and the conversation about *them,* the entity of Benton and Scarpetta and Lucy and anyone else who fell

under their spell. Afterward, Carley wanted nothing else
and Agee wanted more, wanted to be with her, wanted to
make love to her for the rest of his days, and when she'd
finally told him that he must stop writing her e-mails and
leaving her messages, it was too late. The damage was
done. He couldn't always be sure who overheard his conversations or how loud he was, and all it had taken was one
lapse, one voicemail he was leaving on Carley's phone while
his wife happened to be outside his closed office door, about
to come in with a sandwich and a cup of tea.

The marriage ended quickly, and he and Carley maintained infrequent long-distance contact; mostly he kept up
with her in the news as she moved into a variety of media
venues. Then almost a year ago he read a story about plans
for a show, *The Crispin Report,* pegged as hard-biting jour-
nalism and cop shop talk with an emphasis on current cases
and call-ins from viewers, and Agee decided to contact her
with a proposal, maybe more than one. He was lonely. He
hadn't gotten over her. Frankly, he needed money. His
legitimate consulting services were very rarely used anymore, his ties with the FBI having been severed not long
after Benton's were, in part inspired by the situation with
him, which was viewed as sticky by some and as sabotage
by others. For the past five years, Agee's ventures had taken
him elsewhere, a scavenger mostly paid pittances in cash for
services he rendered to industries and individuals and
organizations that profited handsomely from their ability
to manipulate customers, clients, patients, the police, he
didn't care who. Agee had done nothing but bend the knee
to others who were inferior to him, traveling constantly,
quite a lot in France, sinking deeper into invisibility and
debt and despair, and then he met with Carley, whose

prospects were equally perilous, neither of them young any-more.

What someone in her position needed most of all was access and information, he'd pitched to her, and the problem she was going to encounter was that the experts essential to her success wouldn't be willing to appear on camera. The good people don't talk. They can't. Or, like Scarpetta, they have contracts and you don't dare ask. But you could tell, Agee had said. That was the secret he taught Carley. Come onto the set already armed with what you need to know, and don't ask—tell. He could hunt and gather behind the scenes, and supply her with transcripts so her breaking news could be backed up, validated, or at least not disproved.

Of course he would be happy to appear on the air with her whenever she wanted. It would be unprecedented, he'd pointed out. He'd never been on camera before or in photographs and rarely gave interviews. He didn't say it was because he'd never been asked, and she didn't volunteer that she knew that was the reason. Carley wasn't a decent person, and neither was he, but she'd been kind enough to him, as kind as she was capable of being. They tolerated each other and fell into a rhythm, a harmony of professional conspiracy, but it had yet to become anything more, and by now he'd accepted that their night of Bordeaux in the Starr mansion was not to be repeated.

It wasn't a coincidence, because he didn't believe in them, that what brought Agee and Carley together originally would be part of a bigger destiny. She didn't believe in ESP or poltergeists and was neither a sender nor a receiver of telepathy—any information that might come her way too masked by sensory noise. But she trusted what was in the Starrs—specifically, Hannah, Rupe's daughter—and when she disappeared, they instantly seized it as an opportunity, the case they had been waiting for. They had a right to it, had claims to it, because of a prior connection that wasn't random in Agee's mind but an information transfer from Hannah, whom he'd gotten to know at the mansion and had introduced to his paranormal preoccupations and then introduced her to people here and abroad, one of them the man she married. It wasn't inconceivable to him that Hannah might begin to send telepathic signals after she vanished. It wasn't inconceivable that Harvey Fahley would send something next. Not a thought or an image but a message.

What to do about him. Agee was extremely anxious and getting irritated, having replied to Harvey's e-mail about an hour ago and hearing nothing further. There wasn't the luxury of time to wait any longer if Carley was to break the news tonight, and do it with the forensic pathologist who had autopsied Toni sitting right there. What could be better timing? It should be Agee sitting right there. That would be better timing, but he hadn't been invited. He wouldn't be asked when Scarpetta was on the show, couldn't be on the set or in the same building. She refused to appear with him, didn't consider him credible, according to Carley. Maybe Agee would give Scarpetta a lesson in credibility and do a favor for Carley. He needed a transcript.

How to get Harvey on the phone. How to engage him in a conversation. How to hijack his information. Agee contemplated e-mailing him a second time and including his own phone number, asking Harvey to call him, but it wouldn't help if he did. The only way it would suit Agee's purposes would be if Harvey dialed the 1-800 number for the hearing-impaired Web-based telephone service, but then Harvey would know that he was being monitored by a third party, a captioner who was transcribing every word he said in real time. If he was as cautious and traumatized as he seemed to be, he wasn't going to allow any such thing.

If Agee initiated the call, however, then Harvey would have no idea that what he said was being transcribed, was proof, almost as good as a recording but perfectly legal. It was what Agee did all the time when he interviewed sources on Carley's behalf, and on the infrequent occasion when the person complained or claimed he or she had said no such thing, Carley produced the transcript, which did not include Agee's side of the conversation, only what the source said, which was even better. If there was no record of Agee's questions and comments, then what the subject of the interview said could be interpreted rather much any way Carley pleased. Most people just wanted to be important. They didn't care if they were misquoted, as long as she got their name right or, when appropriate, kept them anonymous.

Agee impatiently tapped the space bar of his laptop, waking it up, checking for any new e-mails in his CNN mailbox. Nothing of interest. He had been checking every five minutes, and Harvey wasn't writing him back. Another prick of irritation and anxiety, more intense this time. He reread the e-mail Harvey had sent to him earlier:

Dear Dr. Agee,

I've watched you on *The Crispin Report* and am not writing to go on it. I don't want attention.

My name is Harvey Fahley. I'm a witness
in the case of the murdered jogger who I
just saw on the news has been identified
as Toni Darien. I was driving past
Central Park on 110th Street early this
morning and am positive I saw her being
pulled out of **a yellow cab**. I now
suspect it was her dead body being
pulled out. This was just minutes before
it was found.

Hannah Starr also was last seen in **a
yellow cab**.

I've given my statement to the police,
an investigator named L.A. Bonnell, who
told me I can't talk to anyone about
what I saw. Since you're a forensic
psychiatrist, I believe I can trust that
you'll handle my information
intelligently and in the strictest of
confidence.

My obvious concern is whether the public
should be warned, but I don't feel it's
for me to do it, and anyway, I can't or
I'll get in trouble with the police. But
if someone else is hurt or killed, I'll
never be able to live with myself. I
already feel guilty about not stopping
my car instead of driving past. I should
have stopped to check on her. It was

probably too late, but what if it hadn't
been? I'm really upset about this. I
don't know if you see private patients,
but I might need to talk to someone
eventually.

I'm asking you to please handle my
information as you think proper and
appropriate, but do not reveal it came
from me.

Sincerely, Harvey Fahley

Agee clicked on his sent folder and found the e-mail he'd
written in response forty-six minutes ago, reviewing it
again, wondering if there was something he said in it that
might have discouraged Harvey from answering him:

Harvey:

Please give me a phone number where I
can reach you, and we will handle this
judiciously. In the meantime, I strongly
advise that you not discuss this with
anyone else.

Regards, Dr. Warner Agee

Harvey hadn't answered because he didn't want Agee
to call him. That was likely it. The police had told
Harvey not to talk, and he was afraid to divulge more
than he already had, possibly regretted he'd contacted

Agee to begin with, or maybe Harvey hadn't checked his e-mail in the past hour. Agee couldn't find a telephone listing for Harvey Fahley, had come across one on the Internet, but it was nonworking. He could have said thank you or at the very least acknowledged receiving Agee's e-mail. Harvey was ignoring him. He might contact someone else. Poor impulse control, and next, Harvey divulges valuable information to another source and Agee is cheated again.

He pointed the remote at the TV and pressed the power button, and CNN blinked on. Another commercial announcing Kay Scarpetta's appearance tonight. Agee looked at his watch. In less than an hour. A montage of images: Scarpetta climbing out of a medical examiner's white SUV, her crime scene bag slung over her shoulder; Scarpetta in a white Tyvek disposable jumpsuit on the mobile platform unit, a colossal tractor-trailer with sifting stations set up for mass disasters, such as passenger plane crashes; Scarpetta on the set of CNN.

"What we need is the Scarpetta Factor and here for that is our own Dr. Kay Scarpetta. The best forensic advice on television, right here on CNN." The anchors' standard line these days before segueing into an interview with her. Agee kept hearing it in his memory as if he was hearing it in his bedroom, watching the silent commercial on the silent TV. Scarpetta and her special factor saving the day. Agee watched images of her, images of Carley, a thirty-second spot advertising tonight's show, a show Agee should be on. Carley was frantic about her ratings, was sure she wasn't going to make it another season if something didn't change dramatically, and if she got canceled, what would Agee do? He was a kept man, kept by lesser mortals, kept by Carley, who didn't feel about him the way he felt about her. If the show didn't go on, neither did he.

Agee got off the bed to retrieve his full-shell hearing aids from the bathroom counter, and he looked in the mirror at his bearded face, his receding gray hair, the person staring back at him both familiar and strange. He knew himself and he didn't. *Who are you anymore?* Opening a drawer, he noticed scissors and a razor, and he placed them on a small towel that was beginning to smell sour, and he turned on his hearing aids and the telephone was ringing. Someone complaining about the TV again. He lowered the volume, and CNN went from what had been barely discernible white noise to moderately loud noise that for people with normal hearing would be quite loud and jarring. He returned to the bed to begin his preparations, retrieving two cell phones, one a Motorola with a Washington, D.C., number that was registered to him, the other a disposable Tracfone he'd paid fifteen dollars for at a touristy electronics store in Times Square.

He paired his hearing aid's Bluetooth remote with his Motorola cell phone and on his laptop logged on to the Web-based caption-telephone service. He clicked on *Incoming Calls* at the top of the screen and typed in his D.C. cell phone number. Using the disposable phone, he dialed the 1-800 number for the service, and after the tone was prompted to enter the ten-digit number he wanted to call— his D.C. cell phone number, followed by the pound sign.

The disposable phone in his right hand called the Motorola cell phone in his left, and it rang, and he answered it, holding it against his left ear.

"Hello?" In his normal deep voice, a voice both pleasant and reassuring.

"It's Harvey." In a nervous tenor voice, the voice of someone young, someone very upset. "Are you alone?"

"Yes, I'm alone. How are you? You sound distressed," Agee said.

"I wish I hadn't seen it." The tenor voice faltering, about to cry. "Do you understand? I didn't want to see something like that, to be involved. I should have stopped my car. I should have tried to help. What if she was still alive when I saw her being dragged out of the yellow cab?"

"Tell me exactly what you saw."

Agee talking reasonably, rationally, comfortably settled into his role of psychiatrist, rotating the phones back and forth to his left ear as his conversation with himself was transcribed in real time by a captioner he'd never met or spoken to, someone identified only as operator 5622. Bold black text appeared in the Web browser window on Agee's computer screen as he talked in two different voices on two different phones, interjecting mutterings and noises that sounded like a bad connection while the captioner transcribed only the impersonated Harvey Fahley's dialogue:

". . . When the investigator was talking
to me she said something about the police
knowing Hannah Starr is dead because of
hair recovered, head hair that's
decomposed. (unclear) From where? Uh, she
didn't, the investigator didn't say.
Maybe they already know about a cabdriver
because Hannah was seen getting into one?
Maybe they know a lot they've not
released because of the implication, how

bad it would be for the city. Yes,
exactly. Money. (unclear) But if Hannah's
decomposing head hair was found in a cab
and nobody released that information,
(unclear) bad, really bad. (unclear)
Look, I'm losing you. (unclear) And I
shouldn't be talking anyway. I'm really
scared. I need to get off the phone."

Warner Agee ended the call and highlighted the text,
copying it onto a clipboard and pasting it into a Word document. He attached the file to an e-mail that would land
on Carley's iPhone in a matter of seconds:

Carley:
Appended is a transcript of what a
witness just told me in a phone
interview. As Usual: <u>Not for publication
or release, as we must protect my
source's identity</u>. But I hereby offer
the transcript as proof in the event the
network is questioned. —Warner

He clicked on send.

The set of *The Crispin Report* brought to mind a black hole.
Black acoustical tile, a black table and black chairs on a
black floor beneath a train yard of black-painted light rigs.
Scarpetta supposed the implication was hard news sobriety
and credible drama, which was CNN's style and exactly
what Carley Crispin didn't offer.

"DNA isn't a silver bullet," Scarpetta said, live on the air. "Sometimes it isn't even relevant."

"I'm shocked." Carley, in hot pink that clashed with her coppery hair, was unusually animated tonight. "The most trusted name in forensics doesn't believe DNA is relevant?"

"That's not what I said, Carley. The point I'm making is the same one I've been making for two decades: DNA isn't the only evidence and doesn't take the place of a thorough investigation."

"Folks, you heard it right here!" Carley's face, filler-plumped and paralyzed by Botox, stared into the camera. "DNA's not relevant."

"Again, that's not what I said."

"Dr. Scarpetta. Now, let's be honest. DNA is relevant. In fact, DNA could end up being the most relevant evidence in the Hannah Starr case."

"Carley . . . ?"

"I'm not going to ask you about it," Carley interrupted with a raised hand, trying a new ploy. "I'm citing Hannah Starr as an example. DNA could prove she's dead."

In studio monitors: the same photograph of Hannah Starr that had been all over the news for weeks. Barefoot and beautiful, a low-cut white sundress, on a sidewalk by the beach, smiling wistfully before a backdrop of palm trees and a variegated blue sea.

"And that's what a lot of people in the criminal-justice community have decided," Crispin continued. "Even if you're not going to admit it in public. And by not admitting the truth"—she was beginning to sound accusatory—"you're allowing dangerous conclusions to be made. If she's dead, shouldn't we know it? Shouldn't Bobby Fuller, her poor husband, know it? Shouldn't a formal homicide investigation be opened and warrants gotten?"

In the monitors, another photo that had been in circulation for weeks: Bobby Fuller and his tooth-whitened grin, in tennis clothes, in the cockpit of his four-hundred-thousand-dollar red Porsche Carrera GT.

"Isn't it true, Dr. Scarpetta?" Carley said. "In theory, couldn't DNA prove somebody's dead? If you had DNA from hair recovered from some location, such as a vehicle, for example?"

"It's not possible for DNA to prove a person is dead," Scarpetta said. "DNA is about identity."

"DNA could certainly tell us that the source of the hair found in a vehicle, for example, is Hannah."

"I'm not going to comment."

"And furthermore, if her hair showed evidence of decomposition."

"I can't discuss the facts of this case."

"Can't or won't?" Carley said. "What is it you don't want us to know? Maybe the inconvenient truth that experts like you might just be wrong about what really happened to Hannah Starr?"

Another recycled image on the monitors: Hannah in a Dolce & Gabbana suit, her long blond hair pulled back, glasses on, sitting at a Biedermeier desk in a corner office overlooking the Hudson.

"That her tragic disappearance might just be something entirely different from what everyone, including you, has assumed." Carley's questions, stated as facts, were taking on the tone of an F. Lee Bailey cross-examination.

"Carley, I'm a medical examiner in New York City. I'm sure you understand why I can't have this conversation."

"Technically, you're a private contractor, not a New York City employee."

"I'm an employee and answer directly to the chief medical examiner of New York City," Scarpetta said.

Another photo: the 1950s blue brick façade of the NYC chief medical examiner's office.

"You work pro bono. I believe that's been in the news—you donate your time to the New York office." Carley turned to the camera. "For my viewers who might not know, let me explain that Dr. Kay Scarpetta is a medical examiner in Massachusetts and also works part-time, without pay, for the New York City ME's office." To Scarpetta, "Not that I completely understand how you can work for New York City and the Commonwealth of Massachusetts."

Scarpetta didn't enlighten her.

Carley picked up a pencil as if she might take notes and said, "Dr. Scarpetta, the very fact that you say you can't talk about Hannah Starr is because you believe she's dead. If you didn't believe she was dead, it wouldn't be an issue for you to voice your opinion. She can't be your case unless she's dead."

Not true. Forensic pathologists can, when needed, examine living patients or get involved in cases of missing persons who are presumed dead. Scarpetta wasn't going to offer a clarification.

Instead she said, "It's improper to discuss the details of any case that's under investigation or hasn't been adjudicated. What I agreed to do on your show tonight, Carley, was to have a general discussion about forensic evidence, specifically trace evidence, one of the most common types of which is the microscopic analysis of hair."

"Good. Then let's talk about trace evidence, about hair."

Tapping the pencil on paperwork. "Isn't it a fact that tests done on hair could prove it was shed after someone was dead? If hair was discovered in a vehicle, for example, that had been used to transport a dead body?"

"DNA isn't going to tell you someone is dead," Scarpetta repeated.

"Then hypothetically, what could hair tell us, saying hair identified as Hannah's was recovered from some location, such as a vehicle?"

"Why don't we discuss microscopic hair examination in general. Since this is what you and I agreed we'd talk about tonight."

"In general, then," Carley said. "Tell us how you might be able to determine that hair is from a dead person. You find hair somewhere, let's say inside a vehicle. How can you tell if the person who shed it was alive or dead at the time?"

"Postmortem root damage or lack of it can tell us if head hair was shed by a living person or a dead body," Scarpetta answered.

"Precisely my point." Tapping her pencil like a metronome. "Because according to my sources, there has been hair recovered in the Hannah Starr case, and it definitely showed evidence of the damage you would associate with death and decomposition."

Scarpetta had no idea what Carley was talking about and wondered bizarrely if she might be confusing details of the Hannah Starr case with those from missing toddler Caylee Anthony, whose head hairs recovered from the family car trunk allegedly showed signs of decomposition.

"So, how do you explain hair damaged the way it gets after death if the person isn't dead?" Carley nailed Scarpetta with a stare that looked perpetually startled.

"I don't know what you mean by 'damaged,'" Scarpetta said, and it crossed her mind she should walk off the set.

"Damaged by, let's say insects, for example." Carley tapped the pencil loudly. "Sources have informed me that hair found in the Hannah Starr case shows evidence of damage, the sort of damage you see after death." To the camera, "And this hasn't been released to the public yet. We're discussing it for the first time right here, right now, on my show."

"Insect damage doesn't necessarily mean the person who shed hair is dead." Scarpetta answered the question, avoiding the topic of Hannah Starr. "If you naturally shed hair in your home, in your car, in your garage, the hair can be and in fact likely will be damaged by insects."

"Maybe you can explain to our viewers how insects damage hair."

"They eat it. Microscopically, you can see the bite marks. If you find hair with evidence of this type of damage, you generally assume the hair wasn't shed recently."

"And you assume the person is dead." Carley pointed the pencil at her.

"Based on that finding alone, no, you couldn't draw that conclusion."

In the monitors: microscopic images of two human head hairs magnified 50X.

"Okay, Dr. Scarpetta, we have pictures you asked us to show our viewers," Carley announced. "Tell us exactly what we're looking at."

"Postmortem root banding," Scarpetta explained. "Or, in the words of the eminent trace evidence examiner Nick Petraco, an opaque ellipsoidal band which appears to be composed of a collection of parallel elongated air spaces along the hair shaft nearest the scalp."

"Whew, let's translate for the viewers, how 'bout it."

"In the photos you're looking at, it's the dark area at the bulb-shaped root. See the dark banding? Suffice it to say, this phenomenon doesn't occur in living people."

"And these are Hannah Starr's hairs we're looking at," Carley said.

"No, they're certainly not." If she walked off the set, it would only make matters worse. *Just get through this,* Scarpetta told herself.

"No?" A dramatic pause. "Then whose are they?"

"I'm simply showing examples of what the microscopic analysis of hair can tell us," Scarpetta answered, as if the question was reasonable, when it absolutely wasn't. Carley knew damn well the hair wasn't from the Hannah Starr case. She knew damn well the image was generic, was from a PowerPoint presentation Scarpetta routinely gave at medicolegal death investigation schools.

"They're not Hannah's hairs, and they're not related to her disappearance?"

"They're an example."

"Well, I guess this is what they mean by 'the Scarpetta Factor.' You pull some trick out of your hat to support your theory, which clearly is that Hannah's dead, which is why you're showing us hairs shed by a dead person. Well, I agree, Dr. Scarpetta," Carley said slowly and emphatically. "I believe Hannah Starr is dead. And I believe it's possible what happened to her is connected to the jogger who was just brutally murdered in Central Park, Toni Darien."

In the monitors: a photograph of Toni Darien in tight

pants and a skimpy blouse, bowling lanes in the background; another photograph—this one of her body at the crime scene.

Where the hell did that come from? Scarpetta didn't show her shock. How did Carley get her hands on a scene photograph?

"As we know," Carley Crispin said to the camera, "I have my sources and can't always go into detail about who they are, but I can verify the information. Suffice it to say, I have information that at least one witness has reported to the NYPD that Toni Darien's body was seen being dragged out of a yellow cab early this morning, that apparently a taxi driver was pulling her body out of his yellow cab. Are you aware of this, Dr. Scarpetta?" To the slow tempo of pencil tap-taps.

"I'm not going to talk about the Toni Darien investigation, either." Scarpetta tried not to get distracted by the scene photograph. It looked like one of the photos taken by an OCME medicolegal investigator this morning.

"What you're saying is there's something to talk about," Carley said.

"I'm not saying that."

"Let me remind everyone that Hannah Starr was last seen getting into a yellow taxi after she had dinner with friends in Greenwich Village the day before Thanksgiving. Dr. Scarpetta, you're not going to talk about it, I know. But let me ask you something you should be able to answer. Isn't part of the medical examiner's mission prevention? Aren't you supposed to figure out why somebody died so maybe you can prevent the same thing from happening to someone else?"

"Prevention, absolutely," Scarpetta said. "And prevention

sometimes requires that those of us responsible for public health and public safety exercise extreme caution about the information we release."

"Well, let me ask you this. Why wouldn't it be in the best interest of the public to know there might be a serial killer who's driving a yellow cab in New York City, looking for his next victim? If you had access to a tip like that, shouldn't you publicize it, Dr. Scarpetta?"

"If information is verifiable and would protect the public, yes, I agree with you. It should be released."

"Then why hasn't it been?"

"I wouldn't necessarily know whether such information has or hasn't been, or if it's factual."

"How is it possible you wouldn't know? You get a dead body in your morgue and hear from the police or a credible witness that a yellow taxi might be involved, and you don't think it's your responsibility to pass along the tip to the public so some other poor innocent woman doesn't get brutally raped and murdered?"

"You're straying into an area that is beyond my direct knowledge and jurisdiction," Scarpetta replied. "The function of the medical examiner is to determine cause and manner of death, to supply objective information to those whose job it is to enforce the law. It's not an expectation that the medical examiner should act as an officer of the court or release so-called tips based on information or possibly rumors gathered and generated by others."

The teleprompter was letting Carley know she had a caller on hold. Scarpetta suspected the producer, Alex Bachta, might be trying to derail what was happening, was alerting Carley to quit while she was ahead. Scarpetta's contract had just been about as violated as it could get.

"Well, we have a lot to talk about," Carley said to her viewers. "But first let's take a call from Dottie in Detroit. Dottie, you're on the air. How are things in Michigan? You folks glad the election's over and we've finally been told we're in a recession, in case you didn't know?"

"I voted for McCain and my husband just got laid off from Chrysler and my name's not—" A quiet, breathy voice sounded in Scarpetta's earpiece.

"What's your question?"

"My question's for Kay. You know, I feel close to you, Kay. I just wish you could drop by and have coffee, because I know we'd be good friends and I'd love to offer you spiritual guidance you're not going to get from any lab—"

"What's your question?" Carley cut in.

"What kind of tests they might do to see if a body has begun decomposing. I believe they can test air these days with some kind of robot—"

"I haven't heard anything about a robot," Carley interrupted again.

"I wasn't asking you, Carley. I don't know what to believe anymore except forensic science certainly isn't solving what's wrong with the world. The other morning I was reading an article by Dr. Benton Wesley, who is Kay's highly respected forensic psychologist husband, and according to him, the clearance rate for homicides has dropped thirty percent in the past twenty years and is expected to continue to plummet. Meanwhile, one out of every thirty adults or about that is in prison in this country, so imagine if we caught everybody else who deserves it. Where are we going to put them and how can we afford it? I wanted to know, Kay, if it's true about the robot."

"What you're referring to is a detector that's been dubbed

a mechanical sniffer or electronic nose, and yes, you're right," Scarpetta said. "There is such a thing, and it's used in place of cadaver dogs to search for clandestine graves."

"This question's for you, Carley. It's a pity you're so banal and rude. Just look at how you disgrace yourself night after—"

"Not a question." Carley disconnected the call. "And I'm afraid we're out of time." She stared into the camera and shuffled papers on the desk—papers that were nothing more than a prop. "Join me tomorrow night on *The Crispin Report* for more exclusive details about the shocking disappearance of Hannah Starr. Is she connected to the brutal murder of Toni Darien, whose brutalized body was found in Central Park this morning? Is the missing link a yellow taxi, and should the public be warned? Talking with me again will be former FBI forensic psychiatrist Warner Agee, who believes both women may have been murdered by a violent sexual psychopath who could be a cabdriver in New York City and that city officials may be withholding this information to protect tourism. That's right. Tourism."

"Carley, we're off the air." A cameraman's voice.

"Did we get that last part about tourism? I should have hung up on that woman sooner," Carley said to the dark set. "I'm assuming there were a hell of a lot of callers on hold."

Silence. Then, "We got the part about tourism. A real cliff-hanger, Carley."

"Well, that should get the phones ringing around here," Carley said to Scarpetta. "Thanks so much. That was great. Didn't you think it was great?"

"I thought we had an agreement." Scarpetta removed her earpiece.

"I didn't ask you about Hannah or Toni. I made statements. You can't expect me to ignore credible information. You don't have to answer anything you're uncomfortable with, and you handled yourself perfectly. Why don't you come back tomorrow night? I'll have you and Warner on. I'm going to ask him to work up a profile of the cabdriver," Carley said.

"Based on what?" Scarpetta said heatedly. "Some antiquated anecdotal theory of profiling that isn't based on empirical research? If Warner Agee has something to do with the information you just released, you've got a problem. Ask yourself how he would know it. He's not remotely involved in these cases. And for the record, he was never an FBI profiler."

Scarpetta unclipped her mike, got up from the table, and stepped over cables, heading out of the studio alone. Emerging into a brightly lit long hallway, she passed poster-size photographs of Wolf Blitzer, Nancy Grace, Anderson Cooper, and Candy Crowley, and inside the makeup room she was surprised to discover Alex Bachta sitting on a high swivel chair. He was staring blankly at a TV with the sound turned low as he talked on the phone. She retrieved her coat from a hanger in the closet.

". . . Not that there was any doubt, but I'd agree, yes, a fait accompli. We can't have this sort of . . . I know, I know," Alex said to whoever was on the line. "Got to go."

He looked serious and tired in his rumpled shirt and tie as he hung up. Scarpetta noticed how gray his neatly trimmed beard was getting, how creased his face was, and the bags under his eyes. Carley had that effect on people.

"Don't ask me again," Scarpetta said to him.

Alex motioned for her to shut the door as lights on the phone began to flash.

"I quit," she added.

"Not so fast. Have a seat."

"You violated my contract. More important, you violated my trust, Alex. Where did you get the scene photograph, for God's sake?"

"Carley does her own research. I had nothing to do with it. CNN had nothing to do with it. We had no idea Carley was going to say a fucking thing about yellow cabs and hairs being found. Jesus Christ, I hope it's true. Huge headlines, well, that's great. But it damn well better be true."

"You hope it's true there's a serial killer driving a yellow cab in the city?"

"Not what I mean. Jesus, Kay. A damn hornet's nest, the phones are going crazy. The NYPD deputy commissioner of public information is denying it. Categorically denying it. He said the detail about Hannah Starr's decomposing head hair being found is unfounded, complete crap. Is he right?"

"I'm not going to help you with this."

"Fucking Carley. She's so damn competitive, so damn jealous of Nancy Grace, Bill Kurtis, Dominick Dunne. She'd better have something to back up what she just said, because people are flying all over us. I can't imagine what tomorrow will be like. Interestingly enough, though, the yellow cab connection? Neither denied nor confirmed by NYPD. So, what do you make of that?"

"I'm not going to make anything of it," Scarpetta said. "My job as a forensic analyst isn't to help you work cases on the air."

"It would have been better if we'd had B roll of the mechanical sniffer." Alex shoved his fingers through his hair.

"I didn't know the subject was going to come up. I'd been promised Hannah Starr wouldn't come up. It was never a question that Toni Darien would. Good God. You know she's an OCME case, was at my office this morning. You promised me, Alex. What happened to contracts?"

"I'm trying to envision what it looks like. Rather hard to take it seriously, some crime-busting tool called a sniffer. But then I suppose most police departments don't have access to cadaver dogs."

"You can't bring in experts who are actively working criminal cases and allow this sort of thing to happen."

"If you had explained cadaver dogs. That would have been amazing."

"I would have been happy to go into detail about that, but not the other. You agreed the Starr case was off-limits. You know damn well the Toni Darien case is off-limits."

"Look. You were great tonight, okay?" He met her eyes and sighed. "I know you don't think so and you're upset. I know you're pissed, understandably. So am I."

Scarpetta dropped her coat in a makeup chair and sat. "I probably should have resigned months ago, a year ago. Never done it to begin with. I promised Dr. Edison I would never discuss active cases, and he took me at my word. You've put me in jeopardy."

"I didn't. Carley did."

"No, I did. I put myself in jeopardy when I of all people know better. I'm sure you can find some forensic pathologist or criminalist who'd love to do this and would be happy to voice sensational opinions and speculations instead of being cautiously theoretical and objective the way I am."

"Kay . . ."

"I can't be a Carley. That's not who I am."

"Kay, *The Crispin Report* is in the toilet. Not just the ratings, but she's being blasted by reviewers, by bloggers, and I'm getting complaints from the top, have been getting them for a while. Carley used to be a decent journalist, but no longer, that's for damn sure. She wasn't my idea, and in all fairness to the network, she's known from the start this is an audition."

"Whose idea was she, then? You're the executive producer. What audition?"

"A former White House press secretary, she used to be a huge deal. I don't know what's happened. It was a mistake, and in all fairness, she knew the show was a trial run. For one thing, she promised to use her legitimate connections to get outstanding guests like you."

"She's gotten me because three times now you've put a gun to my head about it."

"Trying to salvage what isn't salvageable. I've tried. You've tried. We've given her every opportunity. Doesn't matter whose idea, none of it matters, and her guests, other than you, suck, are bottom of the barrel, because who wants to go on with her? That fossil of a forensic psychiatrist Dr. Agee, if I have to listen to another second of his pedantic monologues. Bottom line in this business, one season that's not so hot and maybe you try again. Two seasons and you're out. In her case, the answer's obvious. She belongs on some local news broadcast in a small town somewhere. Maybe doing weather or a cooking show or *Ripley's Believe It or Not!* She sure as hell doesn't belong on CNN."

"I assume what you're getting at is you're canceling her," Scarpetta said. "Not good news, especially this time of year and in this economy. Does she know?"

"Not yet. Please don't mention anything. Look, I'll get right to it." He leaned against the edge of the makeup counter, dug his hands into his pockets. "We want you to take her place."

"I hope you're joking. I couldn't possibly. And it's not really what you want, anyway. I'm not a good fit for this sort of theater."

"It's theater, all right. Theater of the absurd," Alex said. "That's what she's turned it into. Took her less than a year to completely fuck it up. We're not at all interested in you doing the same sort of show, doing Carley's bullshit show, hell, no. A crime show in the same time slot, but that's where the similarities end. What we've got in mind is completely different. It's been in discussion for a while now, actually, and all of us here feel the same way. You should have your own show, something perfectly suited to who and what you are."

"Something suited to who and what I am would be a beach house and a good book, or my office on a Saturday morning when no one is around. I don't want a show. I told you I would help out as an analyst only—and only if it didn't interfere with my real life or do harm."

"What we do is real life."

"Remember our early discussions?" Scarpetta said. "We agreed that as long as it didn't interfere with my responsibilities as a practicing forensic pathologist. After tonight, there can be no doubt it's interfering."

"You read the blogs, the e-mails. The response to you is phenomenal."

"I don't read them."

"*The Scarpetta Factor*," Bachta said. "A great name for your new show."

"What you're suggesting is the very thing I'm trying to get away from."

"Why get away from it? It's become a household word, a cliché."

"Which is what I sure as hell don't want to become," she said, trying not to sound as offended as she felt.

"What I mean is, it's the buzz. Whenever something seems unsolvable, people want the Scarpetta Factor."

"Because you started the so-called buzz by having your people say it on the air. By introducing me that way. By introducing what I have to say that way. It's embarrassing and misleading."

"I'm sending a proposal over to your apartment," Alex said. "Take a look and we'll talk."

8

Lights flickered in New Jersey like a million small flames, and planes looked like supernovas, some of them suspended in black space, perfectly still. An illusion, reminding Benton of what Lucy always said: When an aircraft seems motionless, it's either heading directly toward you or directly away. Better know which it is or you're dead.

He leaned forward tensely in his favorite oak chair in front of windows overlooking Broadway and left Scarpetta another message. "Kay, do not walk home alone. Please call me and I'll meet you."

It was the third time he'd tried her phone. She wasn't answering and should have been home an hour ago. His impulse was to grab his shoes, his coat, and run out the door. But that wouldn't be smart. The Time Warner Center and the entire area of Columbus Circle were vast. It was unlikely Benton would find her, and she'd get worried when she came in and discovered him gone. Better to stay put. He got out of his chair and looked south where CNN was headquartered, its gunmetal-gray glass towers checkered with soft white light.

Carley Crispin had betrayed Scarpetta, and city officials were going to be in an uproar. Maybe Harvey Fahley had contacted CNN, had decided to be an iReporter or whatever those people who became self-appointed television journalists were called. Maybe someone else claimed to have witnessed something, to have information, just as Benton had feared and predicted. But the details about decomposing head hairs found in a taxi wouldn't have come from Fahley unless he'd made it up, was outright spinning lies. Who would say something like that? Hannah Starr's hair hadn't been found anywhere.

He called Alex Bachta's cell phone again. This time the producer answered.

"I'm looking for Kay." Benton didn't bother saying hello.

"She left a few minutes ago, walked out with Carley," Alex said.

"With Carley?" Benton said, baffled. "Are you sure?"

"Absolutely. They were leaving at the same time and walked out together."

"Do you know where they were going?"

"You sound worried. Everything all right? Just so you know, the information about the yellow cab and Hannah—"

"I'm not calling about that," Benton cut him off.

"Well, everybody else is. Not our idea. Carley's on her own and she'll have to stand by it. I don't care what her source is. She's accountable."

Benton paced in front of the windows, not interested in Carley or her career. "Kay's not answering her phone," he said.

"I can try to reach Carley for you. Is there a problem?"

"Tell her I'm trying to get hold of Kay and it's best they get in a cab."

"Seems like a weird thing to say, considering. I don't know if I'd recommend a cab right now," Alex said, and Benton wondered if he was trying to be funny.

"I don't want her walking. I'm not trying to alarm anybody," Benton said.

"Then you are worried that this killer might come after—"

"You don't know what I'm worried about, and I don't want to waste time discussing it. I'm asking you to get hold of Kay."

"Hold on. I'm going to try Carley right now," Alex said, and Benton could hear him entering a number on a different phone, leaving Carley a voicemail: ". . . So call me ASAP. Benton's trying to reach Kay. I don't know if you're still with her. But it's urgent." He got back to Benton. "Maybe they forgot to turn their phones back on after the show."

"Here's the phone number for the concierge desk in our building," Benton said. "They can put you through to me if you hear anything. And I'll give you my cell."

He wished Alex hadn't used the word *urgent*. He gave him the numbers and thought about calling Marino next, sitting back down and dropping the phone in his lap, not wanting to talk to him or even hear his voice again tonight, but he needed his help. The lights of high-rises across the Hudson were mirrored in water along the shore, the river dark in the middle, a void, not even a barge in sight, an empty, frigid darkness, what Benton felt in his chest when he thought about Marino. Benton wasn't sure what to do and for a moment did nothing. It angered him that whenever Scarpetta was at risk, Marino was the first person who came to mind, to anybody's mind, as if he was appointed by some higher power to take care of her. Why? Why did he need Marino for anything?

Benton was still angry as hell, and it was at times like this that he felt it most. In some ways he felt it more than he had at the time of the incident. It would be two years this spring, a violation that in fact was criminal. Benton knew all about it, every gory detail, had faced it after it had happened. Marino drunk as hell and crazy, blamed it on booze and the sexual-performance drug he was taking, one factor added to another, didn't matter. Everybody was sorry, couldn't be sorrier. Benton had handled the situation with grace and facility, certainly with humanity, had gotten Marino into treatment, had gotten him a job, and by now Benton should be past it. But he wasn't. It hung over him like one of those planes, bright and huge like a planet, not moving and maybe about to slam into him. He was a psychologist and he had no insight into why he couldn't get out of the way or was in the same damn airspace to begin with.

"It's me," Benton said when Marino answered on the first ring. "Where are you?"

"In my shitcan apartment. You want to tell me what the hell just happened? Where did Carley Crispin get this shit? When Berger finds out, Jesus Christ. She's on the helicopter and doesn't know. Who the hell got to Carley? It's not like she could just pull that info out of nowhere. Someone must have said something. Where the hell did she get the scene photograph? I've been trying to get hold of Bonnell. Big surprise, I'm getting voicemail. I'm sure she's on her phone, probably the commissioner on down the line, everybody wanting to know if we got a serial murderer driving a cab in the city."

Marino had been watching Scarpetta on *The Crispin Report.* That figured. Benton felt a twinge of resentment, then felt nothing. He wasn't going to allow himself to sink into his dark pit.

"I don't know what happened. Someone got to Carley, obviously. Maybe Harvey Fahley, maybe someone else. You sure Bonnell wouldn't—" Benton started to say.

"Are you fucking kidding me? Like she's going to leak details about her own case to CNN?"

"I don't know her, and she was worried about the public not being warned."

"Take it from me, she's not going to be happy about this," Marino said, as if he and Bonnell were new best friends.

"Are you near your computer?"

"Can be. Why? What does the Doc have to say?"

"I don't know. She's not home yet," Benton said.

"You don't know? How come you're not with her?"

"I never go to CNN, never go over there with her. She doesn't like it. You know how she is."

"She walked over by herself?"

"It's six blocks, Marino."

"Doesn't matter. She shouldn't."

"Well, she does. Every time, walks by herself, insists on it—has ever since she started appearing on shows more than a year ago. Won't take a car service and won't let me go with her, assuming I'm in the city the same time she is, and often I'm not." Benton was rambling and sounded irritable. He was annoyed that he was explaining himself. Marino made him feel like a bad husband.

"One of us should be with her when she's got live TV," Marino said. "It's advertised when she's going to be on, advertised on their website, on commercials, days in advance. Someone could be outside the building waiting for her before or after. One of us should be with her, just like I do with Berger. When it's live, it's pretty damn obvious where people are and when."

It was exactly what Benton was worried about. Dodie Hodge. She'd called Scarpetta on TV. Benton didn't know where Dodie was. Maybe in the city. Maybe nearby. She didn't live far from here. Just on the other side of the George Washington Bridge.

"I'll tell you what. I'll let you give Kay a lecture on security and see if she pays more attention to you than she does to me," Benton was saying.

"Probably I should keep an eye on her without her knowing it."

"A quick way to make her hate you."

Marino didn't respond, and he could have. He could say that Scarpetta didn't have it in her to hate him or she would have hated him long before now. She would have begun hating him that spring night in Charleston a year and a half ago when Marino, drunk and enraged, had assaulted her inside her own home. But Benton was quiet. What he'd just said about hate seemed to linger, to hang like one of those planes not moving, and he was sorry he'd said it.

"Dodie Hodge," Benton said. "The caller supposedly from Detroit. I can tell you the reason I know her name is she sent us an anonymous Christmas card. Sent one to Kay and me."

"If that's what you can tell me, then there's other stuff

you can't tell me. Let me guess. From the land of fruit and nuts. Bellevue, Kirby, McLean's. One of your patients, explaining why she'd supposedly read some article you wrote about the shitty clearance rate. All true, though. Another twenty years, nothing will get solved. Everybody will live in forts with machine guns."

"I didn't publish a journal article on that particular topic."

He didn't add that Warner Agee did. Some derivative unoriginal editorial in Benton forgot which newspaper. He had Agee as a Google alert. Out of self-defense, ever since the bullshit had started cropping up in Wikipedia. Dr. Clark hadn't been telling Benton anything he didn't already know.

"She's a patient of yours. True or false?" Marino's voice. Christ, he was loud.

"I can't tell you if she was or wasn't," Benton said.

"Past tense. She's out, then, free as a cuckoo bird. Tell me what you want me to do," Marino said.

"I think it would be a good idea to run her through RTCC." Benton could only imagine what Dr. Clark would say.

"I got to go over there anyway, will probably be there most of tomorrow."

"I'm talking about tonight. Now," Benton said. "Maybe see if that beast of a computer system comes up with anything we should know. They letting you remote-access these days or do you have to go to One Police Plaza?"

"Can't data-mine remote."

"Sorry about that. Hate to put you out."

"Got to work with the analysts, which is a good thing. I ain't a Lucy. Still type with two fingers and don't know a damn thing about disparate data sources, live feeds. What they call the hunt. Am putting on my boots as we speak, heading out on 'the hunt,' just for you, Benton."

Benton was fed up with Marino trying to placate him, trying to win him over as if nothing had happened. Benton wasn't friendly, barely civil, and he knew it and couldn't seem to help it, and it had gotten worse in recent weeks. Maybe it would be better if Marino would just tell him to go fuck himself. Maybe then they could get past it.

"You don't mind me asking, how'd you manage to connect a Christmas card with this Dodie lady who just called from Detroit? Supposedly Detroit," Marino was saying. "The Doc know about the Christmas card?"

"No."

"No to which question?"

"All of them," Benton said.

"This Dodie lady ever met the Doc?"

"Not that I'm aware of. It's not about Kay. It's about me. Calling CNN was for my benefit."

"Yeah, I know, Benton. Everything's about you, but that's not what I asked." Aggression, like a finger poking Benton's chest. *Good. Go ahead and get angry. Fight back.*

"I recognized her voice," Benton answered.

In an earlier century maybe the two of them would have taken it outside and had a slugfest. There was something to be said for primitive behavior. It was purging.

"On a Christmas card? I'm confused," Marino went on.

"A singing card. You open it and a recording plays. A recording of Dodie Hodge singing a rather inappropriate Christmas tune."

"You still got it?"

"Of course. It's evidence."

"Evidence of what?" Marino wanted to know.

"See what you find on the computer."

"I'll ask again. The Doc isn't aware of Dodie Hodge or her card?"

"She's unaware. Let me know what you find at RTCC." Benton couldn't go there himself and take care of it, didn't have the authority, and he resented the hell out of it.

"Meaning I'm going to find something. That's why you're suggesting it," Marino said. "You already know what I'm going to find. You realize how much time your confidentiality crap wastes?"

"I don't know what you'll find. We just need to make sure she isn't dangerous, that she hasn't been arrested somewhere for something," Benton said.

Marino should find a record of Dodie's arrest in Detroit. Maybe there were other things. Benton was being a cop again, only it was by proxy, and the powerlessness he felt was becoming intolerable.

"I'm concerned about unstable individuals who are aggressively interested in well-known people," Benton added.

"Like who besides the Doc? Even though what Dodie did is really about you. Who else? You got other well-known people in mind?"

"For example, movie stars. Hypothetically, a movie star like Hap Judd."

Silence, then Marino said, "Kind of interesting you'd bring him up."

"Why?"

What did Marino know?

"Maybe you should tell me why you brought him up," Marino said.

"As I suggested, see what you find at RTCC." Benton had said too much. "As you know, I'm not in a position to investigate."

He couldn't even ask to see a driver's license when he sat down in a room with a patient. Couldn't pat the person down for a weapon. Couldn't run a background. Couldn't do anything.

"I'll take a look at Dodie Hodge," Marino said. "I'll take a look at Hap Judd. You interested in anything else, let me know. I can run whatever the hell I want. I'm glad I'm not a profiler with all these bullshit limitations. Would drive me batshit."

"If I was still a profiler I wouldn't have limitations and I wouldn't need you to run anything," Benton said testily.

"If I talk to the Doc before you do? Okay if I tell her about Dodie?"

The idea of Marino talking to Scarpetta before Benton did was more than a little irritating.

Benton said, "If for some reason you talk to her before I do, it would be much appreciated if you'd tell her I've been trying to reach her."

"I hear you, and I'm heading out," Marino said. "I'm kind of surprised she's still not home. I could get a couple of marked units to be on the lookout."

"I wouldn't at this point unless you want it all over the news. Remember who she's with. She left with Carley Crispin. Cops roll up on the two of them, what do you suppose the lead will be on Carley's show tomorrow night?"

"My guess is *The Taxi Terror in Manhattan*."

"You making up headlines now?" Benton said.

"Not me. They're already saying it. Talking about the yellow-cab connection. That's probably all we'll be hearing on the news this holiday. Maybe the Doc and Carley stopped for coffee or something."

"I can't imagine why Kay would want to have coffee with her after what she just did."

"Let me know if you need anything else." Marino hung up.

Benton tried Scarpetta again and the call went straight to voicemail. Maybe Alex was right and she'd forgotten to turn her phone back on and no one had reminded her, or maybe the battery was dead. It wasn't like her, no matter the explanation. She must be preoccupied. It wasn't her habit to be out of communication when she was en route and knew he was expecting her within a certain time frame. Alex wasn't answering, either. Benton began studying the recording he'd made of Scarpetta's appearance on *The Crispin Report* an hour earlier while he opened a video file on the computer notebook in his lap, this one a recording he'd made at McLean Hospital in mid-November.

". . . The other morning I was reading an article by Dr. Benton Wesley, who is Kay's highly respected forensic psychologist husband . . ." Dodie's breathy voice, disembodied, sounding from the flat-screen TV.

Benton fast-forwarded the video file on his notebook as he watched Scarpetta on the TV over the nonworking fireplace inside their prewar apartment on Central Park West. She looked stunning, her fine-featured face youthful for her age, her blond hair casual, brushing the collar of a fitted skirt suit, navy with a hint of plum. It was incongruous and disconcerting to look at her, then at the recording of Dodie Hodge playing on the computer in his lap.

". . . You can relate a teeny-weeny bit, can't you? You're almost in my same boat, aren't you, Benton?" A hefty homely woman frumpily dressed, her graying hair in a bun, the Book of Magick in its black cover with yellow stars in front of her. "Of course it's not like having a movie star in the family, but you do have Kay. I hope you'll tell her I never miss her when she's on CNN. Why don't they have you on with her instead of that stuffed shirt Warner Agee, those hearing aids of his like flesh-colored leeches behind his ears?"

"You seem to resent him." Because Dodie had made similar comments before.

Benton watched the recorded image of himself, sitting stiffly, inscrutably, in a proper dark suit and tie. He was tense and Dodie sensed it. She was enjoying his discomfort and seemed to intuit that the subject of Agee might make Benton squirm.

"He had his chance." Dodie smiled but her eyes were flat.

"What chance was that?"

"We have people in common, and he should have been honored . . . "

Benton hadn't given the comment much thought at the time, was too consumed by his desire to get the hell out of the interview room. Now a singing card had been sent and Dodie had called CNN, and he wondered what she'd been implying by her comment about Agee. Who could Benton and Dodie possibly have in common unless it was Warner Agee, and why would she know him? Unless she didn't. Maybe her Detroit lawyer did. The absurd request for Agee to be the expert who evaluated her at McLean was presented by her counsel, someone named Lafourche, slow talking, sounded Cajun, and seemed to have an agenda. Benton had never met him and knew nothing about him, but they'd talked a number of times on the phone when Lafourche would page Benton, track him down to check on how "our girl" was doing, making jokes and cracks about a client "who can tell tales as tall as 'Jack and the Beanstalk.'"

". . . It's a pity you're so banal and rude. . . ." Dodie's voice on the television over the fireplace.

The camera on Scarpetta, absently touching her earpiece as she listened, then returning her hands to the table, folding them placidly. A gesture you'd have to know her as well as Benton did to recognize. She was working hard to control herself. He should have warned her. The hell with HIPAA regulations and confidentiality. He resisted the impulse to rush out into the freezing December night to find his wife. He watched and listened and felt how much he loved her.

9

The lights of Columbus Circle pushed back the darkness of Central Park, and near the gateway leading into it, the Maine Monument's fountain and its gilded sculpture of Columbia Triumphant were deserted.

The red booths of the holiday market were closed, their crowds this season dramatically diminished, and there wasn't a soul milling around the news kiosk, not even the usual cops, just an old man who looked homeless, wrapped in layers, sleeping on a wooden bench. Taxis speeding by were minus advertising in their lighted tops, and gone were long lines of limousines outside apartment buildings and hotels. Everywhere Scarpetta looked she found symbols and signs of dismal times, of the worst times she could recall. She had grown up poor in a marginal part of Miami, but that had felt different because it wasn't everybody. It was just them, the Scarpettas, of struggling Italian immigrant stock.

"Aren't you the lucky one to live right here?" Carley peeked over the turned-up collar of her coat as she and Scarpetta followed the sidewalk in the uneven glow of lamplight.

"Someone pays you well. Or maybe it's Lucy's apartment. She'd be perfect to have on my show to talk about forensic computer investigations. She still good friends with Jaime Berger? I saw them one night at the Monkey Bar. Don't know if they mentioned it. Jaime refuses to be on, and I'm not going to ask again. It really isn't fair. It wasn't anything I did."

Carley didn't seem to have a glimmer that there would be no future shows, at least not with her as the host. Or maybe she was fishing because she suspected what was going on behind the scenes at CNN. It nagged at Scarpetta that when she and Alex had walked out of the makeup room, they'd discovered Carley waiting in the hallway not two feet from the door. Ostensibly, she was just that second leaving and she and Scarpetta should walk together, which hadn't made any sense. Carley didn't live nearby, but in Stamford, Connecticut. She didn't walk or take the train or a cab, always used a car service supplied by the network.

"After she was on *American Morning* last year. I don't know if you saw it." Carley stepped around dirty patches of ice. "That animal abuse case she prosecuted, the pet shop chain. CNN had her on to talk about it, really as a favor. And she got annoyed because she got asked hard questions. So, guess who gets punished? Me. If you asked her, she'd probably go on. I bet you could talk anybody into it you wanted, with the connections you have."

"Why don't we get you a cab," Scarpetta said. "You're going out of your way, and I'm fine to walk alone. It's just up ahead."

She wanted to call Benton so he'd know why she was taking so long and wouldn't worry, but she didn't have her BlackBerry. She must have left it in the apartment, had probably set it down by the sink in the master bath, and it had occurred to her several times now to borrow Carley's phone. But that would mean using it to call a private and unpublished number, and if Scarpetta knew nothing else after tonight, Carley wasn't to be trusted.

"I'm glad Lucy didn't have her fortune invested with Madoff, not that he's the only crook," Carley then said.

A train clattered underfoot and warm air billowed up from a grate. Scarpetta wasn't going to take the bait. Carley was fishing.

"I didn't get out of the market when I should have, waited until the Dow fell below eight thousand," Carley continued. "Here I am, sometimes at the same events as Suze Orman, and did I ask her for advice? How much did Lucy lose?"

As if Scarpetta would tell her, assuming she knew.

"I know she made a fortune in computers and invest-ments, always on the *Forbes* list, in the top hundred. Except now," Carley continued. "I noticed she's not listed anymore. Wasn't she once, well, not that long ago, worth in the bil-lions because of high-speed technologies and all sorts of software she's been inventing since she was practically in diapers? Plus, I'm sure she's been getting good financial advice. Or she was."

"I don't look at *Forbes* lists," Scarpetta said, and she didn't know the answer. Lucy had never been all that forth-coming about her finances, and Scarpetta didn't ask. "I don't talk about my family," she added.

"There certainly are a lot of things you don't talk about."

"And we're here." They had reached Scarpetta's building. "You take care of yourself, Carley. Have a happy holiday and a happy new year."

"Business is business, right? All's fair. Don't forget we're friends." Carley hugged her. She'd never done that before.

Scarpetta entered the polished-marble lobby of her building, digging in her coat pockets for her keys, seeming to remember that's where her BlackBerry had been last. Was she certain? She couldn't remember, tried to reconstruct what she'd done tonight. Had she used her phone at all, maybe taken it out at CNN and left it somewhere? No. She was sure she hadn't.

"You were good on TV." The concierge, young and recently hired, and sharp in his neat blue uniform, smiled at her. "Carley Crispin put you through it, huh? If it had been me, I would have gotten mad. Something just came for you." He reached down behind the desk. Scarpetta remembered his name was Ross.

"Just came?" she said. "At this hour?" Then she remembered. Alex was sending over a proposal.

"The city that never sleeps." Ross handed her a FedEx box.

She boarded the elevator and pressed the button for the twentieth floor, glancing at the airbill, looking at it more closely. She searched for confirmation that the package was from Alex, from CNN, but there was no return address and her own address was unusual:

DR. KAY SCARPETTA
CHIEF MEDICAL EXAMINER of GOTHAM CITY
1111 CENTRAL PARK WEST USA 10023

Referring to her as the chief medical examiner of Gotham City was sarcastic. It was kooky. The handwriting was so precise it looked like a font, almost looked computer-generated, but she could tell it wasn't, and she sensed a mocking intelligence guiding the hand that had held the pen. She wondered how the person knew that she and Benton had an apartment in this building. Their addresses and phone numbers were unpublished and unlisted, and she realized with growing alarm that the sender's copy was still attached to the airbill. The package hadn't been sent by FedEx. *Dear God, don't let this be a bomb.*

The elevator was old, with ornate brass doors and an inlaid wood ceiling, and it climbed excruciatingly slowly, and she imagined a muffled explosion and hurtling down the dark shaft, crashing at the bottom. She smelled a foul tarry chemical odor, like a petroleum-based accelerant, sweet but disgusting. She focused on it, unsure what it was or if it was real. Diesel fuel. Diphorone Pentaperoxide and acetone peroxide and C4 and nitroglycerine. Odors and dangers she knew from working fires and explosions, from teaching at post-blast schools in the late nineties when Lucy was a special agent with ATF, when Scarpetta and Benton were members of its International Response Team. Before Benton was dead, then alive again.

Silver hair, charred flesh and bone, his Breitling watch in a soup of sooty water at that fire scene in Philadelphia where she'd felt her world end. What she'd thought were Benton's remains. His personal effects. Didn't just suspect it, was certain he was dead because she was supposed to be certain. The dirty, foul odor of arson and accelerants. Emptiness yawning before her, impenetrable and forever, nothing left but isolation and pain. She feared nothingness because she knew what it felt like. Year after year of non-existence, her brain going strong but not her heart. How to describe it? Benton still asked her, but not often. He'd been hiding from the Chandonne cartel, from organized criminals, murderous scum, and of course had been protecting her, too. If he was in danger, she was in danger. As if she was in less danger, somehow, with him not around. Not that she was asked. Better if everyone believed he was dead. The Feds said. *Please, God, don't let this be a bomb.* A petroleum, asphalt smell. The offensive fuel odor of coal tar, of naphthenic acid, of napalm. Her eyes watered. She was nauseated.

The brass doors opened and she jostled the package as little as possible. Her hands were shaking. She couldn't leave the FedEx box in the elevator. She couldn't set it down, couldn't get rid of it without placing other residents or building employees at risk. Her fingers fumbled nervously with keys as her heart raced and she hypersalivated, could barely catch her breath. Metal against metal. Friction, static electricity, could set it off. Breathe deeply, slowly, and stay calm. Unlocking the apartment door with a startlingly loud click. *Please, God, don't let this be what I think.*

"Benton?"

She stepped inside, leaving the door open wide.

"Hello? Benton?"

She carefully set the FedEx box on the middle of the coffee table in their empty living room of fine art and mission-style furniture. She imagined expansive windows exploding, a massive glass bomb blowing up and raining razor-sharp shards down twenty stories. She picked up an art-glass sculpture, an undulating bowl in vibrant colors, moved it off the coffee table, set it on the rug, making sure there was a clear path from the doorway to the FedEx box.

"Benton, where are you?"

A stack of paperwork was in his usual Morris recliner by windows overlooking the lights of the Upper West Side and the Hudson. In the distance, planes looked like UFOs above the blazing runways of Teterboro. Lucy was probably flying her helicopter, heading to New York, to Westchester County. Scarpetta didn't like it when Lucy flew after dark. If she lost her engine she could auto-rotate, but how did she see where to set down? What if she lost her engine over miles of trees?

"Benton!"

Scarpetta headed down the hallway toward the master bedroom. She took deep breaths and swallowed repeatedly, trying to slow her heart and settle her gut. She heard a toilet flush.

"Christ, what the hell's going on with your phone?" Benton's voice was followed by him appearing in the bedroom doorway. "Have you gotten any of my messages? Kay? What the hell's the matter?"

"Don't come any closer," she said.

He was still in his suit, simple dark-blue flannel that didn't suggest money because he never wore anything expensive on prison wards or in forensic units, was careful what he telegraphed to prisoners and psychiatric patients. He had taken off his tie and his shoes, and his white shirt was open at the neck and untucked. His silver hair looked the way it did when he'd been running his fingers through it.

"What's happened?" he said, not moving from the doorway. "Something's happened. What?"

"Get your shoes and coat," Scarpetta said, clearing her throat. "Don't come close. I don't know what I've got on me." Desperate to scrub her hands with a solution of bleach, to decon, to take a long, hot shower and remove layers of makeup and shampoo her hair.

"What's happened? Did you run into someone? Did something happen? I've been trying to get hold of you." Benton was a statue in the doorway, his face pale, his eyes looking past her, toward the front door, as if he feared someone had come in with her.

"We need to leave." Her television makeup felt sticky, cloying, like glue. She smelled the smell, thought she did. Tar, sulfur, its molecules trapped in her makeup, in her hairspray, trapped in the back of her nose. The smell of fire and brimstone, of hell.

"The caller from Detroit? I tried to get hold of you," Benton said. "What's going on? Did someone do something?"

She took off her coat, her gloves and dropped them in the hallway, kicking them out of the way, and said, "We need to leave. Now. A suspicious package. It's in the living room. Get warm coats for both of us." *Don't be sick. Don't throw up.*

He disappeared inside the bedroom and she heard him go into his closet, hangers scraping along the rod. He reappeared carrying a pair of hiking boots, a wool coat, and a ski jacket he hadn't worn in so long, it still had a lift ticket attached to the zipper. He handed her the jacket and they hurried down the hallway. Benton's face was hard as he looked at the wide-open door, as he looked at the FedEx box in the living room, at the art glass bowl on the Oriental rug. *Open the windows to minimize pressure and damage if there's an explosion. No, you can't. Do not go into the living room. Do not go near the coffee table. Do not panic.*

Evacuate the apartment, close the door, and keep others from enter-ing. Do not make noise. Do not create shock waves. She shut the door softly, leaving it unlocked so the police could get in. There were two other apartments on this floor.

"You ask the desk how it got here?" Benton said. "I've been up here all night. They didn't call to say anything was delivered."

"I didn't notice certain details until I was already in the elevator. No, I didn't ask. It has a strange odor." She put on his ski jacket and it engulfed her, was almost to her knees. Aspen. When were they there last?

"What sort of odor?"

"A sweet, tarry, rotten-egg sort of smell. I don't know. I might have imagined it. And the airbill, the way it was addressed. I shouldn't have carried it upstairs. Should have left it on the desk and made Ross get out of the way, kept everybody out of the way until the police got here. God, I'm stupid."

"You're not stupid."

"Oh, I'm stupid, all right. Distracted by Carley Crispin and stupid as hell."

She rang the bell of the apartment nearest theirs, a corner unit belonging to a clothing designer she'd seen only in passing. That was New York. You could live next door to someone for years and never have a conversation.

"Don't think he's here," Scarpetta said, ringing the bell, knocking on the door. "I've not seen any sign of him lately."

"How was it addressed?" Benton asked.

She told him about the sender's copy still being attached, about the reference to her being the chief medical examiner of Gotham City. She described the unusual handwriting as she rang the bell one more time. Then they headed to the third apartment, this one lived in by an elderly woman who had been a comedic actress decades ago, best known for a number of appearances on *The Jackie Gleason Show*. Her husband died a year or so ago, and that was the sum of what Scarpetta knew about her, about Judy, except that she had a very nervous toy poodle that began its cacophony of barking the instant Scarpetta rang the bell. Judy looked surprised and not especially pleased when she opened her door. She blocked the doorway, as if hiding a lover or a fugitive, her dog dancing and darting behind her feet.

"Yes?" she said, looking quizzically at Benton, his coat on but in his socks and holding his boots.

Scarpetta explained that she needed to borrow the phone.

"You don't have a phone?" Judy slurred her words a little. She had fine bones but a wasted face. A drinker.

"Can't use cell phones or the phone in our apartment, and we don't have time to explain," Scarpetta said. "We need to use your land line."

"My what?"

"Your house phone, and then you need to come downstairs with us. It's an emergency."

"Certainly not. I'm certainly not going anywhere."

"A suspicious package was delivered. We need to use your phone, and everyone on this floor needs to go downstairs as quickly as possible," Scarpetta explained.

"Why would you bring it up here! Why would you do that?"

Scarpetta smelled booze. No telling what prescriptions she'd find in Judy's medicine cabinet. Irritable depression, substance abuse, nothing to live for. She and Benton stepped inside a paneled living room overwhelmed by fine French antiques and Lladró porcelain figurines of romantic couples in gondolas and carriages, on horseback and swings, kissing and conversing. On a windowsill was an elaborate crystal Nativity scene and on another one an arrangement of Royal Doulton Santas, but no lights or Christmas tree or menorah, only collectibles and photographs from an illustrious past that included an Emmy in a curio cabinet with a Vernis Martin-style finish and hand-painted scenes of cupids and lovers.

"Did something happen inside your apartment?" Judy asked as her dog yapped shrilly.

Benton helped himself to the phone on a giltwood console. He entered a number from memory, and Scarpetta was pretty sure she knew who he was trying to reach. Benton always handled situations efficiently and discreetly, what he referred to as "mainlining," getting information directly to and from the source, which in this instance was Marino.

"They brought a suspicious package up? Why would they do that? What kind of security are they?" Judy continued.

"It's probably nothing. But to be safe," Scarpetta assured her.

"You at headquarters yet? Well, don't bother with that right now," Benton told Marino, adding that there was a remote possibility someone had delivered a dangerous package to Scarpetta.

"I guess someone like you has all sorts of crazies out there." Judy was putting on a full-length coat, sheared chinchilla with scalloped cuffs. Her dog jumped up and down, yapping more frantically as Judy collected her leash from a satinwood étagère.

Benton hunched his shoulder, using the phone hands-free

while he put on his boots, and said, "No, in a neighbor's apartment. Didn't want to use ours and send out an electronic signal when we didn't know what's in it. An alleged FedEx. On the coffee table. Going downstairs right now."

He hung up, and Judy tottered, bending over to snap the leash on the poodle's matching collar, blue leather and an Hermès lock, probably engraved with the neurotic dog's name. They went out the door and got on the elevator. Scarpetta smelled the pungently sweet chemical odor of dynamite. A hallucination. Her imagination. She couldn't possibly smell dynamite. There was no dynamite.

"Do you smell anything?" she asked Benton. "I'm sorry your dog's so upset." It was her way of asking Judy to make the damn thing shut up.

"I don't smell anything," Benton said.

"Maybe my perfume." Judy sniffed her wrists. "Oh. You mean something bad. I hope somebody didn't send you Ant-trax or whatever it's called. Why did you have to bring it upstairs? How's that fair to the rest of us?"

Scarpetta realized her shoulder bag was in the apartment, on the table inside the entryway. Her wallet, her credentials, were in it, and the door was unlocked. She couldn't remember what had happened to her BlackBerry. She should have checked the package before carrying it upstairs. What the hell was wrong with her?

"Marino's on his way but won't get here before the others do," Benton said, not bothering to explain to Judy who Marino was. "He's coming from downtown, from headquarters, from Emergency Operations."

"Why?" Scarpetta watched floors slowly go by.

"RTCC. Doing a data search. Or was going to."

"If this were a co-op, we wouldn't have voted you in."

Judy directed this at Scarpetta. "You get on TV and talk about all these horrible crimes, and look what happens. You bring it home and subject the rest of us. People like you attract kooks."

"We'll hope it's nothing, and I apologize for upsetting you. And your dog," Scarpetta said.

"Slowest damn elevator. Calm down, Fresca, calm down. You know she's all bark. Wouldn't hurt a flea. I don't know where you expect me to go. I suppose the lobby. I don't intend to sit in the lobby all night."

Judy stared straight ahead at the brass elevator doors, her face pinched by displeasure. Benton and Scarpetta didn't talk anymore. Images and sounds Scarpetta hadn't remembered in a long while. Back then, in the late nineties, life had gotten as tragic as it could get, back in the days of ATF. Flying low over scrubby pines and soil so sandy it looked like snow as rotor blades paddled the air and slung sounds in rhythm. Metallic waterways were corrugated by the wind, and startled birds were a dash of pepper flung against the haze, heading for the old blimp station in Glynco, Georgia, where ATF had its explosives range, raid houses, concrete bunkers, and burn cells. She didn't like post-blast schools. Had quit teaching at them after the fire in Philadelphia. Had quit ATF, and so had Lucy, both of them moving on without Benton.

Now he was here in the elevator, as if that part of Scarpetta's past was a nightmare, a surreal dream, one she hadn't gotten over and couldn't. She hadn't taught at a post-blast school since, avoidance, not as objective as she should be. Personally disturbed by bodies blown apart. Flash burns and shrapnel, massive soft-tissue avulsion, bones fragmented, hollow organs lacerated and ruptured, hands gory stumps. She thought about the package she'd carried into the apartment. She hadn't been paying attention, had been too busy fretting about Carley and what Alex had confided, too caught up in what Dr. Edison referred to as her career at CNN. She should have noticed instantly that the airbill had no return address, that the sender's copy was still attached.

"Is it Fresca or Fresco?" Benton was asking Judy.

"Fresca. As in the soda. Had a glass of it in my hand when Bud walked into the apartment with her in a bakery box. For my birthday. That should have been my first clue, all the holes in the top. I thought it was a cake and then she barked."

"I bet she did," said Benton.

Fresca began tugging the leash and barking at a shattering pitch, piercing Scarpetta's ears, stabbing deep into her brain. Hypersalivating, her heart skipping. *Don't get sick.* The elevator stopped, and the heavy brass doors crept open. Red and blue lights flashed through the lobby's front glass door, freezing air sweeping in with half a dozen cops in dark-navy BDUs, tactical jackets, and boots, operator belts heavy with battery holders, mag pouches, batons, flashlights, and holstered pistols. A cop grabbed a luggage cart in each hand and wheeled them out the door. Another made his way straight to Scarpetta as if he knew her. A big man, young, with dark hair and skin, muscular, a patch on his jacket depicting gold stars and the cartoonish red bomb of the bomb squad.

"Dr. Scarpetta? Lieutenant Al Lobo," he said, shaking her hand.

"What's going on here?" Judy demanded.

"Ma'am, we're going to need you to evacuate the

building. If you could just step outside until we're clear in here. For your own safety."

"For how long? Lord, this isn't fair."

The lieutenant eyed Judy as if she looked familiar. "Ma'am, if you'll please go outside. Someone out there will direct you. . . . "

"I can't stay outside in the cold with my dog. This certainly isn't fair." Glaring at Scarpetta.

"What about the bar next door?" Benton suggested. "Okay if she goes over there?"

"They don't allow dogs in the bar," Judy said indignantly.

"I bet if you ask them nicely." Benton walked her as far as the front door.

He returned to Scarpetta and took her hand, and the lobby was suddenly a chaotic, noisy, drafty place, with the elevator doors dinging open and squad members heading upstairs to begin an evacuation immediately above, below, and on either side of Scarpetta and Benton's apartment, or what the lieutenant called "the target." He began machine-gunning questions.

"I'm pretty sure there's no one left on our floor, the twentieth floor," Scarpetta answered. "One neighbor didn't answer and doesn't seem to be home, although you should check again. The other neighbor is her." She meant Judy.

"She looks like someone. One of those old shows like Carol Burnett. Just one floor above you?"

"Two. There are two above ours," Benton said.

Through glass Scarpetta watched more emergency response trucks pull up, white with blue stripes, one of them towing a light trailer. She realized traffic had stopped in both directions. The police had closed off this section of Central Park West. Diesel engines rumbled loudly, approaching sirens wailed, the area around their building beginning to look like a movie set, with trucks and police cars lining the street and halogen lights shining from pedestals and trailers, and red and blue emergency strobes stuttering nonstop.

Members of the bomb squad opened bin doors on the sides of the trucks, grabbing Pelican cases and Roco bags and sacks, and harnesses, and tools, trotting up the steps with armloads and piling them on luggage carts. Scarpetta's stomach had settled down, but there was a cold feeling in it as she watched a female bomb squad tech open a bin and lift out a tunic and trousers, eighty-something pounds of heavily padded tan fire-retardant armor on hangers. A bomb suit. An unmarked black SUV pulled up, and another tech climbed out and let his chocolate Lab bound out of the back.

"I need you to give me as much information as you can about the package," Lobo was saying to the concierge, Ross, standing behind the desk, looking dazed and scared. "But we need to take it outside. Dr. Scarpetta, Benton? If you'll come with us."

The four of them went out to the sidewalk, where the halogen lights were so bright they hurt Scarpetta's eyes and the rumbling of diesel engines resonated like an earthquake. Cops from patrol and the Emergency Service Unit were sealing the perimeter of the building with bright yellow crime-scene tape, and people were assembling by the dozens across the street, inside the deep shadows of the park and sitting on the wall, talking excitedly and taking photographs with cell phones. It was very cold, and arctic blasts bounced off buildings, but the air felt good. Scarpetta's head began to clear, and she could breathe better.

"Describe the package," Lobo said to her. "How big?"

"Midsized FedEx box, I'd say fourteen by eleven and maybe three inches thick. I set it on the middle of the coffee table in the living room. Nothing between it and the door, so it should be easily accessible to you or, if need be, to your robot. I left our door unlocked."

"How heavy would you estimate?"

"Maybe a pound and a half at most."

"Did the contents shift around when you moved it?"

"I didn't move it much. But I'm not aware of anything shifting," she said.

"Did you hear or smell anything?"

"I didn't hear anything. But I might have smelled something. A petroleum-type smell. Tarry but sweet and foul, maybe a sulfurous pyrotechnic smell. I couldn't quite identify it, but an offensive odor that made my eyes water."

"What about you?" Lobo asked Benton.

"I didn't smell anything, but I didn't get close."

"You notice an odor when the package was delivered?" Lobo asked Ross.

"I don't know. I sort of have a cold, like I'm real stopped up."

"The coat I was wearing, and my gloves," Scarpetta said to Lobo. "There're on the hallway floor in the apartment. You might want to bag them, take them with you, to see if there's any sort of residue."

The lieutenant wasn't going to say it, but she'd just given him quite a lot of information. Based on the size and weight of the package, it couldn't contain more than a pound and a half of explosives and wasn't motion-sensitive, unless some creative timing mechanism had been rigged to a tilt switch.

"I didn't notice anything unusual at all." Ross was talking fast, looking at the drama on the street, lights flashing on his boyish face. "The guy put it on the counter and turned around and left. Then I placed it behind the desk instead of in back because I knew Dr. Scarpetta would be returning to the building soon."

"How'd you know that?" Benton asked.

"We have a TV in the break room. We knew she was on CNN tonight. . . ."

"Who's we?" Lobo wanted to know.

"Me, the doormen, one of the runners. And I was here when she left to go over there, to CNN."

"Describe the person who delivered the FedEx," Lobo said.

"Black guy; long, dark coat; gloves; a FedEx cap; a clipboard. Not sure how old but not real old."

"You ever seen him before making deliveries or pickups at this building or in the area?"

"Not that I remember."

"He show up on foot, or did he park a van or truck out front?"

"I didn't see a van or anything," Ross answered. "Usually they park wherever they can get a space and show up on foot. That's pretty much it. What I noticed."

"What you're saying is you got no idea if the guy was really FedEx," Lobo said.

"I can't prove it. But he didn't do anything to make me suspicious. That's pretty much what I know."

"Then what? He set down the package, and what happened next?"

"He left."

"Right that second? He made a beeline to the door? You sure he didn't linger, maybe wander around, maybe go near a stairwell or sit in the lobby?"

ESU cops were getting off the elevator, escorting other residents out of the building.

"You positive the FedEx guy came in and went straight to your desk, then turned around and went straight back out?" Lobo asked Ross.

Ross was staring in astonishment at the caravan coming toward the building, squad cars escorting a fourteen-ton truck-mounted bomb disposal Total Containment Vessel.

He exclaimed, "Holy shhhh . . . Are we having a terrorist attack or something? All this because of that FedEx box? You kidding me?"

"He maybe go over by the Christmas tree there in your lobby? You're sure he didn't go near the elevators?" Lobo persisted. "Ross, you paying attention? Because this is important."

"Holy mother."

The white-and-blue bomb truck, its TCV in back covered by a black tarp, parked directly in front of the building.

"Little things can go a long way. Even the tiniest detail matters," Lobo said. "So I'm asking you again. The FedEx guy. He go anywhere at all, even for a second? To the john? To get a drink of water? He look at what's under the Christmas tree in the lobby?"

"I don't think so. Jesus Christ." Gawking at the bomb truck.

"You don't think so? That's not good enough, Ross. I need to be absolutely sure where he did and didn't go. Do you understand why? I'll tell you why. Anyplace he might have gone, we've got to check to make sure he didn't set some device somewhere nobody's thinking about. Look at me when I'm talking to you. We're going to check the recordings from your security cameras, but it's quicker if you tell me right now what you observed. You sure he wasn't carrying anything else when he entered the lobby? Tell me every detail, the smallest one. Then I'm going to look at the recordings."

"I'm pretty sure he came straight in, handed me the box, and went straight back out," Ross said to him. "But I got no idea if he did anything outside the building or maybe went anywhere else. I didn't follow him. I had no reason to be concerned. The computer for the camera system's in the back. That's all I can think of."

"When he left, which way did he go?"

"I saw him go out this door"—waving a hand at the glass front door—"and that was it."

"This was what time?"

"A little after nine."

"So the last time you saw him was about two hours ago, two hours fifteen."

"I guess."

Benton asked Ross, "Was he wearing gloves?"

"Black ones. They might have been lined with rabbit fur. When he was handing me the box, I think I saw fur sticking out of the gloves."

Lobo suddenly stepped away from them and got on his radio.

"You recall anything else—anything at all—about the way he was dressed?" Benton asked Ross.

"Dark clothes. Seems like he might have had on dark

boots and dark pants. And a long coat, you know, like below his knees. Black. Collar up, gloves on, like I said, maybe fur-lined, and the FedEx cap. That's it."

"Glasses?"

"Sort of tinted ones, flash ones."

"Flash ones?"

"You know. Sort of mirrored. Another thing? I'm just remembering. I thought I smelled cigarettes, maybe matches. Like maybe he'd been smoking."

"I thought you were stopped up, couldn't smell anything," Benton reminded him.

"It just entered my head. I think maybe I did smell something like cigarettes."

"But that's not what you think you smelled," Benton said to Scarpetta.

"No," she answered, not adding that maybe what Ross had detected was sulfur, what smelled like a lighted match, and that was what had reminded him of cigarettes.

"What about this man Ross is describing," Benton said to her. "You see anybody fitting that description when you were walking back here, or maybe earlier, when you headed over to CNN?"

She thought about it but came up with nothing, and it occurred to her. "The clipboard," she asked Ross. "Did he ask you to sign anything?"

"No."

"Then what was the clipboard for?"

Ross shrugged, his breath a white vapor when he talked. "He didn't ask me to do anything. Nothing. Just handed me the package."

"He say specifically to give it to Dr. Scarpetta?" Benton asked.

"He said to make sure she got it, yeah. And he said her name, now that you mention it. He said, 'This is for Dr. Scarpetta. She's expecting it.'"

"FedEx usually that specific, that personal? Isn't that a little unusual? Because I've never heard FedEx make comments like that. How would he know she was expecting something?" Benton said.

"I don't know. I guess it was a little unusual."

"What was on the clipboard?" Scarpetta got back to that.

"I really didn't look. Maybe receipts, package slips. Am I going to get in trouble for this? My wife's pregnant. I don't need any trouble," said Ross, who didn't look nearly old enough to be married and a father.

"I'm wondering why you didn't call the apartment to tell me a package had arrived," Benton said to him.

"Because the FedEx guy said it was for her, like I told you, and I knew she'd be back pretty soon and assumed, now that we're replaying all this, she was expecting it."

"And you knew she'd be back soon because?"

"He was working the desk when I left around eight," Scarpetta answered for Ross, "and he wished me good luck on the show."

"How did you know she was on a show tonight?" Benton asked.

"I've seen commercials, ads for it. Just look." Ross pointed at the top of a building on the other side of Columbus Circle, where news breaks on CNN's scrolling ticker could be seen from blocks away. "Your name's up in freakin' lights."

Below the CNN neon-red marquee, Scarpetta's off-camera comment crawled around the top of the skyscraper:

... connected Hannah Starr and a murdered
jogger and said FBI profiling is "antiquated" and
not based on credible data. On tonight's *Crispin
Report,* Medical Examiner Dr. Kay Scarpetta
connected Hannah Starr and a murdered jogger
and said FBI profiling ...

10

Pete Marino materialized in the middle of the barricaded street, backlit by a blaze of halogen lights, as if he had emerged from the afterlife.

Rotating beacons flashed across his big weathered face and unstylish wire-rimmed glasses, and he was tall and broad in a down jacket, cargo pants, and boots. Pulled low over his bald head was an NYPD cap with an Aviation Unit patch over the bill, an old Bell 47 helicopter that brought to mind *M*A*S*H*. A gift from Lucy, a back-handed one. Marino hated flying.

"I'm assuming you made Lobo's acquaintance," Marino said when he reached Scarpetta and Benton. "He taking good care of you? I don't see no hot chocolate. Right about now bourbon would be good. Let's go sit in my car before you get frostbit."

Marino started walking them to his car, parked north of the bomb truck, which was flooded by halogens on light poles. Cops had removed the tarp and lowered a steel ramp, a special one Scarpetta had seen on other occasions in the past, with serrated tread the size of saw teeth.

If you tripped and fell on the ramp, it would shred you to the bone, but if you stumbled while carrying a bomb, you had a bigger problem. The Total Containment Vessel, or TCV, was mounted on the diamond-steel flatbed and looked like a bright-yellow diving bell sealed shut by a spider yoke that an ESU cop loosened and removed. Beneath it was the lid, about four inches thick, and the ESU cop attached a steel cable to it, using a winch to lower it to the flatbed. He pulled out a wood-framed nylon-webbed tray, placed the winch control on it, and clamped the cable out of the way, making preparations for the bomb tech whose job it would be to lock Scarpetta's suspicious package inside fourteen tons of high-tensile steel before it was driven away to be defeated by New York's finest.

"I'm so sorry about this," Scarpetta said to Marino as they got into his dark-blue Crown Vic, a safe distance from the truck and its TCV. "I'm sure it will turn out to be nothing."

"And I'm sure Benton would agree with me. We're never sure of anything," Marino said. "You and Benton did the right thing."

Benton was looking up at the CNN marquee, neon-red beyond the Trump International Hotel with its shiny silver unisphere, a scaled-down version of the ten-story globe in Flushing Meadows, only this steely representation of the planet was about Donald Trump's expanding universe, not about the space age. Scarpetta watched the news ticker, the same out-of-context nonsense crawling by, and wondered if Carley had orchestrated the timing of it, deciding she must have.

No way Carley would want her ambush launched in

bright lights while she was walking the intended victim home. Wait an hour, then cause Scarpetta trouble with the FBI and maybe make her think twice about going on any television show ever again. *Goddamn it.* Why was behavior like that necessary? Carley knew her ratings were bad, that was why. A desperate and sensational attempt to hang on to her career. And maybe sabotage. Carley had overheard Alex's proposal, knew what was in store for her. Not a suspicion anymore. Scarpetta was convinced.

Marino unlocked his car and said to Scarpetta, "How 'bout you sit up front so you and me can talk. Sorry, Benton, got to stick you in back. Lobo and some of the other bomb guys were just in Mumbai finding out whatever they can so we don't have the same shit happen here. The trend in terrorist tactics, and Benton probably knows this, isn't suicide bombers anymore. It's small groups of highly trained commandos."

Benton didn't answer, and Scarpetta could feel his hostility like static electricity. When Marino tried too hard to be inclusive or friendly, he made the situation worse, and Benton would be rude, and next Marino had to assert himself because he would feel put down and angry. A tedious and ridiculous vacillation, one demeanor, then the other, back and forth, and Scarpetta wished it would stop. Goddamn it, she'd had enough.

"Point is, you couldn't be in better hands. These guys are the best, will take good care of you, Doc." As if Marino had made sure of it personally.

"I feel awful about this." Scarpetta shut her door and reached for the shoulder harness, out of habit, but changed her mind. They weren't going anywhere.

"Last I checked, it wasn't you who did anything." Benton's voice behind her.

Marino started the engine and turned the heat on high. "Probably a box of cookies," he said to Scarpetta. "You and Bill Clinton. Same thing. Wrong address and the bomb squad gets called. Turns out to be cookies."

"Just what I wanted to hear," she said.

"You'd rather it be a bomb?"

"I'd rather none of this had happened." She couldn't help it. She was mortified. She felt guilty, as if all of this was her fault.

"You don't need to apologize," Benton said. "You don't take chances, even if nine times out of ten it's nothing. We'll hope it's nothing."

Scarpetta noticed what was displayed on the screen of the Mobile Data Computer mounted on the dash, a map depicting the Westchester County Airport in White Plains. Maybe it was related to Berger, to her flying in this evening with Lucy, assuming they hadn't already arrived. Strange, though. Didn't make sense for Marino to have the airport map displayed. At the moment, nothing was making sense. Scarpetta was confused and unsettled and felt humiliated.

"Anybody know anything yet?" Benton asked Marino.

"A couple news choppers spotted in the area," he said. "No way this is going to be quiet. You bring in the mother of all bomb trucks and that's it, will be a police escort like a friggin' presidential motorcade when they drive the Doc's package to Rodman's Neck. Me calling Lobo direct cut out a lot of bullshit, but I can't keep this on the QT. Not that you needed the attention, since I see your name up there in lights, bashing the FBI."

"I didn't bash the FBI," Scarpetta said. "I was talking about Warner Agee, and it was off the air and off the record."

"No such thing," Benton said.

"Especially not with Crispy Crispin, claim to fame burning her sources. I don't know why the hell you go on that show," Marino said. "Not that we have time to get into it, but what a friggin' mess. See how deserted the street is right now? If Carley keeps up with her yellow-cab crap, the streets will be this empty from now on, which is probably what she wants. Another scoop, right? Thirty thousand yellow cabs and not a single fare, and crowds of people rioting in a panic on the streets like King Kong's on the loose. Merry Christmas."

"I'm curious about why you have Westchester County Airport on your computer screen." Scarpetta didn't want to discuss her blunders on CNN, and she didn't want to talk about Carley or listen to Marino's hyperbole. "Have you heard from Lucy and Jaime? I would have thought they would have landed by now."

"You and me both," Marino said. "Was doing a MapQuest, trying to figure out the quickest route, not that I'm headed there. It's about them heading here."

"Why would they be heading here? Do they know what's happening?" Scarpetta didn't want her niece showing up in the middle of this.

In Lucy's former life as a special agent and certified fire investigator for ATF, she routinely dealt with explosives and arson. She was good at it, excelled at anything technical and risky, and the more others shied away from something or failed at it, the quicker she was to master it and show them up. Her gifts and fierceness didn't win her friends. While she was emotionally more limber now that she was beyond her twenties, give and take with people still didn't come naturally to her, and respecting boundaries and the law was almost impossible. If Lucy was here, she'd have an opinion and a theory, and maybe a vigilante remedy, and at the moment, Scarpetta wasn't in the mood.

"Not here as in where we're at," Marino was saying. "Here as in them heading back to the city."

"Since when do they need MapQuest to find their way back to the city?" Benton asked from the back.

"A situation I really can't get into."

Scarpetta looked at Marino's familiar rugged profile, looked at what was illuminated on the computer screen mounted above the universal console. She turned around to look at Benton in the backseat. He was staring out his window, watching the squad emerge from the apartment building.

"Everybody's got their cell phones turned off, I assume," Benton said. "What about your radio?"

"It ain't on," Marino said, as if he'd been accused of being stupid.

The bomb tech in the EOD suit and helmet was coming out of the building, shapeless padded arms stretched out, holding a black frag bag.

"They must have seen something on x-ray they didn't like," Benton commented.

"And they're not using Android," Marino said.

"Using who?" Scarpetta said.

"The robot. Nicknamed Android because of the female bomb tech. Her name's Ann Droiden. Weird about people's names, like doctors and dentists with names like

Hurt, Paine, and Puller. She's good. Good-looking, too. All the guys always wanting her to handle their package, if you know what I mean. Must be a tough life, her being the only female on the bomb squad. Reason I'm familiar"—as if he needed to explain why he was going on and on about a pretty bomb tech named Ann—"is she used to work at Two Truck in Harlem where they keep the TCV, and she still drops by now and then to hang out with her old pals at ESU. The Two's not far from my apartment, just a few blocks. I wander over there, have coffee, bring a few treats to their company boxer, nicest damn dog, Mac. A rescue. Whenever I can, if everybody's tied up, I take Mac home so he's not by his lonesome in the quarters all night."

"If they're using her instead of the robot, then whatever's in that box isn't motion-sensitive," Scarpetta said. "They must be certain of that."

"If it was motion-sensitive, I guess we'd be peeling you off the moon, since you carried it up to your apartment," Marino said with his usual diplomacy.

"It could be motion-sensitive and on a timer. Obviously, it's not," Benton said.

Police kept people back, making sure no one was within at least a hundred yards of the bomb tech as she made her way down the building's front steps, her face obscured by a visor. She walked slowly, somewhat stiffly but with surprising agility, toward the truck, its diesel engine throbbing.

"They lost three responders in Nine-Eleven. Vigiano, D'Allara, Curtin, and the bomb squad lost Danny Richards," Marino said. "You can't see it from here, but their names are painted on the bomb truck, on all the trucks at the Two.

They got a little memorial room in there, off the kitchen, a shrine with some of the guys' gear recovered with their bodies. Keys, flashlights, radios, some of it melted. Gives you a different feeling when you seen a guy's melted flashlight, you know?"

Scarpetta hadn't seen Marino in a while. Inevitably, when she came to New York, she was overscheduled and somewhat frantic. It hadn't occurred to her that he might be lonely. She wondered if he was having problems with his girlfriend, Georgia Bacardi, a Baltimore detective he'd gotten serious about last year. Maybe that was over or on its way to being over, and if so, no big surprise. Marino's relationships tended to have the life span of a butterfly. Now Scarpetta felt worse. She felt bad about carrying a package upstairs without examining it first, and she felt guilty about Marino. She should check on him when she was in the city. She should check on him even when she wasn't, a simple phone call or e-mail now and then.

The bomb tech had reached the truck, and her booted feet gripped the serrated tread on the ramp as she climbed up. It was difficult to see past Marino, out the window and down the street, but Scarpetta recognized what was happening, was no stranger to the procedure. The tech would set the frag bag on the tray and slide it back inside the TCV. Using the winch control, she would retract the steel cable to pull the massive steel lid back over the round opening, then replace the spider yoke and tighten it, likely with her bare hands. At most, bomb techs wore thin Nomex gloves or maybe nitrile to protect them from fire or potentially toxic substances. Anything heavily padded would make it impossible to perform the simplest task and probably wouldn't save fingers in a detonation anyway.

When the tech was done, other cops and Lieutenant Lobo convened at the back of the bomb truck, sliding the ramp back in place, covering the containment vessel with the tarp, buttoning up. The truck roared north on the sealed-off street, marked units in front and back, the convoy a moving sea of rapid bursts of light headed for the West Side Highway. From there it would follow a prescribed safe route to the NYPD range at Rodman's Neck, probably to the Cross Bronx and 95 North, whatever would best buffer traffic, buildings, and pedestrians from shock waves, a biological hazard, radiation, or shrapnel, should a device explode en route and somehow defeat its containment.

Lobo was walking toward them. When he reached Marino's car, he climbed into the back next to Benton, a rush of cold air washing in as he said, "I had images sent to your e-mail." He shut his door. "From the security cameras."

Marino began typing on the Toughbook clamped into the pedestal between the front seats, the map of White Plains replaced by a screen asking for his username and password.

"Your FedEx guy's got an interesting tattoo," Lobo said, leaning forward, chewing gum. Scarpetta smelled cinnamon. "A big one on the left side of his neck, kind of hard to see because he's dark-skinned."

Marino opened an e-mail and loaded the attachment. A still from a security video recording filled the screen, a man in a FedEx cap walking toward the concierge desk.

Benton repositioned himself to get a better look and said, "Nope. Got no idea. Don't recognize him."

The man wasn't familiar to Scarpetta, either. African American, high cheekbones, beard and mustache, the FedEx cap pulled low over eyes masked by reflective glasses. The collar of his black wool coat partially obscured a tattoo that covered the left side of his neck, up to his ear, a tattoo of human skulls. Scarpetta counted eight skulls but couldn't see what they were piled on top of, just a linear edge of something.

"Can you enlarge it?" She pointed at the tattoo, at what looked like the edge of a box that with a click of the trackpad got bigger. "Maybe a coffin. Skulls piled inside a coffin. Which immediately makes me wonder if he's served in Iraq or Afghanistan. Skulls, skeletons, skeletons climbing out of coffins, tombstones. Memorials for fallen soldiers, in other words. Usually, each skull represents a lost comrade. Tattoos like this have become popular in the last few years."

"The RTCC can do a search on it," Marino said. "If this guy's in the database for some reason, maybe we can get a hit on his tattoo. We got a whole database of tattoos."

The sharp scent of cinnamon returned, reminding Scarpetta of fire scenes, of the symphony of unexpected odors in places that had burned to the ground. Lobo touched her shoulder and said, "So, nothing about this guy's familiar. Doesn't bring anything to mind."

"No," she said.

"Looks like a mean bastard," Lobo added.

"The concierge, Ross, said there wasn't anything about him that was cause for alarm," Scarpetta said.

"Yeah, that's what he said." Chewing gum. "Course, he also got the job in your building because he was out of work after getting fired by the last building. For leaving the desk unattended. Least he was honest about it. Course, he failed to mention he was charged with possession of a controlled substance last March."

"We sure he's got no connection with this guy?" Benton meant the man on the computer screen.

"Not sure of anything," Lobo said. "But this guy?" Indicating the man with the tattooed neck. "He's probably not FedEx, to state the obvious. You can buy caps like that on eBay, no problem. Or make one. What about when you were walking back from CNN?" Lobo asked Scarpetta. "You see anyone, especially anyone that for some reason caught your eye?"

"A homeless person sleeping on a bench is all that comes to mind."

"Where?" Benton asked.

"Near Columbus Circle. Right there." Scarpetta turned around and pointed.

She realized the emergency vehicles and the curious were gone, and halogen lights had been extinguished, the street returned to incomplete darkness. Soon traffic would resume, residents would reenter the building, and traffic cones, barriers, and yellow tape would vanish as if nothing had happened. She knew of no other city where emergencies could be contained so rapidly and the usual order of things resumed just as fast. The lessons of 9/11. Expertise at a terrible price.

"Nobody in the area now," Lobo said. "Nobody on any benches, but all this activity would have cleared them out. And nobody else caught your eye when you were walking home?"

"No," Scarpetta replied.

"It's just that sometimes when people leave antisocial

presents, they like to hang around and watch or show up after the fact to see the damage they caused."

"Any other photos?" Benton asked, his breath touching Scarpetta's ear and stirring her hair.

Marino clicked on two more video stills, displaying them side by side, full-length shots of the man with the tattoo walking through the apartment building lobby, toward the desk, and away from it.

"No FedEx uniform," Scarpetta observed. "Plain dark pants, black boots, and a black coat buttoned up to his neck. And gloves, and I think Ross was right. I think I see a hint of fur, could be lined with something like rabbit fur."

"Still nothing ringing any bells," Lobo said.

"Not for me," Benton said.

"Or me," Scarpetta agreed.

"Well, whoever he is, he's either the messenger or the sender, and the question of the night is if you know of anybody who might want to hurt you or threaten you," Lobo said to her.

"Specifically, I don't."

"What about in general?"

"In general it could be anyone," she said.

"What about any unusual fan mail, communications sent to your office in Massachusetts or to the ME's office here? Maybe to CNN?"

"Nothing comes to mind."

"Something comes to my mind," Benton said. "The woman who called you on the show tonight. Dodie."

"Exactly," Marino said.

"Exactly?" Lobo said.

"Dodie Hodge, possibly a former patient at McLean's."

Marino always got the name of the hospital wrong. There was no apostrophe S, never had been. "Didn't run her through the RTCC yet because I got interrupted by the Doc's little incident."

"I don't know her," Scarpetta said, and the reminder of the caller who had mentioned Benton by name, referring to some article he'd never written, sent another wave of queasiness through her.

She turned around and said to Benton, "I'm not going to ask."

"I can't say anything," he answered.

"Allow me, since I don't give a shit about protecting nutcases," Marino said to her. "This particular lady checks out of McLean's, and Benton gets a singing Christmas card from her, which is also addressed to you, and next thing you get called on live TV and a package is delivered."

"Is this true?" Lobo asked Benton.

"Can't verify any of it, and I never said she was a patient at McLean."

"You going to tell us she wasn't?" Marino pushed.

"I'm not going to tell you that, either."

"Okay," Lobo said. "How 'bout this. Do we know if this patient, Dodie Hodge, is in this area, maybe in the city right now?"

"Maybe," Benton said.

"Maybe?" Marino said. "Don't you think we should be told if she is?"

"Unless we know she's actually done something illegal or is a threat," Benton started to say. "You know how it works."

"Oh, geez. Regulations that protect everybody but inno- cent people," Marino said. "Yeah, I know how it works.

Whack jobs and juveniles. These days you got eight-year-old kids shooting people. But by all means protect their confidentiality."

"How was the singing card delivered?" Lobo asked.

"FedEx." Benton said that much. "I'm not saying there's no connection. I'm not saying there is. I don't know."

"We'll check with CNN, trace the call Dodie Hodge made to the show," Lobo said. "See where she made it from. And I need a recording of the show, and we're going to want to find her, talk to her. She ever give you any reason to worry she might be dangerous?" he asked Benton. "Never mind. You can't talk about her."

"No, I can't."

"Good. When she blows somebody up, maybe then," Marino said.

"We don't know who left the package, except that it's a black male with a tattoo on his neck," Benton said. "And we don't know what's in the package. We don't know for a fact it's some sort of explosive device."

"We know enough to make me uncomfortable," Lobo said. "What we saw on x-ray. Some wires, button batteries, a microswitch, and what really disturbs me, a small transparent container, sort of like a test tube with some type of stopper in it. No radiation detected, but we didn't use any other detection equipment, didn't want to get that close."

"Great," Marino said.

"Did you smell anything?" Scarpetta asked.

"I didn't approach it," Lobo said. "Those of us who went to your floor worked out of the stairwell, and the tech who entered your apartment was fully contained in the bomb suit. She wasn't going to smell anything unless the odor was really strong."

"You going to deal with it tonight?" Marino asked. "So maybe we know what the hell's in it?"

"We don't render things safe at night. Droiden, who's also a Hazmat tech, is en route to Rodman's Neck, should be there shortly for the transfer from the TCV to a day box. She'll use detectors to determine if there's a possibility of chemical, biological, radiological, or nuclear contamination, if something's off-gassing that they can safely pick up. Like I said, no radiation alarms went off and no evidence of a white powder, but we don't know. On x-ray we did see a vial-like shape that obviously could have something in it, which is of concern. The package will be locked up in a day box, and we'll take care of it first thing in the morning, render it safe so we can see what we're dealing with."

"You and I will be talking," Marino said to Lobo as he got out of the car. "I'll probably be at RTCC all night, seeing what I can find on this Dodie whack job and the tattoo and anything else that comes up."

"Good deal." Lobo shut the door.

Scarpetta watched him walk off toward a dark-blue SUV. She slipped her hands in her pockets for her phone, and was reminded it wasn't her coat and she didn't have her Black-Berry.

"We need to make sure Lucy doesn't hear about this on the news or see a briefing on OEM," she said.

The Office of Emergency Management published constant updates on the Internet, and personnel with a need to know had access to briefings on everything from missing manhole covers to homicides. If Lucy saw that the bomb squad had been dispatched to Central Park West, she would be unnecessarily worried.

"Last I checked they were still in the air," Marino said. "I can call her on the helicopter phone."

"We'll call when we get inside." Benton wanted to get out of the car. He wanted to get away from Marino.

"Don't call the helicopter phone. She doesn't need to be distracted while she's flying," Scarpetta said.

"Tell you what," Marino decided. "Why don't the two of you go inside and try to relax and I'll get hold of them. I got to tell Berger what's going on anyway."

Scarpetta thought she was fine until Benton opened their apartment door.

"Dammit," she exclaimed, taking off the ski jacket and throwing it down on a chair, suddenly so angry she was tempted to yell.

The police had been considerate, not so much as a dirty footprint on the hardwood floor, her handbag undisturbed on the narrow table in the entryway where she'd left it before heading over to CNN. But the millefiori sculpture she'd watched a master glass artisan make on the Venetian island of Murano had been returned to the wrong spot. It wasn't on the coffee table but on the stone-top sofa table, and she pointed this out to Benton, who didn't say a word. He knew when to be silent, and this was one of those times.

"There are fingerprints on it." She held the sculpture up to the light, showing him discernible ridges and furrows, whorls and a tented arc, identifiable patterns of minutiae on the bright-colored glass rim. Evidence of a crime.

"I'll clean it," he said, but she wouldn't give it to him.

"Someone didn't have gloves on." She furiously wiped

the glass with the hem of her silk blouse. "It must have been the bomb tech. Bomb techs don't wear gloves. What's her name. Ann. She didn't have on gloves. She picked it up and moved it." As if the bomb tech named Ann was a burglar. "What else did they touch in here, in our apartment?"

Benton didn't answer because he knew better. He knew what to do and what not to do on the rare occasion Scarpetta got this upset, and she thought she smelled the package again, and then she smelled the embayment, the Laguna Veneta. The shallow salt water and the warmth of the spring sun as she and Benton climbed out of the water taxi at the landing stage in Colonna, following the fondamenta to Calle San Cipriano. Factory visits weren't allowed, but that hadn't stopped her, tugging Benton by the hand past a barge filled with waste glass, to the "Fornace–Entrata Libera" entrance sign and inside, asking for a demonstration in an open space with furnaces like crematoriums and dark-red-painted brick walls and high ceilings. Aldo the artisan was small with a mustache, in shorts and sneakers, from a dynasty of glassblowers, an unbroken lineage stretching back seven hundred years, his ancestors having never left the island, not allowed to venture beyond the lagoon upon penalty of death or having their hands cut off.

Scarpetta had commissioned him on the spot to make something for them, for Benton and her, the happy couple, whatever Aldo liked. It was a special trip, a sacred one, and she wanted to be reminded of the day, of every minute. Benton later said he'd never heard her talk so much, explaining her fascination with the science of glass. Sand and soda lime transitioning into what is neither a liquid nor a solid, but no empirical data that it continues to flow after it's been fashioned into a windowpane or a vase, she'd said in her less-than-perfect Italian. After it's crystallized, only vibrational degrees of freedom remain active, but the form is set. A bowl still looks like a bowl a thousand years later, and prehistoric obsidian blades don't lose their edge. Somewhat of a mystery, maybe why she loved glass. That and what it does to visible light, Scarpetta had said. What happens when color agents are added, such as iron, cobalt, boron, manganese, and selenium for green, blue, purple, amber, and red.

Scarpetta and Benton had returned to Murano the next day to pick up their sculpture after it had been slowly annealed in the kiln and was cool and cocooned in Bubble Wrap. She'd hand-carried it, tucked it in the overhead bin all the way home from a professional trip not at all intended for pleasure, but Benton had surprised her. He'd asked her to marry him. Those days in Italy had become, at least for her, more than memorable. They were an imagined temple where her thoughts retreated when she was both happy and sad, and her temple felt trampled on and sullied as she set the glass sculpture back on the cherry coffee table, where it belonged. She felt violated, as if she'd walked in and discovered their home burglarized, ransacked, a crime scene. She began pacing about, looking for anything else out of place or missing, checking sinks and soaps to see who washed his hands or flushed the toilets.

"No one was in the bathrooms," she announced.

She opened the windows in the living room to get rid of the odor.

"I smell the package. You must smell it," she said.

"I don't smell anything." Benton was standing by the front door with his coat on.

"Yes," she insisted. "You must smell it. It smells like iron. You don't smell it?"

"No," he said. "Maybe you're remembering what you smelled. The package is gone. It's gone and we're safe."

"It's because you didn't touch it and I did. A fungal-metallic odor," she explained. "As if my skin came in contact with iron ions."

Benton reminded her very calmly that she had been wearing gloves when she held the package that might be a bomb.

"But it would have touched my bare flesh between my gloves and the cuffs of my coat when I was holding it." She walked over to him.

The package had left a bouquet on her wrists, an evil perfume, lipid peroxides from the oils on the skin, from sweat, oxidized by enzymes causing corrosion, decomposition. Like blood, she explained. The odor smelled like blood.

"The way blood smells when it's smeared over the skin," she said, and she held up her wrists and Benton sniffed them.

He said, "I don't smell anything."

"Some petroleum-based something, some chemical, I don't know what. I know I smell rust." She couldn't stop talking about it. "There's something in that box that's bad, very bad. I'm glad you didn't touch it."

In the kitchen, she washed her hands, her wrists, her fore-arms with dish detergent and water, as if scrubbing for surgery, as if deconning. She used Murphy Oil Soap on the coffee table where the package had been. She fussed and fumed while Benton silently stood by, watching her, trying not to interfere with her venting, trying to be understanding and rational, and his demeanor only made her more annoyed, more resentful.

"You could at least react to something," she said. "Or maybe you don't care."

"I care very much." He took off his coat. "It's not fair to say I don't. I realize how awful this is."

"I can't tell you care. I never can. I've never been able to tell." As if it was Benton who had left her the package that might be a bomb.

"Would it make you feel better if I lost my temper?" His somber face looked at her.

"I'm taking a shower."

She angrily undressed as she stalked off down the hall to the master bedroom and stuffed her clothes into a dry-cleaning bag. She dropped her underwear into a hamper. She got into the shower, turning on the water as hot as she could stand it, and the steam drove the odor deeper up her nose, into her sinuses, the odor of the package, of fire and brimstone, and the heat and her senses started another slide show. Philadelphia and darkness and hell burning, ladders stretching into the night sky, the sounds of saws cutting holes in the roof and water gushing out of hoses, fifteen hundred gallons a minute, a master stream from the top of the truck for a big fire like that.

Water arched from trucks around the block, and the charred carcass of a car was twisted like an ice cube tray, the tires burned off. Melted aluminum and glass, and beads of copper, scrubbing on walls and deflection of steel, alligatored wood around broken windows, and heavy black smoke. A utility pole looked like a burned match. They said it was a rolling fire, the sort that fools firefighters, not too hot and then so hot it boils your hat. Wading through filthy water, a rainbow of gasoline floating on top of it, flashlights probing the pitch-dark, dripping sounds, water dripping from square ax holes in the tar-paper roof. The thick air smelled like acrid scorched marshmallows, sweet and sharp and sick, as they led her to him, to what was left. Much later they said he was dead when it started, lured there and shot.

Scarpetta turned off the water and stood in the steam, breathing in clouds of it through her nose and mouth. She couldn't see through the glass door, it was so fogged up, but shifting light was Benton walking in. She wasn't ready to talk to him yet.

"I brought you a drink," he said.

The light shifted again, Benton moving past the shower. She heard him pull out the vanity chair, sitting.

"Marino called."

Scarpetta opened the door and reached out for the towel hanging next to it, pulling it inside the shower. "Please shut the bathroom door so it doesn't get cold in here," she said.

"Lucy and Jaime are just a few minutes out from White Plains." Benton got up and shut the door. He sat back down.

"They still haven't landed? What the hell is going on?"

"They got such a late start because of the weather. Just a lot of delays because of weather. He talked to Lucy on the helicopter phone. They're fine."

"I told him not to do that, goddamn it. She doesn't need to be talking on the damn phone when she's flying."

"He said he talked to her just for a minute. He didn't tell her what's happened. He'll fill her in when they're on the ground. I'm sure she'll call you. Don't worry. They're fine." Benton's face looking at her through steam.

She was drying off inside the shower with the glass door half open. She didn't want to come out. He didn't ask her what was wrong, why she was hiding inside the shower like a little kid.

"I've searched everywhere—again—for your phone. It's not in the apartment," he added.

"Did you try calling it?"

"Betting it's on the closet floor in the makeup room at CNN. Where you always hang your coat, if I'm not mistaken."

"Lucy can find it if I ever talk to her again."

"I thought you talked to her earlier today while she was still in Stowe." His way of encouraging her to be reasonable.

"Because I called her." It wasn't possible for Scarpetta to be reasonable right now. "She never calls me, hardly ever these days. Maybe if she ever gets around to calling once in a while, such as when she's delayed because of a blizzard or hasn't landed yet."

Benton looked at her.

"She can find my damn phone then. She sure as hell should, since it was her idea to install a Wide Area Augmentation System-enabled receiver in my BlackBerry, in your BlackBerry, in Jaime's BlackBerry, in Marino's BlackBerry, in the nape of her bulldog's neck, so she can know where we are—or, more precisely, where our phones and her dog are—with a position accuracy of something like ten feet."

Benton was quiet, looking at her through the steamy air. She was still in the shower drying off, which was useless because of the steam. She would dry herself and then sweat.

"Same technology the FAA's considering for use in

flight approaches and autopilot landings, of course." It was as if someone else was talking through her mouth, someone she didn't know or like. "Maybe they're using it in drones, who the hell gives a shit. Except my goddamn phone knows exactly where it goddamn is even if I don't right this goddamn minute, and that sort of tracking is child's play for Lucy. I'll send her an e-mail. Maybe she'll get around to finding my phone." Toweling her hair, about to cry and not sure why. "Maybe she'll call because she's just a little concerned that someone might have left a bomb for me."

"Kay, please don't be so upset. . . ."

"You know I really hate it when someone tells me not to be upset. I spend my entire life not being upset because I'm fucking not allowed to be fucking upset. Well, right now I'm upset and I'm going to feel it because I can't seem to help it. If I could help it I wouldn't be upset now, would I." Her voice shook.

She felt shaky all over, as if she was coming down with something. Maybe she was getting sick. A lot of the staff at the OCME had the flu. It was going around. She closed her eyes, leaning against wet tile that was getting cool.

"I told her to call me before they took off from Vermont." She tried to calm down, to ward off the grief and rage overwhelming her. "She used to call me before she took off and landed or just to say hello."

"You don't know that she didn't call. You can't find your phone. I'm sure she's tried to call." Benton's conciliatory voice, the way he sounded when he was trying to de-escalate a situation that was rapidly becoming explosive. "Let's try to retrace your steps. Do you remember taking it out at any time after leaving the apartment?"

"No."

"But you're sure it was in your coat pocket when you left the apartment."

"I'm not sure of a damn thing right now."

She remembered dropping her coat in one of the makeup chairs when she was talking to Alex Bachta. Maybe it had fallen out then, was still in the chair. She'd send Alex an e-mail, ask him to have someone look for it and keep it locked up until she could retrieve it. She hated that phone, and she'd done something stupid. She'd done something so stupid she almost couldn't believe it. The BlackBerry wasn't password-protected, and she wasn't going to tell Benton. She wasn't going to tell Lucy.

"Lucy will track it down," Benton said. "Marino mentioned you might want to go to Rodman's Neck to see what they find, if you're curious. He'll pick you up whenever you want. First thing, like around seven. I'll go with you."

She wrapped the towel around her and stepped onto a no-slip bamboo mat. Benton, shirtless and barefoot, pajama bottoms on, sat with his back to the vanity. She hated how she felt. She didn't want to feel like this. Benton hadn't done anything to deserve it.

"I think we should find out everything we can from the bomb guys, the labs. I want to know who the hell sent that package and why and what exactly it is." Benton was watching her, the air warm and filmy with steam.

"Yes, the box of cookies some thoughtful patient of yours left for me," she said cynically.

"I guess it could be battery-operated cookies and a test tube-shaped bottle of liquor that smells like an accelerant."

"And Marino wants you to go, too? Not just me? Both

of us?" She combed her hair, but the mirror over the sink was too steamed up to see.

"What's the matter, Kay?"

"I'm just wondering if Marino specifically invited you, that's all." She wiped off the mirror with a washcloth.

"What's wrong?"

"Let me guess. He didn't invite you. Or if he did, he didn't mean it." Combing her hair, looking at her reflection. "I'm not surprised he didn't invite you or didn't mean it if he did. After the way you treated him today. On the conference call. Then in his car."

"Let's don't get started about him." Benton lifted his glass, straight bourbon on the rocks.

She could smell Maker's Mark, reminding her of a case she'd worked in the long-ago past. A man scalded to death in a river of fire when barrels of whisky began bursting in a distillery warehouse engulfed in flames.

"I wasn't friendly or unfriendly," Benton added. "I was professional. Why are you in such a bad mood?"

" '*Why*'?" she asked, as if he couldn't possibly be serious.

"Besides the obvious."

"I'm tired of the cold war you have with Marino. No point in pretending. You have one, and you know it," she said.

"We don't have one."

"I don't think he does anymore; God knows he used to. He honestly seems beyond it, but you don't, and then he gets defensive, gets angry. I find it a remarkable irony, after all those years he had a problem with you."

"Let's be accurate, his problem was with you." Benton's patience was dissipating with the steam. Even he had his limits.

"I'm not talking about me right this minute, but if you're going to bring it up, yes, he had a significant problem with me. But now he doesn't."

"I agree he's better. We'll hope it lasts." Benton played with his drink as if he couldn't make up his mind what to do with it.

In the diffusing steam, Scarpetta could make out a note she'd left for herself on the granite countertop: *Jaime—call Fri. a.m.* In the morning she would have an orchid delivered to One Hogan Place, Berger's office, a belated birthday gesture. Maybe a sumptuous Princess Mikasa. Berger's favorite color was sapphire blue.

"Benton, we're married," Scarpetta said. "Marino couldn't be more aware of that and he's accepted it, probably with relief. I imagine he must be much happier because he's accepted it, has a serious relationship, has made a new life for himself."

She wasn't so sure about Marino's serious relationship or his new life, not after the loneliness she'd sensed earlier when she was sitting next to him in his car. She imagined him dropping by the ESU garage, by the Two, as he called it, in Harlem, to hang out with a rescued dog.

"He's moved on, and now you need to," she was saying. "I want it to end. Whatever you have to do. End it. Don't just pretend. I can see through it, even if I don't say anything. We're all in this together."

"One big happy family," Benton said.

"That's what I mean. Your hostility, your jealousy. I want it to end."

"Have a sip of your drink. You'll feel better."

"Now I'm feeling patronized and getting angry." Her voice was shaking again.

"I'm not patronizing you, Kay." Softly. "And you're already angry. You've been angry for a long time."

"I feel you're patronizing me, and I've not been angry for a long time. I don't understand why you'd say something like that. You're being provocative." She didn't want to fight, hated fighting, but she was pushing things in that direction.

"I'm sorry if it feels I'm patronizing you. I'm not, honest to God. I don't blame you for being angry." He sipped his drink, staring at it, moving the ice around in it. "The last thing I want to be is provocative."

"The problem is you really don't forgive and you certainly don't forget. That's your problem with Marino. You won't forgive him and you certainly won't forget, and in the end, how does that help anything? He did what he did. He was drunk and drugged and crazy and he did something he shouldn't have done. Yes, he did. Maybe I should be the one who doesn't forgive or forget. It was me he goddamn manhandled and abused. But it's the past. He's sorry. So sorry, he avoids me. I go weeks and have no contact with him. He's overly polite when he's around me, around us, overly inclusive toward you, almost obsequious, and all it does is make things more uncomfortable. We'll never get past this unless you allow it. It's up to you."

"It's true I don't forget," he said grimly.

"Not exactly equitable when you consider what some of us have had to forgive and forget," she said, so upset it frightened her. She felt as if she might explode like the package that was hauled away.

His hazel eyes looked at her, watching her carefully. He sat very still, waiting for whatever would come next.

"Especially Marino. Especially Lucy. The secrets you

forced them to keep. It was bad enough for me but so unfair to them, having to lie for you. Not that I'm interested in dredging up the past." But she couldn't stop herself. The past was climbing up and halfway out her throat. She swallowed hard, trying to stop the past from spilling out of her and all over their life, Benton's and her life together.

He watched her, a softness, a sadness, in his eyes that was immeasurable, sweat collecting in the hollow of his neck, disappearing into the silver hair on his chest, trickling down his belly, soaking into the waistband of the polished-cotton gray pajamas she'd bought for him. He was lean and well-defined, with tight muscles and skin, still a striking man, a beautiful man. The bathroom was like a greenhouse, humid and warm from the long shower that had made her feel no less contaminated, no less filthy and foolish. She couldn't wash away the peculiar-smelling package or Carley Crispin's show or the CNN marquee or anything, and she felt powerless.

"Well, don't you have a comment?" Her voice shook badly.

"You know what this is." He got up from the chair.

"I don't want us to argue." Tears welled up in her eyes. "I must be tired. That's all. I'm tired. I'm sorry I'm so tired."

"The olfactory system is one of the oldest parts of our brain, sends information that governs emotions, memory, behavior." He was behind her and slipped his arms around her waist, both of them looking into the hazy mirror. "Individual odor molecules stimulating all sorts of receptors." Kissing the back of her neck, hugging her. "Tell me what you smelled. Tell me in as much detail as you can."

She couldn't see anything in the mirror now, her eyes flooded with tears. She muttered, "Hot pavement. Petroleum. Burning matches. Burning human flesh."

He reached for another towel and rubbed her hair with it, massaging her scalp.

"I don't know. I don't know exactly," she said.

"You don't need to know exactly. It's what it made you feel, that's what we need to know exactly."

"Whoever left that package got what he wanted," she said. "It was a bomb even if it turns out it's not."

11

Lucy hovered the Bell 407 helicopter at the hold line on taxiway Kilo, the wind shoving her around like huge hands as she waited for the tower to clear her to land.

"Not again," she said to Berger, in the left seat, the co-pilot's seat, because she wasn't the sort to ride in back when given the choice. "I don't believe where they put the damn dolly."

Westchester County Airport's west ramp was crowded with parked planes, ranging from single-engine and experimental homebuilt on up to the super-midsize Challenger and ultra-long-range Boeing business jet. Lucy willed herself to stay calm, agitation and flying a dangerous combination, but it didn't take much to set her off. She was volatile, couldn't settle down, and she hated it, but hating something didn't make it go away, and she couldn't get rid of the anger. After all her efforts to manage it and some good things happening, happy things, which had made it easier, now the anger was back out of its bag, maybe more volatile than ever after too much time unattended and ignored. Not gone. She'd just thought it was. "Nobody more intelligent or physically gifted than you or more loved," her Aunt Kay liked to say. "Why are you so aggravated all the time?" Now Berger was saying it. Berger and Scarpetta sounding the same. The same language, the same logic, as if their communications were broadcast over the same frequency.

Lucy calculated the best approach to her dolly, the small wooden platform on wheels parked too close to other aircraft, the tow bar pointed the wrong way. Best plan was a high hover altitude between the wingtips of the Learjet and the King Air at ten o'clock. They'd handle her rotorwash better than the little guys. Then directly over her dolly, a steeper angle of descent than she liked, and she'd have to land with a twenty-eight-knot wind gusting up the tail, assuming the air traffic controller ever got back to her. That much wind blowing up her ass and she had to worry about settling with power, setting down ugly and hard, and exhaust fumes were going to back up into the cabin. Berger would complain about the fumes, get one of her headaches, wouldn't want to fly with Lucy again anytime soon. One more thing they wouldn't do together.

"This is deliberate," Lucy said over the intercom, her arms and legs tense, hands and feet firm on the controls, working the helicopter hard so it basically did nothing but hold its position some thirty feet above ground level. "I'm getting his name and number."

"Tower has nothing to do with where dollies are parked." Berger's voice in Lucy's headset.

"You heard him." Lucy's attention was outside the windscreen. She scanned the dark shapes of aircraft, a thick herd of them, noticing tie-down ropes anchored in the pavement, loosely coiled, frayed ends fluttering in her twenty-million-candlepower NightSun spotlight. "Told me to take the Echo Route. Exactly what I did, sure as hell didn't disregard his instructions. He's jerking me around."

"Tower's got bigger things to worry about than where dollies are parked."

"He can do what he wants."

"Let it go. Not worth it." The rich timbre of Berger's firm voice like fine hardwood. Rain-forest ironwood, mahogany, teak. Beautiful but unyielding, bruising.

"Whenever he's on duty, it's something. It's personal." Lucy hovered, looking out, careful not to drift.

"Doesn't matter. Let it go." Berger the lawyer.

Lucy felt unfairly accused, of what she wasn't sure. She felt controlled and judged and wasn't sure why. The same way her aunt made her feel. The way everybody made her feel. Even when Scarpetta said she wasn't being controlling or judgmental, she had always made Lucy feel controlled and judged. Scarpetta and Berger weren't separated by many years, almost the same age, of an entirely different generation, a full layer of civilization between Lucy and them. She hadn't thought it was a problem, had believed quite the opposite. At last she'd found someone who commanded her respect, someone powerful and accomplished and never boring.

Jaime Berger was compelling, with short, dark brown hair and beautiful features, a genetic thoroughbred who had taken good care of herself and was stunning, really, and wickedly smart. Lucy loved the way Berger looked and moved and expressed herself, loved the way she dressed, her suits or soft corduroys and denim, her politically incorrect fucking fur coat. Lucy still found it hard to believe she'd finally gotten what she'd always wanted, always imagined.

It wasn't perfect. It wasn't close to perfect, and she didn't understand what had happened. They'd been together not quite a year. The last few weeks had been horrid.

Pressing the transmit button on the cyclic, she said over the radio, "Helicopter niner-lima-foxtrot still holding."

After a long pause, the officious voice came back, "Helicopter calling, you were stepped on. Repeat request."

"Helicopter niner-lima-foxtrot still holding," Lucy repeated curtly, and releasing the transmit button, she said to Berger over the intercom, "I wasn't stepped on. You hear any other traffic right this second?"

Berger didn't answer, and Lucy didn't look at her, didn't look anywhere except out the windscreen. One good thing about flying, she didn't have to look at someone if she was angry or hurt. No good deed goes unpunished. How many times had Marino said that to her, only he used the word *favor*, not *deed*. No favor goes unpunished, what he'd been saying since she was a kid and on his nerves something awful. Right about now it felt as if he was her only friend. Unbelievable. It wasn't long ago she wanted to put a bullet in his head just like she'd done to his piece-of-shit son, a fugitive, an Interpol Red Notice, wanted for murder, sitting in a chair, room 511, the Radisson in Szczecin, Poland. Sometimes out of nowhere Rocco Junior was in her mind, sweating and shaking and bug-eyed, dirty food trays everywhere, the air foul from him soiling himself. Begging. And when that didn't work, bribing. After all he'd done to innocent people, pleading for a second chance, for mercy, or trying to buy his way out.

No good deed goes unpunished, and Lucy hadn't done a good deed, wasn't about to, because had she been charitable and let Rocco live, he would have killed his cop father, a hit, payback. Peter Rocco Marino Junior had changed his name to Caggiano, he hated his own father that much, and little Rocco the bad seed had orders, had a precise cold-blooded plan to take out his old man Marino while he was on his yearly fishing trip, minding his own business in his cabin at Buggs Lake. Make it look like a home invasion gone bad. *Well, think again, little Rocco.* When Lucy walked out of that hotel, her ears ringing from the gunshot, all she felt was relief—well, not exactly all. It was something she and Marino didn't talk about. She'd killed his son, a judicious execution that looked like a suicide, black ops, her job, the right thing. But still, it was Marino's son, his only offspring, the last branch on his family tree as far as she knew.

The controller got back to her. "Niner-lima-foxtrot standby."

Fucking loser. Lucy imagined him sitting inside the dark control room, smirking as he looked down on her from the top of his tower.

"Niner-lima-foxtrot," she acknowledged, then to Berger, "Same thing he did last time. Messing with me."

"Don't get worked up."

"I should get his phone number. I'm going to find out who the fuck he is."

"You're getting worked up."

"They better not have lost my car or fucked with it."

"Tower has nothing to do with parking."

"Hope you've got clout with state troopers; I'm going to speed," Lucy said. "We can't be late."

"This was a bad idea. We should have done it another time."

"Another time wouldn't have been your birthday," Lucy said.

She wasn't going to allow herself to feel the sting, not when she was pulling in almost ninety percent torque, a crosswind slamming her tail boom, trying to swing it around while she held it steady with the pedals, making tiny corrections with the cyclic and collective. Berger was admitting it, telling the truth: She hadn't wanted to go to Vermont for her birthday. Not that Lucy needed to be told, good Christ. Alone in front of the fire, looking out at the lights of Stowe, looking out at the snow, and Berger may as well have been in Mexico, she was so distant, so preoccupied. As the head of the New York County DA's Sex Crimes Unit, she supervised what always turned out to be the most heinous cases in the five boroughs, and it was assumed within hours of Hannah Starr's disappearance that she was the victim of foul play, possibly a sex crime. After three weeks of digging, Berger had a very different theory—thanks to Lucy and her forensic computer skills. Lucy's reward? Berger could think of little else. Then the jogger had to die. A surprise getaway Lucy had planned for months, fucked. Another good deed punished.

Lucy, on the other hand, with her own prepossessions and emotions, had been able to sip a grand cru Chablis by the hearth while she undetectably entertained her own shadowed thoughts, very dark shadowed thoughts, fearful thoughts about mistakes she'd made—specifically, the mistake she'd made with Hannah Starr. Lucy couldn't forgive it and couldn't get out from under it, so furious and full of hate it was like being sick, like chronic fatigue or myoneuralgia, always there making her miserable. But she revealed nothing. Berger didn't know, couldn't possibly fathom, what was inside Lucy. Years of deep undercover

with the FBI, ATF, and paramilitary and private investigations, and she controlled what she gave away and what
she kept to herself, had to be impeccably controlled when
the slightest facial tic or gesture could blow a case or get
her killed.

Objectively, ethically, she shouldn't have agreed to do
the forensic computer analysis in the Hannah Starr case,
and she sure as hell should recuse herself now but wasn't
about to, knowing what Hannah deliberately did. Of all
people, Lucy should be the one to take care of such a trav-
esty. She had her own history with Hannah Starr, a far more
devastating one than she'd imagined before she'd started
searching and restoring the entitled pampered bitch's electronic files and e-mail accounts and sat around day after day
looking at e-mails her lover boy husband, Bobby, still sent.
The more Lucy discovered, the more contempt she had, the
more righteous rage. She wouldn't quit now, and no one
could make her.

She hovered over the yellow-painted hold line, listening
to the controller vector some poor Hawker pilot all the hell
over the place. What was wrong with people? When the
economy had begun its free fall, the world seeming to
disintegrate, Lucy had assumed people might behave
better, like they did after 9/11. If nothing else, you get
scared and survival mode kicks in. Chances for survival are
better if you're civilized and don't go out of your way to
piss everybody off unless there's something tangible to be
gained by it. There was nothing tangible to be gained by
what the asshole air traffic controller was doing to Lucy, to
other pilots, and he was doing it because he was anonymous
up there in his tower, the goddamn coward. She was
tempted to confront him, walk over to the tower and press

the intercom button by the locked outer door. Someone would let her in. The people in the tower knew damn well who she was. *Good Christ,* she told herself. *Calm down.* For one thing, there wasn't time.

Once she shut down, she wouldn't refuel. She wasn't going to wait for the fuel truck. It would take forever, might never get to her, the way things were going. She'd lock up the helicopter and grab her car and race to Manhattan. Barring any further delays, they should be in the Village, in her loft, by half past one. That was cutting it close for a two a.m. interview they'd never get again— an interview that might lead to Hannah Starr, whose disappearance had captured the public's morbid imagination since the day before Thanksgiving, when she was allegedly last seen getting into that yellow cab on Barrow Street. Ironically, just blocks from where Lucy lived, Berger had pointed out more than once. *"And you were home that night. Too damn bad you didn't see anything."*

"Helicopter niner-lima-foxtrot," the controller said over the air. "You can proceed to the ramp. Landing is at your own risk. If you're unfamiliar with the airport, you need to inform us."

"Niner-lima-foxtrot," Lucy said with no inflection, the way she sounded before she offed someone or threatened it. She nudged the helicopter forward.

She hover-taxied to the edge of the ramp, made a vertical descent, and set down on her dolly, situated between a Robinson helicopter that reminded her of a dragonfly and a Gulfstream jet that reminded her of Hannah Starr. The wind grabbed the tail boom, and exhaust fumes filled the cabin.

"Unfamiliar?" Lucy chopped the throttle to flight idle

and turned off the low-RPM warning horn. "I'm *unfamiliar*? You hear that? He's trying to make me look like a crappy pilot."

Berger was silent, the smell of fumes strong.

"He does it every damn time now." Lucy reached up and flipped off overhead switches. "Sorry about the exhaust. You okay? Hang in there for two minutes. Really sorry." She should confront the controller. She shouldn't let him get away with it.

Berger took off her headset and opened her window, moving her face as close to it as she could.

"Opening the window makes it worse," Lucy reminded her. She should walk over to the tower and take the elevator up to the top and let him have it inside the control room right in front of his colleagues.

She watched seconds tick by on the digital clock, fifty-something to go, and her anxiety and anger grew. She would find out the name of that damn air traffic controller and would get him. What had she ever done to him or anybody who worked here except act respectfully and mind her own business and tip well and pay her fees? Thirty-one seconds to go. She didn't know his name. She didn't know him. She'd never been anything but professional over the air, no matter how rude he was, and he was always rude to everyone. *Fine. If he wanted a fight, he'd get one. Jesus Christ.* He had no idea who he was tangling with.

Lucy radioed the tower, and the same controller answered her.

"Requesting your supervisor's phone number," Lucy said.

He gave it to her because he had no choice. FAA regs. She wrote it down on her kneeboard. Let him worry. Let him sweat. She radioed the FBO and asked to have her car brought out and her helicopter towed into the hangar. She wondered if her next unpleasant surprise was going to be damage to her Ferrari. Maybe the controller had seen to that, too. She cut the throttle and silenced the warning horn one last time. She took off her headset, hung it on a hook.

"I'm getting out," Berger said inside the dark, stinking cockpit. "You don't need to pick a fight with anyone."

Lucy reached up for the rotor brake, pulled it down. "Hold on until I stop the blades. Remember, we're on the dolly, not the ground. Don't forget that when you step down. Just a few more seconds."

Berger unfastened her four-point harness as Lucy finished the shutdown. Making sure the NG was zero, she flipped off the battery switch. They climbed out, Lucy grabbing their bags and locking up. Berger didn't wait, headed to the FBO, walking fast between aircraft, stepping around tie-downs and dodging a fuel truck, her slender figure in her long mink coat receding and gone. Lucy knew the routine. Berger would dash into the ladies' room, gulp down four Advil or a Zomig, and splash her face with cold water. Under different circumstances, she wouldn't get into the car right now but would give herself a chance to recover, walk around for a while in the fresh air. But there wasn't time.

If they weren't back in Lucy's loft by two a.m., Hap Judd would get spooked, would leave and never contact Berger again. He wasn't the type to tolerate excuses of any sort, would assume an excuse was a ruse. He was being set up, the paparazzi were around the corner, that's exactly what he would think, because he was paranoid as hell and guilty as hell. He'd blow them off. He'd get himself a lawyer, and even the dumbest lawyer would tell him not to talk, and the most promising lead would be lost. Hannah Starr wouldn't be found, soon or ever, and she deserved to be found, for the sake of truth and justice—not her justice. She didn't deserve something she'd denied everybody else. What a joke. The public had no hint. The whole fucking world felt sorry for her.

Lucy never had felt sorry for her but hadn't realized until three weeks ago exactly what she did feel for her. By the time Hannah was reported missing, Lucy was keenly aware of the damage the woman could do and in fact had done, just hadn't recognized it was deliberate. Chalked it up to bad luck, the market, the collapsing economy, and a super-ficial person's superficial advice, a favor that got punished but nothing premeditated and malevolent. Wrong. Wrong. Wrong. Hannah Starr was diabolical; she was evil. If only Lucy had given more weight to her instincts, because the gut feeling she'd gotten the first time she and Hannah had met alone in Florida wasn't good, wasn't close to good, she realized that now. While Hannah was polite and nice, almost flirting, there was something else. Lucy realized that now because she hadn't wanted to realize it then. Maybe it was the way Hannah kept looking at the high-performance boats going by, obnoxiously loud below her glitzy North Miami Beach apartment balcony, so loud Lucy could barely hear herself talk. Greed, unabashed greed. And competi-tiveness.

"Bet you have one of those tucked away somewhere." Hannah's voice, husky, lusty as a 46 Rider XP, triple-stepped hull, inboards at least nine-fifty HP each, headed out to sea, sounding like a Harley full-throttle if your head was next to the Screamin' Eagle pipes.

"I'm not into go-fast boats." Lucy hated them, truth be told.

"No way. You and all your machines? I remember the way you used to drool all over my father's cars. You were the only one he ever let drive his Enzo. I couldn't believe it. You were just a kid. I should think a cigarette boat would be right up your alley."

"Not at all."

"And I thought I knew you."

"They wouldn't get me anywhere I need to go unless I have a secret life of running drugs or errands for the Russian Mafia."

"Secret life? Do tell," Hannah had said.

"I don't have one."

"God, look at it go." Another one leaving a wide swath of lacy white wake, thundering into the inlet from the Intracoastal, under the causeway, toward the Atlantic. "Yet one more of my ambitions. To have one someday. Not a secret life but a boat like that."

"If you have one, better not let me find out. I'm not talking about boats."

"Not me, hon. My life's an open book." Hannah's art deco diamond ring flashed in the sunlight when she placed her hands on the balcony rail, gazing at the aqua water and the powder-blue sky and the long strip of bone-colored beach scattered with furled umbrellas that looked like candy swizzle sticks and feathery palms that were yellowing at the edges of their fronds.

Lucy remembered thinking Hannah could have stepped out of an ad for a five-star resort in her ready-to-wear silk Ungaro, beautiful and blond, with just enough weight to be sexy and just enough years to be credible as a high-level financier. Forty and perfect, one of those precious people untouched by commonness, by hardship, by anything ugly, someone Lucy always avoided at the lavish dinners and parties hosted by Rupe Starr, her father. Hannah had seemed incapable of crime, if for no other reason than she didn't need to bother with anything as untidy as living a lie and stealing people blind. Lucy had misread Hannah's open book, all right, misread it enough to incur incalculable damage. She'd taken a nine-figure hit because of Hannah's little favor. One lie leads to another, and now Lucy was living one, although she had her own definition of lying. It wasn't literally a lie if the end result was truth.

She paused halfway across the ramp, tried Marino on her BlackBerry. Right about now he should be doing surveillance, checking on Hap Judd's whereabouts, making sure he hadn't decided to boogie after his bullshit tap dance about meeting during the wee hours of the morning because he didn't want to be recognized. Didn't want anything ending up on Page Six of the *Post* or all over the Internet. Maybe he should have thought about that before he'd blown off the likes of Jaime Berger the first time she tried to reach him three weeks ago. Maybe he should have thought, period, before running his mouth to a stranger who, what do you know, happened to be a friend of Lucy's, a snitch.

"That you?" Marino's voice in her wireless jawbone. "Was getting worried you'd decided to visit John Denver."

Lucy didn't laugh, not even a smile. She never joked about people who'd been killed in crashes. Planes, helicopters, motorcycles, cars, the space shuttle. Not funny.

"I e-mailed you a MapQuest," Marino said as she resumed walking across the tarmac, hauling luggage over her shoulders. "I know that race car of yours ain't got a GPS."

"Why the hell would I need a GPS to find my way home?"

"Roads being shut down, traffic diverted, because of a little situation that I didn't want to get into while you were flying that death trap of yours. Plus, you got the package with you." He meant Berger, his boss. "You get lost or hung up and are late for your two a.m., guess who gets blamed? She's already going to be pissed when I'm a no-show."

"A no-show? Even better," Lucy said.

All she'd asked was for him to take his time, be maybe thirty or forty minutes late so she could have her chance with Hap Judd. If Marino was sitting there from the get-go, she wouldn't be able to maneuver the interview the way she wanted, and what she wanted was a deconstruction. Lucy had a special talent for interrogation, and she intended to find out what she needed to know so she could take care of things.

"You been keeping up with the news?" Marino said.

"At fuel stops. We know what's all over the Internet about the yellow-cab connection, the stuff about Hannah and the jogger." She assumed that was what he was refer-encing.

"Guess you haven't been monitoring OEM."

"No way. No time. I got diverted twice. One airport was out of Jet-A, another hadn't been plowed. What's going on?"

"A FedEx box left at your aunt's building. She's fine, but you should call her."

"A FedEx box? What are you talking about?" Lucy stopped walking.

"We don't know what's in it. May have something to do with a patient of Benton's. Some whack job who left the Doc a Christmas present. Santa's sleigh had to transport it to Rodman's Neck. Not even an hour ago, headed right at you, to the Cross Bronx Expressway, which you'd be crossing out of White Plains, and why I sent you a map. I routed you way east of the Bronx just in case."

"Shit. Who'd you deal with from the bomb squad? I'll talk to whoever it was." Sixth Precinct, where the bomb squad was headquartered, was in the Village, close to Lucy's loft. She knew a few of the techs.

"Thanks, Special Agent ATF, but it's handled. NYPD will somehow manage without you. I'm doing what needs to be done, not to worry. The Doc will tell you about it. She's fine. This same nut job of Benton's might have a connection with Hollywood." Marino's sarcastic nickname for Hap Judd. "I'm going to check it out at RTCC. But maybe the subject should come up. Her name's Dodie Hodge. A mental patient at McLean's."

"Why would she know him?" Lucy started walking again.

"Might be more of her make-believe, a hallucination, right? But seeing as how there was this incident at your aunt's apartment building, maybe you should ask Hollywood about her. I'll be at RTCC probably all night. Explain it to the boss." He meant Berger. "I don't want her pissed at me. But this is important. I'm going to get to the bottom of it before something worse happens."

"So, where are you? In TriBeCa?" Lucy wove between jet wings, careful of tip extensions sticking up like dorsal fins and communications antennas that could put a person's eye out. She'd once watched a pilot walk into his trailing edge

Junker flap while he was drinking coffee and on the phone, gashed his head wide open.

"Cruised by Hollywood's place a few minutes ago, on my way downtown. Looks like he's home. That's good news. Maybe he'll show up," Marino said.

"You should stake him out, make sure he does. That was our deal." Lucy couldn't stand depending on other people to get the job done. The damn weather. If she'd gotten here earlier, she would have tailed Hap Judd herself and made sure he didn't miss their meeting.

"I got more important things to do right now than bird-dog some pervert who thinks he's the next James Dean. Call if you get detoured and end up lost, Amelia Earhart."

Lucy got off the phone and picked up her pace, thought about checking on her aunt, and then thought about the number she'd written down on her kneeboard. Maybe she should call the supervisor before she left the airport. Maybe it would be better to wait until tomorrow and call the ATC manager or, better yet, complain to the FAA and get the guy sent to refresher training. She was seething as she thought about what he'd broadcast over the tower's frequency, making sure everybody on it heard him accuse her of being an incompetent pilot, accuse her of not knowing her way into an airport she flew in and out of several times a week.

She hangared her helicopter and Citation X jet here, for God's sake. Maybe that was his motivation. To bring her down a notch or two, to rub it in because he'd heard the rumors or was making assumptions about what had happened to her during what everyone was calling the worst financial meltdown since the thirties. Only it wasn't the crash of Wall Street that had done the real damage. Hannah

Starr had. A favor, a gift her father, Rupe, would have wanted Lucy to have. A parting gesture. When Hannah was dating Bobby, that's all she heard. Lucy this and Lucy that.

"He thought you were Einstein. A pretty Einstein but a tomboy. He adored you," Hannah had said to Lucy not even six months ago.

Seductive or making fun, Lucy couldn't tell what Hannah meant or knew or supposed. Rupe had known the facts of Lucy's life, for damn sure. Thin gold-rimmed glasses, fuzzy white hair, and smoky blue eyes, a tiny man in tidy suits and as honest as he was smart. Didn't give a shit who was in Lucy's pants as long as they stayed out of her pockets, as long as it didn't cost her in any way that counted. He understood why women loved women since he loved them, too, said he might very well be a lesbian because if he were a woman, he'd want women. So, what was anybody, anyway? It's what's in your heart, he used to say. Always smiling. A kind, decent man. The father Lucy never had. When he died last May during a business trip to Georgia, from a strain of salmonella infection that ran him down like a cement truck, Lucy had been disbelieving, devastated. How could someone like Rupe be done in by a jalapeño pepper? Was existence contingent on nothing more than the fucking decision to order nachos?

"We miss him terribly. He was my mentor and best buddy." This past June. Hannah on her balcony, watching million-dollar boats roar by. "You did well with him. You can do even better with me."

Lucy told her thanks but no thanks, told her more than once. She wasn't comfortable turning over her entire port-folio to Hannah Starr. No fucking way, Lucy had politely said. At least she'd listened to her gut on that one, but she should have paid attention to what she felt about the favor. *Don't do it.* But Lucy did. Maybe it was her need to impress Hannah because Lucy sensed a competition. Maybe it was her wound, the one Hannah stuck her finger in because she was cunning enough to recognize it. As a child Lucy had been abandoned by her father and as an adult didn't want to be abandoned by Rupe. He had managed her finances from day one and had never been anything but honorable, and he'd cared about her. He was her friend. He would have wanted her to have something special on his way out of this life because she was so special to him.

"A tip he would have given you had he lived long enough," said Hannah, brushing Lucy's fingers as she handed her a business card, her practiced lavish scrawl on the back: *Bay Bridge Finance* and a phone number.

"You were like a daughter to him, and he made me promise to take care of you," Hannah had said.

How could he have promised any such thing? Lucy realized that too late. He'd gotten sick so fast, Hannah never saw him or spoke to him before he died in Atlanta. Lucy hadn't asked that question until nine figures later, and now was certain there had been more to it than the considerable kickback Hannah must have gotten for herding rich people to the slaughter. She'd wanted to hurt Lucy for the sake of hurting her, to maim her, to make her weak.

The air traffic controller couldn't possibly know anything about what had happened to Lucy's net worth, couldn't have the slightest knowledge of her damage and degradation. She was being overly anxious, hypervigilant, and irrational, what Berger called pathological, in a foul mood because a surprise weekend she'd planned for months had been a flop and Berger had been distant and irritable, had rebuffed her in every way that mattered. Berger had ignored her in the town house and on Lucy's way out the door, and onboard the helicopter it hadn't gotten any better. She hadn't talked about anything personal the first half of the flight, then spent the second half sending text messages from the helicopter's cell phone because of Carley Crispin and yellow cabs and who knows what, every slight indirectly leading back to the same damn thing: Hannah. She had taken over Berger's life and taken something else from Lucy, this time something priceless.

Lucy glanced at the control tower, the glass-enclosed top of it blazing like a lighthouse, and imagined the controller, the enemy sitting in front of a radar screen, staring at targets and beacon codes that represented real human beings in real aircraft, everybody doing the best they could to get where they were going safely, while he barked commands and insults. *Piece of shit.* She should confront him. She was going to confront someone.

"So, who towed my dolly out and turned it downwind?" she asked the first line crewman she saw inside the FBO.

"You sure?" He was a skinny, pimply kid in oversized insulated coveralls, marshalling wands in the pockets of his Dickies work coat. He wouldn't look her in the eye.

"Am I sure?" she said, as if she hadn't heard him right.

"You wanna ask my supervisor?"

"No, I don't wanna ask your supervisor. This is the third time I've landed in a tailwind here in the past two weeks, F. J. Reed." She read his name tag. "You know what that means? It means whoever's towing my dolly out of the hangar orients it on the ramp with the tow bar pointed exactly the wrong way—directly downwind, so I land in a tailwind."

"Not me. I would never orientate something downwind."

"There's no *tate*."

"Huh?"

"Orient. As in the Far East," Lucy said. "You know anything about aerodynamics, F. J. Reed? Airplanes, and that includes helicopters, land and take off into the wind, not with the wind on their ass. Crosswinds suck, too. Why? Because wind speed equals airspeed minus ground speed, and the direction of the wind changes the flight trajectory, fucks with the angle of attack. When you're not into the wind on takeoff, it's harder to reach translational lift. When you're landing, you can settle with power, fucking crash. Who's the controller I was talking to? You know the guys in the tower, right, F. J. Reed?"

"I donno anybody in the tower really."

"Really?"

"Yes, ma'am. You're the black chopper with the FLIR and the NightSun. Sort of looks like Homeland Security. But I'd know if you were. We know who comes in and out of here."

Lucy was sure of it. He was the moron who had towed her dolly out and deliberately turned it downwind because the jerk in the control tower had instructed him or at the very least encouraged him to pick on her, to make a fool of her, to humiliate and belittle her.

"Appreciate it. You told me what I need to know," she said.

She stalked off as Berger emerged from the ladies' room, buttoning her mink coat. Lucy could tell she had washed her face, splashed a lot of cold water on it. It didn't take much for Berger to get what she called "sick headaches" and Lucy called migraines. The two of them left the FBO and got into the 599GTB, the twelve-cylinder engine grumbling loudly as Lucy ran her Surefire flashlight along the gleaming Rosso Barchetta paint, the deep red of a fine red wine, looking for the slightest flaw, the faintest sign that there had been any misadventure or mischief with her 611-horsepower supercoupe. She checked the run-flat tires and looked inside the boot, arranging luggage. She tucked herself behind the carbon-fiber steering wheel and scanned the instrument panel, taking note of the mileage, checking the radio station, it'd better be what she'd left it on, making sure nobody took the Ferrari for a joyride during the time she and Berger were away or, as Berger put it, "stuck in Stowe." Lucy thought of the e-mail Marino had sent but didn't look for it. She didn't need his help with navigation, no matter what traffic might have been diverted or roads closed. She should call her aunt.

"I didn't get him," Berger said, her profile clean and lovely in the near dark.

"He'd better hope I don't get him," Lucy said, shifting into first.

"I meant a tip. I didn't tip the valet."

"No tips. Something's not right. Until I figure it out, I'm not nice anymore. How are you feeling?"

"I'm fine."

"Marino says someone, a former psychiatric patient of Benton's, left a package at my aunt's building. The bomb squad had to be called. The package is at Rodman's Neck," Lucy said.

"This is why I never take vacations. I go away and look what happens."

"Name's Dodie Hodge, and Marino says she might have some connection with Hap Judd and he's going to run her through RTCC."

"You come across anything about her?" Berger asked. "All the data searches you've done, I would think you might have if there's anything."

"Not familiar," Lucy said. "We should ask Hap about her, find out how he knows her or if he does. I'm really not liking it that now it appears this asshole is connected to someone who might have just left a package for my aunt."

"It's premature to make any such connection."

"Marino's up to his ears in alligators. He told me to tell you that."

"Implying what?"

"He just said to tell you he's got a lot of stuff to run down. He sounded pretty frantic," Lucy said.

She downshifted back to third after hitting sixty in three seconds flat. Easy goes it on the access road, and hold your horses on Route 120. You can cruise half asleep at a hundred on the Parkway. She wasn't going to tell Berger that Marino wasn't going to make it to the interview.

"Slow down," Berger objected.

"Dammit. I've told Aunt Kay about being on live TV." Taking corners as if she intended to powerslide through them, the manettino controller set to race mode, the power assist shut off. "Same thing you worry about. If you're on live TV, people know where you are. It was obvious she was in the city tonight, and there are plenty of ways we can make it harder for people to do shit like this to her. She should make it hard as hell for people to do shit like this to her."

"Let's don't blame the victim. It's not Kay's fault."

"I've told her repeatedly to stay away from Carley

Crispin, for fuck's sake." Lucy flicked her high beams at some fool creeping in front of her, gunned around him, kicking grit in his eyes.

"It's not her fault. She thinks she's helping," Berger said. "God knows there's so much garbage out there. Juries, especially. Everybody's an expert. Slowly but surely, smart people like Kay have to set the record straight. We all do."

"Helping Carley. That's probably the only person Aunt Kay is helping. And you don't set the record straight with somebody like that. Obviously. Look what just happened. We'll see how many people are still taking taxis in the morning."

"Why are you so hard on her?"

Lucy drove fast and didn't answer.

"Maybe the same reason you're so hard on me," Berger said, looking straight ahead.

"What reason might that be? I see you, what? Two nights a week? I'm sorry you hated your birthday."

"Every one of them," Berger said, the way she sounded when she was trying to ease the tension. "Wait until you're past forty. You'll hate your birthdays, too."

"That's not what I meant."

"I know what you meant."

Lucy drove faster.

"I'm assuming Marino's on his way to your loft?" Berger asked.

"He said he might be a little late." One of those lies that wasn't quite one.

"I don't feel good about this." Berger was thinking about Hannah Starr, about Hap Judd. Preoccupied, obsessed, but not with Lucy. No matter how much Berger reassured her or apologized, things had changed.

Lucy tried to remember exactly when. Summer, maybe, when the city started announcing budget cuts and the planet began wobbling on its axis. Then, in the past few weeks, forget it. And now? Gone. It was feeling gone. It was feeling over. It couldn't be. Lucy wasn't going to let it go. Somehow she had to stop it from leaving her.

"I'll say it again. It's all about the outcome." Lucy reached for Berger's hand, pulled it close, and stroked it with her thumb. "Hap Judd will talk because he's an arrogant sociopath, because he's got nothing but self-interest, and he believes it's in his self-interest."

"Doesn't mean I feel comfortable," Berger said, lacing her fingers in Lucy's. "About a shade away from entrapment. Maybe not even a shade away."

"Here we go again. We're fine. Don't worry. Eric had an eighth of White Widow on him for pain management. Nothing wrong with medical marijuana. As for where he got it? Maybe from Hap. Hap's a pothead."

"Remember who you're talking to. I don't want to know anything about where Eric—or you—get your so-called medical marijuana, and I'm assuming you don't have any, have never had any." Berger had said this before, repeatedly. "I'd better not find out you're growing it indoors somewhere."

"I'm not. I don't do stuff like that anymore. Haven't lit up in years. I promise." Lucy smiled, downshifting onto the exit ramp for I-684 South, Berger's touch reassuring her, bolstering her confidence. "Eric had a few J's. Just happened to be enjoying himself when he just happened to run into Hap, who just happens to frequent the same places, is a creature of habit. Not smart. Makes you easy to find and befriend."

"Yes, so you've said. And I continue to say the following:

What if Eric decides to talk to somebody he shouldn't? Like Hap's lawyer, because he'll get one. After I'm done with him, he will."

"Eric likes me and I give him work."

"Exactly. You trust a handyman."

"A stoner with a record," Lucy said. "Not credible, no one would believe him if it came down to that. Nothing for you to worry about, I promise."

"There's plenty for me to worry about. You induced a famous actor . . ."

"Not exactly Christian Bale, for Christ's sake," Lucy said. "You never even heard of Hap Judd before all this."

"I've heard of him now, and he's famous enough. More to the point, you encouraged him to break the law, to use a controlled substance, and you did it on behalf of a public servant so you could gain evidence against him."

"Wasn't there, not even in New York," Lucy said. "You and I were in Vermont Monday night when Hap and my handyman had so much fun."

"So, that's really why you wanted to steal me away during a workweek."

"I didn't decide your birthday was December seventeenth, and it wasn't my intention for us to get snowed in." Stung again. "But yes, it made sense to have Eric cruise various bars while we were out of town. Especially while you were out of town."

"You didn't just ask him to cruise various bars, you supplied the illegal substance."

"Nope. Eric bought the stuff."

"Where'd he get the money?" Berger said.

"We've been through all this. You're making yourself crazy."

"The defense will claim entrapment, outrageous government conduct."

"And you'll say Hap was predisposed to do what he did."

"Now you're coaching me?" Berger laughed ruefully.
"Don't know why I bothered going to law school. In summary, let's be honest, you had ideas implanted in Hap's
mind that could get him indicted for something we can
never prove. You basically got him stoned and had your
snitch handyman lure him into a conversation about Park
General Hospital, which you got suspicious about because
you hacked into Hap's e-mail account and God knows what
else. Probably the goddamn hospital's, too. Jesus God."

"I got their info fair and square."

"Please."

"Besides, we don't need to prove it," Lucy said. "Isn't
that the point? To scare the shit out of Mr. Hollywood so
he'll do what's right?"

"I don't know why I listen to you," Berger said, holding
Lucy's hand tighter and tucking it against her.

"He could have been honorable. He could have been
helpful. He could have been a normal law-abiding citizen,
but guess what, he's not," Lucy said. "He's brought this
upon himself."

12

Searchlights swept a crisscross of steel bracing at the top of the George Washington Bridge, where a jumper was holding on to cables. He was a big man, maybe in his sixties, the wind whipping his pants legs, his bare ankles fish-belly white in the blazing light, his face dazed. Marino couldn't stop his attention from wandering to the live feed on the flat-screen TV across the room from him.

He wished the cameras would hold steady on the jumper's face. He wanted to see what was there and what was missing. Didn't matter how many times he'd witnessed situations like this. For each desperate person it was different. Marino had watched people die, watched them realize they were going to live, watched people kill and be killed, had looked them in the face and witnessed the moment of recognition that it was over or it wasn't. The look was never exactly the same. Rage, hate, shock, grief, anguish, terror, scorn, amusement, combinations of them, and nothing. As different as people are different.

The windowless blue room where Marino went data mining fairly often these days reminded him of Times

Square, of Niketown. He was surrounded by a dizzying array of images, some dynamic, others static, all bigger than life on flat screens and the two-story data wall comprised of huge Mitsubishi cubes tiled together. An hourglass spun in one of the cubes as the Real Time Crime Center's software searched the more-than-three-terabyte data warehouse for anyone who might match the description of the man in the FedEx cap, a security camera image of him ten feet tall on the wall, and next to it a satellite picture of Scarpetta's granite apartment building on Central Park West.

"He goes, he'll never make it to the water," Marino said from his ergonomic chair at a work station where he was being helped by an analyst named Petrowski. "Jesus. He'll hit the fucking bridge. What was he thinking when he started climbing out on the cables? He was going to land on a car? Take out some poor bastard minding his own business in his MINI Cooper."

"People in his state of mind don't think." Petrowski, a detective in his thirties, in a preppie suit and tie, wasn't particularly interested in what was happening on the GW Bridge at almost two o'clock in the morning.

He was busy entering keywords on a Tattoo Report. *In vino* and *veritas,* and *In vino veritas,* and *bones, skulls,* and now *coffin.* The hourglass twirled like a baton in its quadrant of the data wall near the video image of the man in the FedEx cap and the satellite view of Scarpetta's building. On the flat screen, the jumper was thinking about it, caught in cables like a deranged trapeze artist. Any second, the wind was going to rip him loose. The end.

"We've got nothing very helpful in terms of searching," Petrowski said.

"Yeah, you already told me," Marino said.

He couldn't get a good look at the jumper's face, but maybe he didn't need to. Maybe he knew the feeling. The guy had finally said *Fuck it.* The question was what he'd meant by it. This early morning he either died or stayed in his living hell, so what did he mean when he climbed up on top of the bridge's north tower and ventured out on the cables? Was his intention to exterminate himself or to make a point because he was pissed? Marino tried to determine his socioeconomic status from his grooming, his clothing, his jewelry. Hard to tell. Baggy khakis, no socks, some kind of running shoe, a dark jacket, no gloves. A metal watch, maybe. Kind of slovenly-looking and bald. Probably lost his money, his job, his wife, maybe all three. Marino knew what he felt like. He was pretty sure he did. About a year and a half ago he felt the same way, had thought about going off a bridge, came within an inch of driving his truck through the guardrail, plunging hundreds of feet into Charleston's Cooper River.

"No address except where the victim lives," Petrowski added.

He meant Scarpetta. She was the victim, and it rattled Marino to hear her referred to as a victim.

"The tattoo's unique. It's the best thing we got going." Marino watched the jumper cling to cables high above the upper span of the bridge, high above the black abyss of the Hudson. "Jesus, don't shine the friggin' light in his eyes. How many million candlepower? His hands got to be numb. You imagine how cold those steel cables are? Do yourself a favor, eat your gun next time, buddy. Take a bottle of pills."

Marino couldn't help thinking about himself, reminded

of South Carolina, the blackest period of his life. He'd
wanted to die. He'd deserved to die. He still wasn't a hundred percent sure why he hadn't, why he hadn't ended up
on TV same as this poor bastard on the GW. Marino imagined cops and firefighters, a scuba team, hoisting his
pickup truck out of the Cooper River, him inside, how ugly
that would have been, how unfair to everyone, but when
you're that desperate, that whacked, you don't think about
what's fair. Bloated by decomposition, floaters the worst,
the gases blowing him up and turning him green, eyes
bulging like a frog, lips and ears and maybe his dick nib-
bled off by crabs and fish.

The ultimate punishment would have been to look disgusting like that, to stink so bad he made people gag, a
freakin' horror on the Doc's table. He would have been her
case, her office in Charleston the only show in town. She
would have done him. No way she would have had him
transported hundreds of miles away, no way she would have
brought in another forensic pathologist. She would have
taken care of him. Marino was positive of that. He had seen
her do people she knew in the past, would drape a towel
over their faces, keep their naked dead bodies covered by a
sheet as much as possible, out of respect. Because she was
the best one to take care of them, and she knew it.

". . . It's not necessarily unique, and it probably isn't in
a database," Petrowski was saying.

"What isn't?"

"The tattoo. As for the guy's physical description, that
would include about half the city," Petrowski said. The
jumper on the flat screen may as well have been a movie
he'd already seen. Barely made Petrowski turn his head.
"Black male between the ages of twenty-five and forty-five,

height between five-eight and six-two. No phone number, no address, no license tag, nothing to search on. I can't do much else at this point." As if Marino really shouldn't have come to the eighth floor of One Police Plaza and bothered an RTCC analyst with minutiae like this.

It was true. Marino could have called and asked first. But better to show up with a disk in hand. Like his mother used to say, "Foot in the door, Pete. Foot in the door."

The jumper's foot slipped on a cable and he caught himself.

"Whoa," Marino said to the flat screen, halfway wondering if his thinking the word *foot* had caused the jumper's foot to move.

Petrowski looked where Marino was looking and commented, "They get up there and change their minds. Happens all the time."

"If you really want to end it, why put yourself through it? Why change your mind?" Marino started feeling contempt for the jumper, started feeling pissed. "You ask me, it's bullshit. Nutcakes like this one? They just want attention, want to be on TV, want payback, want something besides death, in other words."

Traffic on the upper level of the bridge was backing up, even at this hour, and on the span directly below the jumper, police were setting up a staging area, laying down an air bag. A negotiator was trying to talk the jumper out of it, and other cops were climbing the tower, trying to get close. Everybody risking his life for someone who didn't give a shit, someone who had said *Fuck it,* whatever that meant. The volume was turned off, and Marino couldn't hear what was being said and didn't need to because it wasn't his case, had nothing to do with him, and he shouldn't be caught up in it. But he was always distracted in the RTCC, where there was too much sensory input and yet not enough. All sorts of images thrown up on the walls but no windows, just blue acoustical panels, curved rows of work stations with dual screens, and gray carpet.

Only when the adjoining conference room's window shades were open, and they weren't right now, was he given a reference point, a view of the Brooklyn Bridge, Downtown Presbyterian, Pace Union, the old Woolworth Building. The New York he remembered from when he was just getting started with the NYPD, was a nothing from Bayonne who gave up boxing, gave up beating the shit out of people, decided to help them instead. He wasn't sure why. He wasn't sure how it happened that he'd ever left New York and ended up in Richmond, Virginia, in the early eighties. At this stage of things it seemed he just woke up one day to discover he was the star detective in the former capital of the Confederacy. The cost of living, a good place to raise a family. What Doris wanted. That was probably the explanation.

What a crock of shit. Their only child, Rocco, left home, got involved in organized crime, and was dead, and Doris ran off with a car salesman and might as well be dead, and during Marino's time in Richmond, it had one of the highest homicide rates per capita in the United States. The drug dealers' rest stop along the I-95 corridor between New York and Miami, where dirtbags did business en route because Richmond had the customer base, seven federal housing projects. Plantations and slavery. What goes around comes around. Richmond was a good place to deal drugs and kill people, because the cops were stupid, that was the word on the street and along the Corridor, up and down the East Coast. Used to offend the hell out of Marino. Not anymore. It was so long ago, and what good did it do to take things personally when they weren't personal. Most things were random.

The older he got, the less he could connect one event in his life to another in a way that showed evidence of something intelligent and caring behind his choices and messes and the messes of those crossing his borders, especially women. How many had he loved and lost or simply fucked? He remembered the first time, clear as day. Bear Mountain State Park on the dock overlooking the Hudson when he was sixteen. But overall, he had no clue, all those times he was drunk, how could he remember? Computers didn't get drunk or forget, had no regrets, didn't care. They connected everything, created logical trees on the data wall. Marino was afraid of his own data wall. He was afraid it didn't make sense, was afraid that almost every decision he'd ever made was a bad one with no rhyme or reason to it, no Master Plan. He didn't want to see how many offshoots went nowhere or were linked to Scarpetta. In a way, she had become the icon in the center of his connections and disconnections. In a way, she made the most sense and the least.

"I keep thinking you can match up images and photographs," Marino said to Petrowski while looking at the jumper on the flat screen. "Like if this FedEx guy's mug shot is in some database and you got his facial features and the tattoo to connect with what we got here from the security camera."

"I see what you're saying. Except I think we've established he's not really FedEx."

"So, you get the computer to do its data-mining thing and match the images."

"We search by keyword or category. Not by image. Maybe someday," Petrowski said.

"Then how come you can Google images like photographs you want and download them?" Marino asked.

He couldn't take his eyes off the jumper. It was true. He must have changed his mind. What had changed it? Fear of heights? Or was it all the fucking attention. *Jesus.* Choppers, cops, and live TV. Maybe he decided to hang around, be on the cover of *People* magazine.

"Because you're searching by keywords, not by the actual image," Petrowski patiently explained. "An image-search application requires a keyword or several keywords, such as, well, see our logo on the wall over there? You search on the keywords *RTCC logo* or *moniker* and the software finds an image or images that includes those same keywords—actually finds the hosting location."

"The wall?" Marino was confused as he looked at the wall with the logo, an eagle and American flags.

"No, the hosting location isn't the wall. It's a database— in our case, a data warehouse because of the massive size and complexity since we started centralizing. Every warrant; offense and incident report; weapon; map; arrest; complaint; C-summons; stop, question, and frisk; juvenile crime; you name it. Same type of link analysis we're doing in counterterrorism," Petrowski said.

"Right. And if you could connect images," Marino said, "you could identify terrorists, different names but the same person, so why aren't we? Okay. They've almost got him. Jesus. Like we should rappel off the bridge for some squirrel like that."

ESU cops in harnesses were suspended by ropes, closing in on three sides.

"We can't. Maybe someday," Petrowski answered, oblivious to the jumper and whether he made it or not. "What we link is public records, like addresses, locations, objects, other large collections of data, but not actual photographs of faces. What you're really getting a hit on is the keywords, not the images of tattoos. Am I making sense? Because I don't feel you're clear on what I've been saying. Maybe if your attention was here in the room with me instead of on the GW Bridge."

"I wish I could see his face better," Marino said to the flat screen with the jumper on it. "Something about him. Like I know him from somewhere."

"From everywhere. A dime a dozen these days. It's selfish as hell. If you want to do yourself in, don't take out other people with you, don't put them at risk, don't cost the taxpayers. They'll slap him in Bellevue tonight. Tomorrow we'll find out he was involved in a Ponzi scam. We've just had a hundred million cut out of our budget, and here we are snatching his ass off a bridge. A week from now, he'll kill himself some other way."

"Naw. He'll be on *Letterman*," Marino said.

"Don't push my button."

"Go back to that Mount Rushmore wino tattoo you had up a minute ago," Marino said, reaching for his coffee as the ESU cops risked their lives to rescue someone who wasn't worth it, was a dime a dozen and probably should have splashed down by now, been picked up by the Coast Guard and escorted to the morgue.

Petrowski clicked on a record he had opened earlier and, using the mouse, dragged an image into a big empty square on a laptop screen. A mug shot appeared on the data wall, a black man with a tattoo covering the right side of his neck: four skulls in an outcropping of rocks, what looked like Mount Rushmore to Marino, and the Latin phrase *In vino veritas.*

"Bottle of wine, fruit of the vine," Marino said, and two ESU cops almost had the jumper. Marino couldn't see his face, couldn't see what he was feeling or if he was talking.

"In wine is truth," Petrowski said. "Think it goes back to ancient Roman times. What the hell's his name. Pliny Something. Maybe Tacitus."

"Mateus and Lancers rosé. Remember those days?"

Petrowski smiled but didn't answer. He was too young, probably had never heard of Mad Dog or Boone's Farm, either.

"Drink a bottle of Lancers in the car, and if you got lucky, you give your date the bottle for a souvenir," Marino went on. "The girls would put candles in them, let all the wax run down, lots of different color candles. What I called a candle fuck. Well, guess you had to be there."

Petrowski and his smile. Marino was never sure what it meant except he figured the guy was wrapped pretty tight. Most computer jockeys were, except Lucy. She wasn't even wrapped, not these days. He glanced at his watch, wondered how she and Berger were making out with Hap Judd as Petrowski arranged images side by side on the data wall. The tattoo on the neck of the man in the FedEx cap was juxtaposed with the tattoo of four skulls and the phrase *In vino veritas.*

"Nope." Marino took another swallow of coffee, black and cold. "Not even close when you really look."

"I tried to tell you."

"I was thinking of patterns, like maybe where he got the tattoo. If we found something that was the same design, I could track down the tattoo artist, show him a picture of this FedEx guy," Marino said.

"It's not in the database," Petrowski said. "Not with those keywords. Not with *coffin,* either, or *fallen comrade* or *Iraq* or anything we've tried. We need a name, an incident, a location, a map, something."

"What about the FBI, their database?" Marino suggested. "That new billion-dollar computer system they got, forget what it's called."

"NGI. Next Generation Identification. Still in development."

"But up and running, I hear." The person Marino had heard it from was Lucy.

"We're talking extremely advanced technology that's spread over a multiyear time frame. I know the early phases have been implemented, which includes IAFIS, CODIS, I think the Interstate Photo System, IPS. Not really sure what else, you know, with the economy being what it is. A lot of stuff's been cut back."

"Well, I hear they got a tattoo database," Marino said.

"Oh, sure."

"So I say we cast a bigger net in our hunt and do a national, maybe even international, search on this FedEx shitbag," Marino suggested. "That's assuming you can't search the FBI database, their NGI, from here."

"No way. We don't share. But I'll shoot them your tattoo. No problem. Well, he's not on the bridge anymore." Petrowski meant the jumper. Was finally curious but only in a bored way.

"That can't be good." Marino looked at the flat screen, realizing he'd missed the big moment. "Shit. I see the ESU guys but not him."

"There he is."

Helicopter searchlights moving over the jumper on the ground, a distant image of his body on the pavement. He'd missed the air bag.

"The ESU guys are going to be pissed" was Petrowski's summary of the situation. "They hate it when that happens."

"What about you send the FBI this photo with the tattoo"—looking at the alleged FedEx guy on the data wall—"while we try a couple other searches. *FedEx.* Maybe *FedEx uniform, FedEx cap.* Anything *FedEx,*" Marino said.

"We can do that." Petrowski started typing.

The hourglass returned to the data wall, twirling. Marino noticed the wall-mounted flat screen had gone black, the police helicopter video feed terminated because the jumper was terminated. He suddenly had an idea why the jumper looked familiar, an actor he'd seen, what was the movie? The police chief who got in trouble with a hooker? What the hell was the movie? Marino couldn't think of the name. Seemed to happen a lot these days.

"You ever seen that movie with Danny DeVito and Bette Midler? What the hell was it called?" Marino said.

"I got no idea." Petrowski watched the hourglass and the reassuring message, *Your report is running.* "What's a movie got to do with anything?"

"Everything's got to do with something. I thought that was the point of this joint." Marino indicated the big blue room.

Eleven records found.

"Now we're cooking," Marino said. "Can't believe I ever used to hate computers. Or the dipshits who work with them."

In the old days, he did hate them and enjoyed ridiculing the people who worked with them. No longer. He was becoming quite accustomed to uncovering critical information through what was called "link analysis," and transmitting it electronically almost instantly. He'd grown quite fond of rolling up on a scene to investigate an incident or interview a complainant and already knowing what a person of interest had done in the past and to whom and what he looked like, who he associated with or was related to, and if he was dangerous to himself or to others. It was a brave new world, Marino liked to say, referencing a book he'd never read but maybe would one of these days.

Petrowski was displaying records on the data wall. Reports on assaults, robberies, a rape, and two shootings in which FedEx was either a reference to packages stolen, words uttered, occupations, or in one case, a fatal pit bull attack. None of the data associated with any of the reports were useful until Marino was looking at a Transit Adjudication Bureau summons, a TAB summons from this past August first, big as life on the data wall. Marino read the last name, the first name, the Edgewater, New Jersey, address, the sex, race, height, and weight.

"Well, what do you know. Look who popped up. I was going to have you run her next," he said as he read the details of the violation:

Subject was observed boarding a NY Transit bus at Southern Boulevard and East 149th Street at 1130 hours and became argumentative with another passenger the subject claimed had taken her seat. Subject began to yell at the passenger. When this officer approached the subject and told her to stop yelling and sit down, she stated, "You can just FedEx your ass to hell because it's not me who did anything. That man over there is a rude son of a bitch."

"Doubt she's got a skull tattoo," Petrowski said ironically. "Don't think she's your man with the package."

"Fucking unbelievable," Marino said. "You print that out for me?"

"You should count how many times per hour you say 'fuck.' In my house, would cost you a lot of quarters."

"Dodie Hodge," Marino said. "The fucking loony tune who called CNN."

13

Lucy's forensic computer investigative agency, Connexions, was located in the same building where she lived, the nineteenth-century former warehouse of a soap-and-candle company on Barrow Street in Greenwich Village, technically the Far West Village. Two- story brick, boldly Romanesque, with rounded arched windows, it was registered as a historic landmark, as was the former carriage house next door that Lucy had purchased last spring to use as a garage.

She was a dream for any preservation commission, since she had not the slightest interest in altering the integrity of a building beyond the meticulous retrofits necessary for her unusual cyber and surveillance needs. More relevant to any nonprofit was her philanthropy, which wasn't without personal benefit, not that Jaime Berger had the slightest faith in altruistic motives being pure, not hardly. She had no idea how much Lucy had donated to de facto conflicts of interest, and she should have an idea, and that bothered her. Lucy should keep nothing from her, but she did, and over recent weeks, Berger had begun to feel an uneasiness about their relationship that was different from misgivings she'd experienced so far.

"Maybe you should get it tattooed on your hand." Lucy held up her hand, palm first. "To cue yourself. Actors like cues. *It all depends.*" She pretended to read something written on the palm of her hand. "Get a tattoo that says *It all depends* and look at it every time you're about to lie."

"I don't need cues, and I'm not lying," Hap Judd replied, maintaining his poise. "People say all kinds of things, and it doesn't necessarily mean they did anything wrong."

"I see," Berger said to Judd as she wished Marino would hurry up. Where the hell was he? "Then what you meant in the bar this past Monday night, the night of December fifteenth, all depends on how one—in this case, me—interprets what you said to Eric Mender. If you stated to him that you can understand being curious about a nineteen-year-old girl in a coma and wanting to see her naked and perhaps touch her in a sexual manner, it's all in the interpretation. I'm trying to figure out how I might interpret a remark like that beyond finding it more than a little troubling."

"Good God, that's what I'm trying to tell you. The interpretation. It's not . . . It's not the way you're thinking. Her picture was all over the news. And it was where I was working then, the hospital she was in happened to be where I had a job," Judd said with less poise. "Yeah, I was curious. People are curious if they're honest. I'm curious for a living, curious about all kinds of things. Doesn't mean I did anything."

Hap Judd didn't look like a movie star. He didn't look

like the type to have roles in big-budget franchises like *Tomb Raider* and *Batman.* Berger couldn't stop thinking that as she sat across from him at the brushed-steel conference table in Lucy's barnlike space of exposed timber beams and tobacco-wood floors, and computer flat screens asleep on paperless desks. Hap Judd was of average height, sinewy verging on too thin, with unremarkable brown hair and eyes, his face Captain America-perfect but bland, the sort of appearance that translated well on film but in the flesh wasn't compelling. Were he the boy next door, Berger would describe him as clean-cut, nice-looking. Were she to rename him, it would be Hapless or Haphazard, because there was something tragically obtuse and reckless about him, and Lucy didn't get that part, or maybe she did, which is why she was torturing him. For the past half-hour, she'd been all over him in a way that caused Berger a great deal of concern. Where the hell was Marino? He should have been here by now. He was supposed to be helping with the interrogation, not Lucy. She was out of bounds, was acting as if she had something personal with Judd, some a priori connection. And maybe she did. Lucy had known Rupe Starr.

"Just because I supposedly said certain things to a stranger in a bar doesn't mean I did anything." Judd had made this point about ten times now. "You have to ask yourself why I said what I supposedly did."

"I'm not asking myself anything. I'm asking you," Lucy said, her laser gaze holding his eyes.

"I'm telling you what I know."

"You're telling us what you want us to hear," Lucy shot back before Berger got a chance to intervene.

"I don't remember everything. I was drinking. I'm a

busy person, have a lot going on. It's inevitable I'm going to forget things," Judd said. "You're not a lawyer. Why's she talking to me like she's a lawyer," he said to Berger. "You're not a real cop, just some assistant or something," he said to Lucy. "Who the hell are you to be asking me all these questions and accusing me?"

"You remember enough to say you didn't do anything." Lucy felt no need to justify herself, sure of herself at her conference table in her loft, a computer open in front of her, a map displayed on it, a grid of some area Berger couldn't make out. "You remember enough to change your story," Lucy added.

"I'm not changing anything. I don't remember that night, whenever it was," Judd answered Lucy as he looked at Berger, as if she might save him. "What the hell do you want from me?"

Lucy needed to back down. Berger had sent her plenty of signals, but she was ignoring them and shouldn't be talking to Hap at all, not unless Berger directly asked her to explain details related to the forensic computer investigation, which they hadn't even gotten to yet. Where was Marino? Lucy was acting like she was Marino, was taking his place, and Berger was beginning to entertain suspicions that hadn't occurred to her before, probably because she knew enough already, and to doubt Lucy further was almost unbearable. Lucy wasn't honest. She knew Rupe Starr and hadn't mentioned it to Berger. Lucy had her own motive and she wasn't a prosecutor, she wasn't law enforcement anymore, and in her own mind had nothing to lose.

Berger had everything to lose, didn't need some celebrity putting dents in her reputation. She had more than her

share of dents, unfairly inflicted. Her relationship with
Lucy hadn't helped. Jesus, it had been anything but helpful. Unkind gossip and vile comments on the Internet. A
dick-hating dyke, the dyke Jew DA Berger had made it to
the top ten on a neo-Nazi hit list, her address and other
personal information posted in hopes someone would *do the
right thing.* Then there were the evangelical Christians
reminding her to pack her bags for her one-way trip to hell.
Berger had never imagined being honest would be so hard
and so punishing. Appearing with Lucy in public, not
hiding or lying, and it had hurt Berger, hurt her far more
than she could have imagined. And for what? To be
deceived. How deep did it go, where would it end? It
would end, don't worry. *It will end,* she kept telling herself.
There would be a conversation at some point and Lucy
would explain herself, and all would be fine. Lucy would
tell her about Rupe.

"What we want is for you to tell the truth." Berger got
a chance to speak before Lucy could jump in. "This is very,
very serious. We're not playing games."

"I don't know why I'm here. I haven't done anything,"
Hap Judd said to her, and she didn't like his eyes.

He was bold the way he stared at her, looking her up and
down, aware of the effect it had on Lucy. He knew what he
was doing, was defiant, and at times Berger sensed he was
amused by them.

"I have a very strong feeling about sending someone to
prison," Berger said.

"I haven't done anything!"

Maybe, maybe not, but he'd also not been helpful. Berger
had given him almost three weeks to be helpful. Three
weeks was a long time when someone was missing, possibly

abducted, possibly dead, or, more likely, busy creating a new identity in South America, the Fiji islands, Australia, God knows where.

"That's not the worst of it," Lucy said to him, her green stare unwavering, her short hair shining rose-gold in the overhead lights. She was ready to pounce again like an exotic cat. "I can't imagine what the inmates would do to a sick fuck like you." She began typing, was in her e-mail now.

"You know what? I almost didn't come at all. I came so close to not coming you wouldn't even believe it," he said to Berger, and the mention of prison had an effect. He wasn't so smug. He wasn't looking at her chest. "This is the shit I get," he said, with no poise left. "I'm not going to sit here and listen to your fucking shit."

He made no move to get up from his chair, a faded denim leg bouncing, sweat stains in the armpits of a baggy white shirt. Berger could see his chest move as he breathed, an unusual silver cross on a leather necklace moving beneath white cotton with each shallow breath. His hands were clenched on the armrests, a chunky silver skull ring shining, his muscles flexed tensely, veins standing out in his neck. He did have to sit here, could no more extricate himself right now than he could avert his gaze from a train wreck about to happen.

"Remember Jeffrey Dahmer?" Lucy said, not looking up as she typed. "Remember what happened to that sick fuck? What the inmates did? Beat him to death with a broom handle, maybe did other things to him with the broom handle. He was into the same sick shit you are."

"Jeffrey Dahmer? You serious?" Judd laughed too loudly. It wasn't really a laugh. He was scared. "She's

fucking crazy," he said to Berger. "I've never hurt anybody in my life. I don't hurt people."

"You mean not yet," Lucy said, a city grid on her screen,
as if she was MapQuesting.

"I'm not talking to her," he said to Berger. "I don't like
her. Fucking make her leave or I'm going to."

"How 'bout I give you a list of people you've hurt?"
Lucy said. "Starting with the family and friends of Farrah
Lacy."

"I don't know who that is, and you can go fuck yourself,"
he snapped.

"You know what a class-E felony is?" Berger asked him.

"I haven't done anything. I haven't hurt anyone."

"Up to ten years in prison. That's what it is."

"In isolation for your own protection," Lucy continued,
ignoring Berger's signals to back off, another screenshot of
a map in front of her.

Berger could make out green shapes that represented
parks, blue shapes that were water, in an area congested
with streets. An alert tone sounded on Berger's BlackBerry.
Someone had just sent her an e-mail at almost three o'clock
in the morning.

"Solitary confinement. Probably Fallsburg," Lucy said.
"They're used to high-profile prisoners. The Son of Sam.
Attica's not so good. He had his throat cut there."

The e-mail was from Marino:

Mental patient possb connected to docs
incident dodie hodge I found something
at rtcc dont forget to ask your witness
if he knows her I'm tied up will explain
later

Berger looked up from her BlackBerry as Lucy continued to terrorize Hap Judd with what happened in prison to people like him.

"Tell me about Dodie Hodge," said Berger. "Your relationship with her."

Judd looked baffled, then angry. He blurted out, "She's a gypsy, a fucking witch. I'm the one who should be here as a victim the way that crazy bitch bothers me. Why the hell are you asking me? What's she got to do with anything? Maybe she's the one accusing me of something. Is she the one behind all this?"

"Maybe I'll answer your questions when you answer mine," Berger said. "Tell me the history of how you know her."

"A psychic, a spiritual adviser. Whatever you want to call her. A lot of people—Hollywood people, really successful people, even politicians—know her, go to her for advice about money, their careers, their relationships. So I was stupid. I talked to her, and she wouldn't stop bothering me. Calls my office in L.A. all the time."

"Then she's stalking you."

"That's what I call it. Yeah, exactly."

"And this started when?" Berger asked.

"I don't know. Last year. Maybe a year ago this past fall. I got referred."

"By whom?"

"Someone in the business who thought I might get something out of it. Career guidance."

"I'm asking for a name," Berger said.

"I got to respect confidentiality. A lot of people go to her. You'd be amazed."

"Go to her, or does she come to you?" Berger said. "Where do the meetings take place?"

"She came to my apartment in TriBeCa. High-profile people aren't going to come to wherever she lives and risk being followed and maybe caught on camera. Or she does readings on the phone."

"And how does she get paid?"

"Cash. Or if it's a phoner, you mail a cashier's check to a P.O. box in New Jersey. Maybe a few times I talked to her on the phone, and then cut her off because she's so damn crazy. Yeah, I'm being stalked. We should talk about me being stalked."

"Does she show up places where you are? Such as your apartment in TriBeCa, where you're filming, places you frequent, such as the bar on Christopher Street here in New York?" Berger asked.

"She leaves messages all the time at my agent's office."

"She calls L.A.? Fine. I'll give you a good contact at the FBI field office in L.A.," Berger said. "The FBI handles stalking. One of their specialties."

Judd didn't reply. He had no interest in talking to the FBI in L.A. He was a cagey bastard, and Berger wondered if the person whose confidentiality he was protecting might be Hannah Starr. Based on what he'd just said, he first met Dodie around the same time his financial transactions with Hannah began. A year ago this past fall.

"The bar on Christopher Street," Berger redirected, not satisfied that Dodie Hodge was related to anything that mattered and annoyed that Marino had interrupted her interrogation of someone she'd begun to strongly dislike.

"You can't prove anything." The defiance was back.

"If you really believe we can't prove anything, why did you bother to show up?"

"Especially since you almost didn't," Lucy interrupted,

busy on her MacBook. Typing e-mails and looking at maps.

"To cooperate," Judd said to Berger. "I'm here to cooperate."

"I see. You couldn't fit cooperation into your busy schedule three weeks ago when you first came to my attention and I tried repeatedly to get hold of you."

"I was in L.A."

"I forgot. They don't have phones in L.A."

"I was tied up, and the messages I got weren't clear. I didn't understand."

"Good, so now you understand and have decided to cooperate," Berger said. "So, let's talk about your little incident this past Monday—specifically, what happened after you left the Stonewall Inn at fifty-three Christopher Street late Monday night. You left with that kid you met, Eric. Remember Eric? The kid you smoked weed with? The kid you talked so openly with?"

"We were high," Judd said.

"Yes, people say things when they're high. You got high and told him wild-ass tales, his words, about what happened at Park General Hospital in Harlem," Berger said.

They were naked beneath a down-filled duvet, unable to sleep, tucked into each other and looking out at the view. The Manhattan skyline wasn't the ocean or the Rockies or the ruins of Rome, but it was a sight they loved, and it was their habit to open the shades at night after turning off the lights.

Benton stroked Scarpetta's bare skin, his chin on top of her head. He kissed her neck, her ears, and her flesh was cool where his lips had been. His chest was pressed against her back, and she could feel the slow beat of his heart.

"I never ask you about your patients," she said.

"Clearly I'm not much of a distraction if you're thinking about my patients," Benton said in her ear.

She pulled his arms around her and kissed his hands. "Maybe you can distract me again in a few minutes. I'd like to raise a hypothetical question."

"You're entitled. I'm surprised you have only one."

"How would someone like your former patient know where we live? I'm not suggesting she left the package." Scarpetta didn't want to say Dodie Hodge's name in bed.

"One might speculate that if someone is sufficiently manipulative, that person might successfully extract information from others," Benton said. "For example, there are staff members at McLean who know where our apartment is, since mail and packages are occasionally sent to me here."

"And staff members would tell a patient?"

"I would hope not, and I'm not saying that's what happened. I'm not even saying this person's ever been to McLean, been a patient there."

He didn't need to say it. Scarpetta had no doubt that Dodie Hodge had been a patient at McLean.

"I'm also not saying she had anything to do with what was left at our building," he added.

He didn't need to say that, either. She knew Benton feared his former patient had left the package.

"What I will say is others might suspect she did, no matter what we discover to the contrary." Benton spoke softly, the intimacy of his tone incongruous with the conversation.

"Marino suspects it and in fact is probably convinced of it, and you're not convinced. That's what you're saying." Scarpetta didn't believe it.

She believed Benton was convinced about this former patient named Dodie who had brazenly called CNN. Benton was convinced she was dangerous.

"Marino might be right. And he might not be," Benton said. "While someone like this particular former patient might be bad news and potentially harmful, it would be even more harmful if the package was sent by someone else and everyone has quit looking because they think they know the answer. And what if they don't? Then what happens? What next? Maybe someone really gets hurt next time."

"We don't know what the package is. It could be nothing. You're getting ahead of yourself."

"It's something. I can already promise you that," he said. "Unless you starred in a Batman movie and didn't tell me, you're not the chief medical examiner of Gotham City. I don't like the tone of that. Not exactly sure why it bothers me as much as it does."

"Because it's snide. It's hostile."

"Maybe. The handwriting interests me. Your description that it was so precise and stylized it looked like a font."

"Whoever wrote the address has a steady hand, maybe an artistic hand," Scarpetta said, and she sensed he was thinking about something else.

He knew something about Dodie Hodge that was causing him to focus on the handwriting.

"You're sure it wasn't generated by a laser printer," Benton said.

"I had quite a long time to look at it on the elevator.

Black ink, ballpoint. There was sufficient variation in the letter formation to make it obvious the address was hand-printed," she said.

"Hopefully there will still be something to look at when we get to Rodman's Neck. The airbill might be our best evidence."

"If we're lucky," she said.

Luck would be a big part of it. Most likely the bomb squad would foil any possible circuitry inside the FedEx box by blasting it with a PAN disrupter, more popularly known as a water cannon, which fires three to four ounces of water, propelled by a modified twelve-gauge shotgun round. The primary target would be the alleged explosive device's power source—the small batteries that showed up on x-ray. Scarpetta could only hope that the batteries weren't directly behind the hand-printed address on the airbill. If they were, there would be nothing left but soggy pulp to look at later this morning.

"We can have a general conversation," Benton then said, sitting up a little, rearranging pillows. "You're familiar with the borderline personality. An individual who has breaks or splits in ego boundaries and, given enough stress, can act out aggressively, violently. Aggression is about competing. Competing for the male, for the female, competing for the person most fit for breeding.Competing for resources, such as food and shelter. Competing for power, because without a hierarchy there can't be social order. In other words, aggression occurs when it's profitable."

Scarpetta thought of Carley Crispin. She thought about the missing BlackBerry. She'd been thinking about her BlackBerry for hours. Anxiety was a tightness around her heart, no matter what she was doing; even while making love she felt fear. She felt anger. She was extremely upset with herself and didn't know how Lucy would handle the truth. Scarpetta had been stupid. How could she be so stupid?

"Unfortunately, these basic primitive drives that might make sense in terms of the survival of a species can become malignant and nonadaptive, can get acted out in grossly inappropriate and unprofitable ways," Benton was saying. "Because when all is said and done, an aggressive act, such as harassing or threatening a prominent person like you, is unprofitable for the initiator. The result will be punishment, a forfeiture of all those things worth competing for. Whether it's commitment to a psychiatric facility or imprisonment."

"So, I'm to conclude that this woman who called me on CNN tonight has a borderline personality disorder, can become violent, given sufficient stress, and is competing with me for the male, which would be you," Scarpetta said.

"She called you to harass me, and it worked," he said. "She wants my attention. The borderline personality thrives on negative reinforcement, on being the eye of the storm. You add some other unfortunate personality disorders to the mix, and you go from the eye of the storm to maybe the perfect storm."

"Transference. All those women patients of yours don't stand a chance. They want what I've got right now."

She wanted it again. She wanted his attention and didn't want to talk anymore about work, about problems, about human beings who were horrors. She wanted to be close to him, to feel that nothing was off-limits, and her yearning for closeness was insatiable because she couldn't have what she wanted. She'd never had what she wanted with Benton, and that was why she still wanted him, wanted him palpably. It was why she'd wanted him to begin with, felt drawn to him, felt an intense desire for him the first time they'd met. She felt the same way now, twenty years later, a desperate attraction that fulfilled her and left her empty, and sex with him was like that, a cycle of taking and giving and filling and emptying and then rearming the mechanism so they could go back for more.

"I do love you, you know," she said into his mouth. "Even when I'm angry."

"You'll always be angry. I hope you'll always love me."

"I want to understand." She didn't and probably couldn't.

When she was reminded, she couldn't understand the choices he'd made, that he could have left her so abruptly, so finally, and never checked on her. She wouldn't have done what he did, but she wasn't going to bring that up again.

"I know I'll always love you." She kissed him and got on top of him.

They rearranged themselves, knew intuitively how to move, the days long past when they needed to consciously calculate which was whose best side or the limits before fatigue and discomfort set in. Scarpetta had heard every permutation of the expected jokes about her skills in anatomy and what a bonus that must be in bed, which was ridiculous, not even that, because she didn't find it amusing. Her patients were with rare exception dead, and their response to her touch therefore moot and not helpful. That didn't mean the morgue hadn't taught her something vital, because certainly it had. It had conditioned her to

refine her senses, to see, smell, and feel the most subtle
nuances in people who could no longer speak, unwilling
people who needed her but could give nothing back. The
morgue had empowered her with strong, capable hands
and strong cravings. She wanted warmth and touch. She
wanted sex.

Afterward, Benton fell asleep, a deep sleep. He didn't stir
when she got out of bed, her mind moving rapidly again,
anxieties and resentments swarming back again. It was a
few minutes past three a.m. She faced a long day that
would inform her as it unfolded, one of those days that was
what she called "unscripted." The range at Rodman's Neck
and her possible bomb, and perhaps the labs, and maybe
the office to dictate autopsy reports and catch up on phone
calls and paperwork. She wasn't scheduled to do autopsies,
but that could always change depending on who was out
and what came in. What to do about her BlackBerry.
Maybe Lucy had answered her. What to do about her niece.
She'd been acting so odd of late, so easily irritated, so impatient, and then what she'd done about the smartphones,
swapping them out and not asking permission, as if that
was generous and considerate. *You should go back to bed and
get some rest. Fatigue and everything seems worse,* Scarpetta told
herself. Going back to sleep wasn't a possibility right now.
She had things to take care of, needed to deal with Lucy,
get it over with. *Tell her what you did. Tell her how stupid her
Aunt Kay is.*

Lucy probably was the most technically gifted person
Scarpetta had ever known, curious about the way everything worked from the day she was born, putting this and
that together and taking them apart, always confident she
could improve the functioning of whatever it was. Such a

proclivity plus a massive insecurity plus an overriding need for power and control and the result was a Lucy, a wizard who could easily destroy just as much as she fixed, depending on her motive and mostly on her mood. Swapping out phones without permission had not been an appropriate act, and Scarpetta still didn't understand why her niece suddenly had done it. In the past she would have asked. She wouldn't have become the self-appointed system administrator for everyone without permission, without so much as a warning, and she was going to be incensed when she learned the truth about Scarpetta's folly, her foolishness. Lucy would say it was like not looking before you cross the street, like walking into the tail rotor.

Scarpetta dreaded the lecture she was certain to get when she confessed to disabling the password on her BlackBerry two days after receiving it, her frustration had been that great. *You shouldn't have, you absolutely shouldn't have*—the thought was caught in a loop in her mind. But every time she'd pulled the device out of its holster she'd had to unlock it. If she didn't use it for ten minutes, it was locked again. Then the last straw, scaring the hell out of herself when her typos had resulted in her entering the password incorrectly six times in a row. Eight failed attempts—it was clearly written in Lucy's instructions—and the BlackBerry rather much self-destructed, everything in it eradicated like those tape recordings in *Mission: Impossible*.

When Scarpetta had e-mailed Lucy that the BlackBerry had been "misplaced," she'd neglected to mention the detail about the password. If someone had her smartphone, it would be a very bad thing, and Scarpetta was deeply afraid of that, and she was afraid of Lucy, and most of all she was afraid of herself. *When did you start becoming so careless?*

You carried a bomb into your apartment and you disabled the password on your smartphone. What the hell's the matter with you? Do something. Fix something. Take care of things. Don't just fret.

She needed to eat, that was part of the problem, her stomach sour from having nothing in it. If she ate something, she'd feel better. She needed to do something with her hands, engage them in an act that was healing, an act besides sex. Preparing food was restorative and soothing. Making one of her favorite dishes, paying attention to details, helped return order and normalcy. It was either cook or clean, and she'd done enough cleaning, could still catch the scent of Murphy Oil Soap as she walked through the living room and into the kitchen. She opened the refrigerator, scanning for inspiration. A frittata, an omelet, she wasn't hungry for eggs or bread or pasta. Something light and healthy, and with olive oil and fresh herbs, like an Insalata Caprese. That would be good. It was a summer dish, to be served only when tomatoes were in season, preferably handpicked from Scarpetta's own garden. But in cities like Boston and New York, wherever there was a Whole Foods or gourmet markets, she could find heirloom tomatoes all year round, rich Black Krims, lush Brandywines, succulent Caspian Pinks, mellow Golden Eggs, sweetly acidic Green Zebras.

She selected a few from a basket on the counter and placed them on a cutting board, quartering them into wedges. She warmed fresh buffalo mozzarella to room temperature by enclosing it in a zip-lock bag and submerging it in hot water for several minutes. Arranging the tomato and the cheese in a circular pattern on a plate, she added leaves of fresh basil and a generous dribble of cold-pressed unfiltered olive oil, finishing with a sprinkle of coarse sea salt. She carried her snack to the adjoining dining room, with its view due west of lighted apartment high-rises and the Hudson, and the distant air traffic in New Jersey.

She took a bite of salad as she opened the browser on her MacBook. Time to deal with Lucy. She'd probably answered her by now. May as well face the music and deal with the missing BlackBerry. It wasn't a trivial worry, nothing trifling about it, and had been on Scarpetta's mind since she'd first noticed it gone, and now it was an obsession. For hours she'd been trying to recall what was on it, trying to imagine what someone might have access to, while a part of her wished she could return to a past when her biggest concern was snooping, someone flipping through a Rolodex or riffling through the call sheets, autopsy protocols, and photographs that routinely were on her desk. In the old days, her answer to most potential indiscretions and leaks was locks. Highly sensitive records went into locked file cabinets, and if there was something on her desk that she didn't want others to see, she locked her office door while she was out. Plain and simple. Just good common sense. All manageable. Just hide the key.

When she was the chief medical examiner of Virginia and her office got its first computer, that, too, was manageable and she'd felt no great fear of the unknown, felt she could handle the bad with the good. Of course, there were glitches in security, but all was fixable and preventable. Cell phones hadn't been a significant problem back then, not at first, when her distrust of them had more to do with the potential use of scanners for eavesdropping and, more mundanely, people developing the uncivilized and reckless habit of having conversations that could be overheard.

Those dangers didn't begin to compare to ones that existed today. There was no adequate description for what she found herself fretting about regularly. Modern technology no longer seemed like her best friend. It bit her often. This time it may have bitten her badly.

Scarpetta's BlackBerry was a microcosm of her personal and professional life, containing phone numbers and e-mail addresses of contacts who would be incensed or compromised if an ill-intended individual got hold of their private information. She was most protective of the families, of those left behind in the wake of a tragic death. In a way, these survivors became her patients, too, depending on her for information, calling her about a detail they suddenly remembered, a question, a theory, simply needing to talk, often at anniversaries or at this time of year, the holidays. The confidences Scarpetta shared with the families and loved ones of decedents were sacred, the most sacred aspect of her work.

How unspeakably awful if the wrong person, a person who worked for a cable news network, for example, came across some of these names, many of them associated with highly publicized cases, a name like Grace Darien. She was the last person Scarpetta had talked to, at about seven-fifteen p.m., after getting off the conference call with Berger, hurrying to get ready for CNN. Mrs. Darien had called Scarpetta's BlackBerry, near hysteria because the press release that identified Toni Darien by name also had stated she'd been sexually assaulted and beaten to death. Mrs. Darien had been confused and panicked, had assumed a blow to the head was different from being beaten to death, and nothing Scarpetta could tell her had been reassuring. Scarpetta hadn't been dishonest. She hadn't been misleading. It wasn't her press release, wasn't her wording, and as difficult as it was, Mrs. Darien needed to understand why Scarpetta couldn't go into any more detail than she already had. She was so sorry, but she simply couldn't discuss the case further.

"Remember what I said?" Scarpetta had been changing her clothes while she talked to her. "Confidentiality is critical, because some details are known only by the killer, the medical examiner, and the police. That's why I can't tell you more at this time."

Here she was, the torchbearer for discretion and ethical conduct, and for all she knew, someone had found Grace Darien's information in a BlackBerry that wasn't password-protected and had contacted the distraught woman. Scarpetta couldn't stop thinking about what Carley had blasted all over the news, the detail about the yellow cab and its allegedly connecting Toni Darien to Hannah Starr, and the false information about Hannah's decomposing head hair being found. Of course a journalist, especially a cold-blooded, desperate one, would want to talk to the Grace Dariens of the world, and the list of possible egregious violations caused by Scarpetta's missing smartphone was getting longer as she remembered more. She continued conjuring up names of contacts she'd been keeping since the beginning of her career, first on paper, then eventually in electronic format, exported from cell phone to cell phone as she upgraded, finally ending up in the device Lucy had bought.

Hundreds of names were in Scarpetta's contacts subfolder, she guessed, many of them people who might never trust her again if someone like Carley Crispin called them on their cell phones, on their direct lines, or at home.

Mayor Bloomberg, Commissioner Kelly, Dr. Edison, count-
less powerful officials here and abroad, in addition to
Scarpetta's extensive network of forensic colleagues and
physicians and prosecutors and defense attorneys, and her
family, friends, doctors, dentist, hairstylist, personal trainer,
housekeeper. Places she shopped. What she ordered on
Amazon, including books she read. Restaurants. Her
accountant. Her private banker. The list got longer the
more she thought about it, longer and more troubling.
Saved voicemails that were visualized on the screen and
could be played without entering a password. Documents
and PowerPoint presentations that included graphic images
she'd downloaded from e-mails—including Toni Darien's
scene photographs. The one Carley had shown on the air
could have come from Scarpetta's phone, and then her anxieties turned to IM, instant messaging, all those
applications that allowed and prompted constant contact.

Scarpetta didn't believe in IM, considered such technologies a compulsion, not an improvement, possibly one of
the most unfortunate and foolhardy innovations in history,
people typing on tiny touch screens and keypads while they
should be paying attention to rather important activities
such as driving, crossing a busy street, operating dangerous
machinery, such as aircraft or trains, or sitting in a class-
room, a lecture hall, attending Grand Rounds or the theater
or a concert, or paying attention to whoever was across from
them in a restaurant or next to them in bed. Not long ago,
she caught a medical student on rotation in the New York
office instant messaging during an autopsy, pushing tiny
keys with latex-sheathed thumbs. She'd kicked him out of
the morgue, expelled him from her tutelage, and encouraged Dr. Edison to ban all electronic devices from any area

beyond the anteroom, but that was never going to happen. It was too late for that, would be turning back the hands on the clock, and no one would comply.

The cops, the medicolegal investigators, the scientists, the pathologists, the anthropologists, the odontologists, the forensic archaeologists, the mortuary, the ID techs and security guards, weren't going to give up their PDAs, iPhones, BlackBerrys, cell phones, and pagers, and despite her continual warnings to her colleagues about disseminating confidential information via instant messaging or even e-mails or, God forbid, taking photographs or making video recordings on these devices, it happened anyway. Even she had fallen prey to sending text messages and downloading images and information far more than was wise, had gotten somewhat lax about it. These days she spent so much time in taxis and airports, the flow of information never pausing, never giving anyone a break, almost none of it password-protected, because she'd gotten frustrated, or maybe because she didn't like feeling controlled by her niece.

Scarpetta clicked on her inbox. The most recent e-mail, sent just minutes ago, was from Lucy, with the provocative subject heading:

FOLLOW THE BREAD CRUMBS

Scarpetta opened it.

Aunt Kay: Attached is a GPS data log of tactical tracking updated every 15 secs. I've included only key times and locations, beginning at approx. 1935 hours when you hung your coat in the

makeup room closet, presumably the
BlackBerry in a pocket. A pic is worth a
thousand words. Go through the slideshow
and form your own conclusion. I know what
mine is. Needless to say, I'm glad you're
safe. Marino told me about the FedEx. -L

The first image in the slideshow was what Lucy called a
"bird's-eye of the Time Warner Center," or basically a close-
on aerial view. This was followed by a map with the street
address, including the latitude and longitude. Unquestion-
ably, Scarpetta's BlackBerry had been at the Time Warner
Center at seven-thirty-five p.m., when she first arrived at
the north tower entrance on 59th Street, was cleared
through security, took the elevator to the fifth floor, walked
down the hallway to the makeup room, and hung her coat
in the closet. At this point, only she and the makeup artist
were in the room, and it wasn't possible anyone could have
gone into the pocket of her coat during the twenty-some
minutes she was in the chair, being touched up and then
just sitting and waiting, watching Campbell Brown on the
television that was always on in there.

As best Scarpetta could recall, a sound technician miked
her at around eight-twenty, which was at least twenty minutes earlier than usual, now that she thought about it, and
she was led to the set and seated at the table. Carley Crispin
didn't appear until a few minutes before nine and sat across
from her, sipped water with a straw, exchanged pleasantries,
and then they were on the air. During the show and until
Scarpetta left the building at close to eleven p.m., the location of her BlackBerry, according to Lucy, remained the
same, with one proviso:

```
If your BB was moved to a different
location at the same address—to another
room or another floor, for example—lat
and long coordinates wouldn't change. So
can't tell. Only know it was in the
building.
```

After that, at almost eleven p.m., when Carley Crispin and Scarpetta left the Time Warner Center, the Black-Berry left the Time Warner Center, too. Scarpetta followed its journey in the log, in the slideshow, clicking on a bird's-eye, this one Columbus Circle, and then another bird's-eye of her apartment building on Central Park West, which was captured at eleven-sixteen p.m. At this point, one might conclude that Scarpetta's Black-Berry was still in her coat pocket and what the WAAS receiver was tracking and recording every fifteen seconds was her own locations as she walked home. But that couldn't be the case. Benton had tried to call her numerous times. If the BlackBerry was in Scarpetta's coat pocket, why didn't it ring? She hadn't turned it off. She almost never did.

More significant, Scarpetta realized, when she'd entered her building, her BlackBerry hadn't. The next images in the slideshow were a series of bird's-eye aerial photos, maps, and addresses that showed a curious journey her BlackBerry had taken, beginning with a return to the Time Warner Center, then following Sixth Avenue and coming to a stop at 60 East 54th Street. Scarpetta enlarged the bird's-eye, studying a cluster of granite grayish buildings tucked amid high-rises, cars, and cabs frozen on the street, recognizing in the background the Museum of

Modern Art, the Seagram Building, the French Gothic spire of Saint Thomas Church.

Lucy's note:

```
60 E. 54th is Hotel Elysée which has,
notably, the Monkey Bar—not "officially
open" unless you're in the know. Like a
private club, very exclusive, very
Hollywood. A hangout for major celebs
and players.
```

Was it possible the Monkey Bar was open now, at three-seventeen a.m.? It would appear, based on the log, that Scarpetta's BlackBerry was still at the East 54th Street address. She remembered what Lucy had said about latitude and longitude. Maybe Carley hadn't gone to the Monkey Bar after all but was in the same building.

Scarpetta e-mailed her niece:

```
Bar still open, or is BB possibly in the
hotel?
```

Lucy's reply:

```
Could be the hotel. I'm in a witness
situation or I'd go there myself.
```

Scarpetta:

```
Marino can, unless he's with you.
```

Lucy:

```
I think I should nuke it. Most of your
data are backed up on the server. You'd
be fine. Marino's not with me.
```

She was saying she could remotely access Scarpetta's
BlackBerry and eradicate most of the data stored on it and
the customization—in essence, return the device to its factory settings. If what Scarpetta suspected was true, it was
a little late for that. Her BlackBerry had been out of her
possession for the past six hours, and if Carley Crispin had
stolen it, she'd had plenty of time to get her hands on a
treasure trove of privileged information and may have
helped herself earlier, explaining the scene photograph she
put on the air. Scarpetta wasn't about to forgive this, and
she would want to prove it.

She wrote:

```
Do not nuke. The BB and what's in it are
evidence. Please keep tracking. Where is
Marino? Home?
```

Lucy's reply:

```
BB hasn't moved from that location in
the past three hours. Marino is at RTCC.
```

Scarpetta didn't answer. She wasn't going to mention
the password problem, not under the circumstances.
Lucy might decide to nuke the BlackBerry, despite what
she'd been instructed, since she didn't seem to need

permission these days. It was rather astonishing what Lucy was privy to, and Scarpetta felt unsettled, was nagged by something she couldn't quite pinpoint. Lucy knew where the BlackBerry was, seemed to know where Marino was, seemed invested in everyone in a way that was different from the past. What else did her niece know, and why was she so intent on keeping tabs on everyone, or at least having the capability? *In case you get kidnapped,* Lucy had said, and she hadn't been joking. *Or if you lose your BlackBerry. If you leave it in a taxi, I can find it,* she'd explained.

It was strange. Scarpetta thought back to when the sleek devices had appeared and marveled over the premeditation, the exactness and cleverness, of how Lucy had managed to surprise them with her gift. A Saturday afternoon, the last Saturday in November, the twenty-ninth, Scarpetta remembered. She and Benton were in the gym working out, had appointments with the trainer, followed up by the steam room, the sauna, then an early dinner and the theater, *Billy Elliot.* They had routines, and Lucy knew them.

She knew the gym in their building was one place they never took their phones. The reception was terrible, and it wasn't necessary, anyway, because they could be reached. Emergency calls could be routed through the fitness club's reception desk. When they had returned to their apartment, the new BlackBerrys were there, a red ribbon around each, on the dining-room table with a note explaining that Lucy, who had a key, had let herself in while they were out and had imported the data from their old cell phones into the new devices. Words to that effect and detailed instructions. She must have done something similar with Berger and Marino.

Scarpetta got up from the dining-room table. She got on the phone.

"Hotel Elysée. How may I help you?" a man with a French accent answered.

"Carley Crispin, please."

A long pause, then, "Ma'am, are you asking me to ring her room? It's quite late."

14

Lucy had finally stopped typing. She'd quit looking at maps and writing e-mails. She was going to say something she shouldn't. Berger could feel it coming and couldn't stop her.

"I've been sitting here wondering what your fans would think," Lucy said to Hap Judd. "I'm trying to get into the mind-set of one of your fans. This movie star I've got a crush on—and now I'm in a fan's mind. And I'm imaging my idol Hap Judd with a latex glove on for a condom, fucking the dead body of a nineteen-year-old girl in a hospital morgue refrigerator."

Hap Judd was stunned, as if he'd been slapped, his mouth open, his face bright red. He was going to erupt.

"Lucy, it's occurred to me, Jet Ranger may need to go out," Berger said, after a pause.

The old bulldog was upstairs in Lucy's apartment and had been out to potty not even two hours ago.

"Not quite yet." Lucy's green eyes met Berger's. Boldness, stubbornness. If Lucy wasn't Lucy, Berger would fire her.

"What about another water, Hap?" Berger said. "Actually, I could use a Diet Pepsi." Berger held Lucy's eyes. Not a suggestion. An order.

She needed a moment alone with her witness, and she needed Lucy to back off and cut it out. This was a criminal investigation, not road rage. What the hell was wrong with her?

Berger resumed with Judd. "We were talking about what you told Eric. He claims you made sexual references about a girl who had just died in the hospital."

"I never said I did something as disgusting as that!"

"You talked about Farrah Lacy to Eric. You told him you suspected inappropriate behavior at the hospital. Staff, funeral home employees engaging in inappropriate behavior with her dead body, perhaps with other dead bodies," Berger said to Judd as Lucy got up from the table and left the room. "Why did you mention all this to someone you didn't know? Maybe because you were desperate to confess, needed to assuage your guilt. When you were talking about what was going on at Park General, you were really talking about yourself. About what you did."

"This is bullshit! Who the hell is setting me up?" Judd was yelling. "Is this about money? Is the little fucker trying to blackmail me or something? Is this some sick lie that insane bitch Dodie Hodge has cooked up?"

"No one is trying to blackmail you. This isn't about money or someone allegedly stalking you. It's about what you did at Park General before you had money, possibly before you had stalkers."

A tone sounded on Berger's BlackBerry next to her on the table. Someone had just sent her an e-mail.

"Dead bodies. Makes me want to puke just thinking about it," Judd said.

"But you've more than thought about it, haven't you," Berger stated.

"What do you mean?"

"You're going to see," she said.

"You're looking for a scapegoat or want to make a name for yourself at my fucking expense."

Berger didn't offer that she'd already made a name for herself and didn't need the help of a second-rate actor.

She said, "I'll repeat myself, what I want is the truth. The truth is therapeutic. You'll feel better. People make mistakes."

He wiped his eyes, his leg bouncing so hard he might fly out of the chair. Berger didn't like him, but she was liking herself less. She was reminded that he had brought this on, could have avoided it had he been helpful when she'd placed that first call three weeks ago. If he'd talked to her, she wouldn't have found it necessary to come up with a plan that rather much had taken on a life of its own. Lucy had made sure it had taken on a life of its own. It had never been Berger's intention to prosecute Hap Judd for what allegedly had happened at Park General Hospital, and she had little or no faith in some handyman pot-smoking snitch named Eric whom she'd never interviewed or met. Marino had talked to Eric. Marino said Eric had told him about Park General, and yes, the information was disconcerting, possibly incriminating. But Berger was interested in a much bigger case.

Hap Judd was a client of Hannah Starr's highly respected and successful money-management company, but he didn't lose his fortune, not a penny of it, to what Berger was calling a Ponzi-by-proxy scam. He was saved when Hannah purportedly pulled his investments out of the stock market this past August 4. That same day exactly two million dollars was wired into his bank account. His original investment of one-fourth that amount made a year earlier had never been in the stock market, but in the pockets of a real-estate investment banking firm, Bay Bridge Finance, whose CEO was recently arrested by the FBI for felony fraud. Hannah would claim ignorance, would say she no more knew about Bay Bridge Finance's Ponzi scheme than did the reputable financial institutions, charities, and banks that were victims of Bernard Madoff and his kind. No doubt Hannah would claim that she was duped like so many others.

But Berger didn't buy it. The timing of the transaction Hannah Starr had instigated on behalf of Hap Judd, apparently without any prompting from him or anyone else, was evidence that she knew exactly what she was involved in and was a conspirator. An investigation into her financial records that had been ongoing since her disappearance the day before Thanksgiving hinted that Hannah, the sole beneficiary of her late father Rupe Starr's fortune and his company, had creative business practices, especially when it came to billing clients. But that didn't make her a criminal. Nothing stood out until Lucy's discovery of that two-million-dollar wire to Hap Judd. Then, suddenly, Hannah's disappearance, which had been assumed to be a predatory crime and therefore Berger's turf, had begun to take on different shadings. Berger had joined forces with other attorneys and analysts in her office's Investigative Division, primarily its Frauds Bureau, and she also had consulted with the FBI.

Hers was a highly classified investigation that the public knew nothing about, because the last thing she wanted transmitted all over the universe was her belief that contrary to popular theories, Hannah Starr wasn't the victim of some sexual psychopath, and if a yellow cab was involved, most likely it was one that had carried her to an FBO where she'd boarded a private plane, which was exactly what was scheduled. She was supposed to have boarded her Gulfstream on Thanksgiving day, bound for Miami, and after that, Saint Barts. She never showed up because she had other plans, more secretive ones. Hannah Starr was a con artist, and very possibly alive and on the lam, and she wouldn't have spared Hap Judd a terrible financial fate unless she'd had more than a professional interest in him. She'd fallen for her celebrity client, and he might just have a clue as to where she was.

"What you never imagined is Eric would call my office Tuesday morning and get my investigator on the phone and repeat everything you told him," Berger said to Judd.

If Marino had shown up for this interview, he could help her at this point. He could repeat what Eric had said to him. Berger was feeling isolated and trivialized. Lucy wasn't respectful and kept things from her, and Marino was too damn busy.

"Ironically," Berger continued, "I'm not sure Eric was suspicious of you as much as he wanted to show off. Wanted to brag about hanging out with a movie star, brag that he had information about a huge scandal, be the next American Idol by ending up all over the news, which seems to be everybody's motivation these days. Unfortunately for you, when we started looking into Eric's story, the Park General scandal? Turns out there's something to it."

"He's just a punk shooting off his mouth." Judd was calmer now that Lucy was out of the room.

"We checked it out, Hap."

"It was four years ago. Something like that, a long time ago, when I worked there."

"Four years, fifty years," Berger said. "There's no statute of limitations. Although I'll admit you've presented the people of New York with an unusual legal challenge. Generally, when we run into a case where human remains have been desecrated, we're talking about archaeology, not necrophilia."

"You wish it was true, but it's not," he said. "I swear. I would never hurt anyone."

"Believe me. Nobody wants something like this to be true," Berger said.

"I came here to help you out." Hands shaking as he wiped his eyes. Maybe he was acting, wanted her to feel sorry for him. "This other thing? It's wrong, fucking wrong, whatever that guy said."

"Eric was quite convincing." If Marino were here, god-damn it, he could help her out. She was furious with him.

"Fucking piece of shit, fuck him. I was joking around after we left the bar. We lit up a blunt. I was joking around about the hospital thing. Just talking big. Jesus Christ, I don't need to do something like that. Why would I do something like that? It was talk, it was weed and talk and maybe some tequila thrown in for good measure. So I'm strung out and in the bar and this guy . . . Fucking nobody piece of shit. Fuck him. I'll sue his ass, fucking ruin him. That's what I get for being nice to some nothing piece-of-shit groupie."

"What makes you think Eric's a groupie?" Berger asked.

"He comes up to me at the bar. You know, I'm minding my own business, having a drink, and he asks me for my autograph. I make the mistake of being nice, and next thing we're walking and he's asking me all this shit about myself, obviously hoping I'm gay, which I'm not, never been even once."

"Is Eric gay?"

"He hangs out at the Stonewall Inn."

"So do you," Berger said.

"I told you, I'm not gay and never have been."

"An unusual venue for you," Berger observed. "The Stonewall Inn is one of the most famous gay establishments in the country, a symbol of the gay rights movement, in fact. Not exactly a hangout for straights."

"If you're an actor, you hang out in all kinds of places so you can play all types of characters. I'm a method actor, you know, I do research. That's my thing, where I get my ideas and figure it out. I'm known for rolling up my sleeves and doing whatever it takes."

"Going to a gay bar is research?"

"I got no problem with where I hang out, because I'm secure with myself."

"What other types of research, Hap? You familiar with the Body Farm in Tennessee?"

Judd looked confused, then incredulous. "What? You're breaking into my e-mail now?"

She didn't answer.

"So I ordered something from them. For research. I'm playing an archaeologist in a movie and we excavate this plague pit, you know, with skeletal remains. Hundreds and thousands of skeletons. It's just research, and I was even going to see if I could go down there to Knoxville so

I have an idea what it's like to be around something like that."

"Be around bodies that are decomposing?"

"If you want to get it right, you've got to see it, smell it, so you can play it. I'm curious what happens, you know, when a body's been in the ground or lying around somewhere. What it looks like after a lot of time passes. I don't have to explain this to you, explain acting to you, my damn career to you. I haven't done anything. You've violated my rights, going into my e-mail."

"I don't recall my saying we'd gone into your e-mail."

"You must have."

"Data searches," she replied, and he was looking her in the eye or looking around but not looking her up and down anymore. He did that only when Lucy was here. "You borrow computers that are connected to a server, you order something online, it's amazing the trail people leave. Let's talk some more about Eric," Berger said.

"The fucking fag."

"He told you he was gay?"

"He was hitting on me, okay? It was obvious, you know, him asking me about myself, my past, and I mentioned I'd had a lot of different jobs, including being a tech at a hospital part-time. Fags hit on me all the time," he added.

"Did you bring up your former hospital job, or did he?"

"I don't remember how it came up. He started asking me about my career, how I'd started out, and I told him about the hospital. I talked about what kinds of things I'd done while I tried to get my acting going good enough to support me. Stuff like helping out as a phlebotomist, collecting specimens, even helping out in the morgue, mopping the floors, rolling bodies in and out of the fridge, whatever they needed."

"Why?" Lucy said as she returned with a Diet Pepsi and a bottle of water.

"What do you mean 'Why'?" Judd craned his head around, and his demeanor changed. He hated her. He made no effort to hide it.

"Why take shit jobs like that?" She popped open the Diet Pepsi can, set it in front of Berger, and sat down.

"All I've got is a high-school diploma," he said, not looking at her.

"Why not be a model or something while you were trying to make it as an actor?" Lucy picked up where she left off, insulting him, taunting him.

A part of Berger paid attention while another part of her was distracted by a second message tone sounding on her BlackBerry. Goddamn it, who was trying to reach her at four o'clock in the morning? Maybe Marino again. Too busy to show up, and now he was interrupting her again. Someone was. Might not be him. She slid the BlackBerry closer as Hap Judd continued to talk, directing his answers to her. Better check her messages, and she subtly entered her password.

"I did some modeling. I did whatever I could to make money and get real-life experience," he said. "I'm not afraid to work. I'm not afraid of anything except people fucking lying about me."

The first e-mail, sent a few minutes ago, was from Marino:

Going to need a search warrant asap re incident involves the doc im emailing facts of the case in a few

"I'm not grossed out by anything," Judd went on. "I'm one of these people who does what it takes. I didn't grow up with anything handed to me."

Marino was saying he was drafting a search warrant that he would be e-mailing to Berger shortly. Then it would be her job to check the accuracy and language and get hold of a judge she could call at any hour, and go to his residence to get the warrant signed. What search warrant, and what was so urgent? What was going on with Scarpetta? Berger wondered if this was related to the suspicious package left at her building last night.

"That's why I can play the roles I do and be convincing. Because I'm not scared, not of snakes or insects," Judd was saying to Berger, who was listening carefully and dealing with e-mails at the same time. "I mean, I could do like Gene Simmons and put a bat in my mouth and breathe fire. I do a lot of my own stunts. I don't want to talk to her. I'm going to leave if I have to talk to her." He glared at Lucy.

The second e-mail, which had just landed, was from Scarpetta:

Re: Search Warrant. Based on my training and experience, I think the search for the stolen data storage device will require a forensic expert.

Clearly Marino and Scarpetta had been in touch with each other, although Berger had no idea what stolen device was involved or what needed to be searched. She couldn't imagine why Scarpetta hadn't given this same instruction to Marino so he could include a forensic expert in the addendum of the warrant he was drafting. Instead, Scarpetta was telling Berger directly that she wanted a civilian to help with the search, someone who knew about data storage devices, such as computers. Then Berger figured it out. Scarpetta needed Lucy to be present at the scene and was asking Berger to make sure that happened. For some reason, it was very important.

"That was quite a stunt you pulled in the hospital morgue," Lucy said to Judd.

"I didn't pull a stunt." Directing everything to Berger. "I was just talking, saying I thought it might be going on, maybe when the funeral homes showed up and because she was really pretty and not all that banged up for someone hurt that bad. I was halfway kidding, although I have wondered what some of these funeral home people are into, and that's the truth. I was suspicious about some of the ones I came across. I think people do all kinds of stuff if they can get away with it."

"I'll quote you on that," Lucy said. "Hap Judd says people do whatever they can get away with. An instant Yahoo! headline."

Berger said to her, "Maybe now's a good time to show him what we've found." She said to Judd, "You've heard of artificial intelligence. This is more advanced than that. I don't suppose you were curious about why we asked you to meet us here."

"Here?" He looked around the room, a blank expression on his Captain America face.

"You mandated the time. I mandated the place. This high-tech minimalist space," Berger said. "See all the computers everywhere? This is a forensic computer investigative firm."

He didn't react.

"That's why I picked this location. And let me clarify. Lucy is an investigative consultant retained by the district attorney's office, but she's quite a lot more than that. Former FBI, ATF, I won't bother with her résumé, would take too long, but your describing her as not a real cop isn't quite accurate."

He didn't seem to understand.

"Let's go back to when you worked at Park General," Berger said.

"I really don't remember—well, almost nothing, not much about that situation."

"What situation?" Berger asked, with what Lucy liked to describe as her "millpond calm." Only when Lucy said it, she didn't mean it as a compliment.

"The girl," he said.

"Farrah Lacy," Berger said.

"Yes, I mean, no. I'm trying to, what I'm saying is it was a long time ago."

"That's the beauty of computers," Berger said. "They don't care if it was a long time ago. Especially Lucy's computers, her neural networking applications, programming constructs that mimic the brain. Let me refresh your memory about your long-ago days at Park General. When you entered the hospital morgue, you had to use your security card. Sound familiar?"

"I guess. I mean, that would be the routine."

"So, every time you used your security card, your security code was entered into the hospital computer system."

"Along with recordings made by the security cameras," Lucy added. "Along with your e-mails, because they resided on the hospital server, which routinely backs up its data, meaning they still have electronic records from when you were there. Including whatever you wrote on— whatever desktop computer you happened to borrow at the hospital. And if you logged in to private e-mail accounts from there, oh, well, those too. Everything's connected. It's just a matter of knowing how. I won't tax you with a lot of computer jargon, but that's what I do in this place. I make connections the same way the neurons in your brain are making them right this minute. Inputs, outputs, from sensory and motor nerves in your eyes, your hands, signal flows that the brain pieces together to accomplish tasks and solve problems. Images, ideas, written messages, conversations. Even screenwriting. All of it interconnected and forming patterns, making it possible to detect, decide, and predict."

"What screenwriting?" Hap Judd's mouth was dry, sounded sticky when he talked. "I don't know what you're talking about."

Lucy started typing. She pointed a remote at a flat screen mounted on a wall. Judd reached for his bottle of water, fumbled with the cap, took a long swallow.

The flat screen divided into windows, each filled by an image: a younger Hap Judd in scrubs walking into the hospital morgue, grabbing latex gloves out of a box, opening the stainless-steel walk-in refrigerator; a newspaper photograph of nineteen-year-old Farrah Lacy, a very pretty, light-skinned African American in a cheerleading outfit, holding pompoms and grinning; an e-mail; a page from a script.

Lucy clicked on the page from the script and it filled the entire screen:

```
CUT TO:
INT. BEDROOM, NIGHT
A beautiful woman in the bed, covers
pulled back, bunched around her bare
feet. She looks dead, hands folded over
her chest in a religious pose. She's
completely nude. An INTRUDER we can't
make out moves closer, closer, closer!
He grips her ankles and slides her limp
body down to the foot of the bed,
parting her legs. We hear the clinks of
his belt being unbuckled.
   INTRUDER
Good news. You're about to go to
heaven.
   As his pants drop to the floor.
```

"Where did you get that? Who the hell gave it to you? You have no right going into my e-mail," Hap Judd said loudly. "And it's not what you think. You're setting me up!"

Lucy clicked the mouse and the flat screen filled with an e-mail:

```
Hey too bad about whats her ass. Fuck
her. I dont mean littereally. Call if U
want a stiff one. Hap
```

"I meant a drink." Words sticking. His voice shook. "I don't remember who . . . Look, it had to be a stiff drink. I was asking someone if they wanted to meet me for a drink."

"I don't know," Lucy said to Berger. "Sounds like he

assumed we interpreted 'stiff one' as something else. Maybe a dead body? You should try spell-check sometime," Lucy said to him. "And you should be careful what you do, what you e-mail, what you text-message on computers that are connected to a server. Like a hospital server. We can sit here all week with you if you want. I've got computer applications that can connect every piece of your entire screwed-up make-believe life."

It was a bluff. At this point, they had very little, not much more than writing he'd done on hospital computers, his e-mails, whatever had resided on the server back then, and some images from security cameras and morgue log entries from the two-week period Farrah Lacy had been hospitalized. There hadn't been time to sift through anything else. Berger had been afraid if she delayed talking to Hap Judd, she'd never get the chance. This was what she called a "blitz attack." If she didn't like the way she felt about it before, now she was really out of her comfort zone. She felt doubt. Serious doubt. The same doubts she'd been feeling all along, only much worse now. Lucy was driving this. She had a destination in mind. She didn't seem to care how she got there.

"I don't want to see anything else," Judd said.

"Just tons of stuff to go through. My eyes are crossed." Lucy tapped the MacBook with an index finger. "All downloaded. Things I doubt you remember, got no idea about. Not sure what the cops would do with this. Ms. Berger? What would the cops do with this?"

"What worries me is what happened while the victim was still alive," Berger said, because she had to play it out. She couldn't stop now. "Farrah was in the hospital two weeks before she died."

"Twelve days, exactly," Lucy said. "On life support, never regained consciousness. Five of those days, Hap was on duty, working at the hospital. You ever go into her room, Hap? Maybe help yourself to her while she was in a coma?"

"You're the one who's sick!"

"Did you?"

"I told you," he said to Berger. "I don't even know who she is."

"Farrah Lacy," Berger repeated the name. "The nineteen-year-old cheerleader whose picture you saw in the news, the *Harlem News.* That same picture we just showed you."

"The same picture you e-mailed to yourself," Lucy said. "Let me guess. You don't remember. I'll remind you. You e-mailed it to yourself the same day it appeared in the news online. You sent the article about the car accident to yourself. I find that very interesting."

She clicked the photograph back on the wall-mounted flat screen. The photograph of Farrah Lacy in her cheerleading uniform. Hap Judd averted his eyes.

He said, "I don't know anything about a car accident."

"Family's coming home from Marcus Garvey Memorial Park in Harlem," Berger said. "A pretty Saturday afternoon in July 2004, some guy talking on his cell phone runs a red light on Lenox Avenue, T-bones them."

"I don't remember," Judd said.

"Farrah had what's called a closed head injury, which is basically an injury to the brain caused by a nonpenetrating wound," Berger said.

"I don't remember. I just sort of remember her being there at the hospital."

"Right. You remember Farrah being a patient in the hospital where you worked. On life support in the ICU.

Sometimes you went into the ICU to draw blood, you remember that?" Berger asked him.

He didn't reply.

"Isn't it true that you had a reputation for being a skilled phlebotomist?" Berger asked.

"He could get blood from a stone," Lucy said. "According to what one of the nurses said to Marino."

"Who the hell's Marino?"

Lucy shouldn't have brought him up. Referencing Berger's investigators or anyone she used in a case was her prerogative, not Lucy's. Marino had talked to a few people at the hospital, over the phone and very carefully. It was a delicate situation. Berger felt a heightened sense of responsibility because of who the potential defendant was. Lucy clearly didn't share her concerns, seemed to want Hap Judd ruined, maybe the same way she'd felt about the air traffic controller a few hours earlier and the linesman she reprimanded in the FBO. Berger had overheard every word through the bathroom door. Lucy was after blood, maybe not just Hap Judd's blood, maybe a lot of people's blood. Berger didn't know why. She didn't know what to think anymore.

"We have a lot of people looking into your situation," Berger said to Judd. "Lucy's been running you and all kinds of data through her computers for days."

Not entirely true. Lucy had spent maybe one day on it remotely from Stowe. Once Marino had begun the process, the hospital was cooperative, e-mailing certain information without protest because it was a personnel issue, a matter pertaining to a former employee, and Marino had suggested as only he could that the more helpful Park General was, the more likely the matter could be resolved diplomatically, discreetly. Warrants and court orders and a former employee who was now famous, and the situation would be all over the news. Unnecessary when maybe nobody was going to be charged with anything in the end, and what a shame to put Farrah Lacy's family through so much pain again, and wasn't it pitiful the way everybody sued these days, Marino had said, or words to that effect.

"Let me refresh your memory," Berger said to Hap Judd. "You went into the ICU, into the room next to Farrah's on the night of July sixth, 2004, to draw blood from a different patient, this one quite elderly. She had terrible veins, so you volunteered to take care of her, since you could get blood from a stone."

"I can show you her chart," Lucy said.

Another bluff. Lucy could show no such thing. The hospital absolutely hadn't given Berger's office access to other patients' confidential information.

"I can pull up the video of you going in there with your gloves on, with your cart, going into her room." Lucy was unrelenting. "I can pull up video of every room you ever went into at Park General, including Farrah's."

"I never did. This is lies, all lies." Judd was slumped down in his chair.

"You sure you didn't go into her room that night while you were up there on the ICU?" Berger said. "You told Eric you did. You said you were curious about Farrah, that she was really pretty, that you wanted to see her naked."

"Fucking lies. He's a fucking liar."

"He'll say the same thing under oath on the witness stand," Berger added.

"It was just talk. Even if I did, it was just to look. I didn't do anything. I didn't hurt anyone."

"Sex crimes are about power," Berger said. "Maybe it made you feel powerful to rape a helpless teenage girl who was unconscious and never going to tell, made you feel big and powerful, especially if you were a struggling actor who could barely get minor roles in soap operas back then. I imagine you were feeling pretty bad about yourself, sticking needles in the arms of sick, cranky people, mopping floors, getting ordered around by nurses, by anybody, really, you were so low on the food chain."

"No," he said, shaking his head side to side. "I didn't do it. I didn't do anything."

"Well, it seems you did, Hap," Berger said. "I'll continue to refresh your memory with a few facts. July seventh, it was in the news that Farrah Lacy was going to be disconnected from life support. At the very time she was disconnected, you came to work even though the hospital hadn't summoned you. You were a per-diem employee, only on duty when you were called. But the hospital didn't call you on the afternoon of July seventh, 2004. You showed up anyway and took it upon yourself to clean the morgue. Mopping the floor, wiping down stainless steel, and this is according to a security guard who's still there and happens to be in a video clip we're about to show you. Farrah died and you headed straight up to the tenth floor, to the ICU, to wheel her body down to the morgue. Sound familiar?"

He stared at the brushed steel tabletop and didn't reply. She couldn't read his affect. Maybe he was in shock. Maybe he was calculating what he was going to say next.

"Farrah Lacy's body was transported by you down to the morgue," Berger repeated. "It was captured on camera. Would you like to see it?"

"This is fucked up. It's not what you're saying." He rubbed his face in his hands.

"We're going to show you that clip right now."

A click of the mouse, and then another click and the video began: Hap Judd in scrubs and a lab coat, wheeling a gurney into the hospital morgue, stopping at the shut stainless-steel refrigerator door. A security guard entering, opening the refrigerator door, looking at the tag on top of the shroud covering the body, and saying, "What are they posting her for? She was brain-dead and had the plug pulled." Hap Judd saying, "Family wants it. Don't ask me. She was fucking beautiful, a cheerleader. Like the dream girl you'd take to the prom." Guard saying, "Oh, yeah?" Hap Judd pulling the sheet down, exposing the dead girl's body, saying, "What a waste." The guard shaking his head, saying, "Get her on in there, I got things to do." Judd wheeling the gurney inside the refrigerator, his reply indistinguishable.

Hap Judd scraped back his chair and got up. "I want a lawyer," he said.

"I can't help you," Berger said. "You haven't been arrested. We don't Mirandize people who haven't been arrested. If you want a lawyer, up to you. No one is stopping you. Help yourself."

"This is so you can arrest me. I assume you're going to, which is why I'm here." He looked uncertain, and he wouldn't look at Lucy.

"Not now," Berger said.

"Why am I here?"

"You're not being arrested. Not now. Maybe you will be, maybe you won't. I don't know," Berger said. "That's not why I asked to talk to you three weeks ago."

"Then what? What do you want?"

"Sit down," Berger said.

He sat back down. "You can't charge me with something like this. You understand? You can't. You got a gun somewhere in here? Why don't you just fucking shoot me."

"Two separate issues," Berger said. "First, we could keep investigating and maybe you'd be charged. Maybe you'd be indicted. What happens after that? You take your chances with a jury. Second, nobody's going to shoot you."

"I'm telling you, I didn't do anything to that girl," Judd said. "I didn't hurt her."

"What about the glove?" Lucy asked pointedly.

"Tell you what. I'm going to ask him about it," Berger said to her.

She'd had enough. Lucy was going to stop it right now.

"I'm going to ask the questions," Berger said, holding Lucy's eyes until she was satisfied she was going to listen this time.

"The guard says he left the morgue, left you alone in there with Farrah Lacy's body." Berger continued her questioning, repeating information Marino had gathered, trying not to think about how unhappy she was with him right now. "He said he checked maybe twenty minutes later and you were just leaving. He asked you what you'd been doing in the morgue all that time and you didn't have an answer. He remembered you had only one surgical glove on and seemed out of breath. Where was the other glove, Hap? In the video we just showed you, you had on two gloves. We can show you other video footage of you going inside the refrigerator and staying in it for almost fifteen minutes with the door open wide. What were you doing in there? Why'd you take off one of your gloves? Did you use it for something, maybe put it over some other part of your body? Maybe put it on your penis?"

"No," he said, shaking his head.

"You want to tell it to a jury? You want a jury of your peers to hear all this?"

He stared down at the table, moving his finger over metal, like a little kid finger-painting. Breathing hard, his face bright red.

"What I'm hearing is you'd like this behind you," Berger said.

"Tell me how." He didn't look up.

Berger had no DNA. She had no eyewitness or any other evidence, and Judd wasn't going to confess. She would never have anything beyond circumstances that weren't much better than innuendo. But that was as much as she needed to destroy Hap Judd. With his degree of celebrity, the accusation was a conviction. If she charged him with desecrating human remains, which was the only charge on the books for necrophilia, his life would be destroyed, and Berger didn't take that lightly. She wasn't known for malicious prosecution, for constructing cases out of a flawed process or from evidence extracted improperly. She'd never resorted to unjustifiable and unreasonable litigation and wasn't about to start now, and she wasn't going to let Lucy push her into it.

"Let's back up three weeks, to when I called your agent. You do remember getting my messages," Berger said. "Your agent said he passed them on to you."

"How do I put this behind me?" Judd looked at her. He wanted a deal.

"Cooperation is a good thing. Collaboration—just like you have to do to make a movie. People working together."

Berger placed her pen on top of her legal pad and folded her hands. "You weren't cooperative or collaborative three weeks ago when I called your agent. I wanted to talk to you, and you couldn't be bothered. I could have sent the cops by your apartment in TriBeCa or tracked you down in L.A. or wherever you were and had you brought in, but I spared you the trauma. I was sensitive because of who you are. Now we're in a different situation. I need your help, and you need mine. Because you've got a problem you didn't have three weeks ago. You hadn't met Eric in the bar three weeks ago. I didn't know about Park General Hospital and Farrah Lacy three weeks ago. Maybe we can help each other."

"Tell me." Fear in his eyes.

"Let's talk about your relationship with Hannah Starr."

He didn't react. He didn't respond.

"You're not going to deny you know Hannah Starr," Berger then said.

"Why would I deny it?" He shrugged.

"And you didn't suspect for even a second that I might be calling about her?" Berger said. "You know she's disappeared, correct?"

"Of course."

"And it didn't occur—"

"Okay. Yeah. But I didn't want to talk about her for privacy reasons," Judd said. "It would have been unfair to her, and I don't see what it has to do with what happened to her."

"You know what happened to her," Berger said, as if he did.

"Not really."

"Sounds to me like you do know."

"I don't want to be involved. It has nothing to do with me," Judd said. "My relationship with her was nobody's business. But she'd tell you I'm not into anything sick. If she were around, she'd tell you that Park General stuff is bullshit. I mean, people who do things like that, it's because they can't have living people, right? She'd tell you I got no problems in that department. I got no problem having sex."

"You were having an affair with Hannah Starr."

"I put a stop to it early on. I tried."

Lucy was staring hard at him.

"You signed on with her investment firm a little over a year ago," Berger said. "I can give you the exact date if you want. You realize, of course, we have an abundance of information because of what's happened."

"Yeah, I know. That's all anybody hears on the news," he said. "And now the other girl. The marathon runner. I can't think of her name. And maybe some serial killer driving a yellow cab. Wouldn't surprise me."

"What makes you think Toni Darien was a marathon runner?"

"I must have heard it on TV, seen it on the Internet or something."

Berger tried to think about any reference to Toni Darien as a marathon runner. She didn't recall that being released to the media, only that she jogged.

"How did you first meet Hannah?" she asked.

"The Monkey Bar, where a lot of Hollywood people hang out," he said. "She was in there one night and we started talking. She was really smart about money, told me all kinds of stuff I didn't know shit about."

"And you know what happened to her three weeks ago," Berger said, and Lucy listened intensely.

"I have a pretty good idea. I think somebody did something. You know, she pissed people off."

"Who did she piss off?" Berger asked.

"You got a phone book? Let me go through it."

"A lot of people," Berger said. "You're saying she pissed
off almost everybody she met?"

"Including me. I admit. She always wanted her way
about everything. She had to have her own way about
absolutely everything."

"You're talking about her as if she's dead."

"I'm not naïve. Most people think something bad happened to her."

"You don't seem upset about the possibility she might
be dead," Berger said.

"Sure it's upsetting. I didn't hate her. I just got tired of
her pushing me and pushing me. Chasing me and chasing
me, if you want me to be honest. She didn't like to be told
no."

"Why did she give you your money back—actually, four
times your original investment? Two million dollars. That's
quite a return on your investment in only a year."

Another shrug. "The market was volatile. Lehman
Brothers was going belly-up. She called me and said she was
recommending I pull out, and I said whatever you think.
Then I got the wire. And later on? Damn if she wasn't right.
I would have lost everything, and I'm not making millions
and millions yet. I'm not A list yet. Whatever I have left
over after expenses, I sure as hell don't want to lose."

"When was the last time you had sex with Hannah?"
Berger was taking notes on the legal pad again, conscious
of Lucy, of her stoniness, of the way she was staring at Hap
Judd.

He had to think. "Uh, okay. I remember. After that call. She told me she was pulling my money out, and could I drop by and she'd explain what was going on. It was just an excuse."

"Drop by where?"

"Her house. I dropped by, and one thing led to another. That was the last time. July, I think. I was heading off to London, and anyway, she has a husband. Bobby. I wasn't all that comfortable at her house when he was there."

"He was there on that occasion? When she asked you to drop by before you headed to London?"

"Uh, I don't remember if he was that time. It's a huge house."

"Their house on Park Avenue."

"He was hardly ever home." Judd didn't answer the question. "Travels all the time in their private jets, back and forth to Europe, all over the place. I got the impression he spends a lot of time in South Florida, that he's into the Miami scene, and they've got this place there on the ocean. He's got an Enzo down there. One of those Ferraris that costs more than a million bucks. I don't really know him. I've met him a few times."

"Where did you meet him and when?"

"When I started investing with their company a little over a year ago. They invited me to their house. I've seen him at their house."

Berger thought about the timing, and she thought about Dodie Hodge again.

"Is Hannah the person who referred you to the fortune-teller, to Dodie Hodge?"

"Okay, yeah. She'd do readings for Hannah and Bobby at the house. Hannah suggested I talk to Dodie, and it was a mistake. The lady's crazy as shit. She got obsessed with me, said I was the reincarnation of a son she'd had in a former life in Egypt. That I was a pharaoh and she was my mother."

"Let me make sure I understand which house you're talking about. The same one you said you visited this past July, when you had sex with Hannah for the last time," Berger said.

"The old man's house, worth, like, eighty million, this huge car collection, unbelievable antiques, statues, Michelangelo paintings on the walls and ceilings, frescoes, whatever you call them."

"I doubt they're Michelangelos," Berger said wryly.

"Like a hundred years old, un-freakin'-believable, practically takes up a city block. Bobby's from money, too. So he and Hannah had a business partnership. She used to tell me they never had sex. Like, not even once."

Berger made a note that Hap Judd continued to refer to Hannah in the past tense. He continued talking about her as if she was dead.

"But the old man got tired of her being this rich little playgirl and said she needed to settle down with someone so he'd know the business was going to be handled right," Judd continued. "Rupe didn't want to leave everything to her if she was still running around, you know, single and partying, and then ended up marrying some schmuck who got his hands on everything. So you can see why she'd screw around on Bobby—even though she used to tell me that sometimes she was afraid of him. It wasn't really screwing around because they didn't have that kind of deal."

"When did you begin having a sexual relationship with Hannah?"

"That first time at the mansion? Let me put it to you this way. She was real friendly. They have an indoor pool, an entire spa like something in Europe. It was me and some other VIP clients, new clients, there for a swim, for drinks and dinner, all these servants everywhere, Dom Pérignon and Cristal flowing like Kool-Aid. So I'm in the pool and she was paying a lot of attention. She started it."

"She started it on your first visit to her father's house a year ago this past August?"

Lucy sat with her arms crossed, staring. She was silent and wouldn't look at Berger.

"It was obvious," Judd said.

"Where was Bobby while she was being obvious?"

"I don't know. Maybe showing off his new Porsche. I do remember that. He'd gotten one of those Carrera GTs, a red one. That picture of him all over the news? That's the car. He was giving people rides up and down Park Avenue. You ask me, you ought to be checking Bobby out. Like, where was he when Hannah disappeared, huh?"

Bobby Fuller was in their North Miami Beach apartment when Hannah disappeared, and Berger wasn't going to offer that.

She said, "Where were you the night before Thanksgiving?"

"Me?" He almost laughed. "Now you're thinking I did something to her? No way. I don't hurt people. That's not my thing."

Berger made a note. Judd was assuming Hannah had been "hurt."

"I asked a simple question," Berger said. "Where were you the night before Thanksgiving, Wednesday, November twenty-sixth?"

"Let me think." His leg was jumping up and down again. "I honestly don't remember."

"Three weeks ago, the Thanksgiving holiday, and you don't remember."

"Wait a minute. I was in the city. Then the next day I flew to L.A. I like to fly on holidays, because the airports aren't crowded. I flew to L.A. Thanksgiving morning."

Berger wrote it down on her legal pad and said to Lucy, "We'll check that out." To Judd, "You remember what airline, what flight you were on?"

"American. Around noon, I don't remember the flight number. I don't celebrate Thanksgiving, don't give a damn about turkey and stuffing and all that. It's nothing to me, which is why I had to think for a minute." His leg bounced rapidly. "I know you probably think it's suspicious."

"What do I think is suspicious?"

"She disappears and the next day I'm on a plane out of here," he said.

15

Marino's Crown Vic was coated with a film of salt, reminding him of his dry, flaky skin this time of year, both him and his car faring similarly during New York winters.

Driving around in a dirty vehicle with scrapes and scuffs on the sides, the cloth seats worn and a small tear in the drooping headliner, had never been his style, and he was chronically self-conscious about it, at times irritated and embarrassed. When he'd seen Scarpetta earlier in front of her building, he'd noticed a big swath of whitish dirt on her jacket from where it had brushed against his passenger door. Now he was about to pick her up, and he wished there was a car wash open along the way.

He'd always been fastidious about what his ride looked like, at least from the outside, whether it was a police car, a truck, a Harley. A man's war wagon was a projection of who he was and what he thought of himself, the exception being clutter, which didn't used to bother him as long as certain people couldn't see it. Admittedly, and he blamed this on his former self-destructive inclinations, he used to be a slob, especially in his Richmond days, the inside of his police car nasty with paperwork, coffee cups, food wrappers, the ashtray so full he couldn't shut it, clothes piled in the back, and a mess of miscellaneous equipment, bags of evidence, his Winchester Marine shotgun commingled in the trunk. No longer. Marino had changed.

Quitting booze and cigarettes had completely razed his former life to the ground, like an old building torn down. What he'd constructed in its place so far was pretty good, but his internal calendar and clock were off and maybe always would be, not only because of how he did and didn't spend his time but because he had so much more of it, by his calculation three to five additional hours per day. He'd figured it out on paper, an assignment Nancy, his therapist, had given to him at the treatment center on Massachusetts' North Shore, June before last. He'd retreated to a lawn chair outside the chapel, where he could smell the sea and hear it crashing against rocks, the air cool, the sun warm on top of his head as he sat there and did the math. He'd never forget his shock. While each smoke supposedly took seven minutes off his life, another two or three minutes were used up just for the ritual: where and when to do it, getting out the pack, knocking a cigarette from it, lighting it, taking the first big hit, then the next five or six drags, putting it out, getting rid of the butt. Drinking was a worse time killer, the day pretty much ending when happy hour began.

"Serenity comes from knowing what you can and can't change," Nancy the therapist had said when he'd presented his findings. "And what you can't change, Pete, is that you've wasted at least twenty percent of your waking hours for the better part of half a century."

It was either wisely fill days that were twenty percent longer or return to his bad ways, which wasn't an option after the trouble they'd caused. He got interested in reading, keeping up with current events, surfing the Net, cleaning, organizing, repairing things, cruising the aisles of Zabar's and Home Depot, and if he couldn't sleep, hanging out at the Two, drinking coffee, taking Mac the dog for walks, and borrowing the ESU's monster garage. He turned his crappy police car into a project, working on it himself with glue and touch-up paint as best he could, and bartering and finagling for a brand-new Code 3 undercover siren and grille and deck lights. He'd sweet-talked the radio repair shop into custom-programming his Motorola P25 mobile radio to scan a wide range of frequencies in addition to SOD, the Special Operations Division. He'd spent his own money on a TruckVault drawer unit that he installed in the trunk to stow equipment and supplies, ranging from batteries and extra ammo to a gear bag packed with his personal Beretta Storm nine-millimeter carbine, a rain suit, field clothes, a soft body armor vest, and an extra pair of Blackhawk zipper boots.

Marino turned on the wipers and squirted a big dose of fluid on the windshield, swiping clean two arches as he drove out of the Frozen Zone, the restricted area of One Police Plaza where only authorized people like him were allowed. Most of the windows in the brown-brick headquarters were dark, especially those on the fourteenth floor, the Executive Command Center, where the Teddy Roosevelt Room and the commissioner's office were located, nobody home. It was after five a.m., had taken a while to type up the warrant and send it to Berger along with a reminder of why he was unable to show up for the interview of Hap Judd, and had it gone okay, and he was sorry not to be there but he had a real emergency on his hands.

He'd reminded her of the possible bomb left at Scarpetta's building, and now he was concerned that the security of the OCME and even the NYPD and district attorney's office might have been breached because the Doc's BlackBerry had been stolen. On it were communications and privileged information that involved the entire New York criminal-justice community. Maybe a slight exaggeration, but he hadn't shown up for Berger, his boss. He'd put Scarpetta first. Berger was going to accuse him of having a problem with his priorities, and it wouldn't be the first time she'd accused him of that. It was the same thing Bacardi accused him of and why they weren't getting along.

At the intersection of Pearl and Finest, he slowed at the white guard booth, the cop inside it a blurry shape waving at him behind fogged-up glass. Marino thought about calling Bacardi like he used to when it didn't matter what time it was or what she was doing. At the beginning of their relationship, nothing was inconvenient, and he talked to her whenever he wanted and told her what was going on, got her input, her wisecracks, her constant comments about missing him and when they would get together next. He felt like ringing up Bonnell—L.A., as he now called her—but he sure as hell couldn't do that yet, and he realized how much he was looking forward to seeing Scarpetta, even if it was work. He'd been surprised, almost didn't believe it, when it was her on the phone saying she had a problem and needed his help, and it pleased him to be reminded that big-shot Benton had his limitations. Benton couldn't do a damn thing about Carley Crispin stealing the Doc's Black-Berry, but Marino could. He would fix her good.

The copper spire of the old Woolworth Building was pointed like a witch's hat against the night sky above the Brooklyn Bridge, where traffic was light but steady, the noise of it like a surging surf, a distant wind. He turned up the volume on his police radio, listening to dispatchers and cops talking their talk, a unique language of codes and chopped-up communication that made no sense to the outside world. Marino had an ear for it, as if he'd been speaking it his entire life, could recognize his unit number no matter how preoccupied he was.

". . . eight-seven-oh-two."

It had the effect of a dog whistle, and he was suddenly alert. He got a spurt of adrenaline, as if someone had mashed down on the gas, and he grabbed the mike.

"Oh-two on the air, K," he transmitted, leaving out his complete unit number, 8702, because he preferred a degree of anonymity whenever he could get it.

"Can you call a number?"

"Ten-four."

The dispatcher gave him a number, and he wrote it down on a napkin as he drove. A New York number that looked familiar, but he couldn't place it. He called it and someone picked up on the first ring.

"Lanier," a woman said.

"Detective Marino, NYPD. The dispatcher just gave me this number. Someone there looking for me?" He cut over to Canal, heading to Eighth Avenue.

"This is Special Agent Marty Lanier with the FBI," she said. "Thanks for getting back to me."

Calling him at almost five a.m.? "What's up?" he said, realizing why the number seemed familiar.

It was the 384 exchange for the FBI's New York field office, which he'd dealt with plenty of times, but he didn't know Marty Lanier or her extension. He'd never heard of her and couldn't imagine why she was tracking him down so early in the morning. Then he remembered. Petrowski had sent photographs to the FBI, the images from the security camera that showed the man with the tattooed neck. He waited to see what Special Agent Lanier wanted.

She said, "We just got information from RTCC that's got you listed as the contact for a data search request. The incident on Central Park West."

It rattled him a little. She was calling about the suspicious package delivered to Central Park West at the very minute he was headed there to pick up Scarpetta.

"Okay," he said. "You found something?"

"Computer got a hit in one of our databases," she said.

The tattoo database, he hoped. He couldn't wait to hear about the asshole in the FedEx cap who'd left the suspicious package for the Doc.

"We can talk about it in person at our field office. Later this morning," Lanier said.

"Later? You saying you got a hit, but it can wait?"

"It's going to have to wait until NYPD deals with the item." She meant the FedEx package. It was locked in the day box at Rodman's Neck, and no one knew what was in it yet. "We don't know if we have a crime reference to One Central Park West," she added.

"Meaning you might have a crime reference to something else?"

"We'll talk when we meet."

"Then why you calling me now like it's an emergency?" It irritated him considerably that the FBI had to call him right away and then wouldn't tell him the details and was making him wait until it was convenient for them to pull together a friggin' meeting.

"I assumed you were on duty, since we just got the information," Lanier explained. "The time stamp on the data search. Looks like you're pulling a midnight."

Bureau cloak-and-dagger BS, he thought, annoyed. It wasn't about Marino pulling a midnight shift. It was about Lanier. She was calling from a 384 exchange because obviously she was at the field office, meaning something was important enough for her to have gone in to work at this hour. Something big was going on. She was explaining to him that she would decide who else should be present at the meeting—translated, Marino wasn't going to know jack shit until he got there, whenever the hell that might be. Much would depend on what the NYPD bomb squad determined about Scarpetta's package.

"So, what's your position with the Bureau?" Marino thought he should ask, since she was jerking him around and telling him what to do.

"At the moment I'm working with the Joint Bank Robbery Task Force. And I'm a principal coordinator for the National Center for the Analysis of Violent Crime," she answered.

Joint Bank Robbery was a catchall task force, the oldest task force in the United States, comprising NYPD investigators and FBI agents who handled everything from bank robberies, kidnappings, and stalking to crimes on the high seas, such as sexual assaults on cruise ships and piracy. Marino wasn't necessarily surprised the JBR Task Force might be involved in a case that the Feds had an interest in, but the National Center for the Analysis of Violent Crime? In other words, a coordinator with the Behavioral Analysis Unit. In other words, Quantico. Marino wasn't expecting that, holy shit. SA Marty Lanier was what he still thought of as a profiler, the same thing Benton used to be. Marino understood a little better why she was being closemouthed over the phone. The FBI was onto something serious.

"You suggesting Quantico's gotten involved in the Central Park West situation?" Marino pushed his luck.

"I'll see you later today" was her answer and how she ended the conversation.

Marino was just a few minutes away from Scarpetta's building, in the low forties on Eighth Avenue, in the heart of Times Square. Illuminated billboards, vinyl banners, signage, and brilliant multicolored data-display screens reminded him of RTCC, and yellow cabs were rolling, but not many people were out, and Marino wondered what the day would bring. Would the public really panic and stay out of taxis because of Carley Crispin and her leak? He seriously doubted it. This was New York. The worst panic he'd ever observed here wasn't even 9/11, it was the economy. It was what he'd been seeing for months, the terrorism on Wall Street, the disastrous financial losses and a chronic fear that it was only going to get worse. Not having two dimes to rub together was a lot more likely to do you in than some serial killer supposedly cruising around in a yellow cab. If you were friggin' broke, you couldn't afford a friggin' cab and were a hell of a lot more worried about ending up a street person than getting whacked while jogging.

At Columbus Circle, the CNN marquee was on to other news that had nothing to do with Scarpetta and *The Crispin*

Report, something about Pete Townshend and The Who on the ticker, bright red against the night. Maybe the FBI was calling an emergency meeting because Scarpetta supposedly had bashed the Bureau in public, had called profiling antiquated. Someone of her status making a statement like that was taken seriously and not easily dismissed. Even if she really hadn't said it or had said it off the record but it was out of context and not what she meant.

Marino wondered what she'd really said and meant, then decided whatever the FBI was up to, it probably had not a damn thing to do with Bureau-bashing, which wasn't new or unusual, anyway. Cops in particular bashed the Bureau all the time. Mostly out of jealousy. If cops really believed the criticisms they slung, they wouldn't beg, borrow, and steal to get on task forces with the FBI or attend special training courses at Quantico. Something else had happened that was unrelated to bad publicity. He kept coming back to the same thing: It had to do with the tattoo, with the man in the FedEx cap. It was going to make Marino crazy that he had to wait for the details.

He parked behind a yellow SUV taxi, a hybrid, the newest thing, New York going green. He got out of his dirty, gas-guzzling Crown Vic and walked into the lobby, and Scarpetta was sitting on the couch, in a heavy shearling coat and boots, dressed for a morning that she assumed would include the range at Rodman's Neck, which was on the water and always windy as hell and cold. Over her shoulder was the black nylon kit bag she routinely carried when she was working, a lot of essentials organized inside. Gloves, shoe covers, coveralls, a digital camera, basic medical supplies. Their lives were like that, never knowing where they might end up or what they were going to find and always feeling like they had to be ready. She had a look on her face, distracted, tired, but smiled the way she did when she was appreciative. She was grateful he'd come to help her out, and that made him feel good. She got up and met him at the door and they walked out together, down the steps, to the dark street.

"Where's Benton?" Marino asked, opening the passenger door. "Be careful of your coat. The car's dirty as hell. All the salt and crap on the road from the snow, no way to keep on top of it. Not like Florida, South Carolina, Virginia. Try finding a car wash, and what good does it do? One block later, it looks like I drove through a chalk quarry." He was self-conscious again.

"I told him not to come," Scarpetta said. "Not that he can help us with my BlackBerry, but not to Rodman's Neck, either. There's a lot going on. He's got things to do."

Marino didn't ask her why or what. He didn't let on how happy he was not to have Benton around, not to be subjected to him and his attitudes. Benton had never been friendly to Marino, not the entire twenty years they'd known each other. They'd never been pals, never socialized, never done a damn thing together. It wasn't like knowing another cop, never had been. Benton didn't fish or bowl or give a rat's ass about motorcycles or trucks; the two of them had never hung out in the bar, trading stories about cases or women, the way guys talk. Truth was, the only thing Marino and Benton had in common was the Doc, and he tried to remember the last time he'd been alone with her. It felt really good to have her to himself. He was going to take care of her problem. Carley Crispin was toast.

Scarpetta said the same thing she always did: "Fasten your seat belt."

He started the car and pulled on his shoulder harness, as much as he hated to strap himself in. One of those old habits, like smoking and drinking, that he might break but never forget or feel particularly good about. So what if he was better off. He couldn't stand wearing a seat belt, and that wasn't going to change, and he just hoped like hell he was never in a situation when he needed to bolt out of his car and oops, oh shit, still had the seat belt on and ended up dead. He wondered if that same special unit was still roaming around doing random checks on cops, out to nail someone's ass for not having his belt on and get him grounded for six months.

"Come on. You must know of situations where these damn things end up killing someone," he said to Scarpetta, who would know the honest answer if anyone did.

"What things?" she said as he pulled away from her building.

"Seat belts. You know, these vehicular straitjackets you're always preaching about, Dr. Worst-Case Scenario. All those years in Richmond? They didn't have cops-turned-snitches driving around, looking to get the rest of us in trouble for not having our seat belts on. No one cared, and I never wore one. Not once. Not even when you used to get in my car and start your nagging about all the different ways I might get hurt or die if I didn't watch out." It put him in a good mood to remember those days, to be driving with her, without Benton. "Remember that time I got in the shoot-out in Gilpin Court? If I hadn't been able to bail out of the car, guess what would have happened?"

"It wasn't your reflex to disengage a seat belt because you had a terrible habit," she said. "And as I recall, you were chasing that particular drug dealer and not the other way around. I don't believe your seat belt was a factor, whether it was fastened or not."

"Historically, cops don't wear seat belts for a reason," he replied. "Going back to the beginning of time, cops don't wear them. You don't wear your belt and you never have the interior light on. Why? Because the only thing worse than having some drone open fire on you while you're belted inside your car is to be belted in and have the interior light on so the asshole can see you better."

"I can give you statistics," Scarpetta said, looking out her window and kind of quiet. "All the dead people who might have been okay if they'd had their belts on. Not sure I can give you a single example of someone who ended up dead because he did have his belt on."

"What about if you go off an embankment and end up in the river?"

"You don't have your belt on, maybe your head hits the windshield. Knocking yourself out isn't very helpful if you're submerged in water. Benton just got a phone call from the FBI," she said. "I don't guess anybody might tell me what's going on."

"Maybe he knows, because I sure as hell don't."

"You heard from them?" she asked, and Marino sensed she was sad.

"Not even fifteen minutes ago while I was on my way to pick you up. Did Benton say anything? Was it a profiler named Lanier?" Marino turned onto Park Avenue and was reminded of Hannah Starr.

The Starrs' mansion wasn't too far from where he and Scarpetta were headed.

"He was on the phone when I left," she said. "All I know is he was talking to the FBI."

"So he didn't say nothing about what she wanted." He assumed it was Marty Lanier, that she'd called Benton after talking with Marino.

"I don't know the answer. He was on the phone when I left," she repeated.

She didn't want to talk about something. Maybe she and Benton had been arguing, or maybe she was edgy and down in the dumps because of her stolen BlackBerry.

"I'm not connecting the dots here," Marino went on, couldn't help himself. "Why would they call Benton? Marty Lanier's an FBI profiler. Why does she need to call a former FBI profiler?"

It gave him secret pleasure to say it out loud, to put a dent in Benton's shiny armor. He wasn't FBI anymore. He wasn't even a cop.

"Benton's been involved in a number of cases that have to do with the FBI." She wasn't defensive about it and was talking quietly and somberly. "But I don't know."

"You're saying the FBI asks his advice?"

"On occasion."

Marino was disappointed to hear it. "That's surprising. I thought him and the Bureau hated each other." As if the Bureau was a person.

"He isn't consulted because he's former FBI. He's consulted because he's a respected forensic psychologist, has been very active in offering his assessments and opinions in criminal cases in New York and elsewhere."

She was looking at Marino from the darkness of the passenger seat, the torn headliner sagging just inches from her hair. He should just order foam-backed cloth and high-temperature glue and replace the damn thing.

"All I can say for sure is it has to do with the tattoo." He retreated from the subject of Benton. "While I was at RTCC, I suggested we cast a wider net and search more than the NYPD data warehouse because we got zip on the tattoo, the skulls, the coffin, on that guy's neck. We did get something on Dodie Hodge. In addition to being arrested in Detroit last month, I found a TAB summons that involved her causing a disturbance on a city bus here in New York, telling someone to FedEx himself to hell. Well, kind of interesting, since the card she sent Benton was in a FedEx envelope, and the guy with the tattoo who delivered your FedEx package had on a FedEx cap."

"Isn't that a little bit like connecting mail because it all has postage stamps?"

"I know. It's probably a stretch," Marino said. "But I can't help but wonder if there's a connection between him and this mental patient who sent you a singing Christmas card and then called you on live TV. And if so, I'm going to be worried because guess what? The guy with the tattooed neck ain't a candidate for a good citizenship award if he's in the FBI's database, right? He's in there because he's been arrested or is wanted for something somewhere, possibly a federal crime."

He slowed down, the Hotel Elysée's red awning up ahead on the left.

Scarpetta said, "I disabled my password on the BlackBerry."

It didn't sound like something she'd do. He didn't know what to say at first and realized she felt embarrassed. Scarpetta was almost never embarrassed.

"I get sick and tired of having to unlock it all the time, too." He could sympathize up to a point. "But no way I wouldn't have a password." He didn't want to sound critical, but what she'd done wasn't smart. It was hard for him to imagine she'd be that careless. "So, what's up with that?"

He started getting nervous as he thought of his own communications with her. E-mails, voicemails, text messages, copies of reports, photographs from the Toni Darien case, including those he'd taken inside her apartment, and his commentary.

"I mean, you're saying Carley could have looked at everything on your friggin' BlackBerry? Shit," he said.

"You wear glasses," Scarpetta said. "You always have your glasses on. I wear reading glasses and don't always have them on. So imagine when I'm walking all over my building or walking outside to pick up a sandwich and need to make a call and can't see to type in the damn password."

"You can make the font bigger."

"This damn present from Lucy makes me feel ninety years old. So I disabled the password. Was it a good idea? No. But I did it."

"You tell her?" Marino said.

"I was going to do something about it. I don't know what I was going to do. I guess I was going to try to adapt, put the password back, and didn't get around to it. I didn't tell her. She can remotely delete everything on it, and I don't want her to do that yet."

"Nope. You get it back and nothing on it links the BlackBerry to you except the serial number? I can still charge Carley with a felony because the value's over two-fifty. But I'd rather make it a bigger deal than that." He'd given it a lot of thought. "If she stole data, I've got more to work with. All the shit you got on your BlackBerry?

Now maybe we make a case for identity theft, a class-C felony, maybe I show intent, make a case for her planning on selling information from the medical examiner's office, making a profit by going public with it. Maybe we give her a nervous breakdown."

"I hope she doesn't do something stupid."

Marino wasn't sure who Scarpetta meant: Carley Crispin or Lucy.

"If there's no data on your phone," he started to reiterate.

"I told her not to nuke it. To use her term."

"Then she won't," Marino said. "Lucy's an experienced investigator, a forensic computer expert who used to be a federal agent. She knows how the system works, and she probably knows you weren't using your damn password, too. Since she set up a network on a server, and don't ask me to speak her jargon about what she set up to supposedly do us a favor. Anyway, she's coming here to bring the warrant by."

Scarpetta was quiet.

"What I'm saying is she probably could check and know about your password, right?" Marino said. "She could know you quit using one, right? I'm sure she checks stuff like that, right?"

"I don't think I'm the one she's been checking on of late," Scarpetta answered.

Marino was beginning to realize why she was acting like something was eating at her, something besides her stolen smartphone or possibly a squabble with Benton. Marino didn't comment, the two of them sitting in his beat-up car in front of one of the nicest hotels in New York City, a doorman looking at them and not venturing outside, leaving them alone. Hotel staff know a cop car when they see one.

"I do think she's been checking on someone, though," Scarpetta then said. "I started thinking about it after going through the GPS log I told you about. Lucy can know where any of us are at any time, if she wants. And I don't think she's been tracking you or me. Or Benton. I don't think it's a coincidence that she suddenly decided we should have these new smartphones."

Marino had his hand on the door handle, not sure what to say. Lucy had been off, been different, been antsy and angry and a little paranoid for weeks, and he should have paid more attention. He should have made the same connection, one that was seeming more obvious the longer the suggestion lingered inside his dark, dirty car. It had never occurred to Marino that Lucy was spying on Berger. It wouldn't have entered his mind because he wouldn't want to believe it. He didn't want any reminder of what Lucy could do when she felt cornered or simply felt justified. He didn't want to remember what she'd done to his son. Rocco was born bad, was a hardened criminal who didn't give a fuck about anyone. If Lucy hadn't taken him out, someone else would have, but Marino didn't like the reminder. He almost couldn't stomach it.

"All Jaime does is work. I can't imagine why Lucy would be that paranoid, and I can't imagine what will happen if Jaime realizes . . . well, if it's true. I hope it's not. But I know Lucy, and I know something's not right and hasn't been right. And you're not saying anything, and this probably isn't the time to discuss it," Scarpetta said. "So, how are we going to handle Carley?"

"When one person works all the time, sometimes the

other person can get a little out of whack. You know, act different," Marino said. "I got the same problem with Bacardi at the moment."

"Are you tracking her with a WAAS-enabled GPS receiver you built into a smartphone that was a present?" Scarpetta said bitterly.

"I'm like you, Doc. Been tempted to throw this new phone in the damn lake," he said seriously, and he felt bad for her. "You know how crappy I type, even on a regular keyboard, and the other day I thought I was hitting the volume button and took a fucking picture of my foot."

"You wouldn't track Bacardi with a GPS even if you thought she was having an affair. That's not what people like us do, Marino."

"Yeah, well, Lucy's not us, and I'm not saying she's doing that." He didn't know it for a fact, but she probably was.

"You work for Jaime. I don't want to ask if there's any basis . . ." She didn't finish.

"There isn't. She's not doing nothing," Marino said. "I can promise you that. If she was screwing around, had something going on the side, believe me, I'd know. And it's not like she doesn't have opportunity. Believe me, I know that, too. I hope it somehow turns out Lucy's really not doing what you're saying. Spying. Jaime finds out something like that, she won't let it go."

"Would you let it go?"

"Hell, no. You got a problem with me, just say it. You think I'm doing something, just say it. But don't give me a free fancy phone so you can spy on me. That's a deal-breaker if you supposedly trust someone."

"I hope it's not a deal-breaker," she said. "How do we do this?" She meant confronting Carley.

They got out of the car.

"I'm going to show my badge to the desk and get her room number," Marino said. "Then we're going to pay her a little visit. Just don't deck her or anything. I don't want to haul you in for assault."

"I wish I could," Scarpetta said. "You have no idea."

16

There was no answer at room 412. Marino thudded the door with his big ham of a fist and started calling out Carley Crispin's name.

"NYPD," he said loudly. "Open up."

He and Scarpetta listened and waited in a hallway that was long and elegant, with crystal sconces and a brown-and-yellow carpet, what looked like a Bijar design.

"I hear the TV," Marino said, knocking with one hand and holding his tackle box field case in the other. "Kind of weird her watching TV at five in the morning. Carley?" he called out. "NYPD. Open up." He motioned for Scarpetta to move away from the door. "Forget it," he said. "She's not going to answer. So now we play hardball."

He slid his BlackBerry out of its holster and had to type in his password, and it reminded Scarpetta of the mess she'd caused and the dismal truth that she wouldn't be standing here at all if Lucy hadn't done something rather terrible. Her niece had set up a server and bought new high-tech smartphones as a ruse. She'd used and deceived everyone. Scarpetta felt awful for Berger. She felt awful for herself—

for everyone. Marino called the number on the business card
the night manager had given to him moments ago, he and
Scarpetta walking toward the elevator. Assuming Carley
was in her room and awake, they didn't want her to hear
what they were saying.

"Yeah, you're going to need to get up here," Marino said
over his phone. "Nope. And I've knocked loud enough to
wake the dead." A pause, then, "Maybe, but the TV's on.
Really. Good to know." He ended the call and said to
Scarpetta, "Apparently, they've had a problem with the TV
being played really loud and other guests complaining."

"That seems a little unusual."

"Carley hard of hearing or something?"

"Not that I'm aware of. I don't think so."

They reached the other end of the hall, near the elevator,
where he pushed open a door that had a lighted exit sign
over it.

"So if you wanted to leave the hotel without going
through the lobby, you could take the stairs. But if you
came back in you'd have to use the elevator," he said, holding the door open, looking down flights of concrete steps.
"No way you can enter the stairs from the street, for the
obvious security reasons."

"You're thinking Carley came here late last night and
left by taking the stairs because she didn't want anyone to
see her?" Scarpetta wanted to know why.

Carley, with her spike heels and fitted skirts, didn't seem
the type to take the stairs or exert herself if she could help it.

"It's not as if she was secretive about staying here,"
Scarpetta pointed out. "Which I also find curious. If you
knew she was here or simply wondered if she might be, like
I did, all you'd have to do is call and ask to be connected

to her room. Most well-known people are unregistered so they can prevent that sort of privacy violation from occurring. This hotel in particular is quite accustomed to having celebrity guests. It goes back to the twenties, is rather much a landmark for the rich and famous."

"Like, who's it famous for?" He set his field case on the carpet.

She didn't know off the top of her head, she said, except that Tennessee Williams had died in the Hotel Elysée in 1983, had choked to death on a bottle cap.

"Figures you'd know who died here," Marino said. "Carley's not all that famous, so I wouldn't add her to the Guess Who Slept or Died Here list. She's not exactly Diane Sawyer or Anna Nicole Smith, and I doubt most people recognize her when she walks down the street. I got to figure out the best way to do this."

He was thinking, leaning against the wall, still in the same clothes he'd been wearing when Scarpetta had seen him last, about six hours ago. A peppery stubble shadowed his face.

"Berger said she can have a warrant here in less than two." He glanced at his watch. "That was almost an hour ago when I talked to her. So maybe another hour and Lucy shows up with the warrant in hand. But I'm not waiting that long. We're going in. We'll find your BlackBerry and get it, and who knows what else is in there." He looked down the length of the quiet hallway. "I listed the necessary facts in the affidavit, pretty much everything and the kitchen sink. Digital storage, digital media, any hard drives, thumb drives, documents, e-mails, phone numbers, with the thought in mind Carley could have downloaded what's on your BlackBerry and printed it or copied it onto a computer. Nothing I like better than snooping on a snoop. And I'm glad Berger thought of Lucy. I don't find something, she sure as hell will."

It hadn't been Berger who had thought of Lucy. It was Scarpetta, and she was less interested in her niece's help at the moment than she was in seeing her. They needed to talk. It really couldn't wait. After Scarpetta had sent the e-mail to Berger suggesting that the paragraph be added to the addendum insuring it was legal for a civilian to assist in searching Carley's room, Scarpetta had talked to Benton. She'd sat down next to him and touched his arm, waking him up. She was going to a scene with Marino, would probably be with him much of the morning, and she had a serious personal matter to take care of, she'd explained. It was best Benton didn't come with them, she'd told him before he could suggest it, and then his cell phone had rung. The FBI calling.

The elevator door opened and the Hotel Elysée's night manager, Curtis, emerged, a middle-aged man with a mustache, dapper in a dark tweed suit. He accompanied them back down the hallway and tried the door of room 412, knocking and ringing the bell, noting the Do Not Disturb light. He commented that it was on most of the time, and he opened the door and ducked his head inside, calling out hello, hello, before stepping back into the hall-way, where Marino asked him to wait. Marino and Scarpetta walked into the room and shut the door, no sign or sound of anyone home. A wall-mounted TV was on, the channel tuned to CNN, the volume low.

"You shouldn't be in here," Marino said to her. "But because these BlackBerrys are so common, I need you to ID it. That's my story, and I'm sticking to it."

They stood just inside the door, looking around a deluxe junior suite that was lived in by someone slovenly, someone possibly antisocial and depressed who had been staying here alone, Scarpetta deduced. The queen-size bed was unmade and strewn with newspapers and men's clothing, and on the side table was a clutter of empty water bottles and coffee cups. To the left of the bed were a bowfront chest of drawers and a large window with the curtains drawn. To the right of that was the sitting area: two blue upholstered French armchairs with books and papers piled on them, a flame mahogany coffee table with a laptop and a small printer, and in plain view on top of a stack of paperwork, a touch-screen device, a BlackBerry in a smoke-gray protective rubberized case called a skin. Next to it was a plastic key card.

"That it?" Marino pointed.

"Looks like it," Scarpetta said. "Mine has a gray cover."

He opened his field case and pulled on surgical gloves, handing her a pair. "Not that we're going to do anything we shouldn't, but this is what I call exigent circumstances."

It probably wasn't. Scarpetta didn't see anything that might suggest someone was trying to escape or get rid of evidence. The evidence appeared to be right in front of her, and no one was here but the two of them.

"I don't suppose I should remind you about fruit of the poisonous tree." She referred to the inadmissibility of evidence gathered during an unreasonable search and seizure. She didn't put on the gloves.

"Naw, I have Berger to remind me. Hopefully she's gotten her favorite judge out of bed by now, Judge Fable, what a name. A legend in his own mind. I went over the whole thing, the fact portion, on speakerphone, with her and a second detective she grabbed as a witness who will swear out the warrant with her in the presence of the judge. What's known as double hearsay, a little complicated but hopefully no problem. Point is, Berger doesn't take chances with affidavits and avoids like the plague being the affiant herself. I don't care whose warrant it is or for what. Hopefully Lucy will roll up soon."

He walked over to the BlackBerry and picked it up by its rubberized edges.

"The only surface good for prints is going to be the display, which I don't want to touch without dusting it first," he decided. "Then I'll swab it for DNA."

He squatted over the field case, retrieving black powder and a carbon-fiber brush, and Scarpetta turned her attention to the men's clothing on the bed, getting close enough to detect a rancid smell, the stench of unclean flesh. She noted that the newspapers were from the past several days, *The New York Times* and *The Wall Street Journal,* and was puzzled by a black Motorola flip phone on a pillow. Scattered on the rumpled linens were a pair of dirty khaki pants, a blue-and-white oxford-cloth shirt, several pairs of socks, pale-blue pajamas, and men's undershorts that were stained yellow in the crotch. The clothing looked as if it hadn't been washed in quite a while, someone wearing the same thing day after day and never sending it out to be laundered. That someone wasn't Carley Crispin. These couldn't be her clothes, and Scarpetta saw no sign of Carley anywhere she looked in this room. Were it not for Scarpetta's BlackBerry being here, Carley wouldn't come to mind for any reason at all.

Scarpetta looked in several wastepaper baskets without digging in them or emptying them on the floor. Crumpled paper, tissues, more newspapers. She walked toward the bathroom, stopping just inside the doorway. The sink and the marble around it, including the marble floor, were covered with cut hair, clumps of gray hair of different lengths, some of it as long as three inches, some as tiny as stubble. On a washcloth were a pair of scissors, a razor, and a can of Gillette shaving cream that had been purchased at a Walgreens, and another hotel key card next to a pair of eyeglasses with old-style square black frames.

At the back of the vanity were a single toothbrush and a tube of Sensodyne toothpaste that was almost used up, and a cleaning kit, an earwax pick. A silver Siemens charger unit was open, and inside it were two Siemens Motion 700 hearing aids, flesh-colored, full-shell in-the-ear type. What Scarpetta didn't see was a remote control, and she walked back into the main room, careful not to touch or disturb anything, resisting the temptation to open the closet or drawers.

"Someone with moderate to severe hearing loss," she said as Marino lifted prints off the BlackBerry. "State-of-the-art hearing aids, background noise reduction, feedback blocker, Bluetooth. You can pair them with your cell phone. Should be a remote control somewhere." Walking around and still not seeing one. "For volume adjustment, to check on the battery power level, that sort of thing. People usually carry them in their pocket or purse. He might have it with him, but he's not wearing his hearing aids. Which doesn't make much sense, or maybe I should say it doesn't bode well."

"Got a couple good ones here," Marino said, smoothing lifting tape on a white card. "I got no idea what you're talking about. Who has hearing aids?"

"The man who shaved his head and beard in the bathroom," she said, opening the room door and stepping back into the hallway, where Curtis the manager was waiting, nervous and ill at ease.

"I don't want to ask anything I shouldn't, but I don't understand what's happening," he said to her.

"Let me ask you a few questions," Scarpetta replied. "You said you came on duty at midnight."

"I work midnight to eight a.m., that's correct," Curtis said. "I haven't seen her since I got here. I can't say I've ever seen her, as I explained a few moments ago. Ms. Crispin checked into the hotel in October, presumably because she wanted a place in the city. I believe because of her show. Not that her reason is any of my business, but that's what I've been told. Truth is, she rarely uses the room herself, and her gentleman friend doesn't like to be disturbed."

This was new information, what Scarpetta was looking for, and she said, "Do you know the name of her gentleman friend or where he might be?"

"I'm afraid I don't. I've never met him because of the hours I work."

"An older man with gray hair and a beard?"

"I've never met him and don't know what he looks like. But I'm told he's a frequent guest on her show. I don't know his name and can't tell you anything else about him except he's very private. I shouldn't say it, but a bit odd. Never speaks to anyone. He goes out and gets food and brings it back in, leaves bags of trash outside his door. Doesn't use room service or the phones or want house-keeping. No one's in the room?" He kept looking at the cracked-open door of room 412.

"Dr. Agee," Scarpetta said. "The forensic psychiatrist

Warner Agee. He's a frequent guest on Carley Crispin's show."

"I don't watch it."

"He's the only frequent guest I can think of who is almost deaf and has gray hair and a beard."

"I don't know. I only know what I just told you. We have a lot of high-profile people who stay here. We don't pry. Our only inconvenience with the man staying in this room is noise. Last night, for example, some of the other guests complained about his TV again. I do know based on notes left for me that several guests called the desk earlier in the evening and complained."

"How early in the evening?" Scarpetta asked.

"Around eight-thirty, quarter of nine."

She was at CNN at that time, and so was Carley. Warner Agee was in the hotel room with the TV turned on loud and other guests complained. The TV was still on when Scarpetta and Marino had walked in a little while ago, tuned to CNN, but the volume had been turned down. She imagined Agee sitting on the messy bed, watching *The Crispin Report* last night. If no one had complained after eight-thirty or a quarter of nine and the TV was on, he must have lowered the volume. He must have put his hearing aids on. Then what happened? He removed them and left the room after shaving his beard and head?

"If someone called asking for Carley Crispin, you wouldn't necessarily know if she's here," Scarpetta said to Curtis. "Just that she's a guest registered under her own name, which is what shows up on the computer when someone at the desk checks. She has a room in her name, but a friend has been staying in it. Apparently, Dr. Agee has. I'm making sure I understand."

"That's correct. Assuming you're right about who her friend is."

"Who is the room billed to?"

"I really shouldn't—"

"The man who was staying in that room, Dr. Agee, isn't there. I'm concerned," Scarpetta said. "For a lot of reasons, I'm very worried. You have no idea where he might be? He's hearing-impaired and doesn't appear to have his hearing aids with him."

"No. I haven't seen him leave. This is most unsettling. I suppose that explains his habit of playing the TV so loud now and then."

"He could have taken the stairs."

The manager looked down the hallway, the exit sign glowing red at the end of it. "This is most disconcerting. What is it you're hoping to find in there?" Looking back at room 412.

Scarpetta wasn't going to give him information. When Lucy showed up with the warrant, he'd get a copy of it and an idea of what they were looking for.

"And if he left by the stairs, no one would have seen him," she continued. "The doormen don't wait on the sidewalk late at night, certainly not when it's this cold. Who is the room billed to?" she again asked.

"To her, to Ms. Crispin. She came in and stopped by the desk around eleven-forty-five last night. Again, I wasn't here. I got here a few minutes later."

"Why would she stop by the desk if she'd been a guest here since October?" Scarpetta asked. "Why wouldn't she just go straight up to her room?"

"The hotel uses magnetic key cards," Curtis said. "No doubt you've had the experience of not using your card for a while and it doesn't work. Whenever new keys are made, we have a record of it on the computer, which includes the checkout date. Ms. Crispin had two new keys made for her."

This was more than a little perplexing. Scarpetta asked Curtis to think about what he was suggesting for a moment. If Carley had a friend—Dr. Warner Agee—staying in her room, she wouldn't leave him with an expired key.

"If he's not registered or paying the bill," she explained, "he wouldn't have the authority to have a new key issued if the old one expired because the checkout date encoded on it had been exceeded. He couldn't extend the reservation himself, I would assume, if he's not the one paying the bill and his name isn't even on the reservation."

"That's true."

"Then maybe we can conclude her key wasn't expired, and maybe that's not really why she had two new ones made," Scarpetta said. "Did she do anything else when she stopped by the front desk last night?"

"If you'll give me a moment. Let me see what I can find out." He got on his phone and made a call. He said to someone, "Do we know if Ms. Crispin was locked out of her room, or did she simply stop by the desk for new keys? And if so, why?" He listened. Then he said, "Of course. Yes, yes, if you would do that right now. I'm sorry to wake him up." He waited.

A call was being made to the desk clerk who would have dealt with Carley late last night, someone who probably was at home, asleep. Curtis kept apologizing to Scarpetta for making her wait. He was getting increasingly distressed, dabbing his brow with a handkerchief and clearing his throat often. Marino's voice drifted out of the room, and she could hear him walking around. He was talking to someone on the phone, but Scarpetta couldn't make out what he was saying.

The manager said, "Yes. I'm still here." Nodding his head. "I see. Well, that makes sense." He tucked his phone back in the pocket of his tweed jacket. "Ms. Crispin came in and went straight to the desk. She said she hadn't been to the hotel for a while and worried her key wouldn't work and her friend was hard of hearing. She worried he might not hear her if she knocked on the door. You see, her reservation was month-to-month, and the last time she renewed it was November twentieth, meaning the key would have expired tomorrow, Saturday. So the reservation needed to be extended if she intended to keep the room, and she went ahead and renewed it and was given two new keys."

"She extended the reservation until January twentieth?"

"Actually, she extended it only through the weekend. She said she likely would be checking out of the room on Monday the twenty-second," Curtis said, staring at the partially opened door of room 412.

Scarpetta could hear Marino moving around in there.

"He never saw her leave," Curtis added. "The person working the desk when she came in saw her take the elevator up, but he didn't see her come back down. And I certainly haven't seen her, either, as I've said."

"Then she must have taken the stairs," Scarpetta said. "Because she's not here and neither is her friend, presumably Dr. Agee. To your knowledge, when Ms. Crispin has been here in the past, has she ever taken the stairs?"

"Most people don't. I've never heard anyone mention she did. Now, some of our high-profile guests try to be very discreet about their comings and goings. But frankly, Ms. Crispin doesn't seem to be what I'd call shy."

Scarpetta thought about the hair clippings in the sink. She wondered if Carley had let herself into the room and might have seen what was in the bathroom. Or maybe Agee was still in the room when she showed up to drop off Scarpetta's stolen BlackBerry. Had they left together? Both of them taking the stairs and leaving Scarpetta's stolen BlackBerry in the room? Scarpetta envisioned Agee with his shaved face and head and no hearing aids and possibly no glasses, sneaking down the stairs with Carley Crispin. It didn't make sense. Something else had happened.

"Does your hotel's computer system keep a log for when rooms are entered and exited by using these magnetic key cards?" Scarpetta thought it unlikely but asked anyway.

"No. Most hotel systems, at least none I know of, would not have something like that. Nor do they have information on the cards."

"No names, addresses, credit card numbers. Nothing like that encoded on the cards," she said.

"Absolutely not," he replied. "Stored on the computer but not the card. The cards open the doors and that's all. We don't have logs. In fact, most hotel cards, at least ones I'm familiar with, don't even have the room number encoded on them, no information of any sort except the checkout date." He looked at room 412 and said, "I guess you didn't find anybody. Nobody's in there."

"Detective Marino is in there."

"Well, I'm glad," Curtis said, relieved. "I didn't want to think the worst about Ms. Crispin or her friend."

He meant he didn't want to think one or both of them were dead inside that room.

"You don't need to wait up here," Scarpetta told him. "We'll let you know when we're done. It may be a while."

The room was quiet when she walked back in and shut the door. Marino had turned off the TV and was standing in the bathroom, holding the BlackBerry in a gloved hand, staring at what was all over the sink and the marble countertop and the floor.

"Warner Agee," she said, pulling on the gloves Marino had given to her earlier. "That's who's been staying in this room. Probably not Carley, probably not ever. It would appear she showed up last night around eleven-forty-five, my guess, for the express purpose of giving Warner Agee my BlackBerry. I need to borrow yours. I can't use mine."

"If that's who did this, not good," Marino said, entering the password on his BlackBerry, handing it to her. "I don't like that. Shaving off all your hair and walking out with no hearing aids or glasses."

"When's the last time you checked OEM, SOD? Anything going on we should know?" She was interested in any updates from the Office of Emergency Management or the Special Operations Division.

Marino got a strange look on his face.

"I can check," she added. "But not if someone's in the hospital or been arrested or taken to a shelter or wandering the streets. I'm not going to know anything unless the person is dead and died in New York City." She entered a number on Marino's BlackBerry.

"The GW Bridge," Marino said. "No way."

"What about the bridge?" As the phone rang in the OCME's Investigations Unit.

"The guy who jumped. Around two a.m. I watched it on a live feed when I was at RTCC. About sixty maybe, bald, no beard. A police chopper was filming the whole friggin' thing."

A medicolegal investigator named Dennis answered the phone.

"Need to check on what's come in," Scarpetta said to him. "We get a case from the GW Bridge?"

"Sure did," Dennis said. "A witnessed descent. ESU tried to talk him down, but he didn't listen. They do have it all on video. The police chopper filmed it, and I said we'd want a copy."

"Good thinking. Do we have any thoughts on an ID?"

"The officer I talked to said they got nothing to go on about that. A white male, maybe in his fifties, his sixties. He had no personal effects that might tell us who he is. No wallet, no phone. You're not going to get a good visual on him. He looks pretty bad. I think the drop from where he was on the bridge is at least a couple hundred feet. You know, like a twenty-story building. You aren't going to want to show anyone his picture."

"Do me a favor," Scarpetta said. "Go downstairs and check his pockets. Check anything that might have come in with him. Take a photo and upload it to me. Call me back while you're still with the body." She gave him Marino's number. "Any other unidentified white males?"

"None that no one has a clue about. We think we know who everybody is so far. Another suicide, a shooting, a pedestrian hit, an OD, guy came in with pills still in his mouth. That's a first for me. Anybody in particular you're looking for?"

"We might have a missing psychiatrist. Warner Agee."

"Why does that sound sort of familiar? Nobody with that name, though."

"Go check the jumper and call me right away."

"He looked familiar," Marino said. "I was watching it happen while I was sitting there, and I kept thinking he looked familiar."

Scarpetta walked back in the bathroom and picked up the key card on top of the vanity, holding it by its edges.

"Let's dust it. And the one on the coffee table. We'll want to get some of the hair and his toothbrush, whatever's needed for an ID. Let's do it now while we're here."

Marino put on a fresh pair of gloves and took the key card from her. He started dusting it while she picked up her BlackBerry and checked her visual voice-mail. There were eleven new calls since she'd used her phone at seven-fifteen last night when she'd talked to Grace Darien before heading over to CNN. Since then, Mrs. Darien had tried to call three more times, between ten and eleven-thirty p.m., no doubt because of what was all over the news, thanks to Carley Crispin. The other eight new calls were listed as *Unknown,* the first one at five past ten p.m., the last one at close to midnight. Benton and Lucy. He'd tried to reach her while she was walking home with Carley, and Lucy probably had tried after hearing the news about the bomb scare. Scarpetta could tell by the green icons next to the new voicemails that none had been accessed, and they could have been. Visual voicemail didn't require the telephone subscriber's password, only the BlackBerry's password, which, of course, was disabled.

Marino changed gloves again and started on the second hotel key card as Scarpetta debated whether she should access her new voicemails remotely, borrowing his phone. She was especially interested in those left by Mrs. Darien,

whose distress would be unimaginable after hearing about
the yellow taxi and the bogus information about Hannah
Starr's hair being found in one. Mrs. Darien probably
thought what a lot of people would, that her daughter had
been killed by some predator who also had killed Hannah,
and if the police had released information sooner, maybe
Toni never would have gotten into a cab. *Don't be stupid
again,* Scarpetta thought. *Don't open any files until Lucy gets
here.* She scrolled through instant messages and e-mails.
Nothing new had been read.

She wasn't seeing any evidence that anyone had looked
at what was on her BlackBerry, but she couldn't be sure.
It wasn't possible for her to tell if someone had looked at
PowerPoint presentations or scene photographs or any
files she'd already perused. But she had no reason to
believe Warner Agee had gotten around to looking at
what was on her BlackBerry, and that was perplexing.
Certainly he would have been curious about phone
messages left by the mother of the murdered jogger.
What rich information for Carley to leak on her show.
Why hadn't he? If Carley had gotten here around eleven-
forty-five, he wasn't dead by then, assuming he was the
man on the GW Bridge some two and a half hours later.
Depression and not caring anymore, she thought. *Maybe that
was it.*

Marino was finished with the key cards, and she got
another pair of gloves from him, their used ones a tidy pile
on the floor, like magnolia petals. She took the key that had
been on the bathroom vanity and tried it on the room door.
The light flashed yellow.

"Nope," she said, and she tried the other key that had
been on the coffee table near her BlackBerry, and the light

flashed green and the lock made a promising click. "The new one," she said. "Carley left my BlackBerry and a new key for him and must have kept a key for herself."

"The only thing I can think of is he wasn't here," Marino said, using a Sharpie to label an evidence bag he neatly arranged with others inside his field case.

Scarpetta was reminded of the old days when he used to deposit evidence, a victim's personal effects, police equipment, in whatever was handy, usually walking out of a crime scene with multiple brown-paper grocery bags or recycled boxes that he would slam shut in the Bermuda Triangle of a trunk that might also have fishing gear, a bowling ball, and a case of beer in it. Somehow he'd managed to never lose or contaminate anything that mattered, and she could recall but a few instances when his lack of discipline posed so much as a minor setback in a case. Mostly he'd always been a threat to himself and anyone who depended on him.

"She shows up and stops by the desk because she doesn't have much choice. She needs to make sure she has a key that works, and she wants to change the reservation, then upstairs she lets herself in and finds him gone." Marino was trying to figure out what Carley had done when she'd gotten here last night. "Unless she decided to use the john while she was here, no reason for her to notice what was in there. All his hair, his hearing aids. Me, personally? I don't think she saw all that or him. I think she left your phone and a new key and then snuck out, taking the stairs, wanting to draw as little attention to herself as possible because she was up to no good."

"So maybe he was out for a while, wandering around." Scarpetta's mind was on Agee. "Thinking about it. Thinking about what he intended to do. Assuming he did something tragic."

Marino snapped shut his field case as his phone rang. Looking at the display, he handed it to Scarpetta. It was the office.

"Nothing in his pockets, which were inside out," Dennis said. "From the police already going through them, looking for something that might ID him, contraband, a weapon, whatever. They put a few things in a bag, some loose change and what looks like a really small remote control. Maybe something that goes to a boom box or satellite radio?"

"Does it have a manufacturer's name on it?" Scarpetta asked.

"Siemens," and Dennis spelled it.

Someone started knocking on the door, and Marino answered it as Scarpetta said to Dennis, "Can you tell if the remote's turned on?"

"Well, there's a little window, you know, a display."

Lucy walked in, handing Marino a manila envelope and taking off her black leather bomber jacket. She was dressed for flying, in cargo pants, a tactical shirt, and lightweight boots with rubber soles. Slung over her shoulder was the dark earth-colored PUSH pack, Practical Utility Shoulder Hold-all, that she carried everywhere, an off-duty bag with multiple mesh and stash pockets and pouches, and probably in one of them a gun. She slipped the pack off her shoulder, unzipped the main compartment, and slid out a MacBook.

"There should be a power button," Scarpetta said, watching Lucy open her computer as Marino directed her attention to Scarpetta's BlackBerry, the two of them talking in low voices that Scarpetta blocked out. "Press it until you think you've turned off the remote," she instructed Dennis. "Did you send a photo?"

"You should have it. I think this thing's off now."

"Then it must have been on while in his pocket," Scarpetta said.

"I'm thinking it was."

"If it had been, the police wouldn't have seen anything in the display that would identify him. You don't see messages like that until you power up whatever it is. Which is what you need to do now. Hold the button down again to power it up and see if you get any sort of system message. Similar to when you power up your phone and your number appears on the display. I think the remote you have belongs to a hearing aid. Actually, two hearing aids."

"There's no hearing aids with the body," Dennis told her. "Of course, they probably would come off when you jump from a bridge."

"Lucy?" Scarpetta said. "Can you log on to my office e-mail and open a file just sent? A photograph. You know my password. It's the same one you enabled for my BlackBerry."

Lucy placed her computer on the console under the wall-mounted TV. She started typing. An image appeared on the computer screen, and she dug into her pack and pulled out a VGA adapter and a display cable. She plugged the adapter into one of the computer's ports.

"I got something in the display. *If lost, please contact Dr. Warner Agee.*" And Dennis recited a phone number. "Now, that's something." His excited voice in Scarpetta's ear. "That makes my night. What's two-oh-two? Isn't that the area code for Washington, D.C.?"

"Call the number and let's see what happens." Scarpetta had a pretty good idea.

Lucy was plugging the cable into the side of the wall-mounted TV when the cell phone rang on the bed inside the hotel room. The ringtone was loud, Bach's Fugue in D Minor, and a gory image of a dead body on a gurney filled the flat screen on the wall.

"That's the guy on the bridge," Marino said, walking closer to the TV. "I recognize the clothes he had on."

The black body pouch was unzipped and spread wide, the shaved and beardless face covered with dark dried blood and deformed beyond recognition. The top of his head was fragmented, blood and brain extruding from the torn tissue edges of his badly lacerated scalp. His left mandible was fractured in at least one place, his jaw gaping and crooked, bared lower teeth bloody and broken and some of them gone, and his left eye was almost completely avulsed, the orb barely attached to the socket. The dark jacket he had on was torn at the shoulder seams, and his left trouser seam was split, and the jagged end of his femur protruded from torn khaki fabric like a snapped-off stick. His ankles were bent at unnatural angles.

"He landed feetfirst and then hit on his left side," Scarpetta said as the cell phone stopped ringing on the bed and Bach's Fugue quit. "I suspect his head struck some abutment on the bridge on his way down."

"He had on a watch," Dennis said over the phone. "It's in the bag with the other effects. Smashed. An old silver metal Bulova on a stretch band that stopped at two-eighteen. I guess we know his time of death. You want me to call the police with the info?"

"I have the police with me," Scarpetta said. "Thank you, Dennis. I'll take care of it from here."

She ended the call, and Marino's BlackBerry started

ringing as she was handing it back to him. He answered
and started walking around.

"Okay," he said, looking at Scarpetta. "But it will probably be just me." He got off the phone and told her, "Lobo.
He just got to Rodman's Neck. I need to head out."

"I've barely gotten started here," she said. "His cause and
manner of death aren't going to be hard. It's the rest of it."

The autopsy she needed to perform on Dr. Warner Agee
was a psychological one, and her niece might just need one,
too. Scarpetta retrieved her kit bag from where she'd left it
on the carpet against the wall, just inside the door. She
pulled out a transparent plastic evidence bag that had a
FedEx envelope and Dodie Hodge's singing Christmas card
inside. Scarpetta hadn't looked at the card. She hadn't listened to it. Benton had given it to her when she'd left
without him earlier this morning.

She said to Marino, "You probably should take this with
you."

17

The lights of Manhattan cast a murky glow along the horizon, turning it a purplish blue like a bruise as Benton traveled south on the West Side Highway, following the Hudson, headed downtown in the dark.

Between warehouses and fences he caught glimpses of the Palmolive Building, and the Colgate clock showed that the time was twenty of seven. The Statue of Liberty was in bas relief against the river and the sky, with her arm held high. Benton's driver cut over on Vestry Street, deeper into the financial district, where the symptoms of the languishing economy were palpable and depressing: restaurant windows covered with brown paper, notices of seized businesses taped to their doors, clearance sales, retail spaces and apartments for rent.

As people moved out, graffiti moved in, spray paint marring abandoned restaurants and stores and metal shutters and blank billboards. Crude, crass scrawls, most of it outrageous and nonsensical, and cartoons everywhere, some of them stunning. The stock market as Humpty Dumpty having his big fall. The U.S.S. *Economy* sinking like the

Titanic. A mural of Freddie Mac as the Grinch in a sleigh piled high with debt, his eight subprime-lender reindeer galloping over the rooftops of foreclosed homes. Uncle Sam bending over so AIG could fuck him in the ass.

Warner Agee was dead. Scarpetta hadn't informed Benton. Marino had. Just a few minutes ago he'd called, not because he knew or could even guess the role Agee had played in Benton's life. Marino simply thought Benton would want to know that the forensic psychiatrist had jumped off a bridge, and Scarpetta's BlackBerry had been found in the hotel room where he had been staying since mid-October, in time for CNN's fall season. Carley Crispin must have worked out an arrangement with Agee—or someone had. She'd bring him to New York and put him up, take care of him, in exchange for information and appearing on her show. For some reason she assumed he was worth it. Benton wondered how much she really believed or if she didn't care about the veracity of Agee's claims as long as she could get away with making a name for herself on prime-time TV. Or was Agee involved in something Benton couldn't imagine? He didn't know, didn't know anything, really, and wondered if he could ever put Warner Agee behind him and why he didn't feel relief or vindication, why he didn't feel something, feel anything at all. He was numb. The way he'd felt when he'd finally emerged from deep cover, from being presumed dead.

The first time he'd walked along the harbor in Boston, the city of his youth, where he'd been hiding in various hovels on and off for six years, and he'd realized he no longer had to be the fictitious man Tom Haviland, he hadn't felt euphoric. He hadn't felt free. He simply hadn't felt. He'd understood completely why some people get out of prison and rob the first convenience store they see so they can go right back. Benton had wanted to go back to being exiled from himself. It had gotten easy to no longer bear the burden of being Benton. He'd gotten good at feeling bad. He'd found meaning and solace in his meaningless existence and suffering even as he'd worked desperately to calculate his way out of it, plotting and planning with surgical precision to eliminate those who made his nonexistence necessary, the organized-crime cartel, the French family of Chandonne.

Spring 2003. Cool, almost cold, the wind blowing off the harbor and the sun out, and Benton was standing on Burroughs Wharf watching the Boston Fire Department's Marine Unit escort a destroyer flying a Norwegian flag, the red fireboats circling the huge shark-gray ship, the firemen in good spirits as they manned deck guns, aiming them up, a plumage of water spraying high in the air, a playful salute. *Welcome to America.* As if the welcome had been for him. *Welcome back, Benton.* But he hadn't felt welcome. Hadn't felt anything. He'd watched the spectacle and pretended it was just for him, the equivalent of pinching himself to see if he was still alive. *Are you?* he kept asking himself. *Who am I?* His mission finally executed in the dark heart of Louisiana, in the bayous and decaying mansions and the ports, where he'd used his brain and his gun to free himself from his oppressors, the Chandonnes and their henchmen, and he'd won. *It's over,* he'd told himself. *You won,* he'd said. It wasn't supposed to feel like this, he kept thinking as he'd walked along the wharf, watching the firemen having fun. His fantasies of the joy he would feel had turned phony and tasteless in the blink of an eye, like biting into a steak and realizing it was plastic, like driving along a sun-scorched highway and never getting one inch closer to a mirage.

He'd found himself terrified of returning to something that was no longer there, found himself just as afraid of having choices as he'd been of having none, just as afraid of having Kay Scarpetta as he'd been afraid of never having her again. Life and its complexities and contradictions. Nothing makes sense and everything does. Warner Agee got what he deserved and he did it to himself and it wasn't his fault and he shouldn't be blamed. A case of meningitis at the age of four had crashed his destiny as surely as if it had been rear-ended by a car and the chain reaction had continued, one collision after the next, not stopping until his body did on the pavement of a bridge. Agee was in the morgue and Benton was in a taxi, both of them sharing one thing in common at this precise point in time: They had a day of reckoning staring them in the eye, were about to meet their Maker.

The FBI occupied six floors inside the Jacob K. Javits Federal Building and Customs Courthouse in the heart of the government center, a complex of modernist glass-and-concrete architecture surrounded by the more traditional columned buildings of the U.S. Courthouse and state office buildings, and blocks away, City Hall, One Police Plaza, One Hogan Place, and the city jail. As was true of most federal centers, this one was cordoned off with yellow tape and fencing, and concrete blast barriers had been strategically placed to prevent vehicles from getting too close. The entire front plaza, a maze of curling green benches and dead grass mounds patched with snow, was inaccessible to the public. To enter the building, Benton had to get out of the taxi at Thomas Paine Park, trot across Lafayette, already busy with traffic. He turned right on Duane Street, also closed to cars, a pop-up barrier with a tire shredder and a guard booth in case you didn't notice the *Do Not Enter* signs.

The forty-one-story glass-and-granite building wasn't open yet, and he pressed a buzzer and identified himself to a uniformed FBI police officer on the other side of the side entrance's glass door. Benton said he was here to see Special Agent Marty Lanier, and after a moment of checking, the officer let him in. Benton handed over a driver's license, emptied his pockets, and walked through the x-ray scanner, having a status no more special than the immigrants who lined up along Worth Street every business day in quest of becoming U.S. citizens. Across a granite lobby was a second checkpoint, this one behind a heavy glass-and-steel door near the elevators, and he went through the same process again, only this time he was required to surrender his driver's license and in exchange was given a key and an ID.

"Any electronic devices, including phones, go in there," the officer said from his booth, pointing at a bank of small lockers above a table, as if Benton had never been here before. "Keep your ID displayed at all times, and you'll get your license back when you return your key."

"Thanks. I'll see if I can remember all that."

Benton pretended to lock up his BlackBerry, tucked it up his sleeve instead. As if there was some great threat he was going to take photographs or a video of a fucking field office. He slipped the locker key in his coat pocket, and inside the elevator he pushed the button for the twenty-eighth floor. The ID with its big V indicating he was a visitor was yet another insult, and he tucked it in his pocket, contemplating whether what he'd done was right when Marino had called about Agee's suicide.

Marino had mentioned he was on his way to Rodman's Neck and he'd see Benton later on at the meeting, whenever the FBI got around to deciding on a time. Benton, having just gotten in the cab, was on his way downtown to the very meeting Marino was talking about, and Benton had chosen to say nothing. He'd rationalized that the information wasn't his to offer. Clearly, Marty Lanier hadn't requested Marino's presence. Benton didn't know whose presence she had requested, but Marino wasn't on the list or he would be here and not on his way to the Bronx. Benton considered that when Marino had talked to Lanier earlier, maybe he'd said something to piss her off.

The elevator doors opened in front of the Executive Management Section, behind glass doors etched with the Department of Justice seal. Benton didn't see any sign of anyone, and he didn't go inside to sit down, preferring to wait in the corridor. He wandered past the typical display cases every Bureau headquarters he'd ever been in boasted—trophies from the hunt, as he thought of them. He took off his coat, looking and listening for any sign of anyone as he idly perused remnants of the Cold War. Hollowed-out rocks and coins and cigarette packs for the clandestine transfer of microfilm. Antitank weapons from the Soviet bloc.

He wandered past FBI movie posters. *"G" Men, The FBI Story, The House on 92nd Street, Thunderheart, Donnie Brasco.* A wall of them that kept on going, and he was constantly amazed by the public's insatiable interest in all things Bureau, not just here but abroad, nothing about FBI agents ever boring unless you were one. Then it was a job, except they owned you. Not just you, but they owned everyone connected to you. When the Bureau had owned him, it had owned Scarpetta, and it had allowed Warner Agee to pry them apart, to tear them from each other, to force them on separate trains bound for different death camps. Benton told himself he didn't miss his old life, didn't miss the fucking FBI. Fucking Agee had done him a fucking favor. Agee was dead. Benton felt a spike of emotion, was startled by it, as if he'd been shocked.

He turned around at the sound of quick footsteps on tile, and a woman he'd never seen before was walking toward him, brunette, compellingly pretty, nice body, mid-thirties, dressed in a soft tawny leather jacket, dark slacks, and boots. The Bureau had a habit of hiring more than its quota of good-looking, accomplished people. Not a stereotype but a fact. It was a wonder they didn't fraternize more, men and women shoulder to shoulder, day in and day out, high-caliber, a little power-drunk, and with a hefty dose of narcissism. They restrained themselves for the most part. When Benton had been an agent, affairs on the job were the exception or so deep undercover they were rarely found out.

"Benton?" She offered her hand and shook his firmly. "Marty Lanier. Security said you were on your way up and I didn't mean to make you wait. You've been here before."

It wasn't a question. She wouldn't ask if she didn't already know the answer and everything else she could possibly find out about him. He had her instantly typed. Smart as hell, hypomanic, didn't know failure. What he called an IPM. In perpetual motion. Benton had his BlackBerry in hand. Didn't care if she saw it. Was blatant about checking his messages. Don't tell him what to do. He wasn't a goddamn visitor.

"We're in the SAC conference room," she said. "We'll get coffee first."

If she was using the special agent in charge's conference room, the meeting wasn't going to be just the two of them. Her accent was shades of Brooklyn or uptown white New Orleans, hard to tell apart. Whatever her dialect, she'd worked to flatten it out.

"Detective Marino's not here," Benton said, tucking the BlackBerry in his pocket.

"He's not essential," she replied, walking.

Benton found the remark annoying.

"I spoke to him earlier, as you know, and in light of the most recent developments, he's more helpful to all involved if he's where he is." She glanced at her watch, a black rubber Luminox popular with Navy SEALs, was probably a member of the Dive Team, another Bureau Wonder Woman. "He should be there soon." She was referring to Rodman's Neck. "Sun rises at oh-seven-hundred plus fifteen or so. The package in question should be rendered safe shortly, and we'll know what it is and how to proceed."

Benton didn't say anything. He was irritated. Feeling hostile.

"I should say *if*. If there's a reason to proceed. Don't know for sure it's germane to other matters." She continued answering questions that hadn't been asked.

Classic FBI, as if new agents go to some Berlitz school of bureaucratic language to learn to double-talk like that. Tell people what you want them to know. Doesn't matter what they need. Mislead or evade or, most commonly, tell them nothing.

"Hard to know what exactly is germane to what at this moment," she added.

He felt as if a glass dome had dropped over him. No point in commenting. He wouldn't be heard. His voice wouldn't carry. He may not even have one.

"I called him originally because he was listed as the contact on a data request electronically sent by RTCC," she was saying. "A tattoo on a subject who delivered the package to your building. That much I explained to you during our brief phone conversation, Benton, and I realize what you don't know is anything else. I apologize for that but can assure you we wouldn't have summoned you out at this early hour if it wasn't a matter of extreme urgency."

They walked down a long corridor, passing interview rooms, each bare with a table and two chairs and a steel handcuff rail, everything beige and blue, what Benton called "federal blue." The blue background of every photo he'd ever seen taken of a director. The blue of Janet Reno's dresses. The blue of George W. Bush's ties. The blue of people who lie until they're blue in the face. Republican blue. There were a hell of a lot of blue Republicans in the FBI. It had always been an ultraconservative organization. No fucking wonder Lucy had been driven out, fired. Benton was an Independent. He wasn't anything anymore.

"Do you have any questions before we join the others?" Lanier stopped before a beige metal door. She entered a code on a keypad and the lock clicked.

Benton said, "I infer you're expecting me to explain to Detective Marino why he was told he should be here. And how it came to pass that we're here for your meeting and he knows nothing about it." Anger simmered.

"You have a long-standing affiliation with Peter Rocco Marino."

It sounded odd hearing someone call him by his full name. Lanier was walking briskly again. Another hallway, this one longer. Benton's anger. It was beginning to boil.

"You worked a number of cases with him in the nineties when you were the unit chief of BSU. What's now BAU," she said. "And then your career was interrupted. I assume you know the news." Not looking at him as they walked. "About Warner Agee. Didn't know him, never met him. Although he's been of interest for a while."

Benton stopped walking, the two of them alone in the middle of an endless empty corridor, a long monotony of dingy beige walls and scuffed gray tile. Depersonalized, institutionalized. Intended to be unprovocative and unimaginative and unrewarding and unforgiving. He placed his hand on her shoulder and was mildly surprised by its firmness. She was small but strong, and when she met his eyes, a question was in hers.

He said, "Don't fuck with me."

A glint in her eyes like metal, and she said, "Please take your hand off me."

He dropped it to his side and repeated what he'd said quietly and with no inflection, "Don't fuck with me, Marty."

She crossed her arms, looking at him, her stance slightly defiant but unafraid.

"You may be the new generation and have briefed yourself up to your eyeballs, but I know more about how it works than you will if you live ten lives," he said.

"No one questions your experience or your expertise, Benton."

"You know exactly what I'm saying, Marty. Don't whistle for me to come like some goddamn dog and then trot me off to a meeting so you can show everybody the tricks the Bureau trained me to perform in the dark ages. The Bureau didn't train me to do a goddamn thing. I trained myself, and you'll never begin to understand what I've been through and why. And who they are."

"'Who they are'?" She didn't seem even slightly put off by him.

"The people Warner was involved with. Because that's what you're getting at, isn't it? Like a moth, Warner took on the shadings of his environment. After a while, you can't tell entities like him from the polluted edifices they cling to. He was a parasite. An antisocial personality disorder. A sociopath. A psychopath. Whatever the hell you people call monsters these days. And just when I was starting to feel sorry for the deaf son of a bitch."

"Can't imagine your feeling sorry for him," she said. "After what he did."

It knocked Benton off guard.

"Suffice it to say, if Warner Agee hadn't lost everything, and I don't just mean financially, and decompensated beyond his ability to control himself, become desperate, in other words?" she went on. "We'd have a hell of a lot more to worry about. As for his hotel room, Carley Crispin might have been paying, but that's for a mundanely practical reason. Agee has no credit cards. They're all expired. He was destitute, and likely was reimbursing Carley in cash, or at least contributing something. I sincerely doubt she has anything to do with this, by the way. For her it was all about the show going on."

"Who did he get involved with." It wasn't a question.

"I have a feeling you know. Find the right pressure points and eventually you disable someone twice your size."

"Pressure points. As in plural. More than one," Benton said.

"We've been working on these people, not sure who they are, but we're getting closer to bringing them down. That's why you're here," she said.

"They're not gone," he said.

She resumed walking.

"I couldn't get rid of all of them," he said. "They've had years to be busy, to cause trouble, to figure out whatever they want."

"Like terrorists," she said.

"They are terrorists. Just a different sort."

"I've read the dossier on what you did get rid of in Louisiana. Impressive. Welcome back. I wouldn't have wanted to be you during all that. I wouldn't have wanted to be Scarpetta. Warner Agee wasn't completely wrong— you were in the most extreme danger imaginable. But his motives couldn't have been more wrong. He wanted you to disappear. It was worse than killing you, really." She said it as if she was describing which was more unpleasant, meningitis or the avian flu. "The rest of it was our fault, although I wasn't around back then, was a fledgling Assistant U.S. Attorney in New Orleans. Signed on with the Bureau a year later, got my master's in forensic psychology after that because I wanted to get involved with behavioral analysis, am the NCAVC coordinator for the New Orleans field office. I won't say I wasn't influenced by the situation down there or by you."

"You were there when I was. When they were. Sam Lanier. The coroner of East Baton Rouge," Benton said. "Related?"

"My uncle. I guess you could say that dealing with the darker side of life runs in the family. I know what happened down there, am actually assigned to the field office in New Orleans. Just got here a few weeks ago. I could get used to this, to New York, if I could ever find a parking place. You should never have been forced out of the Bureau, Benton. I didn't think so at the time."

"At the time?"

"Warner Agee was obvious. His evaluation of you ostensibly on behalf of the Undercover Safeguard Unit. The hotel room in Waltham, Mass. Summer of 2003 when he deemed you no longer fit for duty, suggested a desk job or teaching new agents. I'm quite aware. Again, the right thing for the wrong reason. His opinion had to be allowed, and maybe it was for the best. If you'd stayed, just what do you think you would have done?" She looked at him, stopping at the next shut door.

Benton didn't answer. She entered her code and they walked into the Criminal Division, a rabbit warren of partitioned work spaces, all of them blue.

"Still, it was the Bureau's loss, a very big loss," she said. "I suggest we get coffee in the break room, such as it is." She headed in that direction, a small room with a coffeemaker, a refrigerator, a table, and four chairs. "I won't say what goes around comes around. About Agee," she added, pouring coffee for both of them. "He suicided your career, or tried to, and now he's done the same to his."

"He started self-destructing his career long before now."

"Yes, he did."

"The one who escaped death row in Texas," Benton then said. "I didn't get rid of all of them. I didn't get rid of him, couldn't find him. Is he still alive?"

"What do you take in it?" Opening a Tupperware container of creamer, rinsing a plastic spoon in the sink.

"I didn't get rid of all of them. I didn't get him," Benton said it again.

"If we could ever get rid of all of them," Lanier said, "I'd be out a job."

The NYPD Firearms and Tactics Section on Rodman's Neck was surrounded by a ten-foot-high fence topped with coils of razor wire. Were it not for that unfriendly obstruction and the heavy weapons going off and signs everywhere that said DANGER BLASTING and KEEP AWAY and DON'T EVEN THINK OF PARKING HERE, the southernmost tip of the Bronx, jutting out like a finger into the Long Island Sound, would be, in Marino's opinion, the choicest real estate in the Northeast.

The early morning was gray and overcast, eelgrass and bare trees agitated by the wind as he rode with Lieutenant Al Lobo in a black SUV through what was to Marino a fifty-something-acre theme park of ordnance bunkers, tactical houses, maintenance shops, hangars of emergency response trucks and armored vehicles, and firing ranges indoors and out, including one for snipers. Police and FBI and officers from other agencies went through so many rounds of ammunition that metal drums of their spent brass were as common as trash barrels at a picnic. Nothing was wasted, not even police vehicles totaled in the line of duty or simply driven to death. They ended up out here, were shot and blown up, used in urban simulations, such as riots and suicide bombings.

For all its seriousness, the base had its touches of cop humor, a comic-book motif of brightly painted bombs and rockets and Howitzer rounds buried nose-first in the ground and sticking out of the strangest places. During downtime when the weather was nice, the techs and instructors cooked out in front of their Quonset huts and played cards or with the bomb dogs, or this time of year, sat around and talked while fixing anything electrical that was broken in toys donated to needy families who couldn't afford Christmas. Marino loved the Neck, and as he and Lobo drove and talked about Dodie Hodge, it occurred to Marino that this was the first time he'd ever been here when he didn't hear gunfire, semiautomatics and full auto MP5s, the noise so constant it was calming to him, like being at the movies and hearing popcorn popping.

Even the sea ducks got used to it and maybe came to expect it, eiders and old-squaws swimming by and waddling up on the shore. No wonder some of the best waterfowl shooting was in these parts. The ducks didn't recognize danger in guns going off—pretty damn unsportsmanlike, if you asked Marino. They should call it "sitting duck season," he thought, and he wondered what the constant discharging of weapons and detonations did to fishing, because he'd heard there were some pretty nice black sea bass, fluke, and winter flounder in the sound. One of these days he'd have his own boat and keep it at a marina on City Island. Maybe even live over there.

"I think we should get out here," Lobo said, stopping the Tahoe midway in the explosive demolition range, about a hundred yards downwind of where Scarpetta's package was locked up. "Keep my truck out of the way. They get upset when you accidentally blow up city property."

Marino climbed out, careful where he stepped, the ground uneven with rocks and scrap metal and frag. He was surrounded by a terrain of pits and berms built of sandbags, and rough roadbeds leading to day boxes and observation points of concrete and ballistic glass, and beyond was the water. For as far as he could see, there was water, a few boats far off in the distance and the Yacht Club on City Island. He'd heard stories about vessels coming loose from their moorings and drifting with the tides, ending up on the shores of Rodman's Neck and civilian tow services not fighting over the job of retrieving them, some saying you couldn't pay them enough. Finders keepers, it ought to be. A World Cat 290 with twin Suzuki four-strokes high and dry in sand and cobble, and Marino would brave a hailstorm of bullets and shrapnel as long as he didn't have to give it back.

Bomb tech Ann Droiden was up ahead, in a Tactical Duty Uniform, TDUs, dark-blue canvas seven-pocket pants, probably lined with flannel because of the weather, a parka, ATAC Storm Boots, and amber-tinted wraparound glasses. She didn't wear a hat, and her hands were bare as she clamped the steel tube of a PAN disrupter to a folding stand. She was something to look at but probably too young for Marino. Early thirties, he guessed.

"Try and behave yourself," Lobo said.

"I believe she should be reclassified to a weapon of mass destruction," Marino said, and he always had a hard time not openly gawking at her.

Something about her strong-featured good looks and amazingly agile hands, and he realized she reminded him a little of the Doc, of what she was like when she was that age, when they'd just started working together in Richmond. Back then, for a woman to be the chief of a statewide medical examiner's system as formidable as Virginia's was unheard of, and Scarpetta had been the first female medical examiner Marino had ever met, maybe even ever seen.

"The phone call made from the Hotel Elysée to CNN. It's just a thought I had, and I'll mention it even if it sounds far-fetched, because this lady's, what, in her fifties?" Lobo got back to the conversation they'd started in the SUV.

"What's Dodie Hodge's age got to do with her making the call?" Marino said, and he wasn't sure if he'd done the right thing, leaving Lucy and Scarpetta alone at the Hotel Elysée.

He didn't understand what was going on over there, except that Lucy sure as hell knew how to take care of herself, was probably better at it than Marino, if he was honest. She could shoot a lollipop off its stick at fifty yards. But he was tied in knots, trying to figure things out. According to Lobo, the phone call Dodie Hodge made to CNN last night traced back to the Hotel Elysée. That was the number captured by caller ID, yet Dodie Hodge wasn't a guest at the hotel. The same manager Marino had dealt with earlier said there was no record of anybody by that name ever staying there, and when Marino had provided Dodie's physical description, based on information he'd gotten when he was at RTCC, the manager had said absolutely not. He had no idea who Dodie Hodge was, and furthermore, no outgoing call had been made to *The Crispin Report*'s 1-800 number last night. In fact, no outgoing call had been made from the Hotel Elysée at the precise time—nine-forty-three—when Dodie had called CNN and was put on hold before she was put on the air.

"How much do you know about spoofing?" Lobo said, as

he and Marino walked. "You heard of buying these Spoof-Cards?"

"I've heard of it. Another pain-in-the-ass thing for us to fucking worry about," Marino said.

He wasn't allowed to use his cell phone on the range, nothing that emitted an electronic signal. He wanted to call Scarpetta and tell her about Dodie Hodge. Or maybe he should tell Lucy. Dodie Hodge might have some sort of connection to Warner Agee. He couldn't call anyone, not on the demolition range, where there was at least one possible bomb locked up in a day box.

"Tell me about it," Lobo was saying as they walked and icy wind blasted in from the Sound, through the fence and between berms. "You buy these perfectly legal SpoofCards and can make any number you want appear in the caller ID screen of whoever you're calling and trying to spoof."

Marino contemplated that if Dodie Hodge had a connection to Warner Agee, who obviously had a connection to Carley Crispin, whose show Agee had been on multiple times this fall, and Dodie had called last night, maybe the three of them were connected. This was crazy. How could Agee, Dodie, and Carley be connected, and why? It was like all those offshoots on the data wall at RTCC. You search one name and find fifty others linked to it, reminding him of Saint Henry's Catholic School, of the cluttered tree branches he'd draw on the chalkboard when he was forced to diagram compound sentences in English class.

"A couple months ago," Lobo went on, "my phone rings and there's this number on my caller ID. It's the number for the fucking switchboard at the White House. I'm like, 'What the hell is this?' So I answer and it's my ten-year-old daughter trying to disguise her voice, and she says, 'Please hold for the president.' I'm not amused. This is my cell phone I use for work, and it's like my heart stopped for a minute."

If there was one name all the offshoots had in common, Marino asked himself, what would it be?

"Turns out she got the SpoofCard and the idea from one of her friends, some boy who's maybe eleven," Lobo said. "You go on the Internet, the number for the White House is right there. It's fucked up. Like every time we figure out how to stop this bullshit, there's something else out there to defeat our efforts."

Hannah Starr, Marino decided. Except now it seemed that the one thing everybody had in common was the Doc, he worried. That's why he was walking through the explosives range in the freezing cold at dawn. He turned up the collar of his coat, his ears so cold they were about to fall off.

He said to Lobo, "Seems like if you buy a SpoofCard, you can get traced through the carrier."

Ann Droiden was walking toward the white metal day box with an empty milk jug. She held it under a tank and started filling it with water.

"If the carrier's served with a subpoena, maybe you'll get lucky, but that's assuming you've got a suspect. You got no suspect, how the hell do you know who the fake number traces back to, especially if they don't use their own phone to make the call? It's a fucking nightmare," Lobo said. "So this Dodie Hodge lady, saying she's clever, at least as clever as a ten-year-old, could have spoofed to get us off the scent. Maybe she spoofed when she called *The Crispin Report* last night, and it looks like she's at the Hotel Elysée when, truth is, we don't know where the hell she is. Or maybe she was setting up this Agee guy you were telling me about. Maybe she didn't like him, like a really bad practical joke. But the other thought is what makes you so sure she sent the singing card, for example?"

"She's singing on it."

"Who says?"

"Benton. He should know, since he spent time with her in the bin."

"Doesn't mean she's the one who sent the card. We should be careful of assumptions, that's all. Shit, it's cold. And nothing we do out here lets me wear gloves that are worth a damn."

Droiden set the jug of water on the ground near a big black hard case that held twelve-gauge shotgun cartridges and components of the PAN disrupter, the water cannon. Nearby was a portable metal magazine and several Roco gear and equipment bags, big ones that likely held more equipment and gear, including the bomb disposal suit and helmet she'd be putting on when she was set up and ready to retrieve the package from the day box. She squatted by the open case and picked up a black plastic plug, a screw-on breech, and one of the shotgun cartridges. A diesel engine sounded in the distance—an EMS ambulance showing up, parking on the dirt road, at the ready in case all didn't go according to plan.

"Again," Lobo said, removing a bag from his shoulder, "I'm not saying this Dodie lady used a SpoofCard. I'm just saying that caller ID doesn't mean shit anymore."

"Don't talk to me about it," Droiden said, plugging one end of the tubing. "My boyfriend got spoofed, some asshole he has a restraining order against. She calls him and the caller ID says it's his mother."

"That's too bad," Marino said. He didn't know she had a boyfriend.

"It's like these anonymizers people use so you can't trace their IP, or you do and think they're in another country when they're your next-door neighbor." She inserted the shotgun round into the breech, which she screwed to the plugged back end of the tube. "You can't be sure anything's what it appears to be when it's got to do with phones, with computers. Perps wear cloaks of invisibility. You don't know who's doing what, and even if you do, it's hard to prove. Nobody's accountable anymore."

Lobo had removed a laptop computer from his bag and was turning it on. Marino wondered why a computer was okay out here and not his phone. He didn't ask. He was in overload, like his engine might overheat any minute.

"So I don't need a suit on or anything," he said. "You sure there's nothing in there like anthrax or some chemical that's going to give me cancer?"

"Before I put the package in the day box last night," Droiden said, "I checked it out soup to nuts with the FH Forty, the Twenty-two-hundred R, and APD Two thousand, a high-range ion chamber, a gas monitor, every detector you can think of, in part because of the target."

She meant Scarpetta.

"It was taken seriously, to say the least," Droiden went on. "Not that we're lax out here on any given day, but this is considered special circumstances. Negative for biological agents, at least any known ones like anthrax, ricin, botulism, SEB, and plague. Negative for alpha, beta, gamma, and neutron radiation. No CW agents or irritants. No nerve or blister agents—again, no known ones. No toxic gases, such as ammonia, chlorine, hydrogen sulfide, sulfur dioxide.

No alarms went off, but whatever's in the package is off-gassing something. I could smell it."

"Probably what's in the vial-shaped thing," Marino said.

"Something with a foul smell, a fetid, tarry-type odor," she answered. "Don't know what it is. None of the detectors could identify it."

"At least we know what it's not," Lobo said. "Which is somewhat reassuring. Hopefully it's nothing to worry about."

"Maybe picking up on a contaminant out here?" Marino was thinking about all the different devices that were rendered safe on the range. Decades of bombs and pyrotechnics being shot with water cannons and detonated.

"Like we're saying, we didn't get a reading," Droiden said. "In addition, we account for potential interference vapors that can cause false positives. Devices we've rendered safe out here that might off-gas anything from gasoline to diesel fuel to household bleach? There wouldn't be enough of an interferent vapor at this point for detectable levels. Nothing false-alarmed last night, although cold temperatures aren't ideal, the LCDs sure as hell don't like the weather out here, and we weren't going to carry the frag bag inside any sort of shelter when we don't know what type of device we might be dealing with."

She tilted the PAN disrupter, pointing it almost straight up, and filled it with water, then plugged the front end with a red cap. She leveled the steel tube and tightened the clamps. Reaching back into the open case, she picked out a laser aiming device that slid over the tip of the barrel like a bore sight. Lobo set the laptop on a sandbag, an x-ray of Scarpetta's package on the screen. Droiden would use the image to map a targeting grid that she would align with the laser sight so she could take out the power source—button batteries—with the water cannon.

"Maybe you could hand me the shock tube," she said to Lobo.

He opened the portable magazine, a midsize Army green steel box, and lifted out a reel of what looked like bright yellow plastic-coated twelve-gauge wire, a low-strength det-cord that was safe to handle without fire-retardant clothing or an EOD bomb disposal suit. The inside of the tubing was coated with the explosive HMX, just enough to transmit the necessary shock waves to hit the firing pin inside the breech, which in turn would strike the primer of the cartridge, which would ignite the powder charge, only this shotgun cartridge was a blank. There were no projectiles. What got blasted out of the tube was about five ounces of water traveling at maybe eight hundred feet per second, enough to blow a good-size hole in Scarpetta's FedEx box and take out the power source.

Droiden unrolled several yards of the tube and attached one end to a connector on the breech and the other end to a firing device, what looked like a small green remote control with two buttons, one red, one black. Unzipping two of the Roco bags, she pulled out the green jacket, trousers, and helmet of the bomb suit.

"Now, if you boys will excuse me," she said. "I need to get dressed."

18

Warner Agee's laptop, a Dell several years old, was connected to a small printer, both devices plugged into the wall. Cords ran across the carpet, printouts piled and scattered, making it hard to walk without tripping or stepping on paper.

Scarpetta suspected Agee had worked nonstop in the hotel room Carley apparently had rented for him. He'd been busy doing something not long before he removed his hearing aids and glasses, and left his magnetic key card on the vanity, then took the stairs and likely got into a cab, eventually headed to his death. She wondered what he'd been able to hear those last moments of his life. Probably not the ESU rescuers with their ropes and harnesses and gear, risking their own safety as they tried to reach him. Probably not the traffic on the bridge. Not even the wind. He'd turned off the volume and blurred the picture so it would be easier to descend into nothingness with no turning back. He not only didn't want to be here anymore, for some reason he'd decided it wasn't an option.

"Let's start with the most recent calls," Lucy said, turning her attention to Agee's phone, which she'd plugged into a charger she'd found in an outlet near the bed. "Doesn't look like he spent a lot of time on it. A couple calls yesterday morning, then nothing until six minutes past eight last night. After that, one more call about two and a half hours later, at ten-forty. Starting with this first one at eight-oh-six, I'll do a search and see who it comes back to." She started typing on her MacBook.

"I disabled the password on my BlackBerry." Scarpetta wasn't sure why she said it at this exact moment. It had been on her mind but not on her tongue, and now it was before them, as if it was overripe and had dropped from a tree. "I don't think Warner Agee looked at my BlackBerry. Or that Carley did, unless she got into scene photographs. From what I can tell, any calls, messages, or e-mails that have come in since I used it last haven't been opened."

"I know all about it," Lucy said.

"What's that supposed to mean?"

"Jesus. Like a million people have had this number that called Agee's cell phone. His cell phone's registered to him, by the way, with a D.C. address. A Verizon account, the cheapest low-minute plan. Doesn't appear he was much of a talker, maybe because of his hearing."

"I doubt that's why. His hearing aids are the newest technology, Bluetooth-enabled," Scarpetta said.

She could look around the hotel room and deduce that Warner Agee had spent most of his time in a claustrophobic world that often was silent. She doubted he had friends, and if he had family, he wasn't close to them. She wondered if his only human contact, his only emotional connection in the end, was the woman who had become his self-serving patron: Carley. She gave him work and a roof over his head, it seemed, and now and then showed up with a new key. Scarpetta suspected Agee had no money, and she wondered what had happened to his wallet. Maybe he'd gotten rid of it after leaving the room last night. Maybe he hadn't wanted to be identified but had overlooked the Siemens remote control, which most likely he kept in his pocket as a matter of routine. He may have forgotten about the message on it that would lead someone like Scarpetta directly to him.

"What do you mean, *you know all about it?*" she again asked Lucy. "What do you know? You already knew that no one had gotten into my BlackBerry?"

"Hold on. I'm going to try something." Lucy got on her own BlackBerry and dialed a number she was looking at on her MacBook. She listened for a long moment before ending the call and saying, "It just rang and rang. Bet you it's a disposable phone, explaining why so many different people have had that same number and why voicemail hasn't been set up." She was looking at Agee's cell phone again. "I did some checking," she then said. "When you e-mailed me and I told you I wanted to nuke your BlackBerry and you said no, I checked right then and saw that new messages, e-mails, voicemails hadn't been accessed. That's one reason I didn't just go on and nuke it anyway, regardless of your instructions. Why did you disable the password?"

"How long have you known?"

"Not until you told me you'd lost your phone."

"I didn't lose it."

Lucy was having a hard time looking her in the eye. Not because she was feeling remorse, because that wasn't what

Scarpetta sensed. Her niece was emotional. She was scared, her eyes a dark green like the deep water of a quarry, and her face was unusually defeated and spent. She looked thin, as if she hadn't been working out as much, her trademark strength and fitness at a low ebb. In the course of the several weeks since Scarpetta had seen her last, Lucy had gone from looking fifteen to forty.

Lucy tapped keys and said, "Now I'm looking at this second number that called his phone last night."

"The call made at ten-forty?"

"Right. Comes back as unlisted and unpublished, but the person didn't bother blocking caller ID, which is why it's showing up on Agee's cell phone. Whoever this is, it's the last person he talked to. At least that we know of. So he was still alive and well at ten-forty."

"Alive, but I doubt he was well."

Lucy typed some more on the MacBook and was rolling through files on the Dell laptop as well, able to do about ten tasks at once. She could do almost anything except have a truthful conversation about what was really important in her life.

"He was smart enough to delete his history and empty his cache," she said. "In case you're interested. Won't stop me from finding what he thought he'd gotten rid of. Carley Crispin," she then said. "The unlisted number that called him at ten-forty. It was her. It was Carley. That's her cell phone, an AT&T account. She called Agee, and they talked for about four minutes. Must not have been a good conversation if a couple hours later he jumped off a bridge."

At ten-forty last night Scarpetta was still at CNN, in the makeup room, talking to Alex Bachta with the door shut.

She tried to pinpoint exactly when she'd left. Maybe ten or fifteen minutes later, and she had a sinking feeling that what she'd feared was true. Carley had been eavesdropping and had heard enough to realize what lay ahead. Scarpetta was going to take her place as a talk show host, or that was what Carley would have assumed, at any rate, because it would never occur to her that someone might say no to the sort of offer Alex had made. Carley was going to be let go, and she must have been devastated. Even if she'd hovered outside the door long enough to overhear Scarpetta resisting the notion and voicing why she thought it was a bad idea, Carley had to accept an inevitability she'd fought like hell to prevent: At the age of sixty-one, she was going to have to look for another job, and the odds were almost impossible that she'd find one with a network as well respected and powerful as CNN. In this economy and at her age, she might find nothing.

"Then what?" Scarpetta asked, after describing to Lucy what had happened last night after Carley's show. "Did she step away from the door, perhaps return to her dressing room and make a quick call to Warner? What did she say to him?"

"Maybe that his services were no longer going to be needed," Lucy said. "She loses her show, what would she need him for anymore? If she's not on the air, he wasn't going to be, either."

"Since when do talk-show hosts provide long-term hotel rooms for guests." Scarpetta got around to that. "Especially these days, when everybody is cutting back."

"I don't know."

"I sincerely doubt CNN was reimbursing her. Does she have money? This hotel for two months would cost a fortune, no matter how reasonable a rate they gave her. Why would she spend that kind of money? Why not put him somewhere else, rent him something infinitely less expensive?"

"Don't know."

"Maybe it had to do with the location," Scarpetta considered. "Maybe someone else was involved and funding this. Or him. Someone we know nothing about."

Lucy didn't seem to be listening.

"And if she called at ten-forty to tell Warner he was fired and about to get evicted, then why would she go to the trouble to drop off my BlackBerry?" Scarpetta continued thinking out loud. "Why not just tell him to pack his things and leave the hotel the next day? If she planned to kick him out, why would she bring him my phone? Why would he feel obliged to help her with anything further if she was about to cut him off? Possible Agee was supposed to give my BlackBerry to someone else?"

Lucy didn't answer.

"Why is my BlackBerry so important?"

It was as if Lucy didn't hear a word Scarpetta said.

"Except that it's a conduit to me. To everything about me. To everything about all of us, really," she answered her own question.

Lucy was silent. She wasn't eager to talk further about the stolen BlackBerry, because she didn't want to talk about why she'd bought it to begin with.

"It even knows where I am because of the GPS receiver you put in it," Scarpetta added. "As long as I had it with me, of course. Although I don't think you were particularly worried about where I've been or might be."

Scarpetta started going through computer printouts on

the coffee table, what looked like hundreds of Internet searches for news stories, editorials, references, blogs pertaining to the Hannah Starr case. But it was difficult to concentrate, the most important question a barrier as solid as a concrete wall.

"You don't want to discuss it or own up to what you've done," said Scarpetta.

"Discuss what?" Not looking up.

"Well, we're going to discuss it." As Scarpetta skimmed more news stories that Agee had printed, research he no doubt had been doing for Carley. "You give me a gift I didn't ask for or frankly want, this extremely sophisticated smartphone, and suddenly my entire existence is on some network you created and I'm held hostage by a password. And then you forget to check on me? If you were really so intent on making my life better—making Marino's, Benton's, and Jaime's lives better—why wouldn't you do what any respectable system administrator would do? And check on your users to make sure their passwords are enabled, that the integrity of data is what it ought to be, that there are no breaches in security and no problems?"

"I didn't think you liked it when I checked on you." Lucy rapidly tapped keys on the Dell laptop, going into the downloads folder.

Scarpetta picked up another stack of papers and said, "How does Jaime feel about it when you check on her?"

"This past September he signed an agreement with a D.C. real-estate agency," Lucy said.

"Does Jaime know about the WAAS-enabled GPS receiver?"

"It appears he put his house on the market and moved out of it. It's listed as unfurnished." Lucy went back to her

MacBook and typed something else. "Let's just see if it ever sold."

"Are you going to talk to me?" Scarpetta said.

"Not only hasn't sold, it's a preforeclosure. A condo, two bedrooms, two baths, on Fourteenth Street, not too far from Dupont Circle. Started out at six hundred and twenty thousand, is now a little over five. So, maybe one of the reasons he ended up in this room is he had nowhere else to go."

"Don't try to dodge me, please."

"When he bought it eight years ago, he got it for a little under six. Times were better for him back then, I guess."

"Did you tell Jaime about the GPS?"

"I'd say the guy's broke. Well, now he's dead," Lucy said. "So I guess it doesn't matter if the bank takes his house."

Scarpetta said, "I know about the GPS receiver you installed. But does she? Did you tell Jaime?"

"You lose everything and maybe that's what finally pushes you over the edge, or in Agee's case off the bridge," Lucy said, and her demeanor changed and her voice wavered almost imperceptibly. "What was it you used to read to me when I was a little kid? That poem by Oliver Wendell Holmes. 'The One-Hoss Shay.' *Now in building of chaises, I tell you what / there is always a weakest spot . . . And that's the reason beyond a doubt / That a chaise breaks down, but doesn't wear out . . .* When I was a little kid visiting you in Richmond, living with you on and off and wishing you would keep me. My fucking mother. This time of year, it's always the same thing. Am I coming home for Christmas. I don't hear from her for months, and then she asks me if I'm coming home for Christmas, because what she really wants is to make sure I don't forget to send her a gift.

Send her something expensive, preferably a check. Fuck her."

"What's happened to cause you to distrust Jaime?" Scarpetta said.

"You used to sit next to me in bed in that room down the hall from yours, the room that ended up being mine in your house in Windsor Farms. I loved that house. You'd read to me from a book of his poems. 'Old Ironsides,' 'The Chambered Nautilus,' 'Departed Days.' Trying to explain the facts of life and death to me. You'd say people are like that one-hoss shay. They run for a hundred years and then one day they collapse all at once into a pile of dust." Lucy talked with her hands on both keyboards, files and links opening and closing on laptop screens as she looked at anything other than her aunt. "You said it was the perfect metaphor for death, these people who ended up in your morgue with everything under the sun wrong with them, and yet they kept on going until one day it was that one thing. That one thing that probably had to do with their weakest spot."

Scarpetta said, "I assumed your weakest spot was Jaime."

Lucy said, "And I assumed it was money."

"Have you been spying on her? Is that why you got us these?" Scarpetta indicated the two BlackBerrys on the coffee table, hers and Lucy's. "Are you afraid Jaime is taking money from you? Are you afraid she's like your mother? Help me understand."

"Jaime doesn't need my money, and she doesn't need me." Steadying her voice. "Nobody has what they did. In this economy it melts like ice right before your eyes, like some elaborate ice sculpture that cost a fortune to make and turns into water and evaporates. And you wonder if it ever existed to begin with and what all the excitement was about. I don't have what I did." She hesitated, as if whatever she was thinking was almost impossible for her to say. "It's not about money. It's about something else I got involved in and then I misread everything. Maybe that's as much as I need to say. I started misreading things."

"You do a fine job misreading for someone who quotes poetry so well," Scarpetta said.

Lucy didn't answer.

"What have you misread this time?" Scarpetta was going to make her talk.

But Lucy wouldn't. For a moment the two of them were silent, keys clicking as Lucy typed and the sound of paper moving as Scarpetta sifted through printouts in her lap. She skimmed more Internet searches pertaining to Hannah Starr, and also to Carley Crispin and her failing show, news stories about what one reviewer described as Carley's free fall in the Nielsen ratings, and there were mentions of Scarpetta and the Scarpetta Factor. The only entertainment Carley had provided this season, said a blogger, was the guest appearances of CNN's senior forensic analyst, the intrepid and steely and scalpel-sharp Scarpetta, whose commentaries were dead-on. *"Kay Scarpetta cuts to the heart of the problem with her pointed remarks and is stiff competition—much too stiff—for the flaccid-minded, overblown Carley Crispin."* Scarpetta got up from her chair.

She said to her niece, "Remember one of those visits to Windsor Farms when you were angry with me and formatted everything on my computer and then took it apart? I believe you were ten and misread something I'd said or done, misinterpreted, misunderstood, overreacted, to put it mildly. Are you formatting your relationship with Jaime and in the process of completely dismantling it, and have you asked her if it's merited?"

She opened her kit bag and got out another pair of gloves. Walking past Warner Agee's messy, clothes-strewn bed, she began looking in drawers in the bowfront dresser.

"What has Jaime done that you've possibly misread?" Scarpetta filled the silence.

More men's clothing, none of it folded. Undershorts, undershirts, socks, pajamas, handkerchiefs, and small velvet boxes of cuff links, some of them antique, none expensive. In another drawer were sweatshirts, T-shirts with logos. The FBI Academy, various FBI field offices, the Hostage Rescue and National Response teams, all old and faded and representing memberships Agee had coveted and would never have. She didn't have to know Warner Agee to figure out that what drove him was a desperate need for validation and an unflagging belief that life wasn't fair.

"What might you have misread?" Scarpetta asked again.

"It's not easy to talk about."

"At least try."

"I can't talk about her. Not with you," Lucy replied.

"Not to anyone, let's be honest."

Lucy looked at her.

"It's not easy for you to talk to anyone about anything deeply relevant and profoundly important," Scarpetta said. "You talk incessantly about things that ultimately are heartless, trifling, meaningless. Machines, the invisible intangibles of cyberspace and the people who inhabit these nothing places, people I call shades, who fritter away their time Twittering and chattering and blogging and blathering about nothing to no one."

The bottom dresser drawer was stuck and Scarpetta had

to work her fingers in, trying to dislodge what felt like cardboard and hard plastic.

"I'm real, and I'm here in a hotel room last inhabited by a man who is in a broken heap in the morgue because he decided life was no longer worth it. Talk to me, Lucy, and tell me exactly what's wrong. Tell me in the language of flesh and blood, in the language of feelings. Do you think Jaime doesn't love you anymore?"

The drawer pulled free, and crammed inside were empty Tracfone and SpoofCard packages and instruction booklets and guides, and activation cards that didn't appear to have been used because the PIN strips on the backs hadn't been scratched off. There were printed instructions for a Web-based service that allowed users who can speak but have difficulty hearing to read word-for-word captioned telephone calls in real time.

"Are the two of you not communicating?" She continued asking questions, and Lucy continued her silence.

Scarpetta dug through tangles of chargers and shiny plastic envelopes for recycling prepaid cell phones, at least five of them.

"Are you fighting?"

She returned to the bed and began digging through the dirty clothing on it, pulling back the linens.

"Are you not having sex?"

"Jesus," Lucy blurted out. "For God's sake, you're my aunt."

Scarpetta started opening bedside drawers and said, "I put my hands on naked dead bodies all day long, and having sex with Benton is how we exchange energy and empower each other and belong to each other and communicate with each other and are reminded we exist." Journal articles, more printouts in the drawers, nothing else, still no Trac-fone. "Sometimes we fight. We fought last night."

She got on the floor to look under furniture.

"I used to bathe you and tend to your wounds and listen to your tantrums and fix the messes you made, or at least snatch you out of them one way or other, and sometimes I cried in my goddamn room, you drove me so wild," Scarpetta said. "I've met your long string of partners and dalliances and have quite a good idea exactly what you do with them in bed because we're all the same, have basically the same body parts and use them similarly, and I dare say I've seen and heard a lot that even you can't imagine."

She got up, not seeing any sign of a Tracfone anywhere.

"Why on earth would you be shy around me?" she asked. "And I'm not your mother. Thank God I'm not that wretched sister of mine, who practically gave you away, only I wish she had. I wish she had given you to me and I'd had you all the time from day one. I'm your aunt. I'm your friend. At this stage in our lives, we're colleagues. You can talk to me. Do you love Jaime?"

Lucy's hands were quiet in her lap, and she was staring down at them.

"Do you love her?"

Scarpetta started emptying wastepaper baskets, digging through balled-up paper.

"What are you doing?" Lucy finally asked.

"He had Tracfones, maybe as many as five. Possibly purchased after he moved in two months ago. Just bar codes, no stickers that might say where he bought them. Probably was using them in conjunction with SpoofCards to disguise and fake caller ID. Do you love Jaime?"

"How much time on the Tracfones?"

"Each came with sixty minutes' airtime and/or ninety days' service."

"So, you pick it up in an airport kiosk, a tourist shop, a Target, a Walmart, and pay cash. When you've used up your sixty minutes, instead of adding more airtime, which usually requires a credit card, you toss the phone and get a new one. About a month ago, Jaime stopped wanting me to stay over." Lucy's face was turning red. "First it was one or two nights a week, then three or four. She said it's because she's so frantic with work. Obviously, if you're not sleeping with someone . . ."

"Jaime's always been frantic with work. People like us are always frantic with work," Scarpetta said.

She opened the closet, noting a small wall safe. It was empty, the door open wide.

"That's worse, isn't it? That's the fucking point, isn't it?" Lucy looked miserable, her eyes angry and hurt. "That means it's different for her, doesn't it? You still want Benton no matter how busy you are, even after twenty years, but Jaime doesn't want me and we've barely been together one. So it's not about being fucking busy."

"I agree. It's about something else."

Scarpetta walked her gloved fingers through clothes that had been stylish in the eighties and nineties, pin-striped three-piece and double-breasted suits with wide lapels and pocket kerchiefs, and French-cuffed white shirts that brought to mind caricatures of gangsters during the days of J. Edgar Hoover's FBI. Draped over hangers were five striped ties, and looped around another hanger were two reversible belts—one stitched, the other a crocodile print—that were compatible with the brown and black Florsheim wing-tip dress shoes on the floor.

She said, "When you and I were trying to track my missing BlackBerry, it became patently clear what your WAAS GPS receiver can do. It's why we're sitting in this room. These nights when Jaime has been away from you and you've been tracking her remotely? Did you get information that was helpful?"

At the back of the closet, pushed against the wall, was a very large black hard-sided suitcase, badly scuffed and scratched, a tangle of torn luggage tags and their strings still wrapped around the handle.

"She hasn't gone anywhere," Lucy said. "Was working at the office late and at home. Unless she didn't take her BlackBerry with her, and it doesn't mean someone didn't come to her apartment or she doesn't have something going on with someone in her office."

"Maybe you can hack into the provider that supplies the security cameras for her apartment building, for the district attorney's office, for all of One Hogan Place. Will that be next? Or just install a few cameras in her office, in her conference room, in her penthouse, and spy on her that way. Please don't tell me you did that already."

Scarpetta was wrestling the suitcase out of the closet, noting how heavy it was.

"Jesus Christ. No."

"This isn't about Jaime. It's about you." Scarpetta pressed the clasps on the suitcase, and they sprung open with loud snaps.

The crack of a shotgun blast.

Marino and Lobo took off their hearing protectors and stepped out from behind several tons of concrete blocks and ballistic glass, about three hundred feet up-range from Droiden in her bomb suit. She walked to the pit where Scarpetta's FedEx box had just been shot and knelt to examine what she had defeated. Her helmet turned toward Marino and Lobo, and she gave them a thumbs-up, her bare hand small and pale surrounded by dark-green padding that made her look twice her normal size.

"Like opening a box of Cracker Jacks," Marino said. "Can't wait to see the prize."

He hoped whatever was in Scarpetta's FedEx box was worth all the trouble, and he hoped it wasn't. His career was a chronic conflict he didn't talk about, didn't even like to admit to himself what he really felt. For an investigation to be rewarding meant there needed to be real danger or damage, but what decent human being would hope for such a thing?

"What we got?" Lobo asked her.

Another tech was helping her take off the bomb suit. Droiden had an unpleasant expression on her face as she put her coat back on, zipping it up.

"Something that stinks. That same nasty smell. Not a hoax device, but not like anything I've ever seen. Or smelled, for that matter," she said to Lobo and Marino as the other tech busied himself with the bomb suit, packing it up. "Three AG-ten-type button batteries and aerial repeaters, pyrotechnics. Some kind of greeting card with a voodoo-looking doll attached to the top. A stink bomb."

The FedEx box had been blasted wide open. It was a mass of soggy shredded cardboard, broken glass, the remnants of a small white cloth doll, and what looked like dog fur confined within a berm of dirty sandbags. A recordable voice module not much bigger than a credit card had been blown into several pieces, the mangled button batteries nearby, and as Marino got closer he got a whiff of what Droiden was talking about.

"Smells like a mixture of asphalt, rotten eggs, and dog shit," he said. "What the hell is it?"

"It's whatever was in the vial, a glass vial." Droiden opened a black Roco sack and got out evidence bags, an epoxy-lined aluminum can, face masks, and nitrile gloves. "Not like anything I've ever smelled before, sort of a petroleum-type smell but not. Like tar, sulfur, and dung."

"What was it supposed to do?" Marino asked.

"I think the point was you open the box, and there's a greeting card inside with the doll attached to the top of it. When you open the card, it explodes, causing the glass vial of this stinky liquid to shatter. The voice module's power source, the batteries, was connected to three commercial repeating aerial bombs tied to an electric match, a professional pyrotechnic igniter." She pointed to what was left of three flash firecrackers attached to a thin bridge wire.

"E-matches are very sensitive to current," Lobo told Marino. "A few recorder batteries were all it took. But what someone would have had to do was alter the voice module's slide switch and recorder circuit so the battery current set off the explosion as opposed to playing a recording."

"The average person couldn't do it?" Marino said.

"The average person could definitely do it, as long as he's not stupid and follows directions."

"On the Internet," Marino thought out loud.

"Oh, yeah. You can practically build a fucking atom bomb," Lobo said.

"If the Doc had opened it?" Marino started to ask.

"Hard to say," Droiden said. "Could have injured her,

that's for sure. Maybe blown a few of her fingers off or gotten glass in her face and eyes. Disfigured her. Blinded her. For sure it would have gotten this nasty-smelling liquid all over her."

"I assume that was the point," Lobo said. "Someone wanted this liquid on her, whatever it is. And to mess her up pretty good. Let me take a look at the card."

Marino unzipped his briefcase and gave Lobo the evidence pouch Scarpetta had given to him. Lobo pulled on a pair of gloves and started looking. He opened the Christmas card, an upset Santa on the glossy cover being chased by Mrs. Claus with a rolling pin. A woman's thin, off-tune voice singing. *"Have a Ho-Dee, Do-Dee Christmas . . ."* Lobo peeled back stiff paper and slid out the voice module as the annoying tune continued, *"Stick some mistletoe where it ought to go . . ."* He disconnected the recorder from its batteries, three button batteries, AG10s no bigger than what goes inside a wristwatch. Silence, the wind gusting in from the water and through the fence. Marino couldn't feel his ears anymore, and his mouth was like the Tin Man's, in need of oil. It was getting hard to talk, he was so cold.

"A bare talking module ideal for greeting card mounting." Lobo held the recorder close to Marino to show him. "The kind used by crafters and do-it-yourselfers. Full circuit with a speaker. Ready-made slider switch for auto play, which is the key to the whole thing. The sliding contact closes the firing circuit and triggers the bomb. Ready to order. Hell of a lot easier than making one yourself."

Droiden was plucking bomb parts out of the wet, filthy mess in the pit. She got up and got closer to Marino and Lobo, holding silver, black, and dark-green plastic and metal fragments and black and copper wire in the palm of her nitrile-gloved hand. She took the intact recording module from Lobo and began making a comparison.

"Microscopic examination will confirm," she said, but her meaning was plain.

"Same kind of recorder," Marino said, cupping his big hands around hers to shield the frag from the wind and wishing he could stand there for a long time that close to her. Didn't matter if he'd been up all night and was turning into a chunk of ice, he felt suddenly warm and alert. "Jesus, that stinks. And what is that, dog fur?" With a synthetic rubber-sheathed finger, he prodded several long, coarse hairs. "Why the hell is dog fur in it?"

"Looks like the doll was stuffed with fur. It might be dog fur," she said. "I'm seeing significant similarities in the construction. The circuit board, the slider switch, the record button and microphone speaker."

Lobo was studying the Santa card. He turned it over to see what was on the back.

"Made in China. Recyclable paper. An environmentally friendly Christmas bomb. How nice," he said.

19

Scarpetta dragged the open suitcase across the floor. The twenty-nine accordion file folders inside it, bound by elastic bands and labeled with white stickers that had handwritten dates on them, covered a span of twenty-six years. Most of Warner Agee's career.

"If I talked to Jaime, what do you think she'd tell me about you?" she continued to probe.

"That's easy. I'm pathological." Lucy's anger flashed.

Sometimes her anger was so sudden and intense that Scarpetta could see it like lightning.

"I'm pissed all the time. Want to hurt someone," Lucy said.

Agee must have moved a lot of his personal belongings to the Hotel Elysée, certainly ones that were important to him. Scarpetta picked out the most recent folders and sat on the carpet at her niece's feet.

"Why do you want to hurt someone?" Scarpetta asked her.

"To get back what was fucking taken from me. To redeem myself somehow and get a second chance so I never let anybody do something like that to me again. Do you know what's terrible?" Lucy's eyes blazed. "It's terrible to decide there are some people it's okay to destroy, to kill. And to imagine it, to work it out in your mind, and not feel even a twitch or a twinge. To feel nothing. Like he probably felt." Waving her arm as if Warner Agee was in the room. "That's when the worst happens. When you feel nothing anymore. That's when you do it—you do something you can't take back. It's terrible to know you're really no different from the assholes you're chasing and trying to protect people from."

Scarpetta slipped off the elastic band of the accordion file that appeared to be the most recent one, beginning January first of this year, the end date left blank.

"You are different from them," she said.

"I can't take it back," Lucy said.

"What is it you can't take back?"

The file's six compartments were crammed with papers, receipts, a checkbook, and a brown leather wallet that was worn smooth and curved from years of being carried in a back pocket.

"I can't take back that I did it." Lucy took a deep breath, refusing to cry. "I'm a bad person."

"No, you're not," Scarpetta replied.

Agee's driver's license had expired three years ago. His MasterCard was expired. His Visa and American Express cards were expired.

"I am," Lucy said. "You know what I've done."

"You're not a bad person, and I say that knowing what you've done. Maybe not everything, but plenty," Scarpetta said. "You were FBI, ATF, and like Benton, involved in so much that you really couldn't help and you certainly couldn't talk about and likely still can't. Of course I'm aware, and I'm also aware it's been in the line of duty or for a very sound reason. Like a soldier on the front line. That's what cops are, they're soldiers who go beyond the limits of what's normal so they can somehow keep life normal for the rest of us."

She counted fourteen hundred and forty dollars cash, all twenties, as if they had come from an ATM.

Lucy then said, "Really? What about Rocco Caggiano?"

"What about his father, Pete Marino, if you hadn't?" Scarpetta didn't know the details of what had happened in Poland, and she didn't want to, but she understood the reason. "Marino would be dead," she said. "Rocco was involved in organized crime and would have killed him. It was already set in motion, and you stopped it."

She began looking at receipts for food, toiletries, and transportation, a lot of them from hotels, stores, restaurants, and taxicabs in Detroit, Michigan. Paid in cash.

"I wish I hadn't, that somebody else had. I killed his son. I've done a lot of things I can't take back," Lucy said.

"What can any of us take back? Foolish words, a phrase. People say it all the time, but in fact, we can't take anything back," Scarpetta said. "All we can do is step around the messes we've made and take responsibility and apologize and try to move on."

She was making piles on the floor, digging in the accordion files to see what Agee had thought was important enough about his life to save. She found an envelope of canceled checks. Last January he spent more than six thousand dollars on two Siemens Motion 700 hearing aids and accessories. He'd donated his old ones to Goodwill and gotten a receipt. Soon after, he'd become a subscriber to a Web-based captioning telephone service. No pay stubs or bank records that might indicate where he was getting his money. She pulled out a manila envelope labeled *IAP*. It was thick with newsletters, conference programs, journal articles, all in French, and more receipts and plane tickets. In July 2006 Agee had traveled to Paris to attend a conference at the Institut Anomalous Psychologie.

Scarpetta's conversational French wasn't good, but she could read it fairly well. She scanned a letter from a committee member of the Global Consciousness Project, thanking Agee for agreeing to participate in a discussion on the use of scientific tools in looking for structure in random data during major global events, such as 9/11. The committee member was pleased that he would be seeing Agee again and wondered if his research in psychokinesis was still encountering difficulties in replicating its findings. *The problem, of course, is the raw material of human subjects and the legal and ethical constraints,* she translated.

"Why are you thinking about killing and dying?" she asked Lucy. "Who do you want to kill, and do you wish you were dead?" she said, and again was answered by silence. "You'd better tell me, Lucy. I intend to stay in this room with you for as long as it takes."

"Hannah," Lucy answered.

"You want to kill Hannah Starr?" Scarpetta glanced up at her. "Or you did kill her or you wish she was dead?"

"I didn't kill her. I don't know if she's dead and don't care. I just want her punished. I want to do it personally."

Agee had written the committee member back in French: *While it is true that human subjects are biased and as a result tend to be unreliable, this obstacle can be sidestepped if the subjects in a study are monitored in a way that obviates self-consciousness.*

"Punished for what? What did she do to you that merits your personally taking care of it?" Scarpetta asked.

She opened another accordion file. More on parapsychology. Journal articles. Agee was fluent in French and prominent in the field of paranormal psychology, the study of the "seventh sense," the science of the supernatural. The Paris-based Institute of Anomalous Psychology paid his expenses when he traveled and may have been supplying him with stipends and other fees, including grant monies. The Lecoq Foundation that funded the IAP was keenly interested in Agee's work. There were repeated mentions of Monsieur Lecoq's eagerness to meet with Agee and discuss their "mutual passions and interests."

"She did something to you," Scarpetta continued, and it wasn't a question. Lucy must know Hannah. "What happened? Did you have an affair with her? Did you have sex with her? What?"

"I didn't have sex with her. But . . ."

"But what? You either did or you didn't. Where did you meet her?"

An abstract. *Dans cet article, publié en 2007, Warner Agee, l'un des pionniers de la recherche en parapsychologie, en particulier l'expérience de mort imminente et de sortie hors du corps . . .*

"She wanted me to try something, to start something, to make an overture," Lucy said.

"A physical one."

"She assumed everybody wanted to try something with her, to hit on her," Lucy said. "I didn't. She flirted. She flaunted it. We were alone. I thought Bobby was going to be there, but he wasn't. It was just her, and she teased me. But I didn't. The fucking bitch."

Near-death and out-of-body experiences. People who die and come back to life with paranormal gifts and abilities: healing and mind over matter. The belief that thoughts can control our own bodies and influence physical systems and objects, Scarpetta kept reading . . . *such as electronic devices, noise, and dice, in the same way that lunar phases can influence casino payout rates.*

She asked Lucy, "So, what exactly did Hannah do that was so terrible?"

"I used to tell you about my financial planner."

"The one you called the Money Man."

Agee's tax return for 2007. Income from a retirement fund but no other fees, yet it was clear from correspondence and other paperwork that he was getting money from somewhere or someone. Possibly from the Lecoq Foundation in Paris.

"Her father. Rupe Starr. He was the Money Man," Lucy said. "From the beginning, when I wasn't even twenty yet and started doing so well, he managed me. If it hadn't been for him? Well, I might have given everything away, you know, I was just so happy inventing, dreaming, coming up with ideas I could execute. Creating something out of nothing and making people want it."

2008. No trips to France. Agee was back and forth to Detroit. Where was he getting his cash?

"At one point I was doing some cool digital stuff that I thought might have promise for animation," Lucy was saying, "and this person I'd gotten to know who worked for Apple gave me Rupe's name. You probably know that he was one of the most well-respected and successful money managers on Wall Street."

"I'm wondering why you felt you could never talk to me about him or your money," Scarpetta said.

"You didn't ask."

What was in Detroit besides the failing auto industry? Scarpetta picked up Lucy's MacBook.

"I must have asked." But she couldn't think of an occasion when she had.

"You didn't," Lucy said.

Googling the Lecoq Foundation and finding nothing. Googling Monsieur Lecoq and finding only the expected multiple references to the nineteenth-century French detective novel by Émile Gaboriau. Scarpetta couldn't find any reference to a real person named Monsieur Lecoq who was a wealthy philanthropist invested in paranormal psychology.

"And you certainly don't hesitate to interrogate me about anything else that comes to your mind," Lucy continued. "But you never asked me any specifics about my finances, and if I mentioned the Money Man, you didn't even ask about him."

"Maybe I was afraid." Scarpetta reflected on that sad probability. "So I shied away from the subject by rationalizing that I shouldn't pry."

Googling Motor City Casino Hotel and the Grand Palais in Detroit. Receipts from both hotels over the past few years but no evidence Agee had ever stayed in either of them. Doing what? Gambling? Was he a gambler and got rooms comped, perhaps? How could he afford to be a gambler? A piece of paper from a personalized memo pad: *From the Desk of Freddie Maestro* and what looked like a PIN and

City Bank of Detroit and an address written with a felt-tip pen. Why was the name Freddie Maestro familiar? Was the PIN for an ATM?

"Right," Lucy said. "You can talk about dead bodies and sex but not about someone's net worth. You can dig through some dead person's pockets and dresser drawers and personal files and receipts but not ask me very basic questions about how I make my living and who I'm in business with. You never asked me," Lucy emphasized. "I figured you didn't want to know because you believed I was doing something illegal. Stealing or cheating the government, so I let it go because I sure as hell wasn't going to defend myself to you or anyone."

"I didn't know because I didn't want to know." Scarpetta's own insecurity because she'd grown up poor. "Because I wanted a level playing field." Her own inadequacy because she was powerless when she was a child and her family had no money and her father was dying. "And I can't compete with you when it comes to making money. I'm pretty good at holding on to what I've got, but I've never had the Midas touch or been in the business of business for the sake of business. I'm not particularly good at it."

"Why would you want to compete with me?"

"That's my point. I didn't. I wouldn't because I can't. Maybe I was afraid of losing your respect. And why would you respect my business acumen? If I'd been a brilliant businesswoman, I wouldn't have gone to law school, to med school, spent twelve years of postgraduate education so I could earn less than a lot of Realtors or car salesmen."

"If I was such a brilliant businesswoman we wouldn't be having this conversation," Lucy said.

Googling Michigan on the Internet. The new Las Vegas, and a lot of movies were being filmed there, the state doing what it could to pump money into its hemorrhaging economy. A forty percent tax incentive. And casinos. Michigan had a vocational school for casino dealer training, and some of the organizations supplying tuition assistance included the Veterans Administration, the United Steelworkers, and the United Auto Workers. Come home from Iraq or lose your job at GM and become a blackjack dealer.

"I fucked up. Rupe died last May, and Hannah inherited everything and completely took over. An MBA from Wharton, I'm not saying she isn't smart," Lucy said.

"She took over your account?"

"She tried."

People had to survive any way they could these days, and vices and entertainment were doing well. Movies, the food and beverage industry. Especially liquor. When people feel bad they actively seek feeling good. What did this have to do with Warner Agee? What had he gotten involved in? Scarpetta thought about Toni Darien's dice keychain and High Roller Lanes being like Vegas, as Bonnell had put it. Mrs. Darien said Toni hoped to end up in Paris or Monte Carlo someday, and her MIT-trained father, Lawrence Darien, was a gambler who might have ties to organized crime, according to Marino. Freddie Maestro, Scarpetta remembered. The name of the man who owned High Roller Lanes. He had game arcades and other businesses in Detroit, Louisiana, South Florida, and she couldn't remember where else. Ultimately, he had been Toni Darien's boss. Maybe he knew her father.

"I'd met her a few times, then we had a discussion at her place in Florida and I told her no," Lucy said. "But I let my guard down and acted on a tip she gave me. I dodged a bullet and got a knife in my back. I didn't follow my instincts, and she fucked me. She fucked me good."

"Are you bankrupt?" Scarpetta asked.

Googling *Dr. Warner Agee* with a combination of keywords. *Gambling, casinos, the gaming industry,* and *Michigan.*

"No," Lucy said. "What I have isn't the point. It's not even what I lost. She wanted to hurt me. It gave her pleasure."

"If Jaime's doing such a thorough investigation, how can she not know?"

"Who's doing the thorough investigation, Aunt Kay? It isn't her. Not the electronic information. All of that's from me."

"She has no idea you knew Hannah, that you have this conflict of interest. Because that's exactly what it is." Scarpetta talked as she went through more accordion files.

"She'd boot me out of the process, and that would be completely self-defeating and ridiculous," Lucy answered. "If anybody should be helping, it's me. And I wasn't Hannah's client. I was Rupe's. You know what's in his records? Put it this way: Nothing relevant to what Hannah did to me is going to show up. I've made sure."

Scarpetta said, "That's not right."

"What's not right is what she did."

An article Agee had published in a British journal, *Quantum Mechanics,* two years earlier. Quantum epistemology and measurement. Planck, Bohr, de Broglie, Einstein. The role of human consciousness in the collapse of the wave function. Single photon interference and causality violations in thermodynamics. The elusiveness of human consciousness.

"What the hell are you looking at?" Lucy asked.

"I'm not sure."

Scarpetta flipped pages, skimming, reading, stopping at certain sections.

She said, "Students recruited for studies. The relationship between creative and artistic ability and psi. A study done at Juilliard here in New York. Research at Duke University, Cornell, Princeton. The *Ganzfeld* experiments."

"Psychic phenomena? ESP?" Lucy had a blank expression on her face.

Scarpetta looked up at her and said, "Sensory deprivation. Why do we want to achieve a state of sensory deprivation?"

"It's inversely proportional to perception, to acquiring information," Lucy answered. "The more I deprive my senses, the more I perceive and create. That's why people meditate."

"Then why would we want the opposite for anyone? Overstimulation, in other words?" Scarpetta asked.

"We wouldn't."

"Unless you're in the casino business," Scarpetta said. "Then you would want to seek the most efficient means to overstimulate, to prevent a state of sensory deprivation. You want people to be impulse-driven, to lose their way, so you bombard the visual and auditory environment, the total field, the *Ganzfeld,* and your clients become a confused quarry without the slightest inkling of what's safe and what's not. You blind and deafen them with bright lights and noise so you can take what they've got. So you can steal."

Scarpetta couldn't stop thinking about Toni Darien and her job in a glitzy place of flashing lights and fast-moving images on huge video displays, where people were encouraged to spend money on food, liquor, and games. Bowl badly and play some more. Bowl badly and drink some more. Hap Judd's photograph was hanging in High Roller Lanes. He might have known Toni. He might know a former patient of Benton's, Dodie Hodge. Marino had said something about it to Berger during the conference call last night. Warner Agee might have known Toni Darien's boss, Freddie Maestro. These people might all know one another or be connected somehow. It was almost nine a.m., and Scarpetta was surrounded by the receipts, spent tickets, schedules, publications—the detritus of Agee's self-serving, ill-purposed life. *The soulless bastard.* She got up from the floor.

"We need to go," she said to Lucy. "The DNA Building. Now."

Security camera images of a woman and a man filled multiple flat screens inside the SAC conference room. Since last June, at least nineteen different banks had been robbed by the same pair of brazen bandits the FBI had dubbed Granny and Clyde.

"You getting all this?" Jaime Berger tilted her MacBook so Benton could see what she was looking at, another e-mail just sent.

He nodded. He knew. He was opening messages as they landed on his BlackBerry, the same messages Lucy and Marino were sending Berger, the four of them communicating almost in real time. The package bomb had been viable and the bare voice module recovered from it was the same type used in Dodie Hodge's singing card, only Benton no longer believed the card was from Dodie. She had recorded it and may have penned the address on the airbill, but Benton doubted the hostile holiday ditty was her idea. She wasn't the mastermind who'd scripted anything that had happened thus far, including her call to CNN, the point of that to upset Benton, give him a warning before the next bomb dropped. Literally.

Dodie thrived on drama, but this wasn't her drama, wasn't her show, wasn't even her modus operandi. Benton knew whose it was, he was sure he did, and he should have figured it out before, but he hadn't been looking. He had quit looking because he'd wanted to believe he didn't need to look. Unbelievable to simply say he forgot, but he had. He'd forgotten to keep his scan going, and now the monster was back, had taken on a different shape, a different form, but his personal stamp was as recognizable as a stench. Sadism. Inevitably there had to be sadism, and once it started it wasn't going to stop. Toy with the mouse and torture it within an inch of its life before mauling it to death. Dodie wasn't creative enough, wasn't experienced enough, wasn't deranged or brilliant enough to come up with such a massive and intricate plot on her own. But she was histrionic and borderline, and she'd been willing and able to audition.

At some point, Dodie Hodge had climbed into bed with organized crime. So had Warner Agee, who appeared to be responsible for unethical research projects that were connected to the international gaming industry, to casinos in the United States and abroad, particularly in France. Benton believed that Agee and Dodie were foot soldiers for

the family of Chandonne, had gotten entangled with the
worst one of them, the perversely violent surviving son,
Jean-Baptiste, who had left his DNA in the backseat of a
1991 black Mercedes used in the commission of a bank
robbery in Miami last month. What he was doing in the
car was unknown. Maybe for the thrill of it, had gone
along for the ride, or perhaps was as mundane as his being
chauffeured in the stolen Mercedes for some reason prior
to its being used as a getaway car. Jean-Baptiste certainly
would know his DNA was in the FBI's CODIS database.
He was a convicted murderer and a fugitive. He was getting careless, his compulsions taking over. If his past
history was any indication, he might be abusing alcohol
and drugs.

Three days after the Miami hit, there was another one,
the last of the known nineteen, this time in Detroit. It just
so happened to have occurred on the same day Dodie was
arrested in that city for shoplifting and disturbing the
peace, for making a scene after stuffing three Hap Judd
DVDs down the front of her pants. She was out of control.
With someone like her, it was only a matter of time and
she would have an episode, would lose it, act out, and she
did in Betty's Bookstore Café. It was bad timing, a bad
accident, and certain people had to figure out what to do
with her before she created more of an exposure for those
who couldn't afford it. Someone got her a lawyer in
Detroit, Sebastian Lafourche, originally from Baton Rouge,
Louisiana, where the Chandonnes once had very strong
ties.

Lafourche had suggested that Dodie should be evaluated
by Warner Agee. It wasn't Agee's newfound celebrity status
that was appealing, it was his involvement with organized

crime, with the Chandonne network, even if peripherally. It was like putting a gangster into the hands of a warden who was on the take from the Mob. But the plan didn't work. The DA and McLean wouldn't go for it. The network had to rethink, regroup, and take advantage of an opportunity for mischief and mayhem. Dodie goes to Belmont, and it signals the next act: The enemy has moved into a target's camp, Benton's camp, maybe indirectly Scarpetta's camp. Dodie checked into the hospital and was breathing down Benton's neck, and the toying and torturing continued while laughter rose to the rafters inside the medieval house of Chandonne.

Benton looked across the table at Marty Lanier and said, "This new computer system of yours? Is it able to link data the way RTCC can? Give us something like a decision tree, so we see conditional probabilities? So we can visualize what we're talking about? Because I'm thinking it would help clarify. The roots are deep and the branches are dense and have quite a reach, and it's important to figure out as best we can what's relevant and what isn't. For example? The bank robbery this past August first in the Bronx. That Friday morning at ten-twenty, when American Union was hit." He was looking at his notes. "Not even an hour later, Dodie Hodge was issued a TAB summons on a transit bus at Southern Boulevard and East One-forty-ninth. In other words, she was in the area, a few blocks from the bank that was robbed. Was agitated, hyped up, got into an argument."

"I don't know anything about a TAB summons," said NYPD Detective Jim O'Dell, early forties, thinning red hair, a bit of a paunch.

He sat next to his Joint Bank Robbery Task Force partner,

FBI Special Agent Andy Stockman, late thirties, black hair, plenty of it, and no paunch.

"Came up during data mining when we were looking for anything that had to do with FedEx," Benton said to O'Dell. "When Dodie was confronted by the officer because she was creating a disturbance on the bus, she told him he could FedEx his ass straight to hell, priority overnight. A link RTCC made."

"A weird thing to say. Haven't heard that one before," Stockton said.

"She likes to FedEx things. She's always in a hurry and wants the results of her dramas instantly. I don't know," Benton said impatiently, because Dodie's clichés and hyperbole weren't important and the thought of her irritated the hell out of him. "What matters is a pattern you're going to see repeatedly as we get deeper into this discussion. Impulsiveness. A leader, a Mob boss, who is compulsive and impulsive and is driven by inner forces he ultimately can't control, and the people around him aren't much better. Opposites don't always attract. Sometimes sameness does."

"Birds of a feather," Lanier said.

"Jean-Baptiste and his birds," Benton said. "Yes."

"We need a data wall like they got," O'Dell said to Berger, as if she could do something about it.

"Good luck." Stockton reached for his coffee. "We're paying for our own bottled water up here."

"Seeing the links, the connections would be helpful," Berger agreed.

"You don't know what's there until you do," Benton said. "Especially in something this complex. Because these crimes didn't just start this past June. They go back before

Nine-Eleven, more than a decade, at least my involvement in them does. Not specifically the bank robberies, but the Chandonne family, the massive crime network that used to be theirs."

"What do you mean 'used to be'?" O'Dell said. "Seems they're alive and kicking, if everything I'm hearing is true."

"They're not what they were. You can't begin to understand. Suffice it to say it's different," Benton said. "It's the bad seed taking over the family store and running it into the ground or over a cliff."

"Sounds like the last eight years in the White House," O'Dell quipped.

"The Chandonne family isn't the organized-crime family it was, not even close." Benton had no sense of humor this morning. "In the end, it's disorganized, on its way to complete chaos, with Jean-Baptiste in the driver's seat. His story can end only one way, no matter how many times he tells it or how many different characters he plays. He can keep focused for a while, and maybe he has while his intrusive and obsessional thoughts have continued, because they don't quit. Not with him, and the outcome is predictable. His intrusive thoughts win. He strays a little. He strays a lot. He strays way out of bounds. There is no limit to his destructiveness. Except it always ends in death. Somebody dies. Then multiple people do."

"Sure, we can do a predictive model, put a graph on the wall," Lanier said to O'Dell and Stockman.

"It will take a minute." Stockman started hitting keys on his laptop. "Not just the bank robberies but everything?" He glanced up at Lanier.

"It isn't just bank robberies we're talking about," she

said with a hint of impatience. "I believe that's the point Benton's making and the point of this meeting. The bank robberies are incidental. The tip of the iceberg. Or in keeping with the time of year, the angel on top of the Christmas tree. I want the whole tree."

The reference reminded Benton again of Dodie's stupid song, her breathy off-key voice wishing Scarpetta and him a Ho-Dee, Do-Dee Christmas, a greeting rife with sexually violent innuendo and a hint of what was to come. Scarpetta was going to be lynched, and Benton could shove it up his ass, or something like that, and he imagined Jean-Baptiste Chandonne's delight. Likely the card was his idea, the first taunt that soon would be followed by the next: a FedEx box containing a bomb. Not just an ordinary bomb. Marino's e-mails referred to it as *a stink bomb that might have blown the Doc's fingers off or maybe made her blind.*

"Yeah, it's ridiculous the Feds can't put in something like that," O'Dell was griping. "A damn data wall like RTCC. We need something ten times bigger than a conference room, because this isn't a decision tree, it's a damn decision forest."

Stockman told him, "I'll throw it up on a screen. Sixty inches is as big as one of RTCC's Mitsubishi cubes."

"Don't think so."

"Close enough."

"Nope. It's going to take an IMAX theater."

"Quit complaining and let's get it on the wall so we can see it."

"I'm just saying as complex as this is, we need a two-story wall, at least. All this on one flat screen? You'll have to shrink it as small as newspaper print."

O'Dell and Stockman had spent so much time

together, they tended to bicker and bitch like an old married couple. For the past six months, they'd been working the so-called Granny and Clyde pattern bank robberies in conjunction with other task forces in other FBI field offices, mostly Miami, New York, and Detroit. The Bureau had managed to keep the spree of robberies and their theories about them out of the news, and had done so deliberately and for good reason. They suspected the bandits were pawns in something much bigger and more dangerous. They were pilot fish, small carnivores that swam with sharks.

It was the sharks the Bureau wanted, and Benton was sure he knew what type and family of sharks. French sharks. Chandonne sharks. But the question was what names they were calling themselves now and how to find them. Where was Jean-Baptiste Chandonne? He would be the great white shark, the boss, the debauched head of what was left of the prominent crime family. The father, Monsieur Chandonne, was enjoying his retirement years at La Santé maximum-security prison outside Paris. Jean-Baptiste's brother, the heir apparent, was dead. Jean-Baptiste wasn't wired for a leadership role, but he was motivated, was fueled by violent fantasies and sexually obsessive thoughts, and he lusted for revenge. He could control himself for a while, keep his true inclinations contained for a discrete period of time before the fragile packaging ruptured, exposing neurons and nerves, a bundle of throbbing impulses capable of murder-ous lust and rages and cruel games more explosive than anything the bomb techs had ever rendered safe on their range. Jean-Baptiste had to be rendered safe. It had to happen right now.

Benton believed Jean-Baptiste had sent the package

bomb. He was behind it. He likely had made it. He may have watched it being delivered last night. Maim Scarpetta physically and mentally. Benton imagined Jean-Baptiste outside their building, somewhere in the dark, watching, waiting for Scarpetta to return home from CNN. Benton imagined her reluctantly walking with Carley Crispin, walking past a homeless man bundled in layers of clothing and a quilt on a bench near Columbus Circle. The mention of the homeless man had bothered Benton the first time Scarpetta had brought it up when they were talking to Lobo inside Marino's car. A feeling in Benton's gut, something unsettling. It had continued to disturb him as he'd thought about it more. Whoever was behind the bomb intended it for Scarpetta or for Benton or for both of them and would have found it difficult to resist watching her last night.

Maiming her or maiming Benton. Whoever had been maimed, it may as well have been both of them wounded, ruined, maybe not dead, maybe worse than dead. Jean-Baptiste would have known Benton was in New York, was home last night, waiting for his wife to return from her live appearance on CNN. Jean-Baptiste knew whatever he wanted to know, and he knew what Scarpetta and Benton had together. Jean-Baptiste knew what they had, because he knew what he didn't have and had never had. No one understood apartness better than Jean-Baptiste, and understanding hellish isolation made him understand its antithesis. Darkness and light. Love and hate. Creation and uncreation. The opposites of all things are intimately related. Benton had to find him. Benton had to stop him.

The surest method was to attack vulnerabilities. Benton's credo: You're only as good as the people around you. He kept telling himself, reassuring himself, that Jean-Baptiste had made a mistake. He'd recruited badly, had enlisted small carnivores that were neither strong-minded nor properly programmed and certainly weren't experienced, and he was going to pay for his snap decisions and sick desires and subjective choices. He would be undone by his unsound mind. Granny and Clyde would bring him down. Jean-Baptiste should never have stooped to what by Chandonne standards was petty crime. He should have avoided people unfit for service, people unstable and driven by their own weaknesses and dysfunctions. Jean-Baptiste should have stayed the hell away from small-time character-disordered criminals and banks.

The pattern was the same in each heist, textbook, as if someone had read the manual. The bank branch had been robbed at least once in the past, in some instances more than once, and had no bulletproof partition, known as a "bandit barrier," separating the tellers from the public. The robberies always occurred on a Friday between the hours of nine and eleven a.m., when the branch was likely to have the fewest number of customers and the greatest amount of cash. A benign-looking older woman, who until this morning the FBI had known only as Granny, would walk in, looking like a Sunday-school teacher in a frumpy dress and tennis shoes, her head covered by a scarf or a hat. She always wore tinted glasses in old-style frames. Depending on the weather, she might have on a coat and wool gloves. If the robbery occurred when it was warm, she wore a pair of transparent plastic disposable gloves, the type used by people who work in food service, to obviate leaving her fingerprints or DNA.

Granny always carried a tote deposit bag that she would

begin to unzip as she approached a teller. She would reach inside the bag and pull out a weapon that forensic image enhancement indicated was the same type used each time, a nine-millimeter short-barrel pistol, a toy. The orange tip required by federal law on the barrels of realistic play guns had been removed. She would slide a note to the teller, the same type of note every time, that read: *Empty the drawers in the bag! No dye packs! Or you're dead!* It was written precisely, boldly, on a small piece of paper from a plain white notepad. She'd hold open the deposit bag, and the teller would stuff it full of cash. Granny would zip it up as she hurried outside and got into a car driven by her accomplice, the man the FBI called Clyde. In each instance, the car had been stolen and was found abandoned a short time later in a shopping mall parking lot.

When Benton had first walked into the conference room several hours earlier, he'd instantly recognized Granny and the notes she passed. The handwriting was so perfect it looked like a font. The FBI said it was virtually identical to a typeface called Gotham, the unassuming basic lettering of urban landscapes, the straightforward design commonly seen in signage, the same writing used by whoever had addressed the FedEx envelope that had contained Dodie Hodge's singing card, and possibly the same writing on the address of the FedEx package that contained the bomb. It was hard to know with exactitude about the latter. According to the flurry of e-mails from Marino, the airbill on the bomb had not survived the water cannon. But maybe it didn't matter.

Images of Dodie Hodge in various disguises and her handwriting were all over the SAC conference room's walls, video stills of her in "Aunt Bee" attire, as innocent as Mayberry, walking in and out of banks. Benton would have recognized her anywhere, regardless of her efforts at disguise. She wasn't going to get rid of her big jowly face and thin lips and bulbous nose and the way her ears stuck out. There was only so much she could do about her matronly body and disproportionately thin legs. In the majority of the robberies she was white. In a few she was black. In a recent one this past October, she was brown. A harmless neighbor, a grandmother, innocent and sweet-looking. In some of the stills she was smiling as she hurried out with at most ten thousand dollars inside her fire-resistant tote deposit bag, a different-colored one each time: red, blue, green, black, all offering adequate protection if her written instructions were ignored and a dye pack exploded, spraying an aerosol of red smoke and dye and possibly tear gas.

It was possible Dodie Hodge never would have come to the attention of anyone and would be robbing banks again, maybe robbing them for a long time, had her partner in crime, whose real name was Jerome Wild, not decided to get a distinctive tattoo on his neck when he was at Camp Pendleton last May right before he went AWOL. The tattoo was one he never successfully covered, didn't even make an effort, not with a high collar or a bandana or the professional-quality makeup Dodie used, trace residues of it recovered from the getaway cars. Mineral makeup, Marty Lanier had explained. The FBI labs in Quantico had identified boron nitride, zinc oxide, calcium carbonate, kaolin, magnesium, iron oxides, silica, and mica—the additives and pigments used in technically sophisticated eye shadows, lipsticks, foundations, and powders popular with actors and models.

Jerome Wild's tattoo was large and elaborate, and began just above his left collarbone and ended behind his left ear, and maybe he didn't think it was a problem. He was the getaway driver and never stepped inside the banks, and likely assumed he would never be captured on camera. He assumed wrong. In one of the robberies, a security camera at the corner of another bank across the street captured him clearly behind the wheel of a stolen white Ford Taurus, a hand out the window adjusting the side mirror. He was wearing black gloves lined with rabbit fur.

That photo, which was his downfall, was on a video screen inside the SAC conference room, and it was a face Benton had seen before, just last night, in security stills from Benton and Scarpetta's own building. Jerome Wild in dark glasses and a cap and black-leather rabbit fur-lined gloves. Skeletons climbing out of a coffin covering the left side of his neck. The still from a bank robbery and the still from last night, next to each other in windows on a big flat screen. They were the same man, a pilot fish, a small predator, a recruit who was too unsophisticated and reckless to believe he'd ever get caught or to give it a thought. Wild didn't know or care about tattoo databases, and Jean-Baptiste didn't either, it seemed.

Wild was only twenty-three, was bright and craved excitement and loved taking risks, but he had no values or beliefs. He had no conscience. He certainly wasn't patriotic and didn't give a damn about his country or those who fought for it. When he'd enlisted in the Marines, it was for money, and when he was sent to Camp Pendleton he hadn't served in the Corps long enough to suffer the loss of fallen comrades yet. He hadn't boarded the C-17 yet that was to take him to Kuwait, hadn't done a damn thing except have a good time in California, all expenses paid. The only inspiration required for what was a deeply symbolic and serious tattoo had been the idea of getting a tattoo, any tattoo, as long as it was "cool," according to another soldier who had been interviewed several times now by the FBI.

Wild got his cool tattoo and soon after returned to his birthplace of Detroit for a weekend furlough before he was to be deployed. He never went back to the Marine Corps base. The last reported sighting was by someone who'd gone to high school with him and was fairly certain he recognized Wild in the Grand Palais hotel casino playing the slot machines, and hotel security recordings had confirmed it was him. Playing slots, at the roulette table, at one point walking the floor with a well-dressed elderly man the FBI had identified as Freddie Maestro, believed to have ties to organized crime and the owner of, among other establishments, High Roller Lanes here in New York. Two weeks later in early June, a bank branch near Detroit's Tower Center Mall was robbed by a frumpy white woman in a linen suit who was driven away by a black man in a stolen Chevy Malibu.

Benton was stunned, and he felt foolish. He needed to reexamine his life, and now wasn't a good time to do it, not during a discussion like this with people like this inside an SAC conference room. For all practical purposes, he had gone from being an enforcement agent of the law, an officer of the court, to becoming a fucking academic. A bank robber had been his goddamn patient, and he'd had no idea because he wasn't allowed to do a background check on Dodie Hodge, wasn't allowed to look into anything about who or what she was beyond a loathsome woman with a severe personality disorder who claimed to be the aunt of Hap Judd.

Benton could tell himself all he wanted that even if he'd done a thorough background check on her, what was there to know? Logically, the answer was nothing. He felt angry and humiliated, wishing he was FBI again, wishing he was carrying a gun and a badge and had the imprimatur to find out whatever the hell he wanted. *But you wouldn't have found anything,* he kept telling himself as he sat at the conference table inside a room that was, of course, blue, from the carpet to the walls to the upholstery of the chairs. *Nobody found out anything until you saw her pictures on the wall,* he said to himself. She wasn't recognized. She wasn't searchable by computers.

Dodie had no identifying feature, such as a tattoo, that might end up in a database. She'd never been charged with anything more serious than being disorderly on a bus in the Bronx, and shoplifting and disturbing the peace in Detroit last month, and on neither occasion was there any reason under the sun for anyone to link this fifty-six-year-old bombastic and unpleasant woman to a series of cleverly executed heists that not so coincidentally completely stopped while she was a patient at McLean. Benton reminded himself repeatedly he could have checked her all he wanted and never linked her to Jerome Wild or the Chandonnes. The link was dumb luck. Jean-Baptiste's bad dumb luck, because nothing was ever enough for him. He'd carelessly left his DNA in a stolen Mercedes, had done a number of things of late that went too far. He was decompensating, and now he was before them, before Benton again. Not just a link or a branch but the root.

His mug shot was on a flat screen across the table from

Benton, the last known photograph, taken by the Texas
Department of Justice almost ten years ago. What did the
bastard look like now? Benton couldn't stop staring at the
image on the wall-mounted screen. It seemed the two of
them were looking at each other, squared off, confrontational. The shaved head, the asymmetrical face, one eye
lower than the other and the flesh around them an
inflamed, angry red from a chemical burn that Jean-
Baptiste claimed had made him blind. It hadn't. Two
guards on the Polunsky Unit had found that out the hard
way when Jean-Baptiste slammed them against a concrete
wall and crushed their throats. In the spring of 2003, Jean-
Baptiste walked out of his death-row cell wearing a
uniform and a name tag, a murdered guard's car keys conveniently in a pocket.

"Not an offshoot but a segue," Lanier was saying to
Berger, and the two tended to argue a lot and Benton
really hadn't been listening.

Another e-mail from Marino just landed:

```
On my way to the DNA bldg to meet lucy
and the doc
```

"It will be more obvious when we get a visual. I agree
with Benton. But Jerome's nonviolent," Lanier was saying.
"He's always been nonviolent. So nonviolent he went
AWOL. Went into the military because he couldn't get a
job, and then bailed out because he happened upon an illegal opportunity."

Benton e-mailed Marino:

```
Why?
```

Lanier kept talking. "The Chandonnes' tentacles are in Detroit. Just as they're in Louisiana, Las Vegas, Miami, Paris, Monte Carlo. Port cities. Casino cities. Maybe even Hollywood. Anything that attracts organized crime."

Benton reminded everyone at the table, "But not the father anymore. And not Jean-Baptiste's brother. We carved up the rotten apple in 2003. We didn't get the core, but he's not the same breed."

Marino's e-mailed reply:

```
Toni dariens watch
```

Benton continued, "You're talking about a lust murderer, someone much too compulsive, much too impulse-driven, to successfully run a cartel, to run anything as complex as his family business has been for the better part of a century. We can't work this like an organized-crime case. We have to work it like a repetitive sexual murder case."

"It was a viable bomb," Berger said to Lanier, as if Benton hadn't said anything. "It could have severely injured or even killed Kay. How can you possibly construe that as falling within the rubric of nonviolent?"

"You're missing my point," Lanier told her. "Depends on his intent, and if, in fact, Wild is just the messenger, then he may not have even known what was in the FedEx box."

"That and the guy's MO? In all these bank robberies? There's been nothing violent. He's a coward, stays in the car. Even the gun is fake." Stockman spoke up as he worked on getting the decision tree—the decision forest, as he'd called it—on a flat screen. "I have to agree with Marty that he and Granny . . . this Dodie woman. Sorry.

I've been calling her Granny for the past six months. Anyway, Jerome and Dodie, they're minions."

"Dodie Hodge isn't anybody's minion," Benton said. "She goes along with something if she receives gratification from it. If she's having fun. But she's not a drone. She's cooperative and supervisable only up to a point, which is why Jean-Baptiste made a mistake picking her, picking Jerome, picking anybody he's likely picked. They're all going to be flawed, because he is."

"Then why steal the DVDs, for God's sake?" Berger said to Lanier. "A few Hap Judd movies were worth getting arrested?"

"That wasn't why," Benton said. "She couldn't help herself. And now the network has a problem. One of their bank robbers has just been arrested. They get a lawyer who's in bed with them, and he in turn tries to get a forensic expert who's in bed with them. Instead they ended up with me because of Dodie's histrionics, her narcissism. She wanted to go to the same hospital where the rich and famous go. Again, she's not a minion. She's a bad recruit."

"A bad move stealing those DVDs," Stockman agreed with Berger. "They'd still be robbing banks if she hadn't stuck those damn movies down her pants."

"A bad move shooting off her mouth about Hap Judd," Benton added. "Not that she could help herself, but she's causing problems, creating exposures. We don't know exactly what Hap Judd's involvement in all this is, but he's linked to Dodie, and he's linked to Hannah Starr, and a photograph of him and Freddie Maestro is in High Roller Lanes, which could link Hap to Toni Darien as well. We need to get the tree on the wall, have a visual. I'm going to show you how all this is connected."

"Let's get back to the bomb," Berger said to Lanier. "Just so I'm clear. You're thinking someone else is behind the delivery of this package, Jean-Baptiste is, and that theory is based on?"

"I don't mean to say common sense. . . ." Lanier said.

"You mean to say it, and you just did," Berger answered. "And condescension isn't helpful."

"Let me finish. I don't mean to imply anything even remotely condescending toward you, Jaime. Or toward anyone at this table. From an analytical perspective"—and what Lanier really meant was, *From the perspective of an FBI criminal investigative analyst, a profiler*—"what was done to Dr. Scarpetta, or attempted, is personal." Lanier looked at Benton. "I would say intimately personal." Almost as if to imply that Benton might have been the one who left a bomb for his wife.

"I'm not getting the commonsense part." Berger looked Lanier in the eye.

Berger didn't like her. It probably wasn't about jealousy or insecurity or any of the usual reasons powerful women went after each other. There was a practical problem to be faced. If the FBI took over the entire investigation, including whatever involvement Dodie Hodge or Hap Judd or anyone else being discussed in this room might have with Hannah Starr, it would be the U.S. attorney's office that prosecuted the cases and not the New York County DA, not Berger. *Get over it,* Benton thought. This was fucking bigger than five boroughs. This was federal. It was international. It was dirty and extremely dangerous. If Berger thought about it for a minute, she shouldn't even want to get within a mile of this case.

"The type of bomb, as it's been described," Lanier was saying to Berger. "An implicit threat. Intimidation. Mockery.

And a prior knowledge of the victim and her habits and what was important to her. Dodie Hodge might have served as chief consort, but the bang for the buck, if you'll forgive the pun, would have been Chandonne's."

"I'd like to get over there." Stockman was looking at something on his computer. "Dodie Hodge's place in Edgewater." He started typing an e-mail. "She got a drinking problem? Wine bottles everywhere."

"We need to get in." O'Dell looked at what was on Stockman's computer screen. "See if we find notes, other things linking her to the robberies and who knows what. I mean, it's fine for these guys to look, but they don't know what we know."

"A more pressing concern is Jean-Baptiste," Benton said, because police, the FBI were looking for Dodie, but no one was looking for Chandonne.

"No notes so far but a couple toy guns," O'Dell said to Stockman as agents and cops from the Joint Bank Robbery Task Force searched Dodie's house and sent electronic information in real time. "Bingo," Stockman then said as he read. "Drugs. Looks like Granny does coke. Plus, she's a smoker. Hey, Benton. To your knowledge, does Dodie smoke French cigarettes? Gauloises? I know I didn't pronounce that right."

"She may have had someone staying with her," Stockman said, as he replied to his colleagues in the field.

Benton said, "I'm going to stop listening for a minute."

It was a line that worked almost without exception. When people were arguing and distracted and their agendas were breaking the surface and blowing like whales, if Benton announced he was going to stop listening, everybody stopped talking.

"I'm going to say what I think, and you need to hear this because it will help you understand what you're about to see when these links are made, are on the wall," Benton said. "How are we doing with our tree diagram?" he pointedly asked.

"Anybody besides me need some coffee?" O'Dell said in frustration. "Too damn much going on at once, and I need to visit the little boys' room."

20

On the eighth floor of the OCME's DNA Building, Scarpetta, Lucy, and Marino were alone inside a lab used for scientific training. Criminal cases weren't analyzed in here, but the regulations for working in a clean-room environment still applied.

The three of them were difficult to recognize in disposable protective gowns, hair and shoe covers, masks, gloves, and safety glasses they had donned in the bio vestibule before passing through an air lock into an uncontaminated work space equipped with the latest assay technology, what Marino called contraptions: genomic analyzers, gene amplifiers, centrifuges, vortex mixers, real-time rotary cyclers, and extraction robots for handling large volumes of liquids, such as blood. He moved about restlessly, rustling and making papery sounds, tugging at blue Tyvek and poking and prodding his safety glasses and mask and what he referred to as his "shower cap," constantly readjusting this and that as he griped about his garb.

"You ever put paper shoes on a cat?" His face mask

moved as he talked. "The thing runs around like hell trying to shake them off? That's what I fucking feel like."

"I didn't torture animals, set fires, or wet my bed when I was a kid," Lucy said, picking up a micro USB cable she had sterilized and wrapped.

In front of her on a brown paper-covered counter were two MacBooks that had been wiped off with isopropyl alcohol and enclosed in transparent polypropylene, and the BioGraph watchlike device, which had been swabbed for DNA late yesterday in the evidence exam room down the hall and was now safe for handling. Lucy plugged the cable into the BioGraph and connected it to one of the laptops.

"Like plugging in your iPod or iPhone," she said. "It's syncing with something. What have we got?"

The screen went black and prompted her for a username and password. In a banner at the top was a long string of zeros and ones that Scarpetta recognized as binary code.

"That's odd," she said.

"Very odd," Lucy said. "It doesn't want us to know its name. It's encrypted in binary, which is meant to be a deterrent, to be off-putting. If you're one of these people who surf the Net and somehow find this site, you have to go to some trouble to even have a hint what you've landed on. Even then, you can't get into it unless you're authorized or have a skeleton key."

Skeleton key was one of her euphemisms for hack.

"I'm betting this binary-code address doesn't convert into text that spells *BioGraph,* either." Lucy typed on the other MacBook and opened a file. "If it did, my search engines would have found it, because they sure as hell know how to look for bit strings and their represented words or sequences."

"Jesus," Marino said. "Already I got no damn idea what the hell you're talking about."

He had been slightly nasty from the instant Scarpetta had met him downstairs in the lobby and escorted him to the eighth floor. He was upset about the bomb. He wasn't going to tell her that, but after twenty years, he didn't have to tell her. She knew him better than he knew himself. Marino was irritable because he was scared.

"I'll start over and try to move my lips when I talk this time," Lucy sniped back at him.

"Your mouth is covered. I can't see your lips. I got to take off this cap at least. It's not like I have any hair. I'm starting to sweat."

"Your bald head will shed skin cells," Lucy said. "Probably why you have such a dust problem in your apartment. This so-called watch was designed to sync with a laptop, is interfaceable with just about any kind of computer device because of the micro USB port. Probably because all kinds of people are wearing these so-called watches, collecting data just like Toni Darien was. Let's convert binary to ASCII."

She typed the string of ones and zeros into a field on the other MacBook and hit the return key. Instantly, the code was translated into text that gave Scarpetta pause—in fact, gave her the creeps.

It spelled *Caligula*.

"Wasn't he the Roman emperor who burned down Rome?" Marino said.

"That was Nero," Scarpetta said. "Caligula was probably worse. Probably the most demented, depraved, sadistic emperor in the history of the Roman Empire."

"What I'm waiting for right now," Lucy said, "is to

bypass the username and password. To put it very simply, I've hijacked this site and what's in the BioGraph so the programs on my server can help us out."

"I think I saw a movie about him," Marino said. "He had sex with his sisters and lived in the palace with his horse or something. Maybe he had sex with the horse, too. An ugly bastard. I think he was deformed."

Scarpetta said, "A rather chilling name for a website."

"Come on." Lucy was impatient with the computer, with the programs working invisibly to grant her access to what she wanted.

"I told you about walking back and forth from there by yourself," Marino said to Scarpetta, and he was thinking about the bomb, about what he'd just experienced at Rodman's Neck. "When you're on live TV, you should have security. Maybe you won't argue about it anymore."

He was assuming if he'd escorted her last night, he would have recognized that the FedEx package was suspicious and never would have let her touch it. Marino felt responsible for her safety, had a habit of going overboard about it, when the irony was, the most unsafe she'd ever been was with him not all that long ago.

"Caligula is probably the name of a proprietary project." Lucy was busy on the other MacBook. "That's my guess."

"Thing is, what next?" Marino said to Scarpetta. "I feel like somebody's warming up to something. That singing card Benton got yesterday at Bellevue. Then not even twelve hours later, the FedEx bomb with a voodoo doll. Jesus, it stunk. Can't wait to hear what Geffner says."

Geffner was a trace evidence examiner at the NYPD crime labs in Queens.

"I called him on my way over here and said he better

start looking through the microscope the minute the bomb debris hits the door." Marino glanced at his blue-paper sleeve, shoved it up with a latex-sheathed hand to check his watch. "He should be looking at it now. Hell, we should call him. Jesus. It's almost noon. Like hot asphalt, rotten eggs, and dog shit, like a really filthy fire scene, like someone used an accelerant to burn up a friggin' latrine. I almost gagged, and it takes a lot to make me puke. Plus dog fur. Benton's patient? The whack job who called you on CNN? Hard for me to wrap my mind around her making something like that. Lobo and Ann said it was really nicely done."

As if making a bomb that might blow off a person's hands or worse was to be commended.

Lucy said, "And we're in."

The black screen with the binary banner turned midnight-blue, and CALIGULA appeared across the center in what looked like three-dimensional silvery cast-metal letters. A typeface that was familiar. Scarpetta almost felt queasy.

"Gotham," Lucy said. "That's interesting. The font is Gotham."

Marino's paper gown rustled as he moved closer to see what she meant, his eyes bloodshot behind his safety glasses as he said, "Gotham? I don't see Batman anywhere."

The screen was prompting Lucy to press any key to continue. But she didn't. She was intrigued by the Gotham font and what it might mean.

"Authoritative, practical, what's known as the workman-like typeface of public places," she said. "The sans-serif style you see in names and numbers on signs, walls, buildings, and the Freedom Tower cornerstone at the World

Trade Center site. But the reason the Gotham font has gotten so much attention of late is Obama."

"First I've heard of a font called Gotham," Marino replied. "But then again, I don't get the font newsletter or monthly magazine or go to fucking font conventions."

"Gotham's the typeface the Obama people used during his campaign," Lucy said. "And you should pay attention to fonts, like I've told you how many times? Fonts are part of twenty-first-century documents examination, and you ignore them at your own peril. What they are and why someone might pick them for a specific communication can be telling and significant."

"Why Gotham for this website?" Scarpetta envisioned the FedEx airbill and the immaculate, almost perfect hand-writing on it.

"I don't know, except the typeface is supposed to suggest credibility," Lucy said. "Inspire trust. Subliminally, we're supposed to take this website seriously."

"The name Caligula inspires anything but trust," said Scarpetta.

"Gotham is popular," Lucy said. "It's cool. It's supposed to suggest all the right things if you want to influence someone into taking you or your product or a political candidate or maybe some type of research project seriously."

"Or take a dangerous package seriously," Scarpetta said, suddenly angry. "This typeface looks very similar if not identical to the style of printing on the package I got last night. I don't guess you were able to see the box before it was shot with the PAN disrupter," she asked Marino.

"Like I told you, the batteries they targeted were right behind the address. You said it referenced you as the chief medical examiner of Gotham City. So there's this Gotham reference again. It bother anybody besides me that Hap Judd was in a Batman movie and fucks dead bodies?"

"Why would Hap Judd send Aunt Kay what you're calling a stink bomb?" Lucy said, busy on the other MacBook.

"If the sick prick killed Hannah, maybe? Or maybe he's got to do with Toni Darien, since he's been in High Roller Lanes and probably met her, at the very least. The Doc did Toni's autopsy and might end up being the ME on Hannah's case, too."

"So Aunt Kay gets a bomb delivered? And that's going to prevent Hap Judd from being caught if Hannah's body turns up or for who knows what?" Lucy said, as if Scarpetta wasn't inside the lab with them anymore. "I'm not saying the asshole didn't do something to Hannah or doesn't know where she is."

"Yeah, him and dead bodies," Marino said. "Kind of interesting now that we know Toni may have been dead a few days before she was dumped. Wonder where she was and what fun someone was having with her. He probably did do that dead girl in the hospital fridge. Why else would he be in there fifteen minutes and come out with only one glove on?"

"But I don't think he left a bomb for Aunt Kay thinking that would scare her off the case or two cases or any cases. That's retarded," Lucy said. "And the Gotham font has nothing to do with Batman."

"Maybe it does if the person's into some sort of sicko game," Marino argued.

The odor of fire and brimstone, and Scarpetta kept thinking about the bomb. A stink bomb, a different sort of dirty bomb, an emotionally destructive bomb. Someone who knew Scarpetta. Someone who knew Benton. Someone who knew their history almost as intimately as they did. *Games,* she thought. *Sick games.*

Lucy hit the return key and CALIGULA went away and was replaced by:

Welcome, Toni.

Then:

Do you want to sync data? Yes No

Lucy answered yes and the next message she got was:

Toni, your scales are three days overdue. Would you like to complete them now? Yes No

Lucy clicked on Yes, and the screen faded and was replaced by another one:

Please rate how well these adjectives describe how you felt today.

This was followed by choices such as elated, confused, content, happy, irritable, angry, enthusiastic, inspired, each list of questions followed by a five-point scale, ranging from 1 for *very little or not at all* to 5 for *extreme*.

"If Toni was doing this every day," Marino said, "would it be on her laptop? And maybe that's why it's missing?"

"It wouldn't have been on her laptop. What you're seeing resides on this website's server," Lucy said.

"But she hooked up her watch to her laptop," Marino said.

"Yes. To upload information and to charge it," Lucy said. "The data collected by this watchlike device weren't for her use and wouldn't have lived on her laptop. She not only wouldn't have any use for the data but she wouldn't have the software needed to aggregate it, to sort it, to make it meaningful."

Lucy was being prompted by more questions and was answering them on the screen because she wanted to see what would happen next. She rated her moods as *very little or not at all*. Were Scarpetta answering the questions, she might just rate her own moods as *extreme* right now.

"I don't know," Marino said. "I can't stop thinking this Caligula project might explain why maybe someone went inside her apartment and took her laptop and her phone and who knows what else." His safety glasses looked at Scarpetta and he said, "We don't know it was Toni on the security recording, you're right about that. Just because the person had on what looked like her coat. How hard would that be if you were close to her same size and maybe had on similar running shoes? She wasn't a small person, thin but tall. About five-ten, right? I don't see how it could have been her going into her building Wednesday night at around quarter to six and leaving at seven. You think she's been dead since Tuesday. And now this Caligula thing's saying maybe the same thing. She hasn't done her questionnaire for three days."

"If it's true that someone impersonated her on the security recordings," Lucy said, "then he had her coat or one very similar and the keys to her apartment."

"She was dead at least thirty-six hours," Scarpetta said. "If her apartment keys were in her pocket and her killer knew where she lived, it wouldn't have been hard to take the keys, let himself in, remove what he wanted from the scene, then return her keys to her pocket when he dumped her body in the park. Maybe this person had her coat, too. Maybe she was wearing it when she went out last. It might explain why she didn't seem to be dressed warmly when her body was found. Maybe some of her clothing was missing."

"That's a lot of trouble and a lot of risk," Lucy said. "Somebody didn't plan very well. Seems all the calculating is after the fact, not prior to the crime. Maybe more of an impulse crime and the killer was someone she knew."

"If she'd been communicating with him, that might be the reason for her missing laptop and her phone." Marino was stuck on that. "Text messages stored on her phone. Maybe when you finally get into her e-mail. Maybe she was e-mailing these Caligula people or there are documents on her computer that are incriminating."

"Then why leave the BioGraph device on her body?" Lucy said. "Why take the chance someone might do what we're doing right now?"

Scarpetta said, "It may be that her killer wanted her computer, her phone. But that doesn't mean there was a single rational reason. Maybe the absence of a reason is why the BioGraph wasn't removed from her body."

"There's always a reason," Marino said.

"Not the kind of reason you're talking about, because this may not be the type of crime you're talking about," Scarpetta said, and she thought about her BlackBerry.

She reconsidered the motive for the theft, had a feeling she might be wrong about why Carley Crispin wanted the BlackBerry, that it wasn't simply about what Carley had said when they were walking past Columbus Circle after leaving CNN: *I bet you could talk anybody into it you wanted, with the connections you have."* As if to imply that Scarpetta wouldn't have a problem enticing guests to appear on a TV show, assuming she had her own show, and from that Scarpetta had assigned a motive to her missing smart-phone. Carley wanted information, wanted Scarpetta's contacts, and maybe she did in fact help herself to scene photographs while she'd had the chance. But possibly the BlackBerry ultimately wasn't intended for Carley or even Agee but for someone else. Someone cunning and evil. The last person to have the BlackBerry was Agee, and maybe he would have passed it on to a third party had he not killed himself.

"People commit murder and return to the scene of the crime, not always for the sole reason that they're paranoid and trying to cover their tracks," Scarpetta explained. "Sometimes it's to relive a violent act that was gratifying. Maybe in Toni's case it's more than one motivation. Her phone, her laptop are souvenirs, and they also were a means of impersonating her before her body was found, to throw us off track about her time of death by pretending to be her and using her cell phone to send a text message to her mother at around eight p.m. Wednesday night. Manipulations, games, and fantasy, emotionally driven, sexually driven, sadistically driven. A blend of motivations that created a malignant dis-cord. Like so much in life. It isn't just one thing."

Lucy finished answering the mood rating questions and a *Submit* box appeared on the screen. She clicked on it and got the confirmation that her completed scales had been successfully sent to the site for review. *For review by whom?* Scarpetta wondered. A study sponsor who was a psychol-ogist, a psychiatrist, a neuroscientist, a research assistant, a graduate student. Who the hell knew, but there would be more than one of them. Probably a large faculty of them. These invisible sponsors could be anyone and could exist anywhere and were engaged in a project that obviously was intended to make predictions about human behavior that would prove useful to someone.

"It's an acronym," Lucy said.

On the screen:

THANK YOU FOR PARTICIPATING IN THE CALCULATED INTEGRATION OF GPS UPLOADED LIGHT AND ACTIVITY STUDY.

"CALIGULA," Scarpetta said. "I still don't see why anyone would choose an acronym like that."

"Suffered chronically from nightmares and insomnia." Lucy was skimming through files on her other MacBook, Googles about Caligula. "Used to wander the palace all night long waiting for the sun to come up. The name might have to do with that. If, for example, the study's related to sleep disorders and the effects of light and darkness on moods. His name was derived from the Latin word *caliga,* which means 'little boot.'"

Marino said to Scarpetta, "Your name means 'little shoe.'"

"Come on, guys," Lucy said under her breath, talking to her neural networking programs and search engines. "Sure as hell would be easier if I could take this to my office." She meant the BioGraph device.

"It's all over the Internet about Scarpetta meaning 'little shoe' in Italian," Marino went on, his eyes uneasy behind thick plastic. "The little shoe, the little gumshoe, the little lady with the big kick."

"Now we're cooking," Lucy said.

Data were rolling down her screen, a stew of letters, symbols, numbers.

"I wonder if Toni knew exactly what was being collected by the thing she was wearing on her wrist morning, noon, and night," Lucy said. "Or if whoever killed her did."

"Unlikely she did," Scarpetta said. "The details of what-ever theory researchers hope to prove aren't advertised or disseminated publicly. The subjects themselves don't know the details, only generalities. Otherwise, they can skew the results."

"Must have been something in it for her," Marino said. "Wearing that watch all the time. Answering questions every day."

"She may have had a personal interest in sleep disorders, seasonal affective disorder, who knows what, and saw an ad for a study or someone gave her information. Her mother said she was moody and affected by gloomy weather," Scarpetta said. "Usually people involved in research stud-ies get paid."

She thought about the father, Lawrence Darien, and his aggressive attempts at claiming Toni's personal effects and her dead body. A bioelectrical engineer from MIT. A gam-bler and a drunk with ties to organized crime. When he'd made a scene at the morgue, maybe what he'd really been after was the BioGraph watch.

"Unbelievable what's stored inside this thing." Lucy pulled a stool in front of her MacBooks and sat, looking at raw data that had been stored inside Toni's BioGraph device. "Obviously a combination actigraphy data logger with a highly sensitive accelerometer or bimorph element in a two-layer piezoelectric sensor that basically measures gross motor activity. I'm not seeing anything that strikes me as military or government."

"What would you expect?" Marino asked. "If this was CIA or something."

"Not this. Nothing's encrypted the way I'm used to seeing when it's classified by the government as top secret. Not the usual standard three-block ciphers with the bits and block sizes I associate with algorithms used in symmetric key cryptography. You know, these really long keys, longer than forty bits, that are supposed to be exportable but make it really hard for hackers to break the code. That's not what we've got here. This isn't military or any intelligence-gathering agency. It's private-sector."

"I guess we shouldn't ask why you'd know how the government encrypts its top secret information," Marino commented.

"The purpose of this thing is to gather data for some type of research, not spying, not war, not even terrorists for once," Lucy said as data rolled by. "Not intended for the end user but for researchers. Geeks out there crunching data, but for whom? Sleep schedule variability, sleep quantity, daytime activity patterns, correlated to light exposure. Come on, start aggregating it into some sort of order that's easy to look at." Talking to her programs again. "Give me charts. Give me maps. It's sorting by types of data. A lot of data. A ton of it. Recording data every fifteen seconds. Five thousand seven hundred and sixty times a day this thing was capturing God knows how many different types of data. GPS and pedometer readings. Location data, speed, distance, altitude, and the user's vital signs. Heart rate and SPO-two."

"SPO-two? You must be mistaken," Scarpetta said.

"I'm looking at SPO-two," Lucy said. "Hundreds of thousands of them. SPO-two captured every fifteen seconds."

"I don't see how that's possible," Scarpetta said. "Where's the sensor? You can't measure pulse oximetry, the oxygen saturation of blood, without a sensor of some type. Usually on a fingertip, sometimes a toe, sometimes an earlobe. Has to be a thin part of the person's anatomy so a light can pass through the tissue. A light comprised of both red and infrared wavelengths that determines the oxygenation, the percentage of oxygen saturation, in your blood."

"The BioGraph is Bluetooth-enabled," Lucy said. "So maybe the pulse-oximetry device is Bluetooth-enabled."

"Wireless or otherwise, there had to be one to take these measurements we're seeing," Scarpetta replied. "A sensor she wore virtually all of the time."

A red laser dot moved over names and locations and the branches that connected them on the treelike graph filling the flat screen.

"Imagine Monsieur Chandonne, the father, no longer in power." Benton held a laser pointer, illustrating what he meant as he talked. "And what family associations he has left are scattered. He and a number of his captains are in prison. The Chandonne heir apparent, the brother of Jean-Baptiste, is dead. And law enforcement for the most part has turned its attention to other international troubles. Al Qaida, Iran, North Korea, the global economic disaster. Jean-Baptiste, the surviving child, seizes the opportunity to take over, to start his life again and do it better this time."

"I don't see how," O'Dell said. "He's a lunatic."

"He's not a lunatic," Benton said. "He is extremely intelligent, extremely intuitive, and for a while his intellect can overwhelm his compulsions, his obsessions. The question is how long can that last."

"I totally disagree," O'Dell said to Benton. "This guy a Mob boss? It's not like he can wander around in public without putting a bag over his head. He's an international fugitive, an Interpol Red Notice, and he's deformed, a freak."

"You can disagree all you want. You don't know him," Benton said.

"That genetic condition he has," O'Dell went on. "I can't remember what it's called."

"Congenital hypertrichosis universalis." It was Marty Lanier talking. "Individuals suffering from this very rare condition have an overgrowth of lanugo hair, baby-fine hair, all over their bodies, including areas that usually aren't hairy or excessively hairy. The forehead, the tops of the hands, the elbows. And there may be other deformities, gingival hyperplasia, small teeth widely spaced."

"Like I said, a freak, he looks like a damn werewolf," O'Dell said to everyone at the table. "People who had this condition, it's probably where the legend came from."

"He's not a werewolf, and the condition isn't something from a horror story. It isn't a legend. It's very real," Benton said.

"We don't know how many cases," Lanier added. "Something like fifty, a hundred. Very few reported worldwide."

"*Reported* is the key word," Jaime Berger said, and she was subdued. "You can't count cases if they're not reported, and you can understand why hypertrichosis would have very negative associations and stigmas, implications the sufferer was a monster, was evil."

"And then you treat him accordingly and maybe turn him into that," Lanier added.

"Families hid family members who had this affliction, and Jean-Baptiste was no exception," Benton continued. "He grew up in a basement, in what was essentially a subterranean windowless dungeon of the Chandonne family's seventeenth-century home on Île Saint-Louis in Paris. It's possible the gene Jean-Baptiste inherited traces back to a man in the mid-fifteen hundreds who was born covered with hair and as an infant was presented to King Henri the Second in Paris and raised in the royal palace as a curiosity, an amusement, a pet of sorts. This man married a French woman, and several of their children inherited the disorder. In the late eighteen hundreds, one of their descendants is believed to have married a Chandonne, and a hundred years later the recessive gene became dominant in the form of Jean-Baptiste."

"What I'm trying to get across here," O'Dell said, "is people run screaming from someone who looks like that. How could Jean-Baptiste take over and operate out of the family home in Paris?"

"We don't know where Jean-Baptiste has been living," Benton replied. "We don't know what he's been doing for the past five years. We don't know what he looks like. Laser hair removal, prosthetic dentistry, plastic surgery, the medical technology available these days. We have no idea what he's had done to himself since he escaped from death row. What we do know is you recovered his DNA from the backseat of a stolen Mercedes in Miami, and that unequivocally connects him to the bank robberies being committed by Jerome Wild and Dodie Hodge. Both of them are connected to Detroit, which makes it likely that Jean-Baptiste has connections to Detroit. And Miami. And here."

"The gaming industry," Lanier said. "And maybe the film industry."

"The Chandonne family has had its hands in everything that might be lucrative," Benton said. "The entertainment business, gambling, prostitution, drugs, illegal weapons, counterfeit designer labels, contraband of every sort. Whatever you historically associate with organized crime, Jean-Baptiste will be familiar with it, well versed. It's in his family. It's in his blood. He's had five years to avail himself of a powerful network because of his family connections. He's had access to money. He's been working on whatever has been his plan, and any organized plan requires a recruitment. He needed troops. If he was going to attempt to reestablish the Chandonne crime family or build an empire for himself, to reinvent himself, re-create himself, he needed to enlist a lot of help, and he was going to pick badly. An individual with his history of abuse, his history of psychopathology and extraordinarily violent crimes, isn't going to have what it takes to be a shrewd and successful leader, at least not for long. And he's fueled by his sexually violent compulsions. And he's fueled by vengeance."

The root of the tree graph on the wall was Jean-Baptiste. His name was in the middle of the screen, and all other names branched out from it directly or indirectly.

"So we've got Dodie Hodge and Jerome Wild linked to him." Benton pointed the laser, and the dot moved on names as he mentioned them.

"We should add Hap Judd," Berger said, and she was different, extremely somber. "He's linked to Dodie even though he claims to have nothing to do with her anymore."

Berger wasn't herself, and Benton didn't know what had happened. When everyone had gotten coffee, she'd borrowed the desk of an agent who wasn't in and had made a phone call on a landline. From that point on she'd gotten quiet. She'd stopped offering insights and arguments and had quit pushing back whenever Lanier opened her mouth. Benton had a feeling it didn't have to do with jurisdiction, with a turf battle, with a squabble over who would prosecute what. Jaime Berger seemed defeated. She seemed used up.

"For a period Hap supposedly sought her spiritual advice," Berger said in a flat tone, a monotone. "He stated this when I interviewed him early this morning. He says she's a nuisance, calls his L.A. office frequently, and he avoids her."

"How did he meet Dodie?" Lanier wanted to know.

"Apparently, she was giving spiritual advice, psychic readings, to Hannah Starr," Berger answered. "This isn't unusual. A rather remarkable number of celebrities and very wealthy prominent people, including politicians, seek the counsel of self-proclaimed psychics, gypsies, witches, warlocks, prophets, most of them frauds."

"I assume most of them don't turn out to be bank robbers," Stockman said.

"You'd be surprised what a lot of them turn out to be," Berger said. "Stealing, extortion, financial scams come quite naturally to the profession."

"Dodie Hodge ever been to the Starrs' mansion on Park Avenue?" Lanier asked Berger.

"Hap says yes."

"You consider Hap a suspect in the Hannah Starr case?" O'Dell asked. "He knows where she is or has something to do with it?"

"I consider him the most important suspect at this point," she said, and she sounded worn down, almost detached or maybe broken.

It wasn't about her being tired. It was about something else.

"Hap Judd should be on the wall because of Dodie and because of Hannah." Berger was looking around the table but not really connecting to anyone, almost as if she was addressing a grand jury. "And also Toni Darien. His ties to High Roller Lanes and possibly Freddie Maestro, and we should add Park General Hospital in Harlem, which isn't very far from where Toni's body was found off One hundred and tenth Street."

More branches on the flat screen: Hannah Starr connected to Hap Judd connected to Dodie, and indirectly to Jerome Wild. All the connections now linked to Toni Darien, High Roller Lanes, and Park General Hospital, and linked back to the root, to Jean-Baptiste Chandonne. Berger explained Hap's past at the Harlem hospital, and a young woman who died there named Farrah Lacy, and then Berger got back to Hap's link to the Starrs, his visits to the Park Avenue mansion for at least one dinner and on other occasions for sex. O'Dell interrupted her to point out that Rupe Starr wouldn't have courted a minor actor who had no more to invest than half a million dollars.

"These major players like Rupe," O'Dell explained, "they won't even talk to you unless you got a hell of a lot more than that to hand over."

"This was about a year before Rupe Starr died," Berger said. "By which point Hannah was married to Bobby Fuller."

"Maybe one of those situations where the family starts crowding out the boss, starts running things the way they want," Stockman suggested.

"I know you've looked into Hannah's financials," Berger said, and she meant that the FBI had. "Because of information I passed on that we discovered, that Lucy and I did."

As if everyone would know who Lucy was and, significantly, who she was to Berger.

"A lot of activity in a lot of banks here and abroad," Stockman said. "Starting about two years ago. Then after Rupe Starr died last May, most of the money's been lost."

"Hap claims he was in New York the night before Thanksgiving, when Hannah disappeared. The next day he flew to L.A. We're going to want warrants to search his place in TriBeCa. We should do that without delay. He claims that Hannah and Bobby never had sex," Berger went on, with none of the usual strength in her voice and not a glint of her wry humor. "In his words, not once."

"Yeah, right," O'Dell said sarcastically. "The oldest line in the book. No fire on the hearth so you go elsewhere to get warm."

"Hannah Starr was a socialite, ran with a fast crowd, hobnobbed with the rich and the famous here and abroad but never at the mansion," Berger went on. "She was much more public, would rather be on Page Six of the *Post* than in the family dining room, her style the antithesis of her father's. Her priorities clearly very different. She's the one who first connected to Hap, according to him. They met at the Monkey Bar. Soon after, he was a guest at one of Rupe's dinners and became a client. Hannah personally handled his money. Hap claims Hannah was afraid of Bobby."

"It wasn't Bobby who was in town the night Hannah vanished and then on a plane the very next day," Lanier pointedly said.

"Exactly right," Berger said, looking at Benton. "I'm very concerned about Hap's involvements with everyone. And his proclivities. Kay says Toni Darien was dead for a day and a half before her body was left in the park. She was kept in a cool environment, indoors somewhere. Maybe now that's making sense."

More names were being added to the graph on the wall.

"And Warner Agee and Carley Crispin," Benton said to Stockman. "They should be up there."

"We've got no reason to think Agee or Carley had any association with anybody we've got up here on the wall," O'Dell said.

"We know Carley's connected to Kay," Benton said. "And I'm connected to Agee."

The click of keys. Scarpetta's and Benton's names appeared on the flat screen. It was awful seeing them there. Connected to everyone. Connected to the root, Jean-Baptiste Chandonne.

Benton went on. "And based on what Lucy and Kay found inside Agee's hotel room, I suspect he was involved in the casino business."

Casinos was added to the wall.

"He was using his paranormal interests and influence to research something, manipulate something."

Paranormal was another branch on the tree.

"Maybe doing so under the patronage of a wealthy Frenchman supposedly named Lecoq," Benton continued, and that name appeared next. "Someone—possibly this Monsieur Lecoq—was paying Agee in cash. And possibly Freddie Maestro was, too. So Lecoq and Maestro might be connected, and that would link Detroit to France."

"We don't know who Lecoq is or if he really exists," Lanier said to Benton.

"He exists. But we don't know who he is."

"You thinking this Lecoq guy's the Wolfman?" O'Dell asked Benton.

"Let's don't call him that. Jean-Baptiste Chandonne is no stereotype. He's not a myth. He's a man who could at this point in time be fully capable of looking normal. He could have a number of aliases. In fact, he would have to."

"He speak with a French accent?" Stockman was on his laptop, adding offshoots that appeared on the tree on the wall.

"He can speak with a number of accents or no accent," Benton said. "In addition to French, he's fluent in Italian, Spanish, Portuguese, German, and English. Maybe other languages by now. I don't know."

"Why Carley Crispin?" Stockman asked as he worked on the graph. "And why was she paying for Agee's room? Or was someone else funneling money through her?"

"Probably a type of petty money laundering." Lanier was making notes. "Sounds like a lot of that going on here, even if in relatively small ways. People paying in cash. People paying other people to pay for other people. No credit cards or wire transfers or checks that leave a paper trail. At least not for business that might not be considered legitimate."

"Carley was going to kick him out of his room this weekend." Berger met Benton's eyes, and hers were as impenetrable as stone. "Why?"

"I can offer a theory," Benton said. "Agee e-mailed Carley information allegedly from a witness, and we know it was bogus. He impersonated Harvey Fahley by using a Web captioning service. Lucy found that transcript and a number of other ones on Agee's computer. The producers of *The Crispin Report* are in a hell of a lot of hot water because of what she released on the air last night about Hannah Starr's hair being recovered from a yellow cab. A detail Agee fabricated in a phony phone interview, and Carley fell for it. Or it suited her to fall for it. Either way, she didn't bank on getting into more trouble with the network than she was already in."

"So she fired him," Lanier said to him.

"Why wouldn't she? She also knew she was about to get fired. She wasn't going to need Agee anymore, no matter who was paying for his room. There may be a personal element," Benton said. "We don't know what Carley told Agee when she called him from CNN at close to eleven p.m. last night. The last phone call he got, it seems."

"We got to talk to Carley Crispin," Stockman said. "Too bad Agee's dead. It's sounding to me like he might be the key to everything."

"What he did was stupid as hell," said O'Dell. "He was a forensic psychiatrist. He should have known better. This Harvey Fahley guy was going to deny talking to him."

Berger said, "He has. I spoke to Detective Bonnell while we were getting coffee. She got hold of him after the show last night. He admits e-mailing Agee but claims he never talked to him and never said anything about Hannah's hair being found."

"Harvey Fahley's phone records should show if he talked to him. . . ." O'Dell began.

"A Tracfone made the call, and it's missing," Benton interrupted. "Agee had a drawer full of empty Tracfone boxes. I believe the interview with Fahley was bogus, and so does Lucy. But I doubt it was Agee's conscious intention to get fired."

"An unconscious intention," Lanier offered.

"That's my opinion." Benton believed Warner Agee was ready to self-destruct. "I seriously doubt last night was the first time suicide ever entered his mind. His condo in D.C. is about to be foreclosed on. His credit cards are expired. He relies on others for infusions of cash, is a parasite with nothing but his infirmities and demons to look forward to, and it appears he got tangled up with something that was over his head. He probably knew he was going to get caught."

"Another recruit that would have been a poor choice," Lanier said to everyone as she looked at Benton. "You think Jean-Baptiste would know?"

"What?" Benton's anger flared. "Know that Agee made sure I was exiled from my life and my reward was to be shunned by the FBI, and the reason he was able to do that was because of the Chandonnes?"

Silence inside the FBI conference room.

"Do I think he encountered Jean-Baptiste, that they were somehow acquainted? Yes, I do," Benton said. "Agee the wannabe would have lusted to talk to a so-called monster like Jean-Baptiste Chandonne, and he would have been drawn to him even if he didn't know who he was, saying it was an alias Agee met. He would have been drawn to Jean-Baptiste's psychopathology, to the evil he emanates, and it would be the biggest fucking mistake Warner Agee would fucking ever make."

"Obviously," Lanier said after a pause. "Since he's in the morgue as we speak."

"The Hotel Elysée is very close to the Starr mansion on Park Avenue." Berger's demeanor was calm. Too calm. "Only three or four blocks. You walk out of the hotel and can be at their mansion in five, ten minutes."

Stockman typed, and *Hotel Elysée* and *Starr Mansion* appeared on the flat screen, the newest branches on the tree.

"And you need to put Lucy Farinelli's name up there," Berger said. "Which means you have to add mine, too. Not just because I've been investigating Hannah's disappearance and have interviewed her husband and Hap Judd, but because I'm connected to Lucy. She was a client of Rupe Starr's. Had been for more than a decade. Hard to imagine she never met Hannah and possibly Bobby."

Benton didn't know what she was talking about or where she'd gotten her information. He met her eyes to ask the question because he didn't want to ask it out loud, and the lingering look she gave him was her answer. No. Lucy hadn't told her. Berger had found out some other way.

"Photographs," Berger said to everyone. "Leather-bound volumes in Rupe Starr's rare book room. Parties and dinners with clients over the years. She's in one of the albums. Lucy is."

"You found this out when," Benton said.

"Three weeks ago."

If she'd known that long, then her sudden change in demeanor was related to something else. Bonnell must have relayed other information over the phone that was even more unsettling.

"Nineteen ninety-six. She was twenty, still in college. I didn't see photographs of her in any other albums, possibly because she became an FBI agent after college, would have been extremely careful about appearing at big parties and dinners, and certainly wouldn't have allowed her picture to be taken," Berger went on. "As you know, after Hannah's disappearance was reported by her husband, Bobby, we asked permission to get personal effects, her DNA, from the house on Park Avenue, and I wanted to talk to him."

"He was in Florida when she disappeared, right?" O'Dell said.

"The night she didn't come home from the restaurant," Berger said, "Bobby was in their apartment in North Miami Beach, and we have that confirmed by e-mails sent from the apartment's IP address, and we have confirmation from phone records and the Florida housekeeper, Rosie. She was interviewed. I talked to her myself over the phone, and she confirmed Bobby was there the night of November twenty-sixth, the day before Thanksgiving."

"You know for a fact it was Bobby sending the e-mails and making the phone calls?" Lanier asked. "How do you know Rosie the housekeeper hasn't been doing it and lying to protect her boss?"

"I don't have probable cause or even reasonable suspicion to place him under surveillance when there's no evidence whatsoever of criminal activity on his part," Berger said with no inflection in her voice. "Does that mean I trust him? I don't trust anybody."

"We know what's in Hannah's will?" Lanier asked.

"She's Rupe Starr's only child, and when he died last May he left everything to her," Berger responded. "She revised her will soon after. If she dies, everything goes to a foundation."

"So she cut Bobby out. That strike you as a little unusual?" Stockman said.

"The best prenuptial is to make sure your spouse can't profit by betraying you or killing you," Berger answered. "And now it's moot. Hannah Starr has a few million left and a lot of debt. Supposedly lost almost everything in the market and to Ponzi scams and all the rest this past September."

"She's probably on a yacht in the Mediterranean, having her nails done in Cannes or Monte Carlo," Lanier said. "So Bobby gets nothing. What was your impression of him? Besides your natural inclination not to trust anyone."

"Extremely upset." Berger didn't direct anything to anyone. She continued addressing the table, as if it was a jury. "Extremely worried, stressed, when I talked to him in their home. He's convinced she's the victim of foul play, claims she never would have run off and never would have left him. I was inclined to take that possibility very seriously until Lucy discovered the financial information all of you know about."

"Let's go back to the night Hannah disappeared," O'Dell said. "How did Bobby know she was gone?"

"He tried to call her, and that's reflected in phone records he's made available to us," Berger said. "The following day, Thanksgiving Day, Hannah was to board a private jet for Miami to spend the long weekend with him, and from there go to Saint Barts."

"Alone?" Stockman asked. "Or both of them?"

"She was going to Saint Barts alone," Berger answered.

"So, maybe she was about to skip the country," Lanier said.

"That's what I've wondered," Berger said. "If she did, it wasn't on her private jet, the Gulfstream. She never showed up at the FBO in White Plains."

"This is what Bobby told you?" Benton asked. "We know it's true?"

"He said it, and there's a manifest for the flight. She didn't show up at the FBO. She didn't board the jet, and Bobby wasn't on the manifest for the flight to Saint Barts," Berger answered. "She also wasn't answering the phone. Their New York housekeeper—"

"And her name is?" Lanier asked.

"Nastya." She spelled it, and the name appeared on the wall. "She lives in the mansion and, according to her, Hannah never came home after having dinner in the Village on November twenty-sixth. But apparently this wasn't reason enough to call the police. Sometimes she didn't come home. She'd been at a birthday dinner. One if by Land, Two if by Sea on Barrow Street. She was with a group of friends and supposedly was seen getting into a yellow cab as everyone left the restaurant. That's what we know so far."

"Bobby know she screwed around on him?" O'Dell said.

"'A lot of space in their togetherness' is the way he described it. I don't know what he knows," Berger said. "Maybe what Hap said is true. Bobby and Hannah were business partners more than anything else. He claims he loves her, but we certainly hear that all the time."

"In other words, they have an arrangement. Maybe both of them screw around. He's from money, right?" O'Dell said.

"Not her kind of money. But from a well-off family in California, went to Stanford, got his MBA from Yale, was a successful alternative asset manager, involved in a couple of funds, one U.K.-based, one Monaco-based."

"These hedge fund guys. I mean, some of them were making hundreds of millions," said O'Dell.

"A lot of them aren't now, and some are in jail. What about Bobby?" Stockman said to Berger. "He lose his shirt?"

"Like a lot of these investors, he was counting on energy prices and mining stocks continuing to soar while financials continued to fall. This is what he told me," she replied.

"And then the trend reversed in July," Stockman said.

"He described it as a bloodbath," Berger said. "He can't afford the lifestyle he's grown accustomed to without the Starr fortune, that's for sure."

"So the two of them are more of a merger than a marriage," O'Dell said.

"I can't attest to his real feelings. Who the hell ever knows the truth about what people feel," she said without a trace of emotion. "He seemed distraught when I talked to him, when I met with him. When she didn't show up for her flight on Thanksgiving, he claims he began to panic, called the police, and the police contacted me. Bobby claims he was afraid his wife was the victim of violence and stated that she'd had trouble in the past with being stalked. He flew to New York, met us at the house, walked us through it, at which time we collected a toothbrush of Hannah's to get her DNA in case it turned out to be needed. In the event a body turns up somewhere."

"The photo albums." Benton was still thinking about Lucy and wondering what other secrets she kept. "Why would he show them to you?"

"I inquired about Hannah's clients, if one of them might have targeted her. He said he didn't know who most of her late father's clients, Rupe Starr's clients, were. Bobby suggested we—"

"Who's 'we'?"

"Marino was with me. Bobby suggested we look through the photo albums because it was Rupe's habit to entertain a new client at the mansion, an initiation more than an invitation. If you didn't come to dinner, he didn't take you on. He wanted to have relationships with his clients, and apparently did."

"You saw Lucy's picture from 1996," Benton said, and he could only imagine how Berger felt. "Did Marino see it, too?"

"I recognized her in the photograph. Marino wasn't in the library with me when I found it. He didn't see it."

"Did you ask Bobby about it?" Benton wasn't going to ask her why she'd withheld the information from Marino.

He suspected he knew. Berger was hoping Lucy would tell her the truth, that Berger wouldn't have to confront her. Obviously, Lucy hadn't.

"I didn't show the picture to Bobby or mention it," Berger said. "He wouldn't have known Lucy back then. Hannah and Bobby have been together less than two years."

"Doesn't mean he doesn't know about Lucy," Benton said. "Hannah could have mentioned Lucy to him. I'd be surprised if she didn't. When you were in the library, Jaime, did you pick that particular album off a shelf? Rupe Starr must have dozens of them."

"Scores of them," she said. "Bobby put a stack of them on the table for me."

"Any possibility he wanted you to find the photograph

of Lucy?" Benton had one of his feelings again. Something in his gut that was sending him a message.

"He put them on the table and walked out of the library," Berger replied.

A game. And a cruel one, if Bobby had done it deliberately, Benton thought. If he knew about Berger's private life, he would know it would upset her to discover her partner, her forensic computer expert, had been in the Starr mansion, had been mixed up with those people and had said nothing about it.

"You don't mind my asking," Lanier said to Berger, "why would you allow Lucy to handle the forensic computer part of this investigation if she had ties with the alleged victim? In fact, with the entire Starr family?"

Berger didn't answer at first. Then she said, "I was waiting for her to explain it."

"What is the explanation?" Lanier asked.

"I'm still waiting for it."

"Okay. Well, it could be a problem down the road," Stockman said. "If this goes to court."

"I consider it a problem now." Berger's face was grim. "A much bigger problem than I care to describe."

"Where's Bobby now?" Lanier asked her in a milder tone than she'd used so far.

"It appears back here in the city," Berger said. "He e-mails Hannah. E-mails her daily."

"That's fucked up," O'Dell said.

"Whether it is or it isn't, he's been doing it. We know because obviously we're accessing her e-mail. He e-mailed her late last night and said he'd heard about some development in the case and was returning to New York early this morning. I would expect he's here by now."

"Unless the guy's an imbecile, he must suspect somebody's looking at her e-mails. Makes me suspicious he's doing it for our benefit," O'Dell said.

"My first thought, too," Lanier said.

Games, Benton thought, and the uneasy feeling was stronger.

"I don't know what he suspects. Ostensibly, he's hoping Hannah is alive somewhere and is reading his e-mails to her," Berger said. "I'm assuming he's aware of what was on *The Crispin Report* last night, about Hannah's head hair supposedly being found in a cab. And that's why he's suddenly returning to the city."

"Same thing as hearing she's dead. Damn reporters," Stockman said. "Anything for ratings and don't give a flying flip about what it does to people whose lives they wreck." He said to Benton, "She really say that about us? You know, about the FBI, about profiling being antiquated?"

Stockman meant Scarpetta and what was on the CNN marquee and all over the Internet last night.

"I believe she was misquoted," Benton said blandly. "I think she meant the good ole days were gone and were never all that good."

21

The guard hairs were long and coarse, with four bands of white and black along a shaft that tapered to a point.

"You can do DNA if you want to confirm the species," Geffner was saying over speakerphone. "I know a lab in Pennsylvania, Mitotyping Technologies, that specializes in species determination of animals. But I can tell you already from what I'm looking at. Classic wolf. Great Plains wolf, a subspecies of gray wolf."

"It's not dog, all right, if you say so. I admit it looks like German shepherd fur to me," Scarpetta said from a work station where she could view images Geffner was uploading to her.

Across the lab, Lucy and Marino were monitoring what was going on with the MacBooks, and from where Scarpetta sat, she could see data rapidly aggregating into charts and maps.

"You won't find these banded guard hairs on a German shepherd." Geffner's voice.

"And the finer grayish hairs I'm seeing?" Scarpetta asked.

"Mixed in with the guard hairs. That's just some inner fur. The voodoo-like doll that was glued to the front of the card? It was stuffed with fur, both inner and guard, and some debris mixed in, maybe a little poop and dead leaves and such. An indication the fur hasn't been processed, likely is from their natural habitat, maybe their lair. I've not looked at all of the fur submitted, obviously. But my guess is it's all wolf fur. Guard hairs and hairs from the inner coat."

"Where would someone get it?"

"I did some searching and came up with a few possible sources," Geffner said. "Wildlife preserves, wolf sanctuaries, zoos. Wolf fur is also sold in a well-known witchery in Salem, Massachusetts, called the Hex."

"On Essex Street, in the historic area," Scarpetta said. "I've been in there. A lot of nice oils and candles. Nothing black magic or evil."

"Doesn't have to be evil to be used for evil, I guess," Geffner said. "The Hex sells amulets, potions, and you can buy wolf fur in little gold silk bags. It's supposed to be protective and have healing powers. I doubt anything sold like that would have been processed, so maybe the wolf fur in the doll came from a magic shop."

Lucy was looking at Scarpetta from across the room, as if she was finding something significant that Scarpetta was going to want to see.

As Geffner explained, "Wolves have two layers of fur. The inner, which is the softer sort of wool-like fur that insulates, what I call filler hair. And then this outer coat, the guard layer, coarse hairs that shed water and have the pigmentation you're seeing on the image I sent. The difference in the species is the color. The Great Plains wolf

isn't native to this area. Mostly the Midwest. And you usually don't get wolf fur in criminal cases. Not here in New
York."

"I don't believe I ever have," Scarpetta said. "Here or
anywhere."

Lucy and Marino in their protective garb were standing
and talking tensely. Scarpetta couldn't hear what they were
saying. Something was happening.

"I've seen it for one reason or another." Geffner's easy-
going tenor voice. Not much excited him. He'd been
tracking criminals with a microscope for quite a number
of years. "The crap in people's house. You ever looked at
dust bunnies under the scope? More interesting than
astronomy, a whole universe of information about who and
what goes in and out of a person's residence. All kinds of
hair and fur."

Marino and Lucy were looking at charts rolling by on
the MacBook screens.

"Shit," Marino said loudly, and his safety glasses looked
at Scarpetta. "Doc? You better see this."

And Geffner's voice continued. "Some people raise
wolves or mostly hybrids, a mixture of wolf and canine. But
pure unprocessed wolf fur in a voodoo doll or puppet? More
likely this is connected with the ritualistic motif of the
bomb. Everything I'm researching indicates this is a black-
magic type of thing, although the symbolism is conflicted
and sort of contradictory. Wolves aren't bad. It's just everything else is, including the explosives, the firecrackers,
which would have hurt you or someone, done some real
damage."

"I don't know what you've found." Scarpetta was
reminding him that all she knew so far was that what

Marino had assumed was dog fur and now was identified as wolf fur had been recovered from the bomb debris.

Across the lab, maps were rolling by on one of the MacBooks. Street maps. Photo, elevation, and topographic maps.

"Preliminarily, this is as much as I can tell you." Geffner's voice. "The terrible odor, and there is one. Sort of tarry and sort of like shit, if you'll excuse my French. You familiar with asafoetida?"

"I don't cook Indian food, but I'm familiar enough. An herb rather notorious for its disgusting odor."

Marino rustled as he walked closer to Scarpetta and said, "She had it on the whole time."

"She had on what?" Scarpetta said to him.

"The watch and one of those sensors." The part of his face that showed between the mask and the bouffant cap was flushed and he was sweating.

"Excuse me," she said to Geffner. "I'm sorry. I'm doing about twenty things at once. What about the devil?"

"There's a reason it's called devil's dung," Geffner repeated, "and it might interest you to know that supposedly wolves are attracted to the odor of asafoetida."

The sound of papery feet. Lucy walking across the white-tile floor to a work station, checking various connections and unplugging a large flat-screen monitor. She walked to another work station node and disconnected that monitor.

"Someone went to a fair amount of trouble to grind up asafoetida and what looks like asphalt and mix it with some kind of clear oil like a grapeseed oil, a linseed oil."

Lucy carried the video displays to where Scarpetta sat and set them on her desk. She plugged the monitors into a port hub and the screens began to illuminate, images rolling down slowly and hazily, then sharply defined. Lucy's papery sounds as she returned to her MacBooks, to Marino, the two of them talking. Scarpetta caught the words *fucking slow* and *ordered wrong*. Lucy was aggravated.

"I'm going to do gas chromatography–mass spec. FTIR. But with the microscope so far?" Geffner was saying.

Charts and maps and screen shots rolling by. Vital signs and dates and times. Mobility and exposure to ambient light. Scarpetta scanned data from the BioGraph device, and she looked at the file she'd just opened on the computer screen in front of her. Microscopic images: curled silvery ribbons covered with a rash of rust, and what looked like fragmented bullets.

"Definitely iron filings"—Geffner's voice—"which were readily identifiable visually and with a magnet, and mixed in with this are dull gray particles, also heavy. They sunk to the bottom of a test tube filled with water. Maybe lead."

Toni Darien's vital signs, locations, the weather, dates, and times, captured every fifteen seconds. At two-twelve p.m. this past Tuesday, December 16, the temperature was seventy degrees Fahrenheit, the intensity of ambient white light luminescence was five hundred lux, typical of indoor lighting, her pulse oximetry was ninety-nine percent, her heart rate sixty-four, her pace was five steps, and her location was her apartment on Second Avenue. She was home and awake and walking around. Assuming she was the one wearing the BioGraph device. Scarpetta was going to assume it.

Geffner described, "I'll verify with x-ray fluorescence spectroscopy. Definitely quartz fragments, which I would expect with ground-up asphalt. I've touched a hot tungsten needle to some of the dark-brown and black sticky, viscous semisolid liquid material to see if it softened it, and it did. It does have a characteristic asphalt/petroleum odor."

What Scarpetta had smelled when she'd carried the FedEx box upstairs. Asafoetida and asphalt. She watched charts and maps slowly roll by. She followed Toni Darien's journey as it carried her closer to death. At two-fifteen on December 16, her pace picked up and the temperature dropped to thirty-nine degrees. Humidity eighty-five percent, ambient light eight hundred lux, winds out of the northeast. She was outside, and it was cold and overcast, her pulse oximetry ninety-nine percent as her heart rate began to climb: sixty-five, sixty-seven, seventy, eighty-five, and climbing as minutes passed, heading west on East 86th Street at a pace of thirty-three steps per fifteen seconds. Toni was running.

And Geffner was explaining, "I'm seeing what could be ground peppercorns, their physical properties and morphology characteristic for black, white, and red pepper. I'll verify with GCMS analysis. Asafoetida, iron, lead, pepper, asphalt. The components of a potion that's meant to be a curse."

"Or what Marino's calling a stink bomb." Scarpetta talked to Geffner while she followed Toni Darien west on East 86th Street.

She turned south on Park Avenue, her pulse oximetry ninety-nine percent, her heart rate one hundred and twenty-three beats per minute.

"Ritualistic black magic, but I can't find anything that specifically identifies a certain sect or religion," Geffner was saying. "Not Palo Mayombe or Santeria, nothing I've seen reminds me of what I associate with their rituals and sorcery. I just know your potion wasn't meant to bring any good fortune your way, which gets me back to the contradiction. Wolves are supposed to be favorable, to have great powers of restoring peace and harmony, to have healing powers and bring good luck in hunting."

At four minutes and thirty seconds past three p.m., Toni passed 63rd Street, still jogging south on Park Avenue. The intensity of ambient light was less than seven hundred lux, the relative humidity one hundred percent. It had gotten more overcast and was raining. Her pulse oximetry was the same, her heart rate up to one forty. Grace Darien had said that Toni didn't like to jog in gloomy weather. But she was doing it, running in the cold and rain. Why? Scarpetta kept looking at data as Geffner kept talking.

"The only witchcraft connection I could find is the Navajo word for 'wolf'—*mai-coh*—means 'witch.' A person who can transform himself into something or someone else if he puts on a wolf skin. According to myth, witches or werewolves change shape so they can travel unnoticed. And the Pawnees used wolf skins and fur to protect their treasures and for various magical ceremonies. I've been looking up what I can as we've been moving things along in here. Don't want you to think I'm the world's expert on hexes and mumbo jumbo and folklore."

"I guess the question's going to be if it's the same person who sent the singing Christmas card." Scarpetta was thinking of Benton's former patient Dodie Hodge, and she was looking at data rolling by.

Pulse oximetry the same, but Toni's heart rate was dropping. At the corner of Park and East 58th she must have stopped running. Heart rate one thirty-two, one thirty-one, one thirty, and dropping. She was walking south on Park Avenue in the rain. The time was now eleven past three p.m.

Geffner said, "I think the question is what the person who made your stink bomb might have to do with the Toni Darien homicide."

"Would you please repeat that?" Scarpetta asked as she looked at a GPS screen shot captured by Toni Darien's BioGraph watchlike device at three-fourteen this past Tuesday afternoon. A red arrow on a topographic map pointing to a Park Avenue address.

Hannah Starr's mansion.

"What did you say about Toni Darien?" Scarpetta asked, looking at more GPS screen shots, thinking she was misinterpreting, but she wasn't.

Toni Darien's run had taken her to the Starrs' address. That was why she was jogging in gloomy weather. She was meeting someone.

"More wolf fur," Geffner said. "Fragments of guard hairs."

Pulse oximetry ninety-nine percent. Heart rate eighty-three and dropping. GPS screen shot after screen shot as minutes passed and Toni's heart rate dropped, returning to its resting rate. The sound of shoe covers on tile. Marino and Lucy were walking toward Scarpetta.

"You see where she is?" Lucy's eyes were intense behind the safety glasses. She was making sure Scarpetta understood the significance of the GPS data.

"I'm nowhere near done with analyzing what you submitted in the Darien case." Geffner's voice inside the training lab. "But mixed in with the samples you submitted yesterday are fragments of wolf hair, guard hair, microscopic fragments that are similar to what I just saw when I looked at the fur from the voodoo doll. White, black, coarse. I might not have been able to identify it as wolf fur because it's not intact enough, but it crossed my mind. That or canine. But after seeing what came in with your bomb? That's what I'm thinking it is. In fact, willing to bet."

Marino frowned, and he was very agitated when he said, "You're saying it's not dog fur. It's wolf fur, and it's in both cases? In Toni Darien's case and the bomb case?"

"Marino?" Geffner sounded confused. "That you?"

"I'm here. In the lab with the Doc. What the hell are you talking about? You sure you didn't get something mixed up?"

"I'm going to pretend you didn't say that. The DNA lab I was telling you about, Dr. Scarpetta?"

"I agree," she replied. "We should get the species of wolf identified, make sure they're the same, that the hairs in both cases are from Great Plains wolves."

She listened to him, and she looked at data. Temperature thirty-eight degrees, relative humidity ninety-nine percent, heart rate seventy-seven. Two minutes and fifteen seconds later, at three-seventeen p.m., the temperature was sixty-nine degrees and the humidity was thirty percent: Toni Darien had walked inside Hannah Starr's house.

Detective Bonnell parked in front of a limestone mansion that reminded Berger of Newport, Rhode Island, of massive monuments from an era in America when staggering wealth was made from coal, cotton, silver, and steel, from tangible commodities that scarcely existed anymore.

"I don't get it." Bonnell was staring at the limestone façade of a residence that took up the better part of a city block just a few minutes' walk from Central Park South.

"Eighty million dollars? Who the hell has money like that?" The expression on her face was a mixture of awe and disgust.

"Not Bobby anymore," Berger said. "At least not that we know of. I assume he'll have to sell it, and nobody's going to buy it unless it's some sheikh from Dubai."

"Or if Hannah shows up."

"She and the family fortune are long gone. One way or the other," Berger said.

"Jesus." Bonnell looked at the mansion, and she looked at cars and pedestrians going past. She was looking at everything except Berger. "It makes me think we're really not on the same planet as some people. My place in Queens? I wouldn't know what it's like to live somewhere and not hear assholes yelling and cars honking and sirens morning, noon, and night. The other week, I had a rat. It ran across the bathroom floor and disappeared behind the toilet, and that's all I think about every time I go in there, if you know what I mean. It's probably not true they can come up from the sewer."

Berger unfastened her seat belt and tried Marino on her BlackBerry again. He wasn't answering, and neither was Lucy. If they were still inside the DNA Building, they either weren't getting a signal or weren't allowed to have their cell phones with them, depending on which lab or work space they were in. The OCME's forensic biological sciences facility was probably the largest, most sophisticated one in the world. Marino and Lucy could be anywhere in there, and Berger didn't feel like calling the damn switchboard and tracking them down.

"I'm about to go into the interview on Park Ave," she left Marino another message. "So I might not be able to answer when you call back. Wondering what you found in the lab."

Her voice sounded cool, her tone flat and unfriendly. She was angry with Marino, and she didn't know what she felt about Lucy, grief or fury, love or hate, and something else that was a little bit like dying. What Berger knew about dying, at any rate. She imagined it must be like sliding off the side of a cliff, hanging on until you lose your grip, and on your way down wondering who to blame. Berger blamed Lucy, and she blamed herself. Denial, looking the other way, maybe the same thing Bobby was doing when he continued e-mailing Hannah every day.

For three weeks Berger had known about the photographs taken in 1996 at the very mansion she and Bonnell were about to enter, and Berger's response was to hop aboard avoidance, to pick up the pace and outrun what she couldn't handle. If anybody knew about untruthfulness and its derailments, Berger did. She talked to evasive, unrealistic people all the time, but that hadn't made a difference—knowing better never does when one is about to suffer, about to lose it all—and she'd ridden hard and fast until this morning. Until Bonnell had tracked her down at the FBI field office to pass along information she thought the prosecutor would want to know.

"I'm just going to say this before we go inside," Berger said. "I'm not a weak person, and I'm not a coward. Seeing a few photographs taken twelve years ago is one thing. What you told me is another. I had reason to believe Lucy knew Rupe Starr when she was in college, but no reason to believe she was financially involved with Hannah as recently as six months ago. Now the story has changed and we will act accordingly. I want you to hear this directly, because you don't know me. And this isn't a good way to start."

"I didn't mean to do anything out of line." Bonnell had said this several times. "But what Lucy found in Warner Agee's hotel room, in his computer? Now it involves my case because of him impersonating my witness, Harvey Fahley. And we don't know how deep it's going to get, what all these people are involved in, especially with the implications of organized crime and what you were telling me about the French guy with the genetic disorder."

"You don't have to keep explaining yourself."

"It's not that I wanted to snoop or that I was curious and abused my privileges or position as a police officer. I wouldn't have asked RTCC if I wasn't legitimately concerned about Lucy's credibility. I was going to have to depend on her, and I've heard some things. She was paramilitary once, wasn't she? And got fired from the FBI or ATF. Her helping you out with Hannah Starr had nothing to do with me. But now it does. I'm the lead detective in the Toni Darien case."

"I understand." And Berger did.

"I want to make sure you do," Bonnell said. "You're the DA, the head of the Sex Crimes Unit. I've only been in homicide a year and we've not worked together yet. It's not a good way to start for me, either. But I'm not going to accept a witness at face value, no questions asked, just because she's someone you know—a friend. Lucy will be my witness, so I had to check out a few things."

"She's not my friend."

"She'll end up on the stand if Toni's case goes to court. Or if Hannah's does."

"She's not just a friend. You and I both know what she is," Berger said, and emotions shook inside her. "I'm sure I was on that damn data wall in RTCC for all the world to see. She's more than a friend. I know you're not naïve."

"The analysts out of respect didn't put Lucy's info on the wall. Or anything about you. We were at a work station going through the data, all the links found. I'm not trying to get into your business. I don't care what people do in their personal lives unless it's illegal, and I didn't expect RTCC to turn up what they did about Bay Bridge Finance. That connects Lucy directly to Hannah. I'm not saying it means Lucy's involved in fraud."

"We're going to find out," Berger said.

"If he'll tell us or if he knows." Bonnell meant Bobby. "And he might not, for the same reason Lucy might not. Some people who have that kind of money don't know the details because other people do the investing and management and all the rest. That's what happened to Bernie Madoff's victims. Same thing. They didn't know, and they didn't do anything wrong."

"Lucy isn't the type not to know," Berger said, and she also knew Lucy wasn't the type to let it go.

Bay Bridge Finance was a brokerage that purportedly specialized in portfolio diversification ventures such as timber, mining, petroleum extraction, and real estate, including high-end waterfront apartments in South Florida. Based on what Berger knew about the magnitude of fraud perpetrated by that Ponzi-scamming entity exposed not so long ago, chances were good that Lucy's losses were massive. She intended to find out what she could from Bobby Fuller, not only about Hannah's finances but also her affair with Hap Judd, whose proclivities were deeply disturbing and possibly dangerous. It was time to confront Bobby about Hap and a number of things, to present him with myriad links in hopes he could enlighten them, and he seemed willing. When Berger had reached him on his cell phone less than an hour ago, he'd said he would be happy to talk with Bonnell and her as long as it wasn't in a public place. Like last time, they needed to meet him here.

"Let's go," Berger said to Bonnell, and they got out of the unmarked car.

It was cold and very windy, and dark clouds streamed across the sky the way they did when a front was moving in. Probably a high-pressure system, and tomorrow would be clear skies, what Lucy called "severe clear," but bitterly cold. They followed the walkway off the avenue, and over the mansion's grand entranceway was a green-and-white flag with the Starr coat of arms, a rampant lion and a helmet and the motto *Vivre en espoir,* live in hope. An irony, Berger thought. Hope was the one emotion she didn't feel right now.

She pushed a button on an intercom that had *Starr* on it and *Private Residence.* She burrowed her hands in the pockets of her coat as she and Bonnell waited in silence in the wind, the flag snapping loudly, mindful that they were likely being monitored by closed-circuit cameras and that anything they said might be overheard. The loud click of a deadbolt, and the ornately carved mahogany entry door opened, and then the shape of someone in the black-and-white uniform of a housekeeper showed through spaces in the wrought-iron gate.

Nastya, Berger presumed, was letting them in without

asking who they were over the intercom because she knew, had observed them on a security monitor, and they were expected. Her legal immigration status had been all over the news, and several photographs were in circulation, accompanied by rumors of the services she supplied Bobby besides cooking his dinner and making his bed. The housekeeper the press had dubbed "Nasty" was in her mid-thirties, with pronounced cheekbones, olive skin, and striking blue eyes.

"Please come in." Nastya stepped aside.

The foyer was travertine marble with open arches and a twenty-foot coffered ceiling centered by an antique chandelier of amethyst and smoky-quartz glass. Off to one side, a stairway with an elaborate iron railing curved upstairs, and Nastya asked them to follow her to the library. Berger remembered it was on the third floor, toward the back of the mansion, an enormous interior room where Rupe Starr had spent a lifetime accumulating an antiquarian library worthy of a university or a palace.

"Mr. Fuller had a very long night and a very early morning, and we are so upset by what's been on the news." Nastya stopped on the steps and looked back at Berger. "Is it true?" The sound of her feet on stone as she continued, talking with her back to them and turning her head slightly to the side. "I always worry about who's driving the taxis. You get in, and what do you know, and off you go with a stranger who could take you anywhere. Can I offer you something to drink? Coffee or tea or water or something stronger? It's all right to drink in the library, as long as you don't set something near the books."

"We're fine," Berger replied.

On the third floor they followed a long hallway that was

covered by an antique silk runner in different shades of deep red and rose, and they passed a series of shut doors leading to the library, which smelled mustier than Berger remembered from three weeks ago. The silver chandeliers were electric, the lights turned low, and the room was chilly and unlived-in, as if no one had been in it since Berger was at Thanksgiving. The Florentine leather-bound photo albums she had looked at were still stacked on the library table, and in front of them was the needlework side chair where she had been sitting when she'd found several photographs of Lucy. On a smaller table with a griffin base was an empty crystal glass that she remembered Bobby setting down after drinking several fingers of cognac to settle his nerves. The paneled longcase clock near the fireplace hadn't been wound.

"Remind me again about your situation here," Berger said as she and Bonnell sat on a leather sofa. "You have an apartment on which floor?"

"On the fourth floor in the back," Nastya said, and her eye caught the same details Berger had. The unwound clock and the dirty glass. "I haven't been staying here until today. With Mr. Fuller away . . ."

"In Florida," Berger said.

"He told me you were coming, and I hurried over. I've been in a hotel. He was kind enough to put me in one not far from here so I'm available when needed but not sleeping alone in this place. You can understand why that would be uncomfortable right now."

"Which hotel?" Bonnell asked.

"The Hotel Elysée. The Starr family has used it for years when they have out-of-town guests and business associates who they didn't want staying in the house. It's only a few minutes' walk. You can appreciate why I wouldn't want to stay here right now. Well, it's been very stressful these past weeks. What happened to Hannah and then the media, the vans with their cameras. You never know when they will appear, and it's worse because of that same woman who said those things on CNN last night. Every night, it's all she talks about, and she's constantly bothering Mr. Fuller for interviews. People have no respect. Mr. Fuller gave me time off because why would I want to stay here alone right now?"

"Carley Crispin," Berger said. "She bothers Bobby Fuller?"

"I can't stand her, but I watch because I want to know. But I don't know what to believe," Nastya said. "That was terrible what she said last night. I burst into tears, I was so upset."

"How does she bother Mr. Fuller?" Bonnell asked. "I would imagine he's not easy to reach."

"All I know is she's been here before." Nastya pulled an armchair close and sat. "At a party or two in the past. When she was a White House person, what do you call it? A press secretary. I wasn't here, it was before my time, but you know about Mr. Starr and his famous dinners and parties. That's why there are all these picture books." She indicated the photo albums on the library table. "And many, many more on the shelves. Over thirty years of them, and you probably didn't go through all of them?" she asked, because she hadn't been here the day Berger and Marino had been.

Only Bobby had been home, and Berger hadn't gone through all the albums, only a few. After she found the photographs from 1996, she'd stopped looking.

"Not that it's surprising about Carley Crispin having been to dinners here," Nastya went on proudly. "At one time or another, probably half the famous people in the world have been through this house. But Hannah probably knew her or at least met her. I hate how quiet it's been. Since Mr. Starr died, well, those days are past. And we used to have so many celebrations, so much excitement, so many people. Mr. Fuller is much more private, and he's gone most of the time."

The housekeeper seemed perfectly at ease sitting in a library that she had neither tidied nor cleaned in the last three weeks. Were it not for her uniform, she could be the mistress of the mansion, and it was interesting that she called Hannah Starr by her first name and spoke of her in the past tense. Yet Bobby was Mr. Fuller, and he was late. It was four-twenty, and there was no sign of him. Berger wondered if it was possible he wasn't home, had decided not to meet with them after all. The house was extremely quiet, not even the distant sounds of traffic penetrated the limestone walls, and there were no windows in here, the space like a mausoleum or a vault, perhaps to protect the rare books, art, and antiques from unwanted exposure to sunlight and moisture.

"It's all the more terrible she talks about Hannah the way she does," Nastya went on about Carley Crispin. "Night after night. How do you do that when it's someone you've met?"

"Do you have any idea the last time Carley was here?" Berger asked, getting out her phone.

"I don't know."

"You said she bothers Mr. Fuller." Bonnell got back to that. "She knows him, maybe because of Hannah?"

"I just know she's called here."

"How does she have the number?" Bonnell asked.

Berger wanted to try Bobby's cell phone to see where he was, but she couldn't get a signal in the library.

"I don't know. I don't answer the phone anymore. I'm afraid it might be a reporter. You know, people can find out so much these days. You never know who might somehow get your number," Nastya said as her eyes wandered to an enormous canvas of clipper ships, what looked like a Montague Dawson that filled a mahogany panel of wall between floor-to-ceiling bookcases.

"Why would Hannah take a taxi?" Bonnell asked. "How did she usually get around when she went out to dinner?"

"She drove herself." Nastya's eyes were fixed on the painting. "But if she was going to have a few drinks, she didn't drive. Sometimes clients or friends gave her a ride or she would use a limo. But you know, you live in New York, no matter who you are, you take taxis if that's what you need to do. And sometimes she would if it was last minute. All their cars, a lot of them very old and not driven on the street. Mr. Starr's collection? You've seen it. Maybe when you were here, Mr. Fuller showed it to you?"

Berger hadn't seen it, and she didn't answer.

"In the basement garage," Nastya added.

When Bobby Fuller had shown Berger and Marino around, they hadn't been given a tour of the basement. An antique car collection hadn't seemed important at the time.

"Sometimes one of them gets blocked in," Nastya said.

"Blocked in?" Berger said.

"The Bentley, because Mr. Fuller had been moving things around down there." Nastya's attention returned to the maritime painting. "He's very proud of his cars and spends a lot of time with them."

"Hannah couldn't drive her Bentley to dinner because it was blocked in," Berger repeated.

"The weather was messy, too. And all those cars, and most you can't take out. The Duesenberg. Bugati. Ferrai." She didn't pronounce them right.

"Maybe I'm confused," Berger said. "I thought Bobby wasn't home that night."

22

Scarpetta sat at the work station, alone in the training lab, Lucy and Marino having left moments ago to find Berger and Benton.

She continued to review what Geffner was sending and what was rolling by on the other two monitors, studying multilayered paint chips, one chrome-yellow, the other racecar-red, and data that moved Toni Darien's life minute by minute closer to its end.

"The debris you collected from Toni Darien's head wound and particularly from her hair," Geffner said over speakerphone. "I cross-sectioned the ones you're looking at but haven't had a chance to Melt Mount any of the samples yet, so this is rough, really quick and dirty. You got the images up?"

"I've got them." Scarpetta looked at the paint chips, and she looked at charts and maps and a multitude of graphs.

Thousands of reports from the BioGraph, and she couldn't pause the images or replay them or skip forward, had no choice but to look at data as Lucy's programs sifted through and sorted it. The process wasn't fast enough or facile, and it was confusing. The problem was Caligula. They didn't have the proprietary software that had been developed for the express purpose of aggregating and manipulating the galaxy of data collected by the BioGraph devices.

"The chrome-yellow chip is an oil-based paint, an acrylic melamine and alkyd resin, from an older vehicle," Geffner was explaining. "And then the red chip. That's much newer. You can tell because the pigments are organic-based dyes versus inorganic heavy metals."

Scarpetta had been following Toni Darien through Hannah Starr's house for the past twenty-seven minutes, Toni Darien's minutes, from three-twenty-six p.m. to three-fifty-three p.m. this past Tuesday. During that interval, the ambient temperature of the Park Avenue mansion had remained between sixty-nine and seventy-two as Toni had moved through different areas of it, her pace slow and sporadic, her heart rate not peaking above sixty-seven, as if she was relaxed, maybe walking around and talking to someone. Then the temperature suddenly began to drop. Sixty-nine to sixty-five to sixty-three and falling, while her mobility was constant, ten to twenty paces every fifteen seconds, a leisurely pace. She was walking somewhere in the Starr house where it was cooler.

"Obviously, the paint wasn't transferred from the weapon," Scarpetta said to Geffner. "Unless it was painted with automotive paint."

"More likely a passive transfer." Geffner's voice. "Either from whatever she was struck with or possibly a vehicle that transported her body."

Sixty degrees, fifty-nine, fifty-eight, and falling as Toni continued to move, her pace slow. Eight steps. Three steps.

Seventeen steps. No steps. One step. Four steps. Every fifteen seconds. Temperature fifty-five degrees. It was cool. Her mobility was consistent. She was walking and stopping, maybe talking, maybe looking at something.

"Not from the same source unless it's another passive transfer," Scarpetta said. "A yellow paint chip is from an older vehicle, the red one from a vehicle that's much newer."

"Exactly. The pigments in the chrome-yellow chips are inorganic and contain lead," Geffner said. "I already know I'm going to find lead even though I haven't used micro-FTIR, pryolysis GC–MS. The chips you're looking at are easily distinguishable from each other in terms of age. The newer paint has a thick, clear protective top coat, a thin base coat with red organic pigment, and then three colored primer coats. The chrome-yellow chip has no clear topcoat and a thick base coat, then primer. A couple of black chips? They're new, too. Just the yellow's old."

More charts and maps slowly rolling by. Three-fifty-nine p.m. Toni Darien time. Four-oh-one p.m. Four-oh-three p.m. Her pulse oximetry ninety-nine percent, her heart rate sixty-six, her pace eight to sixteen steps, illumination a consistent three hundred lux. The temperature had dropped to fifty-five. She was walking around someplace cool and dimly lit. Her vital signs indicated she wasn't in any sort of distress.

"They haven't used lead in paint for what?" Scarpetta said. "Twenty-something years?"

"Heavy-metal pigments are the seventies and eighties and earlier because they're not environmentally friendly," he answered. "Consistent with fibers you collected from her wound, her hair, various areas of her body. Synthetic monoacrylic, overdyed black, at least fifteen different types I've seen so far, which I associate with waste fibers, low-end stuff typical of rugs and trunk liners in older vehicles."

"What about fibers from a newer vehicle?" Scarpetta asked.

"So far all I've seen from what you submitted are a lot of the waste fibers."

"Consistent with her body being transported in a car," Scarpetta said. "But not likely a yellow cab."

Four-ten p.m. Toni Darien time, and something happened. Something sudden and swift and devastatingly decisive. In the span of thirty seconds, her pace went from two steps to zero and her mobility stopped. She wasn't moving her arms or legs, any part of her body, and her pulse oximetry had dropped: ninety-eight percent, then ninety-seven. Her heart rate slowed to sixty.

"I anticipated you'd mention that because of what's all over the news," Geffner said. "The average age of a yellow cab in New York City is less than four years old. You can imagine the miles that are put on those things. Not likely, and in fact extremely improbable, the chrome-yellow paint chip came from a yellow cab. Some old vehicle, don't ask me what."

Four-sixteen p.m. Toni Darien time. She became mobile again, but she wasn't walking, her pace register-ing zero on the pedometer built into her watch. Mobile but taking no steps, probably not upright. Someone else was moving her. Pulse oximetry was ninety-five percent, heart rate fifty-seven. Same ambient temperature and illu-mination. She was in the same part of the mansion, and she was dying.

". . . Other trace is rust. And microscopic particulate like sand, rocks, clays, decayed organic matter, plus some insect pieces and parts. In other words, dirt."

Scarpetta imagined Toni Darien being struck from behind, a forceful single blow to the left back of her head. She would have collapsed instantly, fallen to the floor. She wasn't conscious anymore. Four-twenty p.m., and the oxygen saturation of her blood was ninety-four percent and her heart rate was fifty-five. She was mobile again. There was a lot of motion, but her pace remained zero. She wasn't walking. Someone was moving her.

". . . I can send you images of that," Geffner was saying, and Scarpetta was scarcely listening. "Pollen, hair fragments that show insect damage, insect fecal matter, and of course dust mites. A lot of those all over her, and I doubt they came from Central Park. Maybe from whatever she was transported in. Or someplace with a lot of dust."

Charts rolling by. Peaks and bumps on actigraphy graphs. Consistent motion every fifteen seconds, minute after minute. Someone moving her repetitively, rhythmically.

". . . Which are microscopic arachnids, and I would expect an abundance of them in an old carpet or a room with a lot of dust. Dust mites die if there's nothing to feed on anymore, such as sloughed-off skin cells, which is mainly what they're after inside the house . . ."

Four-twenty-nine p.m. Toni Darien time. Pulse oximetry ninety-three percent, heart rate forty-nine beats per minute. She was becoming hypoxic, the low oxygen saturation of her blood beginning to starve her brain as it swelled and bled from its catastrophic injury. Peaks and bumps on actigraphs, her body moving in a rhythm of waves and lines, a repeatable pattern over an extended time measured in seconds, in minutes.

". . . in other words, house dust . . ."

"Thank you," Scarpetta said. "I've got to go," she said to Geffner, and she got off the phone.

The training lab was silent. Graphs and charts and maps rolling by on two large flat screens. She sat mesmerized as the rhythm continued, but different now, in fits and starts and at some intervals extreme and then quiet, and then it would begin again. At five p.m. Toni Darien time, her pulse oximetry was seventy-nine, her heart rate thirty-three. She was in a coma. One minute later the actigraph flatlined because the motion had stopped. Four minutes later there was no further mobility and the ambient illumination suddenly diminished from three hundred lux to less than one. Someone had turned out the lights. At five-fourteen p.m. Toni Darien died in the dark.

Lucy opened the trunk of Marino's car as Benton and a woman climbed out of a black SUV and walked swiftly across Park Avenue. It was past five o'clock, nighttime and cold, and a fitful wind whipped the flag over the Starr mansion entrance.

"Anything?" Benton said, flipping up the collar of his coat.

"We've walked around trying to see in the windows, detect any kind of activity inside. So far nothing," Marino said. "Lucy thinks there's a scrambler, and I think we should go in with a ram and a shotgun and not wait for ESU."

"Why?" the woman's dark shape asked Lucy.

"Do I know you?" Lucy was edgy and unfriendly, frantic inside.

"Marty Lanier, FBI."

"I've been here before," Lucy said, unzipping a bag and sliding open a drawer in the TruckVault Marino had installed in his trunk. "Rupe hated cell phones and didn't allow them in his house."

"Industrial espionage—" Lanier started to suggest.

Lucy cut her off. "He hated them, thought they were rude. If you were inside and tried to use your phone or log on to the Internet, you didn't get a signal. He wasn't committing espionage. He was worried about other people doing it."

"I would think there might be a lot of dead zones in there," Benton said of the limestone building with its tall windows and wrought-iron balconies, reminiscent of *hôtels particuliers,* the grand private homes Lucy associated with the heart of Paris, with the Île Saint-Louis.

She was familiar with the *hôtel* Chandonne inhabited by the corrupt nobility Jean-Baptiste had descended from. The Starr mansion was similar in its style and scale, and somewhere inside were Bonnell and Berger, and Lucy was going to do whatever it took to get in and find them. She surreptitiously tucked a Rabbit Tool inside the bag, then was obvious about packing the thermal imaging scope she had given to Marino for his last birthday, what was basically a handheld FLIR, the same technology she had on her helicopter.

"As much as I hate political considerations," Lanier then said.

"It's a valid point," Benton said, his voice brittle with impatience, and he sounded anxious and frustrated. "We kick in the door and they're sitting in the living room having coffee. My bigger worry is a hostage situation and we cause it to escalate. I'm not armed." He said it to Marino, said it like an accusation.

"You know what I've got," Marino said to Lucy, giving her an unspoken instruction.

Special Agent Lanier acted as if she didn't hear the exchange or notice Lucy grabbing a black soft case about the size of a tennis racket but with *Beretta CX4* embroidered on it. She handed it to Benton and he slipped it over his shoulder, and she shut the trunk. They didn't know who was inside the mansion or nearby but were expecting Jean-Baptiste Chandonne. Either he was Bobby Fuller or someone else, and he worked with others, those who did his bidding, people who were evil and would stoop as low as low got. If Benton had an encounter, he didn't intend to defend himself with bare fists but a compact carbine that shot nine-millimeter rounds.

"I recommend we call ESU and get the entry team here." Lanier was cautious, not wanting to tell NYPD how to do its job.

Marino ignored her, staring at the house as he asked Lucy, "And that was when? You were here last and saw a jamming system when?"

"A couple years back," she said. "He had one since the early nineties, at least. The kind of high-power jamming system that can paralyze RF bands between twenty and three thousand megahertz. The radios NYPD has are eight hundred megahertz and wouldn't be worth shit in there, and neither would cell phones. A little tactical advice? I agree." She looked at Lanier. "Get ESU here now, the A team, because breaking down the door's not the hard part. It's what you do if you're met with resistance, since you don't know who or what the fuck's in there. You force your way in all by yourself and maybe get your ass blown off or get crucified by Mother Blue. Take your pick."

Lucy was the calm voice of reason because inside she was screaming and not about to wait for anyone.

"What Tac are you on if I see anyone?" she asked Marino.

"Tac I," he said.

Lucy walked quickly toward Central Park South, and when she turned the corner, she started to run. At the back of the mansion was an apron of pavers that led to a wooden garage door, a swinging door painted black that opened on the left side, and nearby was a uniform cop Lucy had met earlier. He was probing shrubbery with his flashlight, the four floors above him dark, not a single window lit up.

"Tell you what," Lucy said, unzipping the bag and pulling out the thermal scope. "I'll hang back here and check the windows for heat. You might want to head around to the front. They're thinking of kicking in the door."

"Nobody's called me." The officer's face looked at her, his features indistinguishable in the irregular glow of street-lamps. In a nice way, he was telling Berger's computer nerd to fuck off.

"The A team's en route and nobody's going to call you. You can check with Marino. He's on Tac Ida." Lucy powered on the thermal scope and trained it at windows overhead and they turned murky green in infrared, the draperies across them splotched grayish white. "Maybe some radiant heat from hallways," she said, and the officer was walking off.

Out of sight, gone, on his way to a forced entry that wasn't about to happen where he was going. It was about to happen where he'd just left. Lucy got out the Rabbit

Tool, a handheld hydraulic spreader capable of exerting ten thousand pounds of pressure per square inch. She worked the opposing tips of the jaws between the left side of the garage door and the frame, and started stepping on the foot pump, and wood strained and then several loud pops as iron strap hinges bent and snapped. She grabbed her tools and worked her way through the opening, pulling the door shut behind her so the breach wasn't obvious from the street. She stood inside the cool dark, listening, orienting herself inside the lower level of the Starr garage. The thermal scope wasn't going to help her in here, all it did was detect heat, and she got out her SureFire light and turned it on.

The mansion's alarm system was unarmed, suggesting that when Bonnell and Berger had showed up, the person who let them in must not have reset the security system. *Maybe Nastya,* Lucy thought. She had met her the last time she was here and remembered the housekeeper as a careless and self-important woman, a recent hire of Hannah's, or maybe Nastya was one of Bobby's picks. But it had struck Lucy as peculiar that people like Nastya suddenly were part of Rupe's life. They weren't his type, and the decision likely hadn't been his, and it caused Lucy to wonder what really had happened to him. She didn't think it was possible to murder someone with salmonella, and it wasn't likely there had been a mistake in the diagnosis, not in Atlanta, a city known for its Centers for Disease Control and Prevention. Maybe he'd willed his own death because Hannah and Bobby were cannibalizing his life and he knew what was ahead, which was to have nothing left, to be old and powerless and at their mercy. It was possible. People did that. Got cancer, got in accidents, short-circuiting the inevitable.

She set down her bag and slipped her Glock pistol out of its ankle holster, the long beam of the tactical light probing her surroundings, licking across whitewashed stone walls and terra-cotta tile. Directly left of the garage door was a bay for washing cars, and water slowly dripped from the end of a sloppily coiled hose, and filthy towels were scattered over the floor, a plastic bucket turned on its side, and nearby several gallons of Clorox bleach. There were shoe prints and a lot of tire tracks, and a wheelbarrow and a shovel, both crusty with dried cement.

She followed wheel marks on the floor and more footprints, different treads, different sizes, and a lot of dust, maybe a running shoe, maybe a boot, at least two different people but possibly more. She listened and probed with the light, knowing what the basement was supposed to look like and noting what was different, finding signs everywhere of activity that had nothing to do with anyone maintaining vintage cars anymore. The powerful beam cut across a work area with benches, pressure tools, gauges, air compressors, battery chargers, jacks, cases of oil, and tires, all dusty and randomly placed, as if moved out of the way but unused and unappreciated.

Not at all like the old days, when you could eat off the floor because the garage was Rupe's pride and joy, that and his library, the two areas connected by a hidden door behind a painting of ships. The light moved across thick dust and cobwebs on a lift he'd installed when grease pits weren't legal anymore, were deemed unsafe because of carbon monoxide in the hole when a car engine was running. There didn't used to be a mattress, a bare one near the wall, covered with large brown stains and swipes, what looked like blood, and Lucy saw hairs, long ones, dark ones,

blond ones, and she detected an odor or thought she did.
Nearby was a box of surgical gloves.

About ten steps away was the old grease pit, covered
with a painter's drop cloth that didn't used to be there. The
surrounding floor was crazed with tread marks similar to
others Lucy had seen, and there were spatters and smears of
dried concrete. She squatted to lift an edge of the tarp, and
under it were wide sheets of plywood, and under those her
light illuminated the pit, and at the bottom of it was an
uneven layer of concrete that wasn't very deep, not even
two feet. Whoever had shoveled in the wet cement hadn't
bothered to smooth it, the surface irregular and rough with
mounds and peaks, and she thought she detected an odor
again and was acutely conscious of her gun.

Walking more quickly now, she followed the ramp, staying close to the wall, up to the next level, where Rupe Starr
had kept his cars, and as the incline bent around, Lucy
began to see light. Her boots were quiet on Italian flooring
that used to be immaculate, now dusty and scarred with tire
tracks and scattered with a lot of sand and salt. She heard
voices and stopped. Women's voices. She thought she heard
Berger. Something about being *"blocked in"* and a different
voice saying, *"Well, someone did"* and *"We were originally told,"*
and several times the phrase *"Clearly not true."*

Then, "What friends? And why didn't you tell us this
before?" Berger asked.

This was followed by an accented voice, muffled, a
woman talking fast, and Lucy thought of Nastya and listened for a man, for Bobby Fuller. Where was he? The
message Berger had left Marino while he and Lucy were still
in the training lab without their phones was that Berger and
Bonnell were meeting with Bobby. Supposedly he had flown

in from Fort Lauderdale early this morning because of what he'd heard on the news about Hannah's head hairs being found, and Berger had asked to talk to him again because she had a number of questions. He'd refused to meet her at One Hogan Place or any public place and had suggested the house, this house. Where was he? Lucy had checked, had called the Westchester airport tower, had talked to the same controller who was always so rude.

His name was Lech Peterek, and he was Polish and dour, very unfriendly on the phone because that was who and what he was, had nothing to do with who or what Lucy was. In fact, he didn't seem able to place her until she recited tail numbers, and even then he had been vague. He'd said there was no record of an arrival today from South Florida, not the Gulfstream Bobby Fuller and Hannah Starr routinely flew on—Rupe's Gulfsteam. It was still in its hangar and had been for weeks, the same hangar Lucy used, because it was Rupe who had brokered her purchases of aircraft. It was Rupe who had introduced her to remarkable machines like Bell helicopters and Ferraris. Unlike Hannah, his daughter, he had been well-intentioned, and until his death, Lucy had felt no insecurity about her livelihood and hadn't imagined anyone wanting to ruin it for the hell of it.

She reached the top of the ramp, staying close to the wall in incomplete darkness, the only lights on in the area near the far left corner where the voices came from, but she couldn't see anyone. Berger and probably Bonnell and Nastya were hidden behind vehicles and thick columns that had been boxed in with mahogany and protectively wrapped in black neoprene so precious cars didn't get dings on their doors. Lucy moved closer, listening for distress or any hint of danger, but the voices sounded calm, engaged in an intense conversation that at intervals was confrontational.

"Well, someone has. Obviously." Unmistakably Berger.

"People have always been in and out. They entertain so much. They have always." The accent again.

"You said that had tapered off after Rupe Starr died."

"Yes. Not so much. But still there are a few people who come. I don't know. Mr. Fuller is very private. He and his friends come down here. I don't intrude."

"We're supposed to believe you don't know who's in and out?" The third voice had to be Bonnell.

Rupe Starr's cars. A collection as thoughtful and sentimental as it was impressive and rare. The 1940 Packard like the one his father had owned. The 1957 Thunderbird that had been Rupe's dream when he was in high school and drove a VW Bug. The 1969 Camaro like the one he'd owned after he'd gotten his MBA from Harvard. The 1970 Mercedes sedan he'd rewarded himself with when he'd started doing well on Wall Street. Lucy walked past his prized 1933 Duesenberg Speedster, his Ferrari 355 Spyder, and the last car he'd gotten before his death and hadn't had a chance to restore yet, a 1979 yellow Checker cab because it reminded him of New York in his heyday, he'd said.

The new additions to his collection, the Ferraris, the Porsches, the Lamborghini, had been recent purchases influenced by Hannah and Bobby, including the white Bentley Azure convertible that was parked nose-in against the far wall, Bobby's red Carrera GT blocking it in. Berger, Bonnell, and Nastya were standing by the Bentley's rear fender, talking, their backs to Lucy, not noticing her yet, and she called out hello and told them not to be startled as she reached the Checker cab and noticed a residue of sand on its tires and tracks leading to them. She loudly alerted everyone that she was armed as she continued to walk closer, and they turned around and she recognized the look on Berger's face because she'd seen it before. Fear. Distrust and pain.

"Don't," Berger said, and it was Lucy she feared. "Put the gun down. Please."

"What?" Lucy said, dumbfounded, and she noticed Bonnell's right hand twitch.

"Please put down the gun," Berger said, with no emotion in her tone.

"We've been trying to call, been trying to get you on the radio. Careful, easy does it," Lucy warned Bonnell. "Slowly move your hands away from your body. Hold them out in front of you." Lucy had her pistol ready.

Berger said to her, "Nothing you've done is worth this. Please put it down."

"Easy does it. Be calm. I'm coming closer, and we're going to talk," Lucy said to them as she walked. "You don't know what's happened. We've not been able to get through. Jesus fuck!" she yelled at Bonnell. "Don't fucking move your hand again!"

Nastya muttered something in Russian and began to cry.

Berger stepped closer to Lucy and said, "Give me the gun and we'll talk. Talk about anything you want. Everything's all right. It doesn't matter what you've done. Whether it's money or Hannah."

"I haven't done anything. Listen to me."

"It's all right. Just give me the gun." Berger stared at her while Lucy stared at Bonnell, making sure she didn't go for her weapon.

"It's not all right. You don't know who she is." Lucy

meant Nastya. "Or who any of them are. Toni came here. You don't know because we couldn't get through. The watch Toni was wearing has a GPS in it, and she was here. She came here on Tuesday and died here." Lucy glanced at the yellow Checker cab. "And he kept her here for a while. Or they did."

"No one has been here." Nastya was shaking her head side to side and crying.

"You're a fucking liar," Lucy said. "Where's Bobby?"

"I don't know anything. I just do what I'm told," Nastya cried.

"Where was he Tuesday afternoon?" Lucy said to her. "Where were you and Bobby?"

"I don't come down when they show people the cars."

"Who else was here?" Lucy said, and Nastya didn't answer. "Who was here Tuesday afternoon and all day Wednesday? Who drove out of here at four-something in the morning, yesterday morning? Drove that." Lucy nodded her head at the Checker cab and said to Berger, "Toni's body was in it. We couldn't get through to tell you. The yellow paint chips collected from her body are from something old. An old car painted that color."

Berger said, "Enough damage has been done. Somehow we'll fix it. Please give me the gun, Lucy."

It began to occur to her what Berger meant.

"No matter what you've done, Lucy."

"I've not done anything." Lucy talked to Berger but kept her eyes on Bonnell and Nastya.

"It doesn't matter to me. We'll get past it," Berger said. "But it has to stop now. You can stop it now. Give me the gun."

"Near the Duesenberg over there are boxes," Lucy said.

"The stationary system that has jammed your phones, your radio. If you look, you can see them. They're to my left against that wall. They look like a small washer and dryer with rows of lights in front. Switches for different RF bands, radio frequency bands. Rupe had it installed, and you can see from here it's on. The rows of lights are red because all of the frequencies have been jammed."

Nobody moved and nobody looked. Their eyes were fastened on Lucy as if she might kill them any moment, do to them what Berger had gotten into her head that Lucy did to Hannah. *"And you were home that night. Too damn bad you didn't see anything."* Berger making that remark repeatedly these past few weeks because Lucy's loft was on Barrow Street and Hannah was last seen on Barrow Street, and Berger knew what Lucy could do and didn't trust her, was scared of her, thought she was a stranger, a monster. Lucy didn't know what to say to change it, to roll their lives back to where they used to be, but she wasn't going to let the destruction advance. Not one more inch. She was ending it.

"Jaime, walk over there and look," Lucy said. "Please. Walk over to the boxes and look. Switches designated for different megahertz frequencies."

Berger walked past her but didn't get close, and Lucy didn't look at her. She was busy watching Bonnell's hands. Marino had mentioned that Bonnell hadn't been a homicide detective long, and Lucy could tell she was inexperienced and didn't recognize what was going on because she wasn't listening to her instincts, she was listening to her head and she was panicky. If Bonnell listened to her instincts she would sense that Lucy was being aggressive because Bonnell was, that it wasn't Lucy who had instigated what was now a standoff, a showdown.

"I'm at the boxes," Berger said from the side wall.

"Flip all the switches." Lucy didn't look at her, would be goddamned if she was going to be killed by a fucking cop. "The lights should turn green, and you and Bonnell should see a lot of messages land on your phones. That will tip you off that people have been trying to reach you, that I'm telling you the truth."

The sound of switches being flipped.

Lucy said to Bonnell, "Try your radio. Marino's out front on the street. If the A team hasn't already rammed in the front door, he and the others are just outside. Get on your radio. He's on Tac Ida."

She was telling Bonnell to switch to the point-to-point frequency Tac I, instead of using the standard repeater radio service and going through a dispatcher. Bonnell unclipped her radio from her belt, switched channels, and pressed the transmit button.

"Smoker, do you copy?" she said, watching Lucy. "Smoker, are you on the air?"

"Yeah, I copy, Los Angeles." Marino's tense voice. "What's your twenty?"

"We're in the basement with Hot Shot." Bonnell wasn't answering Marino's question.

He was asking if she was okay, and she was telling him where she was, using personal designations that the two of them must have assigned to each other, and to Lucy. Lucy was Hot Shot, and Bonnell didn't trust her. Bonnell wasn't reassuring Marino that she or anyone was safe. She was doing the opposite.

"Hot Shot's with you?" Marino's voice. "What about the Eagle?"

"Affirm to both."

"Anyone else?"

Bonnell looked at Nastya and answered, "Hazel." Another designation she just made up.

"Tell him I opened the garage door," Lucy said.

Bonnell transmitted it over the air as Berger walked back, looking at her BlackBerry, looking at messages as they landed in a rapid succession of chimes. Earlier calls, some of them from Marino, from Scarpetta. And from Lucy, at least five when she'd realized Berger was on her way here and didn't know what was happening, was missing critical information. Lucy had kept calling, had gotten terrified, had been as frightened as she'd ever been in her life.

"What's your twenty?" Marino's voice asking Bonnell if everyone was all right.

"Not sure who's inside and been having radio problems," Bonnell replied.

"When can we expect you out?"

Lucy said, "Tell him to come through the garage. It's open and they need to come up the ramp to the upper basement level."

Bonnell transmitted the message and said to Lucy, "We're okay." She meant she wasn't going to draw her gun, wasn't going to do something fucking stupid like shoot her.

Lucy lowered the Glock to her side, but she didn't return it to the ankle holster. She and Berger began to walk around, and Lucy showed her the yellow Checker cab and the dirt on tires and the tile floor, but they didn't touch anything. They didn't open its doors but looked through the rear windows at the torn and rotted black carpet, at the tattered and stained black cloth upholstery and folded jump seat. There was a coat on the floor. Green. It looked like a parka. The witness, Harvey Fahley, said he'd seen a yellow taxi. If he wasn't an aficionado of cars, he wouldn't necessarily have noticed that this yellow taxi was about thirty years old with the signature checkerboard trim that contemporary models didn't have. What the average person would notice when driving past in the dark was the chrome-yellow color, the boxy General Motors chassis, and the light on top, which Fahley recalled was turned off, signaling that the taxi wasn't available.

Lucy offered snapshots of information that Scarpetta had relayed over the phone when Lucy and Marino had been on their way here, scared that something awful had happened. Berger and Bonnell weren't answering the police radio or their phones and had no way of knowing that Toni Darien had jogged to this address late last Tuesday, that she likely had died in the basement and it was possible she wasn't the only victim. Lucy and Berger talked and searched and watched for Marino, and Lucy said she was sorry until Berger told her to stop saying it. Both of them were guilty of keeping to themselves things that should have been discussed, neither of them honest, Berger said, as they got to workbenches, two of them plastic, with drawers and bins. Scattered on them were tools and miscellaneous parts, hood ornaments and valves, chrome collars, screws, head bolts. One stick-shift assembly had a large steel knob with blood on it, or maybe rust. They didn't touch it or the spools of fine-gauge wire and what looked like tiny circuit boards that Lucy recognized as recording modules, and a notebook.

It had a black cloth cover with yellow stars on it, and Lucy flipped it open with the barrel of her pistol. A book of magical spells, of recipes and potions for hexing, for protection, winning, and good luck, all handwritten in a perfect script, in Gotham, as precise as a font, and also on the bench were small gold-silk pouches, some emptied of the fur that had been inside them, long black-and-white hairs and clumps of matted undercoat. What looked like wolf fur was scattered on work surfaces and on the floor, which had been cleaned in wide swaths, something recently wiped up or mopped near the orange metallic Lamborghini Diablo VT. The top was down and on the passenger's seat was a pair of Hestra olive nylon mittens with tan cowhide palms, and Lucy imagined Toni Darien entering the mansion upstairs after jogging here.

She imagined Toni feeling comfortable with whoever had greeted her at the door, whoever walked her down to the basement, where it was at most fifty-five degrees. She may have had her coat on as she was given a tour, shown the cars, and she would have been especially impressed with the Lamborghini. She might have gotten behind the wheel and taken off her mittens so she could get the feel of carbon fiber and fantasize, and when she climbed back out, it might have happened then. A pause as she turned away, and someone grabbed an object, perhaps the stick shift, and had struck the back of her head.

"Then she was raped," Berger said.

"She wasn't walking and was being moved around," Lucy told her. "Aunt Kay says it went on for more than an hour. And after she was dead, it started again. Like she was left down here, maybe on that mattress, and then he'd come back. It went on for a day and a half."

"When he first started killing"—Berger meant Jean-Baptiste— "he did it with his brother, Jay. Jay was the handsome one, would have sex with the women, then Jean-Baptiste would beat them to death. He never had sex with them. His excitement was the kill."

"Jay had sex with them. So maybe he found another Jay," Lucy said.

"We need to find Hap Judd right away."

"How did you set it up with Bobby?" Lucy asked, as Marino and four cops dressed like SWAT appeared at the top of the ramp and headed toward them, their hands near their weapons.

"After the meeting at the FBI field office, I called his cell phone," Berger said.

"Then he wasn't home, not in this house," Lucy said. "Unless he'd turned off the frequency jammer and after talking to you turned it back on."

"There's a cognac glass upstairs in the library," Berger said. "It might tell us if Bobby is him." She meant Jean-Baptiste Chandonne again.

Lucy said to Marino as he reached them, "Where's Benton?"

"He and Marty left to pick up the Doc." His eyes were looking everywhere, taking in what was on the mobile benches and the floor, looking at the Checker cab. "Crime Scene's on its way to see if we can figure out what the hell happened down here, and the Doc's bringing the sniffer."

23

Inside what the DNA Building's staff had come to call the Blood Spatter Room, Scarpetta dipped a swab inside a bottle of hexane. She swiped a residue into a petri dish she'd set on the epoxy-tile floor, and pressed the power button on the Lightweight Analyzer for Buried Remains and Decomposition Odor, a LABRADOR.

The e-nose, or sniffer, brought to mind a robotic dog that a creator for the Jetsons might have designed, an S-rod with small speakers on either side of the handle that could pass for ears, and the nose a metal honeycomb of twelve sensors that detected different chemical signatures the same way a canine recognized scents. A battery pack was attached to a strap that Scarpetta slipped over her shoulder, and she tucked the S-rod close to her side and maneuvered the nose over her sample in the petri dish. The LABRADOR responded with an illuminated bar graph on the control console and an audio signal, what sounded like synthesized strums on a harp, a harmonic pattern of tones distinctive for hexane. The e-nose was happy. It had alerted on an alkane hydrocarbon, a simple solvent, and had passed its test. Now it was on to a much more somber assignment.

Scarpetta's premise was simple. It appeared that Toni Darien had been murdered inside the Starr mansion, and the question was where and if other victims had been lured there in the past, or was Toni the only one? She had been in one of the basements, Scarpetta presumed, based on the temperatures registered by the BioGraph device and Scarpetta's own findings, which indicated that the body had been preserved someplace cool and out of the elements. Wherever her body had been, it had left molecules of chemicals and compounds. It had left odors that the human nose wasn't going to pick up but the LABRADOR might, and Scarpetta turned it off and packed it inside a black nylon case. She flipped off ceiling rigs of movable lights that for an instant reminded her of a television set, reminded her of Carley Crispin. Scarpetta put on her coat. She walked out and took a glass staircase down to the lobby and left the building. It was getting close to eight p.m., and the garden in front and its granite benches were empty, windswept, and dark.

She turned right on First Avenue and followed the sidewalk past the Bellevue Hospital Center, heading back to her office, where she was supposed to meet Benton. Her building's front door would be locked, and she took another right at 30th and noticed light spilling onto the street from one of the bays because the metal door was rolled up. Inside was a white van, the engine on and the tailgate open but no one in sight. Using her swipe card, she opened the interior door at the top of the ramp, and inside the familiar merging of white and teal tile, she heard music. Soft rock. Filene must be on duty. It wasn't like her to leave the bay door up.

Scarpetta walked past the floor scale to the mortuary office, not seeing anyone. The chair in front of the Plexiglas window was swiveled to one side, Filene's radio on the floor, her OCME SECURITY jacket hanging on the back of the door. She heard footsteps, and a guard in his dark-blue fatigues appeared from the area of the locker rooms, probably had been in the men's room.

"The bay door's open," she said to him, and she didn't know his name and had never seen him before.

"A delivery," he said, and something about him was familiar.

"From where?"

"Some woman hit by a bus in Harlem."

He was slender but strong, his hands pale and ropy with veins, and wisps of black baby-fine hair strayed from his cap, his eyes masked by gray-tinted glasses. His face was smoothly shaven, his teeth too white and straight, possibly dentures, but he was young for that, and he seemed agitated, excited or nervous, and it occurred to her he might be uneasy working in a morgue after dark. Maybe a temp. As the economy had worsened, so had staffing, and when budgets are severely cut it becomes practical to use more part-time people, more outside vendors, and a lot of staff were out with the flu. Fragmented thoughts raced through her mind at the same time she felt her scalp prickle and her pulse pick up. Her mouth went dry, and she turned to run as he grabbed her arm. The nylon bags she was carrying slipped from her shoulder as she struggled, as he pulled her with shocking force toward the bay where the white van with the open tailgate was parked with the engine on.

The sounds she made weren't intelligible, were too primitive to be words or thoughts, but explosions of panic as she tried to get away, tried to untangle herself from the bags and their shoulder straps, kicking at him and pulling as he yanked open the door that she had just come through moments earlier, and it banged against the wall with such force it sounded like a sledgehammer against cinder block, banging more than once. The long bag with the LABRADOR inside it somehow was caught horizontally in the door frame, and she thought that was why he let go of her, collapsing at her feet, and blood pooled on the ramp and flowed down it. Benton stepped out from behind the white van, holding a carbine, and he ran to her, training the rifle on the man as she backed away from his motionless body.

Blood was pouring out of a wound in his forehead that had exited through the back of his skull, and a spray of blood was on the door frame just inches from where she'd just been. Her face and neck felt cool where they were wet, and she wiped blood and bits of brain tissue off her skin, and she dropped her bags to the white tile floor as a woman walked inside the bay, holding a pistol in both hands, the barrel pointed up. She lowered the gun as she got closer.

"He's down," she said, and it occurred to Scarpetta there might be someone else just shot. "Backups are on the way."

"Make sure we're clear out here," Benton said to the woman as he stepped over the body and the blood on the ramp. "I'll make sure we're clear inside." He said to Scarpetta as his eyes darted around, "Is there anybody else? Do you know if anybody else is inside?"

She said, "How could this happen?"

"Stay with me," he told her.

Benton walked in front of her, checking corridors,

checking the mortuary office, kicking open the doors to the men's locker room and the women's. He kept asking Scarpetta if she was all right. He said there were items at the Starrs' house, clothing, caps, similar to what OCME security wore, in a room in the basement, that it was part of the plan. He repeated it was part of the plan to come here for her, and maybe Berger's coming for *him* had pushed *him* into it. He always had a way of knowing where everyone was and everyone wasn't, Benton kept saying that, kept talking about *him,* and he kept asking her if she was hurt, if she was okay.

Marino had called Benton about the clothes, about what he feared they were for, and when Lanier and Benton got here and saw the open bay door, they immediately mobilized. They were on 30th Street when Hap Judd materialized from the dark and walked into the bay to climb into the van. When he saw them, he ran, and Lanier went after him at the same time Jean-Baptiste Chandonne came out the interior door with Scarpetta.

Benton followed the white-tile corridor, checking the anteroom, checking the main autopsy room. Hap Judd was armed and he was dead, Benton said. Bobby Fuller, who Benton believed was Jean-Baptiste Chandonne, was dead. At the end of the corridor, past the lift that carried bodies up for viewings, there were blood drips on the floor, and then smears, and a door leading to a stairwell, and on the landing was Filene, and next to her a bloody hammer, the kind of hammer used to assemble pine boxes. It appeared the security guard had been dragged back here, and Scarpetta got next to her and pressed her fingers against the side of her neck.

"Get an ambulance," she said to Benton.

She felt the injury at the back of Filene's head, on the right side, an area of swelling that was boggy and bloody. She opened Filene's eyelids to check the pupils, and the right one was dilated and fixed. Her breathing was erratic, her pulse rapid and irregular, and Scarpetta worried the lower brain stem was getting compressed.

"I need to stay here," she told Benton as he called for help. "She may start vomiting or have a seizure. I need to keep her airway clear. I'm right here," she told Filene. "You're going to be okay," Scarpetta told her. "Help is on the way," Scarpetta said.

Six Days Later

Inside the Memorial Room at Two Truck, chairs and benches had been set up near the Coke machine and gun safe because there wasn't enough room in the kitchen for everyone to sit. Scarpetta had brought too much food.

Spinach and egg pappardelle, maccheroni, penne, and spaghetti filled big bowls on the table, and pots of sauces were warming on the stove, a ragù with porcini mushrooms and one with Bolognese and another with prosciutto di Parma. A simple winter tomato sauce was for Marino because he liked it on his lasagna, and that had been his request, with extra meat and extra ricotta. Benton wanted pan-fried veal chops with marsala sauce, and Lucy had asked for her favorite salad with fennel, while Berger was happy with lemon chicken. The air was sharp and pungent with Parmigiano-Reggiano, mushrooms, and garlic, and Lieutenant Al Lobo was worried about crowd control.

"The whole precinct's going to come over here," he said, checking on the bread. "Or maybe all of Harlem. This might be ready."

"It should sound hollow when you tap it," Scarpetta said,

wiping her hands on her apron and taking a look, a wave of fragrant heat rising from the oven.

"Sounds hollow to me." Lobo licked the finger he'd used to tap the bread.

"Same way he checks bombs." Marino walked into the kitchen, Mac the boxer and Lucy's bulldog, Jet Ranger, right behind him, toenails clicking on tile. "He thumps it and if it doesn't blow up, he gets to go home early, all in a day's work. Can they have anything?" Marino was talking about the dogs.

"No," Lucy answered loudly from the Memorial Room. "No people food."

On the other side of an open doorway, she and Berger were arranging strands of white lights on top of the display case containing the personal effects of Joe Vigiano, John D'Allara, and Mike Curtin, the responders from the Two who had died on 9/11. Their gear recovered from the ruins was arranged on shelves, an assortment of handcuffs, keys, holsters, wire cutters, flashlights, D rings and clips from Roco harnesses, melted and bent, and on the floor was a section of steel beam from the World Trade Center. Photos of the three men and other members of the Two who had died on duty were arranged on maple-paneled walls, and over Mac's dog bed was an American flag quilt made by a grammar school. Christmas music accompanied the chatter of police radios, and Scarpetta heard footsteps on the stairs.

Benton had gone out with Bonnell to pick up the last of the food, a frozen chocolate pistachio mousse, a butterless sponge cake, and dry-cured sausages and cheeses. Scarpetta had been heavy on the antipasto because it would keep, and there was nothing better than leftovers when cops are sitting around in their quarters and working in the garage, waiting for emergencies. It was mid-afternoon, Christmas day, cold with snow flurries, and Lobo and Ann Droiden had dropped by from 6th Precinct, everyone gathering at the Two because Scarpetta had decided the holiday dinner should be spent with the people who had done the most for her lately.

Benton appeared in the doorway with a box, his face ruddy from the cold.

"L.A.'s still parking the car. Even cops have no place to park around here. Where would you like it?" He walked in, looking around, not an empty space on a countertop or the kitchen table.

"Here." Scarpetta moved several bowls. "The mousse goes in the freezer for now. And I see you brought wine. Well, I guess you won't be helping out in any emergencies. Is it legal to have wine up here?" she called out to whoever wanted to answer from the Memorial Room, where Lobo and Droiden were with Berger and Lucy.

"Only if it's got a screw cap or comes out of a box," Lobo answered back.

"Anything that costs more than five bucks is contraband," Droiden added.

"Who's on call?" Lucy said. "I'm not. Jaime's not. I think Mac needs to potty."

"He off-gassing again?" Lobo asked.

The brindle boxer was old and arthritic, as was Jet Ranger, both of them rescues, and Scarpetta found the package of treats she'd baked, a healthy cookie made with peanut butter and spelt flour. She whistled and the dogs hurried over to her, not spry but they hadn't lost their enthusiasm, and she said "sit" and then rewarded them.

"If only it were that easy with people," she said, taking off her apron. "Come on," she said to Benton. "Mac needs a little exercise."

Benton got the leash and they put on their coats, and Scarpetta stuffed several plastic bags in a pocket. They took Mac down the scuffed wooden stairs and through the huge garage filled with emergency trucks and gear, hardly any room to walk, and out a side door. Across Tenth Avenue was a small park next to Saint Mary's Church, and she and Benton headed Mac over there because frozen balding grass was better than pavement.

"Status check," Benton said. "You've been cooking for two days."

"I know."

"I don't want to bring it up in there," he said as Mac started sniffing, pulling him toward a bare tree, then toward a bush. "They're going to talk about it all night, anyway. And I think we should let them and in a little while you and I should go home. We should be alone. We haven't been alone all week."

They hadn't slept much, either. It had taken several days to excavate the Starr mansion basement because the electronic nose, the LABRADOR, had gotten as industrious in its sniffing as Mac was right now, leading Scarpetta everywhere, alerting on traces of decomposed blood. For a while she'd feared that there were many bodies in the two levels below the house where Rupe Starr had maintained and kept his cars, but there hadn't been. In the end, only Hannah was down there, beneath concrete in the grease pit, her cause of death not so different from Toni Darien's, except Hannah's injury was more massive and passionate. She'd been struck in the head and face sixteen times, possibly with the same weapon that had been used on Toni, a stick shift with a large steel knob the shape and size of a billiard ball.

The shift assembly was from a hand-built car called a Spyker that Lucy said Rupe had restored and then sold some five years ago, and DNA recovered from it had been contributed by multiple people, three of them positively identified: Hannah, Toni, and the person who Scarpetta believed had beaten them to death, Jean-Baptiste Chandonne, aka Bobby Fuller, an American businessman as fictitious as many of Chandonne's other aliases. Scarpetta didn't perform Chandonne's autopsy, but she'd witnessed it, feeling it was as important to her future as it was to her past. Dr. Edison had taken the case, and the examination had been like any other performed at the NYC OCME, and Scarpetta couldn't help but think how much that might have disappointed Chandonne.

He wasn't any more or less special than anyone, just one more body on a table, only he had more than the usual remnants of cosmetic reconstruction and improvements. His corrective surgeries would have taken years of visits to the OR and long convalescences that must have been torture. Scarpetta could only imagine the misery of full-body-hair laser removal and having every tooth crowned. But perhaps he had been pleased with the end result, because no matter how much she had studied him in the morgue, she'd found very little evidence of his deformities, just railroad tracks of surgical scars revealed when his head was shaved around the entrance and exit wounds caused by the nine-millimeter round Benton had fired through Jean-Baptiste's upper forehead.

Jean-Baptiste Chandonne was dead, and Scarpetta knew

it was him. DNA wasn't wrong, and she could rest assured he would never be on a park bench or in her morgue or in a mansion or anywhere ever again. Hap Judd was dead, and despite how well he had choreographed his paraphilic predilections and ultimate crimes, he'd managed to leave quite a trail of DNA: on the BioGraph watch Toni had started wearing as part of a Chandonne-funded research study called Caligula that her gangster MIT-trained father had gotten her involved with; in her vagina, because latex gloves aren't quite as foolproof as condoms; on the red scarf that had been around her neck; on wadded paper towels Marino had collected from her trash, probably used when Hap thought he was removing any evidence that he'd been inside her apartment; and on two true-crime paperbacks that were in a drawer by her bedside table. The theory was that it had been Hap in the security recordings, his final act.

He put on Toni's parka and a pair of running shoes similar to hers, but he'd gotten the gloves wrong because she'd begun wearing ski mittens, the olive-and-tan Hestras she'd left in the front seat of the Lamborghini, a wireless fingertip pulse oximeter still inside one of them. Hap had entered Toni's building, using the keys he'd taken from her dead body and later returned, and although Scarpetta would never know exactly what he'd had in mind, she suspected it was a combination of purposes. He wanted to remove any evidence that he was connected with her, and there was plenty of it recovered from her cell phone and laptop, both found in his TriBeCa apartment along with her wallet and other items, including chargers that suggested she'd spent time with him there. She'd written him hundreds of text messages, and he'd e-mailed some of his disturbing screenplays to her, and she'd saved them on her hard drive. Text messages from him made it clear their relationship had to be a secret because of his celebrity, and Scarpetta doubted Toni had any idea that her famous boyfriend's sexual fantasies about her were as grotesque as what he wrote and liked to read.

Those individuals who could tell more about the Chandonnes and their network and everything that might have happened were still being rounded up by the FBI. Dodie Hodge and an AWOL Marine named Jerome Wild would soon be on the Top Ten Most Wanted List. Carley Crispin, who had left her fingerprints on Scarpetta's BlackBerry, had retained a prominent lawyer and was no longer on the air and might never be again, certainly not on CNN. The housekeepers Rosie and Nastya were being questioned, and there were stories that Rupe Starr was going to be exhumed, but Scarpetta hoped not, because she didn't think it would prove helpful, would be just another sensation in the news. Benton said that the cast of characters was long, these miscreants that Chandonne had recruited, and it would be quite some time before it was determined who was real, such as Freddie Maestro, and who was just another shape and form of Jean-Baptiste, such as the French philanthropist named Monsieur Lecoq.

"What a good boy you are," Scarpetta praised Mac, thanking him profusely for his deposit.

She picked it up in a plastic bag, and she and Benton walked back across Tenth Avenue, the afternoon light almost gone. The snow was small flakes that didn't stick, but at least it was white stuff, as Benton put it, and it was Christmas, and that was a sign, he said.

"Of what?" she asked. "Scrubbing away our sins? And you can hold this hand. Just don't reach for my other one."

She gave him the hand that didn't have the plastic bag, and then he rang the buzzer outside the Two.

"If our sins were scrubbed away," Benton said, "what would be left?"

"Nothing interesting," she said as the door clicked free. "In fact, I intend to commit as many sins as possible when we get home tonight. Take that as a warning, Special Agent Wesley."

Upstairs in the small kitchen, everyone crowded in because Benton was opening wine and pouring it into plastic glasses, a nice Chianti for whoever could indulge. Marino opened the refrigerator and got out sodas for Lobo and Droiden and a nonalcoholic beer for himself, and by now Bonnell had showed up, and everyone decided it was a good time to have a toast. They wandered into the Memorial Room, and Scarpetta came in last, carrying a basket of fresh bread.

"A family tradition I'd like to tell you about if you'll indulge me," she said. "Memory bread. My mother used to make it when I was a child, and it's called that because when you have a piece, you're supposed to remember something important. It can be from your childhood. It can be from any time or anywhere. So I thought we'd drink a toast and eat some bread and remember what we've been through and who we were, because it's also who we are."

"You sure it's okay to be doing this in here?" Bonnell said. "I don't want to be disrespectful."

"These guys?" Lobo meant his fallen comrades, whose effects didn't look quite so forlorn in the glow of tiny white lights. "They'd be the first ones to want us in here doing this right now. I'm tempted to fix them a plate. I remember how John loved animals." He looked at a photograph of D'Allara while Marino was petting Mac. "We still have his snake pole in his locker."

"Don't think I've ever seen a snake in Manhattan," Berger said.

"Only every day," Lucy said. "We make our living off snakes."

"People let them loose in the park," Droiden said. "Pet pythons they don't want anymore. One time it was an alligator. So, who gets called?"

"We do," everybody said.

Scarpetta passed around the basket of bread and each person pinched off a piece and ate it, and she explained that the secret to memory bread was you could use anything in it you liked. Could be leftover grains coarsely ground or potatoes or cheese or herbs, because people would be better off if they paid attention to what they have and not waste it. Memories are like what you find in the kitchen, she said, all these dribs and drabs in drawers and dark cupboards, bits and pieces that seem extraneous or even bad but in fact might improve something you're making.

"To friends," she said, raising her glass.

Credits

Very special thanks to the following technical advisers:

Dr. Staci Gruber, director, Cognitive and Clinical Neuroimaging Core, McLean Hospital; assistant professor, Department of Psychiatry, Harvard Medical School

Barbara A. Butcher, chief of staff and director of forensic investigations, the City of New York Office of the Chief Medical Examiner

Deputy Commissioner Paul J. Browne, NYPD

Nicholas Petraco, technical leader in criminalistics, NYPD Forensic Investigation Division

Lieutenant-Commander Detective Squad Mark Torre, commanding officer, bomb squad, NYPD

Dr. Louis Schlesinger, professor of forensic psychology, John Jay College of Criminal Justice

Dr. Marcella Fierro, former chief medical examiner of Virginia

Assistant District Attorney Lisa Friel, chief of the Sex Crimes Unit, New York County district attorney's office

The Reverend Lori Bruno, psychic and medium, of Hex: Old World Witchery, Salem, Massachusetts

Other bestselling titles available by mail

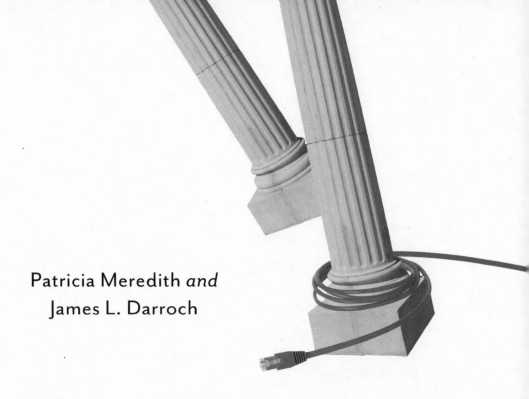

Patricia Meredith *and*
James L. Darroch

Stumbling Giants

Transforming Canada's Banks
for the Information Age

Best wishes

Pat Meredith

UNIVERSITY OF TORONTO PRESS
Toronto Buffalo London

ISBN 978-1-4426-4951-4

∞ Printed on acid-free, 100% post-consumer recycled paper with vegetable-based inks.

Library and Archives Canada Cataloguing in Publication

Meredith, Patricia, 1955–, author
Stumbling giants : transforming Canada's banks for the information age /
Patricia Meredith, James L. Darroch.

Includes bibliographical references and index.
ISBN 978-1-4426-4951-4 (cloth)

1. Banks and banking – Technological innovations – Canada.   2. Financial
services industry – Technological innovations – Canada.   I. Darroch, James
L. (James Lionel), 1951–, author II. Title.

HG2704.M335 2017   332.1'20971   C2017-904807-4

University of Toronto Press acknowledges the financial assistance to its publishing program of the Canada Council for the Arts and the Ontario Arts
Council, an agency of the Government of Ontario.

**Canada Council   Conseil des Arts
for the Arts   du Canada**

**ONTARIO ARTS COUNCIL
CONSEIL DES ARTS DE L'ONTARIO**
an Ontario government agency
un organisme du gouvernement de l'Ontario

Funded by the   Financé par le
Government   gouvernement
of Canada   du Canada

From Patricia Meredith:
For my mother, Gloria Meredith, my husband, Stephen
Karam, and our son, Patrick,
and
For JD, who encouraged me to write the first version of this
book and helped me to see that entrepreneurs can change
the banking industry

From James Darroch:
For my family – my wife, Brenda Blackstock, and our son, Daniel

Contents

Preface
Why We Wrote This Book

In November 2010, Mike Kitchen, a senior executive at Bank of Montreal, presented the *Tech-tonic Shift* scenario to the Payments Roundtable, a group convened by the Payments Task Force, which I (Patricia Meredith) was chairing at the time. Mike painted a bleak picture of the future of banks and other traditional financial institutions. With the rapid adoption of mobile technology, banks were in danger of losing their competitive edge. Profits from transactions would drop, most of their lucrative small payments business would be lost, and, worst of all, their unflinching attachment to outdated systems would prevent them from keeping pace with the new herd of nimble financial technology companies. As Mike described it, this scenario might spell trouble for the banks, but it did not signal their demise; after all, they still had plenty of profitable niche businesses to focus on.

As things turned out, it didn't take long for Mike's story line to start coming true. Within five years, Apple had launched the Apple Pay smartphone app in Canada in partnership with American Express. Apple Pay has created a tsunami in the financial services industry, and for banks in particular. Now, customers can register their payment cards in Apple's mobile wallet to make payments and receive receipts. Google has gone one step further, adding loyalty cards to its mobile wallet, Android Pay. Instead of being the linchpins of financial transactions, the banks are on their way to becoming bit players. They are even paying companies like Apple and Google to give them a role.

By mid-2016, the Canadian banks had caved in to Apple's demands for a share of their payment fees and had agreed to make their services available to the 40 per cent of Canadians with iPhones who are Apple Pay's potential users. As Mike Kitchen and his team had predicted, the end of banking as we know it was in sight. Armed with services such as Apple, Android, Samsung Pay, PayPal, and other offerings by a swarm of innovative financial technology companies, Canadians are no longer hostages to the big banks.

Mike's presentation was music to my ears. It drove home a message that I had been trying to get across since the mid-1990s, namely, that Internet technology, agile new players, and changing customer attitudes were about to turn the banks' business upside down. For fifteen years, they had ignored my entreaties that they shift their attention to the future. They were confident that the music would not stop on their watch and that someone else would deal with the problem in the far distant future.

The working title of this book started out as *The End of Banks: How Canada's Banks Missed the Future and Cost Canadians Dearly*. It reflected my pessimism about the future of Canada's big banks and my frustration with their focus on short-term profits at tremendous cost to consumers, employees, long-term investors, and the Canadian economy. But I struggled to write a succinct conclusion.

Then my co-author, James Darroch, reminded me of the huge role that public policy and regulation have played in shaping this country's financial services industry. We recognized that Canada's unique circumstances demanded a made-in-Canada solution, and that we could hope for such an outcome only if we challenged all those involved in the banking industry, including policy makers, regulators, customers, suppliers, investors, and bankers, to work together to design a financial system for the twenty-first century.

The result is *Stumbling Giants: Transforming Canada's Banks for the Information Age*. The Canadian banks earn a return on equity of about 40 per cent from their domestic retail banking operations. That is high by any standard, and it has given them plenty of money to invest in new technology for the future. Yet, until recently, they gave priority to adding more branches and ATMs, even though such bricks-and-mortar facilities are heading the way of the dinosaur. But the socio-technological revolution is now starting to overwhelm them. Customers expect immediate delivery of financial services, at any place and any time. Direct banks, those without a physical presence and with very little human intervention, can provide these services, and more, at much lower cost. Unlike the banks, they are harnessing such twenty-first-century technologies as the mobile Internet, Cloud computing, and social media. On another front, a new generation of nimble financial technology companies, known as fintechs, are offering innovative lending, wealth management, and payments products.

The 2008 financial crisis was a turning point for banks around the world. But Canada escaped the brunt of the storm. The Canadian banks' good fortune has its roots in the British North America Act, which created Canada in 1867. Under that law, banks are federally regulated, but capital markets are overseen by the provinces. This arrangement has kept the banks strong and capital markets weak. Furthermore, because our banks have been so critical in financing the growth of this nation over the past century and a half, public policy has protected them, putting the emphasis on stability and profitability. Banks have only been allowed to expand into new businesses, including mortgage-backed securities, after they proved they could manage the risks.

These priorities may have served Canada well in the past, but they now cast a shadow over the future. Rather than helping to propel our economy forward, the focus on stability and the aversion to risk are now holding us back. Without significant market-based funding and more access to bank loans, the small businesses that play such a vital role in shaping a competitive economy are increasingly forced to look south of the border for the funds they need to grow. Worse, their founders are tempted to move to Silicon Valley, and their companies will be gobbled up by deep-pocketed rivals from the United States and beyond. Without a super-fast, information-rich payments system, Canada's productivity will sag under the burden of inefficient, paper-based invoices and payments. Companies will be unable to access the data essential for innovative online services. In short, Canada will find itself fenced off from large chunks of the digital world, cut off from some of the most rewarding areas of economic growth.

Canadians still need banks, at a minimum to protect their savings, provide home mortgages, fund loans to small and mid-sized businesses, and support the capital markets for investors and large corporate and government issuers. The banks will always play a key role in helping the Bank of Canada execute its monetary policies. Nonetheless, this book's central theme is that change is long overdue for the banks and the rules that govern them. Boards of directors and long-term investors must force banks to invest in innovation. Government policy needs to find a better balance between stability and innovation. Market-based lending and bank financing for businesses must be encouraged, perhaps with government inducements. The burgeoning array of fintechs, large and small, must have easier access to a modern payments system to spur competition and innovation. Tighter regulation in other areas, such as fuller disclosure of investment management fees, an expanded Canada Pension Plan, and a much stronger Financial Consumer Agency of Canada, will help Canadian consumers take advantage of cheaper alternatives to grow their retirement savings and manage their transactions.

We constantly encounter enthusiastic young bankers who realize that their industry must change if it is to regain its reputation as a vibrant enabler of economic growth. We wrote this book for them in the hope that it will catalyze the industry to transform itself before it is too late. But the dreams of these men and women will not be realized unless a broad cross-section of Canadians – policy makers and regulators, customers, suppliers, investors, and, not least, the bankers themselves – work together to create a banking system better suited to the twenty-first century.

Glossary

ABCP	asset-backed commercial paper
ABM/ATM	automated banking machine / automated teller machine
ABS	asset-backed securities
BCG	Boston Consulting Group
BDC	Business Development Bank of Canada
CBA	Commonwealth Bank of Australia
CDIC	Canada Deposit Insurance Corporation
CFIB	Canadian Federation of Independent Business
CMHC	Canada Mortgage and Housing Corporation
CPA	Canadian Payments Association
E-commerce	electronic commerce, both online and mobile
ETFs	exchange-traded funds
FCAC	Financial Consumer Agency of Canada
GICs	Guaranteed Investment Certificates
GPTs	general purpose technologies
IFT	immediate funds transfer
MBS	mortgage-backed securities
M-commerce	electronic commerce conducted using a mobile device
MSF	merchant service fees – fees paid to a merchant services provider (acquirer or processer) for credit

	and debit card transactions, the largest component of which is the interchange fee, most of which is paid to the financial institution issuing the customer card
NFC	near field communication
OSC	Ontario Securities Commission
OSFI	Office of the Superintendent of Financial Institutions
P2P	person to person, peer to peer, or point to point
POS	point of sale
SMEs	small and mid-sized enterprises

Canada's Big Six Banks

BMO	Bank of Montreal / BMO Financial Group
BNS	Bank of Nova Scotia / Scotiabank
CIBC	Canadian Imperial Bank of Commerce
RBC	Royal Bank of Canada / RBC Financial Group
TD	Toronto-Dominion Bank / TD Canada Trust / TD Bank Group
NBC/BNC	National Bank of Canada / Banque Nationale du Canada

STUMBLING GIANTS

Transforming Canada's Banks for the Information Age

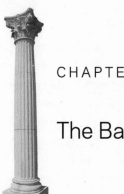

CHAPTER ONE

The Banks Lose Their Way

It is not the most intellectual of the species that survives; it is not the strongest that survives; but the species that survives is the one that is able to adapt to and to adjust best to the changing environment in which it finds itself.[1]

Canadians are proud of their banks, and rightly so. Since Confederation in 1867 the banks have served us well. They have raised deposits and made loans to help finance railroads, pipelines, and seaways. They have supported projects big and small in key industries like mining, forestry, oil and gas, and many others. They have helped consumers buy homes, cars, and vacations and save for their children's education and their own retirement. They have operated a safe, secure, and efficient payments system and have led the world in rolling out debit and credit cards. They support issuers and investors in Canada's capital markets. Beyond our borders, the Canadian banks are highly regarded for their strength and stability. They stood tall in 2008 when most developed countries had to bail out their banks.

But the future of these pillars of our economy looks less bright than their past. As Bill Gates, founder of Microsoft and one of the world's richest men, noted 1994: "We need banking, but we don't need banks anymore."[2] The world he foresaw is already unfolding. Apple, Google, Samsung, Facebook, and a myriad of start-up technology companies, popularly known as fintechs, have launched payment technologies that target some of the banks' most lucrative business. PayPal, which has been processing payments for about fifteen years, would be the largest retail bank in the world, measured by active customers, if it were classified as a financial institution.[3] Similarly, nimble capital markets, both private and public, have displaced banks as the main providers of corporate finance, especially of bonds and derivatives to large corporations and governments.[4] The same applies to an array of new investment products, such as ETFs, and to advice, delivered by one group of fintechs known as robo-advisors.

The big, lumbering banks are bogged down by the physical artefacts of a bygone era: cash, cheques, bricks-and-mortar branches, ATMs, and huge data-processing centres. By contrast, direct or online banks serve customers without a physical presence and with little human intervention. Using mobile apps, Cloud computing, and social networking to reach individual customers in any place, at any time, these direct banks have proven they can exceed customer expectations at a small fraction of the cost of their traditional rivals. The combination of direct banks and targeted fintechs poses a tremendous challenge to the traditional banks.

Although the banks may be stumbling, they have not fallen – at least, not yet. We still need them to finance houses and condos and the tens of thousands of small businesses that are the backbone of our economy. They continue to protect our savings and are necessary for the clearing and settlement of payments through the Bank of Canada. The banks are an indispensable tool in the execution of the Bank of Canada's monetary policy and the government's broad economic agenda. Their role is magnified by the lack of depth and innovation in Canada's provincially regulated capital markets, which are a pale shadow of their U.S. counterparts when it comes to raising funds for companies and projects, especially those rated below investment grade.

Canada's Banks: Big, Profitable, and Trusted ...

A combination of sound management, the structure of the banking system, and prudent actions by regulators sheltered Canada from the write-downs and bailouts that brought many U.S. and European banks to their knees during the 2008 financial crisis.

The Canadian banks remain among the most stable and respected in the world. In 2015, they ranked third in market value among banks in the industrial countries. They were the most profitable, measured by return on equity, among 500 commercial and investment banks ranked by the consultancy McKinsey & Company.[5] Their financial strength stems from public policy that supports stability, as well as from the industry's oligopolistic structure. The six biggest banks – Bank of Montreal (BMO), Bank of Nova Scotia (Scotiabank or BNS), Canadian Imperial Bank of Commerce (CIBC), Royal Bank of Canada (RBC), Toronto-Dominion Bank (TD Bank or TD Canada Trust), and National Bank of Canada (BNC) – have a commanding 70 per cent market share of loans and deposits.[6] Though Canada has a population of just 35 million, the banks' combined profits (net income of $37.5 billion in 2016) are the fourth highest in the world.[7]

The banks go to great pains to remain on good terms with policy makers and regulators, and they work hard to keep their big corporate and government customers happy. That strategy has paid off handsomely. In 2011 the government approved a bid by a consortium of banks and institutional investors for control of TMX Group,[8] which operates Canada's only securities and derivatives exchange. The significance of this deal for the banks is not the expected returns from their investment. Rather, control of TMX enables them to protect the profits that their corporate and investment banking arms earn from companies and governments that are either too small or too unsophisticated to tap more competitive capital markets beyond Canada's borders. From the federal government's perspective, the TMX deal has helped ensure that federally regulated banks have a powerful voice in the provincially regulated domestic capital market.

Domestic retail banking makes up the lion's share of the banks' revenues and profits. This is true even for Bank of Montreal, TD Bank, and Scotiabank, which have expanded into the U.S. and international markets. In 2016:

- The banks' Canadian business made up two-thirds of their total revenues and over 70 per cent of their profits.
- Over 80 per cent of Canadian revenues and profits came from retail banking, wealth management, and creditor (mortgage and loan) insurance for individuals and small and mid-sized businesses.
- Domestic corporate and investment banking, often referred to as wholesale banking, contributed the remaining 20 per cent.[9]

Retail financial services, which include loans, deposits, payments, wealth management, and insurance, are a highly profitable business. In 2016, the six big banks' return on capital from their domestic operations ranged from 30 to 51 per cent, and averaged about 40 per cent.[10] According to Investopedia, even a 15 to 20 per cent return on equity is usually considered high.

Canadians trust their banks, and with good reason. Few other businesses can match the banks' record for safety, stability, and resilience. According to a survey published by Edelman, a large public-relations firm, public trust in the banks rose from 49 per cent of informed respondents between the ages of 35 and 64 to 59 per cent in the five years after the onset of the financial crisis in 2008. The only other G20 country that could boast of rising public confidence in its banks was China.[11] Even so, trust in the Canadian banks is much lower than in their formidable new rivals, technology companies such as Apple, Google, Facebook, Amazon, and PayPal, which garnered a 75 per cent approval rating.

Investors who have put their money into Canadian bank stocks have fared extraordinarily well. The big six as a group have earned a compound annual real return of 10.4 per cent over the past thirty years, almost double the return of the TSX/S&P composite index

Figure 1.1. Common stock performance of Canada's big six banks, 1980–2015

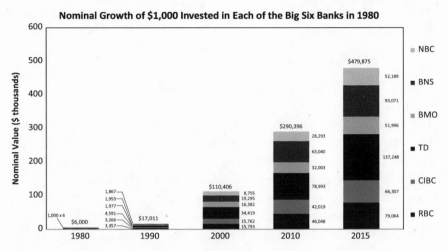

Nominal Growth of $1,000 Invested in Each of the Big Six Banks in 1980

Source: Authors' Analysis

(see figure 1.1). A $1,000 investment in each of the big six banks in early 1980 had ballooned to a staggering $479,875 ($178,562 after inflation) by the end of 2015.

These juicy returns have been driven mostly by the banks' Canadian retail franchises – an oligopoly protected by government regulation. The protection takes many forms. There's the ownership restriction that bars any individual or institution from owning more than 20 per cent of a bank's shares. There's deposit insurance, available only to regulated financial institutions. And there's the banks' stranglehold on access to the Canadian payments system.

These advantages stood the banks in good stead during the financial crisis and for many decades before that. But that is no longer the case. The protective bubble that has long worked in their favour now threatens to hold the banks back as they try to adapt to fast-moving trends that they will ultimately not be able to escape.

Protection is not what the banks need to address the looming threats from online rivals and from the up-and-coming fintechs. Quite the opposite, in fact. The banks would be far better served nowadays if they were exposed to more competition, not less. Only in that way are they likely to take the transformative steps needed to secure their future.

... But Ill Prepared for the Twenty-First Century

The banks' oligopoly may have produced impressive stock market returns, but those have come at the expense of investment in the future. The banking industry beyond Canada's borders has been in the throes of gradual but profound change for several decades. Indeed, advances in digital technology threaten the very business model that has enabled the Canadian banks to thrive for almost 150 years. The old 3–6–3 model of banking – take deposits at 3 per cent, make loans at 6 per cent, and be on the golf course at 3:00 p.m. – no longer holds.

A new generation of direct banks, which serve individual customers through remote channels, has figured out how to provide the services customers want at a fraction of the cost of bricks-and-mortar branches. Far from being masters of their destiny, as they were in the past, Canada's banks are now being buffeted by forces beyond their control. For a start, their once iron grip on their customers is weakening. Debtors can no longer be sure who holds their notes, homeowners cannot be certain who owns their mortgages, and many investors may be surprised at who manages their portfolios. The financial system now abounds with entrepreneurs eager to provide consumer-friendly, mobile, and seamlessly engineered applications that work whenever and wherever we need them – without any help from a bank.[12]

If anything, the banks now face an even tougher struggle to keep abreast of the market than they did ten years ago. The financial crisis has brought a new layer of regulations that improve the banking system's stability. But stricter capital and liquidity requirements and other new rules also add complexity and cost and discourage risk taking, precisely what the banks need least as they confront a flock of nimble and unfamiliar competitors.

The Canadian banks are only now starting to awaken to this difficult environment. In the mid-2000s, when they still had a choice, they opted to keep investing in the old, bricks-and-mortar model. Over the past decade, the banks have added more than 400 branches and 4,000 ATMs in Canada, and more than 2,000 branches outside the country.[13] Rather than supporting customers with modern mobile Internet technology, automated processing, and Cloud computing, they have trained programmers to maintain outdated mainframe computer systems and labour-intensive processes. Rather than investing in automated and innovative services, they have raised fees to cover rising labour costs and boost profits. Significantly, J.D. Power, a consultancy, titled its 2015 survey of Canadian consumers "Retail Banks in Canada Losing Touch with Customers as Profits Climb While Satisfaction Declines."[14] What more evidence do we need that the banks have been moving in the wrong direction?

Much research has gone into explaining why businesses fail to respond to the challenge of disruptive technology. As far as financial services go, the consensus is that mobile devices, Cloud computing, and social networking will ultimately lead to the transformation of the sector as we know it.[15] So it's perhaps not surprising that, far from embracing creative destruction, the Canadian banks and their counterparts in many other parts of the world have chosen to lobby in favour of the status quo. The response of global financial regulators, in the form of the Basel II and III agreements, has reinforced the old business model. But, unfortunately for bankers and regulators, the forces of change are far more powerful than they are.

Why Industries Fail: Creative Destruction ...

Joseph Schumpeter, an Austrian-born economist and political scientist, described creative destruction as "the process of industrial mutation that incessantly revolutionizes the economic structure from within, incessantly destroying the old one, incessantly creating a new one." Spurts in entrepreneurial behaviour periodically disrupt established industries. Such disruptions cause the affected industry to undergo a complete transformation, culminating in the emergence of a new set of more efficient and customer-friendly players.[16] Throughout history, waves of innovation have reinvigorated tired industries, boosted productivity, and spurred economic growth.[17] But experience also suggests that very few incumbents are able to make that transition. As a result, many fall by the wayside.

We have witnessed numerous examples in recent years as the Internet cuts a swath through long-established but sclerotic business models. Take the way in which online news sites such as the *Huffington Post*, *Buzzfeed*, and *Business Insider* have revolutionized the media business. American daily papers lost around $30 billion in advertising spending between 2005 and 2014.[18] Employment at U.S. newspapers sank from 455,700 in 1990 to 225,100 in 2013. Yet during the same period, the number of jobs in Internet publishing and broadcasting soared from 29,400 to 121,200.[19]

Creative destruction explains a key dynamic of industrial change, namely, the transition from a competitive to a monopolistic or oligopolistic market, and back again. Healthy economies and industries go through cycles of destruction that at the same time seem to release a burst of innovation and creativity. After a phase of growth, followed by a period of consolidation, pressure seems to build for a release. But failure to release creativity has inevitably led to rigidity in the system, which C.S. Holling, a conceptual founder of ecological economics, called a "rigidity trap."[20]

It is a normal human reaction to view a forest fire, a plague of locusts, or a bank collapse as an unmitigated disaster that can bring no good. But while such disasters destroy existing structures, they also release trapped resources and nutrients that create new life. In much the same way, the destruction wrought by the 2008 financial crisis also sowed the seeds for thousands of entrepreneurs with innovative ideas to transform long-established lending, investing, and payments mechanisms. Unfortunately for the banks, regulators are trying to put the genie back in the bottle by imposing stricter capital and liquidity ratios. We will examine their response in more detail in subsequent chapters. Suffice it to say for now that this reaction will put the banks in an even deeper hole than the one they already find themselves in.

. . . and General Purpose Technologies

The concept of general purpose technologies, often abbreviated to GPTs, has been developed by the Canadian Institute for Advanced Research's institutions, organizations, and growth program to describe earth-shaking innovations with the potential to transform how business is done across a wide range of sectors.[21] GPTs have four essential attributes: the scope to make vast improvements, many varied uses, applications across a large part of the economy, and the ability to feed off and influence other technologies. Innovations that qualify as GPTs include the printing press, electricity, railways, the internal combustion engine, and, most recently, the computer and the Internet.

One important consequence of technological progress is the accelerating obsolescence of existing capital – whether in the form of machines and equipment or human knowledge.[22] To make matters worse, oligopolies that find favour with government can use their clout to resist adoption of the disruptive new technologies, not only putting a brake on productivity but also catching the industry in a "rigidity trap." The Canadian banks are a prime example.

Since both obsolescence and progress are central to Schumpeter's concept of creative destruction, they have a big impact on how long it takes to adopt a new general purpose technology and the costs of doing so. The norm for new technologies to be understood, adopted, and integrated into production is twenty to thirty years, as was the case with the Internet and the personal computer.[23]

GPTs are not confined to technologies that we can touch or see. They may also apply to ways of thinking about and applying knowledge. In the financial services industry, two GPTs have had an immeasurable impact since the mid-1970s: modern portfolio theory, and information and communications technology. We examine each of them below.

Modern Portfolio Theory

Developed between the 1950s and 1970s at the University of Chicago, modern portfolio theory is based on the concept that assets in an investment portfolio should not be chosen on their individual merits. Rather, each should be judged by how its price changes relative to every other investment in the portfolio.

To grasp the full significance of this theory, we need to understand that investing is a trade-off between risk and expected return. In general, assets with higher expected returns also carry more risk. Modern portfolio theory describes how to assemble a portfolio that provides the highest possible return for a given amount of risk. Conversely, it shows how to create a portfolio with the lowest possible risk for a given expected return.

This general purpose technology laid the foundation for massive growth in the financial services industry, starting in the mid-1970s. Traditional banking activity – in other words, taking deposits and making loans – began to be overshadowed by the bundling of assets, which could be sold to investors as securities in a process known as securitization. This concept paved the way for the creation of entirely new classes of financial instruments: mortgage and other asset-backed securities; high-yield or junk bonds that drove leveraged buyouts and the private equity boom; and derivative instruments, such as interest rate, currency, credit, and liquidity swaps.

Helped by a massive advance in computing technology and falling trade barriers, securitization fuelled the globalization of capital markets. As the world economy became more tightly integrated, new technology and access to new markets propelled cross-border capital flows to unprecedented heights. Between 1990 and 2007, global financial assets almost quadrupled from US$56 trillion to US$206 trillion – that is, a growth rate of roughly 8 per cent a year. The 2008 meltdown brought that explosive growth to an abrupt halt, but the growth has resumed since then, reaching US$294 trillion in 2015.[24]

Not surprisingly, these global trends made themselves felt in Canada's financial services industry. In keeping with the banks' drive to break down barriers and expand their horizons, the Bank Act was amended in 1987 to allow the banks to buy investment dealers. Within a couple of years, five of the six big banks had snapped up Bay Street's largest securities firms. (Only TD Bank did not join the rush to acquire an investment bank.) The acquisitions gave the banks what they needed to take advantage of the trends that were by then sweeping financial markets. Now they too could bypass regulatory barriers; package mortgages, credit card debt, and auto loans into securities; and flex their muscles in capital markets beyond Canada's borders. Because Canadian regulators continued to view these emerging financial conglomerates as banks, they forced them to hold more capital against their securities business than their counterparts in many other countries.[25] As things turned out, this buffer protected the banks when the earth began to shake beneath them in 2008.[26]

Digital Information and Communications Technology

The digital era has unfolded at a dizzying pace, and its impact on transaction and interaction costs has been breathtaking.[27] The Internet, used by a minuscule 0.45 per cent of the world's population in 1994, now reaches more than 45 per cent, or 3.4 billion people – with more coming online every day. Mobile Internet access is exploding even faster, from zero in 2007 to more than 1 billion users in 2012 and an estimated 3 billion by mid-2015.[28] In November 2016, the number of mobile Internet users surpassed the number of desktop users.

The Internet is just the latest in a series of advances in information and communications technology that have transformed the global economy since the late eighteenth century. As box 1.1 shows, each wave has been driven by its own set of technologies and institutions. These waves have done more than just spawn new technologies and industries. Each has transformed the whole structure of the economy and many of the fundamental assumptions of society.

Box 1.1. Waves of technology and economic development

1771 – The Industrial Revolution (the age of machines, factories, and canals)
1829 – The age of steam, coal, iron, and railways
1875 – The age of steel and heavy engineering
1920 – The age of the internal combustion engine and the assembly line
1971 – The age of information and communications technology

Source: Chart based on the concepts of Carlota Perez, see, for example, http://www.carlotaperez.org/pubs

---

Starting in the late 1770s, machines, factories, and canals shaped the Industrial Revolution. The age of steam and coal revolutionized transportation, shrinking distances and opening up new frontiers in trade and human migration. The age of steel ushered in the transformation of cities to their modern form, as well as fundamentally changing the nature of warfare and, with it, the shape of geopolitics. At the turn of the twentieth century, the invention of automobiles, petrochemicals, and mass production techniques transformed vast swathes of our economy and society.

We are now in the midst of yet another revolution, this one of information and communications technology. This shift is different from those of the past two centuries, not least because of the fundamental differences between information and physical resources. Among them:

- Information is *expandable*: It expands as it is used.
- Information is *not resource hungry*: Producing and distributing information requires very little energy or other physical and biological resources.
- Information is *substitutable*: It can, and increasingly does, replace capital, labour, and physical materials.

- Information is *transportable*: It moves as fast as a user needs it to.
- Information is *diffusive*: Information yearns to be free. It leaks universally, pervasively, and continuously. Monopolizing information is almost a contradiction in terms.
- Information is *shareable*: If I sell you my car, you have it and I don't. But if I sell you an idea or give you a fact, we both have it.

The tools of the information age – personal computers, the Internet, downloadable software (now called apps), mobile devices, Cloud computing, and social media – have spawned new industries and transformed services. These inventions have revolutionized traditional activities such as manufacturing and agriculture, leading to huge advances in productivity. And they have been instrumental in transforming national financial markets into global ones.

Computing and Internet technology are also revolutionizing the way financial services are delivered. Over the past twenty years, banking has shifted from somewhere you go to something you do.[29] It is no longer hemmed in by a network of bricks-and-mortar branches and processing centres, nor by such increasingly outdated artefacts as cheques and cash. The banking system that is emerging from the global financial crisis is pervasive, mobile, and seamlessly engineered to work when and where we need it.

Canada's Banks Are Struggling to Adapt

As disruptive change unfolds, it often seems to take place quite slowly, with the full implications only sinking in later. It is worth recalling the oft-told story of the boiled frog. Put a frog in boiling water and it jumps out. Put it in cold water that is slowly brought to a boil and it does not notice the rising temperature until it is too late.

Alas, Canada's big banks find themselves in the same predicament as the frog that seems quite comfortable in cold water – until it is too late. Until very recently, the banks either appeared to be too slow in recognizing the changing temperature or wilfully chose to ignore a mortal threat. Whatever the reason, there is no doubt that they have failed to respond adequately to the disruptive change sweeping their industry.

Let's take a closer look at each explanation for their behaviour.

The Banks Were Too Slow to Recognize Changes around Them

In 1949, Harvard psychologists set up a simple experiment in perception involving about two dozen students. The students were shown a pack of playing cards. But a few of the cards had been doctored. The six of spades was red. The eight of hearts was black. In the first part of the experiment, the cards were flipped over very quickly. The students failed to notice the changes, insisting that the eight of hearts was actually the eight of spades, and that the six of spades was the six of hearts.

The researchers then gave the students a bit more time to see the doctored cards. The result was much the same. The students struggled to square what they were expecting to see with what they in fact saw. Confronted with a red six of spades, some said it looked different, maybe purple or brown or "rusty black." Others were even more confused. "The symbols looked reversed or something," insisted one. Another said, "I can't make the suit out, whatever it is." A third blurted out: "I don't know what colour it is now, or whether it's a spade or a heart. I'm not even sure what a spade looks like."

Some years later, Thomas Kuhn, one of the twentieth century's most influential science historians, sought to explain the students' confusion. As he saw it, the card experiment revealed how people process disruptive information. Their first impulse is to force it into the framework they're most familiar with, in this case, the cards' traditional red and black colours. Humans are programmed, according to Kuhn, to discount or explain away data that do not fit their long-accepted assumptions. The more contradictions – or anomalies – accumulate, the more convoluted the rationalizations become. "In science, as in the playing card experiment, novelty emerges only with difficulty," he noted.[30]

But perceptions quickly change when someone with a more flexible and innovative mindset calls the doctored six of spades what it now is: a red spade. The disruption produces a fresh insight, and the old framework gives way to a new one. This acceptance does not come easily to most people. Indeed, Kuhn suggested that the process can often take a generation to complete. In today's world, however, and especially in the dog-eat-dog world of business, we often do not have the luxury of that much time to accept that something big in our lives has changed.[31] By the time long-established firms become aware that the world around them has shifted, it is often too late for them to catch the innovators who have turned black spades into red ones.

Banks Were Slow to Respond

We recently had an agreeable discussion on disruptive technology with the chief executive of one of the big Canadian banks who, not surprisingly, preferred not to be named. His view was quite straightforward: "It's not going to happen on my watch, and I am not going to do anything about it." Such head-in-the-sand thinking is quite understandable for a business protected from market forces and driven by short-term shareholder returns. Bank executives' incentive to adjust to new circumstances is further dampened by the limited time they typically spend in their jobs and by their compensation packages, which are tied to short-term performance. In other words, they have little incentive to embrace risky and potentially disruptive change and every incentive to stick to the tried-and-trusted ways that make them feel most comfortable.

The wisdom of such lethargy and risk aversion is dubious, given the profound changes in technology, customer attitudes, and regulations that are reshaping the global financial services industry. The 2008 financial crisis and government bailouts may not yet have forced U.S. and European banks to adapt to new realities, but at least they are feeling the pain. On the other hand, the Canadian banks, lauded for their success in riding out the tough times, have felt little pressure to stray from the well-trodden path they have been on for the past several decades.

Their boards of directors and long-term investors have done little to encourage banks to break out of this rut. Equity markets have made it even harder by rewarding banks for earnings growth, even if that growth has meant doubling down on the old, branch-based business model.

Policy makers have continued to emphasize the stability that has been a cornerstone of financial sector policy throughout Canada's history. After Confederation, the federal government needed a stable banking system to help attract foreign investment to the young economy. This was accomplished by a small number of big, profitable banks that were allowed to expand into new businesses only after they had shown they could manage the risks. It was no accident that not a single Canadian bank failed during the Great Depression of the 1930s or the Great Recession eighty years later.[32] But there is a flip side to that success: stability comes at a price, and that price has been innovation.

The Canadian banks are now belatedly starting to feel the heat of competition and new technology. Most have created technology incubators and are looking for nimble fintech partners to help guide them into a more innovative era. The fintechs are, at least for now, only nibbling at the edges. *The biggest threat comes from direct banks, those that serve customers without a physical presence and with little human intervention.* These pioneers offer immediate delivery of financial services at any place, at any time, at a fraction of the cost.

While the banks are making some progress in adapting to the new world of technology-driven financial services, their tentative moves risk being too little too late.

The High Cost of Inaction

Failure to invest for the future is costing Canada dearly. Underinvestment in the payments system costs us at least $8 billion a year in savings we should be making by cutting the use of paper cheques and invoices.[33] Even more significantly, without a digital payments system, Canadian companies and governments cannot capture the savings – estimated at $16 billion to $32 billion a year, or 1 to 2 per cent of GDP – that would come from online delivery of public and private sector services.[34]

On another front, the innovative new technology companies that should be a big part of Canada's economic future are unable to find the financing they need to thrive. The array of fintech start-ups gives Canadians hope that they will no longer be held hostage by the banks, but market-based lending to support them and other new businesses is in short supply. One reason is that the Basel II and III agreements, hammered out in the aftermath of the financial crisis, have forced all banks to hold extra capital and liquidity. Because loans to small and mid-sized businesses usually have the heaviest risk weighting, thus requiring the most capital and reducing return on investment, banks are reluctant to finance many of the most innovative enterprises.[35]

Stability and short-term profitability do not come cheap, as can be seen from the extra costs that stem from Canada's current regulatory regime and the banks' conservative approach to business. The evidence is plentiful and not hard to find. The federal government effectively guarantees most residential mortgages through the Canada Mortgage and Housing Corporation. These guarantees will cost taxpayers dearly if the real estate market turns sour. Small businesses unable to raise financing from Canadian banks are forced to look to family, friends, and angel investors, and to U.S. venture capital funds. Financial advisors, many of them affiliated with the big banks, end up pocketing more than 40 per cent of investment returns that Canadians need for a comfortable retirement.[36] Similarly, the banks regularly raise service charges for routine transactions on their outdated clearing and settlement systems, instead of replacing those systems with ones more suited to a digital world.

There is surely room for a more balanced approach that values stability but at the same time gives banks greater freedom and incentive to take on their innovative direct and fintech rivals. Such an approach would also give Canadian consumers better value for their dollar.

Do the Banks Have a Future?

Peter Drucker noted in 1999 that banks can choose to travel down one of three possible roads.[37] The easiest and usually the most popular option is to keep doing what has worked in the past. But this almost certainly means a steady decline. The Canadian industry may survive with support from the government, providing residential mortgages and small-business loans, protecting savings deposits, and clearing and settling payments. But no matter how hard the banks work to protect the past, it will not be enough to stop new rivals, such as direct banks and fintechs, from scooping up large chunks of their business.

Some would argue that the banks have adapted well to the changing environment over the past thirty years. When their traditional lending and deposit businesses were threatened by securitization in the 1980s, they acquired the country's largest securities dealers. They went on to scoop up independent mutual fund dealers, asset managers, and trust companies to build their wealth management business. They used their vast branch distribution networks to eventually haul in the majority of individual investments. After mortgage brokers won more than half of home-mortgage originations, the banks acquired the "super brokers." Now, the banks have an opportunity to accelerate their participation in digital services by forming partnerships with fintech start-ups. If a fintech partner turns out to be a success, the bank can buy it out. Most of these start-ups focus on a single specialized business, so several acquisitions would be needed to transform the banks' entire model.

But there is a bigger problem. In our view, the main threat to the incumbents is not the fintechs but the direct banks. And, since Scotiabank acquired ING Direct, there are none of those left to buy. But the extraordinary profitability of retail banking, especially the payments business, and the ease of entering this business, especially for companies with good technology and lots of customers, such as Apple, Google, Samsung, and PayPal, make direct banking a tremendous opportunity for them. ING Direct has clearly demonstrated the superiority of a direct bank approach to foreign markets.

In 2011, less than five years after acquiring its customer base, ING sold its U.S. direct bank for US$9 billion.

The second option raised by Peter Drucker is that traditional banks will make way, whether they like it or not, for innovative outsiders and newcomers, in line with Schumpeter's path of "creative destruction." This is unlikely to happen anytime soon. True, there are many who believe that the industry should not be protected from competition, especially in light of its highly publicized excesses and misdeeds. However, in the wake of the global financial crisis, regulators continue to protect banks, at least in Canada, given their importance to the Canadian economy. With regulatory protection, for the foreseeable future bank utilities would survive to clear and settle payments and hold deposits; nevertheless, most other products and services are already being offered by innovative fintechs.

There is a third option. The banks can become innovators themselves as they go through their own process of "creative destruction." That process would start with them transforming their branch-centric operations into a direct bank. Modern technology would enable them to deliver competitive products and services immediately to customers' smartphones. This would be the best outcome for Canadians and their banks, because it would avoid the tremendous costs – human and financial – of options one and two. But an evolutionary transformation of the banking industry can only be achieved through collaboration between the bankers, policy makers, regulators, investors, customers, and suppliers.

A World without Banks

Can you imagine a world without banks? In fact, that world already exists. It has emerged thanks to a new breed of consumer who no longer needs a bank account for everyday living and working. Millions of these people have walked away from the traditional relationship between a bank and its customer, or have never tied the knot in the first place. Instead, they move their money by using prepaid debit cards, gift cards, PayPal, Apple, Android, and Samsung

Pay accounts, and other arrangements that bypass the traditional banking system.

Even when it comes to loans, a growing number of borrowers are turning to sources outside the banking system. Small businesses spurned by the banks are finding support from angel investors, crowdfunding, venture capital, and private equity. Even Canadians hunting for a mortgage are looking for alternatives to the banks. Although the proportion of mortgages provided by lenders other than banks, credit unions, and mortgage-backed securities is only about 2.5 per cent of the market, it is up from 0.8 per cent during the 2008 recession, and volumes are growing by about 25 per cent a year.[38]

In the field of wealth management, a new, low-cost player has emerged in the form of the robo-advisor. Firms like Wealthsimple, Questrade, Nest Wealth, WealthBar, Modern Advisor, and Invisor are a far cry from the old-school broker from RBC Dominion Securities or CIBC Wood Gundy who called each month to discuss your portfolio. Instead, the robo-advisor relies on a set of computer algorithms that tell investors how to divide their portfolios among cash, bonds, equities, and commodities. That advice may or may not be based on a discussion with a human being. And once the asset allocation decisions have been made, the robo-advisor will guide you to the appropriate exchange-traded funds, known as ETFs, which typically levy far lower fees than the mutual funds favoured by the big banks' money managers. The algorithm will also take care of investing future cash flows, rebalancing portfolios as needed, and making use of tax-reduction strategies, all at a price much lower than would be charged by a full-service broker or a mutual fund advisor.

Fintech entrepreneurs are finding ways for consumers to pay for their purchases without ever having to deal with a bank. Imagine that you are shopping, either online or in person. Your shopping app helps find the items you want and compares prices and quality. It checks inventory, promotions, and warranties; tracks your loyalty points; and takes care of payment and delivery. Whether you are buying a ride from Uber or books from Amazon or are dealing with an online retailer supported by PayPal, a couple of clicks are all it takes to complete the transaction. What's more, fintech start-ups like Borrowell, FinanceIt, and LendoGram can even help finance the purchases.

What it all boils down to is that, for the first time, Canadians can shop, pay, borrow, and invest without being held hostage by the big banks. Today's early adopters, most of them millennials without a lot of income or assets, may not be the most desirable customers. But that will surely change as more consumers of all ages and income groups embrace mobile Internet services.

Banks Still Have a Role

Canada's big banks may be stumbling, but they are not yet on their knees. Far from it. They remain essential and powerful cogs in a well-functioning economy. Our financial system, built on strong federally regulated banks and weak provincially controlled capital markets, has so far spawned few alternatives to bank financing for many businesses, especially mid-sized ones. The banks continue to dominate the home mortgage market. An underdeveloped fixed income and securitization market means that many Canadians still invest a big chunk of their savings in bank deposits and guaranteed investment certificates (GICs). Policy makers need the banks to help execute monetary policy and broader economic objectives.

According to the Conference Board of Canada, financial services make up 6.8 per cent of Canada's economy.[39] The big six together employ more than 350,000 people.[40] Their assets amount to double the country's entire economic output. Canadians also have a big stake in the future well-being of their banks through their exposure to bank stocks, either as individual shareholders or through their pension or mutual funds. Alas, those stocks could tumble if investors come to realize how ill-equipped the banks are to face the future. The failure of even one of the banks would be a severe blow to the entire economy.[41]

But no matter how big or important the banks may be, they are undeniably losing their grip on their most loyal and profitable customers. The entry of large technology players, such as Apple,

Google, PayPal, Facebook, and Amazon, into the payments business and the flurry of financial technology entrepreneurs building new lending, investing, and payment vehicles are giving Canadians new ways to manage their money.

Whatever the big banks' shortcomings, the authorities are likely to continue supporting their interests. The government needs the banks to implement monetary policy, support other economic priorities, and overcome the deep-rooted structural defects of Canada's capital markets. Given the importance of the banks to the economy, the best we can hope for is that the upheavals now sweeping the financial services industry will prod them into transforming themselves into businesses more in tune with the fast-moving twenty-first-century marketplace.

CHAPTER TWO

From Branches to Smartphones

Progress is impossible without change, and those who cannot change their minds cannot change anything.

George Bernard Shaw

Our friends Alex and Meg bought a house in June 2011 in Innisfil, Ontario, about an hour's commute from downtown Toronto, where Alex works as a consultant at Deloitte. Realizing in early 2016 that their five-year mortgage would soon be due for renewal, Alex e-mailed his financial advisor at his bank's Innisfil branch, only to receive an auto-reply telling him that the advisor had moved on to another department. The return e-mail suggested that Alex go to the branch to meet with a new advisor. That was not possible, because he leaves home at six in the morning and returns long after the branch has closed for the day.

But a few weeks later, walking through a mall with his two daughters, Alex saw an ad for the bank's mortgage centre, including a toll-free phone number. He duly called. It took half-an-hour of questioning for the customer service representative to realize that Alex wanted to renew an existing mortgage, not apply for a new one. She told him that the only way to do that was to go to the Innisfil branch. The bottom line was that there was no way to renew his mortgage without visiting a bricks-and-mortar office that was usually closed at the times convenient to him.

At any rate, one Saturday morning, Alex drove to the bank. The manager told him that an advisor named Melissa would get back to him. He seemed to be making progress at last. Indeed, Melissa duly followed up, telling him that the rate on a five-year, variable mortgage would be 3.3 per cent. That sounded fine, until Alex heard from his sister that she had been offered a five-year variable deal at just 2.2 per cent. He asked his bank to match that rate or, alternatively, to lower other charges, such as the annual fee on his credit card. Instead, the bank told him that he needed to cough up another $318 for mortgage insurance.

Alex's reaction to the run-around? "Why can't all this be automated? I don't need to talk to a human to roll over a mortgage at a competitive rate. When will the banks start giving their customers what they want?"[1]

Alex's experience with his mortgage highlights the monumental challenge facing Canada's big banks. Their business model is built around their branches. Customers, products, processes, systems, performance measurements, and employee incentives all revolve around the branch. As far as the bank is concerned, the window of opportunity to sell you more products through more channels opens only after you open an account at a branch.

The problem is that's not how customers want to do their banking these days. Most have a smartphone in the palm of their hand that can access services at a time and place of their choosing rather than a time and place that happens to suit the bank. What's more, these customers expect the bank to deliver its services immediately. If I can download a book from Amazon within minutes, why can't a bank deliver a credit card to my phone, instead of sending it by snail mail or forcing me to go to the branch to pick it up?

One Size Fits All

For now, Canada's six big banks all deliver pretty much the same services in much the same way. Their retail strategies essentially have the same three goals:

1. Provide superior client service through relevant and tailored advice.
2. Develop sales expertise, partnerships, and innovative distribution channels.
3. Streamline business processes to improve customer service and efficiency.

Even their marketing slogans are remarkably similar:[2]

- "Always earning the right to be our clients' first choice," and, more recently, "Banking that fits your life." (CIBC)
- ". . . the bank that defines great customer experience – We're here to help." (BMO)
- ". . . the leading bank for our clients. We have a client focused strategy that creates value for all our stakeholders – banking that makes your someday happen." (RBC)
- "Consistently delivering a legendary customer experience in everything we do – America's most convenient bank." (TD)
- ". . . focusing on its core purpose of being the best at helping customers become financially better off – You Are Richer Than You Think." (BNS)

As we tell our MBA students, the main difference between the banks' retail offerings is the colour of their logos – blue, red, green, gold, orange, and claret. But customers don't care about the colour of their bank. What they do care about is the quality, cost, and timeliness of the bank's services.

Banks regularly survey their customers to gauge satisfaction and loyalty. They ask questions like these: How likely is it that you would recommend us (or this product or service) to a friend or colleague? The responses are typically grouped in three categories known as promoters (9–10 out of 10), passives (7–8), and detractors (0–6). A "net promoter score" is calculated by subtracting the percentage of detractors from the percentage of promoters. For example, if 40 per cent of customers recommend a product (rating it a 9 or 10) and

20 per cent do not (a score below 6), the net promoter score is 20. As one would expect, banks with a higher ratio of promoters than detractors tend to gain the most market share.[3]

The most highly rated – and thus fastest-growing – banks typically report net promoter scores between 50 and 80. The most admired retail bank in North America is currently United Services Automobile Association, also known as USAA, a diversified financial services group based in San Antonio, Texas, that serves more than 9 million members of the armed forces and their families. USAA reported a net promoter score of 83 in 2015.[4] ING Direct had the second-highest score. But the average for the large U.S. national banks was close to zero, a clear sign that most fall short in keeping their customers happy.

According to Bain & Company's "Customer Loyalty in Retail Banking" survey, only one Canadian bank boasted a score of 50 or higher in 2015. That distinction went to Tangerine (formerly ING Direct), which overtook President's Choice Financial, a joint venture between CIBC and the Loblaws supermarket chain. PC Financial fell behind in 2015 partly because of its under-investment in mobile. Bain has not disclosed the six big banks' individual net promoter scores since 2012, but the average has hovered around 20. That's hardly a vote of confidence. It means that only about 20 per cent of the banks' customers (promoters less detractors) have been willing to recommend them to friends or colleagues.[5]

While the Canadian banks may trumpet their commitment to superior customer service, they have clearly failed to deliver. Small and mid-sized businesses tend to have an even lower opinion of the banks than individual customers like Alex. Surveys by the Canadian Federation of Independent Business (CFIB) over the past decade consistently show that the vast majority of its members give the banks a score of five or less out of ten. Such poor ratings translate into negative net promoter scores; in other words, all these small-business owners are, in effect, telling others to steer clear of the banks.[6] Credit unions significantly outperform banks when it comes to serving the financial needs of small and mid-sized enterprises, according to the October 2016 CFIB research report, *Battle of the Banks*.[7]

The bottom line is that, in the view of most customers, the banks deliver poor service and unexciting products. And that's even before the customers start sounding off on bank fees.

A New Era Is Unfolding

It is no coincidence that banks with the highest customer satisfaction scores and the lowest expense ratios are those that have not put bricks-and-mortar branches at the centre of their universe. Among the most notable are Tangerine (formerly ING Direct) and President's Choice Financial in Canada, ING Direct and Fidor in Europe, USAA and ING Direct in the United States, and ING Direct in Australia. These banks have automated their processes from end to end to provide immediate delivery of financial services, and they conduct most of – and in some cases all – their business online. These direct banks built their systems, processes, performance measurements, and incentives to support their customers, not their branches. This puts them in a strong position to keep taking advantage of technological advances that improve service and reduce costs.

Let's take a closer look at the difference between banks that put their customers first and those fixated on their branches. Every lending, investment, and payments product today is designed to fill a need. Thus, people don't buy a mortgage; they buy a home. A car loan or lease is merely the means for putting a new car in the driveway. Signing up for a credit card makes sense only if you can use it for shopping. Investing in stocks or exchange-traded funds is designed not simply to make you rich but to finance your retirement or your children's education. Yet the priority for Canadian banks has been to sell the mortgage, car loan, credit card, or mutual fund through as many channels as possible, instead of focusing on the customer's desire to acquire a new home, car, or TV or to ensure a comfortable retirement.

Across the economy, the way services are delivered is changing fast as people adapt to new business models and new ways of paying for their purchases. Companies like Amazon, Uber, OpenTable, Airbnb, and Wealthsimple are using online technology to revolutionize their businesses – shopping, transport, dining, accommodation, and port-folio management, respectively – by interacting in an entirely new way with buyers of their products and services. They are automating the entire process from search to check-out into a seamless experience focused on the customer's end goal. Banks will need to follow suit if they are to have any hope of competing successfully.

Yet, for now, the Canadian banks' approach to using technology remains mired in the past. For the past fifteen to twenty years, their efforts have focused on trying to persuade customers to direct an ever-growing slice of their financial-services business to themselves, at an ever-higher price. The banks have spent hundreds of millions of dollars on databases crammed with information about Canadians with the aim of signing them up for more and more products, from foreign currency and auto insurance to mutual funds and credit cards. This strategy has manifested itself in annoying telemarketing calls in the middle of a family dinner but, most important, in the banks' sprawling branch networks.

Compare these tactics with the approach taken by the new giants of online commerce. When did you last get a telemarketing call from Amazon, at whatever time of the day or night? Instead, it collects data about you, your searches, previous purchases, payments, and other activities, stores them in a massive database, and then uses it to present you with offers that it thinks you might be interested in. Its algorithms are far more sophisticated and intuitive than any system the banks have so far come up with. And unlike the banks, Amazon gets better all the time at understanding each customer's preferences. More than that, it integrates payments and financing, two traditional bank businesses, into its checkout under the banner of Amazon OneClick. It does not ask shoppers to fill in an application form or to visit an office.

Uber, the online ride-sharing service, is another business with a laser-like focus on its customers. Uber is about much more than ride sharing. It is a multinational online transport network, with a platform that can provide a multitude of services. Not only can an Uber car pick you up and drop you off where you want, but it will also transport your parcels, take your kids to school and back, deliver your lunch or dinner, and collect your laundry – all without any cash changing hands. Uber is seeking to use its network to meet just about every transport and logistics need. Why can't banks do the same for financial services?

To illustrate the difference between these customer-centred business models and the banks, let's take the example of a young, growing family. The bank likely discovers that you are starting a family when you buy a registered education savings plan (RESP), which might be months or years after your child is born. By contrast, Amazon is clued in six months before the birth when a pregnant mother orders the book *What to Expect When You Are Expecting*. The timing is important because starting a family is one of those once-in-a-lifetime events that often triggers significant financial transactions, such as a mortgage to buy a house, a line of credit to keep the household finances afloat during maternity leave or to decorate the baby's room, and an RESP to start saving for a child's education. If shopping for bank services was ever different from buying a book, it is certainly no different now. It doesn't take rocket science to appreciate that Amazon has a head start on every Canadian bank.

The surging popularity of online and, more recently, mobile shopping is belatedly forcing the banks to raise their game. Conventional brand marketing and branch-focused campaigns are no longer enough. Instead, the realization is slowly dawning on the banks that they must integrate sales and marketing more closely across multiple platforms to meet customers' specific needs. Instead of just signing up a customer for a mortgage, a bank can build a business around the entire process of buying a home. It can walk the customer through the various steps, answering and anticipating queries, providing access to all the services involved in buying a home (realtor, home inspector, valuer, lawyer, renovator, insurer, and so on), and culminating in a mortgage and a creditor insurance policy.

Crossing the Chasm

Some banks beyond Canada's borders have seen the writing on the wall and are showing that it is possible to switch their focus from branches to customers. Among them are three of Australia's four biggest banks, Texas-based USAA, and Nordea Bank of Finland.

The trailblazer, Commonwealth Bank of Australia, began the shift back in 2008. It invested billions of dollars over five years in new technology and processes that eliminate barriers between products and branches to provide direct service to the customer. Commonwealth Bank has reaped rich rewards from its efforts. Customer satisfaction has improved dramatically. Costs have gone down, and profits have gone up.

United Services Automobile Association (USAA), which has the highest net promoter scores among U.S. retail banks, promises "legendary service and simple tools," which it delivers with one of the lowest cost ratios in the industry. A milestone in USAA's history was the introduction of toll-free phone service to replace mail or telegraph. That forced it to re-engineer its systems and processes to serve customers when they called, rather than when it suited the bank to respond to them. Having made the switch to dealing directly with customers, USAA was able to move from landline to smartphone far more quickly and painlessly than rivals fixated on their branches.

What USAA has learned (and is now teaching others) is that the best way for a bank to win customers' loyalty and at the same time turn a decent profit is to put those customers' preferences ahead of its own. That strategy starts by welcoming new customers in the way *they* find most convenient, rather than in the way that happens to have suited the bank over the years. For more than a century, Canadian banks have, literally, brought customers through the door by flooding every city with branches. Many street intersections have a bank branch on two, and sometimes even all four, corners. But, as our friend Alex's story shows, the emphasis on branches can be more of a turn-off than a come-on when consumers are looking for convenient, easy-to-use services. Banks like USAA, ING Direct, and the three Australian pioneers no longer insist on tying a customer to a branch. Not only do they offer almost all their services online, but they interact with customers from a central hub of information, transaction processing, and decision making.

The Canadian banks, on the other hand, are still wrestling with the dilemma of how to balance centralized information and decentralized service delivery without spending huge amounts of time and money. In our view, the only bank in a position to do this is Scotiabank. Its $3.1 billion acquisition of ING Direct in August 2012 has given it a clear lead over its competitors. At the time of the deal, most observers focused on the benefits of ING Direct's $30 billion retail deposit base, which provided extra stability and diversification of funding, as well as cost-effective funding for future growth. Little attention was paid to the bank's distinct retail brand and its online platform. We believe this will have even wider implications as time goes on. Tangerine's strategy is simple: the customer comes first, and services are delivered via a computer, tablet, or smartphone. This model has given Tangerine impressive customer satisfaction ratings with one-ninth the employees of Scotiabank's traditional branch bank.

Other banks face a far bigger challenge. They have little choice but to try and transform a model deeply wired into their branches into one that responds immediately to customers, wherever they may be. Scotiabank wisely left Tangerine's business model alone after it bought the online bank in 2012. Tangerine remains a separate entity that is run parallel to Scotiabank's long-established branch network. That gives the parent the option to expand the direct-bank operation, possibly by absorbing Scotiabank's branch customers, without having to deal with the cultural issues or costs that would bedevil a top-to-toe transformation from a branch-centred model to a customer-centred one.

CIBC was also well-placed at one time to make the transition, but it blew the opportunity. It was the first Canadian bank to recognize the importance of a direct online operation when it set up its Amicus operation in 1998. Often described as a bank in a box, Amicus serviced customers from kiosks in grocery stores instead of branches. That led to a partnership with supermarket group Loblaws in 1998 under the President's Choice Financial label. CIBC tried to expand this model through partnerships with various U.S. retailers but without success. Amicus became a victim of the dot.com bust and was shut down in 2002. The President's Choice partnership with Loblaws continues, but a lack of investment in its direct platform has erased most of the competitive advantage that CIBC once held.

A Leopard That Changed Its Spots

Canada's banking system is often compared to Australia's. Both are fairly concentrated and, like their Canadian counterparts, the Australian banks are highly profitable.[8] However, there is a big difference in one of the forces driving those profits. Since the mid-1990s, the Australian banks' average cost ratio has shrunk by almost 20 percentage points to an impressive 44 per cent.[9] By comparison, while the Canadian banks have managed to bring down their cost ratios since 2007, their average remains in the low to mid-50s.[10]

Commonwealth Bank of Australia (CBA) has been a global pioneer, significantly improving customer satisfaction scores even as it has brought down costs. In 2013, CBA led its traditional bank rivals in customer satisfaction while it cut its cost ratio by a full percentage point to 45 per cent.[11] And its return on equity that year was a very respectable 18.4 per cent.[12] In fiscal 2016, the cost ratio came down still further to 42 per cent.

CBA owes its success to a new core banking platform that, in the words of its own promotional material, "has resulted in industry-leading features for customers, centred around the only true 24/7 core banking system among the major banks in Australia" – and, it might have added, one of the few anywhere in the world installed by a bank of its size.[13] CBA adds, tellingly, that the new system is "based on the roles and relationships of a customer's financial life – not products or accounts."[14]

The bank launched its four-year overhaul in April 2008 with a plan to modernize systems and transform related operations at a cost of A$580 million. CBA was, in the words on the cover of its 2008 annual report, "Determined to Be Different." Although the decision to commit the time and money was a difficult one, it was likely made easier by the bank's stubbornly low customer satisfaction scores.

To its credit, the bank knew better than to carry out such an ambitious project on its own. Following an internal feasibility study, the board turned for help to two outside consultancies, SAP and Accenture.[15] The results were impressive:

- A 75 per cent reduction in the time taken to bring products to market.
- Simplification of 610 product variations into 18 core products.
- 15 per cent fewer customer balance queries.
- A 36 per cent boost in the product cross-sell rate (from 2.2 to three products per customer).
- A 10 per cent rise in sales and converted referrals per employee.
- One-third fewer processing errors in branches.[16]

The project was not without its challenges. Even after the benefits of the overhaul started to become apparent in 2011, Simon Millet, director of Australian banking at CSC, a large technology consultancy, argued that "there is massive risk and not necessarily much return for taking a big bang approach."[17] CBA ended up spending A$1.3 billion on the new platform, more than double its initial budget. What's more, its spending on technology has continued to soar, jumping by 15 per cent in fiscal 2016, due mainly to application maintenance and further development to keep up with customers' rising expectations for mobile banking.[18]

But CBA has no regrets. As its 2016 annual report noted,

The group's investment in a new core banking system is now delivering market-leading advantages given the dependence of digital banking and related functionality on integrated, real-time systems. It allows us to deliver important benefits to our customers – to businesses who want their payments to be processed in real-time, and to retail customers who value features like instant credit card Lock, Block & Limit. This has again resulted in above-system growth in transaction accounts.[19]

Perhaps the most telling affirmation has come from CBA's Australian rivals, which have proved once again that imitation is the sincerest form of flattery. Most of them have launched similar projects to improve efficiency and customer experience. National Australia Bank began working with Oracle on a transformation project in 2009 and is now spending more than a billion dollars on a new banking platform.[20] Westpac began replacing its technology in 2013 using CSC's Hogan system[21] and in 2015 announced plans to invest A$1.3 billion in a digital-transformation project.[22] The sole holdout is ANZ, which still hopes to keep its customers happy by tweaking existing systems rather than cleaning house.[23]

CBA's initiative has also spurred banks to action far beyond Australia's shores. Joseph Edwin, head of the core banking program at Nordea Bank in Finland, recently outlined for investors how his bank learned from the Australians before embarking on its core banking platform replacement:[24]

> As an important step in the development of more personalized and convenient services to customers in the future, Nordea has signed an agreement with partners to implement the new Core Banking Platform.
>
> - Digitalisation and the rapid change in customers' preferences towards using online and mobile solutions are transforming the banking industry.
> - The new Core Banking Platform is a key part of Nordea's Simplification Program aimed at meeting the bank's 11 million customers' needs going forward. Products and processes are currently being simplified and, as part of the program, the current banking systems will be replaced with new core banking and payment platforms in the coming years.
> - The new Core Banking Platform will be implemented using a solution from Temenos, while Accenture has been chosen to provide the integration and implementation support.
> - The new platform will comprise loans, deposits and transaction accounts for customers in all parts of the bank, and will be provided through a common architecture across the Nordic countries.
> - The migration to the new platform will be done gradually over the coming four to five years.[25]

Mr Edwin's colleague, Jukka Salonen, head of group simplification, summarized the benefits as follows: "Our customers will benefit from much more personalized and convenient services, when we move from different legacy systems to one single platform. Additionally, this will enable us to deliver new digital solutions at a higher speed than today, and we will have a more scalable and resilient platform."[26]

The key message from the Australian banks, Nordea, and other digital pioneers is that today's customers are best served through a single, centralized banking platform rather than the sprawling branch networks that banks relied on in the past to hold their customers close. Not only does this approach reduce costs, it enables the bank to deliver services immediately at any time and any place convenient to the customer.

Canada's big six banks have been slow to get this message. They have been too timid up to now to make the huge commitment of money and time needed to overhaul their technology and invest in continuous maintenance and upgrades. In our view, they have no choice if they are to survive. The question is: Who will go first, and how?

The Sleeping Giants Awaken

The good news is that the Canadian banks are slowly awakening from their slumber. The bad news is that they are taking a blinkered approach, focused on working with fintechs instead of coming to grips with the much more serious challenge posed by the "direct" bank. The fintechs' products may break new ground, but they tend to augment rather than transform the banks' underlying business model. This strategy suggests that the banks are more interested in tinkering with their branch networks than in an all-out assault against the threat that confronts them.

Colleen Johnston, TD's head of technology and marketing, acknowledged that threat in a *Globe and Mail* column in July 2016: "The new killer app in banking isn't just a piece of software, but an elevated customer experience that is pro-active, personal and convenient ... We see the urgency and the need to adapt, and it has motivated us to accelerate our own transformation."[27]

But that transformation is mostly limited to adapting the fintechs' products to the banks' existing operations. Thus, Ms Johnston went on to say: "The new pressure of Fintech has sharpened our focus and allowed us to marshal our efforts. Fintechs have a lot to teach us – and we are listening, learning and using their momentum to drive our own change agenda."[28]

While these efforts may lead to improved products and services, they will not fix the banks' fundamental problem, namely, that their business model, technology, processes, performance measurements, and even employee incentives remain centred on their branches, not their customers.

Unfortunately for the banks, the challenge is becoming ever more urgent. The title of J.D. Power's 2015 survey, "Retail Banks in Canada Losing Touch with Customers as Profits Climb While Satisfaction Declines," sums up their vulnerability.[29] The risk for the banks is that unhappy customers are more likely to seek out other alternatives. This does not necessarily mean that they are about to succumb to a giant new financial technology company. Rather, the newcomers are likely to chip away at bits and pieces – including some of the most profitable bits and pieces – of the banks' business. Unless the banks can step up their game, customers will increasingly be inclined to stitch together their own bundles of financial services, using the growing array of products and services available from the fintechs, big and small. Jeff Marshall, head of Scotiabank's new Digital Factory division, has described this process as "death by a thousand cuts."[30] Another way of looking at it is that customers will become their own aggregators of the services they need rather than allowing a bank to do the job for them, as they have in the past.

The shift to mobile technology is putting pressure on banks to take a mobile-first approach in everything from buying a home to resolving a case of fraud. Overall customer satisfaction levels rose in J.D. Power's and Bain's 2016 retail banking surveys[31] because of the growing popularity of mobile banking. These surveys found that mobile channels are far more likely to please and less likely to annoy than branches or call centres. Specifically, the Bain survey found that apps are one-third more likely than branches to keep customers happy for routine transactions; conversely, a branch visit is 2.3 times more likely than a mobile interaction to annoy a customer. As a result, customers who often use a mobile device for their banking are 40 per cent less likely to switch to another bank than those who rarely use a smartphone or tablet.[32] What the banks have so far failed to understand, however, is that implementing this shift is much easier if it is based on a central technology platform rather than an old-fashioned branch network.

So, how are individual Canadian banks responding to these threats? A recent McKinsey & Company study, "Fintechs Can Help Incumbents, Not Just Disrupt Them," points out that a new era of cooperation is emerging between banks and fintechs in the form of partnerships, licensing agreements, acquisitions, and other deals.[33] We think it is important to highlight some of these initiatives, even though they are too recent to be properly evaluated. We are not convinced that they go far enough to put the banks back into the driver's seat.

Scotiabank

In our view, Scotiabank, with the help of Tangerine, has the best chance among the Canadian banks of reinventing itself. While the parent bank currently has the lowest satisfaction rating of the big six in J.D. Power's 2016 rankings, Tangerine has the highest. This suggests that Scotiabank's most effective strategy for the future may be to make Tangerine the focal point of its entire retail operation, while allowing its old branch-based model to fade away.

Tangerine's progress illustrates how the industry has evolved since the financial crisis. Previously known as ING Direct, it was a wholly-owned subsidiary of the big Dutch ING Group, one of the original disrupters of the global banking industry.[34] ING was a traditional bricks-and-mortar bank prior to the financial crisis, but with one important twist. Unlike many of its global rivals, such as Citibank, HSBC, RBS, and the Canadian banks, it used technology rather than branches to spearhead its drive into new markets. It launched the Canadian online and telephone banking operation in 1997 as a pilot for a broader assault on the North American market.

Ralph Hamers, the Dutch bank's current CEO, takes the view that operations like ING Direct offer a viable alternative to bricks-and-mortar banks. As one commentator noted, "In little over a decade, a huge, drooling St Bernard of a financial services group has turned itself into a greyhound of a bank."[35] That greyhound is now winning the race against many traditional rivals, particularly in Germany, where ING Direct has no branches but more than 8 million customers. The online-only business model has enabled ING Direct to hold its cost ratio to just 43 per cent compared to 52 per cent for the ING Group as a whole.[36] That alone gives it a clear competitive edge.

ING sold its Canadian operation to Scotiabank in 2012. Some interpreted that as an admission of failure. Far from it. The European Commission forced ING to sell assets, including ING Direct in Canada, the United States, and Britain, which meant that the Dutch bank's loss became Scotiabank's gain.

Renamed Tangerine, the online bank has won kudos far and wide. The *Globe and Mail*'s Report on Business ran a story in the summer of 2016 under the headline "Shaking Up Scotiabank: Brian Porter's Vision for a Bank of the Future," saying, "This is the story of a new CEO making dramatic changes, including several executive changes and significant restructuring."[37]

Porter clearly recognizes the importance of Tangerine in his drive to mould all of Scotiabank into a model similar to that of the Australian banks and ING Direct. Here's what he told students at Western University's Ivey Business School in March 2016:

> Tangerine truly is our hidden gem, and is a great example of what a bank-of-the-future can be.
>
> In addition to delivering a great customer experience, Tangerine also delivers great financial results: Its business model serves 2 million customers with less than 1,000 employees.
>
> This is impressive when you consider that we serve the bank's other 21 million customers with almost 90,000 employees.

We're confident that Tangerine will grab an even bigger share of the many millions of "direct ready" Canadians who are interested in banking primarily through mobile or digital channels.

In short, Tangerine acts as our internal "disruptor" and it is a key part of our digital strategy.[38]

Scotiabank has built on the momentum created by Tangerine with a new division specifically charged with accelerating digital transformation.[39] Aptly named Digital Factory, this unit employs 350 people with digital technology and social marketing backgrounds, mostly newcomers to the bank. Digital Factory's mandate is to work with nimble fintech companies and, even more important, to work with Scotiabank's own marketing, technology, operations, and branch personnel to help re-engineer the systems that link customers to the core banking platform. In December 2016, Scotiabank appointed five executives, Digital Banking Leaders, who will drive the bank's digital strategy in its key markets of Canada, Mexico, Peru, Chile, and Columbia.

Part of that strategy involves seeking out strong and innovative partners. Porter mentioned some of them in his Ivey speech: the SCENE loyalty program with Cineplex, a big cinema chain; Kabbage, an Atlanta-based fintech that specializes in digital lending technologies for small businesses; and Sensi-bill, which helps mobile customers manage their receipts.[40] The licensing deal with Kabbage will enable small businesses to apply online for loans of up to $100,000 and receive an answer in minutes. The bank has underscored the importance of these initiatives by hiring a Silicon Valley veteran, Shawn Rose, as executive vice-president for digital banking.[41]

These moves have the potential to align Scotiabank priorities far more closely with those of its customers. A recent poll commissioned by the bank found the following:

- 85 per cent of Canadians prefer to use online and mobile banking channels
- 66 per cent use mobile and digital banking channels at least once a week

- 79 per cent cite convenience as the major reason for using digital
- 85 per cent check account balances and 83 per cent pay bills online

On the other hand, only 16 per cent used digital channels to manage investments, 12 per cent to deposit a cheque, and 3 per cent to apply for a credit card.

Scotiabank remains confident that branches have a role to play, despite the dramatic shift towards online banking, but it also acknowledges that the role of the branch must change. It is trying to achieve that balance by experimenting with new formats centred on digital tools, but with an employee in attendance to help customers make the most of those tools.[42]

CIBC

Forrester's 2016 mobile banking study gives a shout-out to two Canadian banks – Scotiabank and CIBC – as leaders in the charge to mobile banking.[43] CIBC's CEO, Victor Dodig, has embraced innovation as the way for CIBC to meet its goal of being number one in customer satisfaction.[44] His initiatives gained some recognition in 2015 when CIBC emerged as a finalist in the product and service category of the Bank Administration Institute's awards for innovation in retail delivery.[45] Dodig has made it clear that he is well aware of the fintech threat:

> There's always been some sort of innovation in banking, so I think that's been something we've dealt with all the time. What's changed now is these new technologies entering the fore are going to reshape the way people interact with their existing bank, or people are going to choose a completely different banking alternative. And there's a very real risk of being disrupted, so I don't think this is something we should just kind of shove to the side. These new entrants are trying to create banking that's easy, banking that's convenient, banking that's on a client's terms, banking that's frictionless and therefore really, really low cost. And we're trying to do all of that within the existing

footprint we offer. But the way our system's set up today, it's pretty technologically oriented. We've got a leading mobile platform, and we can run it at a relatively low cost. That puts us in good stead.[46]

Recognizing the massive effort needed to adapt, CIBC is beefing up its resources through partnerships, by hiring more young people, and by encouraging them to be creative. After all, the bank can hardly hope to woo millennials as customers if it can't attract them as employees. Dodig disclosed in a recent interview that co-op students played a key role in developing the bank's Apple Watch app.[47]

CIBC is simplifying its delivery structure to focus on providing advice rather than selling products.[48] That means, for example, spending more time developing a retirement plan and less on a hard sell for mutual funds. One way of encouraging that shift is to move as many transactions as possible away from branches and onto a digital platform. Thus, the bank has launched a service to deliver foreign currency to customers' homes and an app to simplify mortgage applications.[49]

CIBC has a long history of collaboration with outsiders, and it is relying on this strategy to help drive its innovation agenda. Its partners have included Loblaws, Telus, Tim Hortons, the Greater Toronto Airports Authority (GTAA), the MaRS Discovery District in Toronto, and the Montreal-based fintech start-up Thinking Capital.[50] Those with MaRS and Thinking Capital could be especially fruitful.

CIBC joined the MaRS fintech cluster to tap into work that might be relevant to banking. Bank executives and co-op students sift through ideas in six-week sessions. One MaRS-related initiative that has already been put into practice is the CIBC Apple Watch app.[51] On another front, Thinking Capital's technology will allow the bank to process small-business loans of between $5,000 and $300,000 much faster than in the past. The plan is for Thinking Capital to fund the loans using bank lines of credit, and to offer incentives for borrowers to move their day-to-day banking business to CIBC. Jon Hountalas, a CIBC executive vice-president, explained that "this partnership is about leveraging innovation to ... attract new business and personal banking relationships to CIBC."[52]

CIBC introduced its Smart Account – a chequing account that automatically adjusts the monthly fee according to usage – as another response to consumer dissatisfaction with traditional flat monthly pricing. While the motivation behind this initiative cannot be faulted, it is far from clear that the pricing is right.

Royal Bank (RBC)

RBC's current chief executive, Dave McKay, is committed to transformation.[53] While Canada's biggest bank has overhauled some aspects of its retail operations, McKay's speech at the 2016 annual meeting put less emphasis on mobile banking than on the bank's growing investor and treasury services (I&TS) business, which contributes far less to revenues and profits than the retail operations.[54] Nonetheless, MacKay did shed some light on RBC's approach to innovation:

> At our innovation lab in Luxembourg, there are currently four client firms at work with our own employees, building new products and platforms, to address real market needs.
>
> This collaborative approach is core to all innovation at RBC. Our strategy is designed to put some of our best people together with some of our best partners to tackle some of the most interesting opportunities in financial technology.
>
> We have already built innovation labs in Toronto, London, Luxembourg, New York, and Orlando, where our work last year produced three commercial patents, and we'll soon open a lab in Silicon Valley and another in the Toronto region.
>
> We've seeded this effort with $100 million of capital to invest in fintech venture funds, and directly with start-ups. This will give us a window on emerging trends and an early opportunity to work with new technologies.[55]

In the same speech, McKay described how RBC is partnering with colleges and universities. For example, the bank has established two research labs to study how artificial intelligence can be applied in banking.[56] While the bank recognizes the challenge posed by fintechs, it also clearly appreciates the opportunities they present.[57]

RBC has won its share of awards, including for best payment innovation and best use of data analytics from Retail Banker International[58] and Euromoney's top award for innovation in global private banking.[59] Perhaps most satisfying for RBC, however, is that it overtook TD Canada Trust in 2016 to become the leading Canadian bank in J.D. Power's rankings of customer satisfaction.

Bank of Montreal (BMO)

Bank of Montreal has recognized the importance of mobile banking, though with mixed results. On the one hand, it announced a new service in July 2016 that will enable customers to open a new account in minutes using a cell phone, without visiting a branch or downloading an app.[60] However, at least one of its initiatives seems more like a gimmick than a giant leap forward. BMO and its U.S. subsidiary, Harris Bancorp, have rolled out a mobile banking feature that enables customers to withdraw cash from an ATM using a smartphone, recognizing that customers will in future carry smartphones but maybe not wallets and cards. BMO has offered customers a $5 incentive to download and use its mobile apps, with an eye on encouraging them to move away from inefficient branch banking.[61]

On the partnership front, BMO has teamed up with Ryerson University's DMZ Group, Canada's top university incubator, in a program known as Next Big Idea in Fintech, which aims to support financial technology start-ups.[62] Cameron Fowler, BMO's head of Canadian personal banking, described the rationale for the tie-up: "The evolving needs of customers are driving a push for innovation and an acceleration of the development of new technologies. Talented entrepreneurs need opportunities, resources and the right environment for their ideas to succeed."[63]

BMO deserves credit for being the first Canadian bank to recognize that robo-advisors are here to stay as an adjunct to traditional money managers. A new service, known as SmartFolio, offers online advice and portfolio management at far lower fees than full-service brokers charge. SmartFolio's chief target is millennials, the group most likely to desert the banks for unconventional financial services intermediaries.[64]

Toronto-Dominion Bank (TD)

Bharat Masrani, who took the reins at TD in 2014, recognizes the importance of online and mobile banking if his bank is to keep its customers happy – and loyal:

> Today, more Canadians do their digital banking with us than any other financial institution in the country. All told, nearly 10.5 million retail banking customers across North America are active online and mobile users – and that represents nearly half of our total retail customer base.
>
> For us, it's not just about developing great technologies; it's about delivering great experiences by leveraging technology. That's how we won in the past 10 years and that's how we are going to win in the future.[65]

TD's innovations include MySpend, an app that helps customers keep track of monthly spending and improve spending habits. Its most notable fintech partnership is a joint venture at Cisco's Internet of Everything Innovation Centre, which opened in Toronto in January 2016. TD also has a lab at the Communitech incubator in Kitchener, Ontario, and a partnership with mobile developer Flybits. Meanwhile, the bank is giving its branches a more intimate feel that puts the emphasis on in-depth conversations and financial advice rather than plain-vanilla banking transactions.

National Bank of Canada (BNC)

National, the smallest of the big six, has kept pace with its larger rivals in the move towards digital and mobile banking, but it has done nothing out of the ordinary. The Quebec-based bank has introduced mobile apps that give customers access to their accounts, calculate mortgage payments, and help locate branches and ATMs.[66]

Its MyIdea app helps customers plan and finance big and small projects.[67]

The Way Forward

In years gone by, Canada's banks were able to adapt to a changing business environment through acquisitions and partnerships. When the four pillars of the financial services industry – banking, investing, trusts, and insurance – crumbled in the late 1980s and early 1990s, the banks scooped up all the major securities dealers and trust companies. These acquisitions paved the way for them to adapt to two significant developments – the fast-growing presence of large corporate and government borrowers in the capital markets, and the migration of bank deposits into equities, fixed income investments, and other investment vehicles such as mutual funds. More recently, as we discuss in chapter 3, the banks have been able to maintain their stranglehold on home mortgage lending by buying up many of the most successful disrupters of that business.

The banks are walking down much the same path again as the digital era unfolds. This time, they are teaming up with a flock of fintech start-ups to understand and assess the new, unfamiliar market centred on tablets, smartphones, and apps. And once again, their end-game appears to be to absorb or partner with the most successful of those digital pioneers. But while such a strategy may have worked well in the past, the odds are that it will be less effective in the future. For a start, no one can predict which technologies will succeed and which will fail. As the banks wait to find out, they could end up being overwhelmed by the winners in the fintech game. Let's not forget that Uber, started as recently as 2009, now has a market capitalization of $70 billion. No Canadian bank could afford to acquire a fintech company of that size.

At the same time, disruptive technology – in the form of the smartphone – is threatening the banks' underlying business model by loosening their control over their customers. The most powerful weapon in the bank-customer relationship used to be the banks' own branches. Today, it's their customers' smartphones. Already powerful technology companies like Apple, Google, Samsung, and PayPal have inserted themselves between the banks and their customers. Among the six Canadian banks, only Scotiabank – thanks to Tangerine – has the direct, customer-centred technology needed for immediate, low-cost delivery of services. With no similar operations available for purchase in Canada, the other five banks have no choice but to build new platforms if they are to maintain their dominance of the financial services industry.

The next five chapters examine the banks' changing retail business in more detail. Retail banks offer three basic products and services: when you and/or your small business need money, they lend you some; when you have money you don't need, they help you invest it; and when you want to exchange money with someone else, they facilitate the transaction.[68] Traditionally, these services have been offered through branches, the core of the banks' present business model. The rest of this book highlights the importance of replacing this model through innovation, investment, and regulation if the Canadian banks are to have any hope of a future as bright as their past.

CHAPTER THREE

Innovation in the Mortgage Market

Innovation is the market introduction of a technical or organizational novelty, not just its invention.

Joseph A. Schumpeter, *The Theory of Economic Development*

From the mid-1980s to the mid-2000s innovation flourished in the home mortgage industry. Government policy supported securitization and expanded mortgage insurance, making it possible for a couple of dozen entrepreneurs to transform the industry. When the 2008 financial crisis hit, the government could use the new tools it had created to pump liquidity into the banking system and manage the fallout.[1] Moreover, consumers have continued to benefit from past innovations.

The next sections trace the following three stages in the evolution of the mortgage industry over the past three decades:

- How a few dozen entrepreneurs transformed the industry with the support of the Canada Mortgage and Housing Corporation (CMHC)
- How foot-dragging by the Canadian banks ended up in their favour during the global financial crisis

- How recent policies set by the Bank of Canada and the finance minister have stalled innovation and effectively nationalized the market for residential mortgages

Competition and Innovation before 2007[2]

The big six banks have long dominated Canada's home financing industry. In the late 1990s, they wrote three out of every four mortgages, and almost all of those originated through their branches. But three developments – the emergence of mortgage brokers, securitization, and automated processing of loans – dramatically changed that cosy world. Mortgage brokers were willing to go to customers at any time and at any place, giving them an edge on the banks, which required home buyers to make an appointment to fill in an application form at a branch during office hours. Securitization made it possible for lenders without a deposit base to access funding at competitive rates. Finally, the advent of computers and communications technology made it possible to process mortgage applications and collect and record payments with only a modest outlay on equipment and staff.

More than 11,000 mortgage brokers were in business by 2007, and they had captured a third of home loan originations. Similarly, the number of lenders offering mortgages through brokers more than doubled to over forty, and four new players entered the mortgage insurance business.

In his ground-breaking book *Breaking Up the Bank*, Lowell Bryan of McKinsey & Company described how credit securitization overturned the traditional commercial banking business.[3] Securitized credit had its origins in a U.S. government-backed program started in the mid-1970s, under which residential mortgages were pooled and guaranteed by Washington's two housing finance giants, "Fannie Mae" (Federal National Mortgage Association) and "Freddie Mac" (Federal Home Loan Mortgage Corporation). Brokers could then market the bundled packages of mortgages as securities to their investor clients. And so, the market in mortgage-backed securities was born.

Securitized credit combines elements of traditional lending and traditional securities, but it also involves new processes and structures. Under the old lending system, one institution (a commercial bank) would originate the loan, structure the terms, absorb the credit risk, fund the asset, and oversee collection of principal payments and interest.[4] Now, several different players are likely to be involved, each having its own role. A mortgage broker might originate the loan. A mortgage bank might underwrite it. An investment bank combines dozens or hundreds of loans into a security. Another business might insure the credit risk, and yet another could sell the mortgage-backed security to an investor and trade it in the secondary market. Finally, a servicing agency will record their principal and interest payments (see figure 3.1).

The fragmented model emerged in Canada only in the mid-1980s, a decade after its appearance in the United States. Independent mortgage brokers and bank mortgage specialists started marketing residential mortgages outside bank branches. CMHC supported new methods of financing, including securities backed by the National Housing Authority (NHA), mortgage-backed securities, and bonds issued by the CMHC itself. Collateralized debt obligations, known as CDOs, funded by asset-backed commercial paper (ABCP), made it possible for companies without a deposit base to get into the business of sub-prime mortgages and unsecured consumer loans. In

Figure 3.1. How securitization has transformed the home mortgage business

Old Model: One Commercial Bank

New Business Model: Several Different Players

Source: Adapted from Lowell Bryan, *Breaking Up the Bank: An Industry under Siege* (Homewood, IL: Dow Jones Irwin, 1988).

addition, independent service providers enabled the flock of new lenders to outsource loan processing and payments administration without having to install their own infrastructure (see figure 3.2).

By the end of 2007, these specialized players had become a fixture in each segment of the residential mortgage business and were starting to eat the banks' lunch. The banks, stuck in their "one-size-fits-all" mould, saw their share of the home mortgage market shrink from 75 per cent in the early 1990s to about 60 per cent.

The newcomers' appeal sprang from one of the timeless tenets of a successful business: they were providing the services that

Figure 3.2. Many specialized players were operating in Canada in 2007

Originating	Underwriting		Servicing
Mortgage Alliance Company	First National	FirstLine Mortgages	MCAP Service Corp.
Home Loans Canada	Maple Trust	MCAP Mortgage	Paradigm Quest
Invis	Bridgewater	ING Direct	
The Mortgage Centre	ResMor Trust Access Mortgage	The Equitable Trust Company	
Mortgage Intelligence	Xceed Mortgages Gibraltar Mortgage	GE Money Wells Fargo Financial	
Enablers:			
filogix Equifax Trans Union Corp. Brascan FIS (Fidelity)	First Canadian Title Mpac Reaves Teranet InContact Portfolio Plus Title Plus	CMHC GE Capital AIG Mortgage Ins.	Marlborough Stirling Sanchez

Source: Why the Frog Does Not Jump out of the Boiling Water, York University, 2009.

their customers wanted. Home buyers now had more options for advice – brokers, specialists, or bank branch personnel. The cost of their mortgages dropped thanks to available and lower-cost securitized financing. The response time to mortgage applications shrank from weeks to hours. The bottom line was that market forces were replacing a stultified hierarchy. The following sections describe some of these new businesses in more detail.

Mortgage Origination and the Role of Brokers

Mortgage brokers have always existed in Canada, but for a long time they were considered lenders of last resort to whom prospective home buyers would turn only if their mortgage application was turned down by the banks. Brokers typically charged fees, making them a high-cost alternative to the banks. But in 1976, Mortgage Centre, a brokerage firm headed by a young entrepreneur named Ivan Wahl, persuaded three well-known lenders – Guaranty Trust, Royal Trust, and Metropolitan Trust – to pay a guaranteed commission if it delivered an agreed volume of high-quality home mortgage applications. The agreed volume represented a threefold increase over Mortgage Centre's previous year's business. But Wahl managed to achieve those volumes by offering customers "no fees, the same rates as the banks and 11 at night service."[5]

Many more independent mortgage brokerages followed in Mortgage Centre's footsteps over the next two decades. Wahl and Brendan Calder, his long-time business partner, franchised Mortgage Centre offices across Canada. Dave Chapman, a London, Ontario realtor, founded Equity Centre in 1985 as part of his flourishing real estate sales office. Four years later, Art Trojan, a former Toronto-Dominion banker, began running his Norlite Mortgage Broker business from Re-Max real estate agency branches.

Life wasn't easy for the brokers in the early days. They had to manually fill in a different application form for each lender. They dropped the forms at a bank or trust company branch and called back a week or two later to find out whether the application had been approved, and at what rate. A week or two was a long time for brokers, real estate agents, and their anxious clients to wait. Even so, the brokers' share of mortgage originations grew from less than 5 per cent in the early 1990s to 18 per cent of first-time home buyers and 14 per cent of all home buyers by 1999.

The advance of communications technology, especially the advent of the Internet, paved the way for three fintech pioneers. Dave Chapman (Centric Systems), Art Trojan (ECNI), and Dave Nichol (Basis 100) saw a way to cut costs and improve customer service. They were able to shorten wait times and reach more lenders by standardizing mortgage applications and sending them electronically. The brokers could access up to ten lenders with a single application, and response times were slashed to two days. By 2007, more than half of all mortgage applications were submitted online, wait times were down to just four hours, and brokers were regularly dealing with up to fifty lenders.

The next step for mortgage brokerage firms was to consolidate into "super-brokers." John Donald, a successful private investor, acquired a 50 per cent stake in Norlite Mortgage Brokers in 2000 and merged it with four regional brokers to create Mortgage Intelligence. Similarly, Dave Nichol and Gordon Dahlen folded regional brokerages across the country into Invis and the Mortgage Alliance. These moves did not go unnoticed by the big banks. CIBC acquired Mortgage Centre through its purchase of Firstline Trust in 1996, and moved its own mortgage specialists into a separate division, Home Loans Canada. By 2007, some 11,000 brokers were originating more than one-third of all residential mortgages in Canada.[6] More than a third of them had ties to one of the five super-brokers – the Mortgage Centre, Invis, Mortgage Intelligence, Home Loans Canada, and Mortgage Alliance Company.

The rise of the mortgage broker took another important step forward in 2004 when the Canadian Institute of Mortgage Professionals created its "accredited mortgage professional" designation. The institute drew up a code of conduct, and many provinces required accreditation before anyone could officially do business as a broker. Mortgage brokers had clearly cemented their position as an important channel for housing finance in Canada.

Most of the big banks (other than CIBC) initially paid little attention to the brokers, regarding them as just another distribution channel for their own products. Only Royal Bank refused to provide mortgages directly to brokers. Gradually, however, the bankers realized that not only were brokers capturing a substantial portion of the revenue on a mortgage (commissions were typically 1 per cent to 1.25 per cent of the principal), but they were also a threat to the banks' drive to capture more of their customers' financial services business. Their responses varied. Bank of Montreal announced in early 2007 that it was getting out of the broker business to focus on building its own network of mortgage specialists. Scotiabank, on the other hand, acquired Maple Trust in 2006 to strengthen its broker business. CIBC had already bet heavily on the broker channel with its acquisition of FirstLine Trust and the creation of Home Loans Canada in 1996.[7] Both TD Canada Trust and National Bank continue to sell mortgages to this day through brokers, figuring that this is the best way to expand their market share.

By 2015, no fewer than 12,000 brokers were drumming up four in every ten residential mortgages in Canada (see figure 3.3). But there is one big difference from the early days. Most of the gains since 2007 have come from mortgage specialists tied to the big banks. The share of independent brokers has stagnated at about 30 per cent of total originations.[8]

Figure 3.3. Residential mortgage originations by brokers, 1999–2015

Source: Authors' Analysis, CMHC Annual Mortgage Consumer Surveys, 1999–2016

Mortgage Underwriting and Funding

Three firms stand out in the transformation of mortgage financing in Canada – GMC Investors, Yield Management Group, and Coventree, Inc. GMC Investors, also led by the entrepreneurial Ivan Wahl, packaged the first mortgage-backed security in Canada back in 1985. Yield Management began applying the latest financial theory to hedging lenders' risk and duration matching of assets and liabilities in the mid-1980s. One of its principals, Alan Jette, later adapted this approach to the CMHC mortgage-backed bond, introduced in 2001. Coventree went a step further, using asset-backed commercial paper to securitize sub-prime mortgages and credit card receivables.

The federal government announced in its 1984 budget that it would sponsor mortgage-backed securities, following the example of Fannie Mae and Freddie Mac in the United States. Previous efforts to start a mortgage-backed securities business in Canada without government guarantees had failed, in large part due to the conservatism of major institutional investors. Less than a year later, Ivan Wahl, with backing from Counsel Corporation, launched GMC (Guaranteed Mortgage Certificates) Investors Corp. The company was a CMHC-approved lender and the only lender in Canada to use mortgage brokers to originate loans. But by May 1985, after GMC had exhausted its bank line of credit, with a government mortgage-backed securities program still nowhere in sight, it was forced to figure out a way to turn the mortgages on its balance sheet into mortgage-backed securities. Citibank agreed to provide a timely payment guarantee, which GMC wrapped around a pool of mortgages, creating what it called a guaranteed mortgage certificate, Canada's first mortgage-backed security. The first certificate, with a face value of $1 million, was sold to the University of Toronto Pension Plan.

The market for mortgage-backed securities initially grew slowly. Many of the reasons behind the rapid expansion of securitization in the United States did not apply north of the border. Canada's nationwide banking system meant that the banks could diversify their mortgage portfolios by region and type of borrower without resorting to structured products. Funding was not an issue because Canadians kept a significant portion of their investments in savings accounts and term deposits, even as Americans were funnelling ever more of their savings into mutual funds. By 2000, fewer than 5 per cent of Canadian residential mortgages were financed in the securitization market.

That same year, however, CMHC decided that, to fulfil its mandate "to enhance the quality, affordability and choice of housing in Canada," it needed to introduce a financial instrument along the lines of the securities issued by Fannie Mae and Freddie Mac. CMHC hired RBC Dominion Securities and Alan Jette (now with TD Bank) to help develop the CMHC mortgage-backed bond. The new security had an electrifying effect on the market. Residential mortgages funded by securities shot up from less than 5 per cent of the total to more than 20 per cent by 2007, and have kept growing ever since (see figure 3.4).

For its part, Coventree played a key role in expanding financing for sub-prime mortgages. Founded in 1998 by Dean Tai, Geoffrey Cornish, and David Allan, all investment bankers who had helped develop the mortgage-backed securities market, Coventree specialized in structured finance using securitization-based technology for sub-prime mortgages, credit card receivables, and home equity

Figure 3.4. Residential mortgage-backed securities, 1992 to 2015

Source: Authors' Analysis, data from CMHC, StatsCan, and Bank of Canada

loans. The company also administered asset-backed commercial paper (ABCP) conduits on behalf of third parties, including the large banks and sub-prime lenders such as Exceed.[9]

Mortgage Processing and Servicing

Three small but innovative companies – Centric Systems, ECNI, and Basis 100 – took advantage of emerging Internet technology and private networks in the early 1990s to improve customer service and reduce costs. By standardizing mortgage applications and sending them electronically, they were able to cut wait times to two days and access up to ten lenders with a single application. By 2007, more than half of all mortgages were originated online through filogix, which had acquired the three start-up companies. Wait times were down to a maximum of four hours, and brokers could access up to fifty potential lenders for a single application.

Other entrepreneurs, such as Rick McGratten of MCAP and John Donald, Dave Chapman, and Kathy Gregory of Paradigm Quest, saw an opportunity to offer these services to new entrants and smaller players that could not afford the infrastructure to process and service mortgages. Both groups set up units to capture this business.

New Business Models

Most of the pieces were in place by the mid-1980s for the creation of Canada's first mortgage bank. Based on the U.S. model, such an institution would originate mortgages through brokers and correspondents (brokers dedicated to a single lender), fund these mortgages in the securities market through mortgage-backed securities and asset-backed commercial paper, and outsource processing and servicing to third-party specialists. In essence, the mortgage bank would exist to warehouse mortgages until they could be bundled up and sold to "securitizers," mostly investment banks.

Starting in 1985, Ivan Wahl and Brendan Calder built a substantial mortgage bank, FirstLine Trust, with backing from Manulife

Financial. The mortgage broking business was ballooning as the Mortgage Centre and other super-brokers expanded across Canada. Mortgage securitization, while still in its infancy, was adequate to meet FirstLine's needs. The broker division, Mortgage Centre, under the direction of Bob Ord, was developing creative new products and innovative marketing techniques, like First Points and Basis Points, to incentivize brokers to sell FirstLine mortgages. For a decade, FirstLine Trust rode a wave of innovation until it was snapped up by CIBC in 1996.

The next big step came in 1988, when Stephen Smith, an investment banker who specialized in mortgages, and Moray Tawze, a Guaranty Trust branch manager, decided to set up a business underwriting loans from mortgage brokers and selling them to Mutual Life. Their company, First National Financial, provided an underwriting service even though it had no capital of its own. First National obtained CMHC-approved lender status after three years, which meant that it could start servicing mortgage loans. Its big break came in 1999, when TD Bank agreed to buy mortgage loans from it on a fully serviced basis. By 2006, First National was selling about 40 per cent of its loans to the banks. It had $24 billion in mortgages under administration and $7.3 billion in annual originations in 2007, making it the largest mortgage lender apart from the five biggest banks.

Meanwhile, three independent investment bankers had formed a new provider of residential mortgages in 1981 through their acquisition of Interior Trust, a small trust company. Interior Trust's initial success attracted the attention of Mutual Life, at that time Canada's third-largest insurer, which acquired a 75 per cent interest in 1985 and renamed it Mutual Trust. Mutual Trust used a tax-efficient, listed mortgage investment fund to grow and, in 1998, spun the business into a newly incorporated company, MCAP Financial, with two divisions, MCAP Mortgage Corporation and MCAP Service Corporation. Bank of Montreal joined Mutual Life as a 40 per cent equity holder in each new business.[10] MCAP Mortgage Corporation originates residential mortgages through brokers for Mutual Life, Bank of Montreal, and other players with large balance sheets.

MCAP Service Corporation provides a service for other lenders by collecting and processing principal, interest, and tax payments and discharging mortgages on repayment.

These players injected a new vibrancy into Canada's mortgage market. The changes have no single explanation, but were rather the result of clusters of innovation in origination, funding, processing, and servicing, as well as new business models that bubbled up over the course of three decades. By 2007, large chunks of the industry had been transformed from the big banks' vertical model to a crowded, competitive marketplace, marking one of the finest examples of successful innovation in the 150-year history of Canadian financial services.

The Financial Crisis: What Did Canada Do Right?

Canada was not entirely immune from the 2008 sub-prime mortgage crisis.

The banks suffered little harm, but Canada's $32 billion market for asset-backed commercial paper froze as it became a victim of the sub-prime meltdown in the United States.[11] Investors and issuers spent years working on a solution to the mess.

Bankers, regulators, and politicians each deserve some of the credit for Canadian banks' stand-out performance during the 2008 meltdown in financial markets. Whatever their contribution, however, none of them can claim to be the banks' true saviour. The reality is that, in many ways, Canada's banking system has lagged five to ten years behind that of the United States[12] and, given their systemic differences, it is not clear that the two would ever be the same. Four aspects are especially relevant. First, the market for home mortgages is quite different in the two countries. Second, Canada's capital markets are less developed than those south of the border. Third, the large investment banks were owned by the commercial banks, bringing them under bank regulations. Fourth, Canada's regulatory system and banking culture have always prized stability above innovation. These differences did not stop innovation in residential mortgage lending in Canada leading up to 2007. But, they did slow innovation down and kept most activities safely under the regulatory umbrella.

The U.S. mortgage industry on the other hand, had evolved into a half-dozen distinct business segments that were only partially regulated. When the crisis hit, little could be done to protect consumers and financial markets from shady practices taking place beyond the reach of regulators. The crisis in the United States was exacerbated by the invention of such exotic but little-understood instruments as collateralized debt obligations – squared – and synthetic and credit default swaps, all so wonderfully portrayed in the movie *The Big Short*.

While the Canadian market had benefited from improved choice, convenience, and cost, it was still in the early stages of this transformation. For example, brokers were originating more than two-thirds of U.S. mortgages by 2007, compared with less than 30 per cent in Canada. These unregulated middlemen received a commission of about 1 per cent for each mortgage they signed up, whether or not the loan was repaid. Furthermore, three-quarters of U.S. home mortgages were securitized, versus only about 20 per cent in Canada. In other words, U.S. lenders typically had no intention of holding the debt to maturity and thus were less concerned about credit risk than they would have been in the old days when the loans remained on their own balance sheets.

Credit-rating agencies, supposedly the financial markets' watchdogs, were attuned to historical default rates based on an entirely different business model and failed to adjust to the new reality of the mortgage business. Finally, investment bankers and securities dealers had little incentive to draw attention to danger signals in the market. After all, they earned commissions on every transaction – and often bonuses, too – giving them an incentive to care more about deal volumes than sound banking practices.

North of the border, the government played a valuable role in keeping the crisis at bay. It pumped liquidity into the Canadian banking system by issuing large volumes of CMHC mortgage-backed bonds, known as CMBs, and CMHC provided insurance on residential mortgages already on the banks' balance sheets. At the same time, the Bank of Canada restricted access to CMBs, making it extremely difficult for non-banks to fund themselves, especially given the collapse of the asset-based commercial paper market. The upshot was that two-thirds of Canada's non-bank mortgage lenders disappeared between 2007 and 2012. And their demise was by no means the last of the fallout. CIBC the largest supplier of broker-originated mortgages, pulled out of mortgage broking in 2010, wound-down FirstLine Trust, and moved its mortgage specialist sales force back into its branches.

These upheavals had the result, for better and worse, of bringing the residential mortgage market back to where it had been in the 1990s, with the six big banks restored to their position as the dominant players. Once again, they now control over 70 per cent of the market. But there is one big difference. Instead of those mortgages being funded by deposits, most are backed by the Government of Canada.

A Nationalization Trap

While Canada may have avoided the extreme excesses of the U.S. sub-prime mortgage market, it was nonetheless moving in a similar direction in the run-up to the 2008 crisis. Going back to 2003, CMHC agreed to allow home buyers to borrow their minimum 5 per cent down payment and 1.5 per cent closing costs. This concession meant that, in practice, buyers needed no down-payment at all, and that the government would insure 95 per cent of any new mortgage. The agency's next move, in 2006, was to allow a zero down payment and to extend amortization periods from a maximum of twenty-five years to as much as forty years. The result of these changes was that more than a third of mortgages issued in 2006 and 2007 had amortization periods longer than twenty-five years and high loan-to-value ratios. By 2008, these riskier mortgages made up 9 per cent of the total mortgage market. Sub-prime mortgages had clearly taken hold in Canada.

But fears that the turmoil in the U.S. mortgage market might spill over the border persuaded the authorities to reverse direction, starting in 2008. These fears were buoyed by a seemingly unstoppable surge in Canadian housing prices. The government's first move was to cut the maximum amortization period on new loans from forty to thirty-five years. Other safeguards followed in quick succession. The minimum down payment on a government-backed mortgage rose from zero to 5 per cent. Minimum credit scores, maximum debt servicing ratios, and tighter loan documentation standards were introduced for the first time.

Canada's mortgage insurance rules looked pretty much the same by 2012 as they had before 2004. The maximum amortization had reverted to twenty-five years, and the government had withdrawn insurance backing on lines of credit secured by homes and had raised the maximum refinancing to 80 per cent of the value of the home. The authorities also capped the CMHCs outstanding insurance commitments at $600 billion, restricted banks' ability to buy bulk insurance to reduce capital requirements, and curtailed the use of government-backed insurance for securities sold to the private sector.

The International Monetary Fund lauded Ottawa in 2012 for its moves to curb CMHC-backed mortgage insurance. But it has urged the government to further reduce its role in the mortgage market in order to share more of the risk with the private sector. The IMF's concerns are twofold: first, the current system exposes the government, and hence taxpayers, to losses in the housing sector; second, it distorts allocation of resources by giving banks a greater incentive to provide mortgages for low-risk homebuyers than for wealth-creating businesses.[13] We share these concerns, and will return to them when we discuss the high level of consumer debt and the Canadian banks' low tolerance for risk in their dealings with small business.

Mortgage markets in the United States and Canada have moved in different directions since the 2008 crisis.[14] Following implementation of the Dodd-Frank law, the private market in residential mortgage-backed securities is slowly returning to the United States. In 2015, 5 per cent of residential mortgages were funded through securitization, and only 13 per cent through bank deposits. The remainder were financed through government-sponsored enterprises, notably Freddie Mac and Fannie Mae. Brokers and agents brought in 62 per cent of residential mortgages, little changed from 2007.

But in Canada, more than a third of mortgages were balance-sheet funded in 2015, and a similar proportion were securitized through NHA mortgage-backed securities and CMHC mortgage-backed bonds. Some 14 per cent were backed by covered bonds, and 15 per cent were issued by non-bank uninsured prime and non-prime mortgage lenders. As in the United States, over 70 per cent of mortgages were either funded or insured by the Government of Canada. Unlike in the United States, private mortgage-backed securities were dormant. Only 28 per cent of mortgages originated with brokers, while 72 per cent were directly provided by banks.[15]

The inescapable conclusion is that the global financial crisis and post-crisis regulatory clampdown have all but killed innovation in Canada's home mortgage market. New entrants captured almost 40 per cent of the market in 2007, but eight years later, over 70 per cent of the market was back in the hands of traditional financial institutions, mainly the big six banks. Restricted access to funding after 2008 forced most of the new entrants to sell or wind down their operations. While securitization and new business models for home mortgages are being resuscitated under a revamped regulatory regime in the United States, Canada has reverted to the bank-dominated business model. The result: change and innovation in this corner of the financial services market have been all but snuffed out, but not reversed.

Another dose of innovation, along the lines of what took place in the 1990s and early 2000s, is badly needed to shrink the government's role in the mortgage market and to help small and mid-sized firms to grow. Canada has shown that its mortgage market can adapt, but the present system does not augur well for change. Bankers' lack of skill in pricing risk, investors' wariness of securitized assets, and conservatively enforced global capital standards have caught Canadian bankers in a "rigidity trap." We will return to this problem in the next chapter.

Consumer Debt Soars

Canadians have become ferocious borrowers. Consumer debt has soared for the past two decades, pushing Canadians even deeper into debt than their American neighbours were at the height of the housing bubble in 2007. From 1980 to 2002, the amount of outstanding home mortgages grew at a compound annual rate of 7.4 per cent and unsecured loans at 8 per cent. The rate of growth has accelerated over the past decade to 9 per cent a year.

The more debt households accumulate and the higher their monthly interest payments, the less money they have to spend on themselves. Canada's household debt-to-income ratio has ballooned from 97 per cent in 1992 to 117 per cent in 2002, 137 per cent in 2007, and 166 per cent in 2015, the highest of the G7 countries (see figure 3.5).[16] By contrast, the U.S. ratio averaged 85 per cent in the 1990s, peaked at 132 per cent in 2007, and retreated to about 100 per cent in June 2015. American consumers focused on paying off their debts in the five years after the financial crisis, although defaults

Figure 3.5. Consumer debt and leverage in Canada, 1980 to 2015

Source: Authors' Analysis, data from StatsCan and Bank of Canada

accounted for about two-thirds of the reduction. Economists view 85 per cent to 95 per cent as the ideal range. Clearly, a long, painful process of adjustment lies ahead for many Canadians.[17]

Besides the financial burden on consumers, soaring household debt has created other points of friction in the marketplace. Fifty-five per cent of Canadians now have a credit card tied to a loyalty program (even though these premium cards are supposedly marketed only to the wealthy). The stampede to premium cards has triggered higher merchant service fees, as Visa, MasterCard, and merchant processors impose surcharges to pay for the extra benefits that the cards offer. The advantages for merchants are less obvious. Quite the contrary. Extra costs imposed by card issuers have fuelled the resentment that many small business owners feel towards the banks.

The surge in consumer debt is not only a cause for concern for policy makers in Ottawa; it also limits the banking industry's growth prospects. Consumer borrowing has propelled bank revenues for the past three decades. But with many of their customers now maxed out on mortgages, credit card debt, and auto and student loans, the banks have limited scope to boost revenues through new lending products and services. Instead, to keep profits rising, they have focused on cost-cutting and higher pricing of the services customers' value most. The trouble is that such a strategy cannot be sustained.

CHAPTER FOUR

Small and Mid-sized Business Blues

Regulation is focused on reducing banks' balance sheets. That means funding the real economy will have to shift to capital markets.

Paul Achleitner, Chairman, Deutsche Bank[1]

Another concern for the banks is their stagnating exposure to small and mid-sized businesses. In their determination to maximize short-term profits and rein in risk, they are failing to fulfil their historical role of channelling deposits into lending activities that support economic growth.[2] As a result, most entrepreneurs are forced to turn to friends, family, and angel investors for the funds they need to start and grow their businesses. Meanwhile, the big banks channel the deposits they have amassed since 2008 into loans to large Canadian and American companies and residential mortgages.[3]

The renewed focus on stability over innovation by global financial regulators has hurt funding for small and medium-sized enterprises (SMEs). In two countries with once vibrant SME sectors, Germany and the United States, many, including President Trump, are concerned that large banks are not meeting the needs of this sector. Ironically, more stringent capital requirements have made lending more expensive for the smaller, local banks that were instrumental in financing smaller businesses. Most governments are looking to capital markets to fund economic growth, but securitization in Canada is dormant. Innovation is necessary to transition our economy from the industrial age to the information age. As with the residential mortgage market, a solution will require government support for securitization, credit enhancement (loan insurance), and coordinated securities regulation to help the capital markets provide the financing necessary for SMEs to build and grow our economy.

Small and mid-sized businesses make an extraordinary contribution to Canada's economy. In 2015, 99.7 per cent of all firms had fewer than 500 employees.[4] In 2015, more than 8.2 million people, equal to almost 70 per cent of the private-sector labour force, worked for small businesses, and 2.3 million more, or 19.8 per cent of the total, were employees of mid-sized businesses.[5] Statistics Canada estimates that these firms made up about 52 per cent of private sector GDP.[6]

One of the most important functions of a well-oiled financial system is to support economic growth by using savings to finance new and existing businesses. In Canada's case, however, the system has come up short. We have been saddled with over-cautious bankers, regulators, and investors. Our venture capital market is extremely small by international standards, and our capital markets are fragmented. These shortcomings have made it difficult for small and mid-sized firms to grow. Encouraging these businesses is especially critical at a time when the manufacturing base is eroding and policy makers are anxious to boost information-based products and services. Canada will not realize its dream of transitioning to a twenty-first century digital economy unless innovative start-ups have access to adequate funding.

SME Financing Is a Global Problem

The challenge of small-business lending is not unique to Canada. Consider Germany where the medium-sized business sector, known collectively as the Mittelstand, is thriving and driving economic growth and prosperity. The lenders to Mittelstand companies are not only the large banks but also two other pillars of the German banking system: cooperative banks and private lenders. According to the *Economist*, "the savings banks and co-operative banks provide about two-thirds of all lending to Mittelstand companies and 43 percent of lending to all companies and households. The Landesbanken, which act as wholesale banks for the savings banks, and DZ Bank and WGZ Bank, which do the same for the co-operative banks, step in to provide more sophisticated services, such as hedging and offshore financing."[7]

The banking system has played a major role in Germany's economic success since the Second World War. But the *Economist* article calls attention to an unintended and unfortunate consequence of a European Union (EU) ruling that Germany unfairly supported the domestic savings banks and that its guarantees were not compliant with the free-competition article of the European Treaty. Until 2005, the Landesbanken could issue debt under a public guarantee – clearly a significant funding advantage, which they have now lost.[8] Furthermore, the banks made some bad investment decisions in the run-up to the new regulations, resulting in a series of cutbacks to Mittelstand lending.

The Mittelstand responded by turning to capital markets as an alternative to bank borrowing, an approach that has worked in the United States. While this tactic was initially successful, recent bond defaults have made it harder for companies to issue public debt.[9] The EU has promoted capital market union and direct investment in securities to offset the wave of banking regulations. But German bankers are eager to reassert their traditional role. They maintain that capital market instruments are too expensive for many Mittelstand firms and do not provide access to companies needing to raise less than 25 million Euros. Georg Fahrenschon, a former finance minister of Bavaria and head of the German Savings Bank Association, made the telling comment that the new regulatory regime "was a real tsunami that landed on the banking sector. In some cases, there are rules that contradict each other. I don't think there is a single expert in the whole world who can judge all the rules in their interdependence."[10] Clearly, the regulations that were designed to foster a safe and sound banking sector are now undermining one of the driving forces of a successful economy. Unfortunately, these same rules apply to the Canadian banks, dampening their willingness to lend to SMEs.

While the Germans look to U.S. securitization as a solution, the reality in the United States is a little different. Capital market innovations are helping to finance small business, but volumes are still small. One example is a recent US$175 million securitization of non-SBA (Small Business Act) loans by OnDeck, an online small business lender. Securitization has emerged as a complement to lending for U.S. community banks – a group similar to the smaller German banks and to Canadian credit unions. Community banks account for less than 20 per cent of U.S. banking assets but more than half of all small business loans.[11] Doyle Mitchell, president and CEO of Industrial Bank in Washington, D.C., neatly summed up the U.S. small business loan situation in recent testimony to the U.S. House Committee on Small Business:

> Federal Reserve data shows that while overall small business lending contracted during the recent recession, lending by a majority of small community banks (those of less than US$250 million in assets) actually increased, and small business lending by banks with asset sizes between US$250 million and US$1 billion declined only slightly. By contrast, small business lending by the largest banks dropped off sharply. The viability of community banks is linked to the success of our small business customers in the communities we serve, and we don't walk away from them when the economy tightens.
>
> The type of small business lending community banks do simply cannot be duplicated by a bank based outside the community. As a recent study by my fellow panelist Marshall Lux noted: "In certain lending markets, the technologies larger institutions can deploy have not yet proven effective substitutes for the skills, knowledge, and interpersonal competencies of many traditional banks ... The exponential growth of regulation in recent years is suffocating community banks' ability to serve their small business customers.[12]

Mr Mitchell's final sentence echoes complaints going back several years. The *American Banker* carried these two headlines in

October 2012: "OCC's Curry Signals Basel III Compromise for Small Banks,"[13] and "Community Banks: Basel III Will Put Us Out of Business."[14] Given the cost of implementing the Internal Ratings-Based approach, most community banks will use the Standardized approach, which leads to more costly loans to SMEs. We can already hear non-bankers' cynical observation about rich bankers yet again asking for favours. However, data on U.S. community banks' profitability published by the Federal Reserve Bank of St Louis show their pre-tax return on equity falling from a range of 15 to 20 per cent before the financial crisis to 5 to 10 per cent in 2012.[15] Despite the economic recovery and low interest rates that should hold down default rates, the community banks' 2015 returns remained well below pre-crisis levels.[16] Unless they can earn returns over their cost of capital, there is little incentive for community banks to expand their small-business lending.

The experience of Germany and the United States shows how new regulations have eroded banks' willingness to support small business. Perhaps Canadian banks could and should have done more for this sector in the past, but our concern is with the future. Given that policy makers and regulators have tended to put stability ahead of innovation, how much small-business lending can we realistically expect the banks to provide? Equally important, do they have the decentralized, local decision-making skills that Doyle Mitchell sees as critical to small-business lending?

Big banks have not been the solution in either Germany or the United States.[17]

In Canada, carving out complementary roles for banks and capital markets is complicated by provincial regulation of capital markets. Experience in Germany and the United States suggests that small local banks are critical to successful small business financing but that new regulation is having the unintended consequence of forcing mid-sized businesses into the bond market. OnDeck's experience shows the potential for securitization, but we suspect that in Canada some sort of government guarantee will be needed to light a fire under this market, especially given the conservative nature of institutional investors, the 2007 challenges with asset-backed commercial paper, and the hangover from the global financial crisis.

Canada's experience with mortgage-backed securities reinforces that view.

Canadian Banks Have Neglected Small Business

The banks have not been effective lenders to small business for decades. The nub of the problem is that they are fixated on risk rather than opportunity. If a business does not qualify for a loan at prime plus 1 per cent or 2 per cent, the rate reserved for the lowest-risk borrowers, then it seldom gets a loan at all. According to a recent Canadian Federation of Independent Business (CFIB) survey, the average small-business borrower pays prime plus 2.01 per cent for a bank loan.[18] In contrast to U.S. practice, banks will typically not approve a loan even if a business is willing to pay prime plus 10 per cent. Since small businesses (especially technology start-ups) are by their very nature risky, the only ones that end up qualifying for loans are those that do not need the money or could easily raise it elsewhere. Just how little interest the Canadian banks have in this business is shown by the fact that two-thirds of their small business customers are sitting on deposits that exceed their loans.[19]

Figure 4.1 illustrates the impact on small-business lending of the different approaches taken by U.S. and Canadian banks. U.S. lenders such as Wells Fargo are prepared to extend small-business loans at rates as high as prime plus 10 per cent to cover their costs and an appropriate risk premium. By contrast, the Canadian banks take no such chances, possibly because they do not trust their own ability to assess and price for risk. Canadian entrepreneurs with any hope of running a successful business are left with no choice but to draw on their own resources. According to the 2016 CFIB survey, three-quarters of respondents use their own equity and assets to build their business. Only about half can secure a bank loan for their business, while more than one-third resort to a personal loan or credit card. Family members and friends provide loans or equity injections for a quarter of all business owners.

Small businesses appear to have got the message. Their demand for bank financing has been steadily declining since the mid-1980s.

Figure 4.1. Small and mid-sized business lending: Canada versus the United States

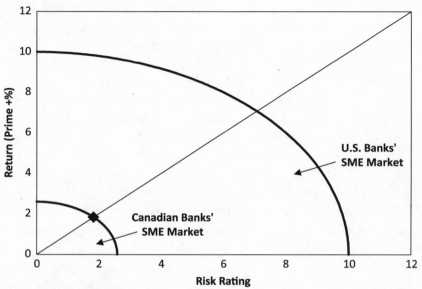

Source: Author's Illustration

More than 70 per cent of small businesses applied for a bank loan between 1983 and 1986. But by 2012, fewer than one-third had asked their main bank for a loan during the previous twelve months. Over the past three years, that proportion has improved, but only slightly. The bad news doesn't end there.

Those who do apply for a loan are increasingly likely to be turned down. Rejection rates on small-business loans climbed from 10.5 per cent of applications in 2000 to 18.4 per cent in 2012, improving to 15.8 per cent in 2015. What's more, those who are approved pay more for both credit lines and term loans. Over the past several years, all the big six Canadian banks have worked with a U.S. consultancy, Nomis Solutions, to introduce price-to-value to credit pricing (the more valuable the service to the customer the higher the price). Their work is bearing fruit – but more for the banks than for their clients. According to the CFIB, the cost of loans at 2.01 per cent over prime is now slightly above 2009 but up significantly from previous surveys in 2000, 2003, and 2006, when average financing costs were 1.53, 1.58 and 1.58 points above prime, respectively. In addition, small businesses must now pay loan application fees just to have the bank consider lending them money.

While this approach may deliver short-term profit for the banks, it is unlikely to enhance small business owners' views of their service. The CFIB asked almost 13,000 business owners in 2015 for their views on the banks. The response was far from reassuring. Every one of the big six scored 5 or less out of 10. Credit unions achieved much higher overall scores – an average of 7.2 – and were best in all four areas: availability and pricing of financing, fees, the quality and consistency of account managers, and quality of service.

The latest CFIB survey reveals that more than three out of ten small-business owners now use personal credit cards to finance their operations. As many of them told the Payments Task Force, this was their way of getting even with the banks for charging exorbitant merchant service fees on their customers' credit card purchases. By using their own cards, business owners can at least collect points of their own to pay for a vacation or a useful piece of merchandise. But there is another, less comforting way to look at this practice: many small businesses in Canada are willing to pay interest charges as high as 20 per cent to obtain the financing they need because they don't have access to regular commercial loans from the banks.

Instead of lending to deserving small firms, the Canadian banks have deployed their deposit windfalls to win back large corporate business from the public debt market. Bank loans as a percentage of total corporate borrowing in Canada fell from 72 per cent in 1990 to 58 per cent in 2000. But the proportion has inched up to 60 per cent since the 2008 financial crisis. It is hard to escape the conclusion that Canada's big banks are much more comfortable lending to big corporations than to small and mid-sized businesses, whether they are innovative technology start-ups or long-established neighbourhood retailers.

There is no easy way to encourage the banks to open the spigots on small-business loans. However, initiatives by the Business

Development Bank of Canada (BDC) may point to a way forward. BDC, a Crown corporation, identifies itself as "the only bank dedicated exclusively to entrepreneurs." It describes its business as follows:

> We offer business loans and advisory services to help Canadian businesses grow, both at home and abroad. Through our subsidiary – BDC Capital, we also offer a full spectrum of specialized financing, including venture capital, equity as well as growth and transition capital...[W]e support more than 42,000 small and medium-sized enterprises across the country, complementing services available from private-sector financial institutions. Ambitious and innovative entrepreneurs are the engine of our economy and it is our role, as Canada's development bank, to help them succeed.[20]

BDC is willing to take on more risk than other lenders, especially in sectors and regions neglected by the big banks. But while it plays a valuable role, its business model would not be appropriate for the banks. It is not regulated, as private-sector banks are, by the Superintendent of Financial Institutions. Nor does it have to comply with the Basel III capital requirements. And as a public institution, it is less motivated by profit and can use government guarantees to fund itself.

Market-Based Financing Is Key[21]

The pattern in home mortgage lending over the past thirty years has followed Joseph Schumpeter's circular model. As discussed in a previous chapter, Schumpeter noticed that healthy economies go through cycles of destruction that release forces leading to creativity and innovation. In other words, a growth spurt is typically followed by a phase of consolidation, then a period of creativity. If, for one reason or another, the creativity is stifled, the result is not innovation but rigidity. This is relevant to the banking system because central bankers and regulators have responded to the financial crisis in a way that has stalled the development of a market in securitized assets. The result has been to prop up the traditional branch-banking model for low-risk assets such as mortgages and to lock the big banks into a "rigidity trap" from which they will struggle to escape.

The good news is that, after a few years of inaction, the securitization market is slowly making a comeback. Policy makers in various parts of the world are now looking for ways to resuscitate the practice of bundling up income streams such as credit-card and car-loan repayments, repackaging them as securities, and selling them in tranches with varying levels of risk. A Bank of England official recently described securitization as "a financing vehicle for all seasons,"[22] and the European Central Bank has watered down rules that threatened to stifle securitization. European issuance of securities backed by car-loan receivables, credit-card debt, and the like doubled between 2010 and 2013, and issuance of paper backed by non-residential mortgages soared from US$4 billion in 2009 to more than US$251 billion in 2016.[23] The market, however, is still a long way from the almost US$3 trillion securitized globally in 2006.

The revival in the securitization market should not come as a surprise. It is less costly to securitize an asset than place it on a bank's balance sheet. The balance sheet route is expensive, partly because of the way banks are regulated and partly because of the economic model they use. For every $100 lent by a typical U.S. bank in 1994, it had to kick in roughly 20 cents for required reserves, and 30 cents for insured deposit premiums. Another $1.20 in pre-tax profit is necessary to support various regulatory requirements. These regulatory costs have become even more burdensome since 2008 for both on-balance-sheet and securitized assets. In any case, simply running a bank is expensive. It takes at least 80 cents per $100 of loans to cover non-interest expenses such as salaries and rents (more for small-business loans, given the need for on-the-ground decision making). That means the bank must earn a minimum spread of 2.5 percentage points between the interest rate it charges borrowers and the rate it pays depositors. By comparison, the equivalent cost to issue a security in the capital markets is less than half a percentage point on the amount financed.[24]

Securities have many advantages over bank loans. They are liquid and tradable in the hands of an investor, while a borrower cannot do much with a loan apart from repaying it. Holders of securities normally have little difficulty in selling if conditions change, or they see a more attractive investment, or they simply want their money back. And given their cost differential, securities are likely to provide better returns than deposits. As deposits decline, securitization will become an increasingly popular way for Canadian banks to lift assets off their balance sheets and move them into the hands of outside investors.

To their credit, regulators have tweaked the securities rules to make securitization safer. One clear improvement is that institutions involved in creating securitized products must retain some of the risk linked to the original loan, ensuring that they still have "skin in the game." The new rules have another safeguard against abuse by discouraging "re-securitizations," in other words, bundling income from securitized products into new securities, as happened at the height of the sub-prime mortgage mania. Finally, investors these days are more disciplined in their approach to asset-backed securities, taking a more sceptical view of opinions issued by credit-rating agencies.

Even so, Canada faces tremendous challenges in resuscitating its securitization market and creating a sub-investment-grade debt market. Unlike the United States, which has large, deep, and innovative capital markets, Canada has much smaller and more conservative markets. Although the coordinated securities regulator is slowly moving forward, new regulations must be adopted by the thirteen provinces and territories. As long as there are opportunities to finance lower-risk residential mortgages and large corporate and government borrowers, banks and investors will take advantage of them rather than lending to small and mid-sized enterprises.

One option is for BDC to rethink the Canada Small Business Financing Program to insure all or part of small and mid-sized business loans in much the same way that CMHC underwrites home mortgages. It would be necessary to develop scalable models to accurately predict cash flows from SME loans, using decision support systems like those being applied in the large corporate market. This would reduce the costs of underwriting SME loans and facilitate the issuance of securities with different risk ratings. It is unlikely, however, that the government would be willing to underwrite relatively risky small-business loans at the same time as it is trying to reduce its exposure to the housing market. On the other hand, carefully considered risk sharing, combined with tax incentives for investors, could create an exciting new investment for individuals saving for retirement that offers both higher risk and higher returns. One of the most significant challenges would be to educate investors on the difference between chasing yield and adjusting their appetite for risk.

Another option worth exploring is an adaptation of the U.S. municipal bond market, which helps cities and towns meet their financial needs. Interest payments on municipal bonds are tax free, which makes them attractive to investors. Bonds offered by small municipalities typically lack liquidity, so banks typically bundle several of them into a single security, which makes them more attractive to investors. Unfortunately, many private mortgage (and other loan) insurers that offered default protection to investors went bankrupt during the financial crisis. Even so, the municipal bond model illustrates how small business issuers might be encouraged to dip their toes into public capital markets.

As in the past, Canada will likely have to rely on foreign investment to nurture small business. The investment could come from venture capital, private equity, and other market-based financing, mostly based in the United States. Nonetheless, there might be an opportunity for the Canadian banks. For more than a century, up to the 1980s, the banks prospered in a country dependent on inward flows of capital to develop its abundant natural resources. Government regulation was instrumental in creating a protected market in which the banks could develop competitive strengths that laid the cornerstone for their expansion beyond Canada's borders. Something similar may be possible again, but this time in the field of small-business financing.[25]

We are among an ever-larger group of Canadians that recognizes the need to find new ways of financing growing businesses. A recent *Globe and Mail* article discusses pressure from the Bank of Canada on the private sector to create a fund to invest in these firms. As one banker notes, "We are good at starting companies in this country but not good at nurturing them. There is agreement that seeing our best small companies snapped up by foreign buyers is a problem, and this fund is one way to deal with that problem."[26] The solution being proposed is a fund modelled on the United Kingdom's Business Growth Fund, an independent company with £2.5 billion in backing from five of the United Kingdom's largest banking groups.

The specifics of how the Business Growth Fund invests are important. As the fund has noted:

- We are looking for management teams with a good track record, a proven business model and a desire to grow
- We make initial investments usually between £2m–£10m for a minority equity stake and a board seat
- We back both privately owned and AIM-listed, profitable companies typically with a turnover of £5m–£100m
- We invest from our own balance sheet so have the flexibility to meet your needs, and we can also provide further funding as the company continues to grow
- We offer long-term funding of up to 10 years, developing a meaningful partnership based on shared goals and objectives from the outset
- We invest in all business sectors with the exception of regulated financial services
- We have a strong local approach. With eight offices across the UK we strive to be close and relevant to the businesses we invest in[27]

The made-in-Canada solution would be designed to meet Canadian needs, according to the *Globe and Mail*: "The plan is to have banks – and potentially pension funds and insurers – put money into a $1-billion-plus private-sector fund that would make $2-million to $20-million debt and equity investments in domestic companies and ensure they have the resources needed to expand globally while remaining based in Canada."[28] The report asserts that the plan has won support from the Bank of Canada's governor, Stephen Poloz, and from CIBC's CEO, Victor Dodig. This discussion suggests that the SME sector needs more assistance than the $1.35 billion Venture Capital Action Plan (VCAP) launched by the federal government and private sector partners in April 2016.

On 9 March 2017, the Canadian Business Growth Fund was announced with initial funding of $500 million and the potential for $1 billion. The fund will have its own management team and board of directors. It will also have offices across Canada. The initial participants are the six large banks, plus Manulife, Sun Life Financial, Great-West Life, HSBC Bank Canada, ATB Financial, Laurentian Bank of Canada, and Canadian Western Bank. Once the fund is formed there will be the opportunity for others to participate. The fund's target is as follows:

> The Canadian Business Growth Fund will make investments in small- and-medium-sized Canadian companies seeking long-term, patient, minority capital to finance continued growth and to allow the scaling up of existing operations. Typical investment amounts in each company will range between $3 million and $20 million. Importantly, the fund will facilitate mentorship and access to talent pools to help these businesses achieve their full potential.[29]

The current low-return environment may provide the impetus needed for investors to play a bigger role in funding small businesses. Life insurance companies and pension funds have been under pressure for some time to find higher-yielding investments. This most likely means that they will need to enhance their risk-management skills and take on more risk. One pioneer in this field is OMERS Ventures, the venture capital arm of the Ontario Municipal Employees Retirement System. The fund was set up to support firms in knowledge-based industries that need extra resources in the form of money and expertise.

Two of the fastest-growing sources of funding for new ventures in Canada are crowdfunding and angel investors. An angel investor is an affluent individual who provides capital for a business start-up, usually in exchange for convertible debt or ownership equity. Crowdfunding involves raising funds through small contributions from the general public using the Internet and social media. The twenty-four groups that belong to the National Angel Capital Organization invested $133.6 million in 283 deals in 2015.[30] These are just the visible angels; countless others work alone or behind the scenes. The Business Development Bank, with $1 billion at its disposal, is emerging as a player in angel investing and a sought-after partner for start-up accelerators such as GrowLab in Vancouver, Toronto-based Extreme, and Communitech in Kitchener, Ontario.

A TD Bank study makes the case for crowdfunding as a crucial source of finance and intelligence for small Canadian ventures.[31] But that can happen only if regulators clarify the rules. As of the time of writing, they had proposed a complicated set of rules that vary from province to province. Already, more than sixty crowdfunding portals, such as Kickstarter or Indiegogo, generate an estimated $3 billion to $5 billion a year globally. Most of the contributions so far take the form of donations, but the market could expand exponentially if it were open to loans or equity financing for small businesses, and were properly regulated.

Crowdfunding was legitimized in the United States by the JOBS Act, which took effect in May 2016 and cleared the way for startups to raise up to $1 million a year, with a minimum of red tape, by selling shares through crowdfunding sites.[32] The Securities and Exchange Commission is now in the process of loosening its rules to allow equity crowdfunding, with strict limits on the amount any individual can invest. The Ontario Securities Commission has also proposed opening the door to equity crowdfunding, but its proposals would limit the amount a company could raise to $1.5 million a year, cap individual investments at $2,500, and require crowdfunding portals to register with the authorities.

While these and other initiatives hold promise, significant concerns remain about continuing access to funds as a start-up takes root. According to the Canadian Venture Capital Association, $2.3 billion in venture capital was invested in 536 Canadian companies in 2015. This represented a 12 per cent increase in value and a 24 per cent jump in transactions over the previous year. However, less than a quarter of the amount, or $530 million, was invested in sixty-four later-stage transactions, another indication of the challenges of taking start-ups to the next stage in Canada. Furthermore, several of the most active venture capital firms are foreign, mostly U.S. based, and the most desirable progression for technology companies is a public share offering on Nasdaq rather than on one of the Toronto exchanges.[33]

Private equity is also playing an important role in small business financing. Investments from this source totalled $22.8 billion, representing 399 deals, in 2015. Although the number of deals was 19 per cent higher than in the previous year, their combined value slumped by 46 per cent.[34] Pension plans and government entities, such as Investissement Quebec, are among the most active players. Over the past few years, growth equity – also known as growth capital or expansion capital – has emerged as a popular way to invest in private companies. A wide range of investors now participate in the growth-equity market, from hedge funds like Tiger Global Management to venture capital firms like Sequoia Capital. Finally, the Canadian Venture Exchange has become a useful vehicle for small businesses to raise funds from the public.

All these financing sources play a valuable role, but they remain too small, at least for the time being, to fill the vast need. The fact is that businesses tailored to the new economy still have a healthy appetite for old-fashioned, plain-vanilla bank loans. The challenge is to bring the banks to the party.

CHAPTER FIVE

Where Are the Customers' Yachts?

An out-of-town visitor was being shown the wonders of the New York financial district. When the party arrived at the Battery, one of his guides indicated some handsome ships riding at anchor. He said: "Look, those are the bankers' and brokers' yachts."

"Yes, but where are the customers' yachts?" asked the naïve visitor.[1]

Over the past fifteen years, financial institutions have made a lot of money managing individuals' investments. Most Canadians have invested the bulk of their retirement savings in mutual funds, largely because their financial advisors have offered them few alternatives. And why would that be? The reason is clear: Canadian mutual funds extract the highest fees in the developed world, even as they produce the lowest returns.[2]

This sad state of affairs has contributed to a situation where many Canadians are not nearly as well prepared for retirement as Americans. Indeed, many experts now refer to a retirement funding crisis north of the border.[3] Even as Canadians were being overcharged by the investment funds industry, U.S. investors started demanding higher returns. Competition since the dot.com bubble burst in 2000 produced a spurt of innovation in U.S. investment products and how they are delivered. Exchange-traded funds (ETFs), tactical asset allocations, and better online advice all made it easier for American savers to earn decent returns on their investments.

To be fair, the fault does not lie entirely on the supply side. Canadians' reluctance to save and their aversion to risk have left them ill-prepared for retirement. Measures now in the pipeline, such as the pending expansion of the Canada Pension Plan (CPP) and improved disclosure of investment advisor fees, will improve matters. But, as the U.S. experience shows, they don't go nearly far enough.

A Story of Meagre Returns[4]

An overhaul of the Bank Act in 1987 cleared the way for Canada's big banks to enter the trust and securities businesses. Over the next five years, they gobbled up almost all of the large trust companies and securities dealers. The banks did not stop there. Twenty years ago, independent firms dominated the mutual fund and asset-management businesses. That is no longer the case. Joined by a handful of big insurance companies, the banks have used their distribution strength and financial muscle to accumulate more than half of the $1.3 trillion in mutual fund assets held by Canadians.[5]

No one would accuse the banks of modesty in promoting their investment services, known these days as "wealth management." TD Bank offers "easy and convenient accounts for reaching your savings goals." Scotiabank promises that "you are richer than you think." And CIBC says that it delivers "what matters," including home ownership and a financially secure retirement. Unfortunately, the banks' achievements have failed to live up to those words. Assuming that Canadians contribute the maximum amount annually to their registered retirement savings plans, or RRSPs, their investment portfolios would typically need to deliver an annual net return (after inflation and fees) of 3.5 per cent to ensure a comfortable retirement.[6] Yet after taking fees into account, real returns over the past fifteen years have been negligible.[7] No wonder so many Canadians see little point in saving or investing for retirement.

For the majority of Canadians with less than $2 million to invest, mutual funds have been almost the only investment product, apart from guaranteed investment certificates (GICs), the banks have promoted. The banks initially set fees on their mutual funds at about 2.5 per cent, based on their normal spread between market investments and the interest they paid on deposits. The management expense ratio, commonly known as MER, on the vast majority of Canadian equity funds ranges between 2 per cent and 3.3 per cent. The MER on bond funds is typically between 1 per cent and 2.3 per cent. These ratios are a stunning almost two percentage points higher than the costs incurred by a typical pension fund. They are driven largely by the banks' high distribution and marketing costs, which make up about 1.5 percentage points of the average for equity and bond funds. We can understand why such fat marketing expenses are necessary, given the poor performance of most mutual funds.[8]

Mutual Fund Economics 101

To better understand mutual fund performance, we examined the ten largest mutual funds with a ten-year track record from May 2002 to April 2012 for twenty-five major asset managers, 250 funds in total. This sample represented 46 per cent of Canada's $813 billion mutual fund market at the end of April 2012. There was nothing special about the period chosen – from five years before to five years after the crisis – and our results were consistent with several other studies over longer time periods.

Players with a predominantly fixed-income fund mix reported fund expenses in a range of 1.7–2 per cent over the decade. Combined expenses for all the funds made up 35–50 per cent of their gross returns, after inflation. Managers with a fund mix skewed towards equities had expenses of 2.5–2.7 per cent, which averaged 45–60 per cent of gross returns. On average for the sample, fund expenses were 2.08 per cent, which represented 41 per cent of real gross returns over the ten years.[9] To make matters worse, fund expenses actually exceeded returns for the five years from 2007 to 2012 (see table 5.1). That trend seems set to continue, given the lower returns projected for equities and bonds in the foreseeable future.

Table 5.1. Ten largest funds by firm no-load investment returns, 2002–2012

April 2012 Asset Manager	Assets Under Management $ billions	Fund Expenses %	Net Real Return 5 years %	Net Real Return 10 years %	Fund Expenses / Gross Real Returns 5 years %	Fund Expenses / Gross Real Returns 10 years %
Banks						
– RBC GAM	69.2	1.67	0.13	2.88	92.8	36.7
– TD AM	43.8	1.71	0.80	3.67	68.1	31.8
– CIBC AM	17.1	1.46	0.14	2.93	91.3	33.3
– BMO AM	15.5	1.79	-0.25	2.73	>100	39.6
– Scotia AM	12.1	1.69	-0.66	2.05	>100	45.2
– NBC	7.2	2.07	-0.25	1.35	>100	60.5
– Desjardins	6.3	2.05	0.18	1.63	91.9	55.7
– HSBC	4.1	1.60	0.40	1.67	80.0	37.2
Total Banks	176.2	1.70	0.20	2.88	89.3	37.2
Total Insurance[10]	44.8	2.56	-0.05	2.64	49.3	49.3
Total Investment Management[11]	162.9	2.36	-0.76	3.09	>100	77.3
Total Top 25 Mutual Fund Players	372.9	2.08	-0.22	2.83	>100	41.4

Source: Authors' Analysis, 2013

Many of the mutual funds in the sample have no extra charges, known as loads, if acquired through the asset manager's captive distribution channel. However, loads apply when a mutual fund is acquired through a non-captive financial advisor. Investors are usually given a choice between a front-end or back-end load (referred to as a deferred sales charge). To avoid load fees, most investors opt for the deferred charge, since the amount is usually reduced in each of the first seven years and eliminated thereafter. Switching charges of up to 2 per cent are also levied at the time of the disposition, regardless of the load option.

In our study, a mutual fund investor who used an independent advisor, opted for the back-end load and had a holding time of three years would have realized a meagre 1 per cent annual return between 2002 and 2012 (table 5.2).[12] That's a far cry from the 3.5 per cent minimum that many personal finance experts believe is needed to fund a comfortable retirement. Total fund expenses, including deferred sales charges, were 3.9 per cent (2.1 per cent, excluding DSC). The reason for the shortfall is not that interest rates are low or stock markets have performed miserably. Returns would probably have been more than adequate, and certainly much higher, were it not for the sky-high charges pocketed by banks, insurance companies, and other fund managers. Retail investors netted just 12 per cent of mutual funds' total returns in the decade to 2012, while fund managers kept a whopping 88 per cent. Over the five years between 2007 and 2012, returns were negative, whether or not deferred sales charges are included.

According to our study, only 23 funds out of a total of 14,905 offered in Canada produced net returns of 4 per cent or more in 2012. In other words, just 1.5 mutual funds out of every 1,000 produced returns for their customers rivalling those of institutional investors like the CPP Investment Board, which manages the Canada Pension Plan. While mutual fund fees have slowly started decreasing, it is hard to think of a more compelling argument for expanding the CPP.

To make matters worse, Canada has the dubious distinction of being the world leader in "closet" indexing, in other words, charging hefty management fees for a supposedly actively managed fund

Table 5.2. Ten largest funds by firm investment returns including load, 2002–2012

April 2012 Asset Manager	Assets under Management $ billions	Fund Expenses %	Net Real Returns with DSC 5 years %	Net Real Returns with DSC 10 years %	Fund Expenses + DSC / Gross Real Returns 5 years %	Fund Expenses + DSC / Gross Real Returns 10 years %
Banks						
– RBC GAM	69.2	3.52	-1.79	0.90	> 100	77.3
– TD AM	43.8	3.38	-0.94	1.88	> 100	62.8
– CIBC AM	17.1	3.31	-1.78	0.95	> 100	75.4
– BMO IM	15.5	3.64	-2.17	0.76	> 100	80.5
– Scotia IM	12.1	3.54	-2.57	0.09	> 100	94.6
– NBC MF	7.2	3.92	-2.17	-0.60	> 100	> 100
– Desjardins	6.3	3.90	-1.74	-0.32	> 100	> 100
– HSBC IM	4.1	3.45	-1.53	-0.28	> 100	> 100
Total Banks	176.2	3.50	-1.67	0.95	> 100	77.3
Total Insurance	44.5	4.26	-1.79	0.85	> 100	84.4
Total Investment Management	152.9	4.21	-2.67	1.11	> 100	77.3
Total Top 25 Mutual Fund Players	372.9	3.88	-2.09	1.00	> 100	78.2

Source: Authors' Analysis, 2013

that in practice hugs a market index. In their paper "Indexing and Active Fund Management: International Evidence," four respected finance professors estimated that about 37 per cent of assets in equity mutual funds sold in Canada are closet indexers. Fees for actively managed funds are typically 1.5 to 2 percentage points above those for passively managed index funds.[13]

Retail investors buy mutual funds in various ways, but all of them carry hefty fees, expenses, or other charges (see figure 5.1). Most investors go through a financial advisor, who typically charges over 2.5 per cent. Full service brokers, the next most popular channel, are also pricey, with fees of slightly above 2.4 per cent.[14] Prior to 1987, bank branches were not in the mutual fund business. Today, mutual funds, which include a 1 per cent trailer fee for the advisor, and mutual fund-wraps, where the advisor manages the client's account for a flat annual fee, coexist with investment deposits (GICs and the like) issued by the bank.[15] In the banks' discount brokerage channel, 11 per cent of the assets are held in mutual funds even though the channel provides limited advice.

Many investor watchdogs advocate unbundling financial advice from selling mutual funds. This could be done by replacing the distribution component of the fund management expense ratio with a fee negotiated directly between financial advisor and client. But such a fee would still not come cheap. The best way to achieve meaningful savings in a fee-based brokerage account is to include products that do not require active management, such as ETFs and index funds. As of September 2016, only BMO Wealth Management among the banks had offered this option to its customers. Discretionary brokerage accounts, the primary way to access ETFs and index funds through an advisor, are usually offered only to wealthy clients with portfolios of $500,000 plus.[16]

Investors can also realize significant savings by using an online discount brokerage account to buy ETFs or index funds. But few bother to go that route, despite the solid advice of personal finance columnists like the *Globe and Mail*'s Rob Carrick. The reason they don't is explained by Nobel prize-winning economists George

Figure 5.1. Cost of ownership across fee-based products and managed asset solutions

*Trading Expense Ratio

1. MER + TER is the management expense ratio plus the trading expense ratio. The trading expense ratio is commissions incurred for buying and selling securities divided by the total assets of the fund. Generally, the higher a fund's TER, the more actively the fund manager has traded in a given year.
2. Mutual Funds A Series are mutual funds sold to retail investors, which normally include a trailing commission of about 1 per cent to the advisor.
3. Mutual Funds F Series are mutual funds sold to institutional investors, which do not pay a trailing commission to the advisor (either a broker or a private asset manager). Instead the advisor charges the investor an annual or quarterly fee for advice, normally about 1 per cent.
4. Currently the only way to buy ETFs and index funds other than doing it yourself through a discount broker is through a discretionary brokerage account, which normally charges about a 1 per cent fee for advice. Separately managed wraps are targeted at wealthy individual investors, who require tailored account management, including tax optimization, private equity investments, etc.
5. Advisor-managed wraps, which charge the investor an annual or quarterly fee, give the advisor the option to buy other investments besides mutual funds.

Source: Investment Funds Institute of Canada submission to OSC 2012

Akerlof and Robert Shiller in their aptly named book *Phishing for Phools: The Economics of Manipulation and Deception*.[17] The problem, say Akerlof and Shiller, is that banks and insurance companies have taken advantage of their reputation for trust, stability, and solid returns on their own shares to persuade their customers to buy very mediocre mutual funds. They have had great success in convincing individual investors that the best way to lift returns and lower risk is through diversification and active stock picking, even though, as we saw in the previous section, this has not been the case at all. As Akerlof and Shiller might say, the banks and insurers have phished Canadian investors for phools. Much more transparency, education, and innovation are needed to address this problem.

A Morningstar analysis in 2015 of mutual fund fees and expenses ranked Canada dead last among twenty-four countries. In other words, Canada had the highest fees. In fact, it was the only country to receive a failing D-grade. The United States came out on top with an A. As the report noted, "The U.S. is marked by a large number of self-directed investors, economies of scale, a high level of price competition, a retirement tax preference that uses the same investments for tax-preferred investments, and one of the highest percentages of assets paying an outside advisory fee not reflected in a fund's total expense ratio." On the other hand, "Canada is on the opposite end for all those factors, plus Canada levies a consumption tax on fund management services."[18]

Regulators Are Trying to Improve Transparency

Regulators are well aware that mutual funds are giving Canadians too little for too much. But despite several years of work, provincial securities watchdogs have yet to agree on an agenda for reform. Late in 2012, the Canadian Securities Administrators, the umbrella group for the patchwork quilt of provincial regulators, published papers on possible standards of conduct for financial advisors and mutual fund fees. Subsequent consultations resulted in "significant disagreement about whether the current regulatory framework for advisors adequately protects investors." The provinces started phasing in new rules in summer 2013 that will eventually require financial advisors to disclose the full amount they are paid each year in fees and commissions for investment advice. This first step towards improved transparency has already persuaded some fund managers to bring down expense ratios.

The changes are scheduled to roll out over a three-year period, which started in July 2014 with a requirement that account statements must include a definition of benchmark performance, and that fees must be disclosed in advance of trades.[19] Provincial securities regulators started phasing in a second round of new rules in July 2016. These require advisors to disclose to clients the full amount paid in fees and commissions each year. Most investors will not see this new disclosure until January 2017.

As of October 2016, regulators were still discussing whether to mandate full disclosure of mutual fund charges, such as management fees, fund operating costs, redemption fees, and short-term trading fees. One argument against such a move is that these minutiae may be too much for the average investor to digest. On the other hand, perhaps the wealth management industry has not done a good enough job of helping Canadians understand what it takes to achieve a comfortable retirement.[20] Regulators, especially the Financial Consumer Agency of Canada (FCAC), should take a greater interest in improving investor protection and financial literacy.[21] To date, the FCAC, which supposedly has jurisdiction over federally regulated financial institutions (banks and insurance companies), has not done much to protect wealth management consumers.

While Canada dithers over reforms, the United Kingdom and Australia have already acted by banning sales commissions for investment advisors, among other measures. In Australia, reforms known as the Future of Financial Advice (FOFA) have encouraged investors to move towards lower-cost products. The use of ETFs almost doubled in the first couple of years after FOFA's implementation, according to the Australian Stock Exchange. Similarly, the United Kingdom's 2012 Retail Distribution Review has changed the way investors pay for financial advice. The Financial Conduct Authority, which regulates the financial industry, noted recently that sales of higher commission financial products had declined noticeably.

While reforms of this kind are desperately needed in Canada, it is far from clear whether they can be implemented. Investment managers in this country are stubbornly pushing back on changes to mutual fund fees, especially the elimination of trailer fees that typically pay advisors 1 per cent a year just for keeping their clients' money in a fund. The Provincial Securities Commissions are still reviewing this issue, even though both the United Kingdom and Australia have banned trailer fees altogether. In June 2015, the OSC announced that it plans to eliminate trailer fees but has not yet set a date for implementation.[22] Instead, it announced another round of consultations, this one of 150 days, rather than the normal 60 or 90 days, in January 2017.[23]

The industry maintains that rival products, such as ETFs, which charge much lower fees, now provide lots of competition to mutual funds and keep financial advisors on their toes. That sounds good in theory, but the fact is that individual investors have not found it easy to access these low-cost products. Almost the only way to buy ETFs until recently was through a discount broker, and most Canadians are not comfortable with "do-it-yourself" investing.

Investors Must Share the Blame

It would be unfair to place all the blame for the inadequacy in Canadians' retirement savings on mutual funds' poor investment returns. Consumers are also at fault. Many have not saved enough or been willing to accept a bit of risk on their investments.

How Canadians Fund Their Retirement

The federal government and the provinces completed a major overhaul of Canada's retirement income system in 1998. The system now consists of two mandatory pillars – Old Age Security (OAS) and the Canada Pension Plan (CPP) – and a voluntary one that includes employer pensions and registered retirement savings plans (RRSPs). The two mandatory pillars are lean by international standards, which makes a well-functioning voluntary component that much more important. Furthermore, many retirees also need a variety of other savings vehicles, such as tax free savings accounts (TFSAs) and real estate investments, to achieve the retirement system's goal of replacing at least half of employment income.

The system has served Canadians well over the years, but it is less likely to do so in the future.[24] The concerns centre especially on middle-income earners and younger people. The system works when the design assumptions hold true, but few are aware of how the math really works. In addition, several trends now making themselves felt will work as headwinds against a comfortable retirement. Our rising life expectancy is especially worrying. As people live longer, they need more income for their retirement years – unless, of course, they choose to work longer.

Several conditions must be met for the retirement system to achieve its goals:[25]

1. Retirement savings must be accumulated throughout the working years, without interruption.
2. Investments must earn at least 3.5 per cent a year, after fees and taking inflation into account, during both the accumulation and disbursement periods.
3. Households should save at least 9 per cent of disposable income for all but the lowest income workers.
4. With few exceptions, no one should expect to retire before age seventy.
5. No one except the wealthiest individuals should retire until they are debt free.

Few, if any, of these conditions are currently being met. A Bank of Montreal report concluded in 2013 that Canadians are not saving enough.[26] In 2008, fully half of Canada's 17.5 million tax filers had neither a company pension nor an RRSP. This proportion has probably fallen farther since then as a result of higher unemployment and increased contract and part-time work. What's more, most Canadians are retiring too early. The average retirement age is now sixty-two and rising only very slowly. It actually declined from sixty-five in 1976 to sixty-one in 1998. According to Ipsos Reid's Canadian Financial Monitor, seniors' households had an average debt of $47,540 in 2012, and that debt was growing faster than for any other age group, with credit card debt up by 2.6 per cent and auto loans by 7.9 per cent.[27] The upshot is that half of all Canadians over age fifty expect to exhaust their retirement savings within ten years of leaving the workforce.[28] At the same time, most employers, including provincial governments, are concerned that their pension plans may not be able to meet their obligations to present and future retirees.

It is also appropriate to question whether the 50 per cent income replacement target is, in fact, adequate these days to fund a healthy and active retirement lifestyle. U.S. research shows that spending drops steadily during the second half of our lives.[29] But, contrary to conventional wisdom, the biggest drop comes before retirement, when children leave home and parents become empty nesters. As couples wait longer to have children, kids stay at home longer, with the result that mortgages are paid off later and parents have less time to save before retirement. What's more, the biggest drop in spending takes place well after retirement. U.S. data suggest that the average eighty-five-year-old spends 66 per cent and the average ninety-year-old 60 per cent of their outlays at age sixty-five.

There are many reasons for the decline in spending: a less active lifestyle, failing health, growing isolation, a fear of depleting funds, and concerns about end-of-life health care expenses. Seniors have good reason to be worried. Outlays on health care as a proportion of economic output have soared by 66 per cent since 1975. The aging population alone is expected to push up health care spending by another 21 per cent by 2030 and by 39 per cent by 2050.[30] If governments are unable to contain health care costs, their only option will be to push more of the costs onto those who can afford to pay, either through higher taxes or through direct payment for treatments such as medical tests or prescription drugs. Factoring in higher health care costs, home care costs (if you want to stay in your own home), expected inflation, and a more active lifestyle, it seems to us that most seniors should be targeting a retirement income equal to 70 per cent of their work earnings, rather than just 50 per cent.

Almost everyone agrees that Canada is in the throes of a retirement crisis, especially for middle-income earners with no employer pension plan. More than six out of ten Canadians do not have a workplace pension, and most of them lack the savings needed to support their lifestyles in retirement. While the rest have the luxury of belonging to a pension plan, many of these plans either do not generate enough income for a comfortable retirement or their solvency is endangered by demographic trends and market upheavals that their designers never imagined.

Clearly, some of the responsibility for this mess rests with individuals who have not saved enough, worked long enough, or paid off their debts. We have not always been so undisciplined. Less than four decades ago, in 1980, Canadians could boast almost the same level of financial assets as their American neighbours and similar investment preferences. But that has changed dramatically. The average Canadian now has only three-quarters of the financial resources of an American, and those are heavily skewed towards low-risk deposits – in other words, assets that earn virtually no return at current rock-bottom interest rates. At almost $50,000 per Canadian adult, the shortfall represents $1 trillion in missing savings.

What went wrong?

Two related culprits must take much of the blame. First, Canadians have sought to avoid risk in recent years by holding large deposits at banks.[31] Second, they have stopped saving, in part because these deposits were not earning the returns they had expected. In other words, one misguided decision has led to another. There is a third explanation, too. Soaring house prices have boosted Canadians' equity in their homes, convincing many of them that there is less need to save.

Canadians Hate Risk

After steadily moving into equity, bond, and other investments during the 1990s, Canadians have more recently changed tack and

Table 5.3. How Canadians invest their savings

	1990	2000	2010	2014
Financial wealth (billions)	$1,017	$1,988	$2,973	$3,605
– Deposits	68%	36%	35%	34%
– Investment Funds	6%	33%	31%	33%
– Securities	23%	25%	17%	NA
– Other fee-based assets	3%	7%	13%	NA

Source: Investment Funds Institute, Investor Economics, September 2015

funnelled a growing proportion of their savings into bank deposits. But putting money into a bank deposit these days is not much different from putting it under the mattress. It may be safe, but the return is close to zero. This shift in savings patterns has its origins in a series of upheavals in financial markets, starting with the 1987 stock market crash and extending to the 2001 dot.com bust and the 2008 meltdown.[32] No fewer than half of the respondents to a 2011 MFS Investor Sentiment Survey agreed with the statement, "Keeping my savings in cash makes me feel more secure."[33] And they have been as good as their word, with those unexciting but secure savings deposits continuing to climb.

As table 5.3 shows, investors of all ages have increasingly put their faith in cash in what appears to be a deliberate and long-term shift in savings patterns. The main driving force appears to be a fear of risk:

- According to the MFS survey, investors held an average of 26 per cent of their portfolios in cash in 2011. Significantly, millennials (the generation born between the early 1980s and the early 2000s) had the highest cash position, at 30 per cent.
- One-quarter of respondents said they liquidated a part of their portfolio in 2010 or 2011 because of market fears. The proportion for millennials was a whopping 52 per cent, far higher than any other age group.
- As noted above, half of investors agreed with the statement, "Keeping my savings in cash makes me feel more secure."

Albert Einstein, a wise man if there ever was one, once said, "The greatest risk in life is taking no risk." In the eighty-nine years from 1926 to 2015, the average annual return on stocks, after taking inflation into account, was 6.9 per cent and on bonds 2.2 per cent. By contrast, deposits yielded a miserly one-half of 1 per cent, far below the annual 3.5 per cent return considered essential for retirement (figure 5.2).[34] Today, real returns on most savings accounts have turned negative, and the situation will only get worse if central bankers lower interest rates even further to keep the economic recovery on track.

The flight to cash deposits may have cost individual savers dearly, but it has meant a huge windfall for the banks. Since 2009, more than $1 trillion has been sitting in accounts insured by the Canadian Deposit Insurance Corporation but earning no after-inflation return. Economists at CIBC concluded in a report titled "Cashing In on Fear" that bank deposits have climbed in recent years to the point where individuals now have the biggest cash buffers on record.[35] Relative to Americans, Canadians are over-weighted in deposits by $420 billion – $340 billion in the big five banks alone. Partly as a result of this windfall, Canadian bank cost structures have become

Figure 5.2. Canadians' return by asset class per year, 1926–2015

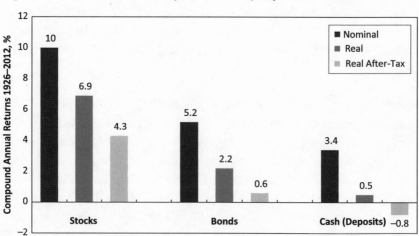

Source: BlackRock Investment Insight, "Cashing In: Rethink the Cost of Cash," 2015

bloated. According to the World Bank, Canada has 80 per cent more bankers per capita than the average OECD country, and these bankers earn almost double on average what workers outside the financial services sector earn.

To show how market structure affects returns on deposits, let's compare Canada with Australia, where a similar bank oligopoly applies. The spread between mortgage and GIC rates is roughly 50 per cent wider among Canada's big six banks than among their four Australian counterparts (figure 5.3). Although mortgage rates are higher in Australia, returns on deposits are much closer to the levels needed to fund a reasonable retirement. This structural difference between Canada and Australia has persisted for the past twenty years, or more. It is also interesting to note that ING Direct Canada, an online bank with a lower cost base and a different business model from the big six, operated with similar spreads to those in Australia, at least until its acquisition by Scotiabank in 2012.

This example from 2013 illustrates the impact of the different approaches. The return on a one-year deposit in Canada was non-existent; in fact, after taking inflation into account, it amounted to a negative 0.15–0.25 per cent. By contrast, the Australian banks were

Figure 5.3. Real posted rates in Australia and Canada for 5-year term, 30 September 2013

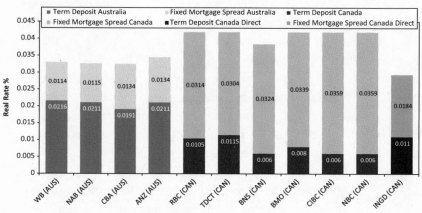

Source: Authors' Analysis, September 2013

paying real interest of more than 1 per cent. Furthermore, the Canadian banks took advantage of falling interest rates to cut savings rates faster than lending rates. That means their net interest margins widened to between 1.84 per cent and 2.85 per cent, depending on the bank, much higher than the Australian banks' margins of 1.39 per cent to 1.54 per cent.[36]

The success of ING Direct and now Tangerine confirms our conclusion that Canadian banks earn huge returns on the backs of savers. ING began offering investment savings accounts in 1997 that paid an interest rate about two percentage points higher than the big bricks-and-mortar banks. Given that the big six made a lot of money by paying low rates on deposits, they were unlikely to match ING's rates. And that's the way it was for almost a decade. But they changed tack in 2007, after ING had scooped in $16 billion in savings, making it the number three player in the business. RBC, TD Canada Trust, and the others belatedly responded by creating their own "high yield" savings accounts.

The Real Estate Bubble Has Helped

Canadians' other "low risk" financial strategy is to invest in houses and condos, partly to make up for the puny returns from savings and mutual funds. They have typically bought the most expensive house they could afford in their fifties, with the idea of cashing out handsomely when they retire. Some 87 per cent of homes owned by baby boomers in growing urban areas have skyrocketed in value. Nearly half of these owners are sitting on gains of 50 per cent or more, especially in cities like Toronto and Vancouver. Many are counting on realizing this gain to help see them through retirement.[37]

This strategy raises a concern. If so many Canadian are planning to sell their homes when they retire, buy a less expensive one, and save the difference, it surely won't be long before housing prices, especially for top-end homes, take a tumble. Ottawa's tighter mortgage lending rules could shrink the number of buyers eligible for financing on the boomers' big homes, forcing them to opt for smaller, less expensive housing. Perversely, this would cut into retirees' gains – and thus the amount available for their retirement – while stoking competition for smaller homes and pushing up prices.

Recognizing this problem, some countries – notably Australia and the United Kingdom – have encouraged the use of "home-equity release" products that enable homeowners to tap into their equity without forcing them to sell. There are two types of equity release plans:

1. A lifetime or reverse mortgage, where the homeowner retains ownership of the property but the property is charged with the repayment of a loan or mortgage, which accrues rolled-up interest until the homeowner's death.
2. A home reversion plan, where the homeowner sells all or part of the property to the equity release provider in return for the right to continue living there rent free.

The trouble is that these plans have not had quite the impact that those who designed them intended. In Australia, reverse mortgages notched up 24 per cent compound annual growth from 2005 to 2011, but fewer than 2 per cent of retirees made use of them. In other words, the initiative resulted in only 42,000 outstanding reverse mortgages in a market with 3.17 million individuals over age sixty-five, 83 per cent of whom are homeowners. More than twenty institutions provide reverse mortgage products, ranging from building societies to major banks, but, as in Canada, these products are considered expensive and confusing. Although legislation introduced in 2012 protects homeowners in Australia from ending up in a negative equity position, governments were promoting reverse mortgages to pay for homecare services.

Similarly, in the United Kingdom, only 2.5 per cent of home-owning seniors have made use of reverse mortgages and similar products, even though more than fifty suppliers are vying for the business.

Significantly, none of the major banks or building societies in Australia and the United Kingdom that offer conventional mortgages is willing to sell lifetime mortgages, reverse mortgages, or home reversion plans under its own brand. The market is entirely in the hands of upstart institutions, because the incumbents consider the reputational risk too high.

These home-equity release products have an even lower penetration in Canada than in Australia and the United Kingdom, despite the fact that Ottawa bases retirement income adequacy assessments on an imputed rental income stream from home ownership. In 2016, there were just two providers of reverse mortgages in Canada, with $2 billion outstanding, even though CMHC provides support through its Home Income Plan.[38]

The Risks of Living Too Long

The life insurance industry, another important provider of wealth management services, faces much the same challenge as the banks. Insurance policies, including annuities, are sold by advisors and brokers who typically earn a commission on every sale. The policies are all too often mired in complexity, a strategy that seems designed to justify high advisors' and brokers' fees.

Complexity adds costs. Insurance policies from a bygone era and the systems that support them must be maintained until the last policyholder dies. New products, especially simple, plain-vanilla policies sold online, are cannibalizing the old products, in the process eating into the profits needed to maintain the old products and systems.

Most Canadians do not have enough insurance to cover the costs of long-term care and critical illness, or the likelihood that they will live far longer than their parents. But these issues are unlikely to be addressed anytime soon given the restrictions on selling insurance policies through bank branches, the plethora of confusing products, and the cost of coverage.

Innovation Is Key

Canadian banks' wealth management business, like the use of their capital for lending, appears caught in a trap. While their strategies have served them well in the past, they are ill-suited to sustaining future growth. The reality is that Canadians are not saving enough, and a large portion of what they are saving is parked in low-risk, low-return deposits or in real estate.

For the time being, the banks are benefiting handsomely from the deposit windfall. Indeed, without it, their earnings would fall dramatically. The more sobering side of the coin is that millions of Canadians will not be able to retire comfortably without higher returns on their savings. Traditional mutual funds are clearly not the answer, but until recently, ordinary investors have not had easy access to new, less costly products, such as ETFs and guaranteed real return funds. Improved transparency as new regulations take hold and innovative products come on the market give us hope that this situation will improve. But unfortunately for the banks, the shifting marketplace will likely mean less revenue for them.

It is instructive to see how American investors are dealing with these problems. Products such as ETFs, index funds, tactical asset allocation funds, and self-directed platforms have made it much easier for them to meet their investment goals. This has resulted in two powerful trends. The first is the dramatic shift from active management of assets to passive investments, in other words, from mutual funds into ETFs and index funds. The second, related trend is that money is moving from high-cost to low-cost investments. In addition, retail investors in the United States have shifted their focus over the past decade from how well an investment performs relative to an index or other funds in that category, known as a relative return, to net real returns. By holding Canadian money managers accountable against a minimum benchmark of an annual 3.5 per cent net real return, investors would undoubtedly help force change on this side of the border.

Exchange-traded funds are currently the most talked-about product in the wealth management business. But ETFs are not for everyone. Because they trade like stocks, there are commission fees on each purchase or sale. This makes them less suitable for individuals on monthly savings plans, or with small amounts to invest. It also means that ETFs are subject to market risk (the prices go up and down with the market), liquidity risk (there may not be an active market, especially for niche ETFs), and concentration risk (certain ETFs may be heavily invested in only a few companies), while some ETFs have no benchmark (active ETFs, for example, may not be designed to follow a specific index).

These pooled funds are like a breath of fresh air in an industry known for exorbitant fees and poor transparency. They have low fees and are easily understood. Yet ETFs have been slow to take off in Canada. In the United States, ETFs and index funds now represent 30 per cent of all retail investments, up from 20 per cent five years ago.[39] But these investments are not sold in bank branches and they don't fit brokers' traditional commission-based compensation plans. Not even Bank of Montreal, the fastest growing ETF distributor, offers these funds through its branch network. Instead, its branches sell high-priced mutual funds whose portfolios hold ETFs. In the case of brokers and dealers, commissions still rule the day. Virtually every product in a client's portfolio, except for individual stocks and bonds, comes with a commission for the advisor. Fee-based accounts, which charge a single annual fee as a percentage of assets, are gaining a foothold, but commission-based products still dominate the market. According to Investor Economics, an independent industry research firm, fee-based accounts, which are more likely to include ETFs, have yet to gain significant traction. They make up only 28 per cent of client assets outside of mutual funds, and an even smaller proportion if mutual funds are included in the calculation.

The good news is that change is on the way. As figure 5.4 shows, ETF sales have picked up steam since 2010. The biggest ETF manager by far is Blackrock's iShares Canada, but several other ETF-only providers have entered the market, among them Horizons Exchange-Traded Funds and Vanguard Investment Management, a large supplier of index funds. Even firms hitherto known for their mutual funds, such as Mackenzie Financial, AGF Management, and CI Financial, have added ETFs to their mix. Most of the banks are also getting on board. Bank of Montreal is now the second-largest player after iShares, with 30 per cent market share. By the end of 2016, Canadians had invested $113.6 billion in ETFs, equal

Figure 5.4. ETFs have started to take off in Canada

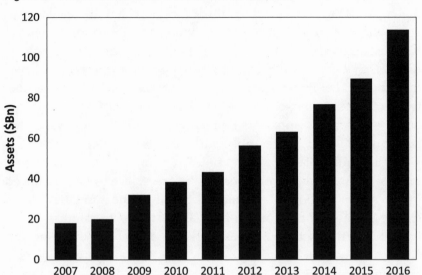

Source: Authors' Analysis, Canadian ETF Association, Industry Statistics

to 8 per cent of investment fund holdings (mutual funds and ETFs collectively).

The mutual fund companies and financial advisors have at last come to realize that ETFs' low cost, tax efficiency, and income benefits make them an attractive investment for their clients. In a fiercely competitive marketplace, it clearly makes more sense to offer what your clients want than to see them drift away. Regulators are now working with the industry to enable mutual fund advisors to sell ETFs. The TMX Group announced in November 2015 that it planned to extend its equities trading and settlement services to the mutual fund industry, which would ultimately reduce costs of selling ETFs to retail investors.[40]

While ETFs still make up a small proportion of most Canadians' investments, there is one niche segment where Canada has emerged as a world leader. We have the highest percentage of actively managed ETFs in the G7, with this type of fund representing 13.7 per cent of total ETF assets, compared with just 1 per cent in the United

States. Unlike a traditional ETF that tracks a specific index, actively managed ETFs are more like mutual funds, with a dedicated manager who may make frequent adjustments to the portfolio. Some have assumed that this is due to differences in regulation, but the reality is that actively managed ETFs charge significantly higher fees than their index-tracking cousins, making them much more attractive to financial advisors. So, even in the world of ETFs, Canadian banks and brokers appear to be taking the short-sighted view that their profitability is more important than their clients' well-being.

In the United States, competition from low-cost ETFs is forcing mutual funds to take another look at their fees. Blackrock announced in November 2015 that it would slash by half the annual expenses charged to investors in one of its ETFs that aims to mimic the performance of the entire U.S. stock market. By the end of the same day, Charles Schwab had matched the price cut. A month later, Vanguard announced fee cuts of as much as 25 per cent on dozens of its funds. Analysts predict that fees on U.S. mutual funds will tumble towards zero.[41] In October 2016, BlackRock slashed its ETF fees again to near-zero in response to a U.S. Department of Labor rule that will require advisers to put the interests of their clients first in picking investment vehicles.[42]

ETFs are not the only threat facing banks and other old-time financial advisors. Over the past few years, the new breed of fintech entrepreneurs has introduced investors to a thoroughly twenty-first century version of the portfolio manager, known as a "robo-advisor." This is a far cry from the traditional financial advisor who meets clients over a coffee to chat about their investments. Robo-advisors are computer algorithms that allocate portfolio assets between cash, bonds, equities, commodities, and so on, based on a pre-determined investment policy that may or may not have been discussed with a human advisor. The robo-advisors typically invest in low-cost ETFs. Their services also include deploying incoming cash flows, rebalancing portfolios, and implementing tax-avoidance strategies, all at a price well below that of full-service brokers and mutual fund advisors. The typical robo-advisor fee is about 0.75 per cent of assets, versus 2.5 per cent (or more) for a traditional investment advisor.

This investment approach has been particularly attractive to millennials. At least nine robo-advisors have set up shop in Canada, among them, Wealthsimple, Portfolio IQ (Questrade), and Invisor. Bank of Montreal joined the fray in late 2015 with an announcement that it would become the first Canadian bank to offer its own robo-advisory service.

J.D. Power, a consultancy, conducts annual customer satisfaction surveys of both full-service retail brokerages and self-directed online or discount brokerages. These surveys consistently find that customer satisfaction with both full-service and self-directed investing is materially lower in Canada than in the United States. The average score for full-service investing in the United States is 804, versus 764 in Canada. Even Canada's highest-ranked players – Edward Jones and Raymond James – would be considered below average by Americans. For self-directed investing, the average U.S. score is 775, compared with 729 north of the border.[43] The *Globe and Mail*'s annual survey of online brokers for 2016 concluded that two small firms – Virtual Broker and Qtrade Investor – performed best in meeting the needs of mainstream investors who are not active traders. The banks' online trading platforms trailed with B and C grades. So even those investors prepared to do their own research and trading must contend with mediocre service.[44]

While the big banks are starting to make progress towards meeting their customers' needs, they still have a long way to go. Until the time comes when investors have access to more self-directed investment vehicles, more price competition, better online tools, more product innovation, lower advisory fees, more transparency, and improved consumer education, they are likely to keep asking, "Where are the customers' yachts?"

CHAPTER SIX

Canada Trails the Third World

As our world changes fundamentally and forever, the opportunities of rising to the challenge far outweigh the risks of falling behind. The time has come to take a longer-term view of how stakeholders, including consumers, can work together to achieve a secure, innovative online payments system that serves the needs of the digital world.

Task Force for the Payments System Review,
The Way We Pay: Transforming the Canadian Payments System

Unprecedented changes are sweeping the global payments industry. The advance of digital technology, the emergence of new players with compelling products, and shifting consumer preferences are combining to disrupt this often hidden yet always critical part of the financial services system.

Like most other countries' economies, Canada's economy depends on the exchange of billions of dollars each day. The payments system enables financial institutions to send large payments to each other securely and to grease the wheels of everyday commerce for businesses, governments, and individuals. The Canadian payments system cleared and settled a total of 7 billion transactions worth $49.6 trillion in 2015, averaging $197 billion each day. The payments business is a gusher of reliable revenues for the banks and a linchpin of customer loyalty.[1] Who will control it in future? If present trends continue, it may not be the banks.

A Hugely Important Business[2]

The payments business is immensely important to banks, including the big Canadian banks. Boston Consulting Group (BCG) defines payments as direct and indirect revenues generated by non-cash payment services. These revenues embrace a host of transactions that we take for granted every day, among them the spread income on transaction account balances, account maintenance fees, transaction fees on debit and credit cards, currency conversion fees, annual card membership fees and penalties, and fees for overdrafts and insufficient funds. BCG estimates that this business contributes 40 per cent to 60 per cent of most banks' retail and wholesale profits.[3] In the case of Canada's big six, the figure is well within this range, given their success in attracting low-interest deposits.

Yet even though payments are the banks' most important business, they have not run it that way. Instead, they have managed the various types of payments in separate silos. Credit cards and lines of credit are part of lending products. Debit cards are either attached to chequing accounts or to alternative distribution channels. Foreign exchange is often managed from the investment banking division. Savings accounts and guaranteed investment certificates are considered part of wealth management. Cash management for businesses is housed in the corporate bank. The technology department is left to develop, maintain, and operate the various systems. The result of this fragmentation is that only the chief executive and a handful of other senior managers have a comprehensive picture of the payments business. Given the way the numbers are reported, it is difficult even for them to fully appreciate the overall contribution to the bottom line.

One result is that the banks have taken a myopic view of the value of this treasure chest. For the past decade, their focus has been on cutting costs to boost profits rather than adapting to the disruptive technologies and changing customer attitudes that are revolutionizing the payments business.

Once a Leader ...

Canada was a world leader for many years in retail point-of-sale (POS) payments, thanks to the banks' success in persuading customers of the benefits of debit and credit cards. Interac, a low-cost, point-of-sale payment option developed in the early 1990s, helped Canada achieve one of the developed world's highest levels of electronic consumer payments. By 2010, shoppers were using credit and debit cards for two-thirds of all their point-of-sale payments, compared with about 40 per cent in most other developed countries.

However, Canada now risks being left behind as others embrace investment and innovation in this critical area of their business. Countries like Norway, Finland, Denmark, Sweden, Australia, and the United Kingdom have all but replaced paper-based payment methods, such as cheques, with online payments. Having eliminated cheques, Sweden is now going cashless.[4] By contrast, in Canada, the rollout of Interac Flash tap-and-go technology and the development of an efficient online debit option have been constrained by uncoordinated decision making on the part of banks and other financial institutions that control Acxsys, the for-profit arm of Interac.

It gets worse. Instead of building a low-cost, convenient online money transfer system for small businesses and individuals similar to B-Pay in Australia or Faster Pay in the United Kingdom, the Canadian banks have chosen to aggressively market their credit cards. The reason is not hard to find: credit cards are far more profitable for the banks than other methods. Interac does offer online transfers for individuals, and this business has mushroomed at an annual rate of 40 per cent over the past six years. But it could have been even more had the banks (except RBC) not dampened demand by slapping a hefty $1.50 fee on every transaction.

Research by the Canadian Payments Association (see table 6.1) shows that from 2008 to 2011, credit card use grew at an annual 7.2 per cent compared with 5.4 per cent for debit cards. In 2011, 14 per cent of retail payments (by value) were made with credit and 16 per cent with debit. By 2013, credit card payments had overtaken debit. According to BCG, credit cards are the dominant payments

Table 6.1. Canadian payments volume

	2008 Volume (millions)	2011 Volume (millions)	2014 Volume (millions)	% Change		% Compound Annual Growth Rate	
				3 year	6 year	3 year	6 year
Cheques	1,350.6	1,186.6	950.3	−20	−30	−7	−6
Debit Card	3,704.4	4,148.1	4,906.9	+18	+32	+6	+5
ABM	880.2	759.3	600.7	−21	−32	−8	−6
Prepaid Card	117.6	147.9	194.5	+32	+65	+10	+9
EFT	1,824.1	2,124.0	2,476.4	+17	+36	+5	+5
Credit Card	2,701.5	3,423.6	4,330.5	+26	+60	+8	+8
E-transfers	10.8	28.7	81.5	+284	+755	+42	+40
Cash	9,662.9	8,494.9	7,172.3	−16	−26	−5	−5
TOTAL	20,252.1	20,313.1	20,713.1				

Source: Payments Canada, Discussion Paper No. 4, November 2016

revenue engine for North American banks, representing 60 per cent of retail payment revenues in 2014. Moreover, credit cards generate the highest return on assets across retail financial products at close to 2.5 per cent, with home-equity loans ranked second at 1.2 per cent. Most of that burden falls on the merchants who accept the cards as payment for the products and services.

The same applies to the loyalty points that have played a key role in marketing credit cards – terrible for merchants but wonderful for banks. According to the 2013 Colloquy Loyalty Census, 90 per cent of Canadian consumers belong to at least one loyalty program. More than half of Canadians would not consider having a credit card that was not affiliated to a suitably rewarding loyalty program. Two-thirds of Canadians agree that programs are worth the hassles of enrolment, opt-ins, presenting a loyalty card upon purchase, referrals, and so on.

Debit and credit cards undoubtedly bring benefits to merchants and consumers. Consumers enjoy payment choice, convenience, and the ability to buy big-ticket items on the spot. Merchants have the advantage of fast, guaranteed payment, as well as lower cash handling costs. Credit cards mean they do not have to extend credit directly to customers for high-priced items. Plastic also generally offers better protection from fraud and theft than cash or cheques.

The downside for merchants is that they are forced to bear a significant portion of the cost of cardholder benefits in the form of interchange fees. Many consumers do not realize that the fancier their card, the higher the fee paid by the merchant for each transaction. Both Visa and MasterCard boosted their interchange revenues in 2008 by introducing premium cards with higher fees.

Interchange fees make up the bulk of the service fees that merchants pay to merchant services providers. Although Visa contends that interchange fees have risen only modestly since the 2008 changes, the Task Force for the Payments System Review concluded that the average merchant service fee levied on smaller merchants soared by as much as 40 per cent between 2007 and 2010. There is strong evidence that providers took advantage of the new fee formula to push up their transaction fees, especially surcharges for premium cards and card-not-present transactions.

New technology and standards have meant even more costs for merchants, especially those that own rather than rent their point-of-sale terminals. Advances in chip and PIN technology, which uses embedded microchips in the card to enhance authentication and reduce fraud, have forced merchants to buy new equipment. They have also had to invest time and money to comply with new standards for payment data security. The upshot, according to documents presented to the Senate Finance Committee, is that Canadian merchants now pay among the highest card interchange fees in the world.[5]

But pressure for change is mounting. As mobile commerce and payment apps proliferate, merchants and their customers now have an opportunity to break free of the banks' grip.

. . . Now a Laggard

Cheques remain more widely used in Canada than in almost any other country. We write almost a billion of these bits of paper each year. Large corporations, small and mid-sized businesses, and governments make up almost 60 per cent of the total volume, with individuals accounting for the remaining 40 per cent. And that suits the Canadian banks very nicely, at least for now. Far from encouraging their customers to replace cheques with digital payments, the banks are investing millions to process more cheques more quickly.

The problem with cheques is that they are inefficient. They involve many manual steps, such as keying in information; printing and mailing; and reconciling payment, invoice, and accounts receivable and payable sub-ledgers. Processing cheques, including the need to transport them physically, causes delays and adds cost.

Yet Canada now trails behind Korea and Malaysia in the race to replace cheques with more efficient electronic payments, especially B2B (businesses and governments paying businesses and/or governments) (see figure 6.1). At the current rate, Canadians will still be writing 800 million cheques a year in 2020, despite the drag on business and government productivity.

The use of cheques shrank by about 5 per cent a year in the decade to 2010, but the rate of decline slowed to about 2 per cent towards the end of the period. The Payments Task Force formed a working group in 2011 with the aim of finding ways to eliminate at least 68 per cent of all remaining cheques by 2020. A big step forward came in 2012 when Public Works and Government Services Canada committed the federal government to stop sending and receiving cheques by 2016. Since then, cheque use has fallen at a compound annual rate of 7 per cent, cutting the proportion of business-to-business payments made by cheque to 42 per cent. Getting rid of cheques entirely was considered unwise, given Canada's heavy reliance on them. Instead, the task force recommended that payment services providers, such as banks, should offer alternative electronic payment methods that deliver greater benefits than the existing cheque-based infrastructure.

Other countries have shown that it is possible to phase out cheques far more quickly. By 2010, northern European countries, including Sweden, Finland, Denmark, Germany, and the United Kingdom had almost completely eliminated cheques. By 2018, cheques are expected to make up a mere 0.8 per cent of personal payments in the United Kingdom. The reduction of cheques for retail purchases

Figure 6.1. Percentage of domestic business-to-business payment flows made by cheque (% USD value of payments)

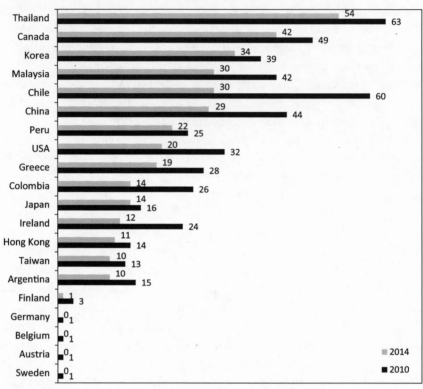

Percent USD value of Payment Transactions

Source: Global Payments Map, 2015, McKinsey & Company: www.mckinsey.com. Copyright © 2017 McKinsey & Company. All rights reserved. Reprinted by permission.

has happened even faster. In 2000, 59.5 per cent of retail payments in the United States were made by cheque. The proportion had plummeted to just 4.3 per cent by 2010. The drop was even more impressive in Australia – from 80 per cent of non-cash retail payments in 1995 to just 3.3 per cent in 2010.

The main reason why Canadians still write so many cheques is that they have few alternatives. While credit and debit cards have done wonders for the popularity of retail point-of-sale technology, progress has been much slower for digital transactions involving businesses, especially small businesses, and government. Canadian financial institutions continue to spend heavily on cheque processing technology, such as image-capturing software at branches and ATMs. These investments encourage all concerned to keep using paper, which is a boon for the banks, considering the reliable revenue and profit stream that old-fashioned cheques provide. While the reluctance to move into the twenty-first century may be understandable, it is also short-sighted because it hampers Canada's competitiveness in an interconnected and increasingly paperless world.

An electronic invoicing and payments (EIP) regime is faster and cheaper. Moving to EIP is a major undertaking that covers all the steps of the purchase-to-pay and order-to-receipt cycles: sending and receiving invoices; dispute handling; acceptance, payment, and collection reconciliation; and archiving. A great deal of time and money is wasted because the steps between purchase and final remittance still use both electronic and physical formats and require manual re-entry of data.

Automation makes it much easier to manage information. It is also essential for any business that wants to deliver its products or services over the Internet. Reconciliation rates and processing times improve. Quality control and responsiveness are enhanced because information can be processed in real time. Simply put, EIP unlocks the potential for a much higher standard of service for both suppliers and their customers.

A study by Billentis, a Swiss e-invoicing and billing services firm, listed the numerous benefits to companies and, by extension, entire economies when they move from paper to electronic invoicing and purchasing:

- Within five to seven years, the twenty-seven member states of the European Union expect to save 243 billion euros a year through enhanced productivity, equal to 1.98 per cent of their combined GDP.
- Organizations are able to reduce the cost of invoicing by 60 to 80 per cent when they move from paper to automated methods.

- Businesses, on average, are able to reduce their costs by the equivalent of 1–2 per cent of revenues by switching from paper to e-invoicing, and by automating related supply chain processes.

Governments, too, gain handsomely from automation. A Capgemini report evaluating a cross-section of sixteen EU members estimated that removing paper would generate a per-unit operating cost reduction of 70 to 75 per cent and a cumulative market impact of over 238 million Euros from 2006 to 2011.[6]

With the help of McKinsey & Company, the Payments Task Force estimated that Canada would notch up direct savings of $7.7 billion a year by automating invoicing and reducing the number of cheques in circulation by 68 per cent.[7] Large enterprises would see the bulk of the savings, about $5 billion, thanks to the elimination of laborious manual processes, such as reconciliation of accounts receivable and payable. Governments would save $1.5 billion on the conversion; but, more importantly, they would no longer have to hire clerks to process the growing demand for pensions and other government payments from retiring baby boomers. Small and midsized businesses and financial institutions would capture savings of $700 million and $600 million, respectively.

The indirect cost to the Canadian economy of paper invoices and cheques is in excess of $7.7 billion annually. By contrast, the Nordic and other European countries have realized cost savings equivalent to 1 per cent to 2 per cent of GDP by automating the delivery of public and private sector services, beginning with payments. This represents $16 to $32 billion in annual cost savings available to governments in Canada (especially the provinces), corporations, and financial institutions. We cannot, however, realize these savings without upgrading our core payments systems so that they are able to carry remittance and other information with the payment. More important, Canada cannot participate fully in the twenty-first century information economy without a digital payments system.

To realize these savings, Canada needs to make significant investments in accounting and processing systems. We also need to replace our payments infrastructure, but the banks have not wanted to make that investment for fear of losing control. Without these costly upgrades, companies and governments cannot implement electronic invoicing and payments, or meet Canadians' expectations for immediate funds transfers. Increasingly, we will not be able to transact with the rest of the digital world, raising the risk that Canada will find itself isolated from full participation in the global information economy.

Impressive progress has been made in the five years since the Task Force for the Payments System Review recommended overhauling the Canadian Payments Association (CPA) and speeding up the move to electronic invoicing and purchasing (see box 6.1). The government amended the Canadian Payments Act in 2014 to put new governance standards in place at the CPA, and an independent board was appointed in 2015. The association published several research studies in 2015, including one outlining the requirements for a new, faster, automated clearing and settlement system that provided the information needed for online processing of invoices. Another investigated the expansion of electronic funds transfers to replace cheques. The association has also continued to develop the international standard for data transmission, known as ISO 20022, which it approved in 2011. In December 2016, Payments Canada announced it was replacing its clearing and settlement systems.

Box 6.1. Task Force for the Payments System Review Recommendations to the Minister of Finance

Recommendations: Government must lead the change

For Canada's payment system to substantially modernize, changes are required in multiple arenas, from consumer behaviours to accounting solutions to the very procedures governments rely upon in delivering services. Industry has not implemented change, in part because of uncertainty and lack of coordination. Therefore, the Government of Canada should lead the change by undertaking the following actions:

- Implement electronic invoicing and payments (EIP) for all government suppliers and recipients of benefits.
- Partner with the private sector to create a mobile ecosystem.
- Propel the building of a digital identification and authentication (DIA) regime to underpin a modernized payments system and protect Canadians' privacy.
- Overhaul the governance, business model, and powers of the Canadian Payments Association and transform the payments infrastructure so that it can innovate to meet the evolving needs of Canadians in a digital economy.

Source: Task Force for the Payments System Review, "Moving Canada into the Digital Age," December 2011, 10. Patricia Meredith chaired this task force. Reproduced with the permission of the Department of Finance, 2017.

Mobile Goes Mainstream

Even as many Canadians continue to pay for their purchases by writing cheques or pulling cash out of their pockets, mobile technology is radically changing their behaviour and their expectations.

More Than Half the World's Population Made a Mobile Payment in 2011

Around the world, mobile phones are driving a dramatic shift in the way people pay their bills and do their banking. According to the World Bank, 98 per cent of the population had a mobile phone subscription by 2015.[8] This means that instead of paying with cash, cheques, or debit and credit cards, the vast majority of consumers can now use a mobile phone to pay for goods or services.

There are seven main types of mobile payment:

- SMS-based (text-based) transactional payments;
- Direct mobile billing;
- In-app payments;
- Mobile commerce and/or Web payments;
- Peer-to-peer payments;
- Near field communications (NFC, tap-and-go, or contactless) payments.

According to Brett King, author of *Bank 3.0*, about half the population of developed countries had made a mobile payment of some sort by 2011 – at a minimum, buying an app or making an in-app purchase from a smartphone would qualify.[9] To put that in perspective, more people made a mobile payment than wrote a cheque. By this simple measurement, mobile payments were already as mainstream as cheques, and that was more than five years ago.

M-Pesa is the world's leading SMS or text-based payment system. It started as a project funded by the U.K. Department for International Development, with the aim of streamlining microfinance loan repayments.[10] M-Pesa's initial goal was quite humble, and no one was prepared for its incredible growth. For example, in Kenya, it addressed a long-time deficiency in the financial system which meant that most people had no access to a modern payments mechanism. The World Bank estimated in 2012 that M-Pesa was processing payments totalling no less than a quarter of Kenya's GDP each year – not surprising, considering that around 92 per cent of the population had signed up.

The GSM Association, which represents mobile operators, has identified 130 similar systems around the globe, with another 93 in the pipeline. In the developing world, where access to bank accounts, branches, and ATMs is limited, SMS-based payments have allowed merchants and consumers to leapfrog banks' costly clearing, settlement, and processing systems.

In Asia, mobile payments have been widely in use for more than a decade. Japan has set the benchmark with 121 million people, or 95 per cent of the total population, now owning a tap-and-go phone. Public transport created the impetus for smart card payments because of the inconvenience of collecting cash fares from commuters in Tokyo and Osaka. The wireless carrier NTT DoCoMo addressed the problem by developing a portable contactless solution and then using its market dominance to encourage more widespread adoption of the new system.

Closer to home, the Starbucks card, powered by a mobile application, now accounts for 40 per cent of purchases at the coffee chain's outlets across North America. With more than 12 million customers actively using its mobile payment app, Starbucks was processing more than 10 million mobile transactions a week in 2016, equal to nearly a quarter of all its North American in-store payments – all this on a platform that did not even exist five years ago. Furthermore, use of the mobile order and pay app increased from 4 per cent of all U.S. transactions in the second quarter of 2016 to 5 per cent in the third quarter. The Starbucks experience is surely proof that consumers are falling over themselves to use this new, convenient form of payment.[11]

Person-to-person (P2P) payments, which allow customers to transfer funds from one bank account or credit card to another via the Internet or a mobile phone, are also rapidly gaining traction. PayPal, a fifteen-year veteran in the non-bank payments business, processed more than $280 billion in P2P payments in 2015, a 27 per cent jump from the previous year.[12] Especially impressive is the surge in mobile payments, from a modest $141 million in 2009 to $4 billion two years later and a head-spinning $50 billion in 2015. The 2015 volume of mobile payments was more than double that of the previous year and equal to one-quarter of all P2P payments processed by PayPal that year. PayPal classifies a mobile payment as a payment across its network from one party to another using a mobile phone.

PayPal's business-to-business (B2B) division, Braintree, which it acquired in the fall of 2013, had recorded more than $50 billion in transactions by the end of 2015. Braintree has 269 million consumer cards on file across forty-six markets – five times the number at the time of its acquisition. While Braintree also handles payment processing for other PayPal services, the company says that the 2015 transaction number was more than four times Braintree's comparable volume two years earlier. In August 2014, PayPal and Braintree launched One Touch payments for mobile apps, its most successful product launch to date. In two years, they have signed up 32 million consumers and 144 merchants, including half of the top 500 U.S. Internet retailers, in 200 markets around the world.[13]

Remittance payments using mobile phones are also exploding. According to the World Bank, 215 million migrants send more than US$600 billion a year to family and friends, many of whom do not have bank accounts. About three-quarters of the total goes to developing countries, with mobile phones playing an ever more important role. Remittance companies, such as Western Union, were on track to process some $55 billion a year in international transactions through mobile devices by 2016, according to Juniper Research, up from $12 billion in 2011 and $330 million in 2008. In 2015, PayPal acquired Xoom, a small mobile remittance player, which enables customers to send money to family members and pay their bills in forty-three countries around the world.

Research by the Federal Reserve Board suggests that many of us make mobile payments without even realizing it.[14] For example, mobile payment users were identified by a general question about whether they have engaged in any mobile payments activities over the past twelve months. In addition, mobile phone users were asked whether they had used their phone for particular mobile payments tasks. Some respondents who answered "no" to the mobile payments question indicated they have done one or more of these mobile payments tasks, indicating that the share of people making mobile payments may be higher than the measure of mobile payments users based on the general definition. In the 2014 survey, 28 per cent of smartphone owners were identified as mobile payments users based on their response to the general question. By comparison, 47 per cent of smartphone owners reported completing at least one mobile payments task, regardless of their answer to the general question about mobile payments.

These examples show beyond any doubt that mobile payments have gone mainstream. New entrants, such as Square, ClearXchange, QuickPay, CashEdge, Venmo, and Dwolla, have capitalized on the inefficiency of sending money from one bank account to another. Under existing wire and automated clearing and settlement systems, a routing number, a bank account number, and a branch code and address are required before one person can send money to another. A combination of complicated interbank agreements, cross-border restrictions, and investments in outdated systems have all held back the banks.

Mobile Wallets: The New Battleground

The mobile payments story can be framed as a battle between banks, wireless carriers, and tech companies. The winners are not yet clear but are set to emerge over the next five years as mobile payments eclipse first cheques, then cards, and eventually cash. Mobile carriers have tried to restrict mobile wallet operations on their networks, but they are unlikely to be successful because the barriers to entry are extremely low. A mobile wallet needs no more than a customer with a mobile phone and Internet access. Of course, users need to be able to deposit funds into the wallet, top them up, and pay. These actions require some level of cooperation and partnership between financial institutions and telecom providers. Given the intense competition in the mobile payments business, it will always be possible to find at least one supplier willing to step forward.

One of the pioneers in mobile wallets is Apple, which launched its Apple Pay service for iPhone users in September 2014. Apple Pay has assembled an impressive array of partners, including the eleven biggest U.S. credit card issuers and retailers such as McDonald's and Walgreens, which together have 220,000 U.S. outlets ready to accept iPhone payments. Card issuers pay 15 cents of every $100 payment to Apple. The banks that issue the cards have been willing to give up a small slice of their fee revenue in the hope that Apple Pay will become ubiquitous. That would drive up transaction volumes – and therefore overall revenue – and could reduce losses to fraud, thanks to Apple Pay's tight security.

The iPhone has a finger scanner, which Apple Pay uses for authentication, as well as iBeacon, which can track shoppers as they walk the aisles. Because Apple stores the payment card (using host card emulation[15] technology) in the secure element of the iPhone, the transaction is considered "card present" and attracts the lowest interchange fees. This was a major breakthrough, as previously all Internet payments were treated as "card not present" and, as such, attracted a much higher fee. Noting that 1.2 billion music lovers already use the Apple iTunes virtual wallet, Carl Icahn wrote in a letter to Apple shareholders, "We believe that a revolutionary payments solution is now a very real opportunity that the company could choose to pursue." Mr Icahn appears to be spot on. By the end of 2015, Apple Pay's digital wallet had more than 12 million active monthly users in the United States. Usage of Apple Pay tripled in 2016, and year-on-year transaction volumes increased 500 per cent. At year end, more than 36 per cent of merchants already accepted Apple Pay.[16]

On another front, Google, the search engine giant, relaunched its mobile wallet, known as Android Pay, in May 2015. Android Pay uses the same fundamental technology as many other mobile payment systems, including Apple Pay, with some Android-specific improvements. Users store their card details using host card emulation. Like Apple Pay, Android users only need to be near a wireless payment terminal to start a transaction. Enter a PIN, pattern, password, or fingerprint to authenticate identity, and you're ready to pay for your purchase. One of Android Pay's major advantages is a common standard for fingerprint sensors, allowing outside developers to access its biometric systems.

Google is initially rolling out Android Pay in the United States, with backing from the major payment networks, such as Visa, MasterCard, American Express, and Discover, plus dozens of financial institutions and retailers with 700,000 outlets around the country. Like Apple Pay, Android Pay uses "tokenization," a new technology that does away with the need for merchants to transfer card details over the Internet. Instead, the system uses a randomly generated token, which helps foil cyber-attacks and other forms of payment fraud.

Android Pay now has its own app that allows users to accrue loyalty points as well as make payments. Google has shown how the app works with the help of a Coca-Cola vending machine adapted to wireless technology. Users approach the payment terminal and choose whether they want to pay for a Coke with a credit card or use loyalty points. App developers will be able to use the Android Pay application program interface for a multitude of purchases, whether in bricks-and-mortar stores or through a smartphone app.

The South Korean electronics group Samsung launched its own mobile wallet service, Samsung Pay, in the summer of 2015. Samsung's advantage is that its technology is compatible with a much larger number of existing payment terminals. Samsung Pay is already available in the United States and was introduced in the United Kingdom, Spain, and China early in 2016. By the end of 2015, both Android and Samsung Pay had more than 5 million active monthly users.[17]

The two credit-card giants, Visa and MasterCard, have introduced mobile wallets of their own. MasterCard's PayPass Wallet and Visa's V.me are designed to be used online, in a mobile phone app, or as tap-and-go. One of the key obstacles to wider acceptance of mobile devices for point-of-sale payments is resistance among consumers, especially older people. They will need to become comfortable with mobile-to-mobile transactions instead of plastic cards and point-of-sale terminals. One hopeful sign is Visa's acquisition of 10 per cent of merchant services aggregator and mobile payments start-up Square in April 2011. Visa will probably try to drive mass adoption of the Square reader, which turns any smartphone into a point-of-sale terminal. That could help change perceptions as shoppers encounter more and more merchants accepting payments through a mobile phone. Success on this front would be a giant shot in the arm for mobile payments.[18]

We can expect to see mobile wallets popping up everywhere. Big retailers, such as Walmart and BestBuy, have launched proprietary in-store gift cards enabled by a mobile app. As with the immensely popular Starbucks app, these cards are mini-mobile wallets that can be used in specific stores.

In the longer term, however, Visa and MasterCard will be hard pressed to compete with these virtual wallets. As Cloud computing and Internet-enabled point-of-sale devices allow more and more retailers to accept payments from phones without having to plug a card into a machine and pay interchange and network fees, they are sure to opt for the easy, convenient, and cheaper route that also provides far more information on their customers. The bottom line is that Visa, MasterCard, and other private networks are rapidly losing their competitive edge as the new mobile payment apps over the Internet gain ever-wider acceptance.

Mobile Payments Take Off

Near field communication, also known as tap-and-go technology, is rapidly gaining momentum as a critical element in mobile payments in the developed world, including Canada. By the end of 2015, five of the six big Canadian banks and several credit unions had launched mobile payment apps.[19] But uptake has been slow, possibly because most Canadians have debit and credit cards that are as easy to tap as their phones.

The Payments Task Force urged banks and wireless carriers in 2011 to come up with ways of encouraging wider use of mobile payments. Canada was already a leader in near field communication, with 11 per cent penetration at the point of sale. Terminals using this technology were found in many of the most popular retail outlets, such as grocery stores, gas stations, restaurants, and coffee shops. This reality demonstrates that Canadians are ready for a revolutionary shift in their payment habits, and yet we have fallen behind in the adoption of mobile payments.

A "mobile payments readiness" index published by MasterCard in 2012 ranked Canada second behind only Singapore. The index took six factors into account: consumer readiness; the economic, technological, and demographic environment; the effectiveness and penetration of consumer financial services; the sophistication and penetration of mobile phone and terminal infrastructure; mobile commerce partnerships among banks, mobile networks, and governments; and the regulatory climate. Canada's high ranking was largely due to collaboration among banks, wireless carriers, and governments, fostered by the Payments Task Force. As the Master-Card study noted:

> The cooperation among banks, mobile networks, and the government makes Canada the leader in the mobile commerce clusters score. Other countries with high mobile commerce clusters scores include Columbia, Japan, Singapore, South Korea and the United Arab Emirates. However, in Canada, cooperation between banks and mobile networks is unique: In 2011, major mobile network Rogers filed to be a bank under the Canada Bank Act. This move has the potential to create big opportunities for mobile near-field communications payments in Canada by integrating the telco and financial services aspects of mobile payments in one entity.[20]

Yet in 2014, Canada dropped to eighth on the MasterCard digital evolution index (which replaced the mobile payments readiness index), having been overtaken by, among others, Sweden, Finland, the United Kingdom, and the United States. Collaboration between the banks and mobile carriers had become more difficult without a catalyst to keep them working together.

A 2012 study by ACI Worldwide and Aite Group, two payments specialists, may help explain the slowing pace of adoption. The study identified a group of consumers, called "smartphonatics," for whom mobile payments are second nature. Only 7 per cent of Canadians fell into this category, the smallest proportion among the fourteen countries studied. Half of all Canadian smartphonatics are Gen Xers (between the ages of thirty-two and forty-six in 2012). About six in ten smartphonatics made mobile payments in the six months prior to the report, and three-quarters did their banking with a mobile device. By contrast, just 12 per cent of non-smartphonatics had made a mobile payment, and 14 per cent had used a mobile device for banking.[21]

The ACI/Aite research suggests that around one in four consumers around the world can be classified as a smartphonatic, with higher numbers found in India and China than in the United States and Europe. According to this research, 80 per cent of smartphonatics have used their smartphone for mobile banking, but just one-third of non-smartphonatics report doing so. Not surprisingly, smartphonatics are generally younger consumers.

Access to a low-cost smartphone and data plan, essential tools for mobile payments, is rapidly becoming a necessity in the information-driven, connected world of today, just as an affordable car became an essential item in the 1950s and 1960s, or a microwave oven in the 1970s and 1980s. But the studies cited above indicate that some barriers still need to be overcome before mobile payments take off in Canada. One is the high cost of mobile phone subscriptions. While the former Conservative government tried on numerous occasions and in various ways to encourage competition and give users more choices, it had very limited success.

In 2010, the Canadian wireless carriers formed a joint venture, known as Zoompass, with the aim of introducing a single mobile payments system. But resistance from the banks ensured that it never got off the ground. A year later, the three large wireless carriers – Bell, Rogers, and Telus – revived the joint venture, renamed EnStream, as a service bureau for mobile phone credentials, serving all credential issuers and mobile operators (figure 6.2). The reincarnated venture is open to financial institutions, retailers, and governments with the aim of linking secure mobile payments and other services to their customers' devices no matter which mobile carrier they use. Customers can change mobile carrier and have their services transferred with their phone number.

CIBC and Rogers belatedly launched Canada's first mobile near field communication payment service in September 2012. Since then, all the other big banks and several credit unions have followed suit. Not every payment app is available on every device or wireless carrier, but the banks are working to fill the gaps. Some have also added special features in the hope of standing out from the pack. The RBC Wallet, for example, offers extra security and protection

Figure 6.2. Canada's credential service manager

Credential Issuers

Source: Enstream, Fall 2011

by storing client information, including card details, on the bank's secure "Cloud" rather than on the phone. This add-on puts RBC's app head-to-head with PayPal's promise to keep its customers' financial information private and protected, no matter where they shop. The problem, however, is that Apple, Android, and Samsung may have little interest in modifying their payments apps to make them compatible with the RBC Wallet. In other words, RBC may find that its supposed competitive advantage turns out to be no advantage at all.

Apple dropped a bombshell in October 2015 when it announced plans to expand Apple Pay to Canada in partnership with American Express. The Silicon Valley giant had talked to the Canadian banks, but the negotiations had dragged on and were seemingly going nowhere. Not only were the banks reluctant to agree to Apple's demand for a 0.15 per cent commission on each transaction, but they were upset that Apple would keep all the data relating to the transaction to itself, except the token number. This would make it almost impossible for the banks to use this data for marketing purposes. For a time, it looked as if the Canadian banks and the most popular credit-card networks might be left out in the cold on mobile payments.

But less than a year later, in May 2016, all the banks agreed to support Apple Pay. Apple agreed to share the data, and the banks agreed to pay the commission. With initial support from Scotiabank, Google introduced Android Pay in Canada in December 2016[22] with similar conditions.

Canadians have valid concerns about mobile payments and Internet technology. Fraud, identity theft, and system failures are a regular feature of the mainstream news. Security and privacy are not yet assured. Consumers will not embrace a new technology until they are sure they can trust it, and that it offers convenience and cost savings. For the time being, online debit transactions enabled by mobile apps remain a laborious process because of the absence of a robust digital identification and authentication regime. Without a way to authenticate the identity of a sender and receiver of information, many consumers are rightly concerned about the security and privacy of their transactions. Improvements are crucial if digital mobile payments are to gain wide popularity.

The federal government and the provinces have been exploring a nationwide digital identification and authentication regime for more than a decade. But, with the exception of British Columbia, they have yet to act. The Payments Task Force brought together government and industry experts from across the country, resulting in the formation of the Digital Identification and Authentication Council of Canada. The new council has begun to move forward to clarify roles and responsibilities and to map out a plan of action. However, without strong endorsement from the federal government, the roll-out could take decades.

In the meantime, the private sector is finding other ways to authenticate transaction information. Mobile phone numbers and Facebook accounts allow merchants to confirm customers' personal details online through social media. Companies like PayPal, Google, Apple, and Amazon store more than enough data about users and their behaviour to develop algorithms that can flag suspicious transactions. Similarly, one of the benefits to RBC of using its Cloud for its mobile payments app is that it can store vast amounts of data about its customers that can be used to offer custom-tailored services and improve security.

It's about the Information

Smartphones and tablets already deliver many of the goods and services we need to manage our daily lives, and much more is undoubtedly to come. Imagine using your phone to take an electrocardiogram when you wake up in the morning and send the results to your doctor, then lock your condo when you leave for work, pay for your subway ride, buy a coffee and a muffin in the food court, swipe a reader to get into your office, book a business trip, vote in the next election ... and much, much more. To echo Samsung's ads, the smartphone is becoming "my life companion."

All this will be made possible by technology companies' interposing themselves between the banks and their customers. The weapon they will use – in fact, are already using – is the payment mechanism bundled into the apps that deliver goods and services. It could be Uber transporting you, your parcels, your lunch, or your dry cleaning. Or it could be OpenTable arranging a restaurant reservation, gathering feedback on the food and service, calculating the appropriate gratuity, and processing your payment so that you don't have to wait for the server to bring your bill. Ground-breaking businesses such as Uber and OpenTable charge a percentage of revenue in return for bundling sales, marketing, and payments. Apple, Android, and Samsung have already set the benchmark by indicating that they will charge 20 to 30 per cent of revenue for data analytics and marketing, sales, and payments.

As mobile technology revolutionizes payments, it is also changing the way we shop for goods and services. Customers, once at the mercy of financial institutions, now have other options and are demanding the convenience, information, and lower prices that competition brings. If their traditional suppliers are unwilling or unable to move with the times, they are not afraid to try the services offered by the likes of Apple and Google. We are fast reaching the point where shoppers now trust these companies more than they trust their banks.

The surge in mobile Internet usage has been astounding. The time Americans spend on smartphones expanded almost fivefold between 2010 and 2014. Tablet usage soared even more, to the point where Americans spent 60 per cent of their online media time on mobile devices. More than one-fifth of millennials, the young adults between eighteen and thirty-four in 2015, no longer use desktop computers outside their work. And mobile usage is growing even faster among their parents and grandparents. While these figures are based on U.S. research, there is little doubt that the trend in Canada is much the same. In November 2016, mobile Internet usage in Canada passed desktop usage for the first time.[23]

A recent Forrester report suggests that 2014 was a tipping point for the mobile phone. In that year, the report notes, "it solidified its position as one of the most disruptive technologies for businesses in decades. Not since the advent of the Internet has a technology forced businesses to completely rethink how they win, serve, and retain customers. Forrester believes that in the future, the new competitive battleground will be the mobile moment. Why? Consumers expect to engage with brands to get any information or service they desire, immediately and in context."[24]

Retail Convergence onto Mobile Smartphones

One of the most striking changes in retailing has been the convergence of searching, comparing, shopping, and rewarding loyalty on mobile phone apps. This is creating a retail revolution. For example, a commuter rushing to the office can use a Starbucks app to order, pick up, and pay for a morning latte without standing in a line.

Howard Schultz, the CEO of Starbucks, made it clear which way the coffee chain was heading when he spoke to investors in January 2014:

> Holiday 2013 was the first in which many traditional bricks and mortar retailers' store foot traffic gave way to online shopping in a major way. Customers researched, compared prices and then bought the brands and items they wanted online, frequently using a mobile device to do so.

This was also the first holiday season in which consumers embraced the convenience and flexibility afforded by physical and digital gift cards with passion. Instead of gifting a particular item, many consumers instead chose to give the gift of choice. Starbucks was prepared for both of these shifts, having invested over many years in the creation and development of proprietary world-class digital and mobile payment and card technology and expertise. This expertise and the assets that support it enabled them to seamlessly process more than 40 million new Starbucks card activations valued at over $610 million in the US and Canada alone in Q1, including over 2 million new Starbucks card activations per day in the days immediately leading up to Christmas and $1.4 billion of Starbucks card loads globally.[25]

Why do mobile payment apps make so much sense for Starbucks – and every other retailer? First, the coffee chain collects billions of dollars in prepaid card balances, which it can invest for its own benefit. Second, an app cuts out the cost of processing small cash and card transactions. Most important, the app is only partly a payment mechanism. It also gives Starbucks invaluable data about customers' habits. It tells Mr Schultz and his colleagues what you buy (say, latte in the morning, Earl Grey tea in the afternoon), when you buy it (8 a.m. and 3 p.m.), and where you buy it. The app also enables Starbucks to reward you instantly for your loyalty and to keep track of those rewards. It can send you an electronic coupon to try out a new product or to offer a muffin with your morning latte.

PayPal took data capture a step further in March 2012 with PayPal Here, a mobile app that enables small businesses to accept almost any form of payment. The core of PayPal Here is an encrypted thumb-sized card reader that turns any iPhone or Android smartphone into a mobile payment device. Small businesses, service providers, and casual sellers can use the app to send invoices or accept credit and debit cards. Although PayPal is not the cheapest point-of-sale service (its merchant fee is typically 2.75 per cent), it is the dominant supplier to online retailers in Canada.

The most impressive part of PayPal's Open Payments Platform, which includes PayPal Here, is the data it collects and stores. Traditional credit card processors store only the date and amount of a purchase. For example, if I spend $100 at Shoppers Drug Mart on 24 January that is the only information transmitted to Visa or MasterCard or Shoppers. But PayPal – as well as Apple, Google, Amazon, Shopify, and their ilk – collect much more than that. They know when and where the purchase took place, and what items were bought. Once a few months of data are stored in the Cloud, merchants can start using it for their own benefit by, for example, offering customers loyalty rewards tailored to their shopping habits. What's more, PayPal can use mobile location sensors to alert a retailer that a particular customer is entering a store, giving the merchant an opportunity to make targeted real-time promotions through the customer's smartphone. As merchants become more adept at using these data-based services, we can foresee the day when, to quote HSBC's chief executive, "the information will become more valuable than the payment transaction."[26]

PayPal's vision does not stop with the Open Payments Platform. It analyses industries as clusters of customers and suppliers. For example, PayPal sees an opening in food services not only to handle mobile payments, coupons, and loyalty points but also to offer restaurants and customers order-ahead and self-checkout services and promotions. Smart point-of-sale systems can be linked to accounting systems to generate daily profit-and-loss statements, automated sales tax filings, and payroll calculations, including tips.

Many entrepreneurs are willing to pay more than the basic 2.75 per cent fee for these services because they cut accounting and administration costs and boost revenue through more effective targeting of prospective customers.

Restaurants are just one example. Many specialized firms will step forward over the next few years to meet the demand for customer and management data combined with payments. The big losers will be the banks. Without access to the data collected at check-out terminals, banks are poorly placed to compete against the likes of PayPal and Apple Pay. Traditional merchant service providers have been rolling out mobile payments applications but without the extra data storage and analysis functions, making them far less useful than services like Smart POS. All the Canadian banks, except Toronto-Dominion, sold their merchant services businesses in the early 2000s because low margins made it difficult to produce a decent return. Players such as Chase Paymentech (owned by JP Morgan Chase), Global Payments, Moneris (an RBC / Bank of Montreal joint venture), and a dozen other merchant service providers will need to invest heavily in the data collection business if they hope to compete successfully against the newcomers. Even if they do, they will find themselves up against hundreds of rivals, each hoping to capture a piece of the mobile retail business.

Data collection is only half of the mobile payments equation. The other half is the potential to change customer behaviour. The smartphone has become an integral part of shopping, both online and at the mall. Customers use their phones these days to find store locations, check for item availability and coupons, read product reviews and seek friends' opinions, make price comparisons, and even send pictures to online competitors such as Amazon before buying. According to a recent Google report, about three-quarters of mobile device users have searched for a product or business on their phone, 27 per cent have made an online purchase with their device, and of those just under half make mobile purchases at least once a month. Internet Retailer 2016 Mobile 500 – the leading guide on charting and analysing mobile data for the retail sector – reported that retailers around the world recorded a staggering $220 billion in sales in 2016 using mobile devices, up 53 per cent.[27] Success in retailing increasingly depends on merchants' engaging with shoppers long before those shoppers reach the store.

Immediate Funds Transfer and Mobile Payments

In a modern economy, we normally pay for goods and services and trade in financial markets by transferring money held in bank accounts. For the better part of the last century, paper cheques were used for most non-cash payments. But cheques have been in decline since the mid-1990s and are rapidly being replaced by a variety of more efficient instruments such as debit and credit cards and automated transfers. The most advanced means of transferring money between bank accounts is immediate funds transfer, known as IFT, which processes payments conveniently, securely, quickly, and at low cost. The recipient can use the funds immediately.

IFT payments through the Canadian banking system are mostly limited to large business transactions, interbank transfers, and specialized financial market transactions such as the purchase of securities.[28] Even so, the popularity of IFT appears to be growing for everyday transactions, such as retail purchases, payments between individuals, and small business accounts payable. E-transfer, an Interac peer-to-peer payment system that resembles IFT, has grown exponentially (figure 6.3).[29] But the benefits to banks of this exciting new technology are minimal because their involvement is minimal. To date, most general-purpose IFT payments are made on systems operated by their upstart rivals, most notably PayPal.

Banks in at least ten countries – Mexico, South Africa, the United Kingdom, China, the Czech Republic, Serbia, the Slovak Republic, Switzerland, Turkey, and Ukraine – have joined forces to set up IFT services within their own borders. Mexico, South Africa, and the United Kingdom have built processing systems specifically designed for IFT. The others have managed to move to IFT by expanding the use of their real-time gross settlement systems.

By contrast, the Canadian banks have so far done little to address the demand for low-cost, online, real-time funds transfer, with the

Figure 6.3. Interac e-transfer: Total volumes and values by fiscal year

Source: Interac, December 2016

notable exception of peer-to-peer e-transfers. In December 2016, Payments Canada (previously the Canadian Payments Association) announced it was poised to roll out a faster and simpler payment system over the next five years. The banks, however, have done so little to modernize their personal and business transaction account systems that it may be too late for them to maintain their dominance of the payments system. Companies with a large customer base and broad distribution networks – whether mobile operators, retailers, or online brands – now find that they have an opportunity to be real players in a business previously accessible only to financial institutions. To put it simply, the mobile phone has enabled an entirely new set of players to enter the payments game.

Blockchain, the technology behind the Bitcoin virtual currency, is potentially even more disruptive. It is a vast, global ledger running on millions of devices and open to anyone. It can be used to move any financial asset, and to store it securely and privately. The trust so essential for such a service comes not from powerful intermediaries like banks but through mass collaboration and clever code. Block-chain acts by consensus without any central bank involvement and has the potential to make all financial markets radically more effi-cient, secure, inclusive, and transparent.

But while the world of payments is changing profoundly, Canada is lagging far behind.

The Future of the Canadian Payments System

Given the importance of the payments business to the Canadian banks, we thought it worthwhile to revisit various scenarios for the future of the Canadian payments system compiled by the Payments Roundtable, a group of users and providers, merchant and consumer groups, technology firms, mobile operators, retail-ers, and government officials, among others. These scenarios, first drawn up in 2011, were framed in the context of two critical vari-ables that the group predicted would shape the payments system in the decade from 2010 to 2020: first, the degree of collaboration between incumbents, regulators, technology companies, retailers, mobile operators, and users; and second, the speed of user adop-tion. As figure 6.4 shows, various permutations of these two vari-ables produced four possible scenarios:

GROUNDHOG DAY

Like the movie of the same name, this scenario reprises the recent past. Canada's payment system moves forward as it has for the past two decades with few changes in its basic infrastructure. The system is fragmented. Governments, financial institutions, businesses, and wireless carriers individually chart their own course and protect their own interests, with few or no common standards.

Regulators respond slowly, generally offering consumers little fraud or identity protection, except when a specific crisis requires a more forceful response. Consumers and businesses are slow to adopt new technology. Concerns about authentication, privacy, and security remain high. With no clear winners emerging, consumers are slow to embrace new technology. Meanwhile, much of the rest

Figure 6.4. Canadian payments system scenarios

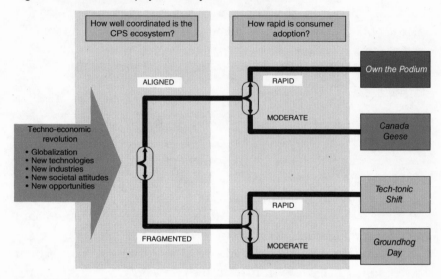

Source: Task Force for the Payments System Review, "The Way We Pay," April 2011, 35.

of the world moves ahead, quickly adopting new technologies and creating a more robust regulatory framework.

TECH-TONIC SHIFT

Technology companies such as Google, Apple, and social networking sites develop alternative payment platforms and become major players. Their success is propelled by enthusiastic customers and cheap new platforms that can easily be scaled up to handle bigger volumes. Government is slow to regulate the fast-moving industry, and competition is fierce. The new entrants take advantage of Cloud computing and collaborative networks to create low-cost businesses. The proliferation of services and applications is phenomenal.

Under this scenario, the old-line financial institutions find themselves under great pressure. Although consumers and businesses benefit from convenient new products, the incidence of fraud rises sharply and security breaches become more common, leading to a proliferation of legal liability cases. In response to mounting consumer pressure to improve security and protect privacy, the government moves to regulate the new entrants more actively. By the end of the decade, new entrants come to terms with the new rules and the market begins to consolidate. Many consumers and businesses use the new and convenient payment options, but some are left behind. In the space of a decade, innovative new technologies and market forces have fuelled a tectonic shift in all kinds of financial transactions.

CANADA GEESE

Like a flock of Canada geese, the payments system is tightly knit, with the efficiency of the group dependent on the behaviour of each constituent part, including incumbents, new entrants, and users. All players understand that it is in their own best interest to agree on rules and standards. Collaboration is spurred by the realization that if they fail to work together, government will wield a heavier regulatory hand.

Because the existing system is reasonably efficient, the incentive to search for and invest in new technology is limited. The cost of meeting regulatory standards and other regulation also put a damper on innovation. Instead, the system encourages gradual, thoughtful, evidence-based reform based on monitoring technologies being tested in other countries. In this way, Canada avoids the risks and disruption of being at the cutting edge but still reaps – albeit belatedly – the benefits of others' fresh thinking.

OWN THE PODIUM

Awareness is growing of the extent of changes wrought by the smartphone. On one hand, the upheaval is disrupting existing business models and ways of working. But it is also creating huge opportunities. Under this scenario, the industry comes together to develop common standards in key areas of the payments business, such as privacy, security, digital ID and authentication, and mobile payments. This collaboration encourages competition and innovation and propels Canada into a world leader in the payments field.

Take one example: The principle that Canadians own their own data could lay the groundwork for a robust digital ID and authentication regime crucial in encouraging rapid consumer adoption. Companies then use Cloud computing and collaborative networks to set up a myriad of payment businesses that meet consumers' needs. Lessons learned in payments quickly flow to other sectors, such as collecting and storing health care records. Under this scenario, Canada becomes a global leader in the new online world by the end of the decade, exporting its expertise and systems to many other countries.

Since these four scenarios for the future of the payments system were published in 2011, some clear patterns have begun to emerge:

- Global adoption of smartphones and tablets connected to the Internet has accelerated.
- The popularity of Cloud computing and data storage has mushroomed.
- New business models are emerging as mobile devices deliver a growing array of services and products.
- There is little sign of a concerted push to develop common rules and standards.
- The Canadian government has been slow to regulate new entrants. Indeed, it has given little indication that it intends to regulate them at all.
- Digital identification and authentication have moved steadily forward, although most provinces have not yet started to roll-out digital identity cards.

Against this background, let us take a closer look at two especially important trends: the rapid adoption of new technology, and the disappointing pace of collaboration.

Adoption of Mobile Technology Is Accelerating

Apple paved the way for mobile apps in July 2007 with the launch of the iPhone and the iOS operating system. The word *app* did not even exist before the iPhone. Now it is as much a part of our every-day life as the microwave and the computer.

- There are now 2 million apps for Apple devices, 2.2 million for Android, 669,000 for Windows, and 600,000 for Amazon.
- More than 140 billion apps have been downloaded for Apple and 280 billion for Google Play (previously known as the Android Marketplace). Users download more than 150 million for Apple and Android each day.
- Revenues from app sales reached US$41 billion in 2015 and are projected to exceed $101 billion in 2020.
- The number of app developers has exploded: 275,000 on Apple Store, 400,000 on Google Play, and 50,000 on Amazon.[30]

The popularity of apps is a clearly burgeoning. The power of exponential growth is illustrated by an ancient fable cited by Ray Kurzweil in his book *The Age of Spiritual Machines*. It tells of a rich ruler who agrees to reward an enterprising subject and thinks he will get off lightly by offering one grain of rice on the first square of a chessboard, then doubling the number of grains on each of the other sixty-three squares. By the thirty-second square, the ruler owes a mound weighing 100,000 kilograms, a large but manageable amount. It's on the second half of the chessboard that the real fun starts. Quickly, 100,000 kilos become 400,000, then 1.6 million, and keep growing. By the sixty-fourth square, the ruler owes 461 billion metric tons, more than 4 billion times as much as on the first thirty-two squares, and equal to 1,000 times the world's entire rice production in 2010.

The growth of the Internet and, with it, the demand for digital payments technology has moved onto the second half of the chessboard.

Canada was once a leader in Internet adoption, but it has been losing ground as the digital revolution goes mobile. Despite expensive broadband and wireless, four out of every five mobile phone users had access to the Internet by 2016. But lacking a coherent digital economy strategy, Canada's shift into the information age has progressed haphazardly. When it comes to payments, collaboration among financial institutions, mobile carriers, technology companies, retailers, users, and regulators, so vital for a big country with a small population, has been sadly lacking. The result is that Canada is likely heading towards either the Groundhog Day or Tech-tonic Shift scenarios, marked by fragmentation and poor regulation. Neither is an especially attractive outcome.

Canadians were early adopters of Internet technology, and they spend more time online than any other nation, including highly wired societies such as China, South Korea, and the United States. According to ComScore, the average Canadian browsed the Web for 36.7 hours a month in 2014. Americans had the second heaviest usage, at 35.2 hours a month. Fully 89 per cent of Canadians had become Internet users by 2015, up from 80 per cent in 2010.[31] A 2012 Statistics Canada survey, the latest available, showed that the number of seniors using the Web, the last hold-outs of the Internet age, grew by 20 per cent in the previous two years with 48 per cent of respondents sixty-five or older saying they were Internet users.[32]

Online shopping has also exploded. The value of orders placed by Canadians hit $30.1 billion in 2014, up 24 per cent from 2013, and Forrester Research has predicted that Canadians will spend more than $39 billion online by 2019, representing 9.5 per cent of all retail purchases. The growth of online shopping reflects not only volumes but also the breadth of goods and services being bought and sold. Some 42 per cent of Canadians reported buying clothing items online, and 40 per cent booked travel. Media sales were also popular, and many respondents bought books, music, apps, and show tickets.

Although the information is a bit dated, other trends for 2012 in the Statistics Canada report show how rapidly and broadly Canadians are adopting new technology:

• Social media usage was up almost 15 per cent, with about two-thirds of Canadians using social media. More than 20 million Canadians had a Facebook page.

- Use of voice or video calling nearly doubled, with 43 per cent of Canadians using a service like Skype or FaceTime, up from 24 per cent in 2010.
- Online video viewing has also grown steadily. Just over half of Canadians downloaded or watched movies or video clips, up almost 20 per cent in two years.[33]

A.T. Kearney's global retail e-commerce index ranked Canada as the eleventh most attractive online retail market in 2015.[34] The survey is based on the following:

- Online market size (40 per cent). Score: 10.6
- Technology adoption and consumer behaviour (20 per cent), including Internet penetration, purchasing trends, and technology adoption. Score: 81.4
- Infrastructure (20 per cent) as measured by the number of credit cards per household and the availability and quality of logistics providers. Score: 88.9
- Growth potential for online retail sales (20 per cent). Score: 23.6

Canada is highly rated on technology adoption, consumer behaviour, and infrastructure but does less well on market size and growth potential. But market size and growth will improve as millennials, who now make up about 23 per cent of the Canadian workforce, become the dominant group, at 40 per cent by 2020. Boomers' representation will shrink from 24 per cent to 13 per cent and Gen Xers' from 37 per cent to 35 per cent.

Although three-quarters of Canadians used a smartphone or tablet to access the Internet by 2016, double the proportion in 2010, mobile phone penetration ranks far behind that in other developed countries, according to the World Bank.[35] That lag is likely due to the high cost of mobile subscriptions in Canada compared with many other countries. Still, despite the high cost, over 90 per cent of younger Canadians aged sixteen to twenty-four were mobile Internet users.

According to a recent Catalyst survey, Canadians consistently cite paying bills and checking bank accounts as two of the top ten things they do on their mobile devices.[36] Over half were using their phones to deposit cheques, an amazing adoption rate for a service that barely existed in 2014. Over 30 per cent of Canadians expect to make more mobile payments in the next year despite concerns about security, especially among people over thirty-five. For those comfortable making mobile payments, the top five methods are, in descending order: PayPal, Starbucks, Apple Pay, Google Wallet, and specific store apps.

In summary, although mobile payments got off to a slow start in Canada, their popularity is sure to accelerate as banks and wireless carriers expand their coverage. With three-quarters of Canadians having access to the Internet through a tablet or smartphone, mobile is already a force to be reckoned with for retailers and bankers. According to a newly released Google report, eight in ten smartphone owners never leave home without their device. Just over half log onto social media every day, and 35 per cent would give up TV before their smartphone.

But Collaboration Is Minimal

Although there has been some collaboration on mobile payments between financial institutions and wireless carriers, this has not extended nearly as far as it should. Time is now running out, and it appears that the Tech-tonic Shift scenario, marked by slow regulation and fierce competition, is the most likely outcome for the Canadian payments system. Sadly, this is also the worst scenario for the banks, because it suggests they will be outflanked quite rapidly by more nimble and innovative newcomers.

Recent developments underscore the threat to the banks. At one end of the spectrum, RBC Financial has launched its own app, RBC Wallet, powered by the RBC Secure Cloud, with the express purpose of maintaining control over its customers. At the other extreme, CIBC signed on to the ill-fated Suretap open payments system, a joint venture between the three dominant telecom operators Rogers, Telus, and Bell. Suretap allowed each bank's customers to load their own cards, and it accepted loyalty cards from most merchants.[37] But the three companies halted the project in May 2016. One of the main reasons for Suretap's failure was that it levied loading fees on cards, while proprietary wallets such as Apple Pay, Android Pay, Samsung Pay, and RBC Wallet charged nothing. Since then, a joint venture between TD Canada Trust and PC Financial has launched an open wallet, known as Ugo, for TD, PC Financial, and certain loyalty cards. But, as of November 2016, Ugo's owners had been unable to attract others to use the wallet.

This fragmented approach could relegate the Canadian banks to the backwaters of the mobile payments business. Unless their approach changes, and changes soon, they have little hope of competing effectively against the likes of Apple, Google, PayPal, and Samsung. In our view, Canadians would respond favourably to a wallet that provides access to public and private sector services, such as medical records, driver's license and insurance records, loyalty cards, payment cards, receipts and record keeping, and so on. Such a solution however, requires close cooperation among governments, financial institutions, retailers, mobile carriers, and users.

The Tech-tonic Shift scenario provides some clues as to how Canada might deal with this challenging environment. It imagines that in 2021 – following a series of disruptions and mounting concerns about the future of Canada's payments industry – the deputy minister of finance will urge the finance minister to convene a new payments task force. The group would be asked to address five vexing issues:

1. Whether and how to complete the phase-out of cash and cheques.
2. Strategies to combat online fraud and strengthen digital identification and authentication.
3. Ways to improve public understanding of the digital payments system.
4. Options for more effective collection of tax online.
5. Ways to streamline the payments system and reduce costs to users.

All in all, it is hard to escape the conclusion that the next five years will be a time of rapid and unsettling change in the payments system.

Addressing those realities will require an inclusive and learning-based approach, with all parties willing to collaborate and learn from one another. One way of meeting this challenge would be to set up an independent organization with a mandate to encourage dialogue, spell out plausible strategies, and propose ways to implement them.

The big question is: Will it be too late?

CHAPTER SEVEN

Long Live the Branch

When the music stops ... things will be complicated. But as long as the music is playing, you've got to get up and dance. We're still dancing.

Charles O. Prince, former Citigroup CEO, July 2007[1]

One might be forgiven for attributing Chuck Prince's infamous remark, made almost a decade ago, to the chief executive of a Canadian bank in 2016.

Since the early 1990s, the Canadian banks have squeezed more and more profit from their retail banking operations by pushing more products through a proliferation of sales channels – branches, ATMs, telephone and online banking, and, most recently, mobile apps. And all the while, they have kept ratcheting up their fees. The banks have talked a good game about using these various outlets to keep customers happy, but in reality they have failed to deliver. As we noted in a previous chapter, their net promoter scores, which measure customer satisfaction, have been abysmal. Yet with their protected oligopoly stifling competition, profits have continued to swell. The banks have been eager enough to learn from agile new competitors, but in the end, those upstarts have been either crushed or acquired by the Bay Street giants.

To put it another way, the banks' formula for success has been to maximize short-term profits by growing and milking their long-established domestic branch banking business rather than transforming themselves into masters of ground-breaking twenty-first-century technologies that would enable them to offer immediate delivery of their services. Even as customers find less use for branches and ATMs, the banks have made the bulk of their investments in those outdated bricks-and-mortar facilities.

At the same time, however, the Canadian banks are no longer the hard-to-tell-apart behemoths that they used to be. They have started to differentiate themselves, largely based on their investments outside Canada. RBC, having tried and failed to make its mark in U.S. retail banking, is now building its global capital markets and wealth management business. TD Bank has become the ninth-largest U.S. commercial bank, thanks to two east coast acquisitions, Commerce Bank and Banknorth. Similarly, Bank of Montreal has become a sizeable player in the U.S. Midwest and the twenty-fourth largest retail bank in the United States with its acquisitions of Chicago's Harris Bancorp in 1984 and Wisconsin-based Marshall & Ilsley in 2011.[2] Scotiabank continues to expand overseas, mostly in Latin and South America and Asia. Only CIBC, until its recent acquisition of Chicago-based Private Bancorp, and National Bank have stuck largely to their home turf.

The banks' thrust to broaden their horizons has, however, come at a price. Their recent investments, especially outside Canada, have yet to produce much value for shareholders.[3] Their protected Canadian businesses produce eye-popping profits – a return on equity of between 30 per cent and 51 per cent on the retail side and between 12 per cent and 31 per cent in wholesale banking. Yet the banks' overall return on equity ranges from only 12 per cent to 20 per cent, suggesting massive cross-subsidization from domestic retail operations to international and wholesale banking activities. This might be considered a sound strategy if the banks were building sustainable customer-focused franchises using the latest technology, but they are not. Instead, they are doubling down on the traditional branch-banking business model at home and in costly foreign acquisitions, an approach that is increasingly open to question.

Both TD Financial and Bank of Montreal have only a modest presence in the rapidly consolidating U.S. market. Industry leaders insist that they must be either number one or number two in each local market to achieve an adequate return for shareholders, although recent returns suggest that even this may not be enough. Likewise, Scotiabank has specialized in exporting traditional banking methods to emerging markets in Latin America and Asia, making it the most international of the big six. But banks in those countries are leap-frogging traditional bricks-and-mortar banking, moving directly to a financial services model dominated by mobile devices and apps, and Scotiabank has been slow to catch up.

Canadian Retail Banking: A Gusher of Profits

Banking in Canada is a protected oligopoly. No one can buy more than 20 per cent of a Canadian bank without approval from the minister of finance. Only regulated financial institutions – in other words, banks and credit unions – have direct access to the payments system and to deposit insurance. The not-so-surprising result is that the industry earns unusually juicy returns. The return on equity for Canadian retail banking averages about 40 per cent, far in excess of their cost of capital and much higher than other countries (see table 7.1). This is true even though Canada has twice as many bankers as the average G20 country, and even though our bankers earn twice as much on average as other Canadian workers.[4]

These numbers may look impressive, but they mask a fundamental weakness: the banks continue to rely on an outdated business model, and their dominance gives them little incentive to change. To illustrate the point, we recall a conversation we had in 2013 with a young business consultant whose firm had just won a multimillion-dollar contract to help one of the big banks redesign its branch account-opening process. After listening to him describe the size and complexity of the project, we asked him what he thought of it. His response was crisp: "I don't know why they don't just write an app." His insight captures the dilemma that the banks face.

Millennials now spend more time using mobile phone apps than surfing the Web. When it comes to millennials' banking, branches

Table 7.1. Canadian banks' retail revenue, profits, and return on equity, 2016

	BMO	TD	BNS	RBC	CIBC	NBC
Retail % of total revenue						
Canada	56.1	58.9	46.2	58.1	71.5	71.9
Other	22.0	27.6	37.3	10.3		
Retail % of Total Net Income						
Canada	61.2	64.4	50.7	61.8	76.1	57.1
Other	23.3	30.8	31.6	5.2		
Retail ROE (%)						
Canada	**n/a**	**41.9**	**30.0**	**32.6**	**51.0**	**n/a**
Other	n/a	8.8	12.8			

a. Retail includes personal and commercial banking, wealth management, and insurance (except RBC international re-insurance business).
b. BMO Canada includes 82.5% of wealth management. The bank did not disclose retail banking ROE for Canada and the United States separately; the combined ROE was 15.9%. In 2012, the last year that Canadian retail banking was disclosed it was 38.9%, in line with the other Canadian banks.
c. In 2015, BNS disclosed domestic retail return on economic equity of 29.7%. In 2016, it revised its disclosure to return on common equity (a less accurate reflection of performance in our view) and restated its 2015 domestic retail return on equity to 21.0%. This suggests to us that domestic retail return on economic equity in 2016 was above 30%.
d. RBC retail income includes personal and commercial banking, 50% of wealth management, and 60% of insurance profits.
e. CIBC retail includes personal and commercial banking and two-thirds of wealth management.

Source: Authors' Analysis, 2016 Fourth Quarter Financial Supplementary Information

are a throwback to the Dark Ages. They expect immediate access to any product or service wherever they happen to be. If they want to open a bank account, they expect to be able to download the application form, complete it online, authenticate their identity, and start making deposits and withdrawals right away. But the Canadian banks don't do things that way. Antiquated regulations – partly designed to stop money laundering and terrorist financing – have made it much easier for the upstart non-banks to provide services in this way.

Online banking is now by far the most popular way for Canadians to handle their day-to-day finances. The Canadian Bankers' Association reports that more than three-quarters of Canadians completed an online banking transaction in 2015, up from 8 per cent in 2000. Some 68 per cent now use the Internet (51 per cent use a PC and 17 per cent a mobile device) as their main means of banking. Furthermore, online banking is popular among all ages. Even half of the over fifty-fives say that they do most of their banking from a computer or mobile device. By contrast, according to the bankers' association, only 12 per cent of Canadians now do most of their banking at a branch, down from 29 per cent in 2000.[5]

Canadians are also rapidly warming to mobile banking (figure 7.1). By 2016, 45 per cent of them were conducting transactions from a smartphone or tablet, up from just 5 per cent in 2010. Almost 40 per cent say their use of mobile banking is growing. That is especially true among young people, but even 21 per cent of those over sixty-five say they are doing more mobile banking. More than half expect to conduct their banking from a mobile device in the near future. The reason is not hard to find. According to research by Bain

Figure 7.1. Canadians are rapidly adopting mobile banking

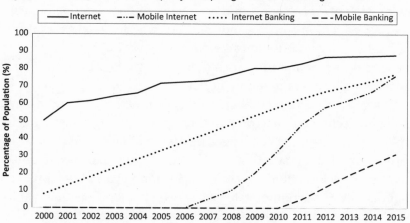

Source: Authors' analysis, Canadian Bankers' Association, World Bank, Catalyst Surveys

& Company, a transaction in a branch is three times more likely to annoy a customer than when it is done from a smartphone or tablet.

The trend is gaining momentum even though online banking is far less user-friendly in Canada than in the United States. Over 30 per cent of new account applications in the United States were completed online in 2015, but almost none in Canada. Opening a bank account north of the border is a laborious process. It requires completing and signing a paper application and signature card so that the bank can comply with "know your client" regulations. The bank must verify two pieces of identification, one of which must be government-issued photo ID. It must photocopy these documents and keep them on file for as long as the account remains open. The good news is that Canadian regulators recently agreed to change their approach to anti-money-laundering and anti-terrorist-financing legislation so that banks can open accounts online and improve their account-opening apps.

It costs an average of $250 to $350 for a bank to open a new account in Canada. That's a lot of money for what ought to be a simple process. It amazes us that the banks are not aggressively reducing these costs by getting rid of signature cards and all the other cumbersome paperwork that they now require. The same is true of many other parts of their business. Maintaining a chequing account costs a bank about $350 a year. Here too, there seems to be scope for big cost savings, which, in turn, would clear the way for lower fees. Why do banks still send out paper statements? Why do they charge fees for wire transfers that prop up a dying part of their business? It all smacks of a business mired in inertia.[6]

This gap between, on the one hand, customers' expectations and emerging technology, and on the other, the banks' ingrained bureaucracy is just one of the challenges the industry faces. Under the old banking model, the size of a bank's branch network was assumed to bear a direct relation to its share of the market and the growth of that market. Sure enough, table 7.2 shows that the Canadian banks eliminated almost 1,500 branches between 1990 and 2005 as more than 95 per cent of transactions moved to ATMs and point-of-sale terminals. Yet, strangely, most started adding branches again in the

Table 7.2. Number of branches and ATMs in Canada, 1990–2015

	BMO	BNS	RBC	TD	CIBC	NBC	Total
Number of Branches							
1990	1,090	1,149	1,617	910	1,527	650	6,943
1995	1,055	1,143	1,577	955	1,390	629	6,749
2000	983	1,131	1,333	1,355	1,197	586	6,585
2005	968	954	1,104	1,014	1,061	457	5,558
2010	910	1,024	1,209	1,127	1,069	442	5,781
2015	939	1,013	1,275	1,165	1,125	452	5,969
Number of ATMs							
1990	1,163	768	3,086	991	1,914	397	8,319
1995	1,763	1,295	3,956	1,966	2,990	624	12,594
2000	1,987	2,136	4,209	2,836	4,310	802	16,820
2005	1,952	2,624	3,906	2,407	3,801	788	15,478
2010	2,076	2,998	4,227	2,733	3,801	869	16,704
2015	3,442	3,567	4,816	2,809	3,936	930	19,500

Big six banks represent: (1) 39.3% of ATMs in Canada in 2000 http://thebankwatch.com/category/atm; (2) 30.3% of ATMs in Canada in 2005 http://thebankwatch.com/category/atm; and (3) 31.6% of ATMs in Canada in 2012 ATM Benchmarking Study 2012 and Industry Report; Interesting facts: http://www.theglobeandmail.com/life/atms-40-years-of-24-hour-dough/article1205709/

Source: Authors' Analysis, Annual reports and links provided above

mid-2000s on the outdated assumption that an expanding bricks-and-mortar network was still necessary to drive growth. This logic makes no sense, given the acceleration in Internet banking since the late 1990s, and overwhelming evidence that the vast majority of customers prefer online to branch banking.[7]

Why Are the Banks Still Spending on Branches?

The handsome returns generated in the banks' protected home market and their limited domestic growth opportunities have spurred them to try and repeat their success beyond Canada's borders. Unfortunately for them, competition has blunted that quest, especially in the United States, where most large banks, other than Wells Fargo, are struggling to earn a double-digit return on equity. Earning an economic return – in other words, a return higher than their cost of capital – has proven a major challenge.

The most fruitful strategy for foreign expansion since the introduction of the Internet in the mid-1990s has been the direct bank, without branches. ING launched a U.S. version of its ING Direct savings bank in 2000. In September 2007, ING Direct acquired 104,000 customers and FDIC-insured assets from the failed virtual bank NetBank. In June 2011, Capital One purchased ING Direct USA from ING for US$9 billion. Not only did ING Direct create value for its shareholders, its net promoter scores were among the highest in the industry. In other words, customers loved it. This direct-banking approach would not only provide Canadian banks with growth but protect them should those mouth-watering Canadian returns decline.

Most of the Canadian banks' foreign forays have ended in failure, or something close to it. RBC tried its hand at retail banking in the United States for ten years but eventually sold its North Carolina-based subsidiary, Centura, at a loss in 2011. TD Bank has sunk more than US$20 billion into an extensive retail network along the eastern seaboard, yet has achieved the number one or two market share in just two small states – Vermont and New Hampshire. Similarly, Bank of Montreal has spent thirty years building a franchise in the Midwest but, after all that time, has gained solid footholds in only Illinois and Wisconsin. Bank of Montreal's business may be an attractive takeover target now that the U.S. market is consolidating, and it faces formidable competition from the likes of Wells Fargo, Bank of America, JP Morgan Chase, Citibank, and US Bancorp.

Bank of Montreal – An Attractive Midwest Franchise

BMO generates 90 per cent of its profits from retail banking and wealth management. It aims to deliver a "great customer experience," yet it continues to tread much the same path as its rivals. It uses the same tools to boost customer loyalty, including using loyalty scores to measure branch employees' performance. BMO's slogan, "Making Money Make Sense," has failed to generate much enthusiasm among existing or prospective customers. All in all, it has done little to distinguish itself from its rivals and has lagged them in revenue growth.

BMO's wealth management business has more to brag about. It has so far been the only bank to promote exchange-traded funds (ETFs) as an alternative to mutual funds and, as noted in an earlier chapter, was the first bank to offer a robo-advisory service. BMO relaunched its Advice-Direct self-serve portfolio management platform in 2011 and developed a new financial planning process to support tactical investing programs. These programs have been very popular with U.S. investors, largely because they focus on producing real positive returns rather than simply doing better than the competition. The payoff has been that BMO is the only one of the big six banks that has expanded its Canadian wealth management business over the past ten years without any major acquisitions.

Even so, most of its growth has come from commercial banking in the U.S. Midwest. After acquiring Harris Bancorp in 1984, BMO made a number of small acquisitions to bolster its presence in the greater Chicago area, whose economy is two-thirds the size of Canada's. The bank took a big step forward in July 2011 with the acquisition of Wisconsin's Marshall & Ilsley Bank for US$4.9 billion. The takeover more than doubled BMO's branch network in the Midwest and substantially strengthened its wealth management business. BMO Harris now operates in eight states. It ranks first or second in Wisconsin and Illinois but has a much smaller footprint in the other six states – Arizona, Florida, Indiana, Kansas, Minnesota, and Missouri.

BMO has not disclosed details of its U.S. retail banking performance since 2012, but as profits have increased marginally, it is likely not covering its cost of capital.[8] We doubt that BMO is willing to double or triple its U.S. investment to achieve a strong competitive position in all eight states. If not, perhaps the time has come for the Canadians to find a buyer for BMO Harris. Such a move would undoubtedly please BMO shareholders eager to see the bank retreat from businesses and regions where it cannot replicate its mouth-watering Canadian returns.

Toronto-Dominion Bank – Falling Behind on the East Coast

TD's growth strategy has also focused on building a regional retail branch-banking bulwark in the United States. It bought control of Maine-based Banknorth for C$5.1 billion in 2005, and spent another C$7 billion over the next two years to acquire Hudson United Bancorp, Interchange Financial Services Corp., plus the 49 per cent of Banknorth that it didn't already own. It then merged Banknorth with New Jersey-based Commerce Bancorp, which it had acquired for C$8.5 billion in 2008, and added another three small Florida banks. Together, this string of acquisitions has given the Canadian bank a network of 1,327 branches in seventeen states stretching along the eastern seaboard from Maine to Florida.

TD makes the bold claim that it is "America's most convenient bank." True, it has won accolades for customer service, based largely on the TD Canada Trust model. But this strategy has yet to translate into respectable financial results. Although revenue and net income have grown at a healthy 20 per cent a year since 2005, expenses have risen even faster. The U.S. bank's cost-to-income ratio deteriorated from 54.7 per cent to 67.3 per cent in 2012, and its return on equity has remained stubbornly low, edging up from 5.4 per cent in 2005 to 8.2 per cent in 2015, still far below the 42.8 per cent return achieved by its Canadian operations. TD noted in its 2012 annual report that its U.S. retail arm needed to earn at least a 9 per cent return on equity to generate a reasonable return to shareholders. Given the extra capital banks are now required to carry under Basel III, our definition of a satisfactory return is more like a sustained 10 to 12 per cent. Whatever the case, there is little doubt that TD's U.S. banking operations produce returns below an acceptable threshold.

The main problem for TD's U.S. operations is scale. Despite the acquisition spree, it is first or second in market share in only two states – Vermont and New Hampshire. TD is among the top four in three other states – Maine, Massachusetts, and New Jersey. Its presence is insignificant in the remaining twelve states. TD has several options for beefing up its mid-Atlantic seaboard operations but only one avenue to gain critical mass for its franchise in south-eastern states, and that is to buy SunTrust Bancorp, with a market value of US$29.5 billion. However, we have serious doubts about the wisdom of spending another US$30 billion or more on traditional U.S. retail banking at a time when the industry is struggling to earn a double-digit return on equity and to compete with the new technology-driven players.

Bank of Nova Scotia – Canada's Only Global Bank

With 21 million customers spread across fifty-five countries, Scotiabank is Canada's most geographically diverse bank by far. It has generated most of its growth beyond Canada's borders through acquisitions, starting in most cases with small, low-cost beachheads in Latin and South America and Asia.[9] Its preferred tactic has been to start off with a 51 per cent stake, then wait and see whether expectations are met, and if so, to buy up the rest.

Scotiabank gained a foothold in the Caribbean more than 150 years ago by financing trade in lumber, rum, and molasses. It now has a market share of more than 15 per cent in the region. Its long history and deep knowledge have helped these operations earn a consistent return on equity of more than 30 per cent, comparable to its Canadian retail operations.

Scotiabank now prefers to be a small fish in a large number of ponds. In most cases, its foreign outposts have a market share below 10 per cent, which means that they have little brand recognition or pricing power and struggle to generate the savings that size typically brings. Since most of Scotiabank's international retail profits have come from its long-standing branch network in the Caribbean, its other overseas businesses appear to have produced a return on equity of less than 10 per cent over the past five years. One cannot help but wonder why Scotiabank has not taken advantage of the direct platform it acquired in ING Direct (now Tangerine) to grow its international operations.

Combining the Caribbean operations with the bank's other international business has produced a return on equity of about 13 per cent over the past five years. Taken together, Scotiabank's international operations appear to offer its shareholders a modest return. Discounting the impressive results from the Caribbean, however, the bank's offshore expansion has been eroding shareholder value for the past decade.

RBC Dumps U.S. Retail for Global Capital Markets

Gord Nixon, who headed Canada's biggest bank for twelve years, sounded a rueful note when he announced his retirement in December 2013: "The one thing we wished we had done differently," Mr. Nixon said, "was deal more quickly with the underperforming assets in the U.S. We had a second-tier franchise in a tough market – the U.S. south-east."[10]

RBC gained a sizeable foothold in U.S. retail banking with its US$3.5 billion acquisition of North Carolina-based Centura Bank in 2001, followed six years later by the acquisition of Alabama National Bancorp for US$1.6 billion. Though RBC Centura had a respectable 439 branches and US$27 billion in assets in 2010, it was no match for SunTrust, a strong regional player with 1,685 branches and US$130 billion in assets. Recognizing that RBC would need to spend heavily to reach the scale necessary to succeed in a highly competitive market, the Canadians finally pulled the plug in 2011, unloading Centura to PNC Financial for US$3.6 billion. The price was less than Centura's book value.

RBC figured that it could generate better returns by investing in its existing businesses, going after carefully targeted wealth management acquisitions, and returning capital to shareholders through dividends and share buybacks. The bank has maintained some U.S. operations to serve the needs of its Canadian retail customers, and it continues to provide banking services to its two remaining U.S. divisions, RBC Wealth Management and RBC Capital Markets.

The wealth management business received a shot in the arm in November 2015 when RBC paid US$5.4 billion for City National Bank, a private bank servicing wealthy individuals, many of them Hollywood stars. RBC is also the world's sixth-largest clearing and custody provider, serving more than 200 investment advisory firms and 4,000 independent advisors. But this is less impressive than it sounds, given that the market is heavily concentrated among the top three players.

RBC has been active in U.S. capital markets for more than a century and has built a significant presence in this business. Indeed, more than 40 per cent of all the bank's capital markets employees are based in the United States, mostly in New York. RBC Capital Markets ranks as the tenth-largest global investment bank. Since 2009, it has expanded its sales and research coverage from nine to thirteen industry sectors and has added more than 270 new borrowing clients, bringing its U.S. loan portfolio to US$65 billion. RBC's capital markets strategy is based on the assumption that securitization will continue to bypass the traditional way that banks raise money for their clients, and that it can make a healthy return as an intermediary between borrowers and investors in securities markets.

According to research by Coalition, the world's largest investment banks chalked up an average return on equity of 6.7 per cent in 2015.[11] As table 7.3 shows, the Canadian banks' capital markets arms averaged a return of 17.4 per cent. In this business, too, they appear to have benefited handsomely from their protected oligopoly.

The banks, supported by a number of large pension funds, wrapped themselves in the maple leaf in 2011 to acquire TMX Group, the company that operates Canada's main securities markets, notably the Toronto Stock Exchange. The banks even named their takeover vehicle Maple Group Acquisition Corp., using it to thwart a proposed deal by TMX to merge with the London Stock Exchange. Rather than face global competition, the banks – with the

Table 7.3. Canadian banks' capital markets business, 2016

	BMO	TD	BNS	RBC	CIBC	BNC
Wholesale % of Total Revenue	20.7	8.8	16.8	20.7	19.4	29.8
Wholesale % of Total Net Income	27.4	10.0	21.3	21.7	25.1	44.6
ROE %	16.2	15.5	12.6	12.2	30.6	n/a

Source: Authors' Analysis, Fourth Quarter 2016 Supplementary Financial Information exception of RBC – have relied for the bulk of their capital markets business on companies and governments that are either too small or too unsophisticated to access the more competitive markets beyond Canada's borders. RBC has paid a price, with the lowest return on capital from the capital markets business among the five banks that disclose this data.

Canada's share of global capital markets is a meagre 3 per cent, and that puts the banks on the horns of a dilemma. Big companies have a choice – they can deal with the global giants based in New York, London, and, increasingly, Beijing and Shanghai. On the other hand, small companies looking for funds are coming to realize that they can market themselves directly to private equity and venture capital investors. Yet the Canadian banks continue to earmark billions of dollars of capital for corporate and investment banking activities, funnelling profits from their Canadian retail franchises to sustain their capital market bragging rights. This is most true for RBC.

CIBC and National Bank Stay at Home

CIBC pulled in its horns after several costly missteps in the early 2000s. Over the course of a decade (mid-2000s to mid-2010s), the bank went from being Canada's second largest to the second smallest of the big six, and by early 2016, it was generating 85 per cent of its revenues and profits from Canada. The bank's CEO, Victor Dodig, said shortly after taking the reins in 2014: "The bank's strategy is to build a strong, innovative, relationship-oriented bank. It has a great team and strong franchise that has proven it can deliver consistent, sustainable results. Our opportunity now is to transform our bank and deliver growth. We will accelerate our transformation by focusing on three bank-wide priorities: Focusing on our clients; innovating for the future; and simplifying our bank."[12]

CIBC had spent much of the previous decade repairing damage done by its earlier mistakes, including several misguided forays into the United States. Its new retail banking strategy is reminiscent of the mid-1990s, when it began rolling out its two retail options – Imperial Service and Convenience Banking. The idea was to assign a personal relationship manager to the 20 per cent of customers with complex financial needs who generated more than four-fifths of the bank's retail profits. The "convenience" bank would provide dramatically streamlined services for the remaining 80 per cent of run-of-the-mill customers. Most of these customers' needs could be met with just seven products delivered online or from kiosks. Simplifying operations in this way meant that the convenience bank could halve operating costs even as it improved customer service.

Innovation was a hallmark of CIBC's strategy in the 1990s. The bank introduced the enormously popular Aerogold Visa card, which at one time boasted a market share of 98 per cent of all Canadian card-holders earning over $75,000 a year. It created Canada's first bank dedicated specifically to mortgages and dominated the mortgage brokerage business, both in origination and underwriting. It forged a partnership with the Loblaws supermarket chain to set up President's Choice Financial, which offered no-fee banking, lower lending and higher savings rates, and cash-back rewards for grocery purchases. It also formed joint ventures with Fiserv, a processing and payments specialist, and Hewlett Packard, the information technology company. These ventures enabled CIBC to outsource paper processing and other outdated systems with the goal of shedding them entirely as they become obsolete. After a fifteen-year hiatus, CIBC seemed to be returning to its innovation roots.

The bank signalled an abrupt U-turn in June 2016, ditching its Canada-only strategy with the proposed purchase of Chicago-based Private Bancorp. We predict that CIBC, like RBC, TD, and BMO before it, will find it difficult to earn a decent return for its shareholders from its new U.S. business, given the fiercely competitive market and the high price (US$5 billion) it paid to close the deal in June 2017. What's more, the challenges of integrating a sizeable acquisition are sure to distract management from its goal of recapturing CIBC's position as Canada's second-largest retail bank.

National Bank is the leading bank in Quebec and the financial institution of choice for many small and mid-sized companies throughout the country. It is the smallest of the big six but has branches in almost every province. National retreated from U.S.

commercial lending in the early 2000s and has focused on Quebec since then. Over the past decade, it has invested heavily in technology and process improvements. These investments are starting to pay off, as National has recently tied with TD for the highest net promoter scores among the big banks.

National has identified commercial banking and wealth management across Canada as specific growth areas to complement its Quebec franchise. It has also built a profitable niche business over the past fifteen years by providing white-label banking services to clients of other financial institutions outside Quebec, such as Investors Group, the mutual fund distributor based in Winnipeg. A subsidiary, National Bank Correspondent Network, offers clearing and back-office services to many independent full-service brokers across the country, and has become an important contributor to the parent's wealth management business. Finally, National has taken advantage of its francophone roots by making modest investments in banks in Cambodia and Mauritius, as well as in a West African banking and insurance group. All in all, National's disciplined strategy has kept it competitive with its bigger, Toronto-based rivals.

Change Is on the Way

A recent Google survey shows that as many as nine out of ten prospective buyers of financial products start their journeys online. For deposits and credit cards, 78 per cent of the research time is spent in front of a screen, up from 58 per cent in 2008. Those looking for mortgages and home loans do 62 per cent of their research online, spending more than eleven hours pondering their options before coming to a decision. More than three-quarters of those surveyed said that they had not heard of the product they finally chose at the time they started their research. According to another recent Google report, almost a third of customers who start their search with a preferred brand in mind end up choosing a different one. These numbers suggest that a bank's battle to win over a customer needs to start long before that individual enters a branch, and that more and more often, the first step is a mobile or online search.

The reality is that anyone who visits a bank branch these days is in a tiny – and dwindling – minority. For most transactions, the branch has become the least preferred channel for day-to-day banking. Why? Because it is inefficient, often inconvenient to get to, and of little use in today's hustle-and-bustle hyper-connected world, where value is measured in speed and responsiveness. For many of the same reasons, use of ATMs has also been sagging since 2010.

The branch has become the most visible evidence of the yawning gap between the services that banks want to push onto their customers and what those customers really want. For the banks, the branch is a vital source of revenue, a change from the past when it was viewed, more accurately, as a cost centre. For the past twenty years, the banks have given high priority to improving branches' financial viability by trying to attract more and more traffic to them. What customers want, however, is nothing more or less than top-notch service. As they see it, they are owed nothing less, given the steady advance in bank fees and charges. Partly for that reason, most now prefer to do their banking online if they possibly can. The irony is that branches are still popping up, mainly because banks are forcing customers into them to sign application forms and signature cards as a come-on to pitch other services. The branch certainly does not offer compelling value to the customer, or a compelling return to the bank.

The banks are now belatedly starting to get that message. Like other retail dinosaurs – think Blockbuster video stores, Barnes & Noble bookstores, and HMV record shops – the bank branch as we know it is very likely to disappear within the next ten years. Canada's six big banks incurred over $1 billion in pre-tax restructuring charges in 2015 and nearly $2 billion over the past two years.[13] Most of these charges were designed to help them cut operating costs and bring down their high cost ratios. They have so far trimmed their branch networks by only 1 to 2 per cent, but there is little doubt that they will wield the axe much more aggressively in the years ahead as they see the writing on those branch walls.

CHAPTER EIGHT

A Banking System for the Twenty-First Century

The biggest risk is not taking any risk ... In a world that's changing really quickly, the only strategy that is guaranteed to fail is not taking risks.

Mark Zuckerberg, Facebook founder

We return to the story of the frog in the boiling water. Like that hapless amphibian, although the Canadian banks have a zest for life, they have not noticed the extent of the danger surrounding them. For too long, government policy, which favours stability over innovation, has protected them. Those policies are now threatened by rapid changes in technology and social attitudes. Regulators continue to protect the status quo, but Canadian consumers, who previously had few other choices to manage their financial affairs, now find they have less and less need for their bank.

So, what can the banks do, not only to survive in the twenty-first century, but to prosper?

Caught in a Trap

In one sense, the banks deserve our sympathy. They are under pressure on several fronts. Stock market investors have ensnared them in expectations of ever-higher quarterly earnings, even as the banks' core businesses are under attack from disruptive technologies. Elsewhere, government policies aimed at promoting stability can no longer protect banks from the rising temperature of the waters around them. If the Canadian banks are to prosper, they must find ways of balancing stability with innovation by having more space to take risks. They must be encouraged to transform their business model to compete with the new generation of direct banks and to collaborate with the up-and-coming fintechs. As Mark Zuckerberg noted, sometimes the biggest risk is not taking any risk.

Clayton Christenson succinctly sums up the banks' predicament in his book *The Innovator's Dilemma*:

Simply put, when the best firms succeeded, they did so because they listened to their customers and invested aggressively in the technology, products and manufacturing capabilities that satisfied their customers' next-generation needs. But, paradoxically, when the best firms subsequently failed, it was for the same reasons – they listened responsively to their customers and invested aggressively in the technology, products and manufacturing capabilities that satisfied their customers' next-generation needs. This is one of the innovator's dilemmas: Blindly following the maxim that good managers should keep close to their customers can sometimes be a fatal mistake.

The conclusion, by established companies, that investing aggressively in disruptive technologies is not a rational decision for them to make, has three bases. First, disruptive products are simpler and cheaper; they generally promise lower margins, not greater profits. Second, disruptive technologies typically are first commercialized in emerging or insignificant markets. And third, leading firms' most profitable customers generally don't want, and indeed initially cannot use, products based on disruptive technologies. By and large, a disruptive technology is initially embraced by the least profitable customers in a market. Hence, most companies with a practiced discipline of listening to their customers and identifying new products that promise greater profitability and growth are rarely able to build a case for investing in disruptive technologies until it is too late.[1]

The innovator's dilemma is especially acute in the area of payments, the banks' most important business. The shift from private networks, proprietary systems, and point-of-sale devices to the mobile public Internet has made the payment process much simpler and cheaper, cutting into the banks' margins and profits. Mobile payments were first introduced in developing countries such as Kenya, Tanzania, Afghanistan, South Africa, and the Philippines. Finally, mobile payments and commerce are being embraced with most gusto by young, technology-savvy customers and less so by the banks' older – and most profitable – customers, who are slower to experiment with new technology and less trusting of open platforms and systems. The risk is that the banks' core payments business will rapidly shrink as their customers age and the new technology is more widely adopted.

Even so, the innovator's dilemma does not fully explain the banks' plight, because it focuses narrowly on changes in technology. The McKinsey Global Institute makes the point that four fundamental disruptive forces – accelerating technological change, urbanization, aging demographics, and globalization – are changing the world more rapidly and profoundly than most of us have yet grasped. The institute estimates that these changes are taking place ten times faster than the pace of change of the nineteenth-century Industrial Revolution, and at 300 times the scale, which means they will have roughly 3,000 times the impact. Much as waves can amplify one another, these trends are gaining strength, magnitude, and influence as they interact. Together, they are producing monumental change.[2] But while Canada is at the cutting edge of most of these changes, the trends do not favour the big six banks' present business model.

As noted in chapter 6, Canadians have been among the earliest adopters and heaviest users of the Internet and mobile technology. According to Statistics Canada's latest available data, 81 per cent of the population lived in urban centres in 2011. That number is expected to rise to 90 per cent by 2030, a similar proportion to that in the United Kingdom and the United States, further complicating the provision of services to the remaining 10 per cent spread across the second-largest land mass in the world. For those outside the major urban centres, mobile and online service delivery will be the only economically feasible option.

What's more, by 2020, as many Canadians will be older than sixty-five as are younger than fourteen. The proportion of working-age Canadians is projected to decline from 69 per cent in 2009 to 60 per cent in 2036, meaning that fewer young people will be available for entry-level jobs in dinosaur businesses like retail banking.

The World Bank focuses on three measures of global integration – trade, people, and finance. It is fair to say that, on all three counts, Canada is one of the most outward-looking countries in the world, with highly advanced communications and information technology, a government active in international organizations, an economy heavily dependent on trade, a population that travels abroad frequently, and a culturally diverse society. Canada's foreign trade makes up more than 60 per cent of GDP, compared with just 30 per cent for the United States. But we cannot expect to maintain this exemplary record in global integration without a strong and innovative financial services sector.

The implications of these changes for the banks are reflected in the attitudes of millennials – those born between 1982 and 2004:

The two biggest challenges facing bank incumbents are customer acquisition and user experience, both of which face reinvention in the light of drastically different consumer preferences. For example, Scratch found that half of all millennials surveyed do not believe their bank offers anything different from competitors, and over two-thirds would rather visit a dentist than hear what their bank has to say. Most believe that the way we access money and pay for goods and services will be totally different in five years, and that start-ups are positioned to overhaul finance. In fact, a third of millennials think that they won't need a bank at all and over two-thirds claim to be more excited about a new offering in financial services from a tech company such as Google or Apple than from their nationwide bank. Additionally, research conducted by the Pew Research Centre reveals that less than a third of millennials believe they will save enough money for retirement or homeownership, far fewer than any other generation.[3]

Emulating other sectors that have been turned upside down by the Internet, the new generation of fintechs are setting up a host of lending, investment, and payment businesses. Of more than 12,000 fintechs identified by McKinsey & Company, almost three-quarters are focused on retail banking, lending, wealth management, and payment systems for small and mid-sized firms. Whether we call them start-ups or upstarts, these pioneers, along with direct banks, are harnessing the mobile Internet, Cloud computing, social media, and modern portfolio theory to disrupt the financial system as we know it. There is no doubt in our minds that retail banking is on the verge of the same kind of earth-shaking disruption as has roiled newspapers, music, travel, and movies, to mention a few.

This entrepreneurial activity in retail financial services is following the pattern of creative destruction described by Joseph Schumpeter and outlined in an earlier chapter. To recap: Schumpeter noticed that healthy economies go through cycles of destruction that seem to release innovation and creativity. After a period of growth and a phase of consolidation, the pressures for a release of some kind can no longer be contained. If those pressures are bottled up, rigidity becomes unavoidable. And that is what is now happening in Canada's financial services sector. Unfortunately, Ottawa's policy of putting stability first, reinforced by the global response by bankers and regulators to the 2008 financial crisis, has strengthened the old branch-banking model and locked the system into a "rigidity trap." Research over the past twenty years has shown that innovation, especially entrepreneurial activity backed by new technology, fosters economic growth. This should send a clear message to policy makers that if Canada's big banks are to prosper, they need to find a better balance between stability and innovation.

But finding the right balance poses a tremendous challenge. Given our underdeveloped (especially for higher-risk issuers) provincially regulated capital markets, the federal government needs strong stable banks to support economic growth and help execute monetary policy. The authorities quite correctly want to ensure access to housing finance and small business loans, and to protect Canadians' savings. But they also dare not lose sight of the fact that the banks have held Canadians hostage for too long. Dissatisfied bank customers are now having their eyes opened to the many benefits that the fintechs offer, especially in wealth management and payments. The new products and services are often more convenient and less costly than anything the banks can currently offer. They also hold out the promise of cementing Canada's participation in the twenty-first-century information economy. Shouldn't we be rushing to embrace regulatory policies and business practices that would allow Canada's financial system to break free of the "rigidity trap" that now threatens to leave us in the dust?

We Need a Catalyst

History has shown that innovation needs a catalyst, often in the form of a crisis. Chances are that without such a shock to the system, the Canadian banks will keep ploughing the same furrow they have ploughed for the past fifteen or twenty years.[4] And why shouldn't they? Healthy profits and rising stock prices are hardly an incentive to pursue wrenching change. It could take a very long time for the message to percolate up and down Bay Street that practices that have served the banks well in the past are unlikely to do so in the future.

The fact is that the environment in which the banks operate is not conducive to rapid change. For a start, the post-2008 world is very different from that of the preceding two decades. Growth is likely to be flat, or "wobbly" as the *Economist* puts it, as the global economy shifts from the industrial age to the information age. Canada is expected to underperform, partly because of the downturn in commodity prices but also because banks, businesses, and governments have not made the investment in technology needed to deliver services over the mobile Internet.[5] Interest rates will likely remain low, perhaps even negative, for some time.

For the past 150 years, government policy has put the emphasis on stability. This stance paid off handsomely during the 2008 crisis, when the banks survived with only moderate support from the Bank of Canada. The banks also play an invaluable role in Canada's capital markets, bringing coherence to the fragmentation created by provincial oversight and the lack of a national securities market. Indeed, the banks now own most of the country's largest securities and derivatives exchange.

But as we have sought to show in earlier chapters, the pressures for change are mounting. It is hard to escape the conclusion that the biggest risk for Canada's big banks right now is to carry on in the risk-averse mode of business as usual. Given the importance of the financial services industry to Canada, policy makers have a responsibility to encourage catalysts that might bring about the change necessary for the Canadian banks to prosper in the information age.

In his presidential address to the American Finance Association in 1993, Michael Jensen identified four "control forces" that push corporations to resolve the problems caused by tensions between managers' decisions and the greater good of society.[6] Each of these forces could play a powerful role in propelling the banks into a new era:

1. *Internal governance*, spearheaded by the board of directors. Up to now, bank directors have been ineffective in nudging the banks to transform themselves. It is not clear that they have even tried. As the well-documented turnover in the Fortune 500 list of top companies shows, directors are notoriously bad at identifying changes that reshape their industry, and at forcing management to act before a crisis strikes.
2. *Capital markets*. Under the Bank Act, no single shareholder may own more than 20 per cent of a Canadian bank without the approval of the minister of finance. As a result, takeovers (hostile or not) are unlikely to propel change. Activist investors, who have driven transformation in many other sectors, have been reluctant to tackle Canada's big banks.
3. *Customers and suppliers*. A business that doesn't keep up with the times risks losing customers and suppliers. This is the most common driver of change but also the most destructive. Bankruptcy or restructuring usually results in huge upheavals, both financial and human, a situation everyone would like to avoid. The danger for the banks is that the lure of new forms of

payment, investing, and lending will prove irresistible to their existing and future customers, especially young ones. The main casualties will be the banks themselves.

4. *Politics and regulation.* Transformative change can only happen within the framework of a supportive political and regulatory environment. But ministers of finance, whatever their political stripe, have so far shown little inclination to address the lack of innovation and competition in the Canadian financial services industry. Instead, the focus has been on stability.

Consumers Have Been Held Hostage

Canadians have a love-hate relationship with the big banks. On one hand, they take justifiable pride in having one of the world's most stable banking systems.[7] But they are tired of high fees, poor service, and products that fall short of their needs. According to a recent study, no fewer than 75 per cent of Canadians are unhappy with their bank.[8] Until recently, there was not much they could do about that. But the emergence of direct banks and nimble financial technology companies, geared to consumers' needs, has raised the prospect of a wider choice at more competitive prices with more user-friendly technology. Today, customers can vote with their fingers, downloading apps for payments and borrowing and investing on their smartphones. The more apps they download, the farther away they move from old-line branch banking.

The banks also have a problem in that they have almost exhausted the growth opportunities from their traditional lending business. Consumers are heavily in debt and cannot afford to borrow more, especially given that interest rates may start rising again.[9] With the introduction of computerized credit scoring in the 1990s, Canadian banks' skill in pricing riskier loans has atrophied to the point where they no longer show much interest in providing small and mid-sized companies with the capital they need. In any case, the tighter capital requirements introduced since the financial crisis have lessened the attraction of this type of lending. Banks have recaptured some of the large corporate and institutional business they lost to the capital markets in the early 2000s, but these customers are bound to return to the markets as soon as they can find cheaper funding.

Growth in the banks' wealth management business will also remain anaemic. Their customers are unlikely to save much in future years without innovative new investment products and services that deliver the 3.5 per cent real returns that Canadians need to afford a comfortable retirement and educate their children. If American money managers can deliver such returns, why can't their Canadian counterparts do the same? New regulations that force banks to disclose their sky-high fees will provide another incentive for their customers to look elsewhere for portfolio management and advice. The banks' wealth management business is vulnerable to low-cost disruptors, such as Blackrock and other ETF distributors and tactical asset allocation funds, not to mention robo-advisors. Finally, the banks have benefited for the past seven years from a massive deposit windfall that could disappear if their customers find other investment alternatives. All in all, the only paths for the banks to expand their wealth management business are either through acquisitions or, for those willing to take some risks, by raising their game using imagination and innovation.

As for the lucrative payments business, technology companies are sure to keep chipping away at the banks' private networks, in the process eroding their huge profit margins. Customers are fed up with the fees banks charge, especially for payment-related services. Their dissatisfaction came through loud and clear in a 2013 forty-eight-hour survey conducted by Yahoo.ca. In response to the question "What more do you want from your bank?" no fewer than 83 per cent of almost 48,000 participants said that bank fees were too high. A cartoon in the *Toronto Star* captured consumer sentiment perfectly: "What do you think will happen if the country gets rid of the nickel?" Response: "The banks will only be able to dime us to death."[10]

Despite this simmering dissatisfaction, the Canadian banks went ahead with hefty fee increases on chequing accounts in April 2016, just two years after bumping up their transaction fees by as much as 500 per cent. It is hard to imagine such tactics winning many hearts or minds. Far from it. The fastest-growing financial institutions right now are the credit unions, which charge lower fees than banks, and three no-fee online banks, Tangerine (owned by Scotiabank), PC Financial (a joint venture between Loblaws and CIBC), and EQ Bank (launched in January 2016). The banks' tactics also risk pushing their customers into the arms of the fintech players, or technology giants such as Apple, Google, Samsung, PayPal, Amazon, and Uber.

As Brett King observed in the subtitle of his book *Bank 3.0,* "Banking is no longer somewhere you go, but something you do." It is far more convenient, faster, and usually cheaper these days to use a mobile device to make a payment, transfer money, apply for a loan, or trade securities than to trek to a bank branch. New technology is alleviating concerns about security and privacy, which, in any case, are less of an issue for the millennial generation than convenience, speed, and cost. This revolution is rapidly making obsolete the branches, ATMs, point-of-sale terminals, computer systems, processing centres, and other infrastructure on which today's banks are built.

Over the past decade and a half, almost all the Canadian banks have sought, at one time or another, to extend their presence into new territory, on the assumption that the old branch-banking model will survive and flourish. All five of the biggest banks, most recently CIBC, have invested tens of billions of dollars in questionable acquisitions beyond Canada's borders. Rather than investing the lucrative returns from their Canadian retail operations in new technology and in innovative products and services, they have doubled down on the old branch-banking model, especially in the United States. Even in Canada, the banks have added hundreds of new branches and ATMs, just at a time when customers are finding less and less use for them.

How the future unfolds will hinge on Canadians' willingness to move to mobile banking technology. As we have described in chapter 7, three-quarters of Canadians preferred online banking to using a branch or ATM, up from 8 per cent in 2000. An ever-growing number of Canadians are embracing mobile devices with data plans, a sure harbinger of a massive swing towards mobile banking.

Smartphone adoption has grown exponentially from 33 per cent of mobile phones in 2010 to 57 per cent in 2012, 68 per cent in 2014, and 81 per cent in 2016. It should therefore come as no surprise that the popularity of mobile banking apps has exploded from 5 per cent in 2010 to 44 per cent in 2016. Now that almost all of us have the means to do our banking, investing, and payments in the palm of our hand, the branches and ATMs that have been such a familiar sight on streets and in shopping malls – indeed, that have been the very essence of a bank – will soon be going the way of the dodo.

Canada has long been an over-banked nation. It is home to almost double the number of bankers relative to population size of other OECD countries (see table 8.1). If their average was applied to Canada, we would have 165,000 fewer jobs in the banking sector, and would spend $14.1 billion less in compensation. Eliminating these jobs would shrink the banks' operating costs from 2.06 per cent to 1.61 per cent of their assets. But these cutbacks would need to be just the starting point if Canada's big banks were truly aiming to become more competitive against the fintech upstarts. They would also need to close branches, haul away ATMs, replace outdated computer systems and huge processing centres, and invest heavily in cutting-edge products and services. Such drastic action is not a choice; it's a do-or-die necessity. Retail banking in Canada, with its 40 per cent return on equity, is far too attractive a business for an ambitious financial services entrepreneur to ignore. In this sense, the banks have set themselves up to become the victims of their own success.

The trouble is, the chances that the Canadian banks will carry out such a far-reaching transformation without a push from their stakeholders are not much higher than zero. Regulators are focused on protecting the status quo. Investors and analysts expect the banks to churn out quarterly earnings growth to justify their share prices. Senior managers – and many other employees – receive bonuses based on meeting those earnings targets. Most employees also own shares in their bank, either directly through stock options and deferred share units or indirectly through pension and mutual funds. It is clearly in their self-interest to work as hard as they can to meet those short-term targets, and – to paraphrase Chuck Prince, the former Citibank CEO – "to keep dancing until the music stops."[11]

Table 8.1. Canada is over-banked: Productivity in Financial Services in the OECD, 2009–10

2009–2010	Total Assets for all Banks US$ tns	Number of Bankers ('000s)	Number Bankers per Capita x 1,000	Number Bankers per 1,000 workers	Average Banker Total Comp US$ 000s	Net Revenue as % of Total Assets	Operating Expense as % of Total Assets	Financials & Insurance as % of GDP
Canada	3.1	354	10.5	19.2	85.5	3.21	2.06	6.6
US.	14.4	2,303	7.5	14.8	77.6	4.66	2.86	8.5
France	8.8	422	6.7	14.7	102.2	1.44	0.90	4.3
Germany	8.1	634	7.7	15.2	88.3	1.65	1.25	4.1
Japan	7.9	302	2.4	4.6	91.4	1.38	0.87	6.0
Italy	4.5	329	5.5	13.2	91.9	2.22	1.40	4.8
Spain	4.2	263	5.7	11.4	93.4	2.34	0.97	4.2
Netherlands	3.9	110	6.7	12.3	202.0	1.53	1.06	7.2
Switzerland	2.3	101	13.0	21.2	211.8	1.92	1.46	10.4
Ireland	2.0	38	5.1	17.3	126.0	1.15	0.44	9.1
Belgium	1.6	66	6.1	13.7	108.9	1.20	0.99	5.9
Korea	1.2	115	2.4	4.7	54.4	2.38	1.17	6.1
Sweden	1.1	45	4.8	9.1	127.2	1.92	1.11	3.5
Mexico	0.4	167	1.6	–	38.7	6.68	3.09	6.9
Poland	0.3	175	4.6	10.1	21.9	4.81	2.65	3.9
Israel	0.3	49	6.5	–	78.7	3.78	2.45	11.9
Chile	0.2	51	3.0	–	3.9	5.24	2.36	4.7

Source: OECD Stats Database, CANSIM 218–0023, US. BEA, Reuters, Kaz Jana Analysis

Without a catalyst of some kind, change of the magnitude required is unlikely to happen. Consumers may be unhappy with bank fees, but not enough of them will take their business elsewhere in the near future to make a significant dent in the banks' bottom line. Short of a financial crisis, the banks' boards of directors are unlikely to act. With no single investor holding more than 5 per cent of a bank's shares, there is also little chance of a shareholder revolt to force change. Like the frog, the Canadian banks are caught in a trap – prisoners of their past success.

A Made-in-Canada Solution

If the banks are unable to do the job themselves, there is one player who can provide the catalyst needed to put them on a different track. Given the banks' importance to the overall economy, the federal government has every incentive to act to safeguard the future health of the industry. The financial services sector represents more than one-third of the Toronto Stock Exchange's main index, and almost every Canadian pension plan has a sizeable holding of bank stocks.[12] Banks are still the primary providers of capital to businesses of all sizes. They underwrite almost three-quarters of all home mortgages and consumer loans. They manage two-thirds of individual savings, covering not only bank accounts but also retirement and education funds. They control the payments system, employ more than 280,000 people in Canada, and make up almost one-tenth of the country's gross domestic product. Given the importance of this industry, it is critical to all Canadians that the banks make a successful transition to the twenty-first century.

Rather than waiting for customers to desert the banks, the federal government should seize the initiative. This would not be the first time that the government has done so. Few of today's senior bankers can forget the United Kingdom's Big Bang of 1986, followed by Canada's "Little Bang" a year later, which allowed banks to enter the securities, investment, and trust industries. These developments were a recognition that powerful external forces were reshaping the industry and were also reflected in sweeping changes to the 1991

Bank Act. In Canada, the Bank Act is regularly reviewed to ensure that banking law keeps pace with the changing environment. It is this history of changes that has ensured stability of the system. The act is normally reviewed every five years. The latest update was scheduled for March 2017, but the federal government has extended the deadline to 2019 to ensure a proper review.

The forces that we have discussed in this book signal an even more dramatic shake-up ahead. But the future of the industry is unclear, is tough to describe, and does not have one right answer. The solution will require the support of multiple stakeholders with widely differing perspectives and priorities. In this situation, a process like the one that catalysed changes to the payments system in 2011 is needed to bring interested parties together to build the financial system that Canada needs for the information age.[13] Bringing together consumers, bankers, technology companies, small and mid-sized businesses, corporations, governments, regulators, and more – stakeholders with very different perspectives and interests – the Payments Task Force created dialogue to explore different futures and look for common ground. Building on this work and the trust it created, a coalition emerged – leaders from across all groups who were ready and willing to build the future they had envisioned. Because of the work done by the task force, the minister of finance was presented with not only a report but also a roadmap – and a community of practice that was prepared to take action.

This process, known as catalytic governance, starts with a dialogue among stakeholders, then goes on to explore alternative future scenarios, develop a shared vision of the future, and create a specific agenda to bring those ideas to fruition. It is an inclusive process that encourages constructive dialogue, creates shared mental maps, and – most importantly – drives communities of practice to action. It creates a system of governance that is inclusive, learning-based, and action-oriented. We will need to include young, tech-savvy bankers and fintechs in this process if we are to move swiftly to create a competitive, made-in-Canada financial system.[14]

The system as it now stands may appear stable, but it is an illusory stability. In the future, public policy will need to recognize that stability cannot be achieved without innovation. It must encourage market-based financing for small and mid-sized businesses and open access to a modern Canadian payments system. It must establish a much stronger voice for consumers by strengthening the mandate of the Financial Consumer Agency of Canada. Finally, it must create a governance system to ensure an effective transition to the information age.

Forcing a real change in direction means putting some hitherto taboo subjects on the table. The authorities should be prepared to consider bank mergers more sympathetically than they did in the late 1990s. This is not because bigger is better but – since not all the existing players will succeed in transitioning from the old model to the new – because allowing the weakest to play on carries the risk of hobbling the entire system.

The good news is that the Canadian banks have recognized these imperatives and are now starting to create small innovation units,[15] as we have described in chapter 2. Although this is undoubtedly a move in the right direction, injecting a little innovation into the old business model will not be enough to equip the banks to compete head-on against the emerging direct banks, let alone the likes of Apple, Google, Samsung, Facebook, and the horde of fintech entrepreneurs threatening death by a thousand cuts.

As we see it, using a catalytic governance approach to the next Bank Act review would bring all key stakeholders together to design and start building the banking industry of the future – in other words, Canada's response to Bill Gates's prediction that "We need banking, but we don't need banks anymore."[16] The banking industry will likely require substantial financial commitments for new technology. Competitors such as fintechs and direct banks must be given access to customers and critical infrastructure. But this would also free the Canadian banks from the "rigidity trap" they now find themselves in and reset the financial system to compete more effectively at a time of rapid and unpredictable change. By transforming themselves before a real crisis hits, Canadian banks may be able to make the transition in much the same way that Canada evolved from a British colony to an independent country without a revolution. Canadian banks could become global technology leaders.

Balancing Innovation and Stability

For more than 150 years, Canadian governments have seen banking as a strategic sector. The regulatory regime has been crafted to achieve six clear objectives:

- Stability to encourage the inward flow of capital
- Federally regulated chartered banks as the dominant financial institutions in Canada
- Canadian control
- An industry that facilitates trade and commerce
- An infrastructure that supports government financing
- A retail network that serves the entire population

While these policies served us well in the industrial age, it is difficult to see that they contribute much in the emerging information age. The goal of public policy should be to promote a globally competitive industry that offers the widest possible choice to Canadians. With a tsunami of new technology threatening to overwhelm the old branch-banking model, the banks have no higher priority than innovation if their survival is to be assured.

Finding the right trade-off between stability and innovation has long been a challenge for public policy, and has been explicitly addressed by virtually all the royal commissions and task forces that have considered the policy framework for the financial sector. We have argued in this book that the banks are caught in a "rigidity trap" largely because they have been too comfortable to feel the pressures for change, and that their comfort is primarily because public policy shields them from competition. But a protected oligopoly focused on growth and profits no longer serves Canadians well. Not only are the banks not taking on enough risk, especially in home mortgage and small business lending, but they are providing expensive and obsolete products and services when cheaper and better options are taking root around them. The inordinately high returns generated by their retail business have boosted their stock prices and made them too complacent about the future. In the absence of a crisis or some other catalyst, they are unlikely to make the investments needed to serve their customers in the information age. Although banks may be less profitable in the future – earning, say, a 20 per cent return on equity rather than 40 per cent – they are necessary and important contributors to Canada's future.

We identify four critical areas below that should be at the top of the list for review, though there may be others.

1. Market-Based Financing for Small and Mid-sized Businesses

Many have argued that one of the primary reasons why Canada lacks innovation is that new ventures lack financial support from banks and capital markets.[17] Innovation and new businesses are vital if the economy is to start roaring again. That is especially true in Ontario, which makes up 40 per cent of total GDP but has lost much of its manufacturing base.

As explained in earlier chapters, lending to small and mid-sized businesses has been dampened by the banks' poor risk-pricing skills and by higher capital requirements imposed after the global financial crisis. To make matters worse, Canada's underdeveloped capital markets have not been able to take up the slack. Instead, Canadian businesses are turning to foreigners for investment capital, as they did in the past to develop our natural resources. The difference between now and then is that twenty-first-century investors are mostly technology-based venture capital and private equity firms. But these foreign investors need a market where they can sell their investments when they want to, and right now the market of choice for fintechs is Nasdaq. This means that many businesses leave Canada long before they reach maturity. Canada needs urgently to foster alternative funding sources so that these businesses continue to benefit the Canadian rather than the U.S. economy. It is thus important, as a first step, to clarify the rules for angel investing, crowdsourcing, venture capital, private equity, and other market-based sources of financing.

But even that is not enough. While market based-financing can meet the needs of a start-up, funding for more mature businesses is also in short supply. That is why many Canadian entrepreneurs move themselves or their businesses, or both, to Silicon Valley and other hospitable locations – or simply sell out as soon as they can, all to the detriment of Canada's economy. To address these short-comings, the University of Toronto's Munk School of Global Affairs' Innovation Policy Lab has urged the federal government and the provinces to provide direct funding for financial technology companies. It cautioned that governments must ponder the lessons learned from past, often unsuccessful, initiatives in this area and must spend the time needed to develop a comprehensive policy to deal with the lack of later-stage financing.[18]

The Business Development Bank could play a significant role. Its mission is to help create and develop strong Canadian businesses through financing, consulting services, and securitization, with a focus on small and mid-sized enterprises. Through a subsidiary, BDC Capital, it already offers a full spectrum of specialized financing, including venture capital, equity, and growth and business transition capital. Using an approach similar to the Canada Mortgage and Housing Corporation's support for home mortgages, the BDC may be able to harness guarantees and securitization to meet the demand for more small-business financing.[19] The government's recent co-insurance model for home mortgages could be an effective way to reduce the risk to taxpayers of underwriting small and mid-sized business loans.

Since the global financial crisis, banks that securitize assets have been obliged to have skin in the game by participating in their own deals. Likewise, any asset-backed security sold to the public must include investors with the expertise and incentive to assess the issue's viability. These rules are designed to reduce reliance on rating agencies and to assure less sophisticated investors that the assets have been properly vetted. At the same time, CMHC is gradually reducing its guarantee on home mortgages from 100 per cent to 80 per cent, following the lead of the United States. These two moves may help kick-start the lethargic Canadian asset-backed securities market, including mortgage-backed securities, which would reduce reliance on government funding for both residential mortgages and small and mid-sized business loans.

On another front, the federal government must continue to push for more effective capital markets regulation. The Supreme Court of Canada has barred Ottawa from unilaterally setting up a national securities regulator. But we hope the government will press ahead with its plan to set up a body with more limited powers – the Cooperative Capital Markets Regulatory Authority. Draft legislation is already in place, and a chairman and a fifteen-member board of directors have been named to oversee the implementation. Participating provinces and territories – so far, Ontario, British Columbia, Saskatchewan, New Brunswick, Prince Edward Island, and Yukon – have agreed to work on enacting the uniform provincial-territorial Capital Markets Act and the complementary federal Capital Markets Stability Act by 30 June 2018. The new regulatory authority is also due to be in business that year.

2. Open Access to a Modern Payments System

The federal government should encourage competition in payments by allowing new entrants easier access to core clearing and settlement infrastructure and by laying the groundwork for a modern payments clearing and settlement system. Giving financial technology companies access to the new system, accompanied by appropriate regulation, would send a very clear message that the government encourages innovation and competition.

A big step forward came in November 2016, when Payments Canada (formerly the Canadian Payments Association) announced plans to replace its small and large clearing and settlement systems with a completely new, faster payments system. This modern system will initially clear and settle transactions in two hours and, shortly thereafter, in one hour. It will operate under revamped standards, making it open to all payments providers and facilitating the transfer of information as well as payments. The cost of the project, estimated at about $1 billion, will be financed by the markets, and the debt will be repaid from future transaction fees. One of the first steps was for Payments Canada to inform the chief executives of the big banks that they will need to upgrade their systems to connect to the new infrastructure or face being cut off at the end of 2019. This means that each bank will have to replace its personal and commercial transaction account systems at a combined cost of several billion dollars.

This bold move is exactly what Canada needs to be competitive. It follows changes made by the federal government to the governance of the Canadian Payments Association (CPA), in line with recommendations by the Payments Task Force. Parliament amended the Canadian Payments Act in December 2014 to enhance the CPA's governance standards. An independent board was put in place in 2015, and it approved a new technology roadmap in September 2016. The minister of finance and the Bank of Canada review and approve the CPA's corporate plan and technology roadmap annually.

If all goes to plan, Canada will have a payments system to be proud of by 2020. More than that, the new mechanism may be just the nudge that the banks need to address their biggest challenge – moving from a branch-banking model to a customer-direct model, as discussed in chapter 2. One reason it has taken so long to modernize Canada's payments system is that new entrants have had difficulty gaining access to the core infrastructure. Under the current rules, each of the twelve direct clearers must be able to connect its system to all the others, as well as with the Canadian Payments Association. Access to the new system must be available at the same price for all participants that meet objective and transparent criteria aimed at safeguarding the system's stability, minimizing operational risk, fostering good conduct, and ensuring user protection.

Access to infrastructure may become a moot point if Blockchain with its global distributed ledger and "trust protocol" with almost unhackable cryptography are adopted. This "Internet of value" would easily allow the transfer of value between parties and significantly reduce the need for the established intermediaries to act as middlemen.

Finally, on the issue of payments, the federal government should encourage banks and wireless carriers to set up a new body that can work with retailers and provincial and local governments, among others, to develop common standards for the delivery of mobile services. Adopting a single set of guidelines for everyone would cut the cost and complexity of mobile products and services to Canadians and help safeguard consumers. A collaborative mobile wallet (the Canadian wallet) would also likely be the best way for the banks and other companies to compete effectively against emerging giants such as Apple, Google, Facebook, and Samsung.

Canada could take a leaf out of the book of Finland, Sweden, and the Netherlands, which decided in the mid-2000s to become their own "creative destroyers." They forced their banks to improve their payments infrastructure, eliminate paper-based payments such as cheques (and more recently in Sweden, cash), and deliver electronic invoicing and payments to businesses and governments. The impact on the banking industry was dramatic. Finland's largest bank, Nordea, closed half of its branches and reduced its workforce significantly. But its revenues continued to grow, as the bank began offering information-based products and services such as weekly cash flow forecasts, daily profit and loss statements, and bigger loans against predicted cash flows to businesses.

3. Strengthen the Financial Consumer Agency of Canada

Consumers need a much stronger voice to restore the balance between highly profitable banks and not-so-competitive services. The Financial Consumer Agency of Canada (FCAC) was created in 2001 in response to a recommendation by the task force on the future of the financial services sector. The task force's 1998 report noted that "the current framework for consumer protection is not as effective as it should be in reducing the information and power imbalance between institutions and consumers."[20] In our view, the statement still holds true today. As we have noted many times in this book, consumer watchdogs have all too often fallen short in holding banks accountable for the quality or price of their services. Many believe that if the federal government cannot give FCAC the necessary to teeth to accomplish its intended mission, then they should kill it because it only gives the banks an excuse for doing nothing.[21]

We propose that the government significantly expand the agency's mandate and funding as a way of signalling a commitment to reform. As with its British and U.S. counterparts, the agency should have the authority to draw up and enforce consumer protection rules for much of the financial system, including financial advisors, credit reporting firms, and mortgage originators, as well as banks, insurers, and credit unions. It should create the tools – among them disclosure requirements, standardized documents, and online resources – that would help Canadians shop more easily for mortgages, credit cards, transaction accounts, and retirement and education savings products.

Another of the agency's priorities should be to strengthen financial literacy. New Zealand has shown the way with effective Web and mobile applications that provide information and simple advice to anyone looking to buy a home, invest for retirement or education, or apply for a credit card. These apps could also encourage consumers to pay down debt and save more for the future.

The financial consumer agency could use social media to help improve the banks' relationship with their customers. Providing tools for consumers to rate the financial services they use would help address the power imbalance. Like hotels, restaurants, books, and other consumer services, banks with lower than, say, a four-star rating would feel the pressure to improve. The number of "likes" that a financial institution gathers on its Facebook page could become as important a measure as its credit rating.

The list of issues for the agency to tackle is a long one, but investments are clearly a high priority. It could mandate improved disclosure of fees for investment management and advice. It could encourage banks to take some of the mystery out of retirement planning by turning their wealth management platforms into more user-friendly financial planning tools. The banks could incorporate investor education into more of their products and services and provide easy-to-understand information on concepts such as net real returns. A code of conduct for wealth management might be an effective way to kick-start this process.

With the help of these reforms and others, a revitalized consumer watchdog could make a real contribution towards shifting the emphasis in banking policy from stability to innovation.

4. A Flexible and Adaptable Governance System

Effective governance is essential to the success of a twenty-first-century financial services industry. The industry will be marked in coming years by rapid, disruptive change, making it all but impossible to predict future trends, and especially future bottlenecks and tensions. To spur innovation, the government must make the financial services industry more accessible to up-and-coming fintechs, without, of course, exposing Canadians to the tremendous risks of an unstable financial system. The solution lies in setting up a governance model that is inclusive, collaborative, flexible, and adaptable while protecting the public interest.

We believe that the model recommended by the Task Force for the Payments System Review achieves these goals. To that end, it proposed the following government actions:

1. Define the banking industry, establish the basis on which its members would be recognized, and set out the principles and objectives of the new governance model, including trust, access, and good value.
2. Create a new oversight body for the financial system to protect the public interest.
3. Encourage the industry to create a broad-based association that would develop and implement strategy and standards. Membership would be mandatory for providers of banking services and voluntary for user groups (consumers, businesses, not-for-profits, and governments) and other interested parties.

This governance structure could also be used to encourage innovation. For example, a broad-based industry association could take on the task of developing standards and codes of conduct for the delivery of mobile services. And because effective leadership and governance in the information age depend less on traditional top-down approaches and more on creating shared meanings and frameworks, this structure would support the industry's ability to adapt to ongoing disruptive change.

All Stakeholders Have a Role

Investors, customers, suppliers, policy makers, regulators, bankers, and directors all have a crucial role to play in nudging the industry forward. Governments must be more proactive, both in directing banks' activities and in encouraging new players to enter the market. Investors, especially long-term players such as the big pension plans, could insist that the banks develop new information-based products and services. They could team up with activist investors to press for initiatives, such as the sale of under-performing units, that would reduce cross-subsidization from Canadian retail banking to foreign and wholesale activities. Customers could demand lower service fees and better returns.

Like the executives they oversee, bank boards are often among the last to respond to new technologies, shifting customer attitudes, and new regulatory trends – until a crisis hits.[22] Boards should give more attention to the longer term, requiring executives to develop plans for innovative products and services and to write-off stranded assets such as branches, ATMs, and outdated computer systems and processing centres.

If all else fails, Canadians could start a grassroots movement for change. They could launch a social media campaign to embarrass the banks into changing their ways, as happened when RBC was forced in April 2013 to abandon its practice of hiring temporary foreign workers. The fact is that ordinary consumers can be a powerful force for change, whether by demanding action from the banks or just quietly moving their business to new, technology-based suppliers. We hope that the banks will get the message before it is too late.

The Banks Have Three Options

As Peter Drucker prophesied over a decade ago, the banks ultimately have just three options:

1. They can do nothing, and continue down the same path they have been on for the past twenty years. The outcome is sure to

be a slow, steady decline, eventually resulting in consolidation of the industry. Given the government's reliance on the banks to support the economy and implement monetary policy, it is very unlikely that the big banks will disappear entirely. As Drucker observed, there are still cotton mills in the United States, but not very many of them and they do not make much money. As the banks' revenues declined, they would seek to save themselves with an aggressive cost-cutting campaign. Expect mass lay-offs, and the closure of many branches and outdated processing facilities. Under this scenario, the banks would increasingly resemble the U.S. savings and loan companies of yesteryear, taking in government-insured deposits and making government-backed mortgage loans. Most of their payments and wealth management business would be lost to more agile and imaginative new entrants.

2. Like the City of London, Canada could make it attractive for new entrants, notably fintech and large technology companies, to enter various facets of the banking business. Competition could be encouraged by enabling non-bank and foreign companies to gain access to the domestic payments system and capital markets. Such a dramatic shift in policy, however, would almost certainly hasten the demise of the Canadian banks, as their old technology would be no match for the Cloud-based applications used on mobile devices. This is true not only for payments, but also for wealth management and loans.

3. The Canadian banks could become their own "creative destroyers." Balancing innovation with stability, the banks could work with policy makers, regulators, customers, suppliers, and investors to rejuvenate the financial services industry. Taking this route would not be painless. It would entail destroying many of the banks' existing businesses, including mutual funds and paper-based transactions. Home mortgages and small and mid-sized business lending would shift to the capital markets. The banks would need to replace much of their existing revenue streams with new information-based services, and, in all likelihood, they would have to develop a new service-delivery

model based largely on mobile technology. The transformation would be reminiscent of the one that engulfed IBM during the 1990s, when the venerable computer maker shifted from selling products to providing services.

Option three would call for a huge leap of faith, and the transition would be painful, lasting at least five years, and perhaps even longer. Not only would the banks need to replace their core systems and processes and migrate their customers from the branch bank to the customer direct bank, they would also have to reinvent their products and services. Rather than charging for transaction processing, they would have to develop valuable information-based services, such as weekly cash-flow forecasts, daily profit-and-loss statements, and bigger loans against predicted cash flows. They could provide wallets to Canadians for not only payments but also loyalty programs, drivers' licences, and health cards, as well as automated record keeping for receipts and other important information. Innovative securitized (and enhanced) SME loans could also help to boost returns for individual investors. The rewards for banks and Canadians would be huge – a financial system built to survive and thrive in the twenty-first century.

The big question is: Are the banks – and their regulators, customers, suppliers, and shareholders – up to the challenge?

Acknowledgments

Patricia Meredith

This book marks the culmination of a very long journey, one that would not have been possible without the support and contributions of many people, only some of whom we can mention here.

For many years, I have tried to understand why industries fail to adapt to disruptive changes in their business environment. In other words, "Why doesn't the frog jump out of the boiling water?" In few sectors is this question more pressing than in the Canadian financial services industry. Sadly, in all likelihood, the Canadian banks will continue to do what they have always done, until that is no longer possible and more innovative firms take their place.

Given the unique separation of banking and securities under the Canadian constitution, the federal government will likely protect the Canadian banks from extinction, but the banks will come to play a much smaller role, as public utilities that provide residential mortgages and loans to small and mid-sized enterprises, and protect savings deposits.

But a much brighter future also beckons – a banking system for the twenty-first century created through collaboration between policy makers, regulators, customers, suppliers, investors, bank executives, and directors. We have written this book in the hope that these stakeholders can come together to create the financial services industry of the future that Canada deserves.

I began my career as a bank analyst in the securities industry about three decades ago, just as that world was starting to change dramatically. Modern financial theory was being used to create new financial instruments, such as mortgage-backed securities, junk bonds, and derivatives. Waves of new information and communications technology accelerated and compounded these changes. With mass adoption of the Internet in the mid-1990s and the introduction of the smartphone in 2007, the branch-centred business model that has served the Canadian retail banking industry so well for more than a hundred years was clearly under threat. A myriad of new technology companies, including titans like Apple, Google, Facebook, PayPal, and Amazon, and nimble innovators such as Lending Tree, Borrowell, Venmo, Square, and Wealthsimple, now provide many of the same services as the banks but with just a few taps on a keyboard and at a fraction of the cost.

Three people made this book possible – my co-author, James Darroch; my mentor, John Donald; and my dear friend Steven Rosell. James and I have been colleagues in the financial services program at the Schulich School of Business where, for the past sixteen years, we have talked about the future of the Canadian banking industry. Working together on this book forced us to crystalize our ideas and find our common vision for the future of the industry. John Donald, a serial financial services entrepreneur, helped me to understand how small companies can topple giants, and gave me a place to write the first draft of this book. Steven Rosell, my friend and co-author of *Catalytic Governance,* helped me find a way to explain without blaming the financial services industry – how it is changing and why the incumbents are slow to respond. With his help, I could create a balanced introduction and move forward with the project.

Since this book has been thirty years in the making, many individuals and organizations have had an important impact:

• The Corporate Strategy Group. Hard working and courageous, these women and men pushed their analytical and

communications skills to make bank executives and directors
aware of the impact of technological, societal, and regulatory
changes on CIBC and the other Canadian banks. Thank you
to Sandra Stewart, Niki Root, Denise Ellis, Lisa Luinenberg,
Michelle Moore, Darell Kletke, Mark Richter, Leigh Merlo,
Heather Sparrow, and Terry Troy and to our assistants: Merlyn
Rodrigues, Nadine Paneranda, and Aimi Lee. I owe a special
thank-you to Leigh and Denise for convening a group to update
me on wholesale banking activities in Canada.

- Al Flood, Holger Kluge, John Hunkin, and other members of
the senior management team of CIBC. For seven years, they
sought to transform CIBC and brought many innovations
to Canadian banking. These included: a mortgage bank and
mortgage-backed securities; a monoline credit card business
with a 98 per cent share of affluent customers in Canada;
Amicus, a new concept in direct banking in partnership with
Loblaws; an integrated corporate and investment bank offering
derivatives and high-yield securities through client service
teams; the separation of the retail bank into a convenience bank
(CIBC) and a relationship bank (Imperial Service); several joint
ventures, including asset management, custody and corporate
trust, items processing, and technology outsourcing to begin
to reduce the bank's reliance on obsolete assets; a world-class
leadership centre; and a corporate centre focused on strategy
and governance. Sadly, these innovations were traded for
short-term shareholder returns when the investment bankers
began managing the bank in 2000. I would also like to thank
my colleague Gwyn Gill, who understood retail banking better
than anyone I have met, because she learned it by working her
way from teller to executive vice-president responsible for retail
customer marketing and strategy.

- My partners at McKinsey & Company, especially Dominic
Barton, Lowell Bryan, Stephen Bear, and their teams, who
worked closely with CIBC on most of these transformative
projects. I learned much about retail banking and global
capital markets from them, and worked on some of the most

interesting projects of my career. More recently, Phil Bruno, Eric Monteiro, and Danish Yusuf helped the Payments Task Force to position Canada's payments system and quantify the benefits of electronic invoicing and payments.

- My colleagues at Monitor Group Canada: Jonathan Goodman, Michael Wenban, Roger Martin, Todd Roberts, Paul Estey, Hugh McKee, Emma Barnes, Cathy Hess, Bruce Terron, and many others who worked with me on large projects involving financial institutions. Over the course of fifteen years, we collaborated on CIBC, TMX Group, CPP-IB, and other assignments for all the Canadian banks and credit unions and several global financial institutions.
- The financial services program at York University. Since most of my students in the Competitive and Organizational Strategy for Financial Institutions program were employed in financial services, they helpfully challenged my biases and frustrations, and helped me to appreciate the inside perspective on some of the banks' actions. Fred Gorbet, the program's former chair, encouraged me to study "why the frog does not jump out of the boiling water" under the enlightened guidance of professors Ellen Auster, Gareth Morgan, and Brenda Zimmerman.
- Former finance minister Jim Flaherty, for giving me the opportunity to chair the Task Force for the Payments System Review. My good friends Barbara Stymiest, former president and CEO of the TMX Group and group head of strategy, treasury, and corporate services at RBC Financial Group; and David Denison, former president and CEO of the CPP-Investment Board. Working with them I developed an in-depth understanding of the Canadian securities and pensions industries. David Dodge, former governor of the Bank of Canada, for his insightful comments on banking and payments.
- The entrepreneurs John Donald, Yousry Bissada, Jake Orbach, Dave Chapman, Art Trojan, and John Bordignon, who founded filogix inc. With them I rediscovered the magic of financial services innovation. Together we created online distribution and "collaborative straight-through processing" for residential

mortgages. One day, with the help of further automation, customers will be able to originate, process, and securitize their own residential mortgage. Brendan Calder and David Allen, also entrepreneurs in the residential mortgage industry, very generously shared their insights with me. More recently, I have worked closely with Aran Hamilton, Ian McNeill, Randy Ostojic, and Ismail Pishori to develop payments- and wealth management-related new ventures.

- Fares Boulos, head of research at CIBC Wood Gundy. When I first predicted in 1988 that the Canadian trust industry would not survive, Fares managed to negotiate a compromise with the investment bankers whose clients were threatening never to deal with Wood Gundy again if we released the report. As a result of his efforts, I changed my conclusion from "would not survive" to "would not prosper"; otherwise the report was issued unchanged. In the early 1990s, we watched the collapse of the Canadian trust industry. This experience gave me the confidence to write this book about an even more important pillar of the Canadian economy – our retail banks.

James Darroch

I have had much luck in my career, but one of the greatest strokes of luck was to be approached by Pat Meredith to join her in this project. My surprise was surpassed only by the joy of having a chance to work with Pat again. I have learned a great deal from her and feel privileged to be part of her work.

Throughout my career, I have had the support of many current and former colleagues and friends at the Schulich School of Business, especially I.A. (Al) Litvak, Dezso J. Horvath, the late Dawson E. Brewer, and the late Sy Friedland. Subsequent work with Al Litvak on banking and public policy was both an academic and a personal joy that few experience. The continuing support of Dezso in his role as dean of the school has also been immensely important. My appreciation of the importance of public policy, first awakened by Jim Gillies, was deepened by years of teaching and working with

Paul Cantor at the Toronto Centre and Fred Gorbet in the financial services program at Schulich.

Senior executives in financial services firms, public policy makers, regulators, lawyers, and industry consultants have generously given their time to help with my research. Space considerations preclude listing all the executives in Toronto, New York, London, and Paris, but some deserve special mention: Corey Jack, David Finnie, Mike Frow, and Michel Maila (whom I met at the Bank of Montreal) were instrumental in developing my appreciation of the relationship between strategy and risk management in financial institutions. Their profound insights forever changed my view of strategy in financial institutions.

* * *

Most important, we would like to thank those who have helped us write this book. Kaz Jana did an excellent job of research, poring over bank annual reports and recasting the data in more useful ways. Alex Walker-Turner and Patrick Meredith-Karam recast our figures to the publisher's format. Our editor, Bernard Simon, did an amazing job of making this book easy to read. Three reviewers, who prefer to remain anonymous, gave us invaluable feedback and helped improve the manuscript immeasurably. And last but not least, our editor, Jennifer DiDomenico at University of Toronto Press provided welcome guidance, encouragement, and constructive criticism as we finalized the project.

Notes

1. The Banks Lose Their Way

1 Leon C. Megginson summarizing his interpretation of the central idea of Darwin's *On the Origin of Species*. Megginson, "Key to Competition is Management," *Petroleum Management* 36(1) (1964).
2 http://www.canajunfinances.com
3 "Special Report on International Banking: Shadow and Substance," *The Economist*, 10 May 2014.
4 This is true globally, largely due to the U.S. capital markets, but not specifically in Canada.
5 According to McKinsey & Company's internal global banking database, Canadian banks' return on tangible equity from 2010 to 2015 was 20 per cent compared with 12 per cent for the top 500 global commercial and investment banks.
6 Calculated from OSFI (banks) and Bank of Canada (industry) reports, dated 31 December 2015, by Bank of Montreal, Nesbitt Burns.
7 According to McKinsey & Company's internal global banking database.
8 Sunny Freeman, "Maple Group Wins Control of TSX Group with 91% of Shares Tendered," *Globe and Mail*, 31 July 2012.
9 Authors' analysis using fourth quarter 2016 Financial Supplements for the six banks.

10 In 2013, some of the Canadian banks stopped disclosing return on equity by line of business. See chapter 7, "Long Live the Branch," table 7.1.

11 According to the Edelman Trust-barometer: http://www.slideshare.net/EdelmanInsights/2015-edelman-trust-barometer-canadian-findings?related+2. As well, Edelman tracks "Trust in Financial Services" (which covers all players in the sector). In Canada, "Trust in the Financial Services Sector" by informed Canadians was 48 per cent in 2008, 62 per cent in 2013, and 51 per cent in 2015.

12 Brett King, *Bank 3.0: Why Banking Is No Longer Somewhere You Go, But Something You Do* (Singapore: John Wiley & Sons, 2013), 15.

13 See chapter 7, "Long Live the Branch," table 7.2.

14 J.D. Power, "Retail Banks in Canada Losing Touch with Customers as Profits Climb While Satisfaction Declines." Available at: http://canada.jdpower.com/press-releases/2015-canadian-retail-banking-satisfaction-study.

15 Clayton Christensen, *The Innovator's Dilemma: When New Technologies Cause Great Firms to Fail* (Boston: Harvard Business Review Press, 1997).

16 In *The Theory of Economic Development* (Cambridge, MA: Harvard University Press, 1934), Joseph Schumpeter describes the evolution of complex business systems. Substantial research now supports this model of creative destruction, including, Philippe Aghion and Peter Howitt, "A Model of Growth through Creative Destruction," *Econometrica* 60 (1992): 323–51.

17 For the past fifteen years, the Institutions, Organizations and Growth Program (previously the Economic Growth and Policy Program) of the Canadian Institute for Advanced Research has focused on these issues, addressed in two books: Elhanan Helpman, ed., *General Purpose Technologies and Economic Growth* (Cambridge, MA: MIT Press, 1998), and Elhanan Helpman, ed., *Institutions and Economic Performance* (Cambridge, MA: MIT Press, 2008).

18 *Economist*, 21 November 2015, 62.

19 Wikipedia, "Decline of Newspapers," 30 April 2015.

20 Frances Westley, Brenda Zimmerman, and Michael Quinn Patton, in *Getting to Maybe: How the World Is Changed* (Toronto: Random House Canada, 2006), 66, point out that the pattern Schumpeter saw in

economies, C.S. Holling, a conceptual founder of ecological economics, saw in natural ecosystems:

> The adaptive cycle tells us that unless we release the resources of time, energy, money and skill locked up in our routines and our institutions on a regular basis, it is hard to create anything new or to look at things from a different perspective. Without those perspectives, and the continuous infusion of novelty and innovation in our lives, our organizations and our systems, there is a slow but definite loss of resilience, and an increase in rigidity.
>
> Holling began his work in resilience by looking at ecosystems, particularly forests. He was fascinated by how often forests that had existed for hundreds of years went through massive change. Protecting them from fires, disease or drought was no way to guarantee their continued existence. Rather, forests seemed to use these massive changes as part of their ongoing evolution.

21 Elhanan Helpman, ed., *General Purpose Technologies and Economic Growth* (Cambridge, MA: MIT Press, 1998), 5.

22 Peter Howitt, "Measurement, Obsolescence and General Purpose Technologies," in Helpman, ed., *General Purpose Technologies and Economic Growth*, 219–51.

23 Philippe Aghion and Peter Howitt, "On the Macroeconomic Effects of Major Technological Change," in Helpman, ed., *General Purpose Technologies and Economic Growth*, 128.

24 Sam Ro, "Here's What the $294 Trillion Market of Global Financial Assets Looks Like," *Business Insider*, 11 February 2015.

25 This was not the case in the United States, where market-based financing (shadow banking) conducted by brokers / dealers, finance companies, asset-backed securities, and government sponsored enterprises (Fannie Mae and Freddie Mac) represented 58 per cent of the $29.5 trillion of financial activity. See Timothy F. Geithner, *Stress Test: Reflections on Financial Crises* (New York: Crown Publishers, 2014), 506.

26 As explained in chapter 3, there were many differences between the U.S. and the Canadian residential mortgage industries that also benefited the Canadian banks.

27 Transaction costs are the costs related to clearing and settling a transaction; while interaction costs are those related to dealing with a customer.

28 Source: Internet Live Stats at www.Internetlivestats.com/internet-users. Internet Society, *Global Internet Report*, 2015: 15.

29 King, *Bank 3.0*, 14.

30 Thomas S. Kuhn, *The Structure of Scientific Revolutions*, 3rd ed. (Chicago: University of Chicago Press, 1996), 64.

31 Kuhn's seminal work, *The Structure of Scientific Revolutions*, is the basis for understanding how "paradigm shifts" take place. On page 151, he quotes Max Planck, surveying his own career in his *Scientific Autobiography*, sadly remarking that "a new scientific truth does not triumph by convincing its opponents and making them see the light, but rather because its opponents eventually die, and a new generation grows up that is familiar with it."

32 In the early 1980s, several small banks in western Canada failed, largely due to heavy real estate exposure and difficulties obtaining title to foreclosed real estate in Alberta. In the late 1950s and early 1960s, a number of banks were allowed to merge when there was concern about their ability to compete given their small size (for example, the Canadian Bank of Commerce and the Imperial Bank of Canada merged in 1961, and the Bank of Toronto merged with the Dominion Bank in 1955).

33 Discussion Paper 2, "The Economic Benefit of Adopting the ISO 20022 Payment Messaging in Canada," released by the Canadian Payments Association (Payments Canada) in November 2015, estimated the benefits of eliminating most cheques in Canada at $4.5 billion. This amount did not include the additional benefits of automating the entire accounts receivable/payable processes.

34 Task Force for the Payment System Review, *Going Digital: Transitioning to Digital Payments*, December 2011: 16–17. Available at: http://paymentsystemreview.ca/wp-content/themes/psr-esp-hub/documents/r03_eng.pdf.

35 As sophisticated lenders, the Canadian banks use the Internal Ratings-Based (IRB) approach to risk-weighting SME loans. According to the General Manager of the Bank for International Settlements, Jaime

Caruana, "The risk weight that determines the funding structure varies from 41% for the IRB approach if the SME is in a portfolio of small retail exposures to 100% under the Standardized approach for an SME (with 5 million euros' sales). Even under the conservative assumption mentioned, the overall funding cost increase from Basel II to Basel III would range from 19 to 47 basis points." Jaime Caruara, "How Much Capital Is Enough?" Available at: http://www.bis.org/speeches/sp141216.pdf.

36 Jim Leach and Jacquie McNish, *The Third Rail: Confronting Our Pension Failures* (Toronto: McClelland & Stewart, 2013), 167. Recent advertisements by Questrade suggest that the fees are in excess of 30 per cent.

37 Peter Drucker, "Innovate or Die," *The Economist*, 23 September 1999.

38 Sunny Freeman, "We Use Other People's Money: The Reality behind Canada's Shadow Mortgage Lenders," *Huffington Post*, 27 June 2016; and Greg McArthur and Jacquie McNish, "Canada's Dirty Subprime Secret," *Globe and Mail*, 14 March 2009.

39 Conference Board of Canada, "An Engine for Growth: 2015 Report Card on Canada's and Toronto's Financial Services Sector," November 2015. The report also states that financial services represent 13.3 per cent of Metropolitan Toronto's gross domestic product (GDP) and 32.2 per cent of its employment.

40 2016 Bank Annual Reports. Approximately 250,000 of those employees work in Canada.

41 Geithner, *Stress Test*, 430.

2. From Branches to Smartphones

1 Interview, 13 June 2016.

2 Bank websites, 9 March 2017.

3 Satmetrix and Bain & Company, "Customer Loyalty in Retail Banking, Global Edition 2012," http://www.bain.com/publications/articles/customer-loyalty-in-retail-banking-2012.aspx and "Customer Behavior and Loyalty in Retail Banking: Mobilizing for Loyalty, Global Edition 2015," http://www.bain.com/publications/articles/customer-loyalty-in-retail-banking-2015-global.aspx.

4 USAA was founded in 1922, when twenty-five army officers agreed to insure each other's vehicles when no one else would. Today this banking and insurance financial group has more than 9 million customers. In November 2016, American Banker awarded USAA "Bank of the Year."

5 Bain & Company, "Customer Behavior, Experience and Loyalty in Retail Banking," *Bain Report*, 18 November 2015:

  http://bain.com/publications/articles/customer-loyalty-in-retail-banking-2015-global.aspx. Bain & Company stopped disclosing individual bank NPSs in 2012 and the big bank average in 2014. However, the best big bank lagged the top performer (Tangerine) by about 40 points in 2016 and PC Financial by 35 points in 2015. Given that the six large banks have clustered close together, this would give the average bank an NPS of about 20.

  It is also worth noting that Canada Trust's customer satisfaction was 20 percentage points higher than that of the banks in the late 1990s, before it was acquired by TD Bank. TD Canada Trust has lost this distinctiveness since then.

6 Canadian Federation of Independent Business, "Battle of the Banks: Credit Unions among the Best for Small Business," October 2016. In this survey, none of the banks had an overall satisfaction score above 5 out of 10, which is necessary for a net promoter score above zero.

7 Queenie Wong, "Battle of the Banks: Credit Unions among the Best for Small Business," *Canadian Federation of Independent Business*, October 2016: http://www.cfib-fcei.ca/cfib-documents/rr3415.pdf.

8 Reserve Bank of Australia, "Financial Stability Review," September 2014, 35: http://www.rba.gov.au/publications/fsr/2014/sep/pdf/0914.pdf.

9 Ibid., Graph B1.

10 Ibid., Graph B2.

11 *Commonwealth Bank of Australia 2013 Annual Report*, 4: https://www.commbank.com.au/content/dam/commbank/about-us/shareholders/pdfs/annual-reports/2013_CBA_Annual_Report_19_August_2013.pdf

12 Ibid., 2.

13 Ibid., 4.

14 Commonwealth Bank of Australia, "Core Banking Transformation," 14 March 2011, 13: https://www.commbank.com.au/about-us/ shareholders/pdfs/2011-asx/Core-Banking-Modernisation-Presentation.pdf.

15 Ibid., 14.

16 Ibid., 5.

17 The remarks were made at a Banktech Conference in Sydney, Australia. "CSC Questions CBA Core Banking Upgrade," 7 July 2011: http://www.theaustralian.com.au/business/ technology/csc-questions-cba-core-banking-upgrade/ story-e6frgakx-1226089681155.

18 Ibid., 17; "Commonwealth Bank Registers Increased IT Spend," *Computerworld from IDG*: http://www.computerworld.com.au/tag/ commonwealth-bank-of-australia/; Aimee Chanthadavong, "Digital Capabilities Sees CommBank's IT Spend up 15 percent in FY16," ZDNet, 10 August 2016: http://www.zdnet.com/article/software-amortisation-drives-commbanks-it-spend-up-15-percent-in-fy16/.

19 *Commonwealth Bank of Australia 2016 Annual Report*, 6: https://www. commbank.com.au/about-us/shareholders/shareholder-information/ annual-reports.html.

20 James Eyers, "Renee Roberts' 20-Year Vision for National Australia Bank's Technology," 27 April 2015: http://www.smh.com.au/ business/banking-and-finance/renee-roberts-20year-vision-for-national-australia-banks-technology-20150425-1mt9of.html.

21 Renal LeMay, "Four Years Later, Westpac Will Finally Shift Core Banking to Celeriti," 11 May 2013: https://delimiter.com.au/2013/ 11/04/four-years-later-westpac-will-finally-shift-core-banking-celeriti/.

22 Bonnie Gardiner, "Westpac Invests $1.3B in Digital Transformation," *CIO from IDG*, 7 September 2015: http://www.cio.com.au/ article/583988/westpac-invests-1-3b-digital-transformation/.

23 Christine St Anne, "ANZ Mulls Core Banking Transformation," *Asia-Pacific Banking & Finance*, 3 June 2016: http://www. australianbankingfinance.com/technology/anz-mulls-core-banking-transformation-/; Beverley Head, "ANZ Bank Rules Out Upgrading Core IT Systems," *The Australian Financial Review Magazine*, 8 July 2016.

24 Commonwealth Bank of Australia, "Core Banking Transformation," 14 March 2011, 13: https://www.commbank.com.au/about-us/shareholders/pdfs/2011-asx/Core-Banking-Modernisation-Presentation.pdf.

25 https://www.nordea.com/Images/33-104789/2016-03-02_Core-Banking-Replacement-Programme_EN.pdf.

26 Bancherul.ro, "Nordea Selects Partners for New Core Banking Platform," 11 September 2015: http://bancherul.ro/nordea-selects-partners-for-new-core-banking-platform--14796.

27 Colleen Johnston, "Banks vs. Fintechs: It's Time to Change the Narrative," *Globe and Mail*, 29 July 2016: https://www.td.com/about-tdbfg/corporate-information/thought-leadership/speech.jsp?id=76.

28 Ibid.

29 J.D. Power, "Retail Banks in Canada Losing Touch with Customers as Profits Climb While Satisfaction Declines," http://canada.jdpower.com/press-releases/2015-canadian-retail-banking-satisfaction-study.

30 Hameet Singh, "How the Banks Are Branching Out," 22 April 2016: http://strategyonline.ca/2016/04/22/how-the-banks-are-branching-out/.

31 Power, "Retail Banks in Canada Losing Touch," http://canada.jdpower.com/press-releases/2015-canadian-retail-banking-satisfaction-study; Bain, "Customer Loyalty in Retail Banking: Global Edition," http://www.bain.com/publications/articles/customer-loyalty-in-retail-banking-2016.aspx

32 J.D. Power, "Customers Finally Adjusting to Shifting Bank Fee Structures; Mobile Adding Value across the Banking Experience," 28 July 2016: http://canada.jdpower.com/press-releases/2016-canadian-retail-banking-satisfaction-study.

33 Miklos Dietz, Jared Moon, and Miklos Radnai, "Fintechs Can Help Incumbents, Not Just Disrupt Them," *McKinsey Quarterly*, July 2016.

34 "ING: Up and at 'em," *The Economist*, 4 October 2014.

35 Lex, *The Financial Times*, 8 May 2015.

36 Ibid.

37 David Berman and Tim Kiladze, "Shaking Up Scotiabank: Brian Porter's Vision for a Bank of the Future," *Globe and Mail*, 22 July 2016.

38 "Brian Porter's Remarks to Students at Ivey Business School, Western University," 31 March 2016: http://www.scotiabank.com/ca/en/0,,10125,00.html.

39 "Scotiabank Creates New Digital Factory to Bring Together Top Tech Minds": http://scotiabank.mwnewsroom.com/press-releases/scotiabank-creates-new-digital-factory-to-bring-to-tsx-bns – 11g067794-001?lang=en-US.

40 Ibid.

41 "Scotiabank Appoints Shawn Rose as Executive Vice President, Digital Banking": http://scotiabank.mwnewsroom.com/press-releases/scotiabank-appoints-shawn-rose-as-executive-vice-p-tsx-bns – 11g103990-001?lang=en-US.

42 "Scotiabank Unveils First of Two New Customer-Centred Branch Formats": http://scotiabank.mwnewsroom.com/press-releases/scotiabank-unveils-first-of-two-new-customer-centr-tsx-bns – 11g101102-001?lang=en-USRBC.

43 Rachel Roizen with Benjamin Ensor, Peter Wannemacher, Aurelie L'Hostis, Alex Causey, and Michael Chirokas, "2016 Canadian Mobile Banking Functionality Benchmark": https://www.forrester.com/report/2016+Canadian+Mobile+Banking+Functionality+Benchmark/-/E-RES129478.

44 Joe Castaldo, "CIBC CEO Victor Dodig on Banking's Tech Revolution," *Canadian Business*, 14 June 2016.

45 Desjardin was another finalist. The winner was the German on-line bank Fidor: http://banknxt.com/53649/innovative-banks-2015/.

46 Ibid.

47 Canada Newswire, "New App Lets Canadians Apply for a Mortgage with a Tap of Their Smartphone": http://news.morningstar.com/all/canada-news-wire/20160517C8245/new-app-lets-canadians-apply-for-a-mortgage-with-a-tap-of-their-smartphone.aspx.

48 CIBC Investor Day Presentation, 7 October 2015, 45: https://www.cibc.com/ca/pdf/investor-day-presentation.pdf.

49 Jessica Galang, "CIBC Launches Online Currency Exchange Service with Home Delivery," *betakit*, 2 November 2015: http://betakit.com/cibc-launches-online-currency-exchange-service-with-home-delivery/.

50　Barbara Shecter, "CIBC Forges 'Fintech' Partnership That Will Offer Faster Loans to Compete with Online Lenders," *Financial Post*, 18 November 2015: http://business.financialpost.com/news/fp-street/cibc-forges-fintech-partnership-that-will-offer-faster-loans-to-compete-with-online-lenders?__lsa=c8ce-8e68.

51　Hameet Singh "How the Banks Are Branching Out," 22 April 2016: http://strategyonline.ca/2016/04/22/how-the-banks-are-branching-out/.

52　Shecter, "CIBC Forges 'Fintech' Partnership."

53　Dave McKay, "Address to Shareholders," 147th Annual Meeting of Royal Bank of Canada, Montreal, 6 April 2016: http://www.rbc.com/newsroom/speeches/20160406-annual-meeting.html.

54　"RBC Makes Sending Money Simple, Instant and Now Free; RBC First to Offer Free Interac e-Transfer Payments for All Personal Chequing Accounts": http://www.rbc.com/newsroom/news/2016/20160503-p2p-interac.html.

55　Ibid., 5–6.

56　"RBC to Boost Focus on AI with New Research Lab," *Globe and Mail*, 18 January 2017.

57　"University of Toronto and RBC Create Startup Accelerator for Young Innovators": http://www.rbc.com/newsroom/news/2016/20160405-onramp.html.

58　"RBC Wins Two Awards from Retail Banker International: RBC Takes Home Best Payment Innovation and Best Use of Data Analytics": http://www.rbc.com/newsroom/news/2016/20160520-rbi-awards.html.

59　"RBC Wins Top Awards for Innovation in Global Private Banking and Wealth Management Survey by Euromoney": http://www.rbc.com/newsroom/news/2016/20160210-innovation-award.html.

60　"BMO Introduces New Way for Canadians to Open Bank Accounts in Minutes Using Their Smartphones": https://newsroom.bmo.com/press-releases/bmo-introduces-new-way-for-canadians-to-open-bank-tsx-bmo-201607151062805001.

61　Ian Hardy, "BMO Will Pay You $5 to Use Its Mobile Banking Apps," 7 July 2016: http://mobilesyrup.com/2016/07/07/bmo-will-pay-you-5-to-use-its-mobile-banking-apps/.

62　"BMO Financial Group Launches 'Next Big Idea in Fintech' with the DMZ at Ryerson University": https://newsroom.bmo.com/

press-releases/bmo-financial-group-launches-next-big-idea-in-fin-tsx-bmo-201604201051233001.

63 Ibid.

64 Alexandra Posadzki, "BMO Becomes First of Big Five to Launch Robo-advisor Service to All Investors," *Globe and Mail*, 18 January 2016.

65 Bharat Masrani, Remarks delivered to the Annual Meeting of Shareholders, Montreal, 31 March 2016: http://www.td.com/document/PDF/investor/Bharat%20Masrani%20AM%202016%20Remarks%20-%20English.pdf.

66 https://www.nbc.ca/en/personal/banking/electronic-solutions/mobile-banking-solutions/smartphone-banking-experience.html.

67 https://www.nbc.ca/en/about-us/news/news-room/press-releases/press-releases-2015/20150119-national-bank-expands-its-suite-of-mobile-banking-solutions-with-two-new-innovative-apps.html.

68 Some would argue four products, as RBC Financial and TD Bank Groups have significant insurance operations.

3. Innovation in the Mortgage Market

1 The federal government issued CMHC mortgage-backed bonds and CMHC-insured bank mortgages so the banks could issue U.S.-covered bonds to increase bank liquidity during the 2008 financial crisis.

2 Much of this section is adapted from Patricia Meredith's PhD dissertation: "Why the Frog Does Not Jump out of the Boiling Water: A Multi-level Exploration of the Limited Responses of the Canadian Banks to Disruptive Changes in the Canadian Residential Mortgage Industry," York University, June 2009. Her research included in-depth long interviews with more than twenty bankers (the CEO, Head of Retail Banking, and Head of Mortgages for each of the six Canadian banks) and all the entrepreneurs mentioned in this short history.

3 Lowell Bryan, *Breaking Up the Bank: An Industry under Siege* (Homewood, IL: Dow Jones Irwin, 1988).

4 There is also the challenge of asset and liability management: Is the duration of the funding matched to the length of the asset? If it is not, and it typically is not, then there is the issue of maturity transformation and who takes that risk and gets the return. Unfortunately, if there was a problem in rolling over the funding and

there is no back up line of credit, then there may be the need for a lender of last resort, like the Bank of Canada.

5 Meredith, "Why the Frog Does Not Jump out of the Boiling Water," PhD diss., York University, 2009, 48.

6 CMHC Annual Mortgage Consumer Surveys, 1999 to 2016.

7 In 2013, CIBC transitioned its brokers from Home Loans Canada to mortgage specialists in its branches and exited the FirstLine Trust broker business.

8 According to industry expert David Allan of TAO Asset Management, in 2015 brokers originated 28 per cent of mortgages in Canada; 72 per cent were originated directly by the lender.

9 Although there was much speculation about poor-quality assets backing the commercial paper, there were no credit losses on Coventree's asset-backed commercial paper.

10 MCAP Financial Corporation holds the remaining 20 per cent interest.

11 A key contributor to the failure of the ABCP market was the inadequate design of the backstop liquidity facilities (something that bankers and rating agencies should have learned from the failure of the commercial paper market in Canada in the 1960s in the wake of the Atlantic Acceptance scandal).

12 Significant differences in public policy regarding home ownership and the structure of the financial system are important. The push to increase home ownership in the United States created fertile ground for investment bankers to use securitization to create new products. Once mortgage-backed securities were established, numerous permutations discussed in the popular movie *The Big Short* were inevitable in the frenzy of innovation. The structure of the U.S. financial system, with national capital markets and a decentralized banking system, created the need for banks to find ways to reduce concentration risk by pooling mortgages nationally. The Canadian financial system, based on national banks and decentralized capital markets, did not have the same concerns about concentration risk or political pressure to increase home ownership.

13 A recent briefing (20 August 2016) by the *Economist*, "Comradely Capitalism: How America Accidentally Nationalized Its Mortgage Market," raises many of the same concerns about the U.S. mortgage market. The government's improvised rescue of the system in 2008–12

left it with a much bigger role in funding mortgages. It is the majority stakeholder in Freddie Mac and Fannie Mae, mortgage companies that were previously privately run (though with an implicit guarantee). They are now in "conservatorship," a type of notionally temporary nationalization that shows few signs of ending.

14 A comparison of the U.S. and Canadian residential mortgage markets, conducted for the authors by TAO Asset Management Group, showed the following:

1. U.S. residential mortgage market – US$ 9.8 trillion
    a. 30% broker originated, 32% agency through correspondent banks, 38% bank or other financial institutions
    b. 82% GSE funded (Freddie 24%, Fannie 37%, Ginnie and other FHFA 21%), 13% bank balance sheet, 5% private RMBS (residential mortgage-backed securities)
2. Canadian residential mortgage market – C$1.35 trillion
    a. 28% broker originated, 72% direct
    b. 36% bank balance sheet funded (conventional fixed 16%, high ratio/HELOC 15%, portfolio insured on balance sheet 5%), 35% NHA MBS, 14% covered bond, 15% non-bank uninsured prime and non-prime (5–8% for B-20 compliant uninsurable, 3–5% subprime, 2% ABCP and one C$300 million Private RMBS)

15 According to CMHC, in 2014, 48 per cent of first-time home buyers and 40 per cent of all purchasers used a mortgage broker (although many of these brokers worked for banks); 49.4 per cent of mortgage originations and 46 per cent of mortgages outstanding were financed with securities.

16 "A Nation of Borrowers," *Financial Post*, 20 January 2016: 1.

17 In June 2017, the C.D. Howe Institute published a commentary, "Spendthrifts and Savers: Are Canadians Acting like They Are "House Poor" or "House Rich," which outlined the economic and policy implications of consumer debt in Canada.

4. Small and Mid-sized Business Blues

1 Eyk Henning and Madeline Nissen, "Deutsche Chairman Paul Achtleitner on the Future of the Bank, Industry," *Wall Street Journal*, 14 May 2015.

2 A *bank* is a financial institution and a financial intermediary that accepts deposits and channels those deposits into lending activities, either directly by lending or indirectly through capital markets. A bank links together customers that have capital deficits and customers with capital surpluses.

3 Although SME loans may offer higher profit margins, they are also costlier to originate and monitor. Although not all SME loans attract the highest risk weighting under the new capital rules (Basel III), most would require more capital backing than residential mortgages and loans to large corporations and governments. The Canadian banks use the Internal Ratings-Based approach rather than the Standardized approach, which can reduce the risk weighting from 100 per cent to 41 per cent if the SME is in a portfolio of small exposures. Even under the conservative assumption mentioned, the overall funding cost increase from Basel II to Basel III would range from 19 to 47 basis points.

4 http://www.ic.gc.ca/eic/site/061.nsf/eng/02715.html. Accessed 8 November 2016.

5 http://www.ic.gc.ca/eic/site/061.nsf/eng/02805.html. Accessed 8 November 2016.

6 www.statcan.gc.ca/pub/11f0027m/11f0027m2012082-eng.pdf.

7 "Germany's Banking System: Old-fashioned but in Favour," *Economist*, 10 November 2012.

8 Ibid.

9 James Shotter and Jim Brundsen, "EU Warned Not to Let Capital Markets Union Hurt Role of Banks," *Financial Times*, 23 August 2015.

10 Ibid.

11 "Testimony of B. Doyle Mitchell, Jr., President and CEO of Industrial Bank, Washington, D.C. On behalf of the Independent Community Bankers of America, before the United States House Committee on Small Business Subcommittee on Economic Growth, Tax and Capital Access Hearing on 'Financing Main Street: How Dodd-Frank Is Crippling Small Lenders and Access to Capital'": http://www.icba.org/docs/default-source/icba/advocacy-documents/testimony/114th-congress/test091715.pdf?sfvrsn=2.

12 Ibid.

13 Donna Borak, "OCC's Curry Signals Basel III Compromise for Small Banks," *American Banker* 177(199) (16 October 2012).

14 Donna Borak, "Community Banks: Basel III Will Put Us Out of Business," *American Banker* 177(204) (23 October 2012).

15 Gary Corner, "Will Community Bank Returns on Equity Return to Precrisis Levels?" *Central Banker* (Spring 2012). Published by the Public Affairs Department of the Federal Reserve Bank of St Louis. Views expressed are not necessarily official opinions of the Federal Reserve Bank of St Louis.

16 The findings of a sharp decline in ROE are supported by Dean F. Amel and Robin A. Prager's study, "Community Bank Performance: How Important Are Managers," *Review of Industrial Organization* 48(2) (March 2016): 149–80. Perhaps even more telling as to the costs of new regulation is the presentation by CenterState Bank on Community Bank performance for Q3 2015.

17 There has been a lively debate around the implications of new banking regulations on SME financing. Jaime Caruana, governor of the Bank of Spain and chair of the Basel Committee on Banking Supervision, raised the issue in 2003 in an address to the European Parliament Workshop on the "Consequences of Basel II for SMEs," Brussels, 10 July 2003: http://www.bis.org/review/r030714d.pdf. As general manager of the Bank for International Settlements, he revisited the issue in 2014 and demonstrated that the increase in funding costs under Basel III would range from 19 to 47 basis points, a not very significant amount. See Jaime Caruana, "How Much Capital Is Enough?": http://www. bis.org/speeches/sp141216.pdf. This is generally confirmed by other studies. See Clara Cardone-Riportella, Antonio Trujillo-Ponce, and Anahi Briozzo, "What Do Basel Capital Accords Mean for SMEs?" (2011): http://e-archivo.uc3m.es/bitstream/handle/10016/10892/wb111004.pdf;jsessionid=1ED399DD39F630A39B6508DA9AAB3304?sequence=1.

However, not all concur with Caruana's assessment of the benign impact of Basel III on SMEs. In fact, the debate over the impact of Basel II and III on SME funding is a hot topic. Humblot does raise concerns over SME bank financing in France. See Thomas Humblot, "Basel III Effects on SMEs' Access to Bank Credit: An Empirical Assessment," CR14-EFI06. (2014): https://hal.archives-ouvertes.fr/hal-01096527/document. Emmanouil Schivas, senior policy adviser at ACCA (the Association of Chartered Certified Accountants) has raised concerns about the potential impact of Basel III by framing the question as "a choice between promoting business growth and safeguarding financial stability": Emmanouil Schivas, "Basel III and SMEs: Getting the Trade-off Right," *Accountancy Futures* (March 2012): http://www.accaglobal. com/content/dam/acca/global/PDF-technical/small-business/ pol-af-gtor.pdf. Clearly, he does not think Basel III got the balance right: "capital regulation alone is oblivious to the realities of lending to SMEs and gives banks incentives to avoid conventional lending altogether. It is therefore important for global regulators to resist complacency and devise further means, outside the framework of Basel III, of monitoring tail risk, as well as to rethink the scope of Basel III and ensure that it applies only to those sectors that stand to benefit from its provisions" (ibid., .8).

The crux of the debate over the impact of Basel III on SMEs is that the impact varies by market depending upon the capital strength and extent of deleveraging of the banks. The topic has been well addressed by Gert Wehinger, who focuses upon the need to assist a transition to non-bank intermediations: especially securitization: Gert Wehringer, "Bank Deleveraging, the Move from Bank to Market-based Financing, and SME Financing," *OECD Journal: Financial Market Trends* (2012): 1: http://www.oecd.org/finance/financial-markets/Bank_deleveraging-Wehinger.pdf.

18 Canadian Federation of Independent Business: Doug Bruce and Queenie Wong, "Battle of the Banks, How Small Businesses Rate Their Banks," 22 May 2013; Queenie Wong, "Battle of the Banks: Credit Unions among the Best for Small Business," October 2016: http:// www.cfib-fcei.ca/cfib-documents/rr3415.pdf; and Queenie Wong, "SME Financing Indicators," October 2016: http://www.cfib-fcei.ca/ cfib-documents/rr3412.pdf.

19 Ibid.

20 https://www.bdc.ca/en/about/pages/default.aspx. Accessed 17 May 2017.

21 There are some important questions regarding risk taking in securitization. One issue is maturity transformation – typically the duration of the loans is longer than the funding instruments'. This creates an issue of interest rate risk when the funding is renewed. Also,

if funding were to dry up, then there may be a need for a lender of last resort, like the Bank of Canada.

22 "The Return of Securitization: Back from the Dead," *Economist*, 11 January 2014.

23 "Securitization in Europe: Limping Along," *Economist*, 25 February 2017.

24 Lowell Bryan and Diana Farrell, *Market Unbound: Unleashing Global Capitalism* (New York: John Wiley & Sons, 1996), 65.

25 James L. Darroch, "Global Competitiveness and Public Policy: The Case of the Canadian Multinational Banks," Special Issue on Canadian Multinationals and International Finance, *Business History* (July 1992); and James L. Darroch, *Canadian Banks and Global Competitiveness* (Montreal and Kingston: McGill-Queen's University Press, 1994), chapter 10, especially 265ff.

26 "Bank of Canada Urges Banks to Set Up National SME Growth Fund," *Globe and Mail*, 7 August 2016.

27 British Growth Fund Website: http://www.businessgrowthfund. co.uk/growth-capital-2/. Retrieved on 17 May 2017.

28 "Bank of Canada Urges Banks to Set Up National SME Growth Fund," *Globe and Mail*, 7 August 2016.

29 Laurentian Bank, "Banks and Insurance Companies Announce Canadian Business Growth Fund of up to $1B":http://www.marketwired.com/ press-release/banks-and-insurance-companies-announce-canadian-business-growth-fund-of-up-to-1b-tsx-lb-2201884.htm.

30 *Backbone Magazine* (November-December 2013): 29.

31 Sonya Gulati, "Crowdfunding: A Kick Starter for Startups," *TD Economics*, 29 January 2014"https://www.td.com/document/PDF/ economics/special/Crowdfunding.pdf

32 Securities and Exchange Commission (SEC), "Investor Bulletin: Crowdfunding for Investors," 16 February 2016: http://www.sec.gov/ oiea/investor-alerts-bulletins/ib_crowdfunding-.html.

33 Canadian Venture Capital / Private Equity Association, *2015 Canadian Venture Capital Market Overview* (March 2016) and discussions with Jim Orlando, OMERS Ventures, on 24 February 2016.

34 In part this decrease was due to the inclusion in 2014 of the Tim Hortons deal, worth $11.8 billion.

5. Where Are the Customers' Yachts?

1 Fred Schwed, Jr, *Where Are the Customers' Yachts? Or a Good Hard Look at Wall Street* (Hoboken, NJ: John Wiley & Sons, 1940, 1955, 1995, 2006), xxxvi.

2 Ajay Chorana, Henri Servaes, and Peter Tufano, "Mutual Fund Fees around the World," *Review of Financial Studies*, 18 July 2007.

3 Not everyone agrees that there is a retirement crisis. For example, the Fraser Institute disputes it.

4 Most of the research for this section was conducted by Kaz Jana and Patricia Meredith for Monitor Deloitte in August 2013.

5 Investment Funds Institute of Canada, "Industry Overview," January 2017.

6 The 3.5 per cent real rate of return assumption was used by the minister of finance to determine the annual tax deductible contribution to a registered retirement savings plan necessary to equalize defined benefit plans with defined contribution plans.

7 For example, from October 2000 to October 2016 the S&P TSX Index was up approximately 35 per cent (market returns), yet investors would have paid more than 2 per cent annually in mutual fund fees for those returns (about 32 per cent in total), leaving very little for their retirement.

8 Recent Questrade advertisements, including "That's 30% of our retirement gone in fees" and "Whose retirement are we funding, ours or our bankers?" have captured customer sentiment.

9 This result is consistent with a U.K. study by David Pitt-Watson, *Tomorrow's Investor: Building the Consensus for a People's Pension in Britain*, RSA Project (December 2010): 5, which estimated that the country's pension members were losing nearly 40 per cent of their savings over the lifetime of their pensions by paying a standard annual fee of 1.5 per cent. Under the current Canadian rate structure, the damage is even greater.

10 The insurance industry includes London Life, Manulife, Great-West Life, Industrial Alliance, IA Clarington, and Canada Life Mutual Funds.

11 The investment management industry includes Investors Group, CI Investments, Mackenzie Financial, Dynamic Funds, Fidelity Investments, MRS McLean Budden (Sun Life), AGF Investments, Invesco (Trimark), Phillips, Hager & North (RBC), Russell Investments, and Franklin Templeton mutual funds.

12 A Dalbar Research study of American investors found the average mutual fund holding time is only three years – likely also true of Canadian investors.

13 Martijn Cremers, Miguel A. Ferreira, Pedro P. Matos, and Laura T. Starks, "Indexing and Active Fund Management: International Evidence," *Journal of Financial Economics* (1 February 2015), Darden Business School Working Paper No. 2558724: https://ssrn.com/abstract=2558724. In March 2016, the Ontario Securities Commission announced that it had "commenced a targeted review of conventional mutual funds that disclose in their prospectus and marketing materials that they pursue active strategies ... Among other data, it considered the funds' active share (a measure of the percentage of a fund's portfolio that overlaps significantly with the composition of the benchmark index)." Clare O'Hara, "Regulators Launch Probe into the 'Closet Indexers' of the Mutual Fund Industry," *Globe and Mail*, 2 March 2016.

14 At the end of 2011, the amount of mutual funds purchased through bank (and credit union) branches (both advice and direct) totalled $244 billion, more than the amount purchased through financial advisors ($235 billion) and considerably more than fund assets held at full service brokerages ($168 billion).

15 Investment Funds Institute of Canada, "Analysis of Factors Influencing Sales, Retention and Redemption of Mutual Fund Units": September 2015 study by Investor Economics.

16 A *discretionary account* is an *investment account* that allows a *broker* to buy and sell securities without the client's consent: www.investopedia.com/terms/d/discretionaryaccount.asp.

17 George A. Akerlof and Robert J. Shiller, *Phishing for Phools: The Economics of Manipulation and Deception* (Princeton, NJ: Princeton University Press, 2015).

18 Morningstar, "2015 Global Fund Investor Experience Study" (February 2016).

19 A benchmark is a standard against which the performance of a security, *mutual fund* or *investment manager* can be measured. Generally, broad market and market-segment stock and bond indexes are used for this purpose: http://www.investopedia.com/terms/b/benchmark. asp#ixzz4OO6zTrFf.

20 The changes are scheduled to roll out over a three-year period, which started in 2014 with account statements that included a definition of *benchmark* and fees being disclosed in advance of trades. As of 31 December 2015, investment firms must provide clients with enhanced account statements that include the opening balance, current market value, original cost, deferred sales charges owing if the fund is sold, account holder, and whether or not the investment is covered by the investor protection fund. As of 30 May 2016, financial advisors and their investment firms have been required to provide investors with a document called "Fund Facts" before the purchase of a mutual fund. A Fund Facts document should include the fund name, portfolio manager, fund fees, trailing commission, minimum amount, top ten investment holdings, investment mix, fund performance over past ten years, and risk rating. As of that date, the Canadian Securities Administrators also offer an online investor education platform to help Canadians become better informed about their investment decisions.

21 As mentioned in chapter 1, banks are federally regulated, and capital markets are provincially overseen. However, in 2001, the federal government created the Financial Consumer Agency of Canada because "the current framework for consumer protection is not as effective as it should be in reducing the information and power imbalance between institutions and consumers." Although this was clearly so for individual investing, to date FCAC has done very little to address the problems, even though it clearly has a mandate over the two largest players – banks and insurers.

22 "Regulators Move Closer to a Ban on Mutual Fund Fees," *Globe and Mail*, 30 June 2016.

23 "Securities Regulators Should Cut the Consultation on Mutual Fund Fees," *Globe and Mail*, 22 January 2017.

24 Jim Leech and Jacquie McNish, *The Third Rail: Confronting Our Pension Failures* (Toronto: McClelland & Stewart, 2013), 167.

25 Ibid., 141–7.

26 Similar reports have been published by most of the other Canadian banks – by CIBC in 2013 and BMO in 2015.

27 "Younger Canadians Put Brakes on Debt in 2012, Older Keep Borrowing," *TD Economics*, 13 February 2013: https://www.td.com/document/PDF/economics/special/YoungerCanadiansPutBrakesOnDebtIn2012.pdf.

28 Tom Hamza, "A Recent Survey Suggests Canadians Are Caught between Low Savings and Unrealistic Attitudes about Tapping into Their Homes," *Investment Executive*, March 2013: http://www.brondesbury.com/Go/327BF31E1C25BCA880/Getting-Real-About-the-House

29 Employee Benefits Research Institute estimates from the Consumption and Activities Survey (2001–2009).

30 MFS U.S. Investing Sentiment Survey, 2015.

31 In the 1980s, when interest rates were very high, Canadians did not move money out of bank deposits into money market funds to the same extent as Americans because there was no cap on the interest rate Canadian banks could pay. Also, the retail fixed income market in Canada, including securitized assets, is much less developed than in the United States. These factors also help to explain the difference.

32 Another part of the problem may be a weak fixed income market in Canada. As this market has always been controlled by the banks, fixed income products have not been developed, promoted, or priced for retail customers.

33 MFS U.S. Investing Sentiment Survey, 2015.

34 BlackRock Investment Insight, "Cashing In: Rethink the Cost of Cash," 4 February 2016.

35 Benjamin Tal and Royce Mendes, "Cashing In on Fear," CIBC Economics, 26 January 2016.

36 We chose Australia for comparison because of the similarities between the two markets: both are protected oligopolies that have evolved from the British banking system. Also, Australians have significantly more retirement savings.

37 Ipsos Reid, "One in four (24%) of Canadians Expect Their Home to Be Their Primary Source of Retirement Income," 19 February 2014.

38 According to FCAC, the CHIP Reverse Mortgage, which is offered by HomeEquity Bank, is the main source of most reverse mortgage products that are available in Canada.

39 "A Great Cost Migration Is Upending the Financial Industry," *Bloomberg View*, 27 October 2016.

40 "New Platforms to Change the Way Mutual Funds Are Traded in Canada," *Globe and Mail*, 16 November 2015.

41 "Fees on Mutual Funds Tumble toward Zero," *Wall Street Journal*, 26 January 2016.

42 "A Great Cost Migration Is Upending the Financial Industry," *Bloomberg View*, 27 October 2016.

43 J.D. Power: "Is Your Next Investment Advisor a Robo-Advisor?" 21 September 2015; "Many Canadian Investors May Be Wondering What They're Paying Their Advisors For," 18 August 2016; and "Investors Adopt More Hands-on Approach to Advisors, Says J.D. Power Full Service Investor Satisfaction Study," 7 April 2016.

44 "Online Broker Survey: Seeking the 'Wow' Factor," *Globe and Mail*, 12 December 2016.

6. Canada Trails the Third World

1 Boston Consulting Group, "Global Payments: Listening to the Customer Voice," 2015. Also, 2011 to 2016 Global Payments Reports.

2 Much of the research for this chapter was conducted by the Task Force for the Payments System Review and reported in *Going Digital: Transitioning to Digital Payments*, December 2011: http://www.fin.gc.ca/n12/data/12-030_1-eng.asp

3 The author has reviewed this analysis for three of the six banks, and all were within the range.

4 "In Sweden, a Cash-Free Future Nears," *New York Times*, 26 December 2015.

5 "Visa and MasterCard Agree to Cut Fees They Charge Merchants Who Accept Credit Cards," *Financial Post*, 4 November 2014.

6 Task Force for the Payments System Review, *Moving Canada into the Digital Age*, December 2011, 4: http://www.fin.gc.ca/n12/data/12-030_1-eng.asp

7   Task Force for the Payments System Review, *Going Digital*, 22. Reducing the number of cheques by 68 per cent would mean approximately 20 per cent of B2B payments were still made by cheque.

8   According to the GSMA Mobile Economy 2016, there were more than 7.6 billion connections (representing 4.7 billion unique subscribers) at the end of 2016. The global subscriber penetration rate now stands at 63 per cent and will reach 5.6 billion people or 70 per cent of the world's population by the end of the decade: http://www.gsma.com/mobileeconomy/.

9   Brett King, *Bank 3.0: Why Banking Is No Longer Somewhere You Go, But Something You Do* (Singapore: John Wiley & Sons, 2013), 330.

10 M-Pesa is a mobile-phone-based money transfer, financing, and microfinancing service launched in 2007 by Vodafone for Safaricom and Vodacom, the largest mobile operators in Kenya and Tanzania.

11 Starbuck's investor presentations file: https://news.starbucks.com/news/investor-day-2016-press-release; https://s21.q4cdn.com/369030626/files/doc_downloads/presentations/SID16_1206_MattR_GerriMF.pdf.

12 According to the *Economist*, PayPal is now the largest retail bank in the world with 143 million customers, 10 million of whom are Canadians. Five million active Canadian customers use their PayPal account at least once a month. Those numbers would make PayPal the third-largest bank in Canada.

13 PayPal and Braintree launch One Touch: http://files.shareholder.com/downloads/AMDA-4BS3R8/4669094691x0x885605/B7B8DD38-FF41-4D27-94EC-84C6E5A3259F/2015_Annual_Report.pdf.

14 http://www.federalreserve.gov/econresdata/mobile-devices/2015-accessing-financial-services.htm#Box3.ResearchNoteMeasuringThe UseOfM-3BD6FE19.

15 Host card emulation (HCE) is a technology that emulates a payment card on a mobile device using only software. This approach offers technical and business benefits to a wide range of mobile industry stakeholders that are active in the near field communication (NFC) payments ecosystem.

16 "Apple Pay Now Available at 36% of U.S. Merchants: Adoption Will Be over 50% by 2018," *Payment Eye*, 16 March 2017.

17 *Fast Company*, 2 March 2016: http://www.fastcompany.com/3057353/fast-feed/apple-pay-leads-mobile-payments-with-12-million-monthly-users.

18 The move by Visa to invest in disruptive payments start-up Square and its recent acquisition of mobile financial services company Fundamo represent strong moves towards mainstream adoption.

19 Although Bank of Montreal has not launched a mobile payments app, it does support Apple Pay for its customers. BMO Harris has announced that it will support Android Pay in the United States.

20 Global Insights, "The Mobile Payments Readiness Index: A Global Market Assessment," MasterCard Worldwide, 2012, 7: https:// mobilereadiness.mastercard.com/globalreport.pdf.

21 Aite Group and ACI Worldwide, "The Global Rise of Smartphonatics: Driving Mobile Payment and Banking Adoption in the United States, EMEA, and Asia-Pacific," 14 May 2012: http://www.aitegroup.com/ report/global-rise-smartphonatics-driving-mobile-payment-and-banking-adoption-united-states-emea-and

22 http://mobilesyrup.com/2016/12/12/android-pay-arrives-in-canada-with-support-currently-limited-to-scotiabank-cards/.

23 "Mobile Internet Use Passes Desktop for the First Time," *Tech Crunch*, 1 November 2016.

24 Forrester Research Inc., "Predictions 2015: Most Brands Will Underinvest in Mobile," 11 November 2014: http://www. telecomnews.co.il/image/users/228328/ftp/my_files/General%20 Files/Predictions%202015-%20Most%20Brands%20Will%20 Underinvest%20In%20Mobile.pdf?id=22286877.

25 http://www.nasdaq.com/aspx/call-transcript.aspx?StoryId=1964831& Title=starbucks-ceo-discusses-f1q-2014-results-earnings-call-transcript.

26 Remarks at the 2010 Canadian Payments Association Conference, June 2010.

27 https://www.digitalcommerce360.com/2016/08/12/2017-mobile-500-next-generation-mobile-commerce/.

28 These payments are made through the Large Value Transfer System (LVTS) and represented 89 per cent of the value of payments but less than 1 per cent of the number of payment transactions in 2016.

29 E-transfers are electronic funds transfers that clear and settle through the small payments system (ACSS – Automated Clearing and Settlement System) once a day (in the wee hours of the morning). Although they appear to the consumer as IFTs, they are not.

30 https://www.statista.com/statistics/276623/number-of-apps-available-in-leading-app-stores/.

31 http://www.internetlivestats.com/internet-users-by-country/.

32 Statistics Canada, "Canadian Internet Use Survey, 2012," released 13 October 2013: https://www.digitalcommerce360.com/2016/08/12/2017-mobile-500-next-generation-mobile-commerce/

33 Ibid.

34 https://www.atkearney.com/news-media/news-releases/news-release/-/asset_publisher/00OIL7Jc67KL/content/the-united-states-tops-a-t-kearney-global-retail-e-commerce-index-for-market-opportunity/10192

35 http://data.worldbank.org/indicator/IT.CEL.SETS.P2

36 Catalyst Reports, "Smartphone Behaviour in Canada and the Implications for Marketers in 2016": http://catalyst.ca/2016-canadian-smartphone-behaviour/.

37 http://mobilesyrup.com/2016/07/14/suretap-wallet-to-be-discontinued-august-26-canada/.

7. Long Live the Branch

1 Michiyo Nakamoto and David Wighton, "Citigroup Chief Stays Bullish on Buy-Outs," *Financial Times*, 9 July 2007. Prince was discussing the large amounts of liquidity fuelling the cheap credit boom.

2 Bank rankings from FRB Statistical Release, Insured Chartered Commercial Banks, 31 December 2016

3 To create economic value for shareholders, investments must earn more than the cost of capital, currently above 10 per cent.

4 See chapter 8, table 8.1.

5 Canadian Bankers' Association, "Issue Brief: How Canadians Bank," 1 March 2017.

6 Brett King, *Bank 3.0: Why Banking Is No Longer Somewhere You Go, But Something You Do* (Singapore: John Wiley & Sons, 2013), 75.

7 According to the Canadian Bankers' Association, under 30 per cent of customers used online banking in 2005 compared with over 75 per cent in 2016.

8 BMO's combined (Canada and United States) ROE has not changed significantly since 2012 when it stopped disclosing the numbers separately. If we assume that it has maintained its Canadian ROE (like the other banks), then its U.S. profitability has not improved substantially.

9 Most of Scotiabank's acquisitions were made using Brady Bonds, which it acquired when its loans to less-developed countries were restructured in the 1980s.

10 "How the Financial Crisis Saved Gord Nixon," *Globe and Mail*, 6 December 2013.

11 "Investment Banks' Return on Equity Declines," *Financial Times*, 21 February 2016: https://www.ft.com/content/0c65e85a-d719-11e5-8887-98e7feb46f27.

12 CIBC, 2015 Annual Report, II.

13 Authors' analysis of 2015 and 2016 annual reports.

8. A Banking System for the Twenty-First Century

1 Clayton M. Christensen, *The Innovator's Dilemma: When New Technologies Cause Great Firms to Fail* (Boston, MA: Harvard Business School Press, 1997), xii–xvii.

2 http://www.mckinsey.com/business-functions/strategy-and-corporate-finance/our-insights/the-four-global-forces-breaking-all-the-trends.

3 "Sorry Banks, Millennials Hate You," *Fast Company*, 24 March 2016: https://www.fastcompany.com/3027197/sorry-banks-millennials-hate-you.

4 According to *Fortune*, 88 per cent of the firms on its 500 list in 1955 had disappeared by 2014.

5 "Canada a Laggard as World's Firms Wake Up to Digital Disruption: Survey," *Globe and Mail*, 5 October 2016; also, Science, Technology and Innovation Council, "Canada's Innovation Challenges and Opportunities," 27 November 2015.

6 Michael C. Jensen, "The Modern Industrial Revolution, Exit, and the Failure of Internal Control Systems," *The Journal of Finance*, 48(3), July 1993.

7 According to McKinsey & Company, Canada has been recognized as having the most stable banking system in the world for the past six years.

8 FIS, "FIS Consumer Banking PACE Index: Understanding Performance Against Customer Expectations (PACE)" (Canada, 2015).

9 *Globe and Mail*, 6 January 2014.

10 Greg Perry, *Toronto Star*, 30 October 2015.

11 Michiyo Nakamoto and David Wighton, "Citigroup Chief Stays Bullish on Buy-Outs," *Financial Times*, 9 July 2007.

12 http://web.tmxmoney.com/indices.php?section=tsx&index=%5ETSX. On 5 May 2016, the financial sector represented 36.4 per cent of the S&P/TSX index.

13 Catalytic governance is a process for leading transformative change that engages a wide range of stakeholders in dialogue and empowers them to envisage and enact a desired future. It was developed from a case study based upon the work of the Task Force for the Payments System Review: see Patricia Meredith, Steven A. Rosell, and Ged R. Davis, *Catalytic Governance: Leading Change in the Information Age* (Toronto: University of Toronto Press, 2016).

14 Some question whether or not all of the stakeholders in an industry can work together without running into competition issues. After consultation with the Competition Bureau and several law firms, the Task Force for the Payments System Review was able to clear this hurdle. As long as the focus was on the industry and not on individual company strategy and pricing, the discussions were encouraged.

15 In March 2016, Scotiabank announced the creation of its Digital Factory, with 350 employees. All the other banks have created similar, but smaller, technology incubators. See "Brian Porter's Remarks to Students at Ivey Business School, Western University," 31 March 2016: http://www.scotiabank.com/ca/en/0,,10125,00.html. Also, "Press Release from Marketwired: Brian Porter Speaks to Ivey Business Students about Scotiabank's Digital Strategy," *Globe and Mail*, 31 March 2016.

16 http://www.canajunfinances.com

17 Dan Breznitz, Shiri Breznitz, and David Wolfe, "Current State of the Financial Technology Innovation Ecosystem in the Toronto Region," A

Report from the Innovation Policy Lab, Munk School of Global Affairs, University of Toronto, Summer 2015.

18 Ibid.

19 The Canada Small Business Financing Loan is a federal-government-guaranteed loan that provides financing to get a business started or help an existing business grow. The CSBF Loan is designed to help businesses purchase, install, renovate, and modernize business equipment and other fixed assets.

20 Task Force on the Future of the Canadian Financial Services Sector (MacKay Task Force), "Change, Challenge, Opportunity," Department of Finance (Canada), September 1998, 15.

21 We believe that FCAC should start with banks where their jurisdiction is clear and that the government should not back off the provision in current pending legislation to clarify that all aspects of banking are under federal jurisdiction.

22 This topic is the focus of Patricia Meredith's third book in her trilogy: *Avoiding Business Failure: Corporate Governance for the Information Age*, in progress with University of Toronto Press.

Suggested Reading

The following works have made a substantial contribution to our thinking and, directly or indirectly, to this book.

Akerlof, George A., and Robert J. Shiller. *Phishing for Phools: The Economics of Manipulation and Deception*. Princeton, NJ: Princeton University Press, 2015

Boston Consulting Group. "Global Payments 2011: Winning after the Storm." 8 February 2011.

Bryan, Lowell. *Breaking Up the Bank: Rethinking an Industry under Siege*. Homewood, IL: Dow Jones Irwin, 1988.

Bryan, Lowell, and Diana Farrell. *Market Unbound: Unleashing Global Capitalism*. New York: John Wiley & Sons, 1996.

Christensen, Clayton. *The Innovator's Dilemma: When New Technologies Cause Great Firms to Fail*. Boston, MA: Harvard Business School Press, 1997.

Darroch, James L. *Canadian Banks and Global Competitiveness*. Montreal and Kingston: McGill-Queen's University Press, 1994.

Geithner, Timothy F. *Stress Test: Reflections on Financial Crises*. New York: Crown Publishing Group, 2014.

Helpman, Elhanan, ed. *General Purpose Technologies and Economic Growth*. Cambridge, MA: MIT Press, 1998.

Jenson, Michael C. "The Modern Industrial Revolution, Exit and the Failure of Internal Control Systems," *The Journal of Finance*, 48(3) (July 1993): 831–80.

King, Brett. *Bank 3.0: Why Banking Is No Longer Somewhere You Go, But Something You Do*. Singapore: John Wiley & Sons, 2013.

Kuhn, Thomas S. *The Structure of Scientific Revolutions*, 3rd ed. Chicago: University of Chicago Press, 1996.

Leech, Jim, and Jacquie McNish. *The Third Rail: Confronting Our Pension Failures*. Toronto: McClelland & Stewart, 2013.

McKinsey & Company, Financial Services Practice. "The Mainstreaming of Alternative Investments: Fueling the New Wave of Growth in Asset Management." June 2012.

Meredith, Patricia. "Why the Frog Does Not Jump Out of the Boiling Water: A Multi-level Exploration of the Limited Responses of the Canadian Banks to Disruptive Changes in the Canadian Residential Mortgage Industry from 1975 to 2008." PhD diss., York University, June 2009.

Meredith, Patricia, Steven A. Rosell, and Ged R. Davis. *Catalytic Governance: Leading Change in the Information Age*. Toronto: University of Toronto Press, 2016.

Schumpeter, Joseph. *The Theory of Economic Development*. Cambridge, MA: Harvard University Press, 1934.

Schwed, Fred, Jr. *Where Are the Customers' Yachts? Or a Good Hard Look at Wall Street*. Hoboken, NJ: John Wiley & Sons, 1940, 1955, 1995, 2006.

Westley, Frances, Brenda Zimmerman, and Michael Quinn Patton. *Getting to Maybe: How the World Is Changed*. Toronto: Random House Canada, 2006.

Index